THE WORKS OF CHARLES DICKENS
STANDARD EDITION

———

Volume XIII

A Tale of Two Cities
The Uncommercial Traveller

LUCIE'S FAREWELL

A
TALE OF TWO CITIES
and
The Uncommercial Traveller

By CHARLES DICKENS

With Frontispiece
and Illustrations by Max Cowper

THE GRESHAM PUBLISHING
COMPANY LIMITED 66 *Chandos*
Street Covent Garden London

Printed in Great Britain

INTRODUCTORY NOTE

A TALE OF TWO CITIES

A Tale of Two Cities was published in weekly instalments in *All the Year Round*, beginning in the first number on April 30, 1859, and ending on November 26 in the same year. It also appeared in monthly parts, through Chapman & Hall, from June to December, 1859. The illustrations were by Phiz.

THE UNCOMMERCIAL TRAVELLER

The Uncommercial Traveller consists of papers on a variety of subjects contributed to *All the Year Round*. Seventeen of them (Nos. I–XVII in this edition) appeared in 1860, from January 28 to October 13; twelve more (Nos. XVIII–XXIX) in 1863, from May 2 to October 24; "The Ruffian" (No. XXX) was published in the issue of October 10, 1868; and seven more (Nos. XXXI–XXXVII) appeared under the general title *New Uncommercial Samples*, from December 5, 1868, to June 5, 1869. A first collection of these papers was issued by Chapman & Hall in 1861, and an enlarged edition in 1868, but several of the papers were included for the first time in the edition of 1875.

A TALE OF TWO CITIES

THIS TALE IS INSCRIBED

TO

THE LORD JOHN RUSSELL

IN REMEMBRANCE

OF

MANY PUBLIC SERVICES

AND

PRIVATE KINDNESSES

PREFACE

WHEN I was acting, with my children and friends, in Mr. Wilkie Collins's drama of *The Frozen Deep*, I first conceived the main idea of this story. A strong desire was upon me then to embody it in my own person; and I traced out in my fancy the state of mind of which it would necessitate the presentation to an observant spectator with particular care and interest.

As the idea became familiar to me, it gradually shaped itself into its present form. Throughout its execution, it has had complete possession of me; I have so far verified what is done and suffered in these pages, as that I have certainly done and suffered it all myself.

Whenever any reference (however slight) is made here to the condition of the French people before or during the Revolution, it is truly made, on the faith of trustworthy witnesses. It has been one of my hopes to add something to the popular and picturesque means of understanding that terrible time, though no one can hope to add anything to the philosophy of Mr. Carlyle's wonderful book.

TAVISTOCK HOUSE, LONDON,
November 1859.

CONTENTS

A TALE OF TWO CITIES

BOOK THE FIRST.   RECALLED TO LIFE

BOOK THE SECOND.   THE GOLDEN THREAD

BOOK THE THIRD. THE TRACK OF A STORM

LIST OF ILLUSTRATIONS

A TALE OF TWO CITIES

BOOK THE FIRST. RECALLED TO LIFE

CHAPTER I

THE PERIOD

IT was the best of times, it was the worst of times, it was the age of wisdom, it was the age of foolishness, it was the epoch of belief, it was the epoch of incredulity, it was the season of Light, it was the season of Darkness, it was the spring of hope, it was the winter of despair, we had everything before us, we had nothing before us, we were all going direct to heaven, we were all going direct the other way—in short, the period was so far like the present period, that some of its noisiest authorities insisted on its being received, for good or for evil, in the superlative degree of comparison only.

There were a king with a large jaw and a queen with a plain face on the throne of England ; there were a king with a large jaw and a queen with a fair face on the throne of France. In both countries it was clearer than crystal to the lords of the State preserves of loaves and fishes that things in general were settled for ever.

It was the year of Our Lord one thousand seven hundred and seventy-five. Spiritual revelations were conceded to England at that favoured period, as at this. Mrs. Southcott had recently attained her five-and-twentieth blessed birthday, of whom a prophetic private in the Life Guards had heralded the sublime appearance by announcing that arrangements were made for the swallowing up of London and Westminster. Even the Cock-lane ghost had been laid only a round dozen of years, after rapping out its messages, as the spirits of this very year last past (supernaturally deficient in originality) rapped out theirs. Mere messages in the earthly order of events had lately come to the English Crown and People from a congress of British subjects in America, which, strange to relate, have proved more important to the human race than any communications yet received through any of the chickens of the Cock-lane brood.

France, less favoured on the whole as to matters spiritual than her sister of the shield and trident, rolled with exceeding smoothness down hill, making paper money and spending it. Under the guidance of her Christian pastors, she entertained herself, besides, with such humane achievements as sentencing a youth to have his hands cut off, his tongue torn out with pincers, and his body burned alive, because he had not kneeled down in the rain to do honour to a dirty procession of monks which passed within his view, at a distance of some fifty or sixty yards. It is likely enough that, rooted in the woods of France and Norway, there were growing trees, when that sufferer was put to death, already marked by the Woodman, Fate, to come down and be sawn into boards, to make a certain movable framework with a sack and a knife in it, terrible in history. It is likely enough that in the rough outhouses of some tillers of the heavy lands adjacent to Paris there were sheltered from the weather that very day rude carts, bespattered with rustic mire, snuffed about by pigs, and roosted in by poultry, which the Farmer, Death, had already set apart to be his tumbrils of the Revolution. But that Woodman and that Farmer, though they work unceasingly, work silently, and no one heard them as they went about with muffled tread : the rather, forasmuch as to entertain any suspicion that they were awake was to be atheistical and traitorous.

In England there was scarcely an amount of order and protection to justify much national boasting. Daring burglaries by armed men, and highway robberies, took place in the capital itself every night ; families were publicly cautioned not to go out of town without removing their furniture to upholsterers' warehouses for security ; the highwayman in the dark was a City tradesman in the light, and, being recognised and challenged by his fellow-tradesman, whom he stopped in his character of " the Captain," gallantly shot him through the head and rode away ; the mail was waylaid by seven robbers, and the guard shot three dead, and then got shot dead himself by the other four, " in consequence of the failure of his ammunition "—after which the mail was robbed in peace ; that magnificent potentate, the Lord Mayor of London, was made to stand and deliver on Turnham Green, by one highwayman, who despoiled the illustrious creature in sight of all his retinue ; prisoners in London gaols fought battles with their turnkeys, and the majesty of the law fired blunderbusses in among them, loaded with rounds of shot and ball ; thieves snipped off diamond crosses from the necks of noble lords at Court drawing-rooms ; musketeers went into St. Giles's to search for contraband goods, and the mob fired on the musketeers, and the musketeers fired on the mob, and nobody thought any of these occurrences much out of the common way. In the midst of them, the hangman, ever busy and ever worse than useless, was in constant requisition ; now stringing up long rows of miscellaneous criminals ; now hanging a housebreaker on Saturday who had been taken on Tuesday ; now burning people in the hand at Newgate by the dozen, and now burning pamphlets at the door of Westminster Hall ; to-day taking the life of an atrocious murderer, and to-morrow of a wretched pilferer who had robbed a farmer's boy of sixpence.

All these things, and a thousand like them, came to pass in and close upon the dear old year one thousand seven hundred and seventy-five. Environed by them, while the Woodman and the Farmer worked unheeded, those two of the large jaws, and those other two of the plain and the fair faces, trod with stir enough, and carried their divine rights with a high hand. Thus did the year one thousand seven hundred and seventy-five conduct their Greatnesses, and myriads of small creatures —the creatures of this chronicle among the rest—along the roads that lay before them.

CHAPTER II

THE MAIL

It was the Dover road that lay, on a Friday night late in November, before the first of the persons with whom this history has business. The Dover road lay, as to him, beyond the Dover mail, as it lumbered up Shooter's Hill. He walked uphill in the mire by the side of the mail, as the rest of the passengers did, not because they had the least relish for walking exercise, under the circumstances, but because the hill, and the harness, and the mud, and the mail, were all so heavy, that the horses had three times already come to a stop, besides once drawing the coach across the road, with the mutinous intent of taking it back to Blackheath. Reins and whip and coachman and guard, however, in combination, had read that article of war which forbade a purpose otherwise strongly in favour of the argument that some brute animals are endued with Reason ; and the team had capitulated and returned to their duty.

With drooping heads and tremulous tails, they mashed their way through the thick mud, floundering and stumbling between whiles, as if they were falling to pieces at the larger joints. As often as the driver rested them and brought them to a stand, with a wary " Wo-ho ! so-ho then ! " the near leader violently shook his head and everything upon it—like an unusually emphatic horse, denying that the coach could be got up the hill. Whenever the leader made this rattle, the passenger started, as a nervous passenger might, and was disturbed in mind.

There was a steaming mist in all the hollows, and it had roamed in its forlornness up the hill, like an evil spirit, seeking rest and finding none. A clammy and intensely cold mist, it made its slow way through the air in ripples that visibly followed and overspread one another, as the waves of an unwholesome sea might do. It was dense enough to shut out everything from the light of the coach-lamps but these its own workings, and a few yards of road ; and the reek of the labouring horses steamed into it, as if they had made it all.

Two other passengers, besides the one, were plodding up the hill by the side of the mail. All three were wrapped to the cheek-bones and over the ears, and wore jack-boots. Not one of the three could have said, from anything he saw, what either of the other two was like ; and each was hidden under almost as many wrappers from the eyes of the mind, as from the eyes of the body, of his two companions. In those days travellers were very shy of being confidential on a short notice, for anybody on the road might be a robber or in league with robbers. As to the latter, when every posting-house and ale-house could produce somebody in "the Captain's" pay, ranging from the landlord to the lowest stable nondescript, it was the likeliest thing upon the cards. So the guard of the Dover mail thought to himself, that Friday night in November, one thousand seven hundred and seventy-five, lumbering up Shooter's Hill, as he stood on his own particular perch behind the mail, beating his feet, and keeping an eye and a hand on the arm-chest before him, where a loaded blunderbuss lay at the top of six or eight loaded horse-pistols, deposited on a sub-stratum of cutlass.

The Dover mail was in its usual genial position that the guard suspected the passengers, the passengers suspected one another and the guard, they all suspected everybody else, and the coachman was sure of nothing but the horses, as to which cattle he could with a clear conscience have taken his oath on the two Testaments that they were not fit for the journey.

"Wo-ho !" said the coachman. " So, then ! One more pull and you're at the top and be damned to you, for I have had trouble enough to get you to it !—Joe ! "

" Halloa ! " the guard replied.

" What o'clock do you make it, Joe ? "

" Ten minutes, good, past eleven."

" My blood ! " ejaculated the vexed coachman, " and not atop of Shooter's yet ! Tst ! Yah ! Get on with you ! "

The emphatic horse, cut short by the whip in a most decided negative, made a decided scramble for it, and the three other horses followed suit. Once more the Dover mail struggled on, with the jack-boots of its passengers squashing along by its side. They had stopped when the coach stopped, and they kept close company with it. If any one of the three had had the hardihood to propose to another to walk on a little ahead into the mist and darkness, he would have put himself in a fair way of getting shot instantly as a highwayman.

The last burst carried the mail to the summit of the hill. The horses stopped to breathe again, and the guard got down to skid the wheel for the descent, and open the coach-door to let the passengers in.

" Tst ! Joe ! " cried the coachman in a warning voice, looking down from his box.

" What do you say, Tom ? "

They both listened.

" I say a horse at a canter coming up, Joe."

" *I* say a horse at a gallop, Tom," returned the guard, leaving his hold of the door, and mounting nimbly to his place. "Gentlemen! In the king's name, all of you!"

With this hurried adjuration he cocked his blunderbuss, and stood on the offensive.

The passenger booked by this history was on the coach-step, getting in; the two other passengers were close behind him, and about to follow. He remained on the step, half in the coach and half out of; they remained in the road below him. They all looked from the coachman to the guard, and from the guard to the coachman, and listened. The coachman looked back and the guard looked back, and even the emphatic leader pricked up his ears and looked back, without contradicting.

The stillness consequent on the cessation of the rumbling and labouring of the coach, added to the stillness of the night, made it very quiet indeed. The panting of the horses communicated a tremulous motion to the coach, as if it were in a state of agitation. The hearts of the passengers beat loud enough perhaps to be heard; but at any rate the quiet pause was audibly expressive of people out of breath, and holding the breath, and having the pulses quickened by expectation.

The sound of a horse at a gallop came fast and furiously up the hill.

"So-ho!" the guard sang out, as loud as he could roar. "Yo there! Stand! I shall fire!"

The pace was suddenly checked, and, with much splashing and floundering, a man's voice called from the mist, "Is that the Dover mail?"

"Never you mind what it is?" the guard retorted. "What are you?"

"*Is* that the Dover mail?"

"Why do you want to know?"

"I want a passenger, if it is."

"What passenger?"

"Mr. Jarvis Lorry."

Our booked passenger showed in a moment that it was his name. The guard, the coachman, and the two other passengers eyed him distrustfully.

"Keep where you are," the guard called to the voice in the mist, "because, if I should make a mistake, it could never be set right in your lifetime. Gentleman of the name of Lorry answer straight."

"What is the matter?" asked the passenger then, with mildly quavering speech. "Who wants me? Is it Jerry?"

("I don't like Jerry's voice, if it is Jerry," growled the guard to himself. "He's hoarser than suits me, is Jerry.")

"Yes, Mr. Lorry."

"What is the matter?"

"A despatch sent after you from over yonder. T. and Co."

"I know this messenger, guard," said Mr. Lorry, getting down into the road—assisted from behind more swiftly than politely by the other two passengers, who immediately scrambled into the coach, shut the door, and pulled up the window. "He may come close; there's nothing wrong."

"I hope there ain't, but I can't make so 'nation sure of that," said the guard, in gruff soliloquy. "Hallo you!"

"Well. And hallo you!" said Jerry, more hoarsely than before.

"Come on at a footpace! d'ye mind me? And if you've got holsters to that saddle o' yourn, don't let me see your hand go nigh 'em. For I'm a devil at a quick mistake, and when I make one it takes the form of Lead. So now let's look at you."

The figures of a horse and rider came slowly through the eddying mist, and came to the side of the mail, where the passenger stood. The rider stooped, and, casting up his eyes at the guard, handed the passenger a small folded paper. The rider's horse was blown, and both horse and rider were covered with mud, from the hoofs of the horse to the hat of the man.

"Guard!" said the passenger, in a tone of quiet business confidence.

The watchful guard, with his right hand at the stock of his raised blunderbuss, his left at the barrel, and his eye on the horseman, answered curtly, "Sir."

"There is nothing to apprehend. I belong to Tellson's Bank. You must know Tellson's Bank in London. I am going to Paris on business. A crown to drink. I may read this?"

"If so be as you're quick, Sir."

He opened it in the light of the coach-lamp on that side, and read—first to himself and then aloud: "'Wait at Dover for Mam'selle.' It's not long, you see, guard. Jerry, say that my answer was, RECALLED TO LIFE."

Jerry started in his saddle. "That's a Blazing strange answer, too," said he, at his hoarsest.

"Take that message back, and they will know that I received this, as well as if I wrote. Make the best of your way. Good-night."

With those words the passenger opened the coach-door and got in; not at all assisted by his fellow-passengers, who had expeditiously secreted their watches and purses in their boots, and were now making a general pretence of being asleep, with no more definite purpose than to escape the hazard of originating any other kind of action.

The coach lumbered on again, with heavier wreaths of mist closing round it as it began the descent. The guard soon replaced his blunderbuss in his arm-chest, and, having looked to the rest of its contents, and having looked to the supplementary pistols that he wore in his belt, looked to a smaller chest beneath his seat, in which there were a few smith's tools, a couple of torches, and a tinder-box. For he was furnished with that completeness that if the coach-lamps had been blown and stormed out, which did occasionally happen, he had only to shut himself up inside, keep the flint and steel sparks well off the straw, and get a light with tolerable safety and ease (if he were lucky) in five minutes.

" Tom ! " softly over the coach-roof.

" Hallo, Joe."

" Did you hear the message ? "

" I did, Joe."

" What did you make of it, Tom ? "

" Nothing at all, Joe."

" That's a coincidence, too," the guard mused, " for I made the same of it myself."

Jerry, left alone in the mist and darkness, dismounted meanwhile, not only to ease his spent horse, but to wipe the mud from his face, and shake the wet out of his hat-brim, which might be capable of holding about half a gallon. After standing with the bridle over his heavily-splashed arm, until the wheels of the mail were no longer within hearing and the night was quite still again, he turned to walk down the hill.

" After that there gallop from Temple Bar, old lady, I won't trust your forelegs till I get you on the level," said this hoarse messenger, glancing at his mare. " ' Recalled to life.' That's a Blazing strange message. Much of that wouldn't do for you, Jerry ! I say, Jerry ! You'd be in a Blazing bad way if recalling to life was to come into fashion, Jerry ! "

CHAPTER III

THE NIGHT SHADOWS

A WONDERFUL fact to reflect upon, that every human creature is constituted to be that profound secret and mystery to every other. A solemn consideration, when I enter a great city by night, that every one of those darkly clustered houses encloses its own secret ; that every room in every one of them encloses its own secret ; that every beating heart in the hundreds of thousands of breasts there is, in some of its imaginings, a secret to the heart nearest it ! Something of the awful-ness even of Death itself is referable to this. No more can I turn the leaves of this dear book that I loved, and vainly hope in time to read it all. No more can I look into the depths of this unfathomable water, wherein, as momentary lights glanced into it, I have had glimpses of buried treasure and other things submerged. It was appointed that the book should shut with a spring, for ever and for ever, when I had read but a page. It was appointed that the water should be locked in an eternal frost, when the light was playing on its surface, and I stood in ignorance on the shore. My friend is dead, my neighbour is dead, my love, the darling of my soul, is dead ; it is the inexorable consolidation and perpetuation of the secret that was always in that individuality, and which I shall carry in mine to my life's end. In any of the burial-places of this city through which I pass is there a sleeper more inscrutable than its busy inhabitants are, in their innermost personality, to me, or than I am to them ?

As to this, his natural and not to be alienated inheritance, the messenger on horseback had exactly the same possessions as the King, the first Minister of State, or the richest merchant in London. So with the three passengers shut up in the narrow compass of one lumbering old mail coach ; they were mysteries to one another, as complete as if each had been in his own coach and six, or his own coach and sixty, with the breadth of a county between him and the next.

The messenger rode back at an easy trot, stopping pretty often at ale-houses by the way to drink, but evincing a tendency to keep his own counsel, and to keep his hat cocked over his eyes. He had eyes that assorted very well with that decoration, being of a surface black, with no depth in the colour or form, and much too near together—as if they were afraid of being found out in something, singly, if they kept too far apart. They had a sinister expression, under an old cocked-hat like a three-cornered spittoon, and over a great muffler for the chin and throat, which descended nearly to the wearer's knees. When he stopped for drink, he moved this muffler with his left hand, only while he poured his liquor in with his right ; as soon as that was done, he muffled again.

"No, Jerry, no!" said the messenger, harping on one theme as he rode. "It wouldn't do for you, Jerry. Jerry, you honest tradesman, it wouldn't suit *your* line of business ! Recalled——! Bust me if I don't think he'd been a-drinking !"

His message perplexed his mind to that degree that he was fain, several times, to take off his hat to scratch his head. Except on the crown, which was raggedly bald, he had stiff, black hair, standing jaggedly all over it, and growing down hill almost to his broad, blunt nose. It was so like smith's work, so much more like the top of a strongly spiked wall than a head of hair, that the best of players at leap-frog might have declined him as the most dangerous man in the world to go over.

While he trotted back with the message he was to deliver to the night watchman in his box at the door of Tellson's Bank, by Temple Bar, who was to deliver it to greater authorities within, the shadows of the night took such shapes to him as arose out of the message, and took such shapes to the mare as arose out of *her* private topics of uneasiness. They seemed to be numerous, for she shied at every shadow on the road.

What time, the mail-coach lumbered, jolted, rattled, and bumped upon its tedious way, with its three fellow-inscrutables inside. To whom, likewise, the shadows of the night revealed themselves, in the forms their dozing eyes and wandering thoughts suggested.

Tellson's Bank had a run upon it in the mail. As the bank passenger —with an arm drawn through the leathern strap, which did what lay in it to keep him from pounding against the next passenger, and driving him into his corner, whenever the coach got a special jolt—

nodded in his place, with half-shut eyes, the little coach-windows, and the coach-lamp dimly gleaming through them, and the bulky bundle of the opposite passenger, became the bank, and did a great stroke of business. The rattle of the harness was the chink of money, and more drafts were honoured in five minutes than even Tellson's, with all its foreign and home connection, ever paid in thrice the time. Then the strong-rooms underground, at Tellson's, with such of their valuable stores and secrets as were known to the passenger (and it was not a little that he knew about them), opened before him, and he went in among them with the great keys and the feebly-burning candle, and found them safe, and strong, and sound, and still, just as he had last seen them.

But though the bank was almost always with him, and though the coach (in a confused way, like the presence of pain under an opiate) was always with him, there was another current of impression that never ceased to run all through the night. He was on his way to dig some one out of a grave.

Now which of the multitude of faces that showed themselves before him was the true face of the buried person the shadows of the night did not indicate ; but they were all the faces of a man of five-and-forty by years, and they differed principally in the passions they expressed, and in the ghastliness of their worn and wasted state. Pride, contempt, defiance, stubbornness, submission, lamentation, succeeded one another ; so did varieties of sunken cheek, cadaverous colour, emaciated hands and figures. But the face was in the main one face, and every head was prematurely white. A hundred times the dozing passenger inquired of this spectre—

" Buried how long ? "

The answer was always the same : " Almost eighteen years."

" You had abandoned all hope of being dug out ? "

" Long ago."

" You know that you are recalled to life ? "

" They tell me so."

" I hope you care to live ? "

" I can't say."

" Shall I show her to you ? Will you come and see her ? "

The answers to this question were various and contradictory. Sometimes the broken reply was, " Wait ! It would kill me if I saw her too soon." Sometimes it was given in a tender rain of tears, and then it was, " Take me to her." Sometimes it was staring and bewildered, and then it was, " I don't know her. I don't understand."

After such imaginary discourse, the passenger in his fancy would dig, and dig, dig—now with a spade, now with a great key, now with his hands—to dig this wretched creature out. Got out at last, with earth hanging about his face and hair, he would suddenly fall away to dust. The passenger would then start to himself, and lower the window, to get the reality of mist and rain on his cheek.

Yet even when his eyes were opened on the mist and rain, on the moving patch of light from the lamps, and the hedge at the roadside retreating by jerks, the night shadows outside the coach would fall into the train of the night shadows within. The real Banking House by Temple Bar, the real business of the past day, the real strong rooms, the real express sent after him, and the real message returned, would all be there. Out of the midst of them the ghostly face would rise, and he would accost it again.

"Buried how long?"

"Almost eighteen years."

"I hope you care to live?"

"I can't say."

Dig—dig—dig—until an impatient movement from one of the two passengers would admonish him to pull up the window, draw his arm securely through the leathern strap, and speculate upon the two slumbering forms, until his mind lost its hold of them, and they again slid away into the bank and the grave.

"Buried how long?"

"Almost eighteen years."

"You had abandoned all hope of being dug out?"

"Long ago."

The words were still in his hearing as just spoken—distinctly in his hearing as ever spoken words had been in his life—when the weary passenger started to the consciousness of daylight, and found that the shadows of the night were gone.

He lowered the window, and looked out at the rising sun. There was a ridge of ploughed land, with a plough upon it where it had been left last night when the horses were unyoked; beyond, a quiet coppice-wood, in which many leaves of burning red and golden yellow still remained upon the trees. Though the earth was cold and wet, the sky was clear, and the sun rose bright, placid, and beautiful.

"Eighteen years!" said the passenger, looking at the sun. "Gracious Creator of day! To be buried alive for eighteen years!"

CHAPTER IV

THE PREPARATION

WHEN the mail got successfully to Dover, in the course of the forenoon, the head drawer at the Royal George Hotel opened the coach-door as his custom was. He did it with some flourish of ceremony, for a mail journey from London in winter was an achievement to congratulate an adventurous traveller upon.

By that time there was only one adventurous traveller left to be congratulated, for the two others had been set down at their respective roadside destinations. The mildewy inside of the coach, with its damp and dirty straw, its disagreeable smell, and its obscurity, was rather like a larger dog-kennel. Mr. Lorry, the passenger, shaking himself out of it in chains of straw, a tangle of shaggy wrapper, flapping hat, and muddy legs, was rather like a larger sort of dog.

"There will be a packet to Calais to-morrow, drawer?"

"Yes, Sir, if the weather holds and the wind sets tolerable fair. The tide will serve pretty nicely at about two in the afternoon, Sir. Bed, Sir?"

"I shall not go to bed till night; but I want a bedroom and a barber."

"And then breakfast, Sir? Yes, Sir. That way, Sir, if you please. Show Concord! Gentleman's valise and hot water to Concord. Pull off gentleman's boots in Concord. (You will find a fine sea-coal fire, Sir.) Fetch barber to Concord. Stir about there, now, for Concord!"

The Concord bed-chamber being always assigned to a passenger by the mail, and passengers by the mail being always heavily wrapped up from head to foot, the room had the odd interest for the establishment of the Royal George, that, although but one kind of man was seen to go into it, all kinds and varieties of men came out of it. Consequently, another drawer, and two porters, and several maids and the landlady, were all loitering by accident at various points of the road between the Concord and the coffee-room, when a gentleman of sixty, formally dressed in a brown suit of clothes, pretty well worn, but very well kept, with large square cuffs and large flaps to the pockets, passed along on his way to his breakfast.

The coffee-room had no other occupant that forenoon than the gentleman in brown. His breakfast-table was drawn before the fire, and as he sat, with its light shining on him, waiting for the meal, he sat so still that he might have been sitting for his portrait.

Very orderly and methodical he looked, with a hand on each knee, and a loud watch ticking a sonorous sermon under his flapped waist-coat, as though it pitted its gravity and longevity against the levity and evanescence of the brisk fire. He had a good leg, and was a little vain of it, for his brown stockings fitted sleek and close and were of a fine texture; his shoes and buckles, too, though plain, were trim. He wore an odd little sleek, crisp, flaxen wig, setting very close to his head, which wig, it is to be presumed, was made of hair, but which looked far more as though it were spun from filaments of silk or glass. His linen, though not of a fineness in accordance with his stockings, was as white as the tops of the waves that broke upon the neighbouring beach, or the specks of sail that glinted in the sunlight far at sea. A face habitually suppressed and quieted was still lighted up under the quaint wig by a pair of moist bright eyes that it must have cost their owner, in years gone by, some pains to drill to the composed and reserved expression of Tellson's Bank. He had a healthy colour in his cheeks, and his face, though lined, bore few traces of anxiety. But perhaps the confidential bachelor clerks in Tellson's Bank were principally occupied with the cares of other people; and perhaps second-hand cares, like second-hand clothes, come easily off and on.

Completing his resemblance to a man who was sitting for his portrait, Mr. Lorry dropped off to sleep. The arrival of his breakfast roused him, and he said to the drawer, as he moved his chair to it—

"I wish accommodation prepared for a young lady who may come here at any time to-day. She may ask for Mr. Jarvis Lorry, or she may only ask for a gentleman from Tellson's Bank. Please to let me know."

"Yes, Sir. Tellson's Bank in London, Sir?"

"Yes."

"Yes, Sir. We have oftentimes the honour to entertain your gentlemen in their travelling backwards and forwards betwixt London and Paris, Sir. A vast deal of travelling, Sir, in Tellson and Company's House."

"Yes. We are quite a French House, as well as an English one."

"Yes, Sir. Not much in the habit of such travelling yourself, I think, Sir?"

"Not of late years. It is fifteen years since we—since I—came last from France."

"Indeed, Sir? That was before my time here, Sir. Before our people's time here, Sir. The George was in other hands at that time, Sir."

"I believe so."

"But I would hold a pretty wager, Sir, that a House like Tellson and Company was flourishing, a matter of fifty, not to speak of fifteen years ago?"

"You might treble that, and say a hundred and fifty, yet not be far from the truth."

"Indeed, Sir!"

Rounding his mouth and both his eyes as he stepped backward from the table, the waiter shifted his napkin from his right arm to his left, dropped into a comfortable attitude, and stood surveying the guest while he ate and drank, as from an observatory or watch-tower, according to the immemorial usage of waiters in all ages.

When Mr. Lorry had finished his breakfast, he went out for a stroll on the beach. The little narrow, crooked town of Dover hid itself away from the beach, and ran its head into the chalk cliffs, like a marine ostrich. The beach was a desert of heaps of sea and stones tumbling wildly about, and the sea did what it liked, and what it liked was destruction. It thundered at the town, and thundered at the cliffs, and brought the coast down, madly. The air among the houses was of so strong a piscatory flavour that one might have supposed sick fish went up to be dipped in it, as sick people went down to be dipped in the sea. A little fishing was done in the port, and a quantity of strolling about by night, and looking seaward: particularly at those times when the tide made, and was near flood. Small tradesmen, who did no business whatever, sometimes unaccountably realised large fortunes, and it was remarkable that nobody in the neighbourhood could endure a lamplighter.

As the day declined into the afternoon, and the air, which had been at intervals clear enough to allow the French coast to be seen, became again charged with mist and vapour, Mr. Lorry's thoughts seemed to cloud too. When it was dark, and he sat before the coffee-room fire, awaiting his dinner as he had awaited his breakfast, his mind was busily digging, digging, digging in the live red coals.

A bottle of good claret after dinner does a digger in the red coals no harm, otherwise than as it has a tendency to throw him out of work. Mr. Lorry had been idle a long time, and had just poured out his last glassful of wine with as complete an appearance of satisfaction as is ever to be found in an elderly gentleman of a fresh complexion who has got to the end of a bottle, when a rattling of wheels came up the narrow street, and rumbled into the inn-yard.

He set down his glass untouched. "This is Mam'selle!" said he.

In a very few minutes the waiter came in to announce that Miss Manette had arrived from London, and would be happy to see the gentleman from Tellson's.

"So soon?"

Miss Manette had taken some refreshment on the road, and required none then, and was extremely anxious to see the gentleman from Tellson's immediately, if it suited his pleasure and convenience.

The gentleman from Tellson's had nothing left for it but to empty his glass with an air of stolid desperation, settle his odd little flaxen wig at the ears, and follow the waiter to Miss Manette's apartment. It was a large, dark room, furnished in a funereal manner with black horsehair, and loaded with heavy dark tables. These had been oiled and oiled until the two tall candles on the table in the middle of the room were gloomily reflected on every leaf, as if *they* were buried in deep graves of black mahogany, and no light to speak of could be expected from them until they were dug out.

The obscurity was so difficult to penetrate that Mr. Lorry, picking his way over the well-worn Turkey carpet, supposed Miss Manette to be, for the moment, in some adjacent room, until, having got past the two tall candles, he saw standing to receive him by the table between them and the fire a young lady of not more than seventeen, in a riding-cloak, and still holding her straw travelling-hat by its ribbon in her hand. As his eyes rested on a short, slight, pretty figure, a quantity of golden hair, a pair of blue eyes that met his own with an inquiring look, and a forehead with a singular capacity (remembering how young and smooth it was) of lifting and knitting itself into an expression that was not quite one of perplexity, or wonder, or alarm, or merely of a bright fixed attention, though it included all the four expressions—as his eyes rested on these things, a sudden vivid likeness passed before him of a child whom he had held in his arms on the passage across that very Channel, one cold time, when the hail drifted heavily and the sea ran high. The likeness passed away, like a breath along the surface of the gaunt pier-glass behind her, on the frame of which a hospital procession of negro cupids, several headless and all cripples, were offering black baskets of Dead Sea fruit to black divinities of the feminine gender—and he made his formal bow to Miss Manette.

"Pray take a seat, Sir." In a very clear and pleasant young voice; a little foreign in its accent, but a very little indeed.

"I kiss your hand, Miss," said Mr. Lorry, with the manners of an earlier date, as he made his formal bow again, and took his seat.

"I received a letter from the Bank, Sir, yesterday, informing me that some intelligence—or discovery——"

"The word is not material, miss; either word will do."

"—respecting the small property of my poor father, whom I never saw—so long dead——"

Mr. Lorry moved in his chair, and cast a troubled look towards the hospital procession of negro cupids. As if *they* had any help for anybody in their absurd baskets!

"—rendered it necessary that I should go to Paris, there to communicate with a gentleman of the Bank, so good as to be despatched to Paris for the purpose."

"Myself."

"As I was prepared to hear, Sir."

She curtseyed to him (young ladies made curtseys in those days), with a pretty desire to convey to him that she felt how much older and wiser he was than she. He made her another bow.

"I replied to the Bank, Sir, that as it was considered necessary, by those who know, and who are so kind as to advise me, that I should go to France, and that as I am an orphan and have no friend who could go with me, I should esteem it highly if I might be permitted to place myself, during the journey, under that worthy gentleman's protection. The gentleman had left London, but I think a messenger was sent after him to beg the favour of his waiting for me here."

"I was happy," said Mr. Lorry, "to be entrusted with the charge. I shall be more happy to execute it."

"Sir, I thank you indeed. I thank you very gratefully. It was told me by the Bank that the gentleman would explain to me the details of the business, and that I must prepare myself to find them of a surprising nature. I have done my best to prepare myself, and I naturally have a strong and eager interest to know what they are."

"Naturally," said Mr. Lorry. "Yes—I——"

After a pause, he added, again settling the crisp flaxen wig at the ears—

"It is very difficult to begin."

He did not begin, but, in his indecision, met her glance. The young forehead lifted itself into that singular expression—but it was pretty and characteristic, besides being singular—and she raised her hand, as if with an involuntary action she caught at, or stayed some passing shadow.

"Are you quite a stranger to me, Sir?"

"Am I not?" Mr. Lorry opened his hands, and extended them outwards with an argumentative smile.

Between the eyebrows and just over the little feminine nose, the line of which was as delicate and fine as it was possible to be, the expression deepened itself as she took her seat thoughtfully in the chair by which she had hitherto remained standing. He watched her as she mused, and the moment she raised her eyes again, went on—

"In your adopted country, I presume, I cannot do better than address you as a young English lady, Miss Manette?"

"If you please, Sir."

"Miss Manette, I am a man of business. I have a business charge to acquit myself of. In your reception of it, don't heed me any more than if I was a speaking machine—truly, I am not much else. I will, with your leave, relate to you, Miss, the story of one of our customers."

"Story!"

He seemed wilfully to mistake the word she had repeated, when he added, in a hurry, "Yes, customers; in the banking business we usually call our connection our customers. He was a French gentleman; a scientific gentleman; a man of great acquirements—a Doctor."

"Not of Beauvais?"

"Why, yes, of Beauvais. Like Monsieur Manette, your father, the gentleman was of Beauvais. Like Monsieur Manette, your father, the gentleman was of repute in Paris. I had the honour of knowing him there. Our relations were business relations, but confidential. I was at that time in our French House, and had been—oh! twenty years."

"At that time—I may ask, at what time, Sir?"

"I speak, Miss, of twenty years ago. He married—an English lady—and I was one of the trustees. His affairs, like the affairs of many other French gentlemen and French families, were entirely in Tellson's hands. In a similar way I am, or I have been, trustee of one kind or other for scores of our customers. These are mere business relations, Miss; there is no friendship in them, no particular interest, nothing like sentiment. I have passed from one to another, in the course of my business life, just as I pass from one of our customers to another in the course of my business day; in short, I have no feelings; I am a mere machine. To go on——"

"But this is my father's story, Sir; and I begin to think"—the curiously roughened forehead was very intent upon him—"that when I was left an orphan through my mother's surviving my father only two years, it was you who brought me to England. I am almost sure it was you."

Mr. Lorry took the hesitating little hand that confidingly advanced to take his, and he put it with some ceremony to his lips. He then conducted the young lady straightway to her chair again, and, holding the chair-back with his left hand, and using his right by turns to rub his chin, pull his wig at the ears, or point what he said, stood looking down into her face while she sat looking up into his.

"Miss Manette, it *was* I. And you will see how truly I spoke of myself just now, in saying I had no feelings, and that all the relations I hold with my fellow-creatures are mere business relations, when you reflect that I have never seen you since. No ; you have been the ward of Tellson's House since, and I have been busy with the other business of Tellson's House since. Feelings ! I have no time for them, no chance of them. I pass my whole life, Miss, in turning an immense pecuniary Mangle."

After this odd description of his daily routine of employment, Mr. Lorry flattened his flaxen wig upon his head with both hands (which was most unnecessary, for nothing could be flatter than its shining surface was before), and resumed his former attitude.

"So far, Miss (as you have remarked), this is the story of your regretted father. Now comes the difference. If your father had not died when he did—— Don't be frightened ! How you start !"

She did, indeed, start. And she caught his wrist with both her hands.

"Pray," said Mr. Lorry, in a soothing tone, bringing his left hand from the back of the chair to lay it on the supplicatory fingers that clasped him in so violent a tremble,—"pray control your agitation—a matter of business. As I was saying——"

Her look so discomposed him that he stopped, wandered, and began anew—

"As I was saying, if Monsieur Manette had not died ; if he had suddenly and silently disappeared ; if he had been spirited away ; if it had not been difficult to guess to what dreadful place, though no art could trace him ; if he had an enemy in some compatriot who could exercise a privilege that I in my own time have known the boldest people afraid to speak of in a whisper, across the water there ; for instance, the privilege of filling up blank forms for the consignment of any one to the oblivion of a prison for any length of time ; if his wife had implored the king, the queen, the court, the clergy, for any tidings of him, and all quite in vain—then the history of your father would have been the history of this unfortunate gentleman, the Doctor of Beauvais."

"I entreat you to tell me more, Sir."

"I will. I am going to. You can bear it ? "

"I can bear anything but the uncertainty you leave me in at this moment."

"You speak collectedly, and you—*are* collected. That's good ! " (Though his manner was less satisfied than his words.) "A matter of business. Regard it as a matter of business—business that must be done. Now if this doctor's wife, though a lady of great courage and spirit, had suffered so intensely from this cause before her little child was born——"

"The little child was a daughter, Sir ? "

"A daughter. A—a—matter of business—don't be distressed. Miss, if the poor lady had suffered so intensely before her little child was born, that she came to the determination of sparing the poor child the inheritance of any part of the agony she had known the pains of, by rearing her in the belief that her father was dead—— No, don't kneel! In Heaven's name, why should you kneel to me?"

"For the truth. Oh dear, good, compassionate Sir, for the truth!"

"A—a matter of business. You confuse me, and how can I transact business if I am confused? Let us be clear-headed. If you could kindly mention now, for instance, what nine times ninepence are, or how many shillings in twenty guineas, it would be so encouraging. I should be so much more at my ease about your state of mind."

Without directly answering to this appeal, she sat so still when he had very gently raised her, and the hands that had not ceased to clasp his wrists were so much more steady than they had been, that she communicated some reassurance to Mr. Jarvis Lorry.

"That's right, that's right. Courage! Business! You have business before you; useful business. Miss Manette, your mother took this course with you. And when she died—I believe broken-hearted—having never slackened her unavailing search for your father, she left you, at two years old, to grow to be blooming, beautiful, and happy, without the dark cloud upon you of living in uncertainty whether your father soon wore his heart out in prison, or wasted there through many lingering years."

As he said the words he looked down, with an admiring pity, on the flowing golden hair, as if he pictured to himself that it might have been already tinged with gray.

"You know that your parents had no great possession, and that what they had was secured to your mother and to you. There has been no new discovery, of money, or of any other property; but——"

He felt his wrist held closer, and he stopped. The expression in the forehead, which had so particularly attracted his notice, and which was now immovable, had deepened into one of pain and horror.

"But he has been—been found. He is alive. Greatly changed, it is too probable; almost a wreck, it is possible; though we will hope the best. Still, alive. Your father has been taken to the house of an old servant in Paris, and we are going there: I, to identify him if I can; you, to restore him to life, love, duty, rest, comfort."

A shiver ran through her frame, and from it through his. She said, in a low, distinct, awe-stricken voice, as if she were saying it in a dream—

"I am going to see his Ghost! It will be his Ghost—not him!"

Mr. Lorry quietly chafed the hands that held his arm. "There, there, there! See now, see now! The best and the worst are known to you now. You are well on your way to the poor wronged gentleman, and, with a fair sea voyage, and a fair land journey, you will be soon at his dear side."

She repeated in the same tone, sunk to a whisper, "I have been free, I have been happy, yet his Ghost has never haunted me!"

"Only one thing more," said Mr. Lorry, laying stress upon it as a wholesome means of enforcing her attention; "he has been found under another name; his own, long forgotten or long concealed. It would be worse than useless now to inquire which; worse than useless to seek to know whether he has been for years overlooked, or always designedly held prisoner. It would be worse than useless now to make any inquiries, because it would be dangerous. Better not to mention the subject, anywhere or in any way, and to remove him—for a while at all events—out of France. Even I, safe as an Englishman, and even Tellson's, important as they are to French credit, avoid all naming of the matter. I carry about me not a scrap of writing openly referring to it. This is a secret service altogether. My credentials, entries, and memoranda are all comprehended in the one line, 'Recalled to Life,' which may mean anything. But what is the matter? She doesn't notice a word! Miss Manette!"

Perfectly still and silent, and not even fallen back in her chair, she sat under his hand, utterly insensible, with her eyes open and fixed upon him, and with that last expression looking as if it were carved or branded into her forehead. So close was her hold upon his arm, that he feared to detach himself lest he should hurt her; therefore he called out loudly for assistance without moving.

A wild-looking woman, whom even in his agitation Mr. Lorry observed to be all of a red colour, and to have red hair, and to be dressed in some extraordinary tight-fitting fashion, and to have on her head a most wonderful bonnet like a Grenadier wooden measure, and good measure too, or a great Stilton cheese, came running into the room in advance of the inn servants, and soon settled the question of his detachment from the poor young lady by laying a brawny hand upon his chest, and sending him flying back against the nearest wall.

("I really think this must be a man!" was Mr. Lorry's breathless reflection, simultaneously with his coming against the wall.)

"Why, look at you all!" bawled this figure, addressing the inn servants. "Why don't you go and fetch things, instead of standing there staring at me? I am not so much to look at, am I? Why don't you go and fetch things? I'll let you know, if you don't bring smelling-salts, cold water, and vinegar, quick, I will."

There was an immediate dispersal for these restoratives, and she softly laid the patient on a sofa, and tended her with great skill and gentleness, calling her "my precious!" and "my bird!" and spreading her golden hair aside over her shoulders with great pride and care.

"And you in brown!" she said, indignantly turning to Mr. Lorry; "couldn't you tell her what you had to tell her without frightening her to death? Look at her, with her pretty pale face and her cold hands. Do you call *that* being a Banker?"

Mr. Lorry was so exceedingly disconcerted by a question so hard to answer, that he could only look on, at a distance, with much feebler sympathy and humility, while the strong woman, having banished the inn servants under the mysterious penalty of "letting them know" something not mentioned if they stayed there staring, recovered her charge by a regular series of gradations, and coaxed her to lay her dropping head upon her shoulder.

" I hope she will do well now," said Mr. Lorry.

" No thanks to you in brown if she does. My darling pretty ! "

" I hope," said Mr. Lorry, after another pause of feeble sympathy and humility, " that you accompany Miss Manette to France ? "

" A likely thing, too ! " replied the strong woman. " If it was ever intended that I should go across salt water, do you suppose Providence would have cast my lot in an island ? "

This being another question hard to answer, Mr. Jarvis Lorry withdrew to consider it.

CHAPTER V

THE WINE-SHOP

A LARGE cask of wine had been dropped and broken in the street. The accident had happened in getting it out of a cart ; the cask had tumbled out with a run, the hoops had burst, and it lay on the stones just outside the door of the wine-shop, shattered like a walnut-shell.

All the people within reach had suspended their business, or their idleness, to run to the spot and drink the wine. The rough, irregular stones of the street, pointing every way, and designed, one might have thought, expressly to lame all living creatures that approached them, had dammed it into little pools ; these were surrounded each by its own jostling group or crowd, according to its size. Some men kneeled down, made scoops of their two hands joined, and sipped, or tried to help women, who bent over their shoulders, to sip, before the wine had all run out between their fingers. Others, men and women, dipped in the puddles with little mugs of mutilated earthenware, or even with handkerchiefs from women's heads, which were squeezed dry into infants' mouths ; others made small mud-embankments, to stem the wine as it ran ; others, directed by lookers-on up at high windows, darted here and there to cut off little streams of wine that started away in new directions ; others devoted themselves to the sodden and lee-dyed pieces of the cask, licking, and even champing the moister wine-rotted fragments with eager relish. There was no drainage to carry off the wine, and not only did it all get taken up, but so much mud got taken up along with it, that there might have been a scavenger in the street, if anybody acquainted with it could have believed in such a miraculous presence.

A shrill sound of laughter and of amused voices—voices of men, women, and children—resounded in the street while this wine game lasted. There was little roughness in the sport, and much playfulness. There was a special companionship in it, an observable inclination on the part of every one to join some other one, which led, especially among the luckier or lighter-hearted, to frolicsome embraces, drinking of healths, shaking of hands, and even joining of hands and dancing, a dozen together. When the wine was gone, and the places where it had been most abundant were raked into a gridiron-pattern by fingers, these demonstrations ceased, as suddenly as they had broken out. The man who had left his saw sticking in the firewood he was cutting set it in motion again; the woman who had left on a door-step the little pot of hot ashes at which she had been trying to soften the pain in her own starved fingers and toes, or in those of her child, returned to it; men with bare arms, matted locks, and cadaverous faces, who had emerged into the winter light from cellars, moved away, to descend again; and a gloom gathered on the scene that appeared more natural to it than sunshine.

The wine was red wine, and had stained the ground of the narrow street in the suburb of Saint Antoine, in Paris, where it was spilled. It had stained many hands, too, and many faces, and many naked feet, and many wooden shoes. The hands of the man who sawed the wood left red marks on the billets; and the forehead of the woman who nursed her baby was stained with the stain of the old rag she wound about her head again. Those who had been greedy with the staves of the cask had acquired a tigerish smear about the mouth; and one tall joker so besmirched, his head more out of a long squalid bag of a night-cap than in it, scrawled upon a wall with his finger dipped in muddy wine-lees—BLOOD.

The time was to come when that wine too would be spilled on the street-stones, and when the stain of it would be red upon many there.

And now that the cloud settled on Saint Antoine, which a momentary gleam had driven from his sacred countenance, the darkness of it was heavy—cold, dirt, sickness, ignorance, and want were the lords in waiting on the saintly presence—nobles of great power all of them; but most especially the last. Samples of a people that had undergone a terrible grinding and re-grinding in the mill, and certainly not in the fabulous mill which ground old people young, shivered at every corner, passed in and out at every doorway, looked from every window, fluttered in every vestige of a garment that the wind shook. The mill which had worked them down was the mill that grinds young people old; the children had ancient faces and grave voices; and upon them, and upon the grown faces, and ploughed into every furrow of age and coming up afresh, was the sign, Hunger. It was prevalent everywhere. Hunger was pushed out of the tall houses in the wretched clothing that hung upon poles and lines; Hunger was patched into them with straw and rag and wood and paper; Hunger was repeated in every fragment of the small modicum of firewood that the man sawed off; Hunger stared down from the smokeless chimneys, and started up from the filthy street that had no offal, among its refuse, of anything to eat. Hunger was the inscription on the baker's shelves, written in every small loaf of his scanty stock of bad bread; at the sausage-shop, in every dead-dog preparation that was offered for sale.   Hunger rattled its dry bones among the roasting chestnuts in the turned cylinder; Hunger was shred into atomies in every farthing porringer of husky chips of potato, fried with some reluctant drops of oil.

Its abiding place was in all things fitted to it.   A narrow winding street, full of offence and stench, with other narrow winding streets diverging, all peopled by rags and nightcaps, and all smelling of rags and nightcaps, and all visible things with a brooding look upon them that looked ill.   In the hunted air of the people there was yet some wild-beast thought of the possibility of turning at bay.   Depressed and slinking though they were, eyes of fire were not wanting among them; nor compressed lips, white with what they suppressed; nor foreheads knitted into the likeness of the gallows-rope they mused about enduring, or inflicting.   The trade signs (and they were almost as many as the shops) were, all, grim illustrations of Want.   The butcher and the porkman painted up only the leanest scrags of meat; the baker, the coarsest of meagre loaves.   The people rudely pictured as drinking in the wine-shops croaked over their scanty measures of thin wine and beer, and were gloweringly confidential together.   Nothing was represented in a flourishing condition save tools and weapons; but the cutler's knives and axes were sharp and bright, the smith's hammers were heavy, and the gunmaker's stock was murderous.   The crippling stones of the pavement, with their many little reservoirs of mud and water, had no footways, but broke off abruptly at the doors. The kennel, to make amends, ran down the middle of the street—when it ran at all, which was only after heavy rains, and then it ran, by many eccentric fits, into the houses.   Across the streets, at wide intervals, one clumsy lamp was slung by a rope and pulley; at night, when the lamplighter had let these down, and lighted, and hoisted them again, a feeble grove of dim wicks swung in a sickly manner overhead, as if they were at sea.   Indeed they were at sea, and the ship and crew were in peril of tempest.

For the time was to come when the gaunt scarecrows of that region should have watched the lamplighter, in their idleness and hunger, so long, as to conceive the idea of improving on his method, and hauling up men by those ropes and pulleys, to flare upon the darkness of their condition.   But the time was not come yet; and every wind that blew over France shook the rags of the scarecrows in vain, for the birds, fine of song and feather, took no warning.

The wine-shop was a corner shop, better than most others in its appearance and degree, and the master of the wine-shop had stood outside it, in a yellow waistcoat and green breeches, looking on at the struggle for the lost wine.   " It's not my affair," said he, with a final shrug of the shoulders.   " The people from the market did it.   Let them bring another."

There, his eyes happening to catch the tall joker writing up his joke, he called to him across the way—

" Say, then, my Gaspard, what do you do there? "

The fellow pointed to his joke with immense significance, as is often the way with his tribe. It missed its mark, and completely failed, as is often the way with his tribe too.

"What now? Are you a subject for the mad hospital?" said the wine-shop keeper, crossing the road, and obliterating the jest with a handful of mud, picked up for the purpose, and smeared over it. "Why do you write in the public streets? Is there—tell me thou—is there no other place to write such words in?"

In his expostulation he dropped his cleaner hand (perhaps accidentally, perhaps not) upon the joker's heart. The joker rapped it with his own, took a nimble spring upward, and came down in a fantastic dancing attitude, with one of his stained shoes jerked off his foot into his hand, and held out. A joker of an extremely, not to say wolfishly practical character, he looked, under those circumstances.

"Put it on, put it on," said the other. "Call wine, wine; and finish there." With that advice he wiped his soiled hand upon the joker's dress, such as it was—quite deliberately, as having dirtied the hand on his account, and then re-crossed the road and entered the wine-shop.

This wine-shop keeper was a bull-necked, martial-looking man of thirty, and he should have been of a hot temperament, for, although it was a bitter day, he wore no coat, but carried one slung over his shoulder. His shirt-sleeves were rolled up, too, and his brown arms were bare to the elbows. Neither did he wear anything more on his head than his own crisply-curling short dark hair. He was a dark man altogether, with good eyes and a good bold breadth between them. Good-humoured looking on the whole, but implacable-looking, too; evidently a man of a strong resolution and a set purpose; a man not desirable to be met rushing down a narrow pass with a gulf on either side, for nothing would turn the man.

Madame Defarge, his wife, sat in the shop behind the counter as he came in. Madame Defarge was a stout woman of about his own age, with a watchful eye that seldom seemed to look at anything, a large hand heavily ringed, a steady face, strong features, and great composure of manner. There was a character about Madame Defarge, from which one might have predicated that she did not often make mistakes against herself in any of the reckonings over which she presided. Madame Defarge, being sensitive to cold, was wrapped in fur, and had a quantity of bright shawl twined about her head, though not to the concealment of her large ear-rings. Her knitting was before her, but she had laid it down to pick her teeth with a toothpick. Thus engaged, with her right elbow supported by her left hand, Madame Defarge said nothing when her lord came in, but coughed just one grain of cough. This, in combination with the lifting of her darkly defined eyebrows over her toothpick by the breadth of a line, suggested to her husband that he would do well to look round the shop among the customers for any new customer who had dropped in while he stepped over the way.

The wine-shop keeper accordingly rolled his eyes about, until they rested upon an elderly gentleman and a young lady who were seated in a corner. Other company were there : two playing cards, two playing dominoes, three standing by the counter lengthening out a short supply of wine. As he passed behind the counter, he took notice that the elderly gentleman said in a look to the young lady, " This is our man."

"What the devil do *you* do in that galley there ? " said Monsieur Defarge to himself ; " I don't know you."

But he feigned not to notice the two strangers, and fell into discourse with the triumvirate of customers who were drinking at the counter.

" How goes it, Jacques ? " said one of these three to Monsieur Defarge. " Is all the spilt wine swallowed ? "

" Every drop, Jacques," answered Monsieur Defarge.

When this interchange of Christian name was effected, Madame Defarge, picking her teeth with her toothpick, coughed another grain of cough, and raised her eyebrows by the breadth of another line.

" It is not often," said the second of the three, addressing Monsieur Defarge, " that many of these miserable beasts know the taste of wine, or of anything but black bread and death. Is it not so, Jacques ? "

" It is so, Jacques," Monsieur Defarge returned.

At this second interchange of the Christian name Madame Defarge, still using her toothpick with profound composure, coughed another grain of cough, and raised her eyebrows by the breadth of another line.

The last of the three now said his say, as he put down his empty drinking vessel and smacked his lips.

" Ah ! So much the worse ! A bitter taste it is that such poor cattle always have in their mouths, and hard lives they live, Jacques. Am I right, Jacques ? "

" You are right, Jacques," was the response of Monsieur Defarge.

This third interchange of the Christian name was completed at the moment when Madame Defarge put her toothpick by, kept her eyebrows up, and slightly rustled in her seat.

" Hold then ! True ! " muttered her husband. " Gentlemen—my wife ! "

The three customers pulled off their hats to Madame Defarge, with three flourishes. She acknowledged their homage by bending her head, and giving them a quick look. Then she glanced in a casual manner round the wine-shop, took up her knitting with great apparent calmness and repose of spirit, and became absorbed in it.

" Gentlemen," said her husband, who had kept his bright eye observantly upon her, " good-day. The chamber, furnished bachelor-fashion, that you wished to see, and were inquiring for when I stepped out, is on the fifth floor. The doorway of the staircase gives on the little courtyard close to the left here,' pointing with his hand, " near to the window of my establishment. But, now that I remember, one of you has already been there, and can show the way. Gentlemen, adieu ! "

They paid for their wine, and left the place. The eyes of Monsieur Defarge were studying his wife at her knitting when the elderly gentleman advanced from his corner, and begged the favour of a word.

"Willingly, Sir," said Monsieur Defarge, and quietly stepped with him to the door.

Their conference was very short, but very decided. Almost at the first word, Monsieur Defarge started and became deeply attentive. It had not lasted a minute, when he nodded and went out. The gentleman then beckoned to the young lady, and they too went out. Madame Defarge knitted with nimble fingers and steady eyebrows, and saw nothing.

Mr. Jarvis Lorry and Miss Manette, emerging from the wine-shop thus, joined Monsieur Defarge in the doorway to which he had directed his other company just before. It opened from a stinking little black court-yard, and was the general public entrance to a great pile of houses, inhabited by a great number of people. In the gloomy tile-paved entry to the gloomy tile-paved staircase Monsieur Defarge bent down on one knee to the child of his old master, and put her hand to his lips. It was a gentle action, but not at all gently done; a very remarkable transformation had come over him in a few seconds. He had no good-humour in his face, nor any openness of aspect left, but had become a secret, angry, dangerous man.

"It is very high; it is a little difficult. Better to begin slowly." Thus Monsieur Defarge, in a stern voice, to Mr. Lorry, as they began ascending the stairs.

"Is he alone?" the latter whispered.

"Alone! God help him, who should be with him!" said the other, in the same low voice.

"Is he always alone, then?"

"Yes."

"Of his own desire?"

"Of his own necessity. As he was, when I first saw him after they found me and demanded to know if I would take him, and, at my peril, be discreet—as he was then, so he is now."

"He is greatly changed?"

"Changed!"

The keeper of the wine-shop stopped to strike the wall with his hand, and muttered a tremendous curse. No direct answer could have been half so forcible. Mr. Lorry's spirits grew heavier and heavier, as he and his two companions ascended higher and higher.

Such a staircase, with its accessories, in the older and more crowded parts of Paris, would be bad enough now; but at that time it was vile indeed to unaccustomed and unhardened senses. Every little habitation within the great foul nest of one high building—that is to say, the room or rooms within every door that opened on the general staircase—left its own heap of refuse on its own landing, besides flinging other refuse from its own windows. The uncontrollable and hopeless mass of decomposition so engendered would have polluted the air, even if poverty and deprivation had not loaded it with their intangible impurities ; the two bad sources combined made it almost insupportable. Through such an atmosphere, by a steep dark shaft of dirt and poison, the way lay. Yielding to his own disturbance of mind, and to his young companion's agitation, which became greater every instant, Mr. Jarvis Lorry twice stopped to rest. Each of these stoppages was made at a doleful grating, by which any languishing good airs that were left uncorrupted seemed to escape, and all spoilt and sickly vapours seemed to crawl in. Through the rusted bars, tastes, rather than glimpses, were caught of the jumbled neighbourhood ; and nothing within range, nearer or lower than the summits of the two great towers of Notre-Dame, had any promise on it of healthy life or wholesome aspirations.

At last the top of the staircase was gained, and they stopped for the third time. There was yet an upper staircase, of a steeper inclination and of contracted dimensions, to be ascended, before the garret story was reached. The keeper of the wine-shop, always going a little in advance, and always going on the side which Mr. Lorry took, as though he dreaded to be asked any question by the young lady, turned himself about here, and, carefully feeling in the pockets of the coat he carried over his shoulder, took out a key.

"The door is locked then, my friend ? " said Mr. Lorry, surprised.

"Ay. Yes," was the grim reply of Monsieur Defarge.

"You think it necessary to keep the unfortunate gentleman so retired ? "

"I think it necessary to turn the key," Monsieur Defarge whispered it closer in his ear, and frowned heavily.

"Why ? "

"Why ! Because he has lived so long locked up that he would be frightened—rave—tear himself to pieces—die—come to I know not what harm—if his door was left open."

"Is it possible ? " exclaimed Mr. Lorry.

"Is it possible !" repeated Defarge, bitterly. "Yes. And a beautiful world we live in, when it *is* possible, and when many other such things are possible, and not only possible, but done—done, see you !—under that sky there, every day. Long live the Devil. Let us go on."

This dialogue had been held in so very low a whisper, that not a word of it had reached the young lady's ears. But by this time she trembled under such strong emotion, and her face expressed such deep anxiety, and, above all, such dread and terror, that Mr. Lorry felt it incumbent on him to speak a word or two of reassurance.

"Courage, dear miss ! Courage ! Business ! The worst will be over in a moment ; it is but passing the room door, and the worst is over. Then all the good you bring to him, all the relief, all the happiness you bring to him, begin. Let our good friend here assist you on that side. That's well, friend Defarge. Come, now. Business, business ! "

They went up slowly and softly. The staircase was short, and they were soon at the top. There, as it had an abrupt turn in it, they came all at once in sight of three men, whose heads were bent down close together at the side of a door, and who were intently looking into the room to which the door belonged, through some chinks or holes in the wall. On hearing footsteps close at hand, these three turned and rose, and showed themselves to be the three of one name who had been drinking in the wine-shop.

"I forgot them in the surprise of your visit," explained Monsieur Defarge. "Leave us, good boys; we have business here."

The three glided by, and went silently down.

There appearing to be no other door on that floor, and the keeper of the wine-shop going straight to this one when they were left alone, Mr. Lorry asked him in a whisper, with a little anger—

"Do you make a show of Monsieur Manette?"

"I show him, in the way you have seen, to a chosen few."

"Is that well?"

"*I* think it is well."

"Who are the few? How do you choose them?"

"I choose them as real men, of my name—Jacques is my name—to whom the sight is likely to do good. Enough; you are English; that is another thing. Stay there, if you please, a little moment."

With an admonitory gesture to keep them back, he stooped, and looked in through the crevice in the wall. Soon raising his head again, he struck twice or thrice upon the door—evidently with no other object than to make a noise there. With the same intention he drew the key across it three or four times, before he put it clumsily into the lock, and turned it as heavily as he could.

The door slowly opened inward under his hand, and he looked into the room and said something. A faint voice answered something. Little more than a single syllable could have been spoken on either side.

He looked back over his shoulder, and beckoned them to enter. Mr. Lorry got his arm securely round the daughter's waist, and held her, for he felt that she was sinking.

"A—a—a—business, business!" he urged, with a moisture that was not of business shining on his cheek. "Come in, come in!"

"I am afraid of it," she answered, shuddering.

"Of it? What?"

"I mean of him. Of my father."

Rendered in a manner desperate by her state and by the beckoning of their conductor, he drew over his neck the arm that shook upon his shoulder, lifted her a little, and hurried her into the room. He set her down just within the door, and held her, clinging to him.

Defarge drew out the key, closed the door, locked it on the inside, took out the key again, and held it in his hand. All this he did methodically, and with as loud and harsh an accompaniment of noise as he could make. Finally, he walked across the room with a measured tread to where the window was. He stopped there, and faced round.

The garret, built to be a depository for firewood and the like, was dim and dark: for the window of dormer shape was in truth a door in the roof, with a little crane over it for the hoisting up of stores from the street, unglazed, and closing up the middle in two pieces, like any other door of French construction. To exclude the cold, one half of this door was fast closed, and the other was opened but a very little way. Such a scanty portion of light was admitted through these means, that it was difficult, on first coming in, to see anything; and long habit alone could have slowly formed in any one the ability to do any work requiring nicety in such obscurity. Yet work of that kind was being done in the garret; for, with his back towards the door, and his face towards the window where the keeper of the wine-shop stood looking at him, a white-haired man sat on a low bench, stooping forward and very busy making shoes.

CHAPTER VI

THE SHOEMAKER

"GOOD-DAY!" said Monsieur Defarge, looking down at the white head that bent low over the shoemaking.

It was raised for a moment, and a very faint voice responded to the salutation, as if it were at a distance—

"Good-day!"

"You are still hard at work, I see?"

After a long silence, the head was lifted for another moment, and the voice replied, "Yes—I am working." This time a pair of haggard eyes had looked at the questioner before the face had dropped again.

The faintness of the voice was pitiable and dreadful. It was not the faintness of physical weakness, though confinement and hard fare no doubt had their part in it. Its deplorable peculiarity was, that it was the faintness of solitude and disuse. It was like the last feeble echo of a sound made long and long ago. So entirely had it lost the life and resonance of the human voice, that it affected the senses like a once beautiful colour faded away into a poor weak stain. So sunken and suppressed it was, that it was like a voice underground. So expressive it was of a hopeless and lost creature, that a famished traveller, wearied out by lonely wandering in a wilderness, would have remembered home and friends in such a tone before lying down to die.

Some minutes of silent work had passed, and the haggard eyes had looked up again, not with any interest or curiosity, but with a dull mechanical perception, beforehand, that the spot where the only visitor they were aware of had stood was not yet empty.

"I want," said Defarge, who had not removed his gaze from the shoemaker, "to let in a little more light here. You can bear a little more?"

The shoemaker stopped his work, looked, with a vacant air of listening, at the floor on one side of him, then similarly at the floor on the other side of him, then upward at the speaker.

"What did you say?"

"You can bear a little more light?"

"I must bear it, if you let it in." (Laying the palest shadow of a stress upon the second word.)

The opened half-door was opened a little further, and secured at that angle for the time. A broad ray of light fell into the garret, and showed the workman with an unfinished shoe upon his lap, pausing in his labour. His few common tools and various scraps of leather were at his feet and on his bench. He had a white beard, raggedly cut, but not very long, a hollow face, and exceedingly bright eyes. The hollowness and thinness of his face would have caused them to look large, under his yet dark eyebrows and his confused white hair, though they had been really otherwise; but they were naturally large, and looked unnaturally so. His yellow rags of shirt lay open at the throat, and showed his body to be withered and worn. He, and his old canvas frock, and his loose stockings, and all his poor tatters of clothes, had, in a long seclusion from direct light and air, faded down to such a dull uniformity of parchment-yellow, that it would have been hard to say which was which.

He had put up a hand between his eyes and the light, and the very bones of it seemed transparent. So he sat, with a steadfastly vacant gaze, pausing in his work. He never looked at the figure before him, without first looking down on this side of himself, then on that, as if he had lost the habit of associating place with sound; he never spoke, without first wandering in this manner, and forgetting to speak.

"Are you going to finish that pair of shoes to-day?" asked Defarge, motioning to Mr. Lorry to come forward.

"What did you say?"

"Do you mean to finish that pair of shoes to-day?"

"I can't say that I mean to. I suppose so. I don't know."

But the question reminded him of his work, and he bent over it again.

Mr. Lorry came silently forward, leaving the daughter by the door. When he had stood for a minute or two by the side of Defarge, the shoemaker looked up. He showed no surprise at seeing another figure, but the unsteady fingers of one of his hands strayed to his lips as he looked at it (his lips and his nails were of the same pale lead-colour), and then the hand dropped to his work, and he once more bent over the shoe. The look and the action had occupied but an instant.

"You have a visitor, you see," said Monsieur Defarge.

"What did you say?"

"Here is a visitor."

The shoemaker looked up as before, but without removing a hand from his work.

"Come!" said Defarge. "Here is Monsieur, who knows a well-made shoe when he sees one. Show him that shoe you are working at. Take it, Monsieur."

Mr. Lorry took it in his hand.

"Tell Monsieur what kind of shoe it is, and the maker's name."

There was a longer pause than usual, before the shoemaker replied—

"I forget what it was you asked me. What did you say?"

"I said, couldn't you describe the kind of shoe, for Monsieur's information?"

"It is a lady's shoe. It is a young lady's walking-shoe. It is in the present mode. I never saw the mode. I have had a pattern in my hand." He glanced at the shoe with some little passing touch of pride.

"And the maker's name?" said Defarge.

Now that he had no work to hold, he laid the knuckles of the right hand in the hollow of the left, and then the knuckles of the left hand in the hollow of the right, and then passed a hand across his bearded chin, and so on in regular changes, without a moment's intermission. The task of recalling him from the vacancy into which he always sank when he had spoken was like recalling some very weak person from a swoon, or endeavouring, in the hope of some disclosure, to stay the spirit of a fast-dying man.

"Did you ask me for my name?"

"Assuredly I did."

"One Hundred and Five, North Tower."

"Is that all?"

"One Hundred and Five, North Tower."

With a weary sound that was not a sigh, nor a groan, he bent to work again, until the silence was again broken.

"You are not a shoemaker by trade?" said Mr. Lorry, looking steadfastly at him.

His haggard eyes turned to Defarge as if he would have transferred the question to him; but as no help came from that quarter, they turned back on the questioner when they had sought the ground.

"I am not a shoemaker by trade? No, I was not a shoemaker by trade. I—I learnt it here. I taught myself. I asked leave to——"

He lapsed away, even for minutes, ringing those measured changes on his hands the whole time. His eyes came slowly back, at last, to the face from which they had wandered; when they rested on it, he started, and resumed, in the manner of a sleeper that moment awake, reverting to a subject of last night.

"I asked leave to teach myself, and I got it with much difficulty after a long while, and I have made shoes ever since."

As he held out his hand for the shoe that had been taken from him, Mr. Lorry said, still looking steadfastly in his face—

"Monsieur Manette, do you remember nothing of me?"

The shoe dropped to the ground, and he sat looking fixedly at the questioner.

"Monsieur Manette"—Mr. Lorry laid his hand upon Defarge's

arm—" do you remember nothing of this man? Look at him. Look at me. Is there no old banker, no old business, no old servant, no old time, rising in your mind, Monsieur Manette?"

As the captive of many years sat looking fixedly, by turns, at Mr. Lorry and at Defarge, some long obliterated marks of an actively intent intelligence in the middle of the forehead gradually forced themselves through the black mist that had fallen on him. They were overclouded again, they were fainter, they were gone; but they had been there. And so exactly was the expression repeated on the fair young face of her who had crept along the wall to a point where she could see him, and where she now stood looking at him, with hands which at first had been only raised in frightened compassion, if not even to keep him off and shut out the sight of him, but which were now extending towards him, trembling with eagerness to lay the spectral face upon her warm young breast, and love it back to life and hope—so exactly was the expression repeated (though in stronger characters) on her fair young face, that it looked as though it had passed like a moving light from him to her.

Darkness had fallen on him in its place. He looked at the two, less and less attentively, and his eyes in gloomy abstraction sought the ground and looked about him in the old way. Finally, with a deep long sigh, he took the shoe up, and resumed his work.

" Have you recognised him, Monsieur?" asked Defarge, in a whisper.

" Yes; for a moment. At first I thought it quite hopeless, but I have unquestionably seen, for a single moment, the face that I once knew so well. Hush! Let us draw further back. Hush!"

She had moved from the wall of the garret, very near to the bench on which he sat. There was something awful in his unconsciousness of the figure that could have put out its hand and touched him as he stooped over his labour.

Not a word was spoken, not a sound was made. She stood, like a spirit, beside him, and he bent over his work.

It happened, at length, that he had occasion to change the instrument in his hand for his shoemaker's knife. It lay on that side of him which was not the side on which she stood. He had taken it up, and was stooping to work again, when his eyes caught the skirt of her dress. He raised them, and saw her face. The two spectators started forward, but she stayed them with a motion of her hand. She had no fear of his striking at her with the knife, though they had.

He stared at her with a fearful look, and after a while his lips began to form some words, though no sound proceeded from them. By degrees, in the pauses of his quick and laboured breathing, he was heard to say—

" What is this?"

With the tears streaming down her face, she put her two hands to her lips, and kissed them to him, then clasped them on her breast, as if she laid his ruined head there.

" You are not the jailer's daughter?"

The Shoemaker's visitor

She sighed " No."

" Who are you ? "

Not yet trusting the tones of her voice, she sat down on the bench beside him. He recoiled, but she laid her hand upon his arm. A strange thrill struck him when she did so, and visibly passed over his frame ; he laid the knife down softly, as he sat staring at her.

Her golden hair, which she wore in long curls, had been hurriedly pushed aside, and fell down over her neck. Advancing his hand by little and little, he took it up and looked at it. In the midst of the action he went astray, and, with another deep sigh, fell to work at his shoemaking.

But not for long. Releasing his arm, she laid her hand upon his shoulder. After looking doubtfully at it, two or three times, as if to be sure that it was really there, he laid down his work, put his hand to his neck, and took off a blackened string with a scrap of folded rag attached to it. He opened this, carefully, on his knee, and it contained a very little quantity of hair : not more than one or two long golden hairs, which he had, in some old day, wound off upon his finger.

He took her hair into his hand again, and looked closely at it. " It is the same. How can it be ? When was it ? How was it ? "

As the concentrating expression returned to his forehead, he seemed to become conscious that it was in hers too. He turned her full to the light, and looked at her.

" She had laid her head upon my shoulder, that night when I was summoned out—she had a fear of my going, though I had none—and when I was brought to the North Tower they found these upon my sleeve. ' You will leave me them ? They can never help me to escape in the body, though they may in the spirit.' Those were the words I said. I remember them very well."

He formed this speech with his lips many times before he could utter it. But when he did find spoken words for it, they came to him coherently, though slowly.

" How was this ?—*Was it you* ? "

Once more the two spectators started, as he turned upon her with a frightful suddenness. But she sat perfectly still in his grasp, and only said, in a low voice, " I entreat you, good gentlemen, do not come near us, do not speak, do not move ! "

" Hark ! " he exclaimed. " Whose voice was that ? "

His hands released her as he uttered this cry, and went up to his white hair, which they tore in a frenzy. It died out, as everything but his shoemaking did die out of him, and he refolded his little packet and tried to secure it in his breast ; but he still looked at her, and gloomily shook his head.

" No, no, no ; you are too young, too blooming. It can't be. See what the prisoner is. These are not the hands she knew, this is not the face she knew, this is not a voice she ever heard. No, no. She was— and He was—before the slow years of the North Tower—ages ago. What is your name, my gentle angel ? "

Hailing his softened tone and manner, his daughter fell upon her knees before him, with her appealing hands upon his breast.

"Oh Sir, at another time you shall know my name, and who my mother was, and who my father, and how I never knew their hard, hard history. But I cannot tell you at this time, and I cannot tell you here. All that I may tell you, here and now, is, that I pray to you to touch me and to bless me. Kiss me, kiss me! Oh my dear, my dear!"

His cold white head mingled with her radiant hair, which warmed and lighted it as though it were the light of Freedom shining on him.

"If you hear in my voice—I don't know that it is so, but I hope it is—if you hear in my voice any resemblance to a voice that once was sweet music in your ears, weep for it, weep for it! If you touch, in touching my hair, anything that recalls a beloved head that lay on your breast when you were young and free, weep for it, weep for it! If, when I hint to you of a Home that is before us, where I will be true to you with all my duty and with all my faithful service, I bring back the remembrance of a Home long desolate, while your poor heart pined away, weep for it, weep for it!"

She held him closer round the neck, and rocked him on her breast like a child.

"If, when I tell you, dearest dear, that your agony is over, and that I have come here to take you from it, and that we go to England to be at peace and at rest, I cause you to think of your useful life laid waste, and of our native France so wicked to you, weep for it, weep for it! And if, when I shall tell you of my name, and of my father who is living, and of my mother who is dead, you learn that I have to kneel to my honoured father, and implore his pardon for having never for his sake striven all day and lain awake and wept all night, because the love of my poor mother hid his torture from me, weep for it, weep for it! Weep for her, then, and for me! Good gentlemen, thank God! I feel his sacred tears upon my face, and his sobs strike against my heart. Oh, see! Thank God for us, thank God!"

He had sunk in her arms, and his face dropped on her breast: a sight so touching, yet so terrible in the tremendous wrong and suffering which had gone before it, that the two beholders covered their faces.

When the quiet of the garret had been long undisturbed, and his heaving breast and shaken form had long yielded to the calm that must follow all storms—emblem to humanity of the rest and silence into which the storm called Life must hush at last—they came forward to raise the father and daughter from the ground. He had gradually dropped to the floor, and lay there in a lethargy, worn out. She had nestled down with him, that his head might lie upon her arm; and her hair drooping over him curtained him from the light.

"If, without disturbing him," she said, raising her hand to Mr. Lorry as he stooped over them, after repeated blowings of his nose, "all could be arranged for our leaving Paris at once, so that, from the very door, he could be taken away——"

"But, consider. Is he fit for the journey?" asked Mr. Lorry.

"More fit for that, I think, than to remain in this city, so dreadful to him."

"It is true," said Defarge, who was kneeling to look on and hear. "More than that; Monsieur Manette is, for all reasons, best out of France. Say, shall I hire a carriage and post-horses?"

"That's business," said Mr. Lorry, resuming on the shortest notice his methodical manners; "and if business is to be done, I had better do it."

"Then be so kind," urged Miss Manette, "as to leave us here. You see how composed he has become, and you cannot be afraid to leave him with me now. Why should you be? If you will lock the door to secure us from interruption, I do not doubt that you will find him, when you come back, as quiet as you leave him. In any case, I will take care of him until you return, and then we will remove him straight."

Both Mr. Lorry and Defarge were rather disinclined to this course, and in favour of one of them remaining. But as there were not only carriage and horses to be seen to, but travelling papers, and as time pressed, for the day was drawing to an end, it came at last to their hastily dividing the business that was necessary to be done, and hurrying away to do it.

Then as the darkness closed in, the daughter laid her head down on the hard ground close at the father's side, and watched him. The darkness deepened and deepened, and they both lay quiet, until a light gleamed through the chinks in the wall.

Mr. Lorry and Monsieur Defarge had made all ready for the journey, and had brought with them, besides travelling cloaks and wrappers, bread and meat, wine, and hot coffee. Monsieur Defarge put this provender, and the lamp he carried, on the shoemaker's bench (there was nothing else in the garret but a pallet bed), and he and Mr. Lorry roused the captive, and assisted him to his feet.

No human intelligence could have read the mysteries of his mind in the scared blank wonder of his face. Whether he knew what had happened, whether he recollected what they had said to him, whether he knew that he was free, were questions which no sagacity could have solved. They tried speaking to him; but he was so confused, and so very slow to answer, that they took fright at his bewilderment, and agreed for the time to tamper with him no more. He had a wild, lost manner of occasionally clasping his head in his hands that had not been seen in him before; yet he had some pleasure in the mere sound of his daughter's voice, and invariably turned to it when she spoke.

In the submissive way of one long accustomed to obey under coercion, he ate and drank what they gave him to eat and drink, and put on the cloak and other wrappings that they gave him to wear. He readily responded to his daughter's drawing her arm through his, and took—and kept—her hand in both his own.

They began to descend; Monsieur Defarge going first with the lamp, Mr. Lorry closing the little procession. They had not traversed many steps of the long main staircase when he stopped, and stared at the roof and round at the walls.

"You remember the place, my father? You remember coming up here?"

"What did you say?"

But before she could repeat the question he murmured an answer, as if she had repeated it.

"Remember? No, I don't remember. It was so very long ago."

That he had no recollection whatever of his having been brought from his prison to that house was apparent to them. They heard him mutter, "One Hundred and Five, North Tower"; and when he looked about him, it evidently was for the strong fortress-walls which had long encompassed him. On their reaching the courtyard he instinctively altered his tread, as being in expectation of a drawbridge; and when there was no drawbridge, and he saw the carriage waiting in the open street, he dropped his daughter's hand and clasped his head again.

No crowd was about the door; no people were discernible at any of the many windows; not even a chance passer-by was in the street. An unnatural silence and desertion reigned there. Only one soul was to be seen, and that was Madame Defarge, who leaned against the door-post, knitting, and saw nothing.

The prisoner had got into a coach, and his daughter had followed him, when Mr. Lorry's feet were arrested on the step by his asking, miserably, for his shoemaking tools and the unfinished shoes. Madame Defarge immediately called to her husband that she would get them, and went, knitting, out of the lamplight, through the courtyard. She quickly brought them down and handed them in, and immediately afterwards leaned against the door-post, knitting, and saw nothing.

Defarge got upon the box, and gave the word "To the Barrier!" The postilion cracked his whip, and they clattered away under the feeble over-swinging lamps.

Under the over-swinging lamps—swinging ever brighter in the better streets, and ever dimmer in the worse—and by lighted shops, gay crowds, illuminated coffee-houses, and theatre-doors, to one of the city gates. Soldiers with lanterns, at the guard-house there. "Your papers, travellers!" "See here then, Monsieur the Officer," said Defarge, getting down, and taking him gravely apart, "these are the papers of Monsieur inside, with the white head. They were consigned to me, with him, at the——" He dropped his voice, there was a flutter among the military lanterns, and one of them being handed into the coach by an arm in uniform, the eyes connected with the arm looked, not an every day or an every night look, at Monsieur with the white head. "It is well. Forward!" from the uniform. "Adieu!" from Defarge. And so, under a short grove of feebler and feebler over-swinging lamps, out under the great grove of stars.

Beneath that arch of unmoved and eternal lights, some so remote from this little earth that the learned tell us it is doubtful whether their rays have even yet discovered it, as a point in space where anything is suffered or done, the shadows of the night were broad and black. All through the cold and restless interval, until dawn, they once more whispered in the ears of Mr. Jarvis Lorry—sitting opposite the buried man who had been dug out, and wondering what subtle powers were for ever lost to him, and what were capable of restoration—the old inquiry—

"I hope you care to be recalled to life?"

And the old answer—

"I can't say."

CHAPTER I

FIVE YEARS LATER

TELLSON'S Bank by Temple Bar was an old-fashioned place, even in the year one thousand seven hundred and eighty. It was very small, very dark, very ugly, very incommodious. It was an old-fashioned place, moreover, in the moral attribute that the partners in the House were proud of its smallness, proud of its darkness, proud of its ugliness, proud of its incommodiousness. They were even boastful of its eminence in those particulars, and were fired by an express conviction that, if it were less objectionable, it would be less respectable. This was no passive belief, but an active weapon which they flashed at more convenient places of business. Tellson's (they said) wanted no elbow-room, Tellson's wanted no light, Tellson's wanted no embellishment. Noakes and Co.'s might, or Snooks Brothers' might ; but Tellson's, thank Heaven !——

Any one of these partners would have disinherited his son on the question of rebuilding Tellson's. In this respect the House was much on a par with the Country, which did very often disinherit its sons for suggesting improvements in laws and customs that had long been highly objectionable, but were only the more respectable.

Thus it had come to pass that Tellson's was the triumphant perfection of inconvenience. After bursting open a door of idiotic obstinacy with a weak rattle in its throat, you fell into Tellson's down two steps, and came to your senses in a miserable little shop, with two little counters, where the oldest of men made your cheque shake as if the wind rustled it, while they examined the signature by the dingiest of windows, which were always under a shower-bath of mud from Fleet Street, and which were made the dingier by their own iron bars proper, and the heavy shadow of Temple Bar. If your business necessitated your seeing " the House," you were put into a species of Condemned Hold at the back, where you meditated on a misspent life, until the House came with its hands in its pockets, and you could hardly blink at it in the dismal twilight. Your money came out of, or went into, wormy old wooden drawers, particles of which flew up your nose and down your throat when they were opened and shut. Your bank-notes had a musty odour, as if they were fast decomposing into rags again. Your plate was stowed away among the neighbouring cesspools, and evil communications corrupted its good polish in a day or two. Your deeds got into extemporised strong-rooms made of kitchens and sculleries, and fretted all the fat out of their parchments into the banking-house air. Your lighter boxes of family papers went up-stairs into a Barmecide room, that always had a great dining-table in it and never had a dinner, and where, even in the year one thousand seven hundred and eighty, the first letters written to you by your old love, or by your little children, were but newly released from the horror of being ogled through the windows by the heads exposed on Temple Bar, with an insensate brutality and ferocity worthy of Abyssinia or Ashantee.

But indeed, at that time, putting to death was a recipe much in vogue with all trades and professions, and not least of all with Tellson's. Death is Nature's remedy for all things, and why not Legislation's ? Accordingly, the forger was put to Death ; the utterer of a bad note was put to Death ; the unlawful opener of a letter was put to Death ; the purloiner of forty shillings and sixpence was put to Death ; the holder of a horse at Tellson's door, who made off with it, was put to Death ; the coiner of a bad shilling was put to Death ; the sounders of three-fourths of the notes in the whole gamut of Crime were put to Death. Not that it did the least good in the way of prevention—it might almost have been worth remarking that the fact was exactly the reverse—but it cleared off (as to this world) the trouble of each particular case, and left nothing else connected with it to be looked after. Thus Tellson's, in its day, like greater places of business, its contemporaries, had taken so many lives, that if the heads laid low before it had been ranged on Temple Bar instead of being privately disposed of, they would probably have excluded what little light the ground floor had, in a rather significant manner.

Cramped in all kinds of dim cupboards and hutches at Tellson's, the oldest of men carried on the business gravely. When they took a young man into Tellson's London house, they hid him somewhere till he was old. They kept him in a dark place, like a cheese, until he had the full Tellson flavour and blue-mould upon him. Then only was he permitted to be seen, spectacularly poring over large books, and casting his breeches and gaiters into the general weight of the establishment.

Outside Tellson's—never by any means in it, unless called in—was an odd-job man, an occasional porter and messenger, who served as the live sign of the house. He was never absent during business hours, unless upon an errand, and then he was represented by his son, a grisly urchin of twelve, who was his express image. People understood that Tellson's, in a stately way, tolerated the odd-job man. The House had always tolerated some person in that capacity, and time and tide had drifted this person to the post. His surname was Cruncher, and on the youthful occasion of his renouncing by proxy the works of darkness, in the easterly parish church of Houndsditch, he had received the added appellation of Jerry.

The scene was Mr. Cruncher's private lodging in Hanging-sword Alley, Whitefriars ; the time, half-past seven of the clock on a windy March morning, Anno Domini seventeen hundred and eighty. (Mr. Cruncher himself always spoke of the year of our Lord as Anna Dominoes : apparently under the impression that the Christian era dated from the invention of a popular game, by a lady who had bestowed her name upon it.)

Mr. Cruncher's apartments were not in a savoury neighbourhood, and were but two in number, even if a closet with a single pane of glass in it might be counted as one. But they were very decently kept. Early as it was, on the windy March morning, the room in which he lay a-bed was already scrubbed throughout ; and between the cups and saucers arranged for breakfast and the lumbering deal table a very clean white cloth was spread.

Mr. Cruncher reposed under a patchwork counterpane, like a Harlequin at home. At first he slept heavily, but by degrees began to roll and surge in bed, until he rose above the surface, with his spiky hair looking as if it must tear the sheets to ribbons. At which juncture he exclaimed, in a voice of dire exasperation—

" Bust me, if she ain't at it agin ! "

A woman of orderly and industrious appearance rose from her knees in a corner, with sufficient haste and trepidation to show that she was the person referred to.

"What ! " said Mr. Cruncher, looking out of bed for a boot. " You're at it agin, are you ? "

After hailing the morn with this second salutation, he threw a boot at the woman as a third. It was a very muddy boot, and may introduce the odd circumstance connected with Mr. Cruncher's domestic economy, that whereas he often came home after banking hours with clean boots, he often got up next morning to find the same boots covered with clay.

"What," said Mr. Cruncher, varying his apostrophe after missing his mark—" what are you up to, Aggerawayter ? "

" I was only saying my prayers."

"Saying your prayers ! You're a nice woman ! What do you mean by flopping yourself down and praying agin me ? "

" I was not praying against you ; I was praying for you."

"You weren't. And if you were, I won't be took the liberty with. Here ! your mother's a nice woman, young Jerry, going a-praying agin your father's prosperity. You've got a dutiful mother, you have, my son. You've got a religious mother, you have, my boy, going and flopping herself down, and praying that the bread-and-butter may be snatched out of the mouth of her only child."

Master Cruncher (who was in his shirt) took this very ill, and, turning to his mother, strongly deprecated any praying away of his personal board.

"And what do you suppose, you conceited female," said Mr. Cruncher, with unconscious inconsistency, "that the worth of *your* prayers may be? Name the price that you put *your* prayers at!"

"They only come from the heart, Jerry. They are worth no more than that."

"Worth no more than that," repeated Mr. Cruncher. "They ain't worth much, then. Whether or no, I won't be prayed agin, I tell you. I can't afford it. I'm not a-going to be made unlucky by *your* sneaking. If you must go flopping yourself down, flop in favour of your husband and child, and not in opposition to 'em. If I had had any but a unnat'ral wife, and this poor boy had had any but a unnat'ral mother, I might have made some money last week instead of being counter-prayed and countermined and religiously circumwented into the worst of luck. B-u-u-ust me!" said Mr. Cruncher, who all this time had been putting on his clothes, "if I ain't, what with piety and one blowed thing and another, been choused this last week into as bad luck as ever a poor devil of a honest tradesman met with! Young Jerry, dress yourself, my boy, and while I clean my boots keep a eye upon your mother now and then, and if you see any signs of more flopping, give me a call. For I tell you,"—here he addressed his wife once more—"I won't be gone agin in this manner. I am as rickety as a hackney-coach, I'm as sleepy as laudanum, my lines is strained to that degree that I shouldn't know, if it wasn't for the pain in 'em, which was me and which somebody else, yet I'm none the better for it in pocket; and it's my suspicion that you've been at it from morning to night to prevent me from being the better for it in pocket, and I won't put up with it, Aggerawayter, and what do you say now!"

Growling, in addition, such phrases as "Ah! yes! You're religious, too. You wouldn't put yourself in opposition to the interests of your husband and child, would you? Not you!" and throwing off other sarcastic sparks from the whirling grindstone of his indignation, Mr. Cruncher betook himself to his boot-cleaning and his general preparation for business. In the meantime his son, whose head was garnished with tenderer spikes, and whose young eyes stood close by one another, as his father's did, kept the required watch upon his mother. He greatly disturbed that poor woman at intervals, by darting out of his sleeping closet, where he made his toilet, with a suppressed cry of "You are going to flop, mother.—Halloa, father!" and, after raising this fictitious alarm, darting in again with an undutiful grin.

Mr. Cruncher's temper was not at all improved when he came to his breakfast. He resented Mrs. Cruncher's saying grace with particular animosity.

"Now, Aggerawayter! What are you up to? At it agin?"

His wife explained that she had merely "asked a blessing."

"Don't do it!" said Mr. Cruncher, looking about, as if he rather expected to see the loaf disappear under the efficacy of his wife's petitions. "I ain't a-going to be blest out of house and home. I won't have my wittles blest off my table. Keep still!"

Exceedingly red-eyed and grim, as if he had been up all night at a party which had taken anything but a convivial turn, Jerry Cruncher worried his breakfast rather than ate it, growling over it like any four-footed inmate of a menagerie. Towards nine o'clock he smoothed his ruffled aspect, and, presenting as respectable and business-like an exterior as he could overlay his natural self with, issued forth to the occupation of the day.

It could scarcely be called a trade, in spite of his favourite description of himself as "a honest tradesman." His stock consisted of a wooden stool made out of a broken-backed chair cut down, which stool young Jerry, walking at his father's side, carried every morning to beneath the banking-house window that was nearest Temple Bar; where, with the addition of the first handful of straw that could be gleaned from any passing vehicle to keep the cold and wet from the odd-job man's feet, it formed the encampment for the day. On this post of his Mr. Cruncher was as well known to Fleet Street and the Temple as the Bar itself—and was almost as ill-looking.

Encamped at a quarter before nine, in good time to touch his three-cornered hat to the oldest of men as they passed in to Tellson's, Jerry took up his station on this windy March morning, with young Jerry standing by him, when not engaged in making forays through the Bar, to inflict bodily and mental injuries of an acute description on passing boys who were small enough for his amiable purpose. Father and son, extremely like each other, looking silently on at the morning traffic in Fleet Street, with their two heads as near to one another as the two eyes of each were, bore a considerable resemblance to a pair of monkeys. The resemblance was not lessened by the accidental circumstance that the mature Jerry bit and spat out straw, while the twinkling eyes of the youthful Jerry were as restlessly watchful of him as of everything else in Fleet Street.

The head of one of the regular indoor messengers attached to Tellson's establishment was put through the door, and the word was given—

"Porter wanted!"

"Hooray, father! Here's an early job to begin with!"

Having thus given his parent God-speed, young Jerry seated himself on the stool, entered on his reversionary interest in the straw his father had been chewing, and cogitated.

"Al-ways rusty! His fingers is al-ways rusty!" muttered young Jerry. "Where does my father get all that iron rust from? He don't get no iron rust here!"

CHAPTER II

A SIGHT

"You know the Old Bailey well, no doubt?" said one of the oldest of clerks to Jerry the messenger.

"Ye-es, Sir," returned Jerry, in something of a dogged manner. "I *do* know the Bailey."

"Just so. And you know Mr. Lorry."

"I know Mr. Lorry, Sir, much better than I know the Bailey. Much better," said Jerry, not unlike a reluctant witness at the establishment in question, "than I, as a honest tradesman, wish to know the Bailey."

"Very well. Find the door where the witnesses go in, and show the door-keeper this note for Mr. Lorry. He will then let you in."

"Into the court, Sir?"

"Into the court."

Mr. Cruncher's eyes seemed to get a little closer to one another, and to interchange the inquiry, "What do you think of this?"

"Am I to wait in the court, Sir?" he asked, as the result of that conference.

"I am going to tell you. The door-keeper will pass the note to Mr. Lorry, and do you make any gesture that will attract Mr. Lorry's attention, and show him where you stand. Then what you have to do is, to remain there until he wants you."

"Is that all, Sir?"

"That's all. He wishes to have a messenger at hand. This is to tell him you are there."

As the ancient clerk deliberately folded and superscribed the note, Mr. Cruncher, after surveying him in silence until he came to the blotting-paper stage, remarked—

"I suppose they'll be trying Forgeries this morning?"

"Treason!"

"That's quartering," said Jerry. "Barbarous!"

"It is the law," remarked the ancient clerk, turning his surprised spectacles upon him. "It is the law."

"It's hard in the law to spile a man, I think. It's hard enough to kill him, but it's wery hard to spile him, Sir."

"Not at all," returned the ancient clerk. "Speak well of the law. Take care of your chest and voice, my good friend, and leave the law to take care of itself. I give you that advice."

"It's the damp, Sir, what settles on my chest and voice," said Jerry. "I leave you to judge what a damp way of earning a living mine is."

"Well, well," said the old clerk; "we all have our various ways of gaining a livelihood. Some of us have damp ways, and some of us have dry ways. Here is the letter. Go along."

Jerry took the letter, and, remarking to himself with less internal deference than he made an outward show of, "You are a lean old one, too," made his bow, informed his son, in passing, of his destination, and went his way.

They hanged at Tyburn in those days, so the street outside Newgate had not obtained one infamous notoriety that has since attached to it. But the jail was a vile place, in which most kinds of debauchery and villainy were practised, and where dire diseases were bred, that came into court with the prisoners, and sometimes rushed straight from the dock at my Lord Chief Justice himself, and pulled him off the bench. It had more than once happened that the Judge in the black cap pronounced his own doom as certainly as the prisoner's, and even died before him. For the rest, the Old Bailey was famous as a kind of deadly inn-yard, from which pale travellers set out continually, in carts and coaches, on a violent passage into the other world, traversing some two miles and a half of public street and road, and shaming few good citizens, if any. So powerful is use, and so desirable to be good use in the beginning. It was famous, too, for the pillory, a wise old institution, that inflicted a punishment of which no one could foresee the extent; also for the whipping-post, another dear old institution, very humanising and softening to behold in action; also for extensive transactions in blood-money, another fragment of ancestral wisdom, systematically leading to the most frightful mercenary crimes that could be committed under heaven. Altogether, the Old Bailey at that date was a choice illustration of the precept that " Whatever is, is right," an aphorism that would be as final as it is lazy, did it not include the troublesome consequence that nothing that ever was, was wrong.

Making his way through the tainted crowd, dispersed up and down this hideous scene of action, with the skill of a man accustomed to make his way quietly, the messenger found out the door he sought, and handed in his letter through a trap in it. For people then paid to see the play at the Old Bailey, just as they paid to see the play in Bedlam—only the former entertainment was much the dearer. Therefore, all the Old Bailey doors were well guarded—except, indeed, the social doors by which the criminals got there, and those were always left wide open.

After some delay and demur, the door grudgingly turned on its hinges a very little way, and allowed Mr. Jerry Cruncher to squeeze himself into court.

"What's on?" he asked, in a whisper, of the man he found himself next to.

"Nothing yet."

"What's coming on?"

"The Treason case."

"The quartering one, eh?"

"Ah!" returned the man, with a relish; "he'll be drawn on a hurdle to be half-hanged, and then he'll be taken down and sliced before his own face, and then his inside will be taken out and burnt while he looks on, and then his head will be chopped off, and he'll be cut into quarters. That's the sentence."

"If he's found Guilty, you mean to say?" Jerry added, by way of proviso.

"Oh! they'll find him guilty," said the other. "Don't you be afraid of that."

Mr. Cruncher's attention was here diverted to the doorkeeper, whom he saw making his way to Mr. Lorry, with the note in his hand. Mr. Lorry sat at a table among the gentlemen in wigs; not far from a wigged gentleman, the prisoner's counsel, who had a great bundle of papers before him; and nearly opposite another wigged gentleman with his hands in his pockets, whose whole attention, when Mr. Cruncher looked at him then or afterwards, seemed to be concentrated on the ceiling of the court. After some gruff coughing and rubbing of his chin and signing with his hand, Jerry attracted the notice of Mr. Lorry, who had stood up to look for him, and who quietly nodded and sat down again.

"What's *he* got to do with the case?" asked the man he had spoken with.

"Blest if I know," said Jerry.

"What have *you* got to do with it, then, if a person may inquire?"

"Blest if I know that either," said Jerry.

The entrance of the Judge, and a consequent great stir and settling down in the court, stopped the dialogue. Presently the dock became the central point of interest. Two jailers, who had been standing there, went out, and the prisoner was brought in and put to the bar.

Everybody present, except the one wigged gentleman who looked at the ceiling, stared at him. All the human breath in the place rolled at him, like a sea, or a wind, or a fire. Eager faces strained round pillars and corners to get a sight of him; spectators in back rows stood up, not to miss a hair of him; people on the floor of the court laid their hands on the shoulders of the people before them, to help themselves at anybody's cost to a view of him — stood a-tiptoe, got upon ledges, stood upon next to nothing, to see every inch of him. Conspicuous among these latter, like an animated bit of the spiked wall of Newgate, Jerry stood, aiming at the prisoner the beery breath of a whet he had taken as he came along, and discharging it to mingle with the waves of other beer, and gin, and tea, and coffee, and what not, that flowed at him, and already broke upon the great windows behind him in an impure mist and rain.

The object of all this staring and blaring was a young man of about five-and-twenty, well-grown and well-looking, with a sunburnt cheek and a dark eye. His condition was that of a young gentleman. He was plainly dressed in black, or very dark gray, and his hair, which was long and dark, was gathered in a ribbon at the back of his neck, more to be out of his way than for ornament. As an emotion of the mind will express itself through any covering of the body, so the paleness which his situation engendered came through the brown upon his cheek, showing the soul to be stronger than the sun. He was otherwise quite self-possessed, bowed to the Judge, and stood quiet.

The sort of interest with which this man was stared and breathed at was not a sort that elevated humanity. Had he stood in peril of a less horrible sentence—had there been a chance of any one of its savage details being spared — by just so much would he have lost in his fascination. The form that was to be doomed to be so shamefully mangled was the sight; the immortal creature that was to be so butchered and torn asunder yielded the sensation. Whatever gloss the various spectators put upon the interest, according to their several arts and powers of self-deceit, the interest was, at the root of it, Ogreish.

Silence in the court! Charles Darnay had yesterday pleaded Not Guilty to an indictment denouncing him (with infinite jingle and jangle) for that he was a false traitor to our serene, illustrious, excellent, and so forth, prince, our Lord the King, by reason of his having, on divers occasions, and by divers means and ways, assisted Lewis, the French King, in his wars against our said serene, illustrious, excellent, and so forth; that was to say, by coming and going between the dominions of our said serene, illustrious, excellent, and so forth, and those of the said French Lewis, and wickedly, falsely, traitorously, and otherwise evil-adverbiously, revealing to the said French Lewis what forces our said serene, illustrious, excellent, and so forth, had in preparation to send to Canada and North America. This much, Jerry, with his head becoming more and more spiky as the law terms bristled it, made out with huge satisfaction, and so arrived circuitously at the understanding that the aforesaid, and over and over again aforesaid, Charles Darnay, stood there before him upon his trial; that the jury were swearing in; and that Mr. Attorney-General was making ready to speak.

The accused, who was (and who knew he was) being mentally hanged, beheaded, and quartered, by everybody there, neither flinched from the situation, nor assumed any theatrical air in it. He was quiet and attentive; watched the opening proceedings with a grave interest; and stood with his hands resting on the slab of wood before him, so composedly, that they had not displaced a leaf of the herbs with which it was strewn. The court was all bestrewn with herbs and sprinkled with vinegar, as a precaution against jail-air and jail-fever.

Over the prisoner's head there was a mirror, to throw the light down upon him. Crowds of the wicked and the wretched had been reflected in it, and had passed from its surface and this earth's together. Haunted in a most ghastly manner that abominable place would have been, if the glass could ever have rendered back its reflections, as the ocean is one day to give up its dead. Some passing thought of the infamy and disgrace for which it had been reserved may have struck the prisoner's mind. Be that as it may, a change in his position making him conscious of a bar of light across his face, he looked up; and when he saw the glass his face flushed, and his right hand pushed the herbs away.

It happened that the action turned his face to that side of the court which was on his left. About on a level with his eyes there sat, in that corner of the Judge's bench, two persons upon whom his look immediately rested ; so immediately, and so much to the changing of his aspect, that all the eyes that were turned upon him, turned to them.

The spectators saw in the two figures a young lady of little more than twenty, and a gentleman who was evidently her father ; a man of a very remarkable appearance in respect of the absolute whiteness of his hair, and a certain indescribable intensity of face : not of an active kind, but pondering and self-communing. When this expression was upon him, he looked as if he were old ; but when it was stirred and broken up—as it was now, in a moment, on his speaking to his daughter —he became a handsome man, not past the prime of life.

His daughter had one of her hands drawn through his arm, as she sat by him, and the other pressed upon it. She had drawn close to him, in her dread of the scene, and in her pity for the prisoner. Her forehead had been strikingly expressive of an engrossing terror and compassion that saw nothing but the peril of the accused. This had been so very noticeable, so very powerfully and naturally shown, that starers who had had no pity for him were touched by her ; and the whisper went about, " Who are they ? "

Jerry, the messenger, who had made his own observations, in his own manner, and who had been sucking the rust off his fingers in his absorption, stretched his neck to hear who they were. The crowd about him had pressed and passed the inquiry on to the nearest attendant, and from him it had been more slowly pressed and passed back ; at last it got to Jerry—

" Witnesses."

" For which side ? "

" Against."

" Against what side ? "

" The prisoner's."

The Judge, whose eyes had gone in the general direction, recalled them, leaned back in his seat, and looked steadily at the man whose life was in his hand, as Mr. Attorney-General rose to spin the rope, grind the axe, and hammer the nails into the scaffold.

CHAPTER III

A DISAPPOINTMENT

MR. ATTORNEY-GENERAL had to inform the jury that the prisoner before them, though young in years, was old in the treasonable practices which claimed the forfeit of his life. That this correspondence with the public enemy was not a correspondence of to-day, or of yesterday, or even of last year, or of the year before. That it was certain the prisoner had, for longer than that, been in the habit of passing and repassing between

France and England, on secret business of which he could give no honest account. That if it were in the nature of traitorous ways to thrive (which happily it never was), the real wickedness and guilt of his business might have remained undiscovered. That Providence, however, had put it into the heart of a person who was beyond fear and beyond reproach to ferret out the nature of the prisoner's schemes, and, struck with horror, to disclose them to his Majesty's Chief Secretary of State and most honourable Privy Council. That this patriot would be produced before them. That his position and attitude were, on the whole, sublime. That he had been the prisoner's friend, but, at once in an auspicious and an evil hour detecting his infamy, had resolved to immolate the traitor he could no longer cherish in his bosom on the sacred altar of his country. That if statues were decreed in Britain, as in ancient Greece and Rome, to public benefactors, this shining citizen would assuredly have had one. That, as they were not so decreed, he probably would not have one. That Virtue, as had been observed by the poets (in many passages which he well knew the jury would have, word for word, at the tips of their tongues; whereat the jury's countenances displayed a guilty consciousness that they knew nothing about the passages), was in a manner contagious; more especially the bright virtue known as patriotism, or love of country. That the lofty example of this immaculate and unimpeachable witness for the Crown, to refer to whom however unworthily was an honour, had communicated itself to the prisoner's servant, and had engendered in him a holy determination to examine his master's table-drawers and pockets, and secrete his papers. That he (Mr. Attorney-General) was prepared to hear some disparagement attempted of this admirable servant; but that, in a general way, he preferred him to his (Mr. Attorney-General's) brothers and sisters, and honoured him more than his (Mr. Attorney-General's) father and mother. That he called with confidence on the jury to come and do likewise. That the evidence of these two witnesses, coupled with the documents of their discovering that would be produced, would show the prisoner to have been furnished with lists of his Majesty's forces, and of their disposition and preparation, both by sea and land, and would leave no doubt that he had habitually conveyed such information to a hostile power. That these lists could not be proved to be in the prisoner's handwriting; but that it was all the same; that, indeed, it was rather the better for the prosecution, as showing the prisoner to be artful in his precautions. That the proof would go back five years, and would show the prisoner already engaged in these pernicious missions within a few weeks before the date of the very first action fought between the British troops and the Americans. That, for these reasons, the jury, being a loyal jury (as he knew they were), and being a responsible jury (as *they* knew they were), must positively find the prisoner Guilty, and make an end of him, whether they liked it or not. That they never could lay their heads upon their pillows; that they never could tolerate the idea of their wives laying their heads upon their pillows; that they never could endure the notion of their children laying their heads upon their pillows ; in short, that there never more could be, for them or theirs, any laying of heads upon pillows at all, unless the prisoner's head was taken off. That head Mr. Attorney-General concluded by demanding of them, in the name of everything he could think of with a round turn it it, and on the faith of his solemn asseveration that he already considered the prisoner as good as dead and gone.

When the Attorney-General ceased, a buzz arose in the court, as if a cloud of great blue-flies were swarming about the prisoner, in anticipation of what he was soon to become. When toned down again, the unimpeachable patriot appeared in the witness-box.

Mr. Solicitor-General then, following his leader's lead, examined the patriot : John Barsad, gentleman, by name. The story of his pure soul was exactly what Mr. Attorney-General had described it to be—perhaps, if it had a fault, a little too exactly. Having released his noble bosom of its burden, he would have modestly withdrawn himself, but that the wigged gentleman with the papers before him, sitting not far from Mr. Lorry, begged to ask him a few questions. The wigged gentleman sitting opposite still looking at the ceiling of the court.

Had he ever been a spy himself ? No, he scorned the base insinuation. What did he live upon ? His property. Where was his property ? He didn't precisely remember where it was. What was it ? No business of anybody's. Had he inherited it ? Yes, he had. From whom ? Distant relation. Very distant ? Rather. Ever been in prison ? Certainly not. Never in a debtors' prison ? Didn't see what that had to do with it. Never in a debtors' prison ?—Come, once again. Never ? Yes. How many times ? Two or three times. Not five or six ? Perhaps. Of what profession ? Gentleman. Ever been kicked ? Might have been. Frequently ? No. Ever kicked down-stairs ? Decidedly not ; once received a kick on the top of a staircase, and fell down-stairs of his own accord. Kicked on that occasion for cheating at dice ? Something to that effect was said by the intoxicated liar who committed the assault, but it was not true. Swear it was not true ? Positively. Ever live by cheating at play ? Never. Ever live by play ? Not more than other gentlemen do. Ever borrow money of the prisoner ? Yes. Ever pay him ? No. Was not this intimacy with the prisoner, in reality a very slight one, forced upon the prisoner in coaches, inns, and packets ? No. Sure he saw the prisoner with these lists ? Certain. Knew no more about the lists ? No. Had not procured them himself, for instance ? No. Expect to get anything by this evidence ? No. Not in regular government pay and employment to lay traps ? Oh dear no. Or to do anything ? Oh dear no. Swear that ? Over and over again. No motives but motives of sheer patriotism ? None whatever.

The virtuous servant, Roger Cly, swore his way through the case at a great rate. He had taken service with the prisoner, in good faith and simplicity, four years ago. He had asked the prisoner, aboard the Calais packet, if he wanted a handy fellow, and the prisoner had engaged him. He had not asked the prisoner to take the handy fellow as an act of charity—never thought of such a thing. He began to have suspicions of the prisoner, and to keep an eye upon him, soon afterwards. In arranging his clothes, while travelling, he had seen similar lists to these in the prisoner's pockets, over and over again. He had taken these lists from the drawer of the prisoner's desk. He had not put them there first. He had seen the prisoner show these identical lists to French gentlemen at Calais, and similar lists to French gentlemen, both at Calais and Boulogne. He loved his country, and couldn't bear it, and had given information. He had never been suspected of stealing a silver tea-pot ; he had been maligned respecting a mustard-pot, but it turned out to be only a plated one. He had known the last witness seven or eight years ; that was merely a coincidence. He didn't call it a particularly curious coincidence ; most coincidences were curious. Neither did he call it a curious coincidence that true patriotism was *his* only motive too. He was a true Briton, and hoped there were many like him.

The blue-flies buzzed again, and Mr. Attorney-General called Mr. Jarvis Lorry.

" Mr. Jarvis Lorry, are you a clerk in Tellson's bank ? "

" I am."

" On a certain Friday night in November one thousand seven hundred and seventy-five, did business occasion you to travel between London and Dover by the mail ? "

" It did."

" Were there any other passengers in the mail ? "

" Two."

" Did they alight on the road in the course of the night ? "

" They did."

" Mr. Lorry, look upon the prisoner. Was he one of those two passengers ? "

" I cannot undertake to say that he was."

" Does he resemble either of these two passengers ? "

" Both were so wrapped up, and the night was so dark, and we were all so reserved, that I cannot undertake to say even that."

" Mr. Lorry, look again upon the prisoner. Supposing him wrapped up as those two passengers were, is there anything in his bulk and stature to render it unlikely that he was one of them ? "

" No."

" You will not swear, Mr. Lorry, that he was not one of them ? "

" No."

" So at least you say he may have been one of them ? "

" Yes.   Except that I remember them both to have been—like myself —timorous of highwaymen, and the prisoner has not a timorous air."

" Did you ever see a counterfeit of timidity, Mr. Lorry ? "

" I certainly have seen that ? "

" Mr. Lorry, look once more upon the prisoner. Have you seen him, to your certain knowledge, before ? "

"I have."

"When?"

"I was returning from France a few days afterwards, and, at Calais, the prisoner came on board the packet-ship in which I returned, and made the voyage with me."

"At what hour did he come on board?"

"At a little after midnight."

"In the dead of the night. Was he the only passenger who came on board at that untimely hour?"

"He happened to be the only one."

"Never mind about 'happening,' Mr. Lorry. He was the only passenger who came on board in the dead of the night?"

"He was."

"Were you travelling alone, Mr. Lorry, or with any companion?"

"With two companions. A gentleman and lady. They are here."

"They are here. Had you any conversation with the prisoner?"

"Hardly any. The weather was stormy, and the passage long and rough, and I lay on a sofa, almost from shore to shore."

"Miss Manette!"

The young lady, to whom all eyes had been turned before, and were now turned again, stood up where she had sat. Her father rose with her, and kept her hand drawn through his arm.

"Miss Manette, look upon the prisoner."

To be confronted with such pity, and such earnest youth and beauty, was far more trying to the accused than to be confronted with all the crowd. Standing, as it were, apart with her on the edge of his grave, not all the staring curiosity that looked on could, for the moment, nerve him to remain quite still. His hurried right hand parcelled out the herbs before him into imaginary beds of flowers in a garden; and his efforts to control and steady his breathing shook the lips from which the colour rushed to his heart. The buzz of the great flies was loud again.

"Miss Manette, have you seen the prisoner before?"

"Yes, Sir."

"Where?"

"On board of the packet-ship just now referred to, Sir, and on the same occasion."

"You are the young lady just now referred to?"

"Oh! most unhappily, I am!"

The plaintive tone of her compassion merged into the less musical voice of the Judge, as he said, somewhat fiercely: "Answer the questions put to you, and make no remark upon them."

"Miss Manette, had you any conversation with the prisoner on that passage across the Channel?"

"Yes, Sir."

"Recall it."

In the midst of a profound stillness, she faintly began—

"When the gentleman came on board——"

(M 982)

"Do you mean the prisoner?" inquired the Judge, knitting his brows.

"Yes, my Lord."

"Then say the prisoner."

"When the prisoner came on board, he noticed that my father," turning her eyes lovingly to him as he stood beside her, "was much fatigued and in a very weak state of health. My father was so reduced that I was afraid to take him out of the air, and I had made a bed for him on the deck near the cabin steps, and I sat on the deck at his side to take care of him. There were no other passengers that night but we four. The prisoner was so good as to beg permission to advise me how I could shelter my father from the wind and weather better than I had done. I had not known how to do it well, not understanding how the wind would set when we were out of the harbour. He did it for me. He expressed great gentleness and kindness for my father's state, and I am sure he felt it. That was the manner of our beginning to speak together."

"Let me interrupt you for a moment. Had he come on board alone?"

"No."

"How many were with him?"

"Two French gentlemen."

"Had they conferred together?"

"They had conferred together until the last moment, when it was necessary for the French gentlemen to be landed in their boat."

"Had any papers been handed about among them, similar to these lists?"

"Some papers had been handed about among them, but I don't know what papers."

"Like these in shape and size?"

"Possibly, but indeed I don't know, although they stood whispering very near to me, because they stood at the top of the cabin steps to have the light of the lamp that was hanging there; it was a dull lamp, and they spoke very low, and I did not hear what they said, and saw only that they looked at papers."

"Now, to the prisoner's conversation, Miss Manette."

"The prisoner was as open in his confidence with me—which arose out of my helpless situation—as he was kind, and good, and useful to my father. I hope," bursting into tears, "I may not repay him by doing him harm to-day."

Buzzing from the blue-flies.

"Miss Manette, if the prisoner does not perfectly understand that you give the evidence which it is your duty to give—which you must give—and which you cannot escape from giving—with great unwillingness, he is the only person present in that condition. Please to go on."

"He told me that he was travelling on business of a delicate and difficult nature, which might get people into trouble, and that he was therefore travelling under an assumed name. He said that this business had, within a few days, taken him to France, and might, at intervals, take him backwards and forwards between France and England for a long time to come."

"Did he say anything about America, Miss Manette? Be particular."

"He tried to explain to me how that quarrel had arisen, and he said that, so far as he could judge, it was a wrong and foolish one on England's part. He added, in a jesting way, that perhaps George Washington might gain almost as great a name in history as George the Third. But there was no harm in his way of saying this; it was said laughingly, and to beguile the time."

Any strongly marked expression of face on the part of a chief actor in a scene of great interest to whom many eyes are directed will be unconsciously imitated by the spectators. Her forehead was painfully anxious and intent as she gave this evidence, and, in the pauses when she stopped for the Judge to write it down, watched its effect upon the counsel for and against. Among the lookers-on there was the same expression in all quarters of the court; insomuch that a great majority of the foreheads there might have been mirrors reflecting the witness, when the Judge looked up from his notes to glare at that tremendous heresy about George Washington.

Mr. Attorney-General now signified to my Lord that he deemed it necessary, as a matter of precaution and form, to call the young lady's father, Doctor Manette; who was called accordingly.

"Doctor Manette, look upon the prisoner. Have you ever seen him before?"

"Once. When he called at my lodgings in London. Some three years, or three years and a half ago."

"Can you identify him as your fellow-passenger on board the packet, or speak to his conversation with your daughter?"

"Sir, I can do neither."

"Is there any particular and special reason for your being unable to do either?"

He answered, in a low voice, "There is."

"Has it been your misfortune to undergo a long imprisonment, without trial, or even accusation, in your native country, Doctor Manette?"

He answered, in a tone that went to every heart, "A long imprisonment."

"Were you newly released on the occasion in question?"

"They tell me so."

"Have you no remembrance of the occasion?"

"None. My mind is a blank, from some time—I cannot even say what time—when I employed myself, in my captivity, in making shoes, to the time when I found myself living in London with my dear daughter here. She had become familiar to me, when a gracious God restored my faculties; but I am quite unable even to say how she had become familiar. I have no remembrance of the process."

Mr. Attorney-General sat down, and the father and daughter sat down together.

A singular circumstance then arose in the case. The object in hand being to show that the prisoner went down, with some fellow-plotter untracked, in the Dover mail on that Friday night in November five years ago, and got out of the mail in the night, as a blind, at a place where he did not remain, but from which he travelled back some dozen miles or more, to a garrison and dockyard, and there collected information, a witness was called to identify him as having been, at the precise time required, in the coffee-room of an hotel in that garrison-and-dockyard town, waiting for another person. The prisoner's counsel was cross-examining this witness with no result, except that he had never seen the prisoner on any other occasion, when the wigged gentleman who had all this time been looking at the ceiling of the court wrote a word or two on a little piece of paper, screwed it up, and tossed it to him. Opening this piece of paper in the next pause, the counsel looked with great attention and curiosity at the prisoner.

"You say again you are quite sure that it *was* the prisoner?"

The witness was quite sure.

"Did you ever see anybody very like the prisoner?"

Not so like (the witness said) as that he could be mistaken.

"Look well upon that gentleman, my learned friend there," pointing to him who had tossed the paper over, "and then look well upon the prisoner. How say you? Are they very like each other?"

Allowing for my learned friend's appearance being careless and slovenly, if not debauched, they were sufficiently like each other to surprise, not only the witness, but everybody present, when they were thus brought into comparison. My Lord being prayed to bid my learned friend lay aside his wig, and giving no very gracious consent, the likeness became much more remarkable. My Lord inquired of Mr. Stryver (the prisoner's counsel) whether they were next to try Mr. Carton (name of my learned friend) for treason. But Mr. Stryver replied to my Lord, no; but he would ask the witness to tell him whether what happened once might happen twice; whether he would have been so confident if he had seen this illustration of his rashness sooner, whether he would be so confident, having seen it; and more. The upshot of which was to smash this witness like a crockery vessel, and shiver his part of the case to useless lumber.

Mr. Cruncher had by this time taken quite a lunch of rust off his fingers in his following of the evidence. He had now to attend while Mr. Stryver fitted the prisoner's case on the jury, like a compact suit of clothes, showing them how the patriot, Barsad, was a hired spy and traitor, an unblushing trafficker in blood, and one of the greatest scoundrels upon earth since accursed Judas—which he certainly did look rather like. How the virtuous servant, Cly, was his friend and partner, and was worthy to be; how the watchful eyes of those forgers and false swearers had rested on the prisoner as a victim, because some family affairs in France, he being of French extraction, did require his making those passages across the Channel—though what those affairs were, a consideration for others who were near and dear to him forbade him, even for his life, to disclose. How the evidence that had been warped and wrested from the young lady, whose anguish in giving it they had witnessed, came to nothing, involving the mere little innocent gallantries and politenesses likely to pass between any young gentleman and young lady so thrown together—with the exception of that reference to George Washington, which was altogether too extravagant and impossible to be regarded in any other light than as a monstrous joke. How it would be a weakness in the government to break down in this attempt to practise for popularity on the lowest national antipathies and fears, and therefore Mr. Attorney-General had made the most of it; how, nevertheless, it rested upon nothing, save that vile and infamous character of evidence too often disfiguring such cases, and of which the State Trials of this country were full. But there my Lord interposed (with as grave a face as if it had not been true), saying that he could not sit upon that Bench and suffer those allusions.

Mr. Stryver then called his few witnesses, and Mr. Cruncher had next to attend while Mr. Attorney-General turned the whole suit of clothes Mr. Stryver had fitted on the jury inside out, showing how Barsad and Cly were even a hundred times better than he had thought them, and the prisoner a hundred times worse. Lastly came my Lord himself, turning the suit of clothes, now inside out, now outside in, but on the whole decidedly trimming and shaping them into grave-clothes for the prisoner.

And now the jury turned to consider, and the great flies swarmed again.

Mr. Carton, who had so long sat looking at the ceiling of the court, changed neither his place nor his attitude, even in this excitement. While his learned friend, Mr. Stryver, massing his papers before him, whispered with those who sat near, and from time to time glanced anxiously at the jury; while all the spectators moved more or less, and grouped themselves anew; while even my Lord himself arose from his seat, and slowly paced up and down his platform, not unattended by a suspicion in the minds of the audience that his state was feverish; this one man sat leaning back, with his torn gown half off him, his untidy wig put on just as it had happened to light on his head after its removal, his hands in his pockets, and his eyes on the ceiling, as they had been all day. Something especially reckless in his demeanour not only gave him a disreputable look, but so diminished the strong resemblance he undoubtedly bore to the prisoner (which his momentary earnestness, when they were compared together, had strengthened), that many of the lookers-on, taking note of him now, said to one another they would hardly have thought the two were so alike. Mr. Cruncher made the observation to his next neighbour, and added, "I'd hold half a guinea that *he* don't get no law-work to do. Don't look like the sort of one to get any, do he?"

Yet this Mr. Carton took in more of the details of the scene than he appeared to take in ; for now, when Miss Manette's head dropped upon her father's breast, he was the first to see it, and to say audibly : "Officer ! look to that young lady. Help the gentleman to take her out. Don't you see she will fall ! "

There was much commiseration for her as she was removed, and much sympathy with her father. It had evidently been a great distress to him to have the days of his imprisonment recalled. He had shown strong internal agitation when he was questioned, and that pondering or brooding look which made him old had been upon him, like a heavy cloud, ever since. As he passed out, the jury, who had turned back and paused a moment, spoke, through their foreman.

They were not agreed, and wished to retire. My Lord (perhaps with George Washington on his mind) showed some surprise that they were not agreed, but signified his pleasure that they should retire under watch and ward, and retired himself. The trial had lasted all day, and the lamps in the court were now being lighted. It began to be rumoured that the jury would be out a long while. The spectators dropped off to get refreshment, and the prisoner withdrew to the back of the dock, and sat down.

Mr. Lorry, who had gone out when the young lady and her father went out, now reappeared, and beckoned to Jerry, who, in the slackened interest, could easily get near him.

"Jerry, if you wish to take something to eat, you can. But keep in the way. You will be sure to hear when the jury comes in. Don't be a moment behind them, for I want you to take the verdict back to the bank. You are the quickest messenger I know, and will get to Temple Bar long before I can."

Jerry had just enough forehead to knuckle, and he knuckled it in acknowledgment of this communication and a shilling. Mr. Carton came up at the moment, and touched Mr. Lorry on the arm.

"How is the young lady ? "

"She is greatly distressed ; but her father is comforting her, and she feels the better for being out of court."

"I'll tell the prisoner so. It won't do for a respectable bank gentleman like you to be seen speaking to him publicly, you know."

Mr. Lorry reddened as if he were conscious of having debated the point in his mind, and Mr. Carton made his way to the outside of the bar. The way out of court lay in that direction, and Jerry followed him, all eyes, ears, and spikes.

"Mr. Darnay ! "

The prisoner came forward directly.

"You will naturally be anxious to hear of the witness, Miss Manette. She will do very well. You have seen the worst of her agitation."

"I am deeply sorry to have been the cause of it. Could you tell her so for me, with my fervent acknowledgments ? "

"Yes, I could. I will, if you ask it."

Mr. Carton's manner was so careless as to be almost insolent. He stood, half turned from the prisoner, lounging with his elbow against the bar.

" I do ask it. Accept my cordial thanks."

" What," said Carton, still only half turned towards him, " do you expect, Mr. Darnay ? "

" The worst."

" It's the wisest thing to expect, and the likeliest. But I think their withdrawing is in your favour."

Loitering on the way out of court not being allowed, Jerry heard no more, but left them—so like each other in feature, so unlike each other in manner—standing side by side, both reflected in the glass above them.

An hour and a half limped heavily away in the thief-and-rascal-crowded passages below, even though assisted off with mutton pies and ale. The hoarse messenger, uncomfortably seated on a form after taking that refection, had dropped into a doze, when a loud murmur and a rapid tide of people setting up the stairs that led to the court carried him along with them.

" Jerry ! Jerry ! " Mr. Lorry was already calling at the door when he got there.

" Here, Sir ! It's a fight to get back again. Here I am, Sir ! "

Mr. Lorry handed him a paper through the throng. " Quick ! Have you got it ? "

" Yes, Sir ! "

Hastily written on the paper was the word " ACQUITTED."

" If you had sent the message, ' Recalled to Life,' again," muttered Jerry, as he turned, " I should have known what you meant, this time."

He had no opportunity of saying, or so much as thinking, anything else, until he was clear of the Old Bailey ; for the crowd came pouring out with a vehemence that nearly took him off his legs, and a loud buzz swept into the street, as if the baffled blue-flies were dispersing in search of other carrion.

CHAPTER IV

CONGRATULATORY

FROM the dimly-lighted passages of the court the last sediment of the human stew that had been boiling there all day was straining off, when Doctor Manette, Lucie Manette, his daughter, Mr. Lorry, the solicitor for the defence, and its counsel, Mr. Stryver, stood gathered round Mr. Charles Darnay—just released—congratulating him on his escape from death.

It would have been difficult, by a far brighter light, to recognise in Doctor Manette, intellectual of face and upright of bearing, the shoe-maker of the garret in Paris. Yet no one could have looked at him twice without looking again, even though the opportunity of observation had not extended to the mournful cadence of his low grave voice, and to the abstraction that overclouded him fitfully, without any apparent reason. While one external cause, and that a reference to his long lingering agony, would always—as on the trial—evoke this condition from the depths of his soul, it was also in its nature to arise of itself, and to draw a gloom over him, as incomprehensible to those unacquainted with his story as if they had seen the shadow of the actual Bastille thrown upon him by a summer sun, when the substance was three hundred miles away.

Only his daughter had the power of charming this black brooding from his mind. She was the golden thread that united him to a Past beyond his misery, and to a Present beyond his misery ; and the sound of her voice, the light of her face, the touch of her hand, had a strong beneficial influence with him almost always. Not absolutely always, for she could recall some occasions on which her power had failed ; but they were few and slight, and she believed them over.

Mr. Darnay had kissed her hand fervently and gratefully, and had turned to Mr. Stryver, whom he warmly thanked. Mr. Stryver, a man of little more than thirty, but looking twenty years older than he was, stout, loud, red, bluff, and free from any drawback of delicacy, had a pushing way of shouldering himself (morally and physically) into companies and conversations, that argued well for his shouldering his way up in life.

He still had his wig and gown on, and he said, squaring himself at his late client to that degree that he squeezed the innocent Mr. Lorry clean out of the group : "I am glad to have brought you off with honour, Mr. Darnay. It was an infamous prosecution, grossly infamous ; but not the less likely to succeed on that account."

"You have laid me under an obligation to you for life—in two senses," said his late client, taking his hand.

"I have done my best for you, Mr. Darnay ; and my best is as good as another man's, I believe."

It clearly being incumbent on some one to say, "Much better," Mr. Lorry said it, perhaps not quite disinterestedly, but with the interested object of squeezing himself back again.

"You think so ? " said Mr. Stryver. "Well ! you have been present all day, and you ought to know. You are a man of business, too."

"And as such," quoth Mr. Lorry, whom the counsel learned in the law had now shouldered back into the group, just as he had previously shouldered him out of it—"as such I will appeal to Doctor Manette to break up this conference and order us all to our homes. Miss Lucie looks ill ; Mr. Darnay has had a terrible day ; we are worn out."

"Speak for yourself, Mr. Lorry," said Stryver ; "I have a night's work to do yet. Speak for yourself."

"I speak for myself," answered Mr. Lorry, "and for Mr. Darnay, and for Miss Lucie, and—— Miss Lucie, do you not think I may speak for us all ? " He asked her the question pointedly, and with a glance at her father.

His face had become frozen, as it were, in a very curious look at Darnay : an intent look, deepening into a frown of dislike and distrust, not even unmixed with fear. With this strange expression on him his thoughts had wandered away.

" My father," said Lucie, softly laying her hand on his.

He slowly shook the shadow off, and turned to her.

" Shall we go home, my father ? "

With a long breath, he answered "Yes."

The friends of the acquitted prisoner had dispersed, under the impression—which he himself had originated—that he would not be released that night. The lights were nearly all extinguished in the passages, the iron gates were being closed with a jar and a rattle, and the dismal place was deserted until to-morrow morning's interest of gallows, pillory, whipping-post, and branding-iron should re-people it. Walking between her father and Mr. Darnay, Lucie Manette passed into the open air. A hackney-coach was called, and the father and daughter departed in it.

Mr. Stryver had left them in the passages, to shoulder his way back to the robing-room. Another person, who had not joined the group, or interchanged a word with any one of them, but who had been leaning against the wall where its shadow was darkest, had silently strolled out after the rest, and had looked on until the coach drove away. He now stepped up to where Mr. Lorry and Mr. Darnay stood upon the pavement.

"So, Mr. Lorry ! Men of business may speak to Mr. Darnay now ? "

Nobody had made any acknowledgment of Mr. Carton's part in the day's proceedings ; nobody had known of it. He was unrobed, and was none the better for it in appearance.

" If you knew what a conflict goes on in the business mind, when the business mind is divided between good-natured impulse and business appearances, you would be amused, Mr. Darnay."

Mr. Lorry reddened, and said, warmly, " You have mentioned that before, Sir. We men of business, who serve a House, are not our own masters. We have to think of the House more than ourselves."

" *I* know, *I* know," rejoined Mr. Carton, carelessly. " Don't be nettled, Mr. Lorry. You are as good as another, I have no doubt : better, I daresay."

" And indeed, Sir," pursued Mr. Lorry, not minding him, " I really don't know what you have to do with the matter. If you'll excuse me, as very much your elder, for saying so, I really don't know that it is your business."

" Business ! Bless you, *I* have no business," said Mr. Carton.

" It is a pity you have not, Sir."

" I think so, too."

" If you had," pursued Mr. Lorry, "perhaps you would attend to it."

" Lord love you, no !—I shouldn't," said Mr. Carton.

" Well, Sir ! " cried Mr. Lorry, thoroughly heated by his indifference, "business is a very good thing, and a very respectable thing. And, Sir, if business imposes its restraints and its silences and impediments, Mr. Darnay as a young gentleman of generosity knows how to make allowance for that circumstance. Mr. Darnay, good-night, God bless you, Sir! I hope you have been this day preserved for a prosperous and happy life.—Chair there!"

Perhaps a little angry with himself, as well as with the barrister, Mr. Lorry bustled into the chair, and was carried off to Tellson's. Carton, who smelt of port wine, and did not appear to be quite sober, laughed then, and turned to Darnay—

"This is a strange chance that throws you and me together. This must be a strange night to you, standing alone here with your counterpart on these street stones?"

"I hardly seem yet," returned Charles Darnay, "to belong to this world again."

"I don't wonder at it; it's not so long since you were pretty far advanced on your way to another. You speak faintly."

"I begin to think I *am* faint."

"Then why the devil don't you dine? I dined, myself, while those numskulls were deliberating which world you should belong to—this, or some other. Let me show you the nearest tavern to dine well at."

Drawing his arm through his own, he took him down Ludgate Hill to Fleet Street, and so, up a covered way, into a tavern. Here they were shown into a little room, were Charles Darnay was soon recruiting his strength with a good plain dinner and good wine; while Carton sat opposite to him at the same table, with his separate bottle of port before him, and his fully half-insolent manner upon him.

"Do you feel, yet, that you belong to this terrestrial scheme again, Mr. Darnay?"

"I am frightfully confused regarding time and place; but I am so far mended as to feel that."

"It must be an immense satisfaction!"

He said it bitterly, and filled up his glass again, which was a large one.

"As to me, the greatest desire I have is to forget that I belong to it. It has no good in it for me—except wine like this—nor I for it. So we are not much alike in that particular. Indeed, I begin to think we are not much alike in any particular, you and I."

Confused by the emotion of the day, and feeling his being there with this Double of coarse deportment to be like a dream, Charles Darnay was at a loss how to answer; finally, answered not at all.

"Now your dinner is done," Carton presently said, "why don't you call a health, Mr. Darnay; why don't you give your toast?"

"What health? What toast?"

"Why, it's on the tip of your tongue. It ought to be, it must be, I'll swear it's there."

"Miss Manette, then!"

"Miss Manette, then!"

A disappointed Drudge

Looking his companion full in the face while he drank the toast, Carton flung his glass over his shoulder against the wall, where it shivered to pieces ; then rang the bell, and ordered in another.

"That's a fair young lady to hand to a coach in the dark, Mr. Darnay !" he said, filling his new goblet.

A slight frown and a laconic "Yes" were the answer.

"That's a fair young lady to be pitied by and wept for by ! How does it feel ? Is it worth being tried for one's life to be the object of such sympathy and compassion, Mr. Darnay ?"

Again Darnay answered not a word.

"She was mightily pleased to have your message, when I gave it her. Not that she showed she was pleased, but I suppose she was."

The allusion served as a timely reminder to Darnay that this disagreeable companion had, of his own free will, assisted him in the strait of the day. He turned the dialogue to that point, and thanked him for it.

"I neither want any thanks, nor merit any," was the careless rejoinder. "It was nothing to do, in the first place ; and I don't know why I did it, in the second. Mr. Darnay, let me ask you a question."

"Willingly, and a small return for your good offices."

"Do you think I particularly like you ?"

"Really, Mr. Carton," returned the other, oddly disconcerted, "I have not asked myself the question."

"But ask yourself the question now."

"You have acted as if you do ; but I don't think you do."

"*I* don't think I do," said Carton. "I begin to have a very good opinion of your understanding."

"Nevertheless," pursued Darnay, rising to ring the bell, "there is nothing in that, I hope, to prevent my calling the reckoning, and our parting without ill-blood on either side."

Carton rejoining, "Nothing in life !" Darnay rang. "Do you call the whole reckoning ?" said Carton. On his answering in the affirmative, "Then bring me another pint of this same wine, drawer, and come and wake me at ten."

The bill being paid, Charles Darnay rose and wished him good-night. Without returning the wish, Carton rose too, with something of a threat of defiance in his manner, and said, "A last word, Mr. Darnay ; you think I am drunk ?"

"I think you have been drinking, Mr. Carton."

"Think ! You know I have been drinking."

"Since I must say so, I know it."

"Then you shall likewise know why. I am a disappointed drudge, Sir. I care for no man on earth, and no man on earth cares for me."

"Much to be regretted. You might have used your talents better."

"May be so, Mr. Darnay ; may be not. Don't let your sober face elate you, however ; you don't know what it may come to. Good-night !"

When he was left alone, this strange being took up a candle, went to a glass that hung against the wall, and surveyed himself minutely in it.

"Do you particularly like the man?" he muttered, at his own image; "why should you particularly like a man who resembles you? There is nothing in you to like; you know that. Ah, confound you! What a change you have made in yourself! A good reason for taking to a man, that he shows you what you have fallen away from, and what you might have been! Change places with him, and would you have been looked at by those blue eyes as he was, and commiserated by that agitated face as he was? Come on, and have it out in plain words! You hate the fellow."

He resorted to his pint of wine for consolation, drank it all in a few minutes, and fell asleep on his arms, with his hair straggling over the table, and a long winding-sheet in the candle dripping down upon him.

CHAPTER V

THE JACKAL

THOSE were drinking days, and most men drank hard. So very great is the improvement Time has brought about in such habits, that a moderate statement of the quantity of wine and punch which one man would swallow in the course of a night, without any detriment to his reputation as a perfect gentleman, would seem, in these days, a ridiculous exaggeration. The learned profession of the law was certainly not behind any other learned profession in its Bacchanalian propensities; neither was Mr. Stryver, already fast shouldering his way to a large and lucrative practice, behind his compeers in this particular, any more than in the drier parts of the legal race.

A favourite at the Old Bailey, and eke at the Sessions, Mr. Stryver had begun cautiously to hew away the lower staves of the ladder on which he mounted. Sessions and Old Bailey had now to summon their favourite, specially, to their longing arms; and shouldering itself towards the visage of the Lord Chief Justice in the Court of King's Bench, the florid countenance of Mr. Stryver might be daily seen, bursting out of the bed of wigs, like a great sunflower pushing its way at the sun from among a rank gardenful of flaring companions.

It had once been noted at the Bar, that while Mr. Stryver was a glib man, and an unscrupulous, and a ready, and a bold, he had not that faculty of extracting the essence from a heap of statements which is among the most striking and necessary of the advocate's accomplishments. But a remarkable improvement came upon him as to this. The more business he got, the greater his power seemed to grow of getting at its pith and marrow; and however late at night he sat carousing with Sydney Carton, he always had his points at his fingers' ends in the morning.

Sydney Carton, idlest and most unpromising of men, was Stryver's great ally. What the two drank together, between Hilary Term and Michaelmas, might have floated a king's ship. Stryver never had a case in hand, anywhere, but Carton was there, with his hands in his pockets, staring at the ceiling of the court; they went the same Circuit, and even there they prolonged their usual orgies late into the night, and Carton was rumoured to be seen at broad day, going home stealthily and unsteadily to his lodgings, like a dissipated cat. At last it began to get about, among such as were interested in the matter, that although Sydney Carton would never be a lion, he was an amazingly good jackal, and that he rendered suit and service to Stryver in that humble capacity.

"Ten o'clock, Sir," said the man at the tavern, whom he had charged to wake him—"ten o'clock, Sir."

"*What's* the matter?"

"Ten o'clock, Sir."

"What do you mean? Ten o'clock at night?"

"Yes, Sir. Your honour told me to call you."

"Oh! I remember. Very well, very well."

After a few dull efforts to get to sleep again, which the man dexterously combated by stirring the fire continuously for five minutes, he got up, tossed his hat on, and walked out. He turned into the Temple, and, having revived himself by twice pacing the pavements of King's Bench Walk and Paper Buildings, turned into the Stryver chambers.

The Stryver clerk, who never assisted at these conferences, had gone home, and the Stryver principal opened the door. He had his slippers on, and a loose bed-gown, and his throat was bare for his greater ease. He had that rather wild, strained, seared marking about the eyes which may be observed in all free livers of his class, from the portrait of Jeffreys downward, and which can be traced, under various disguises of Art, through the portraits of every Drinking Age.

"You are a little late, Memory," said Stryver.

"About the usual time; it may be a quarter of an hour later."

They went into a dingy room lined with books and littered with papers, where there was a blazing fire. A kettle steamed upon the hob, and in the midst of the wreck of papers a table shone, with plenty of wine upon it, and brandy, and rum, and sugar, and lemons.

"You have had your bottle, I perceive, Sydney."

"Two to-night, I think. I have been dining with the day's client; or seeing him dine—it's all one!"

"That was a rare point, Sydney, that you brought to bear upon the identification. How did you come by it? When did it strike you?"

"I thought he was rather a handsome fellow, and I thought I should have been much the same sort of fellow, if I had had any luck."

Mr. Stryver laughed till he shook his precocious paunch.

"You and your luck, Sydney! Get to work, get to work."

Sullenly enough the jackal loosened his dress, went into an adjoining room, and came back with a large jug of cold water, a basin, and a towel or two. Steeping the towels in the water, and partially wringing them out, he folded them on his head in a manner hideous to behold, sat down at the table, and said, "Now I am ready!"

"Not much boiling down to be done to-night, Memory," said Mr. Stryver, gaily, as he looked among his papers.

"How much?"

"Only two sets of them."

"Give me the worst first."

"There they are, Sydney. Fire away!"

The lion then composed himself on his back on a sofa on one side of the drinking-table, while the jackal sat at his own paper-bestrewn table proper on the other side of it, with the bottles and glasses ready to his hand. Both resorted to the drinking-table without stint, but each in a different way; the lion for the most part reclining with his hands in his waistband, looking at the fire, or occasionally flirting with some lighter document; the jackal, with knitted brows and intent face, so deep in his task that his eyes did not even follow the hand he stretched out for his glass, which often groped about, for a minute or more, before it found the glass for his lips. Two or three times the matter in hand became so knotty that the jackal found it imperative on him to get up and steep his towels anew. From these pilgrimages to the jug and basin he returned with such eccentricities of damp head-gear as no words can describe, which were made the more ludicrous by his anxious gravity.

At length the jackal had got together a compact repast for the lion, and proceeded to offer it to him. The lion took it with care and caution, made his selections from it, and his remarks upon it, and the jackal assisted both. When the repast was fully discussed, the lion put his hands in his waistband again, and lay down to meditate. The jackal then invigorated himself with a bumper for his throttle, and a fresh application to his head, and applied himself to the collection of a second meal; this was administered to the lion in the same manner, and was not disposed of until the clocks struck three in the morning.

"And now we have done, Sydney, fill a bumper of punch," said Mr. Stryver.

The jackal removed the towels from his head, which had been steaming again, shook himself, yawned, shivered, and complied.

"You were very sound, Sydney, in the matter of those crown witnesses to-day. Every question told."

"I always am sound; am I not?"

"I don't gainsay it. What has roughened your temper? Put some punch to it and smooth it again."

With a deprecatory grunt, the jackal again complied.

"The old Sydney Carton of old Shrewsbury School," said Stryver, nodding his head over him as he reviewed him in the present and the past, "the old seesaw Sydney. Up one minute and down the next; now in spirits and now in despondency!"

"Ah!" returned the other, sighing: "yes! The same Sydney,

with the same luck. Even then, I did exercises for other boys, and seldom did my own."

"And why not?"

"God knows. It was my way, I suppose."

He sat, with his hands in his pockets and his legs stretched out before him, looking at the fire.

"Carton," said his friend, squaring himself at him with a bullying air, as if the fire-grate had been the furnace in which sustained endeavour was forged, and the one delicate thing to be done for the old Sydney Carton of old Shrewsbury School was to shoulder him into it, "your way is, and always was, a lame way. You summon no energy and purpose. Look at me."

"Oh, botheration!" returned Sydney, with a lighter and more good-humoured laugh, "don't *you* be moral!"

"How have I done what I have done?" said Stryver; "how do I do what I do?"

"Partly through paying me to help you, I suppose. But it's not worth your while to apostrophise me, or the air, about it; what you want to do, you do. You were always in the front rank, and I was always behind."

"I had to get into the front rank; I was not born there, was I?"

"I was not present at the ceremony; but my opinion is you were," said Carton. At this he laughed again, and they both laughed.

"Before Shrewsbury, and at Shrewsbury, and ever since Shrewsbury," pursued Carton, "you have fallen into your rank, and I have fallen into mine. Even when we were fellow-students in the Student Quarter of Paris, picking up French, and French law, and other French crumbs that we didn't get much good of, you were always somewhere, and I was always—nowhere."

"And whose fault was that?"

"Upon my soul, I am not sure that it was not yours. You were always driving and riving and shouldering and pressing, to that restless degree that I had no chance for my life but in rust and repose. It's a gloomy thing, however, to talk about one's own past, with the day breaking. Turn me in some other direction before I go."

"Well then! Pledge me to the pretty witness," said Stryver, holding up his glass. "Are you turned in a pleasant direction?"

Apparently not, for he became gloomy again.

"Pretty witness," he muttered, looking down into his glass. "I have had enough of witnesses to-day and to-night; who's your pretty witness?"

"The picturesque doctor's daughter, Miss Manette."

"*She* pretty?"

"Is she not?"

"No."

"Why, man alive, she was the admiration of the whole court!"

"Rot the admiration of the whole court! Who made the Old Bailey a judge of beauty? She was a golden-haired doll!"

"Do you know, Sydney," said Mr. Stryver, looking at him with sharp eyes, and slowly drawing a hand across his florid face,—"do you know, I rather thought, at the time, that you sympathised with the golden-haired doll, and were quick to see what happened to the golden-haired doll?"

"Quick to see what happened! If a girl, doll or no doll, swoons within a yard or two of a man's nose, he can see it without a perspective-glass. I pledge you, but I deny the beauty. And now I'll have no more drink; I'll get to bed."

When his host followed him out on the staircase with a candle, to light him down the stairs, the day was coldly looking in through its grimy windows. When he got out of the house, the air was cold and sad, the dull sky overcast, the river dark and dim, the whole scene like a lifeless desert. And wreaths of dust were spinning round and round before the morning blast, as if the desert-sand had risen far away, and the first spray of it in its advance had begun to overwhelm the city.

Waste forces within him, and a desert all around, this man stood still on his way across a silent terrace, and saw for a moment, lying in the wilderness before him, a mirage of honourable ambition, self-denial, and perseverance. In the fair city of this vision there were airy galleries from which the loves and graces looked upon him, gardens in which the fruits of life hung ripening, waters of Hope that sparkled in his sight. A moment, and it was gone. Climbing to a high chamber in a well of houses, he threw himself down in his clothes on a neglected bed, and its pillow was wet with wasted tears.

Sadly, sadly, the sun rose; it rose upon no sadder sight than the man of good abilities and good emotions, incapable of their directed exercise, incapable of his own help and his own happiness, sensible of the blight on him, and resigning himself to let it eat him away.

CHAPTER VI

HUNDREDS OF PEOPLE

THE quiet lodgings of Doctor Manette were in a quiet street-corner not far from Soho Square. On the afternoon of a certain fine Sunday when the waves of four months had rolled over the trial for treason, and carried it, as to the public interest and memory, far out to sea, Mr. Jarvis Lorry walked along the sunny streets from Clerkenwell, where he lived, on his way to dine with the Doctor. After several relapses into business-absorption, Mr. Lorry had become the Doctor's friend, and the quiet street-corner was the sunny part of his life.

On this certain fine Sunday Mr. Lorry walked towards Soho, early in the afternoon, for three reasons of habit. Firstly, because, on fine Sundays, he often walked out, before dinner, with the Doctor and Lucie; secondly, because, on unfavourable Sundays, he was accustomed to be with them as the family friend, talking, reading, looking out of window, and generally getting through the day ; thirdly, because he happened to have his own little shrewd doubts to solve, and knew how the ways of the Doctor's household pointed to that time as a likely time for solving them.

A quainter corner than the corner where the Doctor lived was not to be found in London. There was no way through it, and the front windows of the Doctor's lodgings commanded a pleasant little vista of street that had a congenial air of retirement on it. There were few buildings then north of the Oxford Road, and forest-trees flourished, and wild flowers grew, and the hawthorn blossomed, in the now vanished fields. As a consequence, country airs circulated in Soho with vigorous freedom, instead of languishing into the parish like stray paupers without a settlement ; and there was many a good south wall, not far off, on which the peaches ripened in their season.

The summer light struck into the corner brilliantly in the earlier part of the day ; but when the streets grew hot the corner was in shadow, though not in shadow so remote but that you could see beyond it into a glare of brightness. It was a cool spot, staid but cheerful, a wonderful place for echoes, and a very harbour from the raging streets.

There ought to have been a tranquil bark in such an anchorage, and there was. The Doctor occupied two floors of a large still house, where several callings purported to be pursued by day, but whereof little was audible any day, and which was shunned by all of them at night. In a building at the back, attainable by a courtyard where a plane-tree rustled its green leaves, church-organs claimed to be made, and silver to be chased, and likewise gold to be beaten by some mysterious giant who had a golden arm starting out of the wall of the front hall—as if he had beaten himself precious, and menaced a similar conversion of all visitors. Very little of these trades, or of a lonely lodger rumoured to live up-stairs, or of a dim coach-trimming maker asserted to have a counting-house below, was ever heard or seen. Occasionally a stray workman putting his coat on traversed the hall, or a stranger peered about there, or a distant clink was heard across the courtyard, or a thump from the golden giant. These, however, were only the exceptions required to prove the rule that the sparrows in the plane-tree behind the house, and the echoes in the corner before it, had their own way from Sunday morning unto Saturday night.

Doctor Manette received such patients here as his old reputation, and its revival in the floating whispers of his story, brought him. His scientific knowledge, and his vigilance and skill in conducting ingenious experiments, brought him otherwise into moderate request, and he earned as much as he wanted.

These things were within Mr. Jarvis Lorry's knowledge, thoughts, and notice when he rang the door-bell of the tranquil house in the corner on the fine Sunday afternoon.

" Doctor Manette at home ? "

Expected home.

"Miss Lucie at home?"

Expected home.

"Miss Pross at home?"

Possibly at home, but of a certainty impossible for handmaid to anticipate intentions of Miss Pross as to admission or denial of the fact.

"As I am at home myself," said Mr. Lorry, "I'll go up-stairs."

Although the Doctor's daughter had known nothing of the country of her birth, she appeared to have innately derived from it that ability to make much of little means which is one of its most useful and most agreeable characteristics. Simple as the furniture was, it was set off by so many little adornments, of no value but for their taste and fancy, that its effect was delightful. The disposition of everything in the rooms, from the largest object to the least; the arrangement of colours, the elegant variety and contrast obtained by thrift in trifles, by delicate hands, clear eyes, and good sense, were at once so pleasant in themselves, and so expressive of their originator, that, as Mr. Lorry stood looking about him, the very chairs and tables seemed to ask him, with something of that peculiar expression which he knew so well by this time, whether he approved.

There were three rooms on a floor, and the doors by which they communicated being put open that the air might pass freely through them all, Mr. Lorry, smilingly observant of that fanciful resemblance which he detected all around him, walked from one to another. The first was the best room, and in it were Lucie's birds, and flowers, and books, and desk, and work-table, and box of water-colours; the second was the Doctor's consulting-room, used also as the dining-room; the third, changingly speckled by the rustle of the plane-tree in the yard, was the Doctor's bedroom, and there, in a corner, stood the disused shoemaker's bench and tray of tools, much as it had stood on the fifth floor of the dismal house by the wine-shop in the suburb of Saint Antoine in Paris.

"I wonder," said Mr. Lorry, pausing in his looking about, "that he keeps that reminder of his sufferings about him!"

"And why wonder at that?" was the abrupt inquiry that made him start.

It proceeded from Miss Pross, the wild red woman, strong of hand, whose acquaintance he had first made at the Royal George Hotel at Dover, and had since improved.

"I should have thought——" Mr. Lorry began.

"Pooh! You'd have thought!" said Miss Pross; and Mr. Lorry left off.

"How do you do?" inquired that lady then—sharply, and yet as if to express that she bore him no malice.

"I am pretty well, I thank you," answered Mr. Lorry, with meekness; "how are you?"

"Nothing to boast of," said Miss Pross.

"Indeed?"

"Ah! indeed!" said Miss Pross. "I am very much put out about my Ladybird."

"Indeed?"

"For gracious sake say something else besides 'indeed,' or you'll fidget me to death," said Miss Pross, whose character (dissociated from stature) was shortness.

"Really, then?" said Mr. Lorry, as an amendment.

"Really is bad enough," returned Miss Pross, "but better. Yes, I am very much put out."

"May I ask the cause?"

"I don't want dozens of people who are not at all worthy of Ladybird to come here looking after her," said Miss Pross.

"*Do* dozens come for that purpose?"

"Hundreds," said Miss Pross.

It was characteristic of this lady (as of some other people before her time and since) that whenever her original proposition was questioned, she exaggerated it.

"Dear me!" said Mr. Lorry, as the safest remark he could think of.

"I have lived with the darling—or the darling has lived with me, and paid me for it; which she certainly should never have done, you may take your affidavit, if I could have afforded to keep either myself or her for nothing—since she was ten years old. And it's really very hard," said Miss Pross.

Not seeing with precision what was very hard, Mr. Lorry shook his head, using that important part of himself as a sort of fairy cloak that would fit anything.

"All sorts of people who are not in the least degree worthy of the pet are always turning up," said Miss Pross. "When you began it——"

"*I* began it, Miss Pross?"

"Didn't you? Who brought her father to life?"

"Oh! If *that* was beginning it——" said Mr. Lorry.

"It wasn't ending it, I suppose? I say, when you began it, it was hard enough; not that I have any fault to find with Doctor Manette, except that he is not worthy of such a daughter, which is no imputation on him, for it was not to be expected that anybody should be, under any circumstances. But it really is doubly and trebly hard to have crowds and multitudes of people turning up after him (I could have forgiven him), to take Ladybird's affections away from me."

Mr. Lorry knew Miss Pross to be very jealous, but he also knew her by this time to be, beneath the service of her eccentricity, one of those unselfish creatures—found only among women—who will, for pure love and admiration, bind themselves willing slaves to youth when they have lost it, to beauty that they never had, to accomplishments that they were never fortunate enough to gain, to bright hopes that never shone upon their own sombre lives. He knew enough of the world to know that there is nothing in it better than the faithful service of the heart; so rendered and so free from any mercenary taint, he had such an exalted respect for it, that in the retributive arrangements made by his own mind—we all make such arrangements, more or less—he stationed Miss Pross much nearer to the lower angels than many ladies immeasurably better got up both by Nature and Art, who had balances at Tellson's.

"There never was, nor will be, but one man worthy of Ladybird," said Miss Pross; "and that was my brother Solomon, if he hadn't made a mistake in life."

Here again Mr. Lorry's inquiries into Miss Pross's personal history had established the fact that her brother Solomon was a heartless scoundrel who had stripped her of everything she possessed, as a stake to speculate with, and had abandoned her in her poverty for evermore, with no touch of compunction. Miss Pross's fidelity of belief in Solomon (deducting a mere trifle for this slight mistake) was quite a serious matter with Mr. Lorry, and had its weight in his good opinion of her.

"As we happen to be alone for the moment, and are both people of business," he said, when they had got back to the drawing-room and had sat down there in friendly relations, "let me ask you—does the Doctor, in talking with Lucie, never refer to the shoemaking time, yet?"

"Never."

"And yet keeps that bench and those tools beside him?"

"Ah!" returned Miss Pross, shaking her head. "But I don't say he don't refer to it within himself."

"Do you believe that he thinks of it much?"

"I do," said Miss Pross.

"Do you imagine——" Mr. Lorry had begun, when Miss Pross took him up short with—

"Never imagine anything. Have no imagination at all."

"I stand corrected; do you suppose—you go so far as to suppose, sometimes?"

"Now and then," said Miss Pross.

"Do you suppose," Mr. Lorry went on, with a laughing twinkle in his bright eye, as it looked kindly at her, "that Doctor Manette has any theory of his own, preserved through all those years, relative to the cause of his being so oppressed; perhaps, even to the name of his oppressor?"

"I don't suppose anything about it but what Ladybird tells me."

"And that is——?"

"That she thinks he has."

"Now don't be angry at my asking all these questions; because I am a mere dull man of business, and you are a woman of business."

"Dull?" Miss Pross inquired, with placidity.

Rather wishing his modest adjective away, Mr. Lorry replied, "No, no, no. Surely not. To return to business—Is it not remarkable that Doctor Manette, unquestionably innocent of any crime as we are all well assured he is, should never touch upon that question? I will not say with me, though he had business relations with me many years ago, and we are now intimate; I will say with the fair daughter to whom he is so devotedly attached, and who is so devotedly attached to him? Believe me, Miss Pross, I don't approach the topic with you out of curiosity, but out of zealous interest."

"Well! To the best of my understanding, and bad's the best, you'll tell me," said Miss Pross, softened by the tone of the apology, "he is afraid of the whole subject."

"Afraid?"

"It's plain enough, I should think, why he may be. It's a dreadful remembrance. Besides that, his loss of himself grew out of it. Not knowing how he lost himself, or how he recovered himself, he may never feel certain of not losing himself again. That alone wouldn't make the subject pleasant, I should think."

It was a profounder remark than Mr. Lorry had looked for. "True," said he, "and fearful to reflect upon. Yet a doubt lurks in my mind, Miss Pross, whether it is good for Doctor Manette to have that suppression always shut up within him. Indeed, it is this doubt and the uneasiness it sometimes causes me that has led me to our present confidence."

"Can't be helped," said Miss Pross, shaking her head. "Touch that string, and he instantly changes for the worse. Better leave it alone. In short, must leave it alone, like or no like. Sometimes he gets up in the dead of the night, and will be heard, by us overhead there, walking up and down, walking up and down, in his room. Ladybird has learnt to know then that his mind is walking up and down, walking up and down, in his old prison. She hurries to him, and they go on together, walking up and down, walking up and down, until he is composed. But he never says a word of the true reason of his restlessness to her, and she finds it best not to hint at it to him. In silence they go walking up and down together, walking up and down together, till her love and company have brought him to himself."

Notwithstanding Miss Pross's denial of her own imagination, there was a perception of the pain of being monotonously haunted by one sad idea, in her repetition of the phrase, walking up and down, which testified to her possessing such a thing.

The corner has been mentioned as a wonderful corner for echoes; it had begun to echo so resoundingly to the tread of coming feet, that it seemed as though the very mention of that weary pacing to and fro had set it going.

"Here they are!" said Miss Pross, rising to break up the conference; "and now we shall have hundreds of people pretty soon!"

It was such a curious corner in its acoustical properties, such a peculiar Ear of a place, that as Mr. Lorry stood at the open window, looking for the father and daughter whose steps he heard, he fancied they would never approach. Not only would the echoes die away, as though the steps had gone; but echoes of other steps that never came would be heard in their stead, and would die away for good when they seemed close at hand. However, father and daughter did at last appear, and Miss Pross was ready at the street-door to receive them.

Miss Pross was a pleasant sight, albeit wild, and red, and grim, taking off her darling's bonnet when she came up-stairs, and touching it up with the ends of her handkerchief, and blowing the dust off it, and folding her mantle ready for laying by, and smoothing her rich hair with as much pride as she could possibly have taken in her own hair if she had been the vainest and handsomest of women. Her darling was a pleasant sight too, embracing her and thanking her, and protesting against her taking so much trouble for her—which last she only dared to do playfully, or Miss Pross, sorely hurt, would have retired to her own chamber and cried. The Doctor was a pleasant sight too, looking on at them, and telling Miss Pross how she spoilt Lucie, in accents and with eyes that had as much spoiling in them as Miss Pross had, and would have had more if it were possible. Mr. Lorry was a pleasant sight too, beaming at all this in his little wig, and thanking his bachelor stars for having lighted him in his declining years to a Home. But no Hundreds of people came to see the sights, and Mr. Lorry looked in vain for the fulfilment of Miss Pross's prediction.

Dinner-time, and still no Hundreds of people. In the arrangements of the little household, Miss Pross took charge of the lower regions, and always acquitted herself marvellously. Her dinners, of a very modest quality, were so well cooked and so well served, and so neat in their contrivances, half English and half French, that nothing could be better. Miss Pross's friendship being of the thoroughly practical kind, she had ravaged Soho and the adjacent provinces in search of impoverished French, who, tempted by shillings and half-crowns, would impart culinary mysteries to her. From these decayed sons and daughters of Gaul she had acquired such wonderful arts, that the woman and girl who formed the staff of domestics regarded her as quite a Sorceress, or Cinderella's Godmother, who would send out for a fowl, a rabbit, a vegetable or two from the garden, and change them into anything she pleased.

On Sundays, Miss Pross dined at the Doctor's table, but on other days persisted in taking her meals at unknown periods, either in the lower regions, or in her own room on the second floor—a blue chamber, to which no one but her Ladybird ever gained admittance. On this occasion Miss Pross, responding to Ladybird's pleasant face and pleasant efforts to please her, unbent exceedingly, so the dinner was very pleasant too.

It was an oppressive day, and, after dinner, Lucie proposed that the wine should be carried out under the plane-tree, and they should sit there in the air. As everything turned upon her, and revolved about her, they went out under the plane-tree, and she carried the wine down for the special benefit of Mr. Lorry. She had installed herself, some time before, as Mr. Lorry's cup-bearer; and while they sat under the plane-tree, talking, she kept his glass replenished. Mysterious backs and ends of houses peeped at them as they talked, and the plane-tree whispered to them in its own way above their heads.

Still the Hundreds of people did not present themselves. Mr. Darnay presented himself while they were sitting under the plane-tree, but he was only One.

Doctor Manette received him kindly, and so did Lucie. But Miss Pross suddenly became afflicted with a twitching in the head and body, and retired into the house. She was not unfrequently the victim of this disorder, and she called it, in familiar conversation, "a fit of the jerks."

The Doctor was in his best condition, and looked specially young. The resemblance between him and Lucie was very strong at such times, and as they sat side by side, she leaning on his shoulder, and he resting his arm on the back of her chair, it was very agreeable to trace the likeness.

He had been talking all day, on many subjects, and with unusual vivacity. "Pray, Doctor Manette," said Mr. Darnay, as they sat under the plane-tree—and he said it in the natural pursuit of the topic in hand, which happened to be the old buildings of London—"have you seen much of the Tower ? "

"Lucie and I have been there ; but only casually. We have seen enough of it to know that it teems with interest ; little more."

"*I* have been there, as you remember," said Darnay, with a smile, though reddening a little angrily, "in another character, and not in a character that gives facilities for seeing much of it. They told me a curious thing when I was there."

"What was that ? " Lucie asked.

"In making some alterations, the workmen came upon an old dungeon, which had been, for many years, built up and forgotten. Every stone of its inner wall was covered by inscriptions which had been carved by prisoners—dates, names, complaints, and prayers. Upon a corner stone in an angle of the wall, one prisoner, who seemed to have gone to execution, had cut as his last work three letters. They were done with some very poor instrument, and hurriedly, with an unsteady hand. At first they were read as D. I. C. ; but on being more carefully examined, the last letter was found to be G. There was no record or legend of any prisoner with those initials, and many fruitless guesses were made what the name could have been. At length it was suggested that the letters were not initials, but the complete word, DIG. The floor was examined very carefully under the inscription, and, in the earth beneath a stone, or tile, or some fragment of paving, were found the ashes of a paper, mingled with the ashes of a small leathern case or bag. What the unknown prisoner had written will never be read, but he had written something, and hidden it away to keep it from the jailer."

"My father," exclaimed Lucie, "you are ill ! "

He had suddenly started up, with his hand to his head. His manner and his look quite terrified them all.

"No, my dear, not ill. There are large drops of rain falling, and they made me start. We had better go in."

He recovered himself almost instantly. Rain was really falling in large drops, and he showed the back of his hand with rain-drops on it. But he said not a single word in reference to the discovery that had been told of, and as they went into the house the business eye of Mr. Lorry either detected, or fancied it detected, on his face, as it turned towards Charles Darnay, the same singular look that had been upon it when it turned towards him in the passages of the Court House.

He recovered himself so quickly, however, that Mr. Lorry had doubts of his business eye. The arm of the golden giant in the hall was not more steady than he was, when he stopped under it to remark to them that he was not yet proof against slight surprises (if he ever would be), and that the rain had startled him.

Tea-time, and Miss Pross making tea, with another fit of the jerks upon her, and yet no Hundreds of people. Mr. Carton had lounged in, but he made only Two.

The night was so very sultry, that although they sat with doors and windows open, they were overpowered by heat. When the tea-table was done with, they all moved to one of the windows, and looked out into the heavy twilight. Lucie sat by her father ; Darnay sat beside her ; Carton leaned against a window. The curtains were long and white, and some of the thunder-gusts that whirled into the corner caught them up to the ceiling, and waved them like spectral wings.

"The rain-drops are still falling, large, heavy, and few," said Doctor Manette. "It comes slowly."

"It comes surely," said Carton.

They spoke low, as people watching and waiting mostly do ; as people in a dark room, watching and waiting for lightning, always do.

There was a great hurry in the streets, of people speeding away to get shelter before the storm broke ; the wonderful corner for echoes resounded with the echoes of footsteps coming and going, yet not a footstep was there.

"A multitude of people, and yet a solitude !" said Darnay, when they had listened for a while.

"Is it not impressive, Mr. Darnay ?" asked Lucie. "Sometimes I have sat here of an evening, until I have fancied—but even the shade of a foolish fancy makes me shudder to-night, when all is so black and solemn——"

"Let us shudder too. We may know what it is."

'It will seem nothing to you. Such whims are only impressive as we originate them, I think ; they are not to be communicated. I have sometimes sat alone here of an evening, listening, until I have made the echoes out to be the echoes of all the footsteps that are coming by and by into our lives."

"There is a great crowd coming one day into our lives, if that be so," Sydney Carton struck in, in his moody way.

The footsteps were incessant, and the hurry of them became more and more rapid. The corner echoed and re-echoed with the tread of feet; some, as it seemed, under the windows; some, as it seemed, in the room; some coming, some going, some breaking off, some stopping altogether; all in the distant streets, and not one within sight.

"Are all these footsteps destined to come to all of us, Miss Manette, or are we to divide them among us?"

"I don't know, Mr. Darnay; I told you it was a foolish fancy, but you asked for it. When I have yielded myself to it, I have been alone, and then I have imagined them the footsteps of the people who are to come into my life, and my father's."

"I take them into mine!" said Carton. "*I* ask no question and make no stipulations. There is a great crowd bearing down upon us, Miss Manette, and I see them—by the lightning." He added the last words after there had been a vivid flash, which had shown him lounging in the window.

"And I hear them!" he added again, after a peal of thunder. "Here they come, fast, fierce, and furious!"

It was the rush and roar of rain that he typified, and it stopped him, for no voice could be heard in it. A memorable storm of thunder and lightning broke with that sweep of water, and there was not a moment's interval in crash, and fire, and rain, until after the moon rose at midnight.

The great bell of Saint Paul's was striking One in the cleared air, when Mr. Lorry, escorted by Jerry, high-booted and bearing a lantern, set forth on his return-passage to Clerkenwell. There were solitary patches of road on the way between Soho and Clerkenwell, and Mr. Lorry, mindful of footpads, always retained Jerry for this service: though it was usually performed a good two hours earlier.

"What a night it has been! Almost a night, Jerry," said Mr. Lorry, "to bring the dead out of their graves."

"I never see the night myself, master—nor yet I don't expect to—what would do that," answered Jerry.

"Good-night, Mr. Carton," said the man of business. "Good-night, Mr Darnay. Shall we ever see such a night again, together!"

Perhaps. Perhaps see the great crowd of people, with its rush and roar, bearing down upon them too.

CHAPTER VII

MONSEIGNEUR IN TOWN

MONSEIGNEUR, one of the great lords in power at the Court, held his fortnightly reception in his grand hotel in Paris. Monseigneur was in his inner room, his sanctuary of sanctuaries, the Holiest of Holiests to the crowd of worshippers in the suite of rooms without. Monseigneur was about to take his chocolate. Monseigneur could swallow a great many things with ease, and was by some few sullen minds supposed to be rather rapidly swallowing France; but his morning's chocolate could not so much as get into the throat of Monseigneur without the aid of four strong men besides the Cook.

Yes. It took four men, all four ablaze with gorgeous decoration, and the Chief of them unable to exist with fewer than two gold watches in his pocket, emulative of the noble and chaste fashion set by Monseigneur, to conduct the happy chocolate to Monseigneur's lips. One lackey carried the chocolate-pot into the sacred presence; a second milled and frothed the chocolate with the little instrument he bore for that function; a third presented the favoured napkin; a fourth (he of the two gold watches) poured the chocolate out. It was impossible for Monseigneur to dispense with one of these attendants on the chocolate and hold his high place under the admiring heavens. Deep would have been the blot upon his escutcheon if his chocolate had been ignobly waited on by only three men; he must have died of two.

Monseigneur had been out at a little supper last night, where the Comedy and the Grand Opera were charmingly represented. Monseigneur was out at a little supper most nights, with fascinating company. So polite and so impressible was Monseigneur, that the Comedy and the Grand Opera had far more influence with him in the tiresome articles of state affairs and state secrets than the needs of all France. A happy circumstance for France, as the like always is for all countries similarly favoured!—always was for England (by way of example) in the regretted days of the merry Stuart who sold it.

Monseigneur had one truly noble idea of general public business, which was, to let everything go on in its own way; of particular public business Monseigneur had the other truly noble idea that it must all go his way—tend to his own power and pocket. Of his pleasures, general and particular, Monseigneur had the other truly noble idea, that the world was made for them. The text of his order (altered from the original by only a pronoun, which is not much) ran: "The earth and the fulness thereof are mine, saith Monseigneur."

Yet Monseigneur had slowly found that vulgar embarrassments crept into his affairs, both private and public; and he had, as to both classes of affairs, allied himself perforce with a Farmer-General. As to finances public, because Monseigneur could not make anything at all of them, and must consequently let them out to somebody who could; as to finances private, because Farmer-Generals were rich, and Monseigneur, after generations of great luxury and expense, was growing poor. Hence Monseigneur had taken his sister from a convent, while there was yet time to ward off the impending veil, the cheapest garment she could wear, and had bestowed her as a prize upon a very rich Farmer-General, poor in family. Which Farmer-General, carrying an appropriate cane with a golden apple on the top of it, was now among the company in the outer rooms, much prostrated before by mankind—always excepting superior mankind of the blood of Monseigneur, who, his own wife included, looked down upon him with the loftiest contempt.

A sumptuous man was the Farmer-General. Thirty horses stood in his stables, twenty-four male domestics sat in his halls, six body-women waited on his wife. As one who pretended to do nothing but plunder and forage where he could, the Farmer-General—howsoever his matrimonial relations conduced to social morality—was at least the greatest reality among the personages who attended at the hotel of Monseigneur that day.

For the rooms, though a beautiful scene to look at, and adorned with every device of decoration that the taste and skill of the time could achieve, were, in truth, not a sound business; considered with any reference to the scarecrows in the rags and nightcaps elsewhere (and not so far off, either, but that the watching towers of Notre Dame, almost equidistant from the two extremes, could see them both), they would have been an exceedingly uncomfortable business— if that could have been anybody's business, at the house of Monseigneur. Military officers destitute of military knowledge; naval officers with no idea of a ship; civil officers without a notion of affairs; brazen ecclesiastics, of the worst world worldly, with sensual eyes, loose tongues, and looser lives; all totally unfit for their several callings, all lying horribly in pretending to belong to them, but all nearly or remotely of the order of Monseigneur, and therefore foisted on all public employments from which anything was to be got—these were to be told off by the score and the score. People not immediately connected with Monseigneur or the State, yet equally unconnected with anything that was real, or with lives passed in travelling by any straight road to any true earthly end, were no less abundant. Doctors who made great fortunes out of dainty remedies for imaginary disorders that never existed smiled upon their courtly patients in the ante-chambers of Monseigneur. Projectors who had discovered every kind of remedy for the little evils with which the State was touched, except the remedy of setting to work in earnest to root out a single sin, poured their distracting babble into any ears they could lay hold of at the reception of Monseigneur. Unbelieving Philosophers who were re-modelling the world with words, and making card-towers of Babel to scale the skies with, talked with Unbelieving Chemists who had an eye on the transmutation of metals, at this wonderful gathering accumulated by Monseigneur. Exquisite gentlemen of the finest breeding, which was at that remarkable time—and has been since—to be known by its fruits of indifference to every natural subject of human interest, were in the most exemplary state of exhaustion at the hotel of Monseigneur. Such homes had these various notabilities left behind them in the fine world of Paris, that the spies among the assembled devotees of Monseigneur—forming a goodly half of the polite company —would have found it hard to discover among the angels of that sphere one solitary wife who, in her manners and appearance, owned to being a Mother. Indeed, except for the mere act of bringing a troublesome creature into this world—which does not go far towards the realisation of the name of mother—there was no such thing known to the fashion. Peasant women kept the unfashionable babies close, and brought them up, and charming grandmammas of sixty dressed and supped as at twenty.

The leprosy of unreality disfigured every human creature in attendance upon Monseigneur. In the outermost room were half-a-dozen exceptional people who had had, for a few years, some vague misgiving in them that things in general were going rather wrong. As a promising way of setting them right, half of the half-dozen had become members of a fantastic sect of Convulsionists, and were even then considering within themselves whether they should foam, rage, roar, and turn cataleptic on the spot—thereby setting up a highly intelligible finger-post to the Future, for Monseigneur's guidance. Besides these Dervishes were other three who had rushed into another sect, which mended matters with a jargon about " the Centre of Truth ": holding that Man had got out of the Centre of Truth—which did not need much demonstration—but had not got out of the Circumference, and that he was to be kept from flying out of the Circumference, and was even to be shoved back into the Centre, by fasting and seeing of spirits. Among these, accordingly, much discoursing with spirits went on— and it did a world of good which never became manifest.

But the comfort was that all the company at the grand hotel of Monseigneur were perfectly dressed. If the Day of Judgment had only been ascertained to be a dress day, everybody there would have been eternally correct. Such frizzling and powdering and sticking up of hair, such delicate complexions artificially preserved and mended, such gallant swords to look at, and such delicate honour to the sense of smell, would surely keep anything going, for ever and ever. The exquisite gentlemen of the finest breeding wore little pendent trinkets that chinked as they languidly moved ; these golden fetters rang like precious little bells ; and what with that ringing, and with the rustle of silk and brocade and fine linen, there was a flutter in the air that fanned Saint Antoine and his devouring hunger far away.

Dress was the one unfailing talisman and charm used for keeping all things in their places. Everybody was dressed for a Fancy Ball that was never to leave off. From the Palace of the Tuileries, through Monseigneur and the whole Court, through the Chambers, the Tribunals of Justice, and all society (except the scarecrows), the Fancy Ball descended to the Common Executioner, who, in pursuance of the charm, was required to officiate " frizzled, powdered, in a gold-laced coat, pumps, and white silk stockings." At the gallows and the wheel—the axe was a rarity—Monsieur Paris, as it was the episcopal mode among his brother Professors of the provinces, Monsieur Orleans, and the rest, to call him, presided in this dainty dress. And who among the company at Monseigneur's reception in that seventeen hundred and eightieth year of our Lord could possibly doubt that a system rooted in a frizzled hangman, powdered, gold-laced, pumped, and white-silk stockinged, would see the very stars out !

Monseigneur, having eased his four men of their burdens and taken his chocolate, caused the doors of the Holiest of Holiests to be thrown open, and issued forth. Then what submission, what cringing and fawning, what servility, what abject humiliation ! As to bowing down in body and spirit, nothing in that way was left for Heaven—which may have been one among other reasons why the worshippers of Monseigneur never troubled it.

Bestowing a word of promise here and a smile there, a whisper on one happy slave and a wave of the hand on another, Monseigneur affably passed through his rooms to the remote region of the Circumference of Truth. There Monseigneur turned, and came back again, and so in due course of time got himself shut up in his sanctuary by the chocolate sprites, and was seen no more.

The show being over, the flutter in the air became quite a little storm, and the precious little bells went ringing down-stairs. There was soon but one person left of all the crowd, and he, with his hat under his arm and his snuff-box in his hand, slowly passed among the mirrors on his way out.

" I devote you," said this person, stopping at the last door on his way, and turning in the direction of the sanctuary, " to the Devil ! "

With that, he shook the snuff from his fingers as if he had shaken the dust from his feet, and quietly walked down-stairs.

He was a man of about sixty, handsomely dressed, haughty in manner, and with a face like a fine mask—a face of a transparent paleness ; every feature in it clearly defined ; one set expression on it. The nose, beautifully formed otherwise, was very slightly pinched at the top of each nostril. In those two compressions, or dints, the only little change that the face ever showed resided. They persisted in changing colour sometimes, and they would be occasionally dilated and contracted by something like a faint pulsation ; then they gave a look of treachery, and cruelty, to the whole countenance. Examined with attention, its capacity of helping such a look was to be found in the line of the mouth, and the lines of the orbits of the eyes, being much too horizontal and thin ; still, in the effect the face made, it was a handsome face, and a remarkable one.

Its owner went down-stairs into the courtyard, got into his carriage, and drove away. Not many people had talked with him at the reception ; he had stood in a little space apart, and Monseigneur might have been warmer in his manner. It appeared, under the circumstances, rather agreeable to him to see the common people dispersed before his horses, and often barely escaping from being run down. His man drove as if he were charging an enemy, and the furious recklessness of the man brought no check into the face, or to the lips of the master. The complaint had sometimes made itself audible, even in that deaf city and dumb age, that, in the narrow streets without foot ways, the fierce patrician custom of hard driving endangered and maimed the mere vulgar in a barbarous manner. But few cared enough for that to think of it a second time, and, in this matter, as in all others, the common wretches were left to get out of their difficulties as they could.

With a wild rattle and clatter, and an inhuman abandonment of consideration not easy to be understood in these days, the carriage dashed through streets and swept round corners, with women screaming before it, and men clutching each other and clutching children out of its way. At last, swooping at a street corner by a fountain, one of its wheels came to a sickening little jolt, and there was a loud cry from a number of voices, and the horses reared and plunged.

But for the latter inconvenience the carriage probably would not have stopped ; carriages were often known to drive on, and leave their wounded behind, and why not? But the frightened valet had got down in a hurry, and there were twenty hands at the horses' bridles.

"What has gone wrong?" said Monsieur, calmly looking out.

A tall man in a nightcap had caught up a bundle from among the feet of the horses, and had laid it on the basement of the fountain, and was down in the mud and wet, howling over it like a wild animal.

"Pardon, Monsieur the Marquis!" said a ragged and submissive man, "it is a child."

"Why does he make that abominable noise? Is it his child?"

"Excuse me, Monsieur the Marquis—it is a pity—yes."

The fountain was a little removed ; for the street opened, where it was, into a space some ten or twelve yards square. As the tall man suddenly got up from the ground, and came running at the carriage, Monsieur the Marquis clapped his hand for an instant on his sword-hilt.

"Killed!" shrieked the man, in wild desperation, extending both arms at their length above his head, and staring at him. "Dead!"

The people closed round, and looked at Monsieur the Marquis. There was nothing revealed by the many eyes that looked at him but watchfulness and eagerness ; there was no visible menacing or anger. Neither did the people say anything ; after the first cry, they had been silent, and they remained so. The voice of the submissive man who had spoken was flat and tame in its extreme submission. Monsieur the Marquis ran his eyes over them all, as if they had been mere rats come out of their holes.

He took out his purse.

"It is extraordinary to me," said he, "that you people cannot take care of yourselves and your children. One or the other of you is for ever in the way. How do I know what injury you have done my horses. See! Give him that."

He threw out a gold coin for the valet to pick up, and all the heads craned forward that all the eyes might look down at it as it fell. The tall man called out again with a most unearthly cry, "Dead!"

He was arrested by the quick arrival of another man, for whom the rest made way. On seeing him, the miserable creature fell upon his shoulder, sobbing and crying, and pointing to the fountain, where some women were stooping over the motionless bundle, and moving gently about it. They were as silent, however, as the men.

"I know all, I know all," said the last comer. "Be a brave man, my Gaspard! It is better for the poor little plaything to die so than to live. It has died in a moment without pain. Could it have lived an hour as happily?"

"You are a philosopher, you there," said the Marquis, smiling, "How do they call you?"

"They call me Defarge."

"Of what trade?"

"Monsieur the Marquis, vendor of wine."

"Pick up that, philosopher and vendor of wine," said the Marquis, throwing him another gold coin, "and spend it as you will. The horses there; are they right?"

Without deigning to look at the assemblage a second time, Monsieur the Marquis leaned back in his seat, and was just being driven away with the air of a gentleman who had accidentally broken some common thing, and had paid for it, and could afford to pay for it, when his ease was suddenly disturbed by a coin flying into his carriage, and ringing on its floor.

"Hold!" said Monsieur the Marquis. "Hold the horses! Who threw that?"

He looked to the spot where Defarge the vendor of wine had stood, a moment before; but the wretched father was grovelling on his face on the pavement in that spot, and the figure that stood beside him was the figure of a dark, stout woman, knitting.

"You dogs!" said the Marquis, but smoothly, and with an unchanged front, except as to the spots on his nose; "I would ride over any of you very willingly, and exterminate you from the earth. If I knew which rascal threw at the carriage, and if that brigand were sufficiently near it, he should be crushed under the wheels."

So cowed was their condition, and so long and hard their experience of what such a man could do to them, within the law and beyond it, that not a voice, or a hand, or even an eye was raised. Among the men, not one. But the woman who stood knitting looked up steadily, and looked the Marquis in the face. It was not for his dignity to notice it; his contemptuous eyes passed over her, and over all the other rats; and he leaned back in his seat again, and gave the word "Go on!"

He was driven on, and other carriages came whirling by in quick succession—the Minister, the State-Projector, the Farmer-General, the Doctor, the Lawyer, the Ecclesiastic, the Grand Opera, the Comedy, the whole Fancy Ball in a bright continuous flow came whirling by, The rats had crept out of their holes to look on, and they remained looking on for hours; soldiers and police often passing between them and the spectacle, and making a barrier behind which they slunk, and through which they peeped. The father had long ago taken up his bundle and hidden himself away with it, when the women who had

tended the bundle while it lay on the base of the fountain sat there
watching the running of the water and the rolling of the Fancy Ball—
when the one woman who had stood conspicuous, knitting, still knitted
on with the steadfastness of Fate.   The water of the fountain ran, the
swift river ran, the day ran into evening, so much life in the city ran
into death according to rule, time and tide waited for no man, the rats
were sleeping close together in their dark holes again, the Fancy Ball
was lighted up at supper, all things ran their course.

CHAPTER VIII

MONSEIGNEUR IN THE COUNTRY

A BEAUTIFUL landscape, with the corn bright in it, but not abundant.
Patches of poor rye where corn should have been, patches of poor peas
and beans, patches of most coarse vegetable substitutes for wheat.   On
inanimate nature, as on the men and women who cultivated it, a prevalent tendency towards an appearance of vegetating unwillingly—a
dejected disposition to give up, and wither away.

Monsieur the Marquis in his travelling carriage (which might have
been lighter), conducted by four post-horses and two postilions, fagged
up a steep hill.   A blush on the countenance of Monsieur the Marquis
was no impeachment of his high breeding ; it was not from within ; it
was occasioned by an external circumstance beyond his control—the
setting sun.

The sunset struck so brilliantly into the travelling carriage when it
gained the hill-top, that its occupant was steeped in crimson.   "It will
die out," said Monsieur the Marquis, glancing at his hands, "directly."

In effect, the sun was so low that it dipped at the moment.   When
the heavy drag had been adjusted to the wheel, and the carriage slid
down hill, with a cinderous smell, in a cloud of dust, the red glow departed quickly ; the sun and the Marquis going down together, there
was no glow left when the drag was taken off.

But there remained a broken country, bold and open, a little village
at the bottom of the hill, a broad sweep and rise beyond it, a church-
tower, a windmill, a forest for the chase, and a crag with a fortress on
it used as a prison.   Round upon all these darkening objects, as the
night drew on, the Marquis looked, with the air of one who was coming
near home.

The village had its one poor street, with its poor brewery, poor tannery,
poor tavern, poor stable-yard for relays of post-horses, poor fountain,
all usual poor appointments.   It had its poor people too.   All its people
were poor, and many of them were sitting at their doors, shredding
spare onions and the like for supper, while many were at the fountain,
washing leaves, and grasses, and any such small yieldings of the earth
that could be eaten.   Expressive signs of what made them poor were

not wanting—the tax for the state, the tax for the church, the tax for the lord, tax local and tax general, were to be paid here and to be paid there, according to solemn inscription in the little village, until the wonder was that there was any village left unswallowed.

Few children were to be seen, and no dogs. As to the men and women, their choice on earth was stated in the prospect—Life on the lowest terms that could sustain it, down in the little village under the mill; or captivity and Death in the dominant prison on the crag.

Heralded by a courier in advance, and by the cracking of his postilions' whips, which twined snake-like about their heads in the evening air, as if he came attended by the Furies, Monsieur the Marquis drew up in his travelling carriage at the posting-house gate. It was hard by the fountain, and the peasants suspended their operations to look at him. He looked at them, and saw in them, without knowing it, the slow, sure filing down of misery-worn face and figure that was to make the meagreness of Frenchmen an English superstition which should survive the truth through the best part of a hundred years.

Monsieur the Marquis cast his eyes over the submissive faces that drooped before him, as the like of himself had drooped before Monseigneur of the Court—only the difference was, that these faces drooped merely to suffer and not to propitiate—when a grizzled mender of the roads joined the group.

"Bring me hither that fellow!" said the Marquis to the courier.

The fellow was brought, cap in hand, and the other fellows closed round to look and listen, in the manner of the people at the Paris fountain.

"I passed you on the road?"

"Monseigneur, it is true. I had the honour of being passed on the road."

"Coming up the hill, and at the top of the hill, both?"

"Monseigneur, it is true."

"What did you look at, so fixedly?"

"Monseigneur, I looked at the man."

He stooped a little, and with his tattered blue cap pointed under the carriage. All his fellows stooped to look under the carriage.

"What man, pig? And why look there?"

"Pardon, Monseigneur; he swung by the chain of the shoe—the drag."

"Who?" demanded the traveller.

"Monseigneur, the man."

"May the Devil carry away these idiots! How do you call the man? You know all the men of this part of the country. Who was he?"

"Your clemency, Monseigneur! He was not of this part of the country. Of all the days of my life, I never saw him."

"Swinging by the chain? To be suffocated?"

"With your gracious permission, that was the wonder of it, Monseigneur. His head hanging over—like this!"

He turned himself sideways to the carriage, and leaned back, with his face thrown up to the sky, and his head hanging down; then recovered himself, fumbled with his cap, and made a bow.

"What was he like?"

"Monseigneur, he was whiter than the miller. All covered with dust, white as a spectre, tall as a spectre!"

The picture produced an immense sensation in the little crowd; but all eyes, without comparing notes with other eyes, looked at Monsieur the Marquis. Perhaps to observe whether he had any spectre on his conscience.

"Truly, you did well," said the Marquis, felicitously sensible that such vermin were not to ruffle him, "to see a thief accompanying my carriage, and not open that great mouth of yours. Bah! Put him aside, Monsieur Gabelle!"

Monsieur Gabelle was the Postmaster and some other taxing functionary united; he had come out with great obsequiousness to assist at this examination, and had held the examined by the drapery of his arm in an official manner.

"Bah! Go aside!" said Monsieur Gabelle.

"Lay hands on this stranger if he seeks to lodge in your village to-night, and be sure that his business is honest, Gabelle."

"Monseigneur, I am flattered to devote myself to your orders."

"Did he run away, fellow?—where is that Accursed?"

The accursed was already under the carriage with some half-dozen particular friends, pointing out the chain with his blue cap. Some half-dozen other particular friends promptly hauled him out, and presented him breathless to Monsieur the Marquis.

"Did the man run away, Dolt, when we stopped for the drag?"

"Monseigneur, he precipitated himself over the hill-side, head first, as a person plunges into the river."

"See to it, Gabelle.—Go on!"

The half-dozen who were peering at the chain were still among the wheels, like sheep; the wheels turned so suddenly that they were lucky to save their skins and bones; they had very little else to save, or they might not have been so fortunate.

The burst with which the carriage started out of the village and up the rise beyond was soon checked by the steepness of the hill. Gradually it subsided to a foot-pace, swinging and lumbering upward among the many sweet scents of a summer night. The postilions, with a thousand gossamer gnats circling about them in lieu of the Furies, quietly mended the points to the lashes of their whips; the valet walked by the horses; the courier was audible, trotting on ahead into the dim distance.

At the steepest point of the hill there was a little burial-ground, with a cross and a new large figure of Our Saviour on it; it was a poor figure in wood, done by some inexperienced rustic carver, but he had studied the figure from the life—his own life, maybe—for it was dreadfully spare and thin.

To this distressful emblem of a great distress that had long been growing worse, and was not at its worst, a woman was kneeling. She turned her head as the carriage came up to her, rose quickly, and presented herself at the carriage-door.

"It is you, Monseigneur! Monseigneur, a petition."

With an exclamation of impatience, but with his unchangeable face, Monseigneur looked out.

"How, then! What is it? Always petitions!"

"Monseigneur. For the love of the great God! My husband, the forester."

"What of your husband, the forester? Always the same with you people. He cannot pay something."

"He has paid all, Monseigneur. He is dead."

"Well! He is quiet. Can I restore him to you?"

"Alas, no, Monseigneur! But he lies yonder, under a little heap of poor grass."

"Well?"

"Monseigneur, there are so many little heaps of poor grass!"

"Again, well?"

She looked an old woman, but was young. Her manner was one of passionate grief; by turns she clasped her veinous and knotted hands together with wild energy, and laid one of them on the carriage door—tenderly, caressingly, as if it had been a human breast, and could be expected to feel the appealing touch.

"Monseigneur, hear me! Monseigneur, hear my petition! My husband died of want; so many die of want; so many more will die of want."

"Again, well? Can I feed them?"

"Monseigneur, the good God knows; but I don't ask it. My petition is, that a morsel of stone or wood, with my husband's name, may be placed over him to show where he lies. Otherwise the place will be quickly forgotten, it will never be found when I am dead of the same malady; I shall be laid under some other heap of poor grass. Monseigneur, they are so many, they increase so fast, there is so much want. Monseigneur! Monseigneur!"

The valet had put her away from the door, the carriage had broken into a brisk trot, the postilions had quickened the pace, she was left far behind, and Monseigneur, again escorted by the Furies, was rapidly diminishing the league or two of distance that remained between him and his château.

The sweet scents of the summer night rose all around him, and rose, as the rain falls, impartially, on the dusty, ragged, and toil-worn group at the fountain not far away; to whom the mender of roads, with the aid of the blue cap without which he was nothing, still enlarged upon his man like a spectre, as long as they could bear it. By degrees, as they could bear no more, they dropped off one by one, and lights twinkled in little casements; which lights, as the casements darkened, and more stars came out, seemed to have shot up into the sky instead of having been extinguished.

The shadow of a large, high-roofed house, and of many overhanging trees, was upon Monsieur the Marquis by that time ; and the shadow was exchanged for the light of a flambeau, as his carriage stopped, and the great door of his château was opened to him.

"Monsieur Charles, whom I expect ; is he arrived from England ? "

"Monseigneur, not yet."

CHAPTER IX

THE GORGON'S HEAD

IT was a heavy mass of building, that château of Monsieur the Marquis, with a large stone courtyard before it, and two stone sweeps of staircase meeting in a stone terrace before the principal door. A stony business altogether, with heavy stone balustrades, and stone urns, and stone flowers, and stone faces of men, and stone heads of lions, in all directions. As if the Gorgon's head had surveyed it, when it was finished, two centuries ago.

Up the broad flight of shallow steps Monsieur the Marquis, flambeau preceded, went from his carriage, sufficiently disturbing the darkness to elicit loud remonstrance from an owl in the roof of the great pile of stable building away among the trees. All else was so quiet, that the flambeau carried up the steps, and the other flambeau held at the great door, burnt as if they were in a close room of state, instead of being in the open night-air. Other sound than the owl's voice there was none, save the falling of a fountain into its stone basin ; for it was one of those dark nights that hold their breath by the hour together, and then heave a long low sigh, and hold their breath again.

The great door clanged behind him, and Monsieur the Marquis crossed a hall grim with certain old boar-spears, swords, and knives of the chase ; grimmer with certain heavy riding-rods and riding-whips, of which many a peasant, gone to his benefactor Death, had felt the weight when his lord was angry.

Avoiding the larger rooms, which were dark and made fast for the night, Monsieur the Marquis, with his flambeau-bearer going on before, went up the staircase to a door in a corridor. This, thrown open, admitted him to his own private apartment of three rooms : his bed-chamber and two others. High vaulted rooms with cool uncarpeted floors, great dogs upon the hearths for the burning of wood in winter time, and all luxuries befitting the state of a marquis in a luxurious age and country. The fashion of the last Louis but one, of the line that was never to break—the fourteenth Louis—was conspicuous in their rich furniture ; but it was diversified by many objects that were illustrations of old pages in the history of France.

A supper-table was laid for two in the third of the rooms—a round room, in one of the château's four extinguisher-topped towers—a small,

Monsieur le Marquis

lofty room, with its window wide open, and the wooden jalousie-blinds closed, so that the dark night only showed in slight horizontal lines of black, alternating with their broad lines of stone colour.

"My nephew," said the Marquis, glancing at the supper preparation; "they said he was not arrived?"

Nor was he; but he had been expected with Monseigneur.

"Ah! It is not probable he will arrive to-night; nevertheless, leave the table as it is. I shall be ready in a quarter of an hour."

In a quarter of an hour Monseigneur was ready, and sat down alone to his sumptuous and choice supper. His chair was opposite to the window, and he had taken his soup, and was raising his glass of Bordeaux to his lips, when he put it down.

"What is that?" he calmly asked, looking with attention at the horizontal lines of black and stone colour.

"Monseigneur? That?"

"Outside the blinds. Open the blinds."

It was done.

"Well?"

"Monseigneur, it is nothing. The trees and the night are all that are here."

The servant who spoke had thrown the blinds wide, had looked out into the vacant darkness, and stood, with that blank behind him, looking round for instructions.

"Good," said the imperturbable master. "Close them again."

That was done too, and the Marquis went on with his supper. He was halfway through it, when he again stopped with his glass in his hand, hearing the sound of wheels. It came on briskly, and came up to the front of the château.

"Ask who is arrived."

It was the nephew of Monseigneur. He had been some few leagues behind Monseigneur, early in the afternoon. He had diminished the distance rapidly, but not so rapidly as to come up with Monseigneur on the road. He had heard of Monseigneur, at the posting-houses, as being before him.

He was to be told (said Monseigneur) that supper awaited him then and there, and that he was prayed to come to it. In a little while he came. He had been known in England as Charles Darnay.

Monseigneur received him in a courtly manner, but they did not shake hands.

"You left Paris yesterday, Sir?" he said to Monseigneur, as he took his seat at table.

"Yesterday. And you?"

"I come direct."

"From London?"

"Yes."

"You have been a long time coming," said the Marquis, with a smile.

"On the contrary; I come direct."

"Pardon me! I mean, not a long time on the journey; a long time intending the journey."

"I have been detained by"—the nephew stopped a moment in his answer—"various business."

"Without doubt," said the polished uncle.

So long as a servant was present, no other words passed between them. When coffee had been served and they were alone together, the nephew, looking at the uncle and meeting the eyes of the face that was like a fine mask, opened a conversation.

"I have come back, Sir, as you anticipate, pursuing the object that took me away. It carried me into great and unexpected peril; but it is a sacred object, and if it had carried me to death, I hope it would have sustained me."

"Not to death," said the uncle; "it is not necessary to say to death."

"I doubt, Sir," returned the nephew, "whether, if it had carried me to the utmost brink of death, you would have cared to stop me there."

The deepened marks in the nose, and the lengthening of the fine straight lines in the cruel face, looked ominous as to that; the uncle made a graceful gesture of protest, which was so clearly a slight form of good breeding, that it was not reassuring.

"Indeed, Sir," pursued the nephew, "for anything I know, you may have expressly worked to give a more suspicious appearance to the suspicious circumstances that surrounded me."

"No, no, no," said the uncle, pleasantly.

"But, however that may be," resumed the nephew, glancing at him with deep distrust, "I know that your diplomacy would stop me by any means, and would know no scruple as to means."

"My friend, I told you so," said the uncle, with a fine pulsation in the two marks. "Do me the favour to recall that I told you so, long ago."

"I recall it."

"Thank you," said the Marquis—very sweetly indeed.

His tone lingered in the air, almost like the tone of a musical instrument.

"In effect, Sir," pursued the nephew, "I believe it to be at once your bad fortune, and my good fortune, that has kept me out of a prison in France here."

"I do not quite understand," returned the uncle, sipping his coffee. "Dare I ask you to explain?"

"I believe that if you were not in disgrace with the Court, and had not been overshadowed by that cloud for years past, a *lettre de cachet* would have sent me to some fortress indefinitely."

"It is possible," said the uncle, with great calmness. "For the honour of the family, I could even resolve to incommode you to that extent. Pray excuse me!"

"I perceive that, happily for me, the Reception of the day before yesterday was, as usual, a cold one," observed the nephew.

"I would not say happily, my friend," returned the uncle, with refined politeness ; " I would not be sure of that. A good opportunity for consideration, surrounded by the advantages of solitude, might influence your destiny to far greater advantage than you influence it for yourself. But it is useless to discuss the question. I am, as you say, at a disadvantage. These little instruments of correction, these gentle aids to the power and honour of families, these slight favours that might so incommode you, are only to be obtained now by interest and importunity. They are sought by so many, and they are granted (comparatively) to so few ! It used not to be so, but France in all such things is changed for the worse. Our not remote ancestors held the right of life and death over the surrounding vulgar. From this room, many such dogs have been taken out to be hanged ; in the next room (my bedroom), one fellow, to our knowledge, was poniarded on the spot for professing some insolent delicacy respecting his daughter—*his* daughter ? We have lost many privileges ; a new philosophy has become the mode ; and the assertion of our station, in these days, might (I do not go so far as to say would, but might) cause us real inconvenience. All very bad, very bad ! "

The Marquis took a gentle little pinch of snuff, and shook his head, as elegantly despondent as he could becomingly be of a country still containing himself, that great means of regeneration.

"We have so asserted our station, both in the old time and in the modern time also," said the nephew, gloomily, "that I believe our name to be more detested than any name in France."

"Let us hope so," said the uncle. " Detestation of the high is the involuntary homage of the low."

"There is not," pursued the nephew, in his former tone, "a face I can look at, in all this country round about us, which looks at me with any deference on it but the dark deference of fear and slavery."

"A compliment," said the Marquis, "to the grandeur of the family, merited by the manner in which the family has sustained its grandeur. Hah ! " And he took another gentle little pinch of snuff, and lightly crossed his legs.

But when his nephew, leaning an elbow on the table, covered his eyes thoughtfully and dejectedly with his hand, the fine mask looked at him sideways with a stronger concentration of keenness, closeness, and dislike than was comportable with its wearer's assumption of indifference.

"Repression is the only lasting philosophy. The dark deference of fear and slavery, my friend," observed the Marquis, "will keep the dogs obedient to the whip, as long as this roof," looking up to it, "shuts out the sky."

That might not be so long as the Marquis supposed. If a picture of the château as it was to be a very few years hence, and of fifty like it as they too were to be a very few years hence, could have been shown to him that night, he might have been at a loss to claim his own from the ghastly, fire-charred, plunder-wrecked ruins. As for the roof he vaunted, he might have found *that* shutting out the sky in a new way—to wit, for ever, from the eyes of the bodies into which its lead was fired, out of the barrels of a hundred thousand muskets.

"Meanwhile," said the Marquis, "I will preserve the honour and repose of the family, if you will not. But you must be fatigued. Shall we terminate our conference for the night?"

"A moment more."

"An hour, if you please."

"Sir," said the nephew, "we have done wrong, and are reaping the fruits of wrong."

"*We* have done wrong?" repeated the Marquis, with an inquiring smile, and delicately pointing, first to his nephew, then to himself.

"Our family; our honourable family, whose honour is of so much account to both of us, in such different ways. Even in my father's time we did a world of wrong, injuring every human creature who came between us and our pleasure, whatever it was. Why need I speak of my father's time, when it is equally yours? Can I separate my father's twin-brother, joint inheritor, and next successor, from himself?"

"Death has done that!" said the Marquis.

"And has left me," answered the nephew, "bound to a system that is frightful to me, responsible for it, but powerless in it; seeking to execute the last request of my dear mother's lips, and obey the last look of my dear mother's eyes, which implored me to have mercy and to redress; and tortured by seeking assistance and power in vain."

"Seeking them from me, my nephew," said the Marquis, touching him on the breast with his forefinger—they were now standing by the hearth—"you will for ever seek them in vain, be assured."

Every fine straight line in the clear whiteness of his face was cruelly, craftily, and closely compressed, while he stood looking quietly at his nephew, with his snuff-box in his hand. Once again he touched him on the breast, as though his finger were the fine point of a small sword, with which, in delicate finesse, he ran him through the body, and said—

"My friend, I will die, perpetuating the system under which I have lived."

When he had said it, he took a culminating pinch of snuff, and put his box in his pocket.

"Better to be a rational creature," he added then, after ringing a small bell on the table, "and accept your natural destiny. But you are lost, Monsieur Charles, I see."

"This property and France are lost to me," said the nephew, sadly; "I renounce them."

"Are they both yours to renounce? France may be, but is the property? It is scarcely worth mentioning; but, is it yet?"

"I had no intention, in the words I used, to claim it yet. If it passed to me from you, to-morrow——"

"Which I have the vanity to hope is not probable."

"—or twenty years hence——"

"You do me too much honour," said the Marquis; "still, I prefer that supposition."

" —I would abandon it, and live otherwise and elsewhere. It is little to relinquish. What is it but a wilderness of misery and ruin !"

" Hah !" said the Marquis, glancing round the luxurious room.

" To the eye it is fair enough, here ; but seen in its integrity, under the sky, and by the daylight, it is a crumbling tower of waste, mismanagement, extortion, debt, mortgage, oppression, hunger, nakedness, and suffering."

" Hah !" said the Marquis again, in a well-satisfied manner.

" If it ever becomes mine, it shall be put into some hands better qualified to free it slowly (if such a thing is possible) from the weight that drags it down, so that the miserable people who cannot leave it, and who have been long wrung to the last point of endurance, may, in another generation, suffer less ; but it is not for me. There is a curse on it, and on all this land."

" And you ? " said the uncle. " Forgive my curiosity ; do you, under your new philosophy, graciously intend to live ? "

" I must do, to live, what others of my countrymen, even with nobility at their backs, may have to do some day—work."

" In England, for example ? "

" Yes. The family honour, Sir, is safe from me in this country. The family name can suffer from me in no other, for I bear it in no other."

The ringing of the bell had caused the adjoining bed-chamber to be lighted. It now shone brightly, through the door of communication. The Marquis looked that way, and listened for the retreating step of his valet.

" England is very attractive to you, seeing how indifferently you have prospered there," he observed then, turning his calm face to his nephew with a smile.

" I have already said, that for my prospering there I am sensible I may be indebted to you, Sir. For the rest, it is my Refuge."

" They say, those boastful English, that it is the Refuge of many. You know a compatriot who has found a Refuge there? A Doctor ? "

" Yes."

" With a daughter ? "

" Yes."

" Yes," said the Marquis. " You are fatigued. Good-night !"

As he bent his head in his most courtly manner, there was a secrecy in his smiling face, and he conveyed an air of mystery to those words, which struck the eyes and ears of his nephew forcibly. At the same time the thin straight lines of the setting of the eyes, and the thin straight lips, and the markings in the nose, curved with a sarcasm that looked handsomely diabolic.

" Yes," repeated the Marquis. " A Doctor with a daughter. Yes. So commences the new philosophy ! You are fatigued. Good-night !"

It would have been of as much avail to interrogate any stone face outside the château as to interrogate that face of his. The nephew looked at him, in vain, in passing on to the door.

"Good-night!" said the uncle. "I look to the pleasure of seeing you again in the morning. Good repose! Light Monsieur my nephew to his chamber there!—And burn Monsieur my nephew in his bed, if you will," he added to himself, before he rang his little bell again, and summoned his valet to his own bedroom.

The valet come and gone, Monsieur the Marquis walked to and fro in his loose chamber-robe, to prepare himself gently for sleep, that hot still night. Rustling about the room, his softly-slippered feet making no noise on the floor, he moved like a refined tiger—looked like some enchanted marquis of the impenitently wicked sort, in story, whose periodical change into tiger form was either just going off, or just coming on.

He moved from end to end of his voluptuous bedroom, looking again at the scraps of the day's journey that came unbidden into his mind: the slow toil up the hill at sunset, the setting sun, the descent, the mill, the prison on the crag, the little village in the hollow, the peasants at the fountain, and the mender of roads with his blue cap pointing out the chain under the carriage. That fountain suggested the Paris fountain, the little bundle lying on the step, the women bending over it, and the tall man with his arms up, crying "Dead!"

"I am cool now," said Monsieur the Marquis, "and may go to bed."

So, leaving only one light burning on the large hearth, he let his thin gauze curtains fall around him, and heard the night break its silence with a long sigh as he composed himself to sleep.

The stone faces on the outer walls stared blindly at the black night for three heavy hours; for three heavy hours the horses in the stables rattled at their racks, the dogs barked, and the owl made a noise with very little resemblance in it to the noise conventionally assigned to the owl by men-poets. But it is the obstinate custom of such creatures hardly ever to say what is set down for them.

For three heavy hours the stone faces of the château, lion and human, stared blindly at the night. Dead darkness lay on all the landscape, dead darkness added its own hush to the hushing dust on all the roads. The burial-place had got to the pass that its little heaps of poor grass were undistinguishable from one another; the figure on the cross might have come down, for anything that could be seen of it. In the village, taxers and taxed were fast asleep. Dreaming, perhaps, of banquets, as the starved usually do, and of ease and rest, as the driven slave and the yoked ox may, its lean inhabitants slept soundly, and were fed and freed.

The fountain in the village flowed unseen and unheard, and the fountain at the château dropped unseen and unheard—both melting away, like the minutes that were falling from the spring of Time— through three dark hours. Then the gray water of both began to be ghostly in the light, and the eyes of the stone faces of the château were opened.

Lighter and lighter, until at last the sun touched the tops of the

still trees, and poured its radiance over the hill. In the glow the
water of the château fountain seemed to turn to blood, and the stone
faces crimsoned. The carol of the birds was loud and high, and on
the weather-beaten sill of the great window of the bed-chamber of
Monsieur the Marquis one little bird sang its sweetest song with all
its might. At this the nearest stone face seemed to stare amazed,
and, with open mouth and dropped under-jaw, looked awe-stricken.

Now the sun was full up, and movement began in the village.
Casement windows opened, crazy doors were unbarred, and people
came forth shivering—chilled, as yet, by the new sweet air. Then
began the rarely lightened toil of the day among the village population.
Some to the fountain; some to the fields; men and women here, to
dig and delve; men and women there, to see to the poor live stock,
and lead the bony cows out, to such pasture as could be found by the
roadside. In the church and at the cross, a kneeling figure or two;
attendant on the latter prayers, the led cow, trying for a breakfast
among the weeds at its foot.

The château awoke later, as became its quality, but awoke gradually
and surely. First the lonely boar-spears and knives of the chase had
been reddened as of old; then had gleamed trenchant in the morning
sunshine; now doors and windows were thrown open, horses in their
stables looked round over their shoulders at the light and freshness
pouring in at doorways, leaves sparkled and rustled at iron-grated
windows, dogs pulled hard at their chains, and reared impatient to be
loosed.

All these trivial incidents belonged to the routine of life, and the
return of morning. Surely not so the ringing of the great bell of the
château, nor the running up and down the stairs; nor the hurried
figures on the terrace; nor the booting and tramping here and there
and everywhere, nor the quick saddling of horses and riding away?

What winds conveyed this hurry to the grizzled mender of roads,
already at work on the hill-top beyond the village, with his day's
dinner (not much to carry) lying in a bundle that it was worth no
crow's while to peck at, on a heap of stones? Had the birds, carrying
some grains of it to a distance, dropped one over him as they sow
chance seeds? Whether or no, the mender of roads ran, on the sultry
morning, as if for his life, down the hill, knee-high in dust, and never
stopped till he got to the fountain.

All the people of the village were at the fountain, standing about in
their depressed manner, and whispering low, but showing no other
emotions than grim curiosity and surprise. The led cows, hastily
brought in and tethered to anything that would hold them, were
looking stupidly on, or lying down chewing the cud of nothing
particularly repaying their trouble, which they had picked up in their
interrupted saunter. Some of the people of the château, and some of
those of the posting-house, and all the taxing authorities, were armed
more or less, and were crowded on the other side of the little street in
a purposeless way, that was highly fraught with nothing. Already

the mender of roads had penetrated into the midst of a group of fifty particular friends, and was smiting himself in the breast with his blue cap. What did all this portend, and what portended the swift hoisting-up of Monsieur Gabelle behind a servant on horseback, and the conveying away of the said Gabelle (double-laden though the horse was) at a gallop, like a new version of the German ballad of Leonora?

It portended that there was one stone face too many up at the château.

The Gorgon had surveyed the building again in the night, and had added the one stone face wanting; the stone face for which it had waited through about two hundred years.

It lay back on the pillow of Monsieur the Marquis. It was like a fine mask, suddenly startled, made angry, and petrified. Driven home into the heart of the stone figure attached to it was a knife. Round its hilt was a frill of paper, on which was scrawled—

"*Drive him fast to his tomb. This, from* JACQUES."

CHAPTER X

TWO PROMISES

MORE months, to the number of twelve, had come and gone, and Mr. Charles Darnay was established in England as a higher teacher of the French language who was conversant with French literature. In this age he would have been a Professor; in that age he was a Tutor. He read with young men who could find any leisure and interest for the study of a living tongue spoken all over the world, and he cultivated a taste for its stores of knowledge and fancy. He could write of them, besides, in sound English, and render them into sound English. Such masters were not at that time easily found; Princes that had been, and Kings that were to be, were not yet of the Teacher class, and no ruined nobility had dropped out of Tellson's ledgers to turn cooks and carpenters. As a tutor, whose attainments made the student's way unusually pleasant and profitable, and as an elegant translator who brought something to his work besides mere dictionary knowledge, young Mr. Darnay soon became known and encouraged. He was well acquainted, moreover, with the circumstances of his country, and those were of ever-growing interest. So, with great perseverance and untiring industry, he prospered.

In London he had expected neither to walk on pavements of gold, nor to lie on beds of roses; if he had had any such exalted expectation, he would not have prospered. He had expected labour, and he found it, and did it, and made the best of it. In this his prosperity consisted.

A certain portion of his time was passed at Cambridge, where he read with undergraduates as a sort of tolerated smuggler who drove a contraband trade in European languages, instead of conveying Greek and Latin through the Custom-house. The rest of his time he passed in London.

Now, from the days when it was always summer in Eden, to these days when it is mostly winter in fallen latitudes, the world of a man has invariably gone one way—Charles Darnay's way—the way of the love of a woman.

He had loved Lucie Manette from the hour of his danger. He had never heard a sound so sweet and dear as the sound of her compassionate voice ; he had never seen a face so tenderly beautiful as hers when it was confronted with his own on the edge of the grave that had been dug for him. But he had not yet spoken to her on the subject ; the assassination at the deserted château far away beyond the heaving water and the long, long, dusty roads—the solid stone château which had itself become the mere mist of a dream—had been done a year, and he had never yet, by so much as a single spoken word, disclosed to her the state of his heart.

That he had his reasons for this he knew full well. It was again a summer day when, lately arrived in London from his college occupation, he turned into the quiet corner in Soho, bent on seeking an opportunity of opening his mind to Doctor Manette. It was the close of the summer day, and he knew Lucie to be out with Miss Pross.

He found the Doctor reading in his arm-chair at a window. The energy which had at once supported him under his old sufferings and aggravated their sharpness had been gradually restored to him. He was now a very energetic man indeed, with great firmness of purpose, strength of resolution, and vigour of action. In his recovered energy he was sometimes a little fitful and sudden, as he had at first been in the exercise of his other recovered faculties ; but this had never been frequently observable, and had grown more and more rare.

He studied much, slept little, sustained a great deal of fatigue with ease, and was equably cheerful. To him now entered Charles Darnay, at sight of whom he laid aside his book and held out his hand.

"Charles Darnay ! I rejoice to see you. We have been counting on your return these three or four days past. Mr. Stryver and Sydney Carton were both here yesterday, and both made you out to be more than due."

"I am obliged to them for their interest in the matter," he answered, a little coldly as to them, though very warmly as to the Doctor. "Miss Manette——"

"Is well," said the Doctor, as he stopped short, "and your return will delight us all. She has gone out on some household matters, but will soon be home."

"Doctor Manette, I knew she was from home. I took the opportunity of her being from home to beg to speak to you."

There was a blank silence.

"Yes?" said the Doctor, with evident constraint. "Bring your chair here, and speak on."

He complied as to the chair, but appeared to find the speaking on less easy.

"I have had the happiness, Doctor Manette, of being so intimate here," so he at length began, "for some year and a half, that I hope the topic on which I am about to touch may not——"

He was stayed by the Doctor's putting out his hand to stop him. When he had kept it so a little while, he said, drawing it back—

"Is Lucie the topic?"

"She is."

"It is hard for me to speak of her at any time. It is very hard for me to hear her spoken of in that tone of yours, Charles Darnay."

"It is a tone of fervent admiration, true homage, and deep love, Doctor Manette!" he said deferentially.

There was another blank silence before her father rejoined—

"I believe it. I do you justice; I believe it."

His constraint was so manifest, and it was so manifest, too, that it originated in an unwillingness to approach the subject, that Charles Darnay hesitated.

"Shall I go on, Sir?"

Another blank.

"Yes, go on."

"You anticipate what I would say, though you cannot know how earnestly I say it, how earnestly I feel it, without knowing my secret heart, and the hopes and fears and anxieties with which it has long been laden. Dear Doctor Manette, I love your daughter fondly, dearly, disinterestedly, devotedly. If ever there were love in the world, I love her. You have loved yourself; let your old love speak for me!"

The Doctor sat with his face turned away, and his eyes bent on the ground. At the last words he stretched out his hand again, hurriedly, and cried—

"Not that, Sir! Let that be! I adjure you, do not recall that!"

His cry was so like a cry of actual pain, that it rang in Charles Darnay's ears long after he had ceased. He motioned with the hand he had extended, and it seemed to be an appeal to Darnay to pause. The latter so received it, and remained silent.

"I ask your pardon," said the Doctor, in a subdued tone, after some moments. "I do not doubt your loving Lucie; you may be satisfied of it."

He turned towards him in his chair, but did not look at him, or raise his eyes. His chin dropped upon his hand, and his white hair overshadowed his face—

"Have you spoken to Lucie?"

"No."

"Nor written?"

"Never."

"It would be ungenerous to affect not to know that your self-denial is to be referred to your consideration for her father. Her father thanks you."

He offered his hand ; but his eyes did not go with it.

"I know," said Darnay, respectfully, "how can I fail to know, Doctor Manette, I who have seen you together from day to day, that between you and Miss Manette there is an affection so unusual, so touching, so belonging to the circumstances in which it has been nurtured, that it can have few parallels, even in the tenderness between a father and child. I know, Dr. Manette—how can I fail to know— that, mingled with the affection and duty of a daughter who has become a woman, there is in her heart towards you all the love and reliance of infancy itself. I know that, as in her childhood she had no parent, so she is now devoted to you with all the constancy and fervour of her present years and character, united to the trustfulness and attachment of the early days in which you were lost to her. I know perfectly well that if you had been restored to her from the world beyond this life, you could hardly be invested, in her sight, with a more sacred character than that in which you are always with her. I know that when she is clinging to you, the hands of baby, girl, and woman, all in one, are round your neck. I know that in loving you she sees and loves her mother at her own age, sees and loves you at my age, loves her mother broken-hearted, loves you through your dreadful trial and in your blessed restoration. I have known this, night and day, since I have known you in your home."

Her father sat silent, with his face bent down. His breathing was a little quickened ; but he repressed all other signs of agitation.

"Dear Doctor Manette, always knowing this, always seeing her and you with this hallowed light about you, I have forborne, and forborne, as long as it was in the nature of man to do it. I have felt, and do even now feel, that to bring my love—even mine—between you, is to touch your history with something not quite as good as itself. But I love her. Heaven is my witness that I love her !"

"I believe it," answered her father, mournfully. "I have thought so before now. I believe it."

"But do not believe," said Darnay, upon whose ear the mournful voice struck with a reproachful sound, "that if my fortune were so cast as that, being one day so happy as to make her my wife, I must at any time put any separation between her and you, I could or would breathe a word of what I now say. Besides that I should know it to be hopeless, I should know it to be a baseness. If I had any such possibility, even at a remote distance of years, harboured in my thoughts, and hidden in my heart—if it ever had been there—if it ever could be there—I could not now touch this honoured hand."

He laid his own upon it as he spoke.

"No, dear Doctor Manette. Like you, a voluntary exile from France ; like you, driven from it by its distractions, oppressions, and miseries ; like you, striving to live away from it by my own exertions, and trusting in a happier future, I look only to sharing your fortunes, sharing your life and home, and being faithful to you to the death,— not to divide with Lucie her privilege as your child, companion, and friend ; but to come in aid of it, and bind her closer to you, if such a thing can be."

His touch still lingered on her father's hand. Answering the touch for a moment, but not coldly, her father rested his hands upon the arms of his chair, and looked up for the first time since the beginning of the conference. A struggle was evidently in his face ; a struggle with that occasional look which had a tendency in it to dark doubt and dread.

"You speak so feelingly and so manfully, Charles Darnay, that I thank you with all my heart, and will open all my heart—or nearly so. Have you any reason to believe that Lucie loves you ? "

"None. As yet, none."

"Is it the immediate object of this confidence, that you may at once ascertain that, with my knowledge ? "

"Not even so. I might not have the hopefulness to do it for weeks ; I might (mistaken or not mistaken) have that hopefulness to-morrow."

"Do you seek any guidance from me ? "

"I ask none, Sir. But I have thought it possible that you might have it in your power, if you should deem it right, to give me some."

"Do you seek any promise from me ? "

"I do seek that."

"What is it ? "

"I well understand that, without you, I could have no hope. I well understand that, even if Miss Manette held me at this moment in her innocent heart—do not think I have the presumption to assume so much—I could retain no place in it against her love for her father."

"If that be so, do you see what, on the other hand, is involved in it ? "

"I understand equally well that a word from her father in any suitor's favour would outweigh herself and all the world. For which reason, Doctor Manette," said Darnay, modestly but firmly, "I would not ask that word to save my life."

"I am sure of it. Charles Darnay, mysteries arise out of close love, as well as out of wide division ; in the former case, they are subtle and delicate, and difficult to penetrate. My daughter Lucie is, in this one respect, such a mystery to me ; I can make no guess at the state of her heart."

"May I ask, Sir, if you think she is——" As he hesitated, her father supplied the rest.

"Is sought by any other suitor ? "

"It is what I meant to say."

Her father considered a little before he answered—

"You have seen Mr. Carton here, yourself. Mr. Stryver is here too, occasionally. If it be at all, it can only be by one of these."

"Or both," said Darnay.

"I had not thought of both ; I should not think either likely. You want a promise from me. Tell me what it is."

"It is, that if Miss Manette should bring to you at any time, on her own part, such a confidence as I have ventured to lay before you, you will bear testimony to what I have said, and to your belief in it. I hope you may be able to think so well of me as to urge no influence against me. I say nothing more of my stake in this; this is what I ask. The condition on which I ask it, and which you have an undoubted right to require, I will observe immediately."

"I give the promise," said the Doctor, "without any condition. I believe your object to be, purely and truthfully, as you have stated it. I believe your intention is to perpetuate, and not to weaken, the ties between me and my other and far dearer self. If she should ever tell me that you are essential to her perfect happiness, I will give her to you. If there were—Charles Darnay, if there were——"

The young man had taken his hand gratefully; their hands were joined as the Doctor spoke.

"—any fancies, any reasons, any apprehensions, anything whatsoever, new or old, against the man she really loved — the direct responsibility thereof not lying on his head — they should all be obliterated for her sake. She is everything to me; more to me than suffering, more to me than wrong, more to me—— Well! This is idle talk."

So strange was the way in which he faded into silence, and so strange his fixed look when he had ceased to speak, that Darnay felt his own hand turn cold in the hand that slowly released and dropped it.

"You said something to me," said Doctor Manette, breaking into a smile. "What was it you said to me?"

He was at a loss how to answer, until he remembered having spoken of a condition. Relieved as his mind reverted to that, he answered—

"Your confidence in me ought to be returned with full confidence on my part. My present name, though but slightly changed from my mother's, is not, as you will remember, my own. I wish to tell you what that is, and why I am in England."

"Stop!" said the Doctor of Beauvais.

"I wish it, that I may the better deserve your confidence, and have no secret from you."

"Stop!"

For an instant the Doctor even had his two hands at his ears; for another instant, even had his two hands laid on Darnay's lips.

"Tell me when I ask you, not now. If your suit should prosper, if Lucie should love you, you shall tell me on your marriage morning. Do you promise?"

"Willingly."

"Give me your hand. She will be home directly, and it is better she should not see us together to-night. Go! God bless you!"

It was dark when Charles Darnay left him, and it was an hour later and darker when Lucie came home; she hurried into the room alone—for Miss Pross had gone straight up-stairs—and was surprised to find his reading-chair empty.

"My father!" she called to him. "Father dear!"

Nothing was said in answer, but she heard a low hammering sound in his bedroom. Passing lightly across the intermediate room, she looked in at his door and came running back frightened, crying to herself, with her blood all chilled, "What shall I do! What shall I do!"

Her uncertainty lasted but a moment; she hurried back, and tapped at his door, and softly called to him. The noise ceased at the sound of her voice, and he presently came out to her, and they walked up and down together for a long time.

She came down from her bed to look at him in his sleep that night. He slept heavily, and his tray of shoemaking tools, and his old unfinished work, were all as usual.

CHAPTER XI

A COMPANION PICTURE

"SYDNEY," said Mr. Stryver, on that self-same night, or morning, to his jackal, "mix another bowl of punch; I have something to say to you."

Sydney had been working double tides that night, and the night before, and the night before that, and a good many nights in succession, making a grand clearance among Mr. Stryver's papers before the setting in of the Long Vacation. The clearance was effected at last; the Stryver arrears were handsomely fetched up; everything was got rid of until November should come with its fogs atmospheric and fogs legal, and bring grist to the mill again.

Sydney was none the livelier and none the soberer for so much application. It had taken a deal of extra wet-towelling to pull him through the night; a correspondingly extra quantity of wine had preceded the towelling; and he was in a very damaged condition, as he now pulled his turban off and threw it into the basin in which he had steeped it at intervals for the last six hours.

"Are you mixing that other bowl of punch?" said Stryver the portly, with his hands in his waistband, glancing round from the sofa where he lay on his back.

"I am."

"Now, look here! I am going to tell you something that will rather surprise you, and that perhaps will make you think me not quite as shrewd as you usually do think me. I intend to marry."

"*Do* you?"

"Yes. And not for money. What do you say now?"

"I don't feel disposed to say much. Who is she?"

"Guess."

"Do I know her?"

"Guess."

"I am not going to guess, at five o'clock in the morning, with my brains frying-and sputtering in my head. If you want me to guess, you must ask me to dinner."

"Well then, I'll tell you," said Stryver, coming slowly into a sitting posture. "Sydney, I rather despair of making myself intelligible to you, because you are such an insensible dog."

"And you," returned Sydney, busy concocting the punch, "are such a sensitive and poetical spirit."

"Come!" rejoined Stryver, laughing boastfully, "though I don't prefer any claim to being the soul of Romance (for I hope I know better), still I am a tenderer sort of fellow than *you*."

"You are a luckier, if you mean that."

"I don't mean that. I mean I am a man of more—more——"

"Say gallantry, while you are about it," suggested Carton.

"Well! I'll say gallantry. My meaning is that I am a man," said Stryver, inflating himself at his friend as he made the punch, "who cares more to be agreeable, who takes more pains to be agreeable, who knows better how to be agreeable, in a woman's society, than you do."

"Go on," said Sydney Carton.

"No; but before I go on," said Stryver, shaking his head in his bullying way, "I'll have this out with you. You've been at Dr. Manette's house as much as I have, or more than I have. Why, I have been ashamed of your moroseness there! Your manners have been of that silent and sullen and hang-dog kind, that, upon my life and soul, I have been ashamed of you, Sydney!"

"It should be very beneficial to a man in your practice at the bar to be ashamed of anything," returned Sydney; "you ought to be much obliged to me."

"You shall not get off in that way," rejoined Stryver, shouldering the rejoinder at him; "no, Sydney, it's my duty to tell you—and I tell you to your face to do you good—that you are a de-vilish ill-conditioned fellow in that sort of society. You are a disagreeable fellow."

Sydney drank a bumper of the punch he had made, and laughed.

"Look at me!" said Stryver, squaring himself; "I have less need to make myself agreeable than you have, being more independent in circumstances. Why do I do it?"

"I never saw you do it yet," muttered Carton.

"I do it because it's politic; I do it on principle. And look at me! I get on."

"You don't get on with your account of your matrimonial intentions," answered Carton, with a careless air; "I wish you would keep to that. As to me—will you never understand that I am incorrigible?" He asked the question with some appearance of scorn.

"You have no business to be incorrigible," was his friend's answer, delivered in no very soothing tone.

"I have no business to be, at all, that I know of," said Sydney Carton. "Who is the lady?"

"Now, don't let my announcement of the name make you uncomfortable, Sydney," said Mr. Stryver, preparing him with ostentatious friendliness for the disclosure he was about to make, "because I know you don't mean half you say; and if you meant it all, it would be of no importance. I make this little preface, because you once mentioned the young lady to me in slighting terms."

" I did ? "

" Certainly ; and in these chambers."

Sydney Carton looked at his punch and looked at his complacent friend ; drank his punch and looked at his complacent friend.

" You made mention of the young lady as a golden-haired doll. The young lady is Miss Manette. If you had been a fellow of any sensitiveness or delicacy of feeling in that kind of way, Sydney, I might have been a little resentful of your employing such a designation ; but you are not. You want that sense altogether ; therefore I am no more annoyed when I think of the expression than I should be annoyed by a man's opinion of a picture of mine, who had no eye for pictures ; or of a piece of music of mine, who had no ear for music."

Sydney Carton drank the punch at a great rate ; drank it by bumpers, looking at his friend.

" Now you know all about it, Syd," said Mr. Stryver. " I don't care about fortune ; she is a charming creature, and I have made up my mind to please myself ; on the whole, I think I can afford to please myself. She will have in me a man already pretty well off, and a rapidly rising man, and a man of some distinction : it is a piece of good fortune for her, but she is worthy of good fortune. Are you astonished ? "

Carton, still drinking the punch, rejoined, " Why should I be astonished ? "

" You approve ? "

Carton, still drinking the punch, rejoined, " Why should I not approve ? "

" Well ! " said his friend Stryver, "you take it more easily than I fancied you would, and are less mercenary on my behalf than I thought you would be ; though, to be sure, you know well enough by this time that your ancient chum is a man of a pretty strong will. Yes, Sydney, I have had enough of this style of life, with no other as a change from it ; I feel that it is a pleasant thing for a man to have a home when he feels inclined to go to it (when he doesn't, he can stay away), and I feel that Miss Manette will tell well in any station, and will always do me credit. So I have made up my mind. And now, Sydney, old boy, I want to say a word to *you* about *your* prospects. You are in a bad way, you know ; you really are in a bad way. You don't know the value of money, you live hard, you'll knock up one of these days, and be ill and poor ; you really ought to think about a nurse."

The prosperous patronage with which he said it made him look twice as big as he was, and four times as offensive.

" Now, let me recommend you," pursued Stryver, "to look it in the face. I have looked it in the face, in my different way ; look it in the

face, you, in your different way. Marry. Provide somebody to take
care of you. Never mind your having no enjoyment of women's
society, nor understanding of it, nor tact for it. Find out somebody.
Find out some respectable woman with a little property—somebody in
the landlady way, or lodging-letting way—and marry her, against a
rainy day. That's the kind of thing for *you*. Now think of it,
Sydney."

" I'll think of it," said Sydney.

CHAPTER XII

THE FELLOW OF DELICACY

Mr. Stryver, having made up his mind to that magnanimous bestowal
of good fortune on the Doctor's daughter, resolved to make her
happiness known to her before he left town for the Long Vacation.
After some mental debating of the point, he came to the conclusion
that it would be as well to get all the preliminaries done with, and
they could then arrange at their leisure whether he should give her his
hand a week or two before Michaelmas Term, or in the little Christmas
vacation between it and Hilary.

As to the strength of his case, he had not a doubt about it, but
clearly saw his way to the verdict. Argued with the jury on substantial worldly grounds—the only grounds ever worth taking into
account—it was a plain case, and had not a weak spot in it. He
called himself for the plaintiff, there was no getting over his evidence,
the counsel for the defendant threw up his brief, and the jury did not
even turn to consider. After trying it, Stryver, C.J., was satisfied
that no plainer case could be.

Accordingly, Mr. Stryver inaugurated the Long Vacation with a
formal proposal to take Miss Manette to Vauxhall Gardens ; that
failing, to Ranelagh ; that unaccountably failing too, it behoved him
to present himself in Soho, and there declare his noble mind.

Towards Soho, therefore, Mr. Stryver shouldered his way from the
Temple, while the bloom of the Long Vacation's infancy was still upon
it. Anybody who had seen him projecting himself into Soho while he
was yet on Saint Dunstan's side of Temple Bar, bursting in his full-
blown way along the pavement, to the jostlement of all weaker people,
might have seen how safe and strong he was.

His way taking him past Tellson's, and he both banking at Tellson's
and knowing Mr. Lorry as the intimate friend of the Manettes, it
entered Mr. Stryver's mind to enter the bank, and reveal to Mr. Lorry
the brightness of the Soho horizon. So he pushed open the door with
the weak rattle in its throat, stumbled down the two steps, got past
the two ancient cashiers, and shouldered himself into the musty back

closet where Mr. Lorry sat at great books ruled for figures, with perpendicular iron bars to his window, as if that were ruled for figures too, and everything under the clouds were a sum.

"Halloa!" said Mr. Stryver. "How do you do? I hope you are well!"

It was Stryver's grand peculiarity that he always seemed too big for any place, or space. He was so much too big for Tellson's, that old clerks in distant corners looked up with looks of remonstrance, as though he squeezed them against the wall. The House itself, magnificently reading the paper quite in the far-off perspective, lowered displeased, as if the Stryver head had been butted into its responsible waistcoat.

The discreet Mr. Lorry said, in a sample tone of the voice he would recommend under the circumstances, "How do you do, Mr. Stryver? How do you do, Sir?" and shook hands. There was a peculiarity in his manner of shaking hands, always to be seen in any clerk at Tellson's who shook hands with a customer when the House pervaded the air. He shook in a self-abnegating way, as one who shook for Tellson and Co.

"Can I do anything for you, Mr. Stryver?" asked Mr. Lorry, in his business character.

"Why, no, thank you; this is a private visit to yourself, Mr. Lorry; I have come for a private word."

"Oh indeed!" said Mr. Lorry, bending down his ear, while his eye strayed to the House afar off.

"I am going," said Mr. Stryver, leaning his arms confidentially on the desk; whereupon, although it was a large double one, there appeared to be not half desk enough for him,—"I am going to make an offer of myself in marriage to your agreeable little friend, Miss Manette, Mr. Lorry."

"Oh dear me!" cried Mr. Lorry, rubbing his chin, and looking at his visitor dubiously.

"Oh dear me, Sir?" repeated Stryver, drawing back. "Oh dear you, Sir? What may your meaning be, Mr. Lorry?"

"My meaning," answered the man of business, "is, of course, friendly and appreciative, and that it does you the greatest credit, and —in short, my meaning is everything you could desire. But—really, you know, Mr. Stryver——" Mr. Lorry paused, and shook his head at him in the oddest manner, as if he were compelled against his will to add, internally, "you know there really is so much too much of you!"

"Well!" said Stryver, slapping the desk with his contentious hand, opening his eyes wider, and taking a long breath, "if I understand you, Mr. Lorry, I'll be hanged!"

Mr. Lorry adjusted his little wig at both ears as a means towards that end, and bit the feather of a pen.

"D—n it all, Sir!" said Stryver, staring at him, "am I not eligible?"

"Oh dear yes! Yes. Oh yes, you're eligible!" said Mr. Lorry. "If you say eligible, you are eligible."

"Am I not prosperous?" asked Stryver.

"Oh! if you come to prosperous, you are prosperous," said Mr. Lorry.

"And advancing?"

"If you come to advancing, you know," said Mr. Lorry, delighted to be able to make another admission, "nobody can doubt that."

"Then what on earth is your meaning, Mr. Lorry?" demanded Stryver, perceptibly crestfallen.

"Well! I—— Were you going there now?" asked Mr. Lorry.

"Straight!" said Stryver, with a plump of his fist on the desk.

"Then I think I wouldn't, if I was you."

"Why?" said Stryver. "Now, I'll put you in a corner," forensically shaking a forefinger at him. "You are a man of business and bound to have a reason. State your reason. Why wouldn't you go?"

"Because," said Mr. Lorry, "I wouldn't go on such an object without having some cause to believe that I should succeed."

"D—n me!" cried Stryver, "but this beats everything."

Mr. Lorry glanced at the distant House, and glanced at the angry Stryver.

"Here's a man of business—a man of years—a man of experience—in a Bank," said Stryver; "and having summed up three leading reasons for complete success, he says there's no reason at all! Says it with his head on!" Mr. Stryver remarked upon the peculiarity as if it would have been infinitely less remarkable if he had said it with his head off.

"When I speak of success, I speak of success with the young lady; and when I speak of causes and reasons to make success probable, I speak of causes and reasons that will tell as such with the young lady. The young lady, my good Sir," said Mr. Lorry, mildly tapping the Stryver arm, "the young lady. The young lady goes before all."

"Then you mean to tell me, Mr. Lorry," said Stryver, squaring his elbows, "that it is your deliberate opinion that the young lady at present in question is a mincing Fool?"

"Not exactly so. I mean to tell you, Mr. Stryver," said Mr. Lorry, reddening, "that I will hear no disrespectful word of that young lady from any lips; and that if I knew any man—which I hope I do not—whose taste was so coarse, and whose temper was so overbearing, that he could not restrain himself from speaking disrespectfully of that young lady at this desk, not even Tellson's should prevent my giving him a piece of my mind."

The necessity of being angry in a suppressed tone had put Mr. Stryver's blood-vessels into a dangerous state when it was his turn to be angry; Mr. Lorry's veins, methodical as their courses could usually be, were in no better state now it was his turn.

"That is what I mean to tell you, Sir," said Mr. Lorry. "Pray let there be no mistake about it."

Mr. Stryver sucked the end of a ruler for a little while, and then stood hitting a tune out of his teeth with it, which probably gave him the toothache. He broke the awkward silence by saying—

"This is something new to me, Mr. Lorry. You deliberately advise me not to go up to Soho and offer myself—myself, Stryver, of the King's Bench bar?"

"Do you ask me for my advice, Mr. Stryver?"

"Yes, I do."

"Very good. Then I give it, and you have repeated it correctly."

"And all I can say of it is," laughed Stryver, with a vexed laugh, "that this—ha, ha! beats everything past, present, and to come."

"Now understand me," pursued Mr. Lorry. "As a man of business, I am not justified in saying anything about this matter, for, as a man of business, I know nothing of it. But as an old fellow who has carried Miss Manette in his arms, who is the trusted friend of Miss Manette and of her father too, and who has a great affection for them both, I have spoken. The confidence is not of my seeking, recollect. Now, you think I may not be right?"

"Not I!" said Stryver, whistling. "I can't undertake to find third parties in common sense; I can only find it for myself. I suppose sense in certain quarters; you suppose mincing bread-and-butter nonsense. It's new to me, but you are right, I dare say."

"What I suppose, Mr. Stryver, I claim to characterise for myself. And understand me, Sir," said Mr. Lorry, quickly flushing again, "I will not—not even at Tellson's—have it characterised for me by any gentleman breathing."

"There! I beg your pardon!" said Stryver.

"Granted. Thank you. Well, Mr. Stryver, I was about to say— it might be painful to you to find yourself mistaken; it might be painful to Doctor Manette to have the task of being explicit with you; it might be very painful to Miss Manette to have the task of being explicit with you. You know the terms upon which I have the honour and happiness to stand with the family. If you please, committing you in no way, representing you in no way, I will undertake to correct my advice by the exercise of a little new observation and judgment expressly brought to bear upon it. If you should then be dissatisfied with it, you can but test its soundness for yourself; if, on the other hand, you should be satisfied with it, and it should be what it now is, it may spare all sides what is best spared. What do you say?"

"How long would you keep me in town?"

"Oh! it is only a question of a few hours. I could go to Soho in the evening, and come to your chambers afterwards."

"Then I say yes," said Stryver; "I won't go up there now—I am not so hot upon it as that comes to; I say yes, and I shall expect you to look in to-night. Good-morning."

Then Mr. Stryver turned and burst out of the Bank, causing such a concussion of air on his passage through, that to stand up against it bowing behind the two counters required the utmost remaining strength of the two ancient clerks. Those venerable and feeble persons were always seen by the public in the act of bowing, and were popularly believed, when they had bowed a customer out, still to keep on bowing in the empty office until they bowed another customer in.

The barrister was keen enough to divine that the banker would not have gone so far in his expression of opinion on any less solid ground than moral certainty. Unprepared as he was for the large pill he had to swallow, he got it down. "And now," said Mr. Stryver, shaking his forensic forefinger at the Temple in general, when it was down, "my way out of this is to put you all in the wrong."

It was a bit of the art of an Old Bailey tactician, in which he found great relief. "You shall not put me in the wrong, young lady," said Mr. Stryver; "I'll do that for you."

Accordingly, when Mr. Lorry called that night as late as ten o'clock, Mr. Stryver, among a quantity of books and papers littered out for the purpose, seemed to have nothing less on his mind than the subject of the morning. He even showed surprise when he saw Mr. Lorry, and was altogether in an absent and preoccupied state.

"Well!" said that good-natured emissary, after a full half-hour of bootless attempts to bring him round to the question. "I have been to Soho."

"To Soho?" repeated Mr. Stryver, coldly. "Oh, to be sure! What am I thinking of!"

"And I have no doubt," said Mr. Lorry, "that I was right in the conversation we had. My opinion is confirmed, and I reiterate my advice."

"I assure you," returned Mr. Stryver, in the friendliest way, "that I am sorry for it on your account, and sorry for it on the poor father's account. I know this must always be a sore subject with the family; let us say no more about it."

"I don't understand you," said Mr. Lorry.

"I dare say not," rejoined Stryver, nodding his head in a soothing and final way; "no matter, no matter."

"But it does matter," Mr. Lorry urged.

"No, it doesn't; I assure you it doesn't. Having supposed that there was sense where there is no sense, and a laudable ambition where there is not a laudable ambition, I am well out of my mistake, and no harm is done. Young women have committed similar follies often before, and have repented them in poverty and obscurity often before. In an unselfish aspect, I am sorry that the thing is dropped, because it would have been a bad thing for me in a worldly point of view; in a selfish aspect, I am glad that the thing has dropped, because it would have been a bad thing for me in a worldly point of view—it is hardly necessary to say I could have gained nothing by it. There is no harm at all done. I have not proposed to the young lady, and, between ourselves, I am by no means certain, on reflection, that I ever should have committed myself to that extent. Mr. Lorry, you cannot control the mincing vanities and giddinesses of empty-headed girls; you must not expect to do it, or you will always be disappointed. Now, pray say no more about it. I tell you, I regret it on account of others, but I am satisfied on my own account. And I am really very much obliged to you for allowing me to sound you, and for giving me your advice ; you know the young lady better than I do ; you were right, it never would have done."

Mr. Lorry was so taken aback, that he looked quite stupidly at Mr. Stryver shouldering him towards the door, with an appearance of showering generosity, forbearance, and good-will on his erring head. "Make the best of it, my dear Sir," said Stryver ; "say no more about it ; thank you again for allowing me to sound you ; good-night ! "

Mr. Lorry was out in the night before he knew where he was. Mr. Stryver was lying back on his sofa, winking at his ceiling.

CHAPTER XIII

THE FELLOW OF NO DELICACY

IF Sydney Carton ever shone anywhere, he certainly never shone in the house of Doctor Manette. He had been there often, during a whole year, and had always been the same moody and morose lounger there. When he cared to talk, he talked well ; but the cloud of caring for nothing, which overshadowed him with such a fatal darkness, was very rarely pierced by the light within him.

And yet he did care something for the streets that environed that house, and for the senseless stones that made their pavements. Many a night he vaguely and unhappily wandered there, when wine had brought no transitory gladness to him ; many a dreary daybreak revealed his solitary figure lingering there, and still lingering there when the first beams of the sun brought into strong relief removed beauties of architecture in spires of churches and lofty buildings, as perhaps the quiet time brought some sense of better things, else forgotten and unattainable, into his mind. Of late the neglected bed in the Temple Court had known him more scantily than ever ; and often when he had thrown himself upon it no longer than a few minutes, he had got up again, and haunted that neighbourhood.

On a day in August, when Mr. Stryver (after notifying to his jackal that " he had thought better of that marrying matter ") had carried his delicacy into Devonshire, and when the sight and scent of flowers in the City streets had some waifs of goodness in them for the worst, of health for the sickliest, and of youth for the oldest, Sydney's feet still trod those stones. From being irresolute and purposeless, his feet became animated by an intention, and in the working out of that intention they took him to the Doctor's door.

He was shown up-stairs, and found Lucie at her work, alone. She had never been quite at her ease with him, and received him with some little embarrassment as he seated himself near her table. But, looking

51

Sydney Carton's last confidence

up at his face in the interchange of the first few commonplaces, she observed a change in it.

"I fear you are not well, Mr. Carton!"

"No. But the life I lead, Miss Manette, is not conducive to health. What is to be expected of, or by, such profligates?"

"Is it not—forgive me; I have begun the question on my lips—a pity to live no better life?"

"God knows it is a shame!"

"Then why not change it?"

Looking gently at him again, she was surprised and saddened to see that there were tears in his eyes. There were tears in his voice too, as he answered—

"It is too late for that. I shall never be better than I am. I shall sink lower, and be worse."

He leaned an elbow on her table, and covered his eyes with his hand. The table trembled in the silence that followed.

She had never seen him softened, and was much distressed. He knew her to be so, without looking at her, and said—

"Pray forgive me, Miss Manette. I break down before the knowledge of what I want to say to you. Will you hear me?"

"If it will do you any good, Mr. Carton, if it would make you happier, it would make me very glad!"

"God bless you for your sweet compassion!"

He unshaded his face after a little while, and spoke steadily.

"Don't be afraid to hear me. Don't shrink from anything I say. I am like one who died young. All my life might have been."

"No, Mr. Carton. I am sure that the best part of it might still be; I am sure that you might be much, much worthier of yourself."

"Say of you, Miss Manette, and although I know better—although in the mystery of my own wretched heart I know better—I shall never forget it!"

She was pale and trembling. He came to her relief with a fixed despair of himself which made the interview unlike any other that could have been holden.

"If it had been possible, Miss Manette, that you could have returned the love of the man you see before you—self-flung away, wasted, drunken, poor creature of misuse as you know him to be—he would have been conscious this day and hour, in spite of his happiness, that he would bring you to misery, bring you to sorrow and repentance, blight you, disgrace you, pull you down with him. I know very well that you can have no tenderness for me; I ask for none; I am even thankful that it cannot be."

"Without it, can I not save you, Mr. Carton? Can I not recall you —forgive me again!—to a better course? Can I in no way repay your confidence? I know this is a confidence," she modestly said, after a little hesitation, and in earnest tears, "I know you would say this to no one else. Can I turn it to no good account for yourself, Mr. Carton?"

He shook his head.

"To none. No, Miss Manette, to none. If you will hear me through a very little more, all you can ever do for me is done. I wish you to know that you have been the last dream of my soul. In my degradation I have not been so degraded but that the sight of you with your father, and of this home made such a home by you, has stirred old shadows that I thought had died out of me. Since I knew you, I have been troubled by a remorse that I thought would never reproach me again, and have heard whispers from old voices impelling me upward, that I thought were silent for ever. I have had unformed ideas of striving afresh, beginning anew, shaking off sloth and sensuality, and fighting out the abandoned fight. A dream, all a dream, that ends in nothing, and leaves the sleeper where he lay down; but I wish you to know that you inspired it."

"Will nothing of it remain? Oh Mr. Carton, think again! Try again!"

"No, Miss Manette; all through it, I have known myself to be quite undeserving. And yet I have had the weakness, and have still the weakness, to wish you to know with what a sudden mastery you kindled me, heap of ashes that I am, into fire—a fire, however, inseparable in its nature from myself, quickening nothing, lighting nothing, doing no service, idly burning away."

"Since it is my misfortune, Mr. Carton, to have made you more unhappy than you were before you knew me——"

"Don't say that, Miss Manette, for you would have reclaimed me, if anything could. You will not be the cause of my becoming worse."

"Since the state of your mind that you describe is, at all events, attributable to some influence of mine—this is what I mean, if I can make it plain—can I use no influence to serve you? Have I no power for good, with you, at all?"

"The utmost good that I am capable of now, Miss Manette, I have come here to realise. Let me carry through the rest of my misdirected life the remembrance that I opened my heart to you, last of all the world; and that there was something left in me at this time which you could deplore and pity."

"Which I entreated you to believe, again and again, most fervently, with all my heart, was capable of better things, Mr. Carton!"

"Entreat me to believe it no more, Miss Manette. I have proved myself, and I know better. I distress you; I draw fast to an end. Will you let me believe, when I recall this day, that the last confidence of my life was reposed in your pure and innocent breast, and that it lies there alone, and will be shared by no one?"

"If that will be a consolation to you, yes."

"Not even by the dearest one ever to be known to you?"

"Mr. Carton," she answered, after an agitated pause, "the secret is yours, not mine; and I promise to respect it."

"Thank you. And again, God bless you."

He put her hand to his lips, and moved towards the door.

"Be under no apprehension, Miss Manette, of my ever resuming this conversation by so much as a passing word. I will never refer to it again. If I were dead, that could not be surer than it is henceforth. In the hour of my death, I shall hold sacred the one good remembrance—and shall thank and bless you for it—that my last avowal of myself was made to you, and that my name, and faults, and miseries were gently carried in your heart. May it otherwise be light and happy!"

He was so unlike what he had ever shown himself to be, and it was so sad to think how much he had thrown away, and how much he every day kept down and perverted, that Lucie Manette wept mournfully for him as he stood looking back at her.

"Be comforted!" he said, "I am not worth such feeling, Miss Manette. An hour or two hence, and the low companions and low habits that I scorn but yield to will render me less worth such tears as those than any wretch who creeps along the streets. Be comforted! But, within myself, I shall always be, towards you, what I am now, though outwardly I shall be what you have heretofore seen me. The last supplication but one I make to you is, that you will believe this of me."

"I will, Mr. Carton."

"My last supplication of all is this, and with it I will relieve you of a visitor with whom I well know you have nothing in unison, and between whom and you there is an impassable space. It is useless to say it, I know, but it rises out of my soul. For you, and for any dear to you, I would do anything. If my career were of that better kind that there was any opportunity or capacity of sacrifice in it, I would embrace any sacrifice for you and for those dear to you. Try to hold me in your mind, at some quiet times, as ardent and sincere in this one thing. The time will come, the time will not be long in coming, when new ties will be formed about you—ties that will bind you yet more tenderly and strongly to the home you so adorn—the dearest ties that will ever grace and gladden you. Oh Miss Manette, when the little picture of a happy father's face looks up in yours, when you see your own bright beauty springing up anew at your feet, think now and then that there is a man who would give his life to keep a life you love beside you!'

He said "Farewell!" said a last "God bless you!" and left her.

CHAPTER XIV

THE HONEST TRADESMAN

To the eyes of Mr. Jeremiah Cruncher, sitting on his stool in Fleet Street with his grisly urchin beside him, a vast number and variety of objects in movement were every day presented. Who could sit upon anything in Fleet Street during the busy hours of the day, and not be dazed and deafened by two immense processions, one ever tending westward with the sun, the other ever tending eastward from the sun, both ever tending to the plains beyond the range of red and purple where the sun goes down !

With his straw in his mouth, Mr. Cruncher sat watching the two streams, like the heathen rustic who has for several centuries been on duty watching one stream—saving that Jerry had no expectation of their ever running dry. Nor would it have been an expectation of a hopeful kind, since a small part of his income was derived from the pilotage of timid women (mostly of a full habit and past the middle term of life) from Tellson's side of the tides to the opposite shore. Brief as such companionship was in every separate instance, Mr. Cruncher never failed to become so interested in the lady as to express a strong desire to have the honour of drinking her very good health. And it was from the gifts bestowed upon him towards the execution of this benevolent purpose that he recruited his finances, as just now observed.

Time was when a poet sat upon a stool in a public place and mused in the sight of men. Mr. Cruncher, sitting on a stool in a public place, but not being a poet, mused as little as possible, and looked about him.

It fell out that he was thus engaged in a season when crowds were few, and belated women few, and when his affairs in general were so unprosperous as to awaken a strong suspicion in his breast that Mrs. Cruncher must have been "flopping" in some pointed manner, when an unusual concourse pouring down Fleet Street westward attracted his attention. Looking that way, Mr. Cruncher made out that some kind of funeral was coming along, and that there was popular objection to this funeral, which engendered uproar.

"Young Jerry," said Mr. Cruncher, turning to his offspring, "it's a buryin'."

"Hooroar, father !" cried Young Jerry.

The young gentleman uttered this exultant sound with mysterious significance. The elder gentleman took the cry so ill that he watched his opportunity, and smote the young gentleman on the ear.

"What d'ye mean ? What are you hoooroaring at ? What do you want to conwey to your own father, you young Rip ? This boy is a-getting too many for *me !*" said Mr. Cruncher, surveying him. "Him and his hooroars ! Don't let me hear no more of you, or you shall feel some more of me. D'ye hear ?"

"I warn't doing no harm," Young Jerry protested, rubbing his cheek.

"Drop it then," said Mr. Cruncher ; "I won't have none of *your* no harms. Get a-top of that there seat, and look at the crowd."

His son obeyed, and the crowd approached ; they were bawling and hissing round a dingy hearse and dingy mourning coach, in which mourning coach there was only one mourner, dressed in the dingy trappings that were considered essential to the dignity of the position. The position appeared by no means to please him, however, with an increasing rabble surrounding the coach, deriding him, making grimaces at him, and incessantly groaning and calling out: "Yah! Spies! Tst! Yaha! Spies!" with many compliments too numerous and forcible to repeat.

Funerals had at all times a remarkable attraction for Mr. Cruncher; he always pricked up his senses, and became excited when a funeral passed Tellson's. Naturally, therefore, a funeral with this uncommon attendance excited him greatly, and he asked of the first man who ran against him—

"What is it, brother? What's it about?"

"*I* don't know," said the man. "Spies! Yaha! Tst! Spies!"

He asked another man. "Who is it?"

"*I* don't know," returned the man, clapping his hands to his mouth nevertheless, and vociferating in a surprising heat and with the greatest ardour, "Spies! Yaha! Tst, tst! Spi-ies!"

At length a person better informed on the merits of the case tumbled against him, and from this person he learned that the funeral was the funeral of one Roger Cly.

"Was He a spy?" asked Mr. Cruncher.

"Old Bailey spy," returned his informant. "Yaha! Tst! Yah! Old Bailey Spi-i-ies!"

"Why, to be sure!" exclaimed Jerry, recalling the trial at which he had assisted. "I've seen him. Dead, is he?"

"Dead as mutton," returned the other, "and can't be too dead. Have 'em out, there! Spies! Pull 'em out, there! Spies!"

The idea was so acceptable in the prevalent absence of any idea, that the crowd caught it up with eagerness, and loudly repeating the suggestion to have 'em out, and to pull 'em out, mobbed the two vehicles so closely that they came to a stop. On the crowd's opening the coach doors, the one mourner scuffled out of himself and was in their hands for a moment; but he was so alert, and made such good use of his time, that in another moment he was scouring away up a by-street, after shedding his cloak, hat, long hatband, white pocket-handkerchief, and other symbolical tears.

These the people tore to pieces and scattered far and wide with great enjoyment, while the tradesmen hurriedly shut up their shops; for a crowd in those times stopped at nothing, and was a monster much dreaded. They had already got the length of opening the hearse to take the coffin out, when some brighter genius proposed instead its being escorted to its destination amidst general rejoicing. Practical suggestions being much needed, this suggestion too was received with acclamation, and the coach was immediately filled with eight inside and a dozen out, while as many people got on the roof of the hearse as could by any exercise of ingenuity stick upon it. Among the first of these volunteers was Jerry Cruncher himself, who modestly concealed his spiky head from the observation of Tellson's in the further corner of the mourning coach.

The officiating undertakers made some protest against these changes in the ceremonies; but the river being alarmingly near, and several

voices remarking on the efficacy of cold immersion in bringing refractory members of the profession to reason, the protest was faint
and brief. The remodelled procession started, with a chimney-sweep
driving the hearse—advised by the regular driver, who was perched
beside him, under close inspection, for the purpose—and with a pieman,
also attended by his cabinet minister, driving the mourning coach. A
bear-leader, a popular street character of the time, was impressed as
an additional ornament, before the cavalcade had gone far down the
Strand; and his bear, who was black and very mangy, gave quite an
Undertaking air to that part of the procession in which he walked.

Thus, with beer-drinking, pipe-smoking, song-roaring, and infinite
caricaturing of woe, the disorderly procession went its way, recruiting
at every step, and all the shops shutting up before it. Its destination
was the old church of Saint Pancras, far off in the fields. It got there
in course of time; insisted on pouring into the burial-ground; finally,
accomplished the interment of the deceased Roger Cly in its own way,
and highly to its own satisfaction.

The dead man disposed of, and the crowd being under the necessity
of providing some other entertainment for itself, another brighter
genius (or perhaps the same) conceived the humour of impeaching
casual passers-by as Old Bailey spies, and wreaking vengeance on
them. Chase was given to some scores of inoffensive persons who had
never been near the Old Bailey in their lives, in the realisation of this
fancy, and they were roughly hustled and maltreated. The transition
to the sport of window-breaking, and thence to the plundering of public-
houses, was easy and natural. At last, after several hours, when
sundry summer-houses had been pulled down, and some area-railings
had been torn up, to arm the more belligerent spirits, a rumour got
about that the Guards were coming. Before this rumour the crowd
gradually melted away, and perhaps the Guards came, and perhaps
they never came, and this was the usual progress of a mob.

Mr. Cruncher did not assist at the closing sports, but had remained
behind in the churchyard, to confer and condole with the undertakers.
The place had a soothing influence on him. He procured a pipe from
a neighbouring public-house, and smoked it, looking in at the railings
and maturely considering the spot.

"Jerry," said Mr. Cruncher, apostrophising himself in his usual
way, "you see that there Cly that day, and you see with your own
eyes that he was a young 'un and a straight-made 'un."

Having smoked his pipe out, and ruminated a little longer, he turned
himself about, that he might appear, before the hour of closing, on his
station at Tellson's. Whether his meditations on mortality had touched
his liver, or whether his general health had been previously at all amiss,
or whether he desired to show a little attention to an eminent man, is
not so much to the purpose, as that he made a short call upon his
medical adviser—a distinguished surgeon—on his way back.

Young Jerry relieved his father with dutiful interest, and reported
No job in his absence. The bank closed, the ancient clerks came out,

the usual watch was set, and Mr. Cruncher and his son went home to tea.

"Now, I tell you where it is!" said Mr. Cruncher to his wife, on entering. "If, as a honest tradesman, my wenturs goes wrong to-night, I shall make sure that you've been praying again me, and I shall work you for it just the same as if I seen you do it."

The dejected Mrs. Cruncher shook her head.

"Why, you're at it afore my face!" said Mr. Cruncher, with signs of angry apprehension.

"I am saying nothing."

"Well, then; don't meditate nothing. You might as well flop as meditate. You may as well go again me one way as another. Drop it altogether."

"Yes, Jerry."

"Yes, Jerry," repeated Mr. Cruncher, sitting down to tea. "Ah! It *is* yes, Jerry. That's about it. You may say yes, Jerry."

Mr. Cruncher had no particular meaning in these sulky corrobora-tions, but made use of them, as people not unfrequently do, to express general ironical dissatisfaction.

"You and your yes, Jerry," said Mr. Cruncher, taking a bite out of his bread-and-butter, and seeming to help it down with a large invisible oyster out of his saucer. "Ah! I think so. I believe you."

"You are going out to-night?" asked his decent wife, when he took another bite.

"Yes, I am."

"May I go with you, father?" asked his son, briskly.

"No, you mayn't. I'm a-going—as your mother knows—a-fishing. That's where I'm going to. Going a-fishing."

"Your fishing-rod gets rayther rusty; don't it, father?"

"Never you mind."

"Shall you bring any fish home, father?"

"If I don't, you'll have short commons to-morrow," returned that gentleman, shaking his head; "that's questions enough for you; I ain't a-going out till you've been long a-bed."

He devoted himself during the remainder of the evening to keeping a most vigilant watch on Mrs. Cruncher, and sullenly holding her in conversation that she might be prevented from meditating any petitions to his disadvantage. With this view, he urged his son to hold her in conversation also, and led the unfortunate woman a hard life by dwelling on any causes of complaint he could bring against her, rather than he would leave her for a moment to her own reflections. The devoutest person could have rendered no greater homage to the efficacy of an honest prayer than he did in this distrust of his wife. It was as if a professed unbeliever in ghosts should be frightened by a ghost story.

"And mind you!" said Mr. Cruncher. "No games to-morrow! If I, as a honest tradesman, succeed in providing a jinte of meat or two, none of your not touching of it, and sticking to bread. If I, as a honest tradesman, am able to provide a little beer, none of your declaring on water. When you go to Rome, do as Rome does. Rome will be a ugly customer to you if you don't. *I'*m your Rome, you know."

Then he began grumbling again—

"With your flying into the face of your own wittles and drink! I don't know how scarce you mayn't make the wittles and drink here, by your flopping tricks and your unfeeling conduct. Look at your boy: he *is* your'n, ain't he? He's as thin as a lath. Do you call yourself a mother, and not know that a mother's first duty is to blow her boy out?"

This touched Young Jerry on a tender place, who adjured his mother to perform her first duty, and, whatever else she did or neglected, above all things to lay especial stress on the discharge of that maternal function so affectingly and delicately indicated by his other parent.

Thus the evening wore away with the Cruncher family, until Young Jerry was ordered to bed, and his mother, laid under similar injunctions, obeyed them. Mr. Cruncher beguiled the earlier watches of the night with solitary pipes, and did not start upon his excursion until nearly one o'clock. Towards that small and ghostly hour, he rose up from his chair, took a key out of his pocket, opened a locked cupboard, and brought forth a sack, a crowbar of convenient size, a rope and chain, and other fishing tackle of that nature. Disposing these articles about him in skilful manner, he bestowed a parting defiance on Mrs. Cruncher, extinguished the light, and went out.

Young Jerry, who had only made a feint of undressing when he went to bed, was not long after his father. Under cover of the darkness he followed out of the room, followed down the stairs, followed down the court, followed out into the streets. He was in no uneasiness concerning his getting into the house again, for it was full of lodgers, and the door stood ajar all night.

Impelled by a laudable ambition to study the art and mystery of his father's honest calling, Young Jerry, keeping as close to house fronts, walls, and doorways, as his eyes were close to one another, held his honoured parent in view. The honoured parent, steering northward, had not gone far, when he was joined by another disciple of Izaak Walton, and the two trudged on together.

Within half an hour from the first starting, they were beyond the winking lamps, and the more than winking watchmen, and were out upon a lonely road. Another fisherman was picked up here—and that so silently, that if Young Jerry had been superstitious, he might have supposed the second follower of the gentle craft to have, all of a sudden, split himself into two.

The three went on, and Young Jerry went on, until the three stopped under a bank overhanging the road. Upon the top of the bank was a low brick wall, surmounted by an iron railing. In the shadow of bank and wall the three turned out of the road, and up a blind lane, of which the wall—there risen to some eight or ten feet high—formed one side. Crouching down in a corner, peeping up the lane, the next object that Young Jerry saw was the form of his honoured parent, pretty well defined against a watery and clouded moon, nimbly scaling an iron gate. He was soon over, and then the second fisherman got over, and then the third. They all dropped softly on the ground within the gate, and lay there a little—listening perhaps. Then they moved away on their hands and knees.

It was now Young Jerry's turn to approach the gate, which he did, holding his breath. Crouching down again in a corner there, and looking in, he made out the three fishermen creeping through some rank grass ! and all the grave-stones in the churchyard—it was a large churchyard that they were in—looking on like ghosts in white, while the church tower itself looked on like the ghost of a monstrous giant. They did not creep far, before they stopped and stood upright. And then they began to fish.

They fished with a spade, at first. Presently the honoured parent appeared to be adjusting some instrument like a great corkscrew. Whatever tools they worked with, they worked hard, until the awful striking of the church clock so terrified Young Jerry that he made off, with his hair as stiff as his father's.

But his long-cherished desire to know more about these matters not only stopped him in his running away, but lured him back again. They were still fishing perseveringly, when he peeped in at the gate for the second time ; but now they seemed to have got a bite. There was a screwing and complaining sound down below, and their bent figures were strained, as if by a weight. By slow degrees the weight broke away the earth upon it, and came to the surface. Young Jerry very well knew what it would be ; but when he saw it, and saw his honoured parent about to wrench it open, he was so frightened, being new to the sight, that he made off again, and never stopped until he had run a mile or more.

He would not have stopped then, for anything less necessary than breath, it being a spectral sort of race that he ran, and one highly desirable to get to the end of. He had a strong idea that the coffin he had seen was running after him ; and, pictured as hopping on behind him, bolt upright, upon its narrow end, always on the point of overtaking him and hopping on at his side—perhaps taking his arm —it was a pursuer to shun. It was an inconsistent and ubiquitous fiend too, for, while it was making the whole night behind him dreadful, he darted out into the roadway to avoid dark alleys, fearful of its coming hopping out of them like a dropsical boy's-kite without tail and wings. It hid in doorways too, rubbing its horrible shoulders against doors, and drawing them up to its ears, as if it were laughing. It got into shadows on the road, and lay cunningly on its back to trip him up. All this time it was incessantly hopping on behind and gaining on him, so that when the boy got to his own door he had reason for being half dead. And even then it would not leave him, but followed him up-stairs with a bump on every stair, scrambled into bed with him, and bumped down, dead and heavy, on his breast when he fell asleep.

From his oppressed slumber Young Jerry in his closet was awakened after daybreak and before sunrise by the presence of his father in the family room. Something had gone wrong with him ; at least so Young Jerry inferred, from the circumstance of his holding Mrs. Cruncher by the ears, and knocking the back of her head against the head-board of the bed.

"I told you I would," said Mr. Cruncher, "and I did."

"Jerry, Jerry, Jerry !" his wife implored.

"You oppose yourself to the profit of the business," said Jerry, "and me and my partners suffer. You was to honour and obey ; why the devil don't you ? "

"I try to be a good wife, Jerry," the poor woman protested, with tears.

"Is it being a good wife to oppose your husband's business? Is it honouring your husband to dishonour his business ? Is it obeying your husband to disobey him on the wital subject of his business ? "

"You hadn't taken to the dreadful business then, Jerry."

"It's enough for you," retorted Mr. Cruncher, "to be the wife of a honest tradesman, and not to occupy your female mind with calculations when he took to his trade or when he didn't. A honouring and obeying wife would let his trade alone altogether. Call yourself a religious woman ? If you're a religious woman, give me a irreligious one ! You have no more nat'ral sense of duty than the bed of this here Thames river has of a pile, and similarly it must be knocked into you."

The altercation was conducted in a low tone of voice, and terminated in the honest tradesman's kicking off his clay-soiled boots, and lying down at his length on the floor. After taking a timid peep at him lying on his back, with his rusty hands under his head for a pillow, his son lay down too, and fell asleep again.

There was no fish for breakfast, and not much of anything else. Mr. Cruncher was out of spirits, and out of temper, and kept an iron pot-lid by him as a projectile for the correction of Mrs. Cruncher, in case he should observe any symptoms of her saying Grace. He was brushed and washed at the usual hour, and set off with his son to pursue his ostensible calling.

Young Jerry, walking with the stool under his arm at his father's side along sunny and crowded Fleet Street, was a very different Young Jerry from him of the previous night, running home through darkness and solitude from his grim pursuer. His cunning was fresh with the day, and his qualms were gone with the night—in which particulars it is not improbable that he had compeers in Fleet Street and the City of London, that fine morning.

"Father," said Young Jerry, as they walked along, taking care to keep at arm's-length and to have the stool well between them, "what's a Resurrection-Man ? "

Mr Cruncher came to a stop on the pavement before he answered, "How should I know?"

"I thought you knowed everything, father," said the artless boy.

"Hem! Well," returned Mr. Cruncher, going on again, and lifting off his hat to give his spikes free play, "he's a tradesman."

"What's his goods, father?" asked the brisk Young Jerry.

"His goods," said Mr. Cruncher, after turning it over in his mind, "is a branch of Scientific goods."

"Persons' bodies, ain't it, father?" asked the lively boy.

"I believe it is something of that sort," said Mr. Cruncher.

"Oh father, I should so like to be a Resurrection-Man when I'm quite growed up!"

Mr. Cruncher was soothed, but shook his head in a dubious and moral way. "It depends upon how you dewelop your talents. Be careful to dewelop your talents, and never to say no more than you can help to nobody, and there's no telling at the present time what you may not come to be fit for." As Young Jerry, thus encouraged, went on a few yards in advance, to plant the stool in the shadow of the Bar, Mr. Cruncher added to himself: "Jerry, you honest tradesman, there's hopes wot that boy will yet be a blessing to you, and a recompense to you for his mother!"

CHAPTER XV

KNITTING

THERE had been earlier drinking than usual in the wine-shop of Monsieur Defarge. As early as six o'clock in the morning sallow faces peeping through its barred windows had descried other faces within, bending over measures of wine. Monsieur Defarge sold a very thin wine at the best of times, but it would seem to have been an unusually thin wine that he sold at this time. A sour wine, moreover, or a souring, for its influence on the mood of those who drank it was to make them gloomy. No vivacious Bacchanalian flame leaped out of the pressed grape of Monsieur Defarge; but a smouldering fire that burnt in the dark lay hidden in the dregs of it.

This had been the third morning in succession on which there had been early drinking at the wine-shop of Monsieur Defarge. It had begun on Monday, and here was Wednesday come. There had been more of early brooding than drinking; for many men had listened and whispered and slunk about there from the time of the opening of the door who could not have laid a piece of money on the counter to save their souls. These were to the full as interested in the place, however, as if they could have commanded whole barrels of wine; and they glided from seat to seat, and from corner to corner, swallowing talk in lieu of drink, with greedy looks.

Notwithstanding an unusual flow of company, the master of the wine-shop was not visible. He was not missed; for nobody who crossed the threshold looked for him, nobody asked for him, nobody wondered to see only Madame Defarge in her seat, presiding over the distribution of wine, with a bowl of battered small coins before her, as much defaced and beaten out of their original impress as the small coinage of humanity from whose ragged pockets they had come.

A suspended interest and a prevalent absence of mind were perhaps observed by the spies who looked in at the wine-shop, as they looked in at every place, high and low, from the king's palace to the criminal's jail. Games at cards languished, players at dominoes musingly built towers with them, drinkers drew figures on the tables with spilt drops of wine, Madame Defarge herself picked out the pattern on her sleeve with her toothpick, and saw and heard something inaudible and invisible a long way off.

Thus Saint Antoine in this vinous feature of his, until mid-day. It was high noontide when two dusty men passed through his streets and under his swinging lamps, of whom one was Monsieur Defarge; the other a mender of roads in a blue cap. All adust and athirst, the two entered the wine-shop. Their arrival had lighted a kind of fire in the breast of Saint Antoine, fast spreading as they came along, which stirred and flickered in flames of faces at most doors and windows. Yet no one had followed them, and no man spoke when they entered the wine-shop, though the eyes of every man there were turned upon them.

"Good-day, gentlemen!" said Monsieur Defarge.

It may have been a signal for loosening the general tongue. It elicited an answering chorus of "Good-day!"

"It is bad weather, gentlemen," said Defarge, shaking his head.

Upon which every man looked at his neighbour, and then all cast down their eyes and sat silent. Except one man, who got up and went out.

"My wife," said Defarge aloud, addressing Madame Defarge; "I have travelled certain leagues with this good mender of roads, called Jacques. I met him—by accident—a day and a half's journey out of Paris. He is a good child, this mender of roads, called Jacques. Give him to drink, my wife!"

A second man got up and went out. Madame Defarge set wine before the mender of roads called Jacques, who doffed his blue cap to the company, and drank. In the breast of his blouse he carried some coarse dark bread; he ate of this between whiles, and sat munching and drinking near Madame Defarge's counter. A third man got up and went out.

Defarge refreshed himself with a draught of wine—but he took less than was given to the stranger, as being himself a man to whom it was no rarity—and stood waiting until the countryman had made his breakfast. He looked at no one present, and no one now looked at him,—not even Madame Defarge, who had taken up her knitting, and was at work.

"Have you finished your repast, friend?" he asked, in due season.

"Yes, thank you."

"Come, then! You shall see the apartment that I told you you could occupy. It will suit you to a marvel."

Out of the wine-shop into the street, out of the street into a court-yard, out of the courtyard up a steep staircase, out of the staircase into a garret—formerly the garret where a white-haired man sat on a low bench, stooping forward and very busy, making shoes.

No white-haired man was there now; but the three men were there who had gone out of the wine-shop singly. And between them and the white-haired man afar off was the one small link that they had once looked in at him through the chinks in the wall.

Defarge closed the door carefully, and spoke in a subdued voice—

"Jacques One, Jacques Two, Jacques Three! This is the witness encountered by appointment, by me, Jacques Four. He will tell you all. Speak, Jacques Five!"

The mender of roads, blue cap in hand, wiped his swarthy forehead with it, and said, "Where shall I commence, Monsieur?"

"Commence," was Monsieur Defarge's not unreasonable reply, "at the commencement."

"I saw him then, Messieurs," began the mender of roads, "a year ago this running summer, underneath the carriage of the Marquis, hanging by the chain. Behold the manner of it. I leaving my work on the road, the sun going to bed, the carriage of the Marquis slowly ascending the hill, he hanging by the chain—like this."

Again the mender of roads went through the whole performance, in which he ought to have been perfect by that time, seeing that it had been the infallible resource and indispensable entertainment of his village during a whole year.

Jacques One struck in, and asked if he had ever seen the man before.

"Never," answered the mender of roads, recovering his per-pendicular.

Jacques Three demanded how he afterwards recognised him then.

"By his tall figure," said the mender of roads, softly, and with his finger at his nose. "When Monsieur the Marquis demands that evening, 'Say, what is he like?' I make response, 'Tall as a spectre.'"

"You should have said, short as a dwarf," returned Jacques Two.

"But what did I know? The deed was not then accomplished, neither did he confide in me. Observe! Under those circumstances even, I do not offer my testimony. Monsieur the Marquis indicates me with his finger, standing near our little fountain, and says, 'To me! Bring that rascal!' My faith, Messieurs, I offer nothing."

"He is right there, Jacques," murmured Defarge to him who had interrupted. "Go on!"

"Good!" said the mender of roads, with an air of mystery. "The tall man is lost, and he is sought—how many months? Nine, ten, eleven?"

" No matter, the number," said Defarge. " He is well hidden, but at last he is unluckily found. Go on ! "

" I am again at work upon the hill-side, and the sun is again about to go to bed. I am collecting my tools to descend to my cottage down in the village below, where it is already dark, when I raise my eyes, and see coming over the hill six soldiers. In the midst of them is a tall man with his arms bound—tied to his sides—like this ! "

With the aid of his indispensable cap, he represented a man with his elbows bound fast at his hips, with cords that were knotted behind him.

" I stand aside, Messieurs, by my heap of stones, to see the soldiers and their prisoner pass (for it is a solitary road, that, where any spectacle is well worth looking at), and at first, as they approach, I see no more than that they are six soldiers with a tall man bound, and that they are almost black to my sight—except on the side of the sun going to bed, where they have a red edge, Messieurs. Also, I see that their long shadows are on the hollow ridge on the opposite side of the road, and are on the hill above it, and are like the shadows of giants. Also, I see that they are covered with dust, and that the dust moves with them as they come, tramp, tramp ! But when they advance quite near to me, I recognise the tall man, and he recognises me. Ah, but he would be well content to precipitate himself over the hill-side once again, as on the evening when he and I first encountered, close to the same spot ! "

He described it as if he were there, and it was evident that he saw it vividly ; perhaps he had not seen much in his life.

" I do not show the soldiers that I recognise the tall man ; he does not show the soldiers that he recognises me ; we do it, and we know it, with our eyes. ' Come on ! ' says the chief of that company, pointing to the village, ' bring him fast to his tomb ! ' and they bring him faster. I follow. His arms are swelled because of being bound so tight, his wooden shoes are large and clumsy, and he is lame. Because he is lame, and consequently slow, they drive him with their guns—like this ! "

He imitated the action of a man's being impelled forward by the butt-ends of muskets.

" As they descend the hill like madmen running a race, he falls. They laugh and pick him up again. His face is bleeding and covered with dust, but he cannot touch it ; thereupon they laugh again. They bring him into the village ; all the village runs to look ; they take him past the mill, and up to the prison ; all the village sees the prison gate open in the darkness of the night, and swallow him—like this ! "

He opened his mouth as wide as he could, and shut it with a sounding snap of his teeth. Observant of his unwillingness to mar the effect by opening it again, Defarge said, " Go on, Jacques."

" All the village," pursued the mender of roads, on tiptoe and in a low voice, " withdraws ; all the village whispers by the fountain ; all the village sleeps ; all the village dreams of that unhappy one, within the locks and bars of the prison on the crag, and never to come out of it, except to perish. In the morning, with my tools upon my shoulder, eating my morsel of black bread as I go, I make a circuit by the prison, on my way to my work. There I see him, high up, behind the bars of a lofty iron cage, bloody and dusty as last night, looking through. He has no hand free to wave to me ; I dare not call to him ; he regards me like a dead man."

Defarge and the three glanced darkly at one another. The looks of all of them were dark, repressed, and revengeful, as they listened to the countryman's story ; the manner of all of them, while it was secret, was authoritative too. They had the air of a rough tribunal ; Jacques One and Two sitting on the old pallet-bed, each with his chin resting on his hand, and his eyes intent on the road-mender ; Jacques Three, equally intent, on one knee behind them, with his agitated hand always gliding over the network of fine nerves about his mouth and nose ; Defarge standing between them and the narrator, whom he had stationed in the light of the window, by turns looking from him to them, and from them to him.

"Go on, Jacques," said Defarge.

"He remains up there in his iron cage some days. The village looks at him by stealth, for it is afraid. But it always looks up, from a distance, at the prison on the crag ; and in the evening, when the work of the day is achieved and it assembles to gossip at the fountain, all faces are turned towards the prison. Formerly they were turned towards the posting-house ; now they are turned towards the prison. They whisper at the fountain, that although condemned to death he will not be executed ; they say that petitions have been presented in Paris, showing that he was enraged and made mad by the death of his child ; they say that a petition has been presented to the King himself. What do I know ? It is possible. Perhaps yes, perhaps no."

"Listen then, Jacques," Number One of that name sternly interposed. "Know that a petition was presented to the King and Queen. All here, yourself excepted, saw the King take it, in his carriage in the street, sitting beside the Queen. It is Defarge whom you see here, who, at the hazard of his life, darted out before the horses, with the petition in his hand."

"And once again listen, Jacques !" said the kneeling Number Three, his fingers ever wandering over and over those fine nerves, with a strikingly greedy air, as if he hungered for something—that was neither food nor drink ; "the guard, horse and foot, surrounded the petitioner, and struck him blows. You hear ? "

"I hear, Messieurs."

"Go on then," said Defarge.

"Again ; on the other hand, they whisper at the fountain," resumed the countryman, "that he is brought down into our country to be executed on the spot, and that he will very certainly be executed. They even whisper that because he has slain Monseigneur, and because Monseigneur was the father of his tenants—serfs—what you will—he will be executed as a parricide. One old man says at the fountain, that his right hand, armed with the knife, will be burnt off before his face; that into wounds which will be made in his arms, his breast, and his legs there will be poured boiling oil, melted lead, hot resin, wax, and sulphur; finally, that he will be torn limb from limb by four strong horses. That old man says, all this was actually done to a prisoner who made an attempt on the life of the late King, Louis Fifteen. But how do I know if he lies? I am not a scholar."

"Listen once again then, Jacques!" said the man with the restless hand and the craving air. "The name of that prisoner was Damiens, and it was all done in open day, in the open streets of this city of Paris; and nothing was more noticed in the vast concourse that saw it done than the crowd of ladies of quality and fashion, who were full of eager attention to the last—to the last, Jacques, prolonged until nightfall, when he had lost two legs and an arm, and still breathed! And it was done—why, how old are you?"

"Thirty-five," said the mender of roads, who looked sixty.

"It was done when you were more than ten years old; you might have seen it."

"Enough!" said Defarge, with grim impatience. "Long live the Devil! Go on."

"Well! Some whisper this, some whisper that; they speak of nothing else; even the fountain appears to fall to that tune. At length, on Sunday night when all the village is asleep, come soldiers, winding down from the prison, and their guns ring on the stones of the little street. Workmen dig, workmen hammer, soldiers laugh and sing; in the morning, by the fountain, there is raised a gallows forty feet high, poisoning the water."

The mender of roads looked *through* rather than *at* the low ceiling, and pointed as if he saw the gallows somewhere in the sky.

"All work is stopped, all assemble there, nobody leads the cows out, the cows are there with the rest. At midday, the roll of drums. Soldiers have marched into the prison in the night, and he is in the midst of many soldiers. He is bound as before, and in his mouth there is a gag—tied so, with a tight string, making him look almost as if he laughed." He suggested it, by creasing his face with his two thumbs, from the corners of his mouth to his ears. "On the top of the gallows is fixed the knife, blade upwards, with its point in the air. He is hanged there forty feet high—and is left hanging, poisoning the water."

They looked at one another, as he used his blue cap to wipe his face, on which the perspiration had started afresh while he recalled the spectacle.

"It is frightful, Messieurs. How can the women and the children draw water! Who can gossip of an evening, under that shadow! Under it, have I said? When I left the village, Monday evening as the sun was going to bed, and looked back from the hill, the shadow struck across the church, across the mill, across the prison—seemed to strike across the earth, Messieurs, to where the sky rests upon it!"

The hungry man gnawed one of his fingers as he looked at the other three, and his finger quivered with the craving that was on him.

"That's all, Messieurs. I left at sunset (as I had been warned to do), and I walked on, that night and half next day, until I met (as I was warned I should) this comrade. With him I came on, now riding and now walking, through the rest of yesterday and through last night. And here you see me!"

After a gloomy silence the first Jacques said, "Good! You have acted and recounted faithfully. Will you wait for us a little, outside the door?"

"Very willingly," said the mender of roads, whom Defarge escorted to the top of the stairs, and, leaving seated there, returned.

The three had risen, and their heads were together when he came back to the garret.

"How say you, Jacques?" demanded Number One. "To be registered?"

"To be registered, as doomed to destruction," returned Defarge.

"Magnificent!" croaked the man with the craving.

"The château, and all the race?" inquired the first.

"The château and all the race," returned Defarge. "Extermination."

The hungry man repeated, in a rapturous croak, "Magnificent!" and began gnawing another finger.

"Are you sure," asked Jacques Two, of Defarge, "that no embarrassment can arise from our manner of keeping the register? Without doubt it is safe, for no one beyond ourselves can decipher it; but shall we always be able to decipher it—or, I ought to say, will she?"

"Jacques," returned Defarge, drawing himself up, "if Madame my wife undertook to keep the register in her memory alone, she would not lose a word of it—not a syllable of it. Knitted in her own stitches and her own symbols, it will always be as plain to her as the sun. Confide in Madame Defarge. It would be easier for the weakest poltroon that lives to erase himself from existence, than to erase one letter of his name or crimes from the knitted register of Madame Defarge."

There was a murmur of confidence and approval, and then the man who hungered asked: "Is this rustic to be sent back soon? I hope so. He is very simple; is he not a little dangerous?"

"He knows nothing," said Defarge; "at least nothing more than would easily elevate him to a gallows of the same height. I charge myself with him; let him remain with me; I will take care of him and set him on his road. He wishes to see the fine world—the King, the Queen, and Court; let him see them on Sunday."

"What?" exclaimed the hungry man, staring. "Is it a good sign that he wishes to see Royalty and Nobility?"

"Jacques," said Defarge; "judiciously show a cat milk, if you wish her to thirst for it. Judiciously show a dog his natural prey, if you wish him to bring it down one day."

Nothing more was said, and the mender of roads, being found already dozing on the topmost stair, was advised to lay himself down on the pallet-bed and take some rest. He needed no persuasion, and was soon asleep.

Worse quarters than Defarge's wine-shop could easily have been found in Paris for a provincial slave of that degree. Saving for a mysterious dread of Madame by which he was constantly haunted, his life was very new and agreeable. But Madame sat all day at her counter, so expressly unconscious of him, and so particularly determined not to perceive that his being there had any connection with anything below the surface, that he shook in his wooden shoes whenever his eye lighted on her. For he contended with himself that it was impossible to foresee what that lady might pretend next ; and he felt assured that if she should take it into her brightly ornamented head to pretend that she had see him do a murder and afterwards flay the victim, she would infallibly go through with it until the play was played out.

Therefore, when Sunday came, the mender of roads was not enchanted (though he said he was) to find that Madame was to accompany Monsieur and himself to Versailles. It was additionally disconcerting to have Madame knitting all the way there, in a public conveyance ; it was additionally disconcerting yet to have Madame in the crowd in the afternoon, still with her knitting in her hands as the crowd waited to see the carriage of the King and Queen.

" You work hard, Madame," said a man near her.

" Yes," answered Madame Defarge ; " I have a good deal to do."

" What do you make, Madame ? "

" Many things."

" For instance——"

" For instance," returned Madame Defarge, composedly, " shrouds."

The man moved a little further away, as soon as he could, and the mender of roads fanned himself with his blue cap, feeling it mightily close and oppressive. If he needed a King and Queen to restore him, he was fortunate in having his remedy at hand ; for soon the large-faced King and the fair-faced Queen came in their golden coach, attended by the shining Bull's Eye of their Court, a glittering multitude of laughing ladies and fine lords ; and in jewels and silks and powder and splendour and elegantly spurning figures and handsomely disdainful faces of both sexes the mender of roads bathed himself, so much to his temporary intoxication, that he cried Long live the King, Long live the Queen, Long live everybody and everything ! as if he had never heard of ubiquitous Jacques in his time. Then there were gardens, courtyards, terraces, fountains, green banks, more King and Queen, more Bull's Eye, more lords and ladies, more Long live they all ! until he absolutely wept with sentiment. During the whole of this scene, which lasted some three hours, he had plenty of shouting and weeping and sentimental company, and throughout Defarge held him by the collar, as if to restrain him from flying at the objects of his brief devotion and tearing them to pieces.

"Bravo!" said Defarge, clapping him on the back when it was over, like a patron; "you are a good boy!"

The mender of roads was now coming to himself, and was mistrustful of having made a mistake in his late demonstrations; but no.

"You are the fellow we want," said Defarge in his ear; "you make these fools believe that it will last for ever. Then they are the more insolent, and it is the nearer ended."

"Hey!" cried the mender of the roads reflectively; "that's true."

"These fools know nothing. While they despise your breath, and would stop it for ever and ever, in you or in a hundred like you rather than in one of their own horses or dogs, they only know what your breath tells them. Let it deceive them, then, a little longer; it cannot deceive them too much."

Madame Defarge looked superciliously at the client, and nodded in confirmation.

"As to you," said she, "you would shout and shed tears for anything, if it made a show and a noise. Say! Would you not?"

"Truly, Madame, I think so. For the moment."

"If you were shown a great heap of dolls, and were set upon them to pluck them to pieces and despoil them for your own advantage, you would pick out the richest and the gayest. Say! Would you not?"

"Truly yes, Madame."

"Yes. And if you were shown a flock of birds, unable to fly, and were set upon them to strip them of their feathers for your own advantage, you would set upon the birds with the finest feathers, would you not?"

"It is true, Madame."

"You have seen both dolls and birds to-day," said Madame Defarge, with a wave of her hand towards the place where they had last been apparent; "now, go home!"

CHAPTER XVI

STILL KNITTING

MADAME DEFARGE and Monsieur her husband returned amicably to the bosom of Saint Antoine, while a speck in a blue cap toiled through the darkness, and through the dust, and down the weary miles of avenue by the wayside, slowly tending towards that point of the compass where the château of Monsieur the Marquis, now in his grave, listened to the whispering trees. Such ample leisure had the stone faces, now, for listening to the trees and to the fountain, that the few village scarecrows who, in their quest for herbs to eat and fragments of dead stick to burn, strayed within sight of the great stone courtyard and terrace staircase, had it borne in upon their starved fancy that the expression of the faces was altered. A rumour just lived in the village —had a faint and bare existence there, as its people had—that when the knife struck home, the faces changed, from faces of pride to faces of anger and pain ; also, that when that dangling figure was hauled up forty feet above the fountain, they changed again, and bore a cruel look of being avenged, which they would henceforth bear for ever. In the stone face over the great window of the bed-chamber where the murder was done, two fine dints were pointed out in the sculptured nose, which everybody recognised, and which nobody had seen of old ; and on the scarce occasions when two or three ragged peasants emerged from the crowd to take a hurried peep at Monsieur the Marquis petrified, a skinny finger would not have pointed to it for a minute, before they all started away among the moss and leaves, like the more fortunate hares who could find a living there.

Château and hut, stone face and dangling figure, the red stain on the stone floor, and the pure water in the village well—thousands of acres of land—a whole province of France—all France itself—lay under the night sky, concentrated into a faint hair-breadth line. So does a whole world, with all its greatnesses and littlenesses, lie in a twinkling star. And as mere human knowledge can split a ray of light and analyse the manner of its composition, so sublimer intelligences may read in the feeble shining of this earth of ours every thought and act, every vice and virtue, of every responsible creature on it.

The Defarges, husband and wife, came lumbering under the starlight, in their public vehicle, to that gate of Paris whereunto their journey naturally tended. There was the usual stoppage at the barrier guard-house, and the usual lanterns came glancing forth for the usual examination and inquiry. Monsieur Defarge alighted, knowing one or two of the soldiery there, and one of the police. The latter he was intimate with, and affectionately embraced.

When Saint Antoine had again enfolded the Defarges in his dusky wings, and they, having finally alighted near the Saint's boundaries, were picking their way on foot through the black mud and offal of his streets, Madame Defarge spoke to her husband—

" Say then, my friend ; what did Jacques of the police tell thee ? "

" Very little to-night, but all he knows. There is another spy commissioned for our quarter. There may be many more, for all that he can say, but he knows of one."

" Eh well ! " said Madame Defarge, raising her eyebrows with a cool business air. " It is necessary to register him. How do they call that man ? "

" He is English."

" So much the better. His name ? "

" Barsad," said Defarge, making it French by pronunciation. But he had been so careful to get it accurately, that he then spelt it with perfect correctness.

" Barsad," repeated Madame. " Good. Christian name ? "

"John."

"John Barsad," repeated Madame, after murmuring it once to herself. "Good. His appearance; is it known?"

"Age, about forty years; height, about five feet nine; black hair; complexion dark; generally, rather handsome visage; eyes dark, face thin, long, and sallow; nose aquiline, but not straight, having a peculiar inclination towards the left cheek; expression, therefore, sinister."

"Eh my faith. It is a portrait!" said Madame, laughing. "He shall be registered to-morrow."

They turned into the wine-shop, which was closed (for it was midnight), and where Madame Defarge immediately took her post at her desk, counted the small moneys that had been taken during her absence, examined the stock, went through the entries in the book, made other entries of her own, checked the serving man in every possible way, and finally dismissed him to bed. Then she turned out the contents of the bowl of money for the second time, and began knotting them up in her handkerchief, in a chain of separate knots, for safe keeping through the night. All this while Defarge, with his pipe in his mouth, walked up and down, complacently admiring, but never interfering; in which condition, indeed, as to the business and his domestic affairs, he walked up and down through life.

The night was hot, and the shop, close shut and surrounded by so foul a neighbourhood, was ill-smelling. Monsieur Defarge's olfactory sense was by no means delicate, but the stock of wine smelt much stronger than it ever tasted, and so did the stock of rum and brandy and aniseed. He whiffed the compound of scents away, as he put down his smoked-out pipe.

"You are fatigued," said Madame, raising her glance as she knotted the money. "There are only the usual odours."

"I am a little tired," her husband acknowledged.

"You are a little depressed too," said Madame, whose quick eyes had never been so intent on the accounts, but they had had a ray or two for him. "Oh, the men, the men!"

"But, my dear!" began Defarge.

"But, my dear!" repeated Madame, nodding firmly; "but, my dear! You are faint of heart to-night, my dear!"

"Well, then," said Defarge, as if a thought were wrung out of his breast, "it *is* a long time."

"It is a long time," repeated his wife; "and when is it not a long time? Vengeance and retribution require a long time; it is the rule."

"It does not take a long time to strike a man with lightning," said Defarge.

"How long," demanded Madame, composedly, "does it take to make and store the lightning? Tell me."

Defarge raised his head thoughtfully, as if there were something in that too.

"It does not take a long time," said Madame, "for an earthquake to swallow a town. Eh well! Tell me how long it takes to prepare the earthquake?"

"A long time, I suppose," said Defarge.

"But when it is ready, it takes place, and grinds to pieces everything before it. In the meantime, it is always preparing, though it is not seen or heard. That is your consolation. Keep it."

She tied a knot with flashing eyes, as if it throttled a foe.

"I tell thee," said Madame, extending her right hand, for emphasis, "that although it is a long time on the road, it is on the road and coming. I tell thee it never retreats, and never stops. I tell thee it is always advancing. Look around and consider the lives of all the world that we know, consider the faces of all the world that we know, consider the rage and discontent to which the Jacquerie addresses itself with more and more of certainty every hour. Can such things last? Bah! I mock you."

"My brave wife," returned Defarge, standing before her with his head a little bent, and his hands clasped at his back, like a docile and attentive pupil before his catechist, "I do not question all this. But it has lasted a long time, and it is possible—you know well, my wife, it is possible—that it may not come during our lives."

"Eh well! How then?" demanded Madame, tying another knot, as if there were another enemy strangled.

"Well!" said Defarge, with a half-complaining and half-apologetic shrug. "We shall not see the triumph."

"We shall have helped it," returned Madame, with her extended hand in strong action. "Nothing that we do is done in vain. I believe, with all my soul, that we shall see the triumph. But, even if not, even if I knew certainly not, show me the neck of an aristocrat and tyrant, and still I would——"

Then Madame, with her teeth set, tied a very terrible knot indeed.

"Hold!" cried Defarge, reddening a little as if he felt charged with cowardice; "I too, my dear, will stop at nothing."

"Yes! But it is your weakness that you sometimes need to see your victim and your opportunity to sustain you. Sustain yourself without that. When the time comes, let loose a tiger and a devil; but wait for the time with the tiger and the devil chained—not shown—yet always ready."

Madame enforced the conclusion of this piece of advice by striking her little counter with her chain of money as if she knocked its brains out, and then gathering the heavy handkerchief under her arm in a serene manner, and observing that it was time to go to bed.

Next noontide saw the admirable woman in her usual place in the wine-shop, knitting away assiduously. A rose lay beside her, and if she now and then glanced at the flower, it was with no infraction of her usual pre-occupied air. There were a few customers, drinking or not drinking, standing or seated, sprinkled about. The day was very hot, and heaps of flies, who were extending their inquisitive and adventurous perquisitions into all the glutinous little glasses near Madame, fell dead at the bottom. Their decease made no impression on the other flies out promenading, who looked at them in the coolest manner (as if they themselves were elephants, or something as far removed), until they met the same fate. Curious to consider how heedless flies are!—perhaps they thought as much at Court that sunny summer day.

A figure entering at the door threw a shadow on Madame Defarge which she felt to be a new one. She laid down her knitting, and began to pin her rose in her head-dress, before she looked at the figure.

It was curious. The moment Madame Defarge took up the rose, the customers ceased talking, and began gradually to drop out of the wine-shop.

"Good-day, Madame," said the newcomer.

"Good-day, Monsieur."

She said it aloud, but added to herself, as she resumed her knitting : "Hah ! Good-day, age about forty, height about five feet nine, black hair, generally rather handsome visage, complexion dark, eyes dark, thin, long, and sallow face, aquiline nose, but not straight, having a peculiar inclination towards the left cheek, which imparts a sinister expression ! Good-day, one and all !"

"Have the goodness to give me a little glass of old cognac, and a mouthful of cool, fresh water, Madame."

Madame complied with a polite air.

"Marvellous cognac this, Madame !"

It was the first time it had ever been so complimented, and Madame Defarge knew enough of its antecedents to know better. She said, however, that the cognac was flattered, and took up her knitting. The visitor watched her fingers for a few moments, and took the opportunity of observing the place in general.

"You knit with great skill, Madame."

"I am accustomed to it."

"A pretty pattern too !"

"*You* think so ?" said Madame, looking at him with a smile.

"Decidedly. May one ask what it is for ?"

"Pastime," said Madame, still looking at him with a smile, while her fingers moved nimbly.

"Not for use ?"

"That depends. I may find a use for it one day. If I do— well," said Madame, drawing a breath and nodding her head with a stern kind of coquetry, "I'll use it !"

It was remarkable ; but the taste of Saint Antoine seemed to be decidedly opposed to a rose on the head-dress of Madame Defarge. Two men had entered separately, and had been about to order drink, when, catching sight of that novelty, they faltered, made a pretence of looking about as if for some friend who was not there, and went away. Nor of those who had been there when this visitor entered was there one left. They had all dropped off. The spy had kept his eyes open, but had been able to detect no sign. They had lounged away in a poverty-stricken, purposeless, accidental manner, quite natural and unimpeachable.

"JOHN," thought Madame, checking off her work as her fingers knitted, and her eyes looked at the stranger. "Stay long enough, and I shall knit 'BARSAD' before you go."

"You have a husband, Madame?"

"I have."

"Children?"

"No children."

"Business seems bad?"

'Business is very bad; the people are so poor."

"Ah, the unfortunate, miserable people! So oppressed, too—as you say."

"As *you* say," Madame retorted, correcting him, and deftly knitting an extra something into his name that boded him no good.

"Pardon me; certainly it was I who said so, but you naturally think so. Of course."

"*I* think?" returned Madame, in a high voice. "I and my husband have enough to do to keep this wine-shop open, without thinking. All we think, here, is how to live. That is the subject *we* think of, and it gives us, from morning to night, enough to think about, without embarrassing our heads concerning others. *I* think for others? No, no."

The spy, who was there to pick up any crumbs he could find or make, did not allow his baffled state to express itself in his sinister face, but stood with an air of gossiping gallantry, leaning his elbow on Madame Defarge's little counter, and occasionally sipping his cognac.

"A bad business this, Madame, of Gaspard's execution. Ah! the poor Gaspard!" With a sigh of great compassion.

"My faith!" returned Madame, coolly and lightly, "if people use knives for such purposes, they have to pay for it. He knew beforehand what the price of his luxury was; he has paid the price."

"I believe," said the spy, dropping his soft voice to a tone that invited confidence, and expressing an injured revolutionary susceptibility in every muscle of his wicked face,—"I believe there is much compassion and anger in this neighbourhood touching the poor fellow? Between ourselves."

"Is there?" asked Madame, vacantly.

"Is there not?"

"—Here is my husband!" said Madame Defarge.

As the keeper of the wine-shop entered at the door, the spy saluted him by touching his hat, and saying, with an engaging smile, "Goodday, Jacques!" Defarge stopped short, and stared at him.

"Good-day, Jacques!" the spy repeated, with not quite so much confidence, or quite so easy a smile under the stare.

"You deceive yourself, Monsieur," returned the keeper of the wineshop. "You mistake me for another. That is not my name. I am Ernest Defarge."

" It is all the same," said the spy, airily, but discomfited too ; " good-day ! "

" Good-day ! " answered Defarge, drily.

" I was saying to Madame, with whom I had the pleasure of chatting when you entered, that they tell me there is—and no wonder !—much sympathy and anger in Saint Antoine touching the unhappy fate of poor Gaspard."

" No one has told me so," said Defarge, shaking his head. " I know nothing of it."

Having said it, he passed behind the little counter, and stood with his hand on the back of his wife's chair, looking over that barrier at the person to whom they were both opposed, and whom either of them would have shot with the greatest satisfaction.

The spy, well used to his business, did not change his unconscious attitude, but drained his little glass of cognac, took a sip of fresh water, and asked for another glass of cognac. Madame Defarge poured it out for him, took to her knitting again, and hummed a little song over it.

" You seem to know this quarter well ; that is to say, better than I do ? " observed Defarge.

" Not at all, but I hope to know it better. I am so profoundly interested in its miserable inhabitants."

" Hah ! " muttered Defarge.

" The pleasure of conversing with you, Monsieur Defarge, recalls to me," pursued the spy, " that I have the honour of cherishing some interesting associations with your name."

" Indeed ! " said Defarge, with much indifference.

" Yes, indeed. When Doctor Manette was released, you, his old domestic, had the charge of him, I know. He was delivered to you. You see I am informed of the circumstances."

" Such is the fact, certainly," said Defarge. He had had it conveyed to him, in an accidental touch of his wife's elbow as she knitted and warbled, that he would do best to answer, but always with brevity.

" It was to you," said the spy, " that his daughter came ; and it was from your care that his daughter took him, accompanied by a neat brown Monsieur ; how is he called ?—in a little wig—Lorry—of the bank of Tellson and Company—over to England."

" Such is the fact," repeated Defarge.

" Very interesting remembrances ! " said the spy. " I have known Dr. Manette and his daughter in England."

" Yes ? " said Defarge.

" You don't hear much about them now ? " said the spy.

" No," said Defarge.

" In effect," Madame struck in, looking up from her work and her little song, " we never hear about them. We received the news of their safe arrival, and perhaps another letter, or perhaps two ; but, since then, they have gradually taken their road in life—we, ours—and we have held no correspondence."

"Perfectly so, Madame," replied the spy. "She is going to be married."

"Going?" echoed Madame. "She was pretty enough to have been married long ago. You English are cold, it seems to me."

"Oh! You know I am English."

"I perceive your tongue is," returned Madame; "and what the tongue is, I suppose the man is."

He did not take the identification as a compliment; but he made the best of it, and turned it off with a laugh. After sipping his cognac to the end, he added—

"Yes, Miss Manette is going to be married. But not to an Englishman; to one who, like herself, is French by birth. And speaking of Gaspard (ah, poor Gaspard! It was cruel, cruel!), it is a curious thing that she is going to marry the nephew of Monsieur the Marquis, for whom Gaspard was exalted to that height of so many feet; in other words, the present Marquis. But he lives unknown in England, he is no Marquis there; he is Mr. Charles Darnay. D'Aulnais is the name of his mother's family."

Madame Defarge knitted steadily, but the intelligence had a palpable effect upon her husband. Do what he would, behind the little counter, as to the striking of a light and the lighting of his pipe, he was troubled, and his hand was not trustworthy. The spy would have been no spy if he had failed to see it, or to record it in his mind.

Having made at least this one hit, whatever it might prove to be worth, and no customers coming in to help him to any other, Mr. Barsad paid for what he had drunk, and took his leave: taking occasion to say, in a genteel manner, before he departed, that he looked forward to the pleasure of seeing Monsieur and Madame Defarge again. For some minutes after he had emerged into the outer presence of Saint Antoine, the husband and wife remained exactly as he had left them, lest he should come back.

"Can it be true," said Defarge, in a low voice, looking down at his wife as he stood smoking with his hand on the back of her chair: "what he has said of Ma'amselle Manette?"

"As he has said it," returned Madame, lifting her eyebrows a little, "it is probably false. But it may be true."

"If it is——" Defarge began, and stopped.

"If it is?" repeated his wife.

"—And if it does come, while we live to see it triumph—I hope, for her sake, Destiny will keep her husband out of France."

"Her husband's destiny," said Madame Defarge, with her usual composure, "will take him where he is to go, and will lead him to the end that is to end him. That is all I know."

"But it is very strange—now, at least, is it not very strange," said Defarge, rather pleading with his wife to induce her to admit it, "that, after all our sympathy for Monsieur her father, and herself, her husband's name should be proscribed under your hand at this moment, by the side of that infernal dog's who has just left us?"

"Stranger things than that will happen when it does come," answered Madame. "I have them both here, of a certainty; and they are both here for their merits; that is enough."

She rolled up her knitting when she had said those words, and presently took the rose out of the handkerchief that was wound about her head. Either Saint Antoine had an instinctive sense that the objectionable decoration was gone, or Saint Antoine was on the watch for its disappearance; howbeit, the Saint took courage to lounge in very shortly afterwards, and the wine-shop recovered its habitual aspect.

In the evening, at which season of all others Saint Antoine turned himself inside out, and sat on doorsteps and window-ledges, and came to the corners of vile streets and courts for a breath of air, Madame Defarge, with her work in her hand, was accustomed to pass from place to place and from group to group: a Missionary—there were many like her—such as the world will do well never to breed again. All the women knitted. They knitted worthless things; but the mechanical work was a mechanical substitute for eating and drinking; the hands moved for the jaws and the digestive apparatus—if the bony fingers had been still, the stomachs would have been more famine-pinched.

But as the fingers went, the eyes went, and the thoughts. And as Madame Defarge moved on from group to group, all three went quicker and fiercer among every little knot of women that she had spoken with, and left behind.

Her husband smoked at his door, looking after her with admiration. "A great woman," said he, "a strong woman, a grand woman, a frightfully grand woman!"

Darkness closed around, and then came the ringing of church bells and the distant beating of the military drums in the Palace Court-yard, as the women sat knitting, knitting. Darkness encompassed them. Another darkness was closing in as surely, when the church bells, then ringing pleasantly in many an airy steeple over France, should be melted into thundering cannon; when the military drums should be beating to drown a wretched voice, that night all potent as the voice of Power and Plenty, Freedom and Life. So much was closing in about the women who sat knitting, knitting, that they their very selves were closing in around a structure yet unbuilt, where they were to sit knitting, knitting, counting dropping heads.

CHAPTER XVII

ONE NIGHT

NEVER did the sun go down with a brighter glory on the quiet corner in Soho than one memorable evening when the Doctor and his daughter sat under the plane-tree together. Never did the moon rise with a milder radiance over great London than on that night when it found them still seated under the tree, and shone upon their faces through its leaves.

Lucie was to be married to-morrow. She had reserved this last evening for her father, and they sat alone under the plane-tree.

"You are happy, my dear father?"

"Quite, my child."

They had said little, though they had been there a long time. When it was yet light enough to work and read, she had neither engaged herself in her usual work, nor had she read to him. She had employed herself in both ways, at his side under the tree, many and many a time; but this time was not quite like any other, and nothing could make it so.

"And I am very happy to-night, dear father. I am deeply happy in the love that Heaven has so blessed—my love for Charles, and Charles's love for me. But if my life were not to be still consecrated to you, or if my marriage were so arranged as that it would part us, even by the length of a few of these streets, I should be more unhappy and self-reproachful now than I can tell you. Even as it is——"

Even as it was, she could not command her voice.

In the sad moonlight she clasped him by the neck, and laid her face upon his breast. In the moonlight, which is always sad, as the light of the sun itself is—as the light called human life is—at its coming and its going.

"Dearest dear! Can you tell me, this last time, that you feel quite, quite sure no new affections of mine, and no new duties of mine, will ever interpose between us? *I* know it well, but do you know it? In your own heart, do you feel quite certain?"

Her father answered, with a cheerful firmness of conviction he could scarcely have assumed, "Quite sure, my darling! More than that," he added, as he tenderly kissed her; "my future is far brighter, Lucie, seen through your marriage, than it could have been—nay, than it ever was—without it."

"If I could hope *that*, my father!——"

"Believe it, love! Indeed it is so. Consider how natural and how plain it is, my dear, that it should be so. You, devoted and young, cannot fully appreciate the anxiety I have felt that your life should not be wasted——"

She moved her hand towards his lips, but he took it in his, and repeated the word.

"—wasted, my child—should not be wasted, struck aside from the natural order of things—for my sake. Your unselfishness cannot entirely comprehend how much my mind has gone on this; but only ask yourself, how could my happiness be perfect, while yours was incomplete?"

"If I had never seen Charles, my father, I should have been quite happy with you."

He smiled at her unconscious admission that she would have been unhappy without Charles, having seen him, and replied—

" My child, you did see him, and it is Charles. If it had not been Charles, it would have been another. Or, if it had been no other, I should have been the cause, and then the dark part of my life would have cast its shadow beyond myself, and would have fallen on you."

It was the first time, except at the trial, of her ever hearing him refer to the period of his suffering. It gave her a strange and new sensation while his words were in her ears, and she remembered it long afterwards.

" See ! " said the Doctor of Beauvais, raising his hand towards the moon. " I have looked at her from my prison-window, when I could not bear her light. I have looked at her when it has been such torture to me to think of her shining upon what I had lost, that I have beaten my head against my prison-walls. I have looked at her in a state so dull and lethargic, that I have thought of nothing but the number of horizontal lines I could draw across her at the full, and the number of perpendicular lines with which I could intersect them." He added in his inward and pondering manner, as he looked at the moon, " It was twenty either way, I remember, and the twentieth was difficult to squeeze in."

The strange thrill with which she heard him go back to that time deepened as he dwelt upon it ; but there was nothing to shock her in the manner of his reference. He only seemed to contrast his present cheerfulness and felicity with the dire endurance that was over.

" I have looked at her, speculating thousands of times upon the unborn child from whom I had been rent. Whether it was alive. Whether it had been born alive, or the poor mother's shock had killed it. Whether it was a son who would some day avenge his father. (There was a time in my imprisonment when my desire for vengeance was unbearable.) Whether it was a son who would never know his father's story ; who might even live to weigh the possibility of his father's having disappeared of his own will and act. Whether it was a daughter who would grow to be a woman."

She drew closer to him, and kissed his cheek and his hand.

" I have pictured my daughter, to myself, as perfectly forgetful of me—rather, altogether ignorant of me, and unconscious of me. I have cast up the years of her age, year after year. I have seen her married to a man who knew nothing of my fate. I have altogether perished from the remembrance of the living, and in the next generation my place was a blank."

" My father ! Even to hear that you had such thoughts of a daughter who never existed, strikes to my heart as if I had been that child."

" You, Lucie ? It is out of the consolation and restoration you have brought to me that these remembrances arise, and pass between us and the moon on this last night.—What did I say just now ? "

" She knew nothing of you. She cared nothing for you."

" So ! But on other moonlight nights, when the sadness and the silence have touched me in a different way—have affected me with something as like a sorrowful sense of peace as any emotion that had pain for its foundations could—I have imagined her as coming to me in my cell, and leading me out into the freedom beyond the fortress. I have seen her image in the moonlight often, as I now see you; except that I never held her in my arms; it stood between the little grated window and the door. But you understand that that was not the child I am speaking of?"

"The figure was not; the—the—image; the fancy?"

"No. That was another thing. It stood before my disturbed sense of sight, but it never moved. The phantom that my mind pursued was another and more real child. Of her outward appearance I know no more than that she was like her mother. The other had that likeness too—as you have—but was not the same. Can you follow me, Lucie? Hardly, I think? I doubt you must have been a solitary prisoner to understand these perplexed distinctions."

His collected and calm manner could not prevent her blood from running cold, as he thus tried to anatomise his old condition.

"In that more peaceful state I have imagined her, in the moonlight, coming to me and taking me out to show me that the home of her married life was full of her loving remembrance of her lost father. My picture was in her room, and I was in her prayers. Her life was active, cheerful, useful; but my poor history pervaded it all."

"I was that child, my father. I was not half so good, but in my love that was I."

"And she showed me her children," said the Doctor of Beauvais, "and they had heard of me, and had been taught to pity me. When they passed a prison of the State, they kept far from its frowning walls, and looked up at its bars, and spoke in whispers. She could never deliver me; I imagined that she always brought me back after showing me such things. But then, blessed with the relief of tears, I fell upon my knees, and blessed her."

"I am that child, I hope, my father. Oh my dear, my dear, will you bless me as fervently to-morrow?"

"Lucie, I recall these old troubles in the reason that I have to-night for loving you better than words can tell, and thanking God for my great happiness. My thoughts, when they were wildest, never rose near the happiness that I have known with you, and that we have before us."

He embraced her, solemnly commended her to Heaven, and humbly thanked Heaven for having bestowed her on him. By and by they went into the house.

There was no one bidden to the marriage but Mr. Lorry; there was even to be no bridesmaid but the gaunt Miss Pross. The marriage was to make no change in their place of residence; they had been able to extend it, by taking to themselves the upper rooms formerly belonging to the apocryphal invisible lodger, and they desired nothing more.

Doctor Manette was very cheerful at the little supper. They were only three at table, and Miss Pross made the third. He regretted that

Charles was not there; was more than half disposed to object to the loving little plot that kept him away; and drank to him affectionately.

So the time came for him to bid Lucie good-night, and they separated. But in the stillness of the third hour of the morning Lucie came down-stairs again, and stole into his room, not free from un-shaped fears, beforehand.

All things, however, were in their places; all was quiet; and he lay asleep, his white hair picturesque on the untroubled pillow, and his hands lying quiet on the coverlet. She put her needless candle in the shadow at a distance, crept up to his bed, and put her lips to his; then leaned over him, and looked at him.

Into his handsome face the bitter waters of captivity had worn; but he covered up their tracks with a determination so strong, that he held the mastery of them even in his sleep. A more remarkable face in its quiet, resolute, and guarded struggle with an unseen assailant was not to be beheld in all the wide dominions of sleep that night.

She timidly laid her hand on his dear breast, and put up a prayer that she might ever be as true to him as her love aspired to be, and as his sorrows deserved. Then she withdrew her hand, and kissed his lips once more, and went away. So the sunrise came, and the shadows of the leaves of the plane-tree moved upon his face as softly as her lips had moved in praying for him.

CHAPTER XVIII

NINE DAYS

THE marriage-day was shining brightly, and they were ready outside the closed door of the Doctor's room, where he was speaking with Charles Darnay. They were ready to go to church: the beautiful bride, Mr. Lorry, and Miss Pross—to whom the event, through a gradual process of reconcilement to the inevitable, would have been one of absolute bliss, but for the yet lingering consideration that her brother Solomon should have been the bridegroom.

"And so," said Mr. Lorry, who could not sufficiently admire the bride, and who had been moving round her to take in every point of her quiet, pretty dress; "and so it was for this, my sweet Lucie, that I brought you across the Channel, such a baby! Lord bless me! How little I thought what I was doing! How lightly I valued the obligation I was conferring on my friend Mr. Charles!"

"You didn't mean it," remarked the matter-of-fact Miss Pross, "and therefore how could you know it? Nonsense!"

"Really? Well; but don't cry," said the gentle Mr. Lorry.

"I am not crying," said Miss Pross; "*you* are."

"I, my Pross?" (By this time Mr. Lorry dared to be pleasant with her, on occasion.)

"You were, just now; I saw you do it, and I don't wonder at it. Such a present of plate as you have made 'em is enough to bring tears into anybody's eyes. There's not a fork or a spoon in the collection," said Miss Pross, "that I didn't cry over, last night after the box came, till I couldn't see it."

"I am highly gratified," said Mr. Lorry, "though, upon my honour, I had no intention of rendering those trifling articles of remembrance invisible to any one. Dear me! This is an occasion that makes a man speculate on all he has lost. Dear, dear, dear! To think that there might have been a Mrs. Lorry, any time these fifty years almost!"

"Not at all!" From Miss Pross.

"You think there never might have been a Mrs. Lorry?" asked the gentleman of that name.

"Pooh!" rejoined Miss Pross; "you were a bachelor in your cradle."

"Well!" observed Mr. Lorry, beamingly adjusting his little wig, "that seems probable too."

"And you were cut out for a bachelor," pursued Miss Pross, "before you were put in your cradle."

"Then, I think," said Mr. Lorry, "that I was very unhandsomely dealt with, and that I ought to have had a voice in the selection of my pattern. Enough! Now, my dear Lucie," drawing his arm soothingly round her waist, "I hear them moving in the next room, and Miss Pross and I, as two formal folks of business, are anxious not to lose the final opportunity of saying something to you that you wish to hear. You leave your good father, my dear, in hands as earnest and as loving as your own; he shall be taken every conceivable care of; during the next fortnight, while you are in Warwickshire and thereabouts, even Tellson's shall go to the wall (comparatively speaking) before him. And when, at the fortnight's end, he comes to join you and your beloved husband, on your other fortnight's trip in Wales, you shall say that we have sent him to you in the best health and in the happiest frame. Now I hear Somebody's step coming to the door. Let me kiss my dear girl with an old-fashioned bachelor blessing, before Somebody comes to claim his own."

For a moment he held the fair face from him to look at the well-remembered expression on the forehead, and then laid the bright golden hair against his little brown wig, with a genuine tenderness and delicacy which, if such things be old-fashioned, were as old as Adam.

The door of the Doctor's room opened, and he came out with Charles Darnay. He was so deadly pale—which had not been the case when they went in together—that no vestige of colour was to be seen in his face. But in the composure of his manner he was unaltered, except that to the shrewd glance of Mr. Lorry it disclosed some shadowy indication that the old air of avoidance and dread had lately passed over him, like a cold wind.

He gave his arm to his daughter, and took her down-stairs to the chariot which Mr. Lorry had hired in honour of the day. The rest followed in another carriage, and soon, in a neighbouring church, where no strange eyes looked on, Charles Darnay and Lucie Manette were happily married.

Besides the glancing tears that shone among the smiles of the little group when it was done, some diamonds, very bright and sparkling, glanced on the bride's hand, which were newly released from the dark obscurity of one of Mr. Lorry's pockets. They returned home to breakfast, and all went well, and in due course the golden hair that had mingled with the poor shoemaker's white locks in the Paris garret were mingled with them again in the morning sunlight, on the threshold of the door at parting.

It was a hard parting, though it was not for long. But her father cheered her, and said at last, gently disengaging himself from her enfolding arms, "Take her, Charles! She is yours!"

And her agitated hand waved to them from a chaise window, and she was gone.

The corner being out of the way of the idle and curious, and the preparations having been very simple and few, the Doctor, Mr. Lorry, and Miss Pross, were left quite alone. It was when they turned into the welcome shade of the cool old hall that Mr. Lorry observed a great change to have come over the Doctor, as if the golden arm uplifted there had struck him a poisoned blow.

He had naturally repressed much, and some revulsion might have been expected in him when the occasion for repression was gone. But it was the old scared lost look that troubled Mr. Lorry; and through his absent manner of clasping his head and drearily wandering away into his own room when they got up-stairs, Mr. Lorry was reminded of Defarge the wine-shop keeper, and the starlight ride.

"I think," he whispered to Miss Pross, after anxious consideration, "I think we had best not speak to him just now, or at all disturb him. I must look in at Tellson's; so I will go there at once and come back presently. Then we will take him a ride into the country, and dine there, and all will be well."

It was easier for Mr. Lorry to look in at Tellson's than to look out of Tellson's. He was detained two hours. When he came back he ascended the old staircase alone, having asked no question of the servant; going thus into the Doctor's rooms, he was stopped by a low sound of knocking.

"Good God!" he said, with a start. "What's that?"

Miss Pross, with a terrified face, was at his ear. "Oh me, oh me! All is lost!" cried she, wringing her hands. "What is to be told to Ladybird? He doesn't know me, and is making shoes!"

Mr. Lorry said what he could to calm her, and went himself into the Doctor's room. The bench was turned towards the light, as it had been when he had seen the shoemaker at his work before, and his head was bent down, and he was very busy.

"Doctor Manette. My dear friend, Doctor Manette!"

The Doctor looked at him for a moment—half inquiringly, half as if he were angry at being spoken to—and bent over his work again.

He had laid aside his coat and waistcoat; his shirt was open at the throat, as it used to be when he did that work; and even the old haggard, faded surface of face had come back to him. He worked hard—impatiently—as if in some sense of having been interrupted.

Mr. Lorry glanced at the work in his hand, and observed that it was a shoe of the old size and shape. He took up another that was lying by him, and asked what it was?

"A young lady's walking shoe," he muttered, without looking up. "It ought to have been finished long ago. Let it be."

"But, Doctor Manette. Look at me!"

He obeyed, in the old mechanically submissive manner, without pausing in his work.

"You know me, my dear friend? Think again. This is not your proper occupation. Think, dear friend!"

Nothing would induce him to speak more. He looked up, for an instant at a time, when he was requested to do so; but no persuasion would extract a word from him. He worked, and worked, and worked, in silence, and words fell on him as they would have fallen on an echoless wall, or on the air. The only ray of hope that Mr. Lorry could discover was, that he sometimes furtively looked up without being asked. In that there seemed a faint expression of curiosity or perplexity—as though he were trying to reconcile some doubts in his mind.

Two things at once impressed themselves on Mr. Lorry, as important above all others; the first, that this must be kept secret from Lucie; the second, that it must be kept secret from all who knew him. In conjunction with Miss Pross, he took immediate steps towards the latter precaution, by giving out that the Doctor was not well, and required a few days of complete rest. In aid of the kind deception to be practised on his daughter, Miss Pross was to write, describing his having been called away professionally, and referring to an imaginary letter of two or three hurried lines in his own hand, represented to have been addressed to her by the same post.

These measures, advisable to be taken in any case, Mr. Lorry took in the hope of his coming to himself. If that should happen soon, he kept another course in reserve, which was to have a certain opinion that he thought the best on the Doctor's case.

In the hope of his recovery, and of resort to this third course being thereby rendered practicable, Mr. Lorry resolved to watch him attentively, with as little appearance as possible of doing so. He therefore made arrangements to absent himself from Tellson's for the first time in his life, and took his post by the window in the same room.

He was not long in discovering that it was worse than useless to speak to him, since, on being pressed, he became worried. He abandoned that attempt on the first day, and resolved merely to keep himself always before him, as a silent protest against the delusion into which he had fallen, or was falling. He remained, therefore, in his seat near the window, reading and writing, and expressing, in as many pleasant and natural ways as he could think of, that it was a free place.

Doctor Manette took what was given him to eat and drink, and worked on, that first day, until it was too dark to see—worked on, half an hour after Mr. Lorry could not have seen, for his life, to read or write. When he put his tools aside as useless, until morning, Mr. Lorry rose and said to him—

" Will you go out ? "

He looked down at the floor on either side of him in the old manner, looked up in the old manner, and repeated in the old low voice—

" Out ? "

" Yes ; for a walk with me. Why not ? "

He made no effort to say why not, and said not a word more. But Mr. Lorry thought he saw, as he leaned forward on his bench in the dusk, with his elbows on his knees and his head in his hands, that he was in some misty way asking himself, " Why not ? " The sagacity of the man of business perceived an advantage here, and determined to hold it.

Miss Pross and he divided the night into two watches, and observed him at intervals from the adjoining room. He paced up and down for a long time before he lay down ; but when he did finally lay himself down, he fell asleep. In the morning he was up betimes, and went straight to his bench and to work.

On this second day Mr. Lorry saluted him cheerfully by his name, and spoke to him on topics that had been of late familiar to them. He returned no reply, but it was evident that he heard what was said, and that he thought about it, however confusedly. This encouraged Mr. Lorry to have Miss Pross in with her work several times during the day ; at those times they quietly spoke of Lucie, and of her father then present, precisely in the usual manner, and as if there were nothing amiss. This was done without any demonstrative accompaniment, not long enough, or often enough to harass him ; and it lightened Mr. Lorry's friendly heart to believe that he looked up oftener, and that he appeared to be stirred by some perception of inconsistencies surrounding him.

When it fell dark again, Mr. Lorry asked him as before—

" Dear Doctor, will you go out ? "

As before, he repeated, " Out ? "

" Yes ; for a walk with me. Why not ? "

This time Mr. Lorry feigned to go out when he could extract no answer from him, and, after remaining absent for an hour, returned. In the meanwhile the Doctor had removed to the seat in the window, and had sat there looking down at the plane-tree ; but on Mr. Lorry's return he slipped away to his bench.

The time went very slowly on, and Mr. Lorry's hope darkened, and his heart grew heavier again, and grew yet heavier and heavier every day. The third day came and went, the fourth, the fifth. Five days, six days, seven days, eight days, nine days.

With a hope ever darkening, and with a heart always growing heavier and heavier, Mr. Lorry passed through this anxious time. The secret was well kept, and Lucie was unconscious and happy ; but he could not fail to observe that the shoemaker, whose hand had been a little out at first, was growing dreadfully skilful, and that he had never been so intent on his work, and that his hands had never been so nimble and expert, as in the dusk of the ninth evening.

CHAPTER XIX

AN OPINION

WORN out by anxious watching, Mr. Lorry fell asleep at his post. On the tenth morning of his suspense he was startled by the shining of the sun into the room where a heavy slumber had overtaken him when it was dark night.

He rubbed his eyes and roused himself ; but he doubted, when he had done so, whether he was not still asleep. For going to the door of the Doctor's room and looking in, he perceived that the shoemaker's bench and tools were put aside again, and that the Doctor himself sat reading at the window. He was in his usual morning dress, and his face (which Mr. Lorry could distinctly see), though still very pale, was calmly studious and attentive.

Even when he had satisfied himself that he was awake, Mr. Lorry felt giddily uncertain for some few moments whether the late shoemaking might not be a disturbed dream of his own ; for did not his eyes show him his friend before him in his accustomed clothing and aspect, and employed as usual ; and was there any sign within their range that the change of which he had so strong an impression had actually happened ?

It was but the inquiry of his first confusion and astonishment, the answer being obvious. If the impression were not produced by a real corresponding and sufficient cause, how came he, Jarvis Lorry, there ? How came he to have fallen asleep, in his clothes, on the sofa in Dr. Manette's consulting-room, and to be debating these points outside the Doctor's bedroom door in the early morning ?

Within a few minutes Miss Pross stood whispering at his side. If he had had any particle of doubt left, her talk would of necessity have resolved it ; but he was by that time clear-headed, and had none. He advised that they should let the time go by until the regular breakfast-hour, and should then meet the Doctor as if nothing unusual had occurred. If he appeared to be in his customary state of mind, Mr. Lorry would then cautiously proceed to seek direction and guidance from the opinion he had been, in his anxiety, so anxious to obtain.

Miss Pross submitting herself to his judgment, the scheme was worked out with care. Having abundance of time for his usual methodical toilet, Mr. Lorry presented himself at the breakfast-hour in his usual white linen, and with his usual neat leg. The Doctor was summoned in the usual way, and came to breakfast.

So far as it was possible to comprehend him without overstepping those delicate and gradual approaches which Mr. Lorry felt to be the only safe advance, he at first supposed that his daughter's marriage had taken place yesterday. An incidental allusion, purposely thrown out, to the day of the week, and the day of the month, set him thinking and counting, and evidently made him uneasy. In all other respects, however, he was so composedly himself that Mr. Lorry determined to have the aid he sought. And that aid was his own.

Therefore, when the breakfast was done and cleared away, and he and the Doctor were left together, Mr. Lorry said, feelingly—

"My dear Manette, I am anxious to have your opinion, in confidence, on a very curious case in which I am deeply interested; that is to say, it is very curious to me; perhaps to your better information it may be less so."

Glancing at his hands, which were discoloured by his late work, the Doctor looked troubled, and listened attentively. He had already glanced at his hands more than once.

"Doctor Manette," said Mr. Lorry, touching him affectionately on the arm, "the case is the case of a particularly dear friend of mine. Pray give your mind to it, and advise me well for his sake—and, above all, for his daughter's—his daughter's, my dear Manette."

"If I understand," said the Doctor, in a subdued tone, "some mental shock——?"

"Yes!"

"Be explicit," said the Doctor. "Spare no detail."

Mr. Lorry saw that they understood one another, and proceeded.

"My dear Manette, it is the case of an old and a prolonged shock, of great acuteness and severity to the affections, the feelings, the—the—as you express it—the mind. The mind. It is the case of a shock under which the sufferer was borne down, one cannot say for how long, because I believe he cannot calculate the time himself, and there are no other means of getting at it. It is the case of a shock from which the sufferer recovered, by a process that he cannot trace himself—as I once heard him publicly relate in a striking manner. It is the case of a shock from which he has recovered, so completely as to be a highly intelligent man, capable of close application of mind, and great exertion of body, and of constantly making fresh additions to his stock of knowledge, which was already very large. But, unfortunately, there has been," he paused and took a deep breath—"a slight relapse."

The Doctor, in a low voice, asked, "Of how long duration?"

"Nine days and nights."

"How did it show itself? I infer," glancing at his hands again, "in the resumption of some old pursuit connected with the shock?"

"That is the fact."

"Now, did you ever see him," asked the Doctor, distinctly and collectedly, though in the same low voice, "engaged in that pursuit originally?"

"Once."

"And when the relapse fell on him, was he in most respects—or in all respects—as he was then?"

"I think in all respects."

"You spoke of his daughter. Does his daughter know of the relapse?"

"No. It has been kept from her, and I hope will always be kept from her. It is known only to myself, and to one other who may be trusted."

The Doctor grasped his hand, and murmured, "That was very kind. That was very thoughtful!" Mr. Lorry grasped his hand in return, and neither of the two spoke for a little while.

"Now, my dear Manette," said Mr. Lorry, at length, in his most considerate and most affectionate way, "I am a mere man of business, and unfit to cope with such intricate and difficult matters. I do not possess the kind of information necessary; I do not possess the kind of intelligence; I want guiding. There is no man in this world on whom I could so rely for right guidance as on you. Tell me, how does this relapse come about? Is there danger of another? Could a repetition of it be prevented? How should a repetition of it be treated? How does it come about at all? What can I do for my friend? No man ever can have been more desirous in his heart to serve a friend than I am to serve mine, if I knew how. But I don't know how to originate, in such a case. If your sagacity, knowledge, and experience could put me on the right track, I might be able to do so much; unenlightened and undirected, I can do so little. Pray discuss it with me; pray enable me to see it a little more clearly, and teach me how to be a little more useful."

Doctor Manette sat meditating after these earnest words were spoken, and Mr. Lorry did not press him.

"I think it probable," said the Doctor, breaking silence with an effort, "that the relapse you have described, my dear friend, was not quite unforeseen by its subject."

"Was it dreaded by him?" Mr. Lorry ventured to ask.

"Very much." He said it with an involuntary shudder.

"You have no idea how such an apprehension weighs on the sufferer's mind, and how difficult—how almost impossible—it is for him to force himself to utter a word upon the topic that oppresses him."

"Would he," asked Mr. Lorry, "be sensibly relieved if he could prevail upon himself to impart that secret brooding to any one, when it is on him?"

"I think so. But it is, as I have told you, next to impossible. I even believe it—in some cases—to be quite impossible."

"Now," said Mr. Lorry, gently laying his hand on the Doctor's arm again, after a short silence on both sides, "to what would you refer this attack?"

"I believe," returned Doctor Manette, "that there had been a strong and extraordinary revival of the train of thought and remembrance that was the first cause of the malady. Some intense associations of a most distressing nature were vividly recalled, I think. It is probable that there had long been a dread lurking in his mind that those associations would be recalled—say, under certain circumstances—say, on a particular occasion. He tried to prepare himself in vain; perhaps the effort to prepare himself made him less able to bear it."

"Would he remember what took place in the relapse?" asked Mr. Lorry, with natural hesitation.

The Doctor looked desolately round the room, shook his head, and answered, in a low voice, "Not at all."

"Now, as to the future," hinted Mr. Lorry.

"As to the future," said the Doctor, recovering firmness, "I should have great hope. As it pleased Heaven in its mercy to restore him so soon, I should have great hope. He yielding under the pressure of a complicated something, long dreaded and long vaguely foreseen and contended against, and recovering after the cloud had burst and passed, I should hope that the worst was over."

"Well, well! That's good comfort. I am thankful!" said Mr. Lorry.

"I am thankful!" repeated the Doctor, bending his head with reverence.

"There are two other points," said Mr. Lorry, "on which I am anxious to be instructed. I may go on?"

"You cannot do your friend a better service." The Doctor gave him his hand.

"To the first, then. He is of a studious habit, and unusually energetic; he applies himself with great ardour to the acquisition of professional knowledge, to the conducting of experiments, to many things. Now, does he do too much?"

"I think not. It may be the character of his mind to be always in singular need of occupation. That may be, in part, natural to it; in part, the result of affliction. The less it was occupied with healthy things, the more it would be in danger of turning in the unhealthy direction. He may have observed himself, and made the discovery."

"You are sure that he is not under too great a strain?"

"I think I am quite sure of it."

"My dear Manette, if he were overworked now——"

"My dear Lorry, I doubt if that could easily be. There has been a violent stress in one direction, and it needs a counterweight."

"Excuse me, as a persistent man of business. Assuming for a moment that he *was* overworked; it would show itself in some renewal of this disorder?"

"I do not think so. I do not think," said Doctor Manette, with the firmness of self-conviction, "that anything but the one train of association would renew it. I think that, henceforth, nothing but some extraordinary jarring of that chord could renew it. After what has happened, and after his recovery, I find it difficult to imagine any such violent sounding of that string again. I trust, and I almost believe, that the circumstances likely to renew it are exhausted."

He spoke with the diffidence of a man who knew how slight a thing would overset the delicate organisation of the mind, and yet with the confidence of a man who had slowly won his assurance out of personal endurance and distress. It was not for his friend to abate that confidence. He professed himself more relieved and encouraged than he really was, and approached his second and last point. He felt it to be the most difficult of all ; but, remembering his old Sunday morning conversation with Miss Pross, and remembering what he had seen in the last nine days, he knew that he must face it.

"The occupation resumed under the influence of this passing affliction so happily recovered from," said Mr. Lorry, clearing his throat, "we will call—Blacksmith's work, Blacksmith's work. We will say, to put a case and for the sake of illustration, that he had been used, in his bad time, to work at a little forge. We will say that he was unexpectedly found at his forge again. Is it not a pity that he should keep it by him ? "

The Doctor shaded his forehead with his hand, and beat his foot nervously on the ground.

"He has always kept it by him," said Mr. Lorry, with an anxious look at his friend. "Now, would it not be better that he should let it go ? "

Still the Doctor, with shaded forehead, beat his foot nervously on the ground.

"You do not find it easy to advise me ? " said Mr. Lorry. "I quite understand it to be a nice question. And yet I think——" And there he shook his head, and stopped.

"You see," said Doctor Manette, turning to him after an uneasy pause, "it is very hard to explain, consistently, the innermost workings of this poor man's mind. He once yearned so frightfully for that occupation, and it was so welcome when it came—no doubt it relieved his pain so much, by substituting the perplexity of the fingers for the perplexity of the brain, and by substituting, as he became more practised, the ingenuity of the hands for the ingenuity of the mental torture—that he has never been able to bear the thought of putting it quite out of his reach. Even now, when I believe he is more hopeful of himself than he has ever been, and even speaks of himself with a kind of confidence, the idea that he might need that old employment, and not find it, gives him a sudden sense of terror, like that which one may fancy strikes to the heart of a lost child."

He looked like his illustration, as he raised his eyes to Mr. Lorry's face.

"But may not—mind ! I ask for information, as a plodding man of business who only deals with such material objects as guineas, shillings, and bank-notes—may not the retention of the thing involve the retention of the idea? If the thing were gone, my dear Manette, might not the fear go with it? In short, is it not a concession to the misgiving to keep the forge?"

There was another silence.

"You see, too," said the Doctor, tremulously, "it is such an old companion."

"I would not keep it," said Mr. Lorry, shaking his head; for he gained in firmness as he saw the Doctor disquieted. "I would recommend him to sacrifice it. I only want your authority. I am sure it does no good. Come! Give me your authority, like a dear good man. For his daughter's sake, my dear Manette!"

Very strange to see what a struggle there was within him!

"In her name, then, let it be done; I sanction it. But I would not take it away while he was present. Let it be removed when he is not there; let him miss his old companion after an absence."

Mr. Lorry readily engaged for that, and the conference was ended. They passed the day in the country, and the Doctor was quite restored. On the three following days he remained perfectly well, and on the fourteenth day he went away to join Lucie and her husband. The precaution that had been taken to account for his silence Mr. Lorry had previously explained to him, and he had written to Lucie in accordance with it, and she had no suspicions.

On the night of the day on which he left the house Mr. Lorry went into his room with a chopper, saw, chisel, and hammer, attended by Miss Pross carrying a light. There, with closed doors, and in a mysterious and guilty manner, Mr. Lorry hacked the shoemaker's bench to pieces, while Miss Pross held the candle as if she were assisting at a murder—for which, indeed, in her grimness, she was no unsuitable figure. The burning of the body (previously reduced to pieces convenient for the purpose) was commenced without delay in the kitchen fire; and the tools, shoes, and leather were buried in the garden. So wicked do destruction and secrecy appear to honest minds, that Mr. Lorry and Miss Pross, while engaged in the commission of their deed and in the removal of its traces, almost felt, and almost looked, like accomplices in a horrible crime.

CHAPTER XX

A PLEA

When the newly-married pair came home, the first person who appeared to offer his congratulations was Sydney Carton. They had not been at home many hours when he presented himself. He was not improved in habits, or in looks, or in manner; but there was a certain rugged air of fidelity about him, which was new to the observation of Charles Darnay.

He watched his opportunity of taking Darnay aside into a window, and of speaking to him when no one overheard.

"Mr. Darnay," said Carton, "I wish we might be friends."

"We are already friends, I hope."

"You are good enough to say so, as a fashion of speech; but I don't mean any fashion of speech. Indeed, when I say I wish we might be friends, I scarcely mean quite that, either."

Charles Darnay—as was natural—asked him, in all good-humour and good-fellowship, what he did mean.

"Upon my life," said Carton, smiling, "I find that easier to comprehend in my own mind than to convey to yours. However, let me try. You remember a certain famous occasion when I was more drunk than—than usual?"

"I remember a certain famous occasion when you forced me to confess that you had been drinking."

"I remember it too. The curse of those occasions is heavy upon me, for I always remember them. I hope it may be taken into account one day, when all days are at an end for me! Don't be alarmed; I am not going to preach."

"I am not at all alarmed. Earnestness in you is anything but alarming to me."

"Ah!" said Carton, with a careless wave of his hand, as if he waved that away. "On the drunken occasion in question (one of a large number, as you know) I was insufferable about liking you, and not liking you. I wish you would forget it."

"I forgot it long ago."

"Fashion of speech again! But, Mr. Darnay, oblivion is not so easy to me as you represent it to be to you. I have by no means forgotten it, and a light answer does not help me to forget it."

"If it was a light answer," returned Darnay, "I beg your forgiveness for it. I had no other object than to turn a slight thing, which, to my surprise, seems to trouble you too much, aside. I declare to you, on the faith of a gentleman, that I have long dismissed it from my mind. Good Heaven, what was there to dismiss! Have I had nothing more important to remember in the great service you rendered me that day?"

"As to the great service," said Carton, "I am bound to avow to you, when you speak of it in that way, that it was mere professional claptrap. I don't know that I cared what became of you when I rendered it.—Mind! I say when I rendered it; I am speaking of the past."

"You make light of the obligation," returned Darnay, "but I will not quarrel with *your* light answer."

"Genuine truth, Mr. Darnay, trust me! I have gone aside from my purpose; I was speaking about our being friends. Now, you know me; you know I am incapable of all the higher and better flights of men.   If you doubt it, ask Stryver, and he'll tell you so."

" I prefer to form my own opinion, without the aid of his."

" Well !   At any rate you know me as a dissolute dog, who has never done any good, and never will."

" I don't know that you ' never will.' "

" But I do, and you must take my word for it.   Well !   If you could endure to have such a worthless fellow, and a fellow of such indifferent reputation, coming and going at odd times, I should ask that I might be permitted to come and go as a privileged person here ; that I might be regarded as a useless (and I would add, if it were not for the resemblance I detected between you and me, an unornamental) piece of furniture, tolerated for its old service, and taken no notice of. I doubt if I should abuse the permission.   It is a hundred to one if I should avail myself of it four times in a year.   It would satisfy me, I dare say, to know that I had it."

" Will you try ? "

" That is another way of saying that I am placed on the footing I have indicated.   I thank you, Darnay.   I may use that freedom with your name ? "

" I think so, Carton, by this time."

They shook hands upon it, and Sydney turned away.   Within a minute afterwards he was, to all outward appearance, as unsubstantial as ever.

When he was gone, and in the course of an evening passed with Miss Pross, the Doctor, and Mr. Lorry, Charles Darnay made some mention of this conversation in general terms, and spoke of Sydney Carton as a problem of carelessness and recklessness.   He spoke of him, in short, not bitterly or meaning to bear hard upon him, but as anybody might who saw him as he showed himself.

He had no idea that this could dwell in the thoughts of his fair young wife ; but when he afterwards joined her in their own rooms, he found her waiting for him with the old pretty lifting of the forehead strongly marked.

" We are thoughtful to-night ! " said Darnay, drawing his arm about her.

" Yes, dearest Charles," with her hands on his breast, and the inquiring and attentive expression fixed upon him ; " we are rather thoughtful to-night, for we have something on our mind to-night."

" What is it, my Lucie ? "

" Will you promise not to press one question on me, if I beg you not to ask it ? "

" Will I promise ?   What will I not promise to my Love ? "

What, indeed, with his hand putting aside the golden hair from the cheek, and his other hand against the heart that beat for him !

" I think, Charles, poor Mr. Carton deserves more consideration and respect than you expressed for him to-night."

" Indeed, my own ?   Why so ? "

"That is what you are not to ask me. But I think—I know—he does."

"If you know it, it is enough. What would you have me do, my Life?"

"I would ask you, dearest, to be very generous with him always, and very lenient on his faults when he is not by. I would ask you to believe that he has a heart he very, very seldom reveals, and that there are deep wounds in it. My dear, I have seen it bleeding."

"It is a painful reflection to me," said Charles Darnay, quite astounded, "that I should have done him any wrong. I never thought this of him."

"My husband, it is so. I fear he is not to be reclaimed; there is scarcely a hope that anything in his character or fortunes is reparable now. But I am sure that he is capable of good things, gentle things, even magnanimous things."

She looked so beautiful in the purity of her faith in this lost man, that her husband could have looked at her as she was for hours.

"And oh, my dearest Love!" she urged, clinging nearer to him, laying her head upon his breast, and raising her eyes to his, "remember how strong we are in our happiness, and how weak he is in his misery!"

The supplication touched him home. "I will always remember it, dear Heart! I will remember it as long as I live."

He bent over the golden head, and put the rosy lips to his, and folded her in his arms. If one forlorn wanderer then pacing the dark streets could have heard her innocent disclosure, and could have seen the drops of pity kissed away by her husband from the soft blue eyes so loving of that husband, he might have cried to the night—and the words would not have parted from his lips for the first time—

"God bless her for her sweet compassion!"

CHAPTER XXI

ECHOING FOOTSTEPS

A WONDERFUL corner for echoes, it has been remarked, that corner where the Doctor lived. Ever busily winding the golden thread which bound her husband, and her father, and herself, and her old directress and companion, in a life of quiet bliss, Lucie sat in the still house in the tranquilly resounding corner, listening to the echoing footsteps of years.

At first there were times, though she was a perfectly happy young wife, when her work would slowly fall from her hands, and her eyes would be dimmed. For there was something coming in the echoes, something light, afar off, and scarcely audible yet, that stirred her heart too much. Fluttering hopes and doubts—hopes of a love as yet unknown to her; doubts of her remaining upon earth to enjoy that new delight—divided her breast. Among the echoes then there would arise the sound of footsteps at her own early grave; and thoughts of the husband who would be left so desolate, and who would mourn for her so much, swelled to her eyes, and broke like waves.

That time passed, and her little Lucie lay on her bosom. Then, among the advancing echoes, there was the tread of her tiny feet and the sound of her prattling words. Let greater echoes resound as they would, the young mother at the cradle-side could always hear those coming. They came, and the shady house was sunny with a child's laugh, and the Divine friend of children, to whom in her trouble she had confided hers, seemed to take her child in His arms, as He took the child of old, and made it a sacred joy to her.

Ever busily winding the golden thread that bound them all together, weaving the service of her happy influence through the tissue of all their lives, and making it predominate nowhere, Lucie heard in the echoes of years none but friendly and soothing sounds. Her husband's step was strong and prosperous among them; her father's firm and equal. Lo, Miss Pross, in harness of string, awakening the echoes, as an unruly charger, whip-corrected, snorting and pawing the earth under the plane-tree in the garden!

Even when there were sounds of sorrow among the rest, they were not harsh nor cruel. Even when golden hair, like her own, lay in a halo on the pillow round the worn face of a little boy, and he said, with a radiant smile, "Dear papa and mamma, I am very sorry to leave you both, and to leave my pretty sister; but I am called, and I must go!" those were not tears all of agony that wetted his young mother's cheek, as the spirit departed from her embrace that had been entrusted to it. Suffer them and forbid them not. They see my Father's face. Oh Father, blessed words!

Thus the rustling of an Angel's wings got blended with the other echoes, and they were not wholly of earth, but had in them that breath of heaven. Sighs of the winds that blew over a little garden-tomb were mingled with them also, and both were audible to Lucie, in a hushed murmur—like the breathing of a summer sea asleep upon a sandy shore—as the little Lucie, comically studious at the task of the morning, or dressing a doll at her mother's footstool, chattered in the tongues of the Two Cities that were blended in her life.

The echoes rarely answered to the actual tread of Sydney Carton. Some half-dozen times a year, at most, he claimed his privilege of coming in uninvited, and would sit among them through the evening, as he had once done often. He never came there heated with wine. And one other thing regarding him was whispered in the echoes, which has been whispered by all true echoes for ages and ages.

No man ever really loved a woman, lost her, and knew her with a blameless though an unchanged mind when she was a wife and a mother, but her children had a strange sympathy with him—an instinctive delicacy of pity for him. What fine hidden sensibilities are touched in such a case, no echoes tell ; but it is so, and it was so here. Carton was the first stranger to whom little Lucie held out her chubby arms, and he kept his place with her as she grew.   The little boy had spoken of him, almost at the last.   " Poor Carton !   Kiss him for me ! "

Mr. Stryver shouldered his way through the law, like some great engine forcing itself through turbid water, and dragged his useful friend in his wake, like a boat towed astern.   As the boat so favoured is usually in a rough plight, and mostly under water, so Sydney had a swamped life of it.   But easy and strong custom, unhappily so much easier and stronger in him than any stimulating sense of desert or disgrace, made it the life he was to lead ; and he no more thought of emerging from his state of lion's jackal, than any real jackal may be supposed to think of rising to be a lion.   Stryver was rich ;   had married a florid widow with property and three boys, who had nothing particularly shining about them but the straight hair of their dumpling heads.

These three young gentlemen Mr. Stryver, exuding patronage of the most offensive quality from every pore, had walked before him like three sheep to the quiet corner in Soho, and had offered as pupils to Lucie's husband, delicately saying, " Halloa ! here are three lumps of bread-and-cheese towards your matrimonial picnic, Darnay ! "   The polite rejection of the three lumps of bread-and-cheese had quite bloated Mr. Stryver with indignation, which he afterwards turned to account in the training of the young gentlemen, by directing them to beware of the pride of Beggars, like that tutor-fellow.   He was also in the habit of declaiming to Mrs. Stryver, over his full-bodied wine, on the arts Mrs. Darnay had once put in practice to " catch " him, and on the diamond-cut-diamond arts in himself, Madam, which had rendered him " not to be caught."   Some of his King's Bench familiars, who were occasionally parties to the full-bodied wine and the lie, excused him for the latter by saying that he had told it so often that he believed it himself—which is surely such an incorrigible aggravation of an originally bad offence as to justify any such offender's being carried off to some suitably retired spot, and there hanged out of the way.

These were among the echoes to which Lucie, sometimes pensive, sometimes amused and laughing, listened in the echoing corner, until her little daughter was six years old.   How near to her heart the echoes of her child's tread came, and those of her own dear father's, always active and self-possessed, and those of her dear husband's, need not be told.   Nor how the lightest echo of their united home, directed by herself with such a wise and elegant thrift that it was more abundant than any waste, was music to her.   Nor how there were echoes all about her, sweet in her ears, of the many times her father had told her that he found her more devoted to him married (if that could be) than single, and of the many times her husband had said to her that no cares and duties seemed to divide her love for him or her help to him, and asked her, " What is the magic secret, my darling, of your being everything to all of us, as if there were only one of us, yet never seeming to be hurried, or to have too much to do?"

But there were other echoes from a distance that rumbled menacingly in the corner all through this space of time. And it was now, about little Lucie's sixth birthday, that they began to have an awful sound, as of a great storm in France with a dreadful sea rising.

On a night in mid-July, one thousand seven hundred and eighty-nine, Mr. Lorry came in late from Tellson's, and sat himself down by Lucie and her husband in the dark window. It was a hot, wild night, and they were all three reminded of the old Sunday night when they had looked at the lightning from the same place.

"I began to think," said Mr. Lorry, pushing his brown wig back, "that I should have to pass the night at Tellson's. We have been so full of business all day, that we have not known what to do first, or which way to turn. There is such an uneasiness in Paris, that we have actually a run of confidence upon us! Our customers over there seem not to be able to confide their property to us fast enough. There is positively a mania among some of them for sending it to England."

"That has a bad look," said Darnay.

"A bad look, you say, my dear Darnay? Yes, but we don't know what reason there is in it. People are so unreasonable! Some of us at Tellson's are getting old, and we really can't be troubled out of the ordinary course without due occasion."

"Still," said Darnay, "you know how gloomy and threatening the sky is."

"I know that, to be sure," assented Mr. Lorry, trying to persuade himself that his sweet temper was soured, and that he grumbled, "but I am determined to be peevish after my long day's botheration. Where is Manette?"

"Here he is," said the Doctor, entering the dark room at the moment.

"I am quite glad you are at home; for these hurries and forebodings by which I have been surrounded all day long have made me nervous without reason. You are not going out, I hope!"

"No; I am going to play backgammon with you, if you like," said the Doctor.

"I don't think I do like, if I may speak my mind. I am not fit to be pitted against you to-night. Is the teaboard still there, Lucie? I can't see."

"Of course, it has been kept for you."

"Thank ye, my dear. The precious child is safe in bed?"

"And sleeping soundly."

"That's right; all safe and well! I don't know why anything should be otherwise than safe and well here, thank God; but I have been so put out all day, and I am not as young as I was! My tea, my dear! Thank ye. Now, come and take your place in the circle, and let us sit quiet, and hear the echoes about which you have your theory."

"Not a theory; it was a fancy."

"A fancy, then, my wise pet," said Mr. Lorry, patting her hand. "They are very numerous and very loud, though, are they not? Only hear them!"

Headlong, mad, and dangerous footsteps to force their way into anybody's life, footsteps not easily made clean again if once stained red, the footsteps raging in Saint Antoine afar off, as the little circle sat in the dark London window.

Saint Antoine had been, that morning, a vast dusky mass of scarecrows heaving to and fro, with frequent gleams of light above the billowy heads, where steel blades and bayonets shone in the sun. A tremendous roar arose from the throat of Saint Antoine, and a forest of naked arms struggled in the air like shrivelled branches of trees in a winter wind, all the fingers convulsively clutching at every weapon or semblance of a weapon that was thrown up from the depths below, no matter how far off.

Who gave them out, whence they last came, where they began, through what agency they crookedly quivered and jerked, scores at a time, over the heads of the crowd, like a kind of lightning, no eye in the throng could have told; but muskets were being distributed—so were cartridges, powder, and ball, bars of iron and wood, knives, axes, pikes, every weapon that distracted ingenuity could discover or devise. People who could lay hold of nothing else set themselves with bleeding hands to force stones and bricks out of their places in walls. Every pulse and heart in Saint Antoine was on high-fever strain and at high-fever heat. Every living creature there held life as of no account, and was demented with a passionate readiness to sacrifice it.

As a whirlpool of boiling waters has a centre point, so all this raging circled round Defarge's wine-shop, and every human drop in the caldron had a tendency to be sucked towards the vortex where Defarge himself, already begrimed with gunpowder and sweat, issued orders, issued arms, thrust this man back, dragged this man forward, disarmed one to arm another, laboured and strove in the thickest of the uproar.

"Keep near to me, Jacques Three," cried Defarge; "and do you, Jacques One and Two, separate and put yourselves at the head of as many of these patriots as you can. Where is my wife?"

"Eh well! Here you see me!" said Madame, composed as ever, but not knitting to-day. Madame's resolute right hand was occupied with an axe, in place of the usual softer implements, and in her girdle were a pistol and a cruel knife.

"Where do you go, my wife?"

"I go," said Madame, "with you at present. You shall see me at the head of women by and by."

"Come, then!" cried Defarge, in a resounding voice. "Patriots and friends, we are ready! The Bastille!"

With a roar that sounded as if all the breath in France had been shaped into the detested word, the living sea rose, wave on wave, depth on depth, and overflowed the city to that point. Alarm-bells ringing, drums beating, the sea raging and thundering on its new beach, the attack begun.

Deep ditches, double drawbridge, massive stone walls, eight great towers, cannon, muskets, fire and smoke. Through the fire and through the smoke—in the fire and in the smoke, for the sea cast him up against a cannon, and on the instant he became a cannonier— Defarge of the wine-shop worked like a manful soldier, Two fierce hours.

Deep ditch, single drawbridge, massive stone walls, eight great towers, cannon, muskets, fire and smoke. One drawbridge down! "Work, comrades all, work! Work, Jacques One, Jacques Two, Jacques One Thousand, Jacques Two Thousand, Jacques Five-and-Twenty Thousand; in the name of all the Angels or the Devils—which you prefer—work!" Thus Defarge of the wine-shop, still at his gun, which had long grown hot.

"To me, women!" cried Madame his wife. "What! We can kill as well as the men when the place is taken!" And to her, with a shrill thirsty cry, trooping women variously armed, but all armed alike in hunger and revenge.

Cannon, muskets, fire and smoke; but still the deep ditch, the single drawbridge, the massive stone walls, and the eight great towers. Slight displacements of the raging sea, made by the falling wounded. Flashing weapons, blazing torches, smoking waggon-loads of wet straw, hard work at neighbouring barricades in all directions, shrieks, volleys, execrations, bravery without stint, boom, smash, and rattle, and the furious sounding of the living sea; but still the deep ditch, and the single drawbridge, and the massive stone walls, and the eight great towers, and still Defarge of the wine-shop at his gun, grown doubly hot by the service of Four fierce hours.

A white flag from within the fortress, and a parley—this dimly perceptible through the raging storm, nothing audible in it—suddenly the sea rose immeasurably wider and higher, and swept Defarge of the wine-shop over the lowered drawbridge, past the massive stone outer walls, in among the eight great towers surrendered!

So resistless was the force of the ocean bearing him on, that even to draw his breath or turn his head was as impracticable as if he had been struggling in the surf at the South Sea, until he was landed in the outer courtyard of the Bastille. There, against an angle of the wall, he made a struggle to look about him. Jacques Three was nearly at his side; Madame Defarge, still heading some of her women, was visible in the inner distance, and her knife was in her hand. Everywhere was tumult, exultation, deafening and maniacal bewilderment, astounding noise, yet furious dumb show.

"The Prisoners!"

"The Records!"

"The secret cells!"

"The instruments of torture!"

"The Prisoners!"

Of all these cries, and ten thousand incoherencies, "The Prisoners!"
was the cry most taken up by the sea that rushed in, as if there were
an eternity of people, as well as of time and space. When the foremost billows rolled past, bearing the prison officers with them, and
threatening them all with instant death if any secret nook remained
undisclosed, Defarge laid his strong hand on the breast of one of these
men—a man with a gray head, who had a lighted torch in his hand—
separated him from the rest, and got him between himself and the
wall.

"Show me the North Tower!" said Defarge. "Quick!"

"I will faithfully," replied the man, "if you will come with me.
But there is no one there."

"What is the meaning of One Hundred and Five, North Tower?"
asked Defarge. "Quick!"

"The meaning, Monsieur?"

"Does it mean a captive, or a place of captivity? Or do you mean
that I shall strike you dead?"

"Kill him!" croaked Jacques Three, who had come close up.

"Monsieur, it is a cell."

"Show it me!"

"Pass this way then."

Jacques Three, with his usual craving on him, and evidently disappointed by the dialogue taking a turn that did not seem to promise
bloodshed, held by Defarge's arm as he held by the turnkey's. Their
three heads had been close together during this brief discourse, and
it had been as much as they could do to hear one another even then,
so tremendous was the noise of the living ocean in its irruption into
the fortress, and its inundation of the courts and passages and staircases. All around outside, too, it beat the walls with a deep, hoarse
roar, from which, occasionally, some partial shouts of tumult broke
and leaped into the air like spray.

Through gloomy vaults where the light of day had never shone,
past hideous doors of dark dens and cages, down cavernous flights of
steps, and again up steep rugged ascents of stone and brick, more like
dry waterfalls than staircases, Defarge, the turnkey, and Jacques
Three, linked hand and arm, went with all the speed they could make.
Here and there, especially at first, the inundation started on them and
swept by; but when they had done descending, and were winding and
climbing up a tower, they were alone. Hemmed in here by the
massive thickness of walls and arches, the storm within the fortress
and without was only audible to them in a dull, subdued way, as if
the noise out of which they had come had almost destroyed their sense
of hearing.

The turnkey stopped at a low door, put a key in a clashing lock,
swung the door slowly open, and said, as they all bent their heads and
passed in—

"One Hundred and Five, North Tower!"

There was a small, heavily-grated, unglazed window high in the wall, with a stone screen before it, so that the sky could only be seen by stooping low and looking up. There was a small chimney, heavily barred across, a few feet within. There was a heap of old feathery wood-ashes on the hearth. There was a stool, and table, and a straw bed. There were the four blackened walls, and a rusted iron ring in one of them.

"Pass that torch slowly along these walls, that I may see them," said Defarge to the turnkey.

The man obeyed, and Defarge followed the light closely with his eyes.

"Stop!—Look here, Jacques!"

"A. M.!" croaked Jacques Three, as he read greedily.

"Alexandre Manette," said Defarge in his ear, following the letters with his swart forefinger, deeply engrained with gunpowder. "And here he wrote 'a poor physician.' And it was he, without doubt, who scratched a calendar on this stone. What is that in your hand? A crowbar? Give it me!"

He had still the linstock of his gun in his own hand. He made a sudden exchange of the two instruments, and turning on the worm-eaten stool and table, beat them to pieces in a few blows.

"Hold the light higher!" he said, wrathfully, to the turnkey. "Look among those fragments with care, Jacques. And see! Here is my knife," throwing it to him; "rip open that bed, and search the straw. Hold the light higher, you!"

With a menacing look at the turnkey he crawled upon the hearth, and, peering up the chimney, struck and prised at the sides with the crowbar, and worked at the iron grating across it. In a few minutes some mortar and dust came dropping down, which he averted his face to avoid; and in it, and in the old wood-ashes, and in a crevice in the chimney into which his weapon had slipped or wrought itself, he groped with a cautious touch.

"Nothing in the wood, and nothing in the straw, Jacques?"

"Nothing."

"Let us collect them together, in the middle of the cell. So! Light them, you!"

The turnkey fired the little pile, which blazed high and hot. Stooping again to come out at the low-arched door, they left it burning, and retraced their way to the courtyard, seeming to recover their sense of hearing as they came down, until they were in the raging flood once more.

They found it surging and tossing, in quest of Defarge himself. Saint Antoine was clamorous to have its wine-shop keeper foremost in the guard upon the governor who had defended the Bastille and shot the people. Otherwise the governor would not be marched to the Hôtel de Ville for judgment. Otherwise the governor would escape, and the people's blood (suddenly of some value, after many years of worthlessness) be unavenged.

In the howling universe of passion and contention that seemed to encompass this grim old officer, conspicuous in his gray coat and red decoration, there was but one quite steady figure, and that was a woman's. "See, there is my husband!" she cried, pointing him out. "See Defarge!" She stood immovable close to the grim old officer, and remained immovable close to him; remained immovable close to him through the streets, as Defarge and the rest bore him along; remained immovable close to him when he was got near his destination, and began to be struck at from behind; remained immovable close to him when the long-gathering rain of stabs and blows fell heavy; was so close to him when he dropped dead under it, that, suddenly animated, she put her foot upon his neck, and with her cruel knife—long ready— hewed off his head.

The hour was come when Saint Antoine was to execute his horrible idea of hoisting up men for lamps to show what he could be and do. Saint Antoine's blood was up, and the blood of tyranny and domination by the iron hand was down—down on the steps of the Hôtel de Ville, where the governor's body lay—down on the sole of the shoe of Madame Defarge, where she had trodden on the body to steady it for mutilation. "Lower the lamp yonder!" cried Saint Antoine, after glaring round for a new means of death; "here is one of his soldiers to be left on guard!" The swinging sentinel was posted, and the sea rushed on.

The sea of black and threatening waters, and of destructive up-heaving of wave against wave, whose depths were yet unfathomed and whose forces were yet unknown. The remorseless sea of turbulently swaying shapes, voices of vengeance, and faces hardened in the furnaces of suffering until the touch of pity could make no mark on them.

But in the ocean of faces where every fierce and furious expression was in vivid life, there were two groups of faces—each seven in number —so fixedly contrasting with the rest, that never did sea roll which bore more memorable wrecks with it. Seven faces of prisoners, suddenly released by the storm that had burst their tomb, were carried high overhead: all scared, all lost, all wondering and amazed, as if the Last Day were come, and those who rejoiced around them were lost spirits. Other seven faces there were, carried higher, seven dead faces, whose drooping eyelids and half-seen eyes awaited the Last Day. Impassive faces, yet with a suspended—not an abolished—expression on them; faces, rather, in a fearful pause, as having yet to raise the dropped lids of the eyes, and bear witness with the bloodless lips, "THOU DIDST IT!"

Seven prisoners released, seven gory heads on pikes, the keys of the accursed fortress of the eight strong towers, some discovered letters and other memorials of prisoners of old time, long dead of broken hearts—such and such-like the loudly echoing footsteps of Saint Antoine escort through the Paris streets in mid-July, one thousand seven hundred and eighty-nine. Now, Heaven defeat the fancy of

Madame Defarge

Lucie Darnay, and keep these feet far out of her life ! For they are headlong, mad, and dangerous ; and in the years so long after the breaking of the cask at Defarge's wine-shop door, they are not easily purified when once stained red.

CHAPTER XXII

THE SEA STILL RISES

HAGGARD Saint Antoine had had only one exultant week in which to soften his modicum of hard and bitter bread to such extent as he could with the relish of fraternal embraces and congratulations, when Madame Defarge sat at her counter, as usual, presiding over the customers. Madame Defarge wore no rose in her head, for the great brotherhood of Spies had become, even in one short week, extremely chary of trusting themselves to the Saint's mercies. The lamps across his streets had a portentously elastic swing with them.

Madame Defarge, with her arms folded, sat in the morning light and heat, contemplating the wine-shop and the street. In both there were several knots of loungers, squalid and miserable, but now with a manifest sense of power enthroned on their distress. The raggedest nightcap, awry on the wretchedest head, had this crooked significance in it : "I know how hard it has grown for me, the wearer of this, to support life in myself ; but do you know how easy it has grown for me, the wearer of this, to destroy life in you ? " Every lean bare arm that had been without work before had this work always ready for it now, that it could strike. The fingers of the knitting women were vicious, with the experience that they could tear. There was a change in the appearance of Saint Antoine ; the image had been hammering into this for hundreds of years, and the last finishing blows had told mightily on the expression.

Madame Defarge sat observing it with such suppressed approval as was to be desired in the leader of the Saint Antoine women. One of her sisterhood knitted beside her. The short, rather plump wife of a starved grocer, and the mother of two children withal, this lieutenant had already earned the complimentary name of The Vengeance.

"Hark !" said The Vengeance. "Listen, then ! Who comes ? "

As if a train of powder laid from the outermost bound of the Saint Antoine Quarter to the wine-shop door had been suddenly fired, a fast-spreading murmur came rushing along.

"It is Defarge," said Madame. "Silence, patriots ! "

Defarge came in breathless, pulled off a red cap he wore, and looked around him. "Listen, everywhere !" said Madame again. "Listen to him !" Defarge stood, panting, against a background of eager eyes and open mouths, formed outside the door ; all those within the wine-shop had sprung to their feet.

"Say then, my husband. What is it?"

"News from the other world!"

"How, then?" cried Madame, contemptuously. "The other world?"

"Does everybody here recall old Foulon, who told the famished people that they might eat grass, and who died, and went to Hell?"

"Everybody!" from all throats.

"The news is of him. He is among us!"

"Among us!" from the universal throat again. "And dead?"

"Not dead! He feared us so much—and with reason—that he caused himself to be represented as dead, and had a grand mock-funeral. But they have found him alive, hiding in the country, and have brought him in. I have seen him but now, on his way to the Hôtel de Ville, a prisoner. I have said that he had reason to fear us. Say all! *Had* he reason?"

Wretched old sinner of more than threescore years and ten, if he had never known it yet, he would have known it in his heart of hearts if he could have heard the answering cry.

A moment of profound silence followed. Defarge and his wife looked steadfastly at one another. The Vengeance stooped, and the jar of a drum was heard as she moved it at her feet behind the counter.

"Patriots!" said Defarge, in a determined voice, "are we ready?"

Instantly Madame Defarge's knife was in her girdle; the drum was beating in the streets, as if it and a drummer had flown together by magic; and The Vengeance, uttering terrific shrieks, and flinging her arms about her head like all the forty Furies at once, was tearing from house to house, rousing the women.

The men were terrible, in the bloody-minded anger with which they looked from windows, caught up what arms they had, and came pouring down into the streets; but the women were a sight to chill the boldest. From such household occupations as their bare poverty yielded, from their children, from their aged and their sick crouching on the bare ground famished and naked, they ran out with streaming hair, urging one another, and themselves, to madness with the wildest cries and actions. Villain Foulon taken, my sister! Old Foulon taken, my mother! Miscreant Foulon taken, my daughter! Then a score of others ran into the midst of these, beating their breasts, tearing their hair, and screaming, Foulon alive! Foulon, who told the starving people they might eat grass! Foulon, who told my old father that he might eat grass, when I had no bread to give him! Foulon, who told my baby it might suck grass, when these breasts were dry with want! Oh mother of God, this Foulon! Oh Heaven, our suffering! Hear me, my dead baby and my withered father: I swear on my knees, on these stones, to avenge you on Foulon! Husbands, and brothers, and young men, Give us the blood of Foulon, Give us the head of Foulon, Give us the heart of Foulon, Give us the body and soul of Foulon, Rend Foulon to pieces, and dig him into the ground, that grass may grow from him! With these cries, numbers of the women, lashed into blind frenzy, whirled about, striking and tearing at their own friends until they dropped into a passionate swoon, and were only saved by the men belonging to them from being trampled under foot.

Nevertheless, not a moment was lost ; not a moment ! This Foulon was at the Hôtel de Ville, and might be loosed. Never, if Saint Antoine knew his own sufferings, insults, and wrongs ! Armed men and women flocked out of the Quarter so fast, and drew even these last dregs after them with such a force of suction, that within a quarter of an hour there was not a human creature in Saint Antoine's bosom but a few old crones and the wailing children.

No. They were all by that time choking the Hall of Examination where this old man, ugly and wicked, was, and overflowing into the adjacent open space and streets. The Defarges, husband and wife, The Vengeance, and Jacques Three were in the first press, and at no great distance from him in the Hall.

" See ! " cried Madame, pointing with her knife. " See the old villain bound with ropes. That was well done to tie a bunch of grass upon his back. Ha, ha ! That was well done. Let him eat it now ! " Madame put her knife under her arm, and clapped her hands as at a play.

The people immediately behind Madame Defarge, explaining the cause of her satisfaction to those behind them, and those again explaining to others, and those to others, the neighbouring streets resounded with the clapping of hands. Similarly, during two or three hours of drawl, and the winnowing of many bushels of words, Madame Defarge's frequent expressions of impatience were taken up, with marvellous quickness, at a distance : the more readily because certain men who had by some wonderful exercise of agility climbed up the external architecture to look in from the windows, knew Madame Defarge well, and acted as a telegraph between her and the crowd outside the building.

At length the sun rose so high that it struck a kindly ray, as of hope or protection, directly down upon the old prisoner's head. The favour was too much to bear ; in an instant the barrier of dust and chaff that had stood surprisingly long went to the winds, and Saint Antoine had got him !

It was known directly to the furthest confines of the crowd. Defarge had but sprung over a railing and a table, and folded the miserable wretch in a deadly embrace—Madame Defarge had but followed and turned her hand in one of the ropes with which he was tied—The Vengeance and Jacques Three were not yet up with them, and the men at the windows had not yet swooped into the Hall, like birds of prey from their high perches—when the cry seemed to go up, all over the city, " Bring him out ! Bring him to the lamp ! "

Down, and up, and head foremost on the steps of the building ; now on his knees ; now on his feet ; now on his back ; dragged, and struck at, and stifled by the bunches of grass and straw that were thrust into his face by hundreds of hands ; torn, bruised, panting, bleeding, yet always entreating and beseeching for mercy ; now full of vehement agony of action, with a small clear space about him as the people drew one another back that they might see ; now a log of dead wood drawn through a forest of legs, he was hauled to the nearest street corner where one of the fatal lamps swung, and there Madame Defarge let him go—as a cat might have done to a mouse—and silently and composedly looked at him while they made ready, and while he besought her, the women passionately screeching at him all the time, and the men sternly calling out to have him killed with grass in his mouth. Once he went aloft, and the rope broke, and they caught him shrieking ; twice he went aloft, and the rope broke, and they caught him shrieking ; then the rope was merciful, and held him, and his head was soon upon a pike, with grass enough in the mouth for all Saint Antoine to dance at the sight of.

Nor was this the end of the day's bad work, for Saint Antoine so shouted and danced his angry blood up, that it boiled again on hearing when the day closed in that the son-in-law of the despatched, another of the people's enemies and insulters, was coming into Paris under a guard five hundred strong, in cavalry alone. Saint Antoine wrote his crimes on flaring sheets of paper, seized him—would have torn him out of the breast of an army to bear Foulon company—set his head and heart on pikes, and carried the three spoils of the day in Wolf-procession through the streets.

Not before dark night did the men and women come back to the children, wailing and breadless. Then the miserable bakers' shops were beset by long files of them, patiently waiting to buy bad bread ; and while they waited with stomachs faint and empty, they beguiled the time by embracing one another on the triumphs of the day, and achieving them again in gossip. Gradually these strings of ragged people shortened and frayed away ; and then poor lights began to shine in high windows, and slender fires were made in the streets, at which neighbours cooked in common, afterwards supping at their doors.

Scanty and insufficient suppers those, and innocent of meat, as of most other sauce to wretched bread. Yet human fellowship infused some nourishment into the flinty viands, and struck some sparks of cheerfulness out of them. Fathers and mothers who had had their full share in the worst of the day played gently with their meagre children ; and lovers, with such a world around them and before them, loved and hoped.

It was almost morning when Defarge's wine-shop parted with its last knot of customers, and Monsieur Defarge said to Madame his wife, in husky tones, while fastening the door—

"At last it is come, my dear !"

"Eh well !" returned Madame. "Almost."

Saint Antoine slept, the Defarges slept ; even The Vengeance slept with her starved grocer, and the drum was at rest. The drum's was the only voice in Saint Antoine that blood and hurry had not changed. The Vengeance, as custodian of the drum, could have wakened him up and had the same speech out of him as before the Bastille fell, or old Foulon was seized ; not so with the hoarse tones of the men and women in Saint Antoine's bosom.

CHAPTER XXIII

FIRE RISES

THERE was a change on the village where the fountain fell, and where the mender of roads went forth daily to hammer out of the stones on the highway such morsels of bread as might serve for patches to hold his poor ignorant soul and his poor reduced body together. The prison on the crag was not so dominant as of yore ; there were soldiers to guard it, but not many ; there were officers to guard the soldiers, but not one of them knew what his men would do—beyond this : that it would probably not be what he was ordered.

Far and wide lay a ruined country, yielding nothing but desolation. Every green leaf, every blade of grass and blade of grain, was as shrivelled and poor as the miserable people. Everything was bowed down, dejected, oppressed, and broken. Habitations, fences, domesticated animals, men, women, children, and the soil that bore them—all worn out.

Monseigneur (often a most worthy individual gentleman) was a national blessing, gave a chivalrous tone to things, was a polite example of luxurious and shining life, and a great deal more to equal purpose ; nevertheless, Monseigneur as a class had, somehow or other, brought things to this. Strange that Creation, designed expressly for Monseigneur, should be so soon wrung dry and squeezed out ! There must be something short-sighted in the eternal arrangements, surely ! Thus it was, however ; and the last drop of blood having been extracted from the flints, and the last screw of the rack having been turned so often that its purchase crumbled, and it now turned and turned with nothing to bite, Monseigneur began to run away from a phenomenon so low and unaccountable.

But this was not the change on the village, and on many a village like it. For scores of years gone by Monseigneur had squeezed it and wrung it, and had seldom graced it with his presence except for the pleasures of the chase—now found in hunting the people ; now found in hunting the beasts for whose preservation Monseigneur made edifying spaces of barbarous and barren wilderness. No. The change consisted in the appearance of strange faces of low caste, rather than in the disappearance of the high-caste, chiselled, and otherwise beatified and beatifying features of Monseigneur.

For in these times, as the mender of roads worked, solitary, in the dust, not often troubling himself to reflect that dust he was and to dust he must return, being for the most part too much occupied in thinking how little he had for supper and how much more he would eat if he had it—in these times, as he raised his eyes from his lonely labour, and viewed the prospect, he would see some rough figure approaching on foot, the like of which was once a rarity in those parts, but was now a frequent presence. As it advanced, the mender of roads would discern without surprise that it was a shaggy-haired man, of almost barbarian aspect, tall, in wooden shoes that were clumsy even to the eyes of a mender of roads, grim, rough, swart, steeped in the mud and dust of many highways, dank with the marshy moisture of many low grounds, sprinkled with the thorns and leaves and moss of many byways through woods.

Such a man came upon him, like a ghost, at noon in the July weather, as he sat on his heap of stones under a bank, taking such shelter as he could get from a shower of hail.

The man looked at him, looked at the village in the hollow, at the mill, and at the prison on the crag. When he had identified these objects in what benighted mind he had, he said, in a dialect that was just intelligible—

"How goes it, Jacques?"

"All well, Jacques."

"Touch then!"

They joined hands, and the man sat down on the heap of stones.

"No dinner?"

"Nothing but supper now," said the mender of roads, with a hungry face.

"It is the fashion," growled the man. "I meet no dinner anywhere."

He took out a blackened pipe, filled it, lighted it with flint and steel, pulled at it until it was in a bright glow, then suddenly held it from him, and dropped something into it from between his finger and thumb that blazed and went out in a puff of smoke.

"Touch then." It was the turn of the mender of roads to say it this time, after observing these operations. They again joined hands.

"To-night?" said the mender of roads.

"To-night," said the man, putting the pipe in his mouth.

"Where?"

"Here."

He and the mender of roads sat on the heap of stones looking silently at one another, with the hail driving in between them like a pigmy charge of bayonets, until the sky began to clear over the village.

"Show me!" said the traveller then, moving to the brow of the hill.

"See!" returned the mender of roads, with extended finger. "You go down here, and straight through the street, and past the fountain——"

"To the Devil with all that!" interrupted the other, rolling his eye over the landscape. "*I* go through no streets and past no fountains. Well?"

"Well! About two leagues beyond the summit of that hill above the village."

"Good. When do you cease to work?"

"At sunset."

"Will you wake me before departing? I have walked two nights

without resting. Let me finish my pipe, and I shall sleep like a child.
Will you wake me?"

"Surely."

The wayfarer smoked his pipe out, put it in his breast, slipped off
his great wooden shoes, and lay down on his back on the heap of
stones. He was fast asleep directly.

As the road-mender plied his dusty labour, and the hail-clouds, rolling away, revealed bright bars and streaks of sky which were responded to by silver gleams upon the landscape, the little man (who
wore a red cap now, in place of his blue one) seemed fascinated by the
figure on the heap of stones. His eyes were so often turned towards
it, that he used his tools mechanically, and, one would have said, to
very poor account. The bronze face, the shaggy black hair and beard,
the coarse woollen red cap, the rough medley dress of homespun stuff
and hairy skins of beasts, the powerful frame attenuated by spare living,
and the sullen and desperate compression of the lips in sleep, inspired
the mender of roads with awe. The traveller had travelled far, and his
feet were footsore, and his ankles chafed and bleeding ; his great shoes,
stuffed with leaves and grass, had been heavy to drag over the many
long leagues, and his clothes were chafed into holes, as he himself was
into sores. Stooping down beside him, the road-mender tried to get a
peep at secret weapons in his breast or where not ; but in vain, for he
slept with his arms crossed upon him, and set as resolutely as his lips.
Fortified towns with their stockades, guard-houses, gates, trenches,
and drawbridges, seemed to the mender of roads to be so much air as
against this figure. And when he lifted his eyes from it to the horizon
and looked around, he saw in his small fancy similar figures, stopped
by no obstacle, tending to centres all over France.

The man slept on, indifferent to showers of hail and intervals of
brightness, to sunshine on his face and shadow, to the pattering lumps
of dull ice on his body and the diamonds into which the sun changed
them, until the sun was low in the west, and the sky was glowing.
Then the mender of roads, having got his tools together and all things
ready to go down into the village, roused him.

"Good!" said the sleeper, rising on his elbow   "Two leagues
beyond the summit of the hill?"

"About."

"About. Good!"

The mender of roads went home, with the dust going on before him
according to the set of the wind, and was soon at the fountain, squeezing
himself in among the lean kine brought there to drink, and appearing
even to whisper to them in his whispering to all the village. When the
village had taken its poor supper, it did not creep to bed, as it usually
did, but came out of doors again, and remained there. A curious
contagion of whispering was upon it, and also, when it gathered
together at the fountain in the dark, another curious contagion of
looking expectantly at the sky in one direction only. Monsieur Gabelle,
chief functionary of the place, became uneasy ; went out on his house-

top alone, and looked in that direction too ; glanced down from behind his chimneys at the darkening faces by the fountain below, and sent word to the sacristan, who kept the keys of the church, that there might be need to ring the tocsin by and by.

The night deepened. The trees environing the old château, keeping its solitary state apart, moved in a rising wind, as though they threatened the pile of building massive and dark in the gloom. Up the two terrace flights of steps the rain ran wildly, and beat at the great door, like a swift messenger rousing those within ; uneasy rushes of wind went through the hall, among the old spears and knives, and passed lamenting up the stairs, and shook the curtains of the bed where the last Marquis had slept. East, West, North, and South, through the woods, four heavy-treading, unkempt figures crushed the high grass and cracked the branches, striding on cautiously to come together in the courtyard. Four lights broke out there, and moved away in different directions, and all was black again.

But not for long. Presently the château began to make itself strangely visible by some light of its own, as though it were growing luminous. Then a flickering streak played behind the architecture of the front, picking out transparent places, and showing where balustrades, arches, and windows were. Then it soared higher, and grew broader and brighter. Soon, from a score of the great windows, flames burst forth, and the stone faces awakened, stared out of fire.

A faint murmur arose about the house from the few people who were left there, and there was a saddling of a horse and riding away. There was spurring and splashing through the darkness, and bridle was drawn in the space by the village fountain, and the horse in a foam stood at Monsieur Gabelle's door. " Help, Gabelle ! Help, every one !" The tocsin rang impatiently, but other help (if that were any) there was none. The mender of roads, and two hundred and fifty particular friends, stood with folded arms at the fountain, looking at the pillar of fire in the sky. " It must be forty feet high," said they, grimly, and never moved.

The rider from the château, and the horse in a foam, clattered away through the village, and galloped up the stony steep, to the prison on the crag. At the gate a group of officers were looking at the fire ; removed from them, a group of soldiers. " Help, gentlemen-officers ! The château is on fire ; valuable objects may be saved from the flames by timely aid ! Help, help !" The officers looked towards the soldiers, who looked at the fire ; gave no orders ; and answered, with shrugs and biting of lips, " It must burn."

As the rider rattled down the hill again and through the street, the village was illuminating. The mender of roads, and the two hundred and fifty particular friends, inspired as one man and woman by the idea of lighting up, had darted into their houses, and were putting candles in every dull little pane of glass. The general scarcity of everything occasioned candles to be borrowed in a rather peremptory manner of Monsieur Gabelle ; and in a moment of reluctance and hesitation on that functionary's part, the mender of roads, once so submissive to authority, had remarked that carriages were good to make bonfires with, and that post-horses would roast.

The château was left to itself to flame and burn. In the roaring and raging of the conflagration, a red-hot wind, driving straight from the infernal regions, seemed to be blowing the edifice away. With the rising and falling of the blaze, the stone faces showed as if they were in torment. When great masses of stone and timber fell, the face with the two dints in the nose became obscured : anon struggled out of the smoke again, as if it were the face of the cruel Marquis, burning at the stake and contending with the fire.

The château burned ; the nearest trees, laid hold of by the fire, scorched and shrivelled ; trees at a distance, fired by the four fierce figures, begirt the blazing edifice with a new forest of smoke. Molten lead and iron boiled in the marble basin of the fountain ; the water ran dry ; the extinguisher tops of the towers vanished like ice before the heat, and trickled down into four rugged wells of flame. Great rents and splits branched out in the solid walls, like crystallisation ; stupefied birds wheeled about and dropped into the furance ; four fierce figures trudged away, East, West, North, and South, along the night-enshrouded roads, guided by the beacon they had lighted, towards their next destination. The illuminated village had seized hold of the tocsin, and, abolishing the lawful ringer, rang for joy.

Not only that ; but the village, light-headed with famine, fire, and bell-ringing, and bethinking itself that Monsieur Gabelle had to do with the collection of rent and taxes—though it was but a small instalment of taxes, and no rent at all, that Gabelle had got in those latter days— became impatient for an interview with him, and, surrounding his house, summoned him to come forth for personal conference. Where-upon Monsieur Gabelle did heavily bar his door, and retire to hold counsel with himself. The result of that conference was, that Gabelle again withdrew himself to his house-top behind his stack of chimneys, this time resolved, if his door were broken in (he was a small Southern man of retaliative temperament), to pitch himself head foremost over the parapet, and crush a man or two below.

Probably Monsieur Gabelle passed a long night up there, with the distant château for fire and candle, and the beating at his door, combined with the joy-ringing, for music ; not to mention his having an ill-omened lamp slung across the road before his posting-house gate, which the village showed a lively inclination to displace in his favour. A trying suspense, to be passing a whole summer night on the brink of the black ocean, ready to take that plunge into it upon which Monsieur Gabelle had resolved ! But the friendly dawn appearing at last, and the rush-candles of the village guttering out, the people happily dispersed, and Monsieur Gabelle came down, bringing his life with him for that while.

Within a hundred miles, and in the light of other fires, there were other functionaries less fortunate, that night and other nights, whom the rising sun found hanging across once peaceful streets where they had been born and bred ; also, there were other villagers and townspeople less fortunate than the mender of roads and his fellows, upon whom the functionaries and soldiery turned with success, and whom they strung up in their turn.   But the fierce figures were steadily wending East, West, North, and South, be that as it would ; and whosoever hung, fire burned.   The altitude of the gallows that would turn to water and quench it no functionary, by any stretch of mathematics, was able to calculate successfully.

CHAPTER XXIV

DRAWN TO THE LOADSTONE ROCK

IN such risings of fire and risings of sea—the firm earth shaken by the rushes of an angry ocean which had now no ebb, but was always on the flow, higher and higher, to the terror and wonder of the beholders on the shore—three years of tempest were consumed.   Three more birthdays of little Lucie had been woven by the golden thread into the peaceful tissue of the life of her home.

Many a night and many a day had its inmates listened to the echoes in the corner, with hearts that failed them when they heard the thronging feet.   For the footsteps had become to their minds as the footsteps of a people, tumultuous under a red flag and with their country declared in danger, changed into wild beasts, by terrible enchantment long persisted in.

Monseigneur, as a class, had dissociated himself from the phenomenon of his not being appreciated : of his being so little wanted in France, as to incur considerable danger of receiving his dismissal from it and this life together.   Like the fabled rustic who raised the Devil with infinite pains, and was so terrified at the sight of him that he could ask the Enemy no question, but immediately fled, so Monseigneur, after boldly reading the Lord's Prayer backwards for a great number of years, and performing many other potent spells for compelling the Evil One, no sooner beheld him in his terrors than he took to his noble heels.

The shining Bull's Eye of the Court was gone, or it would have been the mark for a hurricane of national bullets.   It had never been a good eye to see with—had long had the mote in it of Lucifer's pride, Sardan-apalus's luxury, and a mole's blindness—but it had dropped out and was gone.   The Court, from that exclusive inner circle to its outermost rotten ring of intrigue, corruption, and dissimulation, was all gone together.   Royalty was gone ; had been besieged in its Palace and "suspended," when the last tidings came over.

The August of the year one thousand seven hundred and ninety-two was come, and Monseigneur was by this time scattered far and wide.

As was natural, the headquarters and great gathering-place of

Monseigneur, in London, was Tellson's Bank. Spirits are supposed to haunt the places where their bodies most resorted, and Monseigneur without a guinea haunted the spot where his guineas used to be. Moreover, it was the spot to which such French intelligence as was most to be relied upon came quickest. Again, Tellson's was a munificent house, and extended great liberality to old customers who had fallen from their high estate. Again, those nobles who had seen the coming storm in time, and, anticipating plunder or confiscation, had made provident remittances to Tellson's, were always to be heard of there by their needy brethren. To which it must be added that every newcomer from France reported himself and his tidings at Tellson's, almost as a matter of course. For such variety of reasons, Tellson's was at that time, as to French intelligence, a kind of High Exchange ; and this was so well known to the public, and the inquiries made there were in consequence so numerous, that Tellson's sometimes wrote the latest news out in a line or so and posted it in the Bank windows, for all who ran through Temple Bar to read.

On a steaming, misty afternoon Mr. Lorry sat at his desk, and Charles Darnay stood leaning on it, talking with him in a low voice. The penitential den once set apart for interviews with the House was now the news-exchange, and was filled to overflowing. It was within half an hour or so of the time of closing.

"But although you are the youngest man that ever lived," said Charles Darnay, rather hesitating, "I must still suggest to you——"

"I understand. That I am too old?" said Mr. Lorry.

"Unsettled weather, a long journey, uncertain means of travelling, a disorganised country, a city that may not be even safe for you."

"My dear Charles," said Mr. Lorry, with cheerful confidence, "you touch some of the reasons for my going, not for my staying away. It is safe enough for me ; nobody will care to interfere with an old fellow of hard upon fourscore when there are so many people there much better worth interfering with. As to its being a disorganised city, if it were not a disorganised city there would be no occasion to send somebody from our House here to our House there, who knows the city and the business, of old, and is in Tellson's confidence. As to the uncertain travelling, the long journey, and the winter weather, if I were not prepared to submit myself to a few inconveniences for the sake of Tellson's, after all these years, who ought to be?"

"I wish I were going myself," said Charles Darnay, somewhat restlessly, and like one thinking aloud.

"Indeed! You are a pretty fellow to object and advise!" exclaimed Mr. Lorry. "You wish you were going yourself? And you a Frenchman born? You are a wise counsellor."

"My dear Mr. Lorry, it is because I am a Frenchman born that the thought (which I did not mean to utter here, however) has passed through my mind often. One cannot help thinking, having had some sympathy for the miserable people, and having abandoned something to them,"—he spoke here in his former thoughtful manner—"that one might be listened to, and might have the power to persuade to some restraint. Only last night, after you had left us, when I was talking to Lucie——"

"When you were talking to Lucie," Mr. Lorry repeated. "Yes. I wonder you are not ashamed to mention the name of Lucie! Wishing you were going to France at this time of day!"

"However, I am not going," said Charles Darnay, with a smile. "It is more to the purpose that you say you are."

"And I am, in plain reality. The truth is, my dear Charles," Mr. Lorry glanced at the distant House, and lowered his voice, "you can have no conception of the difficulty with which our business is transacted, and of the peril in which our books and papers over yonder are involved. The Lord above knows what the compromising consequences would be to numbers of people if some of our documents were seized or destroyed ; and they might be, at any time, you know, for who can say that Paris is not set afire to-day, or sacked to-morrow ! Now, a judicious selection from these with the least possible delay, and the burying of them, or otherwise getting of them out of harm's way, is within the power (without loss of precious time) of scarcely any one but myself, if any one. And shall I hang back when Tellson's knows this and says this —Tellson's, whose bread I have eaten these sixty years—because I am a little stiff about the joints ? Why, I am a boy, Sir, to half a dozen old codgers here !"

"How I admire the gallantry of your youthful spirit, Mr. Lorry."

"Tut ! Nonsense, Sir !—And, my dear Charles," said Mr. Lorry, glancing at the House again, "you are to remember, that getting things out of Paris at this present time, no matter what things, is next to an impossibility. Papers and precious matters were this very day brought to us here (I speak in strict confidence ; it is not business-like to whisper it, even to you) by the strangest bearers you can imagine, every one of whom had his head hanging on by a single hair as he passed the Barriers. At another time our parcels would come and go as easily as in business-like Old England ; but now everything is stopped."

"And do you really go to-night ?"

"I really go to-night, for the case has become too pressing to admit of delay."

"And do you take no one with you ?"

"All sorts of people have been proposed to me, but I will have nothing to say to any of them. I intend to take Jerry. Jerry has been my bodyguard on Sunday nights for a long time past, and I am used to him. Nobody will suspect Jerry of being anything but an English bull-dog, or of having any design in his head but to fly at anybody who touches his master."

"I must say again that I heartily admire your gallantry and youthfulness."

"I must say again, nonsense, nonsense ! When I have executed this little commission, I shall perhaps accept Tellson's proposal to retire and live at my ease, Time enough then to think about growing old."

This dialogue had taken place at Mr. Lorry's usual desk, with Monseigneur swarming within a yard or two of it, boastful of what he would do to avenge himself on the rascal people before long. It was too much the way of Monseigneur under his reverses as a refugee, and it was much too much the way of native British orthodoxy to talk of this terrible Revolution as if it were the one only harvest ever known under the skies that had not been sown—as if nothing had ever been done, or omitted to be done, that had led to it—as if observers of the wretched millions in France, and of the misused and perverted resources that should have made them prosperous, had not seen it inevitably coming, years before, and had not in plain words recorded what they saw. Such vapouring, combined with the extravagant plots of Monseigneur for the restoration of a state of things that had utterly exhausted itself, and worn out Heaven and earth as well as itself, was hard to be endured without some remonstrance by any sane man who knew the truth. And it was such vapouring all about his ears, like a troublesome confusion of blood in his own head, added to a latent uneasiness in his mind, which had already made Charles Darnay restless, and which still kept him so.

Among the talkers was Stryver, of the King's Bench Bar, far on his way to State promotion, and, therefore, loud on the theme, broaching to Monseigneur his devices for blowing the people up and exterminating them from the face of the earth, and doing without them, and for accomplishing many similar objects akin in their nature to the abolition of eagles by sprinkling salt on the tails of the race. Him Darnay heard with a particular feeling of objection ; and Darnay stood divided between going away that he might hear no more, and remaining to interpose his word, when the thing that was to be went on to shape itself out.

The House approached Mr. Lorry, and laying a soiled and unopened letter before him, asked if he had yet discovered any traces of the person to whom it was addressed ? The House laid the letter down so close to Darnay that he saw the direction—the more quickly because it was his own right name. The address, turned into English, ran—

"Very pressing. To Monsieur heretofore the Marquis St. Evremond, of France. Confided to the cares of Messrs. Tellson and Co., Bankers, London, England."

On the marriage morning Dr. Manette had made it his one urgent and express request to Charles Darnay that the secret of this name should be—unless he, the Doctor, dissolved the obligation—kept inviolate between them. Nobody else knew it to be his name ; his own wife had no suspicion of the fact ; Mr. Lorry could have none.

"No," said Mr. Lorry, in reply to the House ; "I have referred it, I think, to everybody now here, and no one can tell me where this gentleman is to be found."

The hands of the clock verging upon the hour of closing the Bank, there was a general set of the current of talkers past Mr. Lorry's desk. He held the letter out inquiringly ; and Monseigneur looked at it, in the person of this plotting and indignant refugee ; and This, That, and The Other, all had something disparaging to say, in French or in English, concerning the Marquis who was not to be found.

" Nephew, I believe—but in any case degenerate successor—of the polished Marquis who was murdered," said one. " Happy to say I never knew him."

" A craven who abandoned his post," said another—this Monseigneur had been got out of Paris, legs uppermost and half suffocated, in a load of hay—" some years ago."

" Infected with the new doctrines," said a third, eyeing the direction through his glass in passing ; " set himself in opposition to the last Marquis, abandoned the estates when he inherited them, and left them to the ruffian herd. They will recompense him now, I hope, as he deserves."

" Hey ? " cried the blatant Stryver. " Did he though ? Is that the sort of fellow ? Let us look at his infamous name. D—n the fellow ! "

Darnay, unable to restrain himself any longer, touched Mr. Stryver on the shoulder, and said—

" I know the fellow."

" Do you, by Jupiter ? " said Stryver. " I am sorry for it."

" Why ? "

" Why, Mr. Darnay ? D'ye hear what he did ? Don't ask why, in these times."

" But I do ask why."

" Then I tell you again, Mr. Darnay, I am sorry for it. I am sorry to hear you putting any such extraordinary questions. Here is a fellow who, infected by the most pestilent and blasphemous code of devilry that ever was known, abandoned his property to the vilest scum of the earth that ever did murder by wholesale, and you ask me why I am sorry that a man who instructs youth knows him ? Well, but I'll answer you. I am sorry because I believe there is contamination in such a scoundrel. That's why."

Mindful of the secret, Darney with great difficulty checked himself, and said : " You may not understand the gentleman."

" I understand how to put *you* in a corner, Mr. Darnay," said Bully Stryver, " and I'll do it. If this fellow is a gentleman, I *don't* under-stand him. You may tell him so, with my compliments. You may also tell him from me that, after abandoning his worldly goods and position to this butcherly mob, I wonder he is not at the head of them. But no, gentlemen," said Stryver, looking all round, and snapping his fingers, " I know something of human nature, and I tell you that you'll never find a fellow like this fellow trusting himself to the mercies of such precious *protégés*. No, gentlemen ; he'll always show 'em a clean pair of heels very early in the scuffle, and sneak away."

With those words, and a final snap of his fingers, Mr. Stryver shouldered himself into Fleet Street, amidst the general approbation of his hearers. Mr. Lorry and Charles Darnay were left alone at the desk, in the general departure from the Bank.

"Will you take charge of the letter?" said Mr. Lorry. "You know where to deliver it?"

"I do."

"Will you undertake to explain that we suppose it to have been addressed here on the chance of our knowing where to forward it, and that it has been here some time?"

"I will do so. Do you start for Paris from here?"

"From here, at eight."

"I will come back to see you off."

Very ill at ease with himself, and with Stryver and most other men, Darnay made the best of his way into the quiet of the Temple, opened the letter, and read it. These were its contents—

"Prison of the Abbaye, Paris,
"*June* 21, 1792.

"Monsieur heretofore the Marquis,

"After having long been in danger of my life at the hands of the village, I have been seized, with great violence and indignity, and brought a long journey on foot to Paris. On the road I have suffered a great deal. Nor is that all ; my house has been destroyed—razed to the ground.

"The crime for which I am imprisoned, Monsieur heretofore the Marquis, and for which I shall be summoned before the tribunal, and shall lose my life (without your so generous help), is, they tell me, treason against the majesty of the people, in that I have acted against them for an emigrant. It is in vain I represent that I have acted for them, and not against, according to your commands. It is in vain I represent that, before the sequestration of emigrant property, I had remitted the imposts they had ceased to pay ; that I had collected no rent ; that I had had recourse to no process. The only response is, that I have acted for an emigrant, and where is that emigrant?

"Ah ! most gracious Monsieur heretofore the Marquis, where is that emigrant? I cry in my sleep where is he? I demand of Heaven, will he not come to deliver me? No answer. Ah ! Monsieur heretofore the Marquis, I send my desolate cry across the sea, hoping it may perhaps reach your ears through the great bank of Tilson known at Paris !

"For the love of Heaven, of justice, of generosity, of the honour of your noble name, I supplicate you, Monsieur heretofore the Marquis, to succour and release me. My fault is, that I have been true to you. Oh Monsieur heretofore the Marquis, I pray you be you true to me !

"From this prison here of horror, whence I every hour tend nearer and nearer to destruction, I send you, Monsieur heretofore the Marquis, the assurance of my dolorous and unhappy service.

"Your afflicted,
"Gabelle."

The latent uneasiness in Darnay's mind was roused to vigorous life by this letter. The peril of an old servant and a good one, whose only crime was fidelity to himself and his family, stared him so reproachfully in the face that, as he walked to and fro in the Temple considering what to do, he almost hid his face from the passers-by.

He knew very well that, in his horror of the deed which had culminated the bad deeds and bad reputation of the old family house, in his resentful suspicions of his uncle, and in the aversion with which his conscience regarded the crumbling fabric that he was supposed to uphold, he had acted imperfectly. He knew very well that, in his love for Lucie, his renunciation of his social place, though by no means new to his own mind, had been hurried and incomplete. He knew that he ought to have systematically worked it out and supervised it, and that he had meant to do it, and that it had never been done.

The happiness of his own chosen English home, the necessity of being always actively employed, the swift changes and troubles of the time which had followed on one another so fast, that the events of this week annihilated the immature plans of last week, and the events of the week following made all new again ; he knew very well, that to the force of these circumstances he had yielded—not without disquiet, but still without continuous and accumulating resistance. That he had watched the times for a time of action, and that they had shifted and struggled until the time had gone by, and the nobility were trooping from France by every highway and byway, and their property was in course of confiscation and destruction, and their very names were blotting out, was as well known to himself as it could be to any new authority in France that might impeach him for it.

But he had oppressed no man, he had imprisoned no man ; he was so far from having harshly exacted payment of his dues, that he had relinquished them of his own will, thrown himself on a world with no favour in it, won his own private place there, and earned his own bread. Monsieur Gabelle had held the impoverished and involved estate on written instructions to spare the people, to give them what little there was to give—such fuel as the heavy creditors would let them have in the winter, and such produce as could be saved from the same grip in the summer—and no doubt he had put the fact in plea and proof, for his own safety, so that it could not but appear now.

This favoured the desperate resolution Charles Darnay had begun to make, that he would go to Paris.

Yes. Like the mariner in the old story, the winds and streams had driven him within the influence of the Loadstone Rock, and it was drawing him to itself, and he must go. Everything that arose before his mind drifted him on, faster and faster, more and more steadily, to the terrible attraction. His latent uneasiness had been, that bad aims were being worked out in his own unhappy land by bad instruments, and that he, who could not fail to know that he was better than they, was not there, trying to do something to stay bloodshed, and assert the claims of mercy and humanity. With this uneasiness half stifled, and half reproaching him, he had been brought to the pointed comparison of himself with the brave old gentleman in whom duty was so strong; upon that comparison (injurious to himself) had instantly followed the sneers of Monseigneur, which had stung him bitterly, and those of Stryver, which above all were coarse and galling, for old reasons. Upon those had followed Gabelle's letter: the appeal of an innocent prisoner, in danger of death, to his justice, honour, and good name.

His resolution was made. He must go to Paris.

Yes. The Loadstone Rock was drawing him, and he must sail on, until he struck. He knew of no rock; he saw hardly any danger. The intention with which he had done what he had done, even although he had left it incomplete, presented it before him in an aspect that would be gratefully acknowledged in France on his presenting himself to assert it. Then that glorious vision of doing good, which is so often the sanguine mirage of so many good minds, arose before him, and he even saw himself in the illusion with some influence to guide this raging Revolution that was running so fearfully wild.

As he walked to and fro with his resolution made, he considered that neither Lucie nor her father must know of it until he was gone. Lucie should be spared the pain of separation; and her father, always reluctant to turn his thoughts towards the dangerous ground of old, should come to the knowledge of the step, as a step taken, and not in the balance of suspense and doubt. How much of the incompleteness of his situation was referable to her father, through the painful anxiety to avoid reviving old associations of France in his mind, he did not discuss with himself. But that circumstance too had had its influence in his course.

He walked to and fro, with thoughts very busy, until it was time to return to Tellson's and take leave of Mr. Lorry. As soon as he arrived in Paris he would present himself to this old friend, but he must say nothing of his intention now.

A carriage with post-horses was ready at the Bank door, and Jerry was booted and equipped.

"I have delivered that letter," said Charles Darnay to Mr. Lorry. "I would not consent to your being charged with any written answer, but perhaps you will take a verbal one?"

"That I will, and readily," said Mr. Lorry, "if it is not dangerous."

"Not at all. Though it is to a prisoner in the Abbaye."

"What is his name?" said Mr. Lorry, with his open pocket-book in his hand.

"Gabelle."

"Gabelle. And what is the message to the unfortunate Gabelle in prison?"

"Simply, 'that he has received the letter, and will come.'"

"Any time mentioned?"

"He will start upon his journey to-morrow night."

"Any person mentioned?"

"No."

He helped Mr. Lorry to wrap himself in a number of coats and cloaks, and went out with him from the warm atmosphere of the old Bank into the misty air of Fleet Street. "My love to Lucie, and to little Lucie," said Mr. Lorry at parting, "and take precious care of them till I come back." Charles Darnay shook his head and doubtfully smiled as the carriage rolled away.

That night—it was the fourteenth of August—he sat up late, and wrote two fervent letters; one was to Lucie, explaining the strong obligation he was under to go to Paris, and showing her, at length, the reasons that he had for feeling confident that he could become involved in no personal danger there; the other was to the Doctor, confiding Lucie and their dear child to his care, and dwelling on the same topics with the strongest assurances. To both he wrote that he would dispatch letters in proof of his safety immediately after his arrival.

It was a hard day, that day of being among them, with the first reservation of their joint lives on his mind. It was a hard matter to preserve the innocent deceit of which they were profoundly unsuspicious. But an affectionate glance at his wife, so happy and busy, made him resolute not to tell her what impended (he had been half moved to do it, so strange it was to him to act in anything without her quiet aid), and the day passed quickly. Early in the evening he embraced her, and her scarcely less dear namesake, pretending that he would return by and by (an imaginary engagement took him out, and he had secreted a valise of clothes ready), and so he emerged into the heavy mist of the heavy streets, with a heavier heart.

The unseen force was drawing him fast to itself now, and all the tides and winds were setting straight and strong towards it. He left his two letters with a trusty porter, to be delivered half an hour before midnight, and no sooner; took horse for Dover; and began his journey. "For the love of Heaven, of justice, of generosity, of the honour of your noble name!" was the poor prisoner's cry with which he strengthened his sinking heart, as he left all that was dear on earth behind him, and floated away for the Loadstone Rock.

BOOK THE THIRD. THE TRACK OF A STORM

CHAPTER I

IN SECRET

THE traveller fared slowly on his way who fared towards Paris from England in the autumn of the year one thousand seven hundred and ninety-two. More than enough of bad roads, bad equipages, and bad horses he would have encountered to delay him, though the fallen and unfortunate King of France had been upon the throne in all his glory; but the changed times were fraught with other obstacles than these. Every town-gate and village taxing-house had its band of citizen-patriots, with their national muskets in a most explosive state of readiness, who stopped all comers and goers, cross-questioned them, inspected their papers, looked for their names in lists of their own, turned them back, or sent them on, or stopped them and laid them in hold, as their capricious judgment or fancy deemed best for the dawning Republic One and Indivisible, of Liberty, Equality, Fraternity, or Death.

A very few French leagues of his journey were accomplished, when Charles Darnay began to perceive that for him along these country roads there was no hope of return until he should have been declared a good citizen at Paris. Whatever might befall now, he must on to his journey's end. Not a mean village closed upon him, not a common barrier dropped across the road behind him, but he knew it to be another iron door in the series that was barred between him and England. The universal watchfulness so encompassed him, that if he had been taken in a net, or were being forwarded to his destination in a cage, he could not have felt his freedom more completely gone.

This universal watchfulness not only stopped him on the highway twenty times in a stage, but retarded his progress twenty times in a day, by riding after him and taking him back, riding before him and stopping him by anticipation, riding with him and keeping him in charge. He had been days upon his journey in France alone, when he went to bed tired out, in a little town on the high road, still a long way from Paris.

Nothing but the production of the afflicted Gabelle's letter from his prison of the Abbaye would have got him on so far. His difficulty at the guard-house in this small place had been such, that he felt his journey to have come to a crisis. And he was, therefore, as little surprised as a man could be to find himself awakened, at the small inn to which he had been remitted until morning, in the middle of the night.

Awakened by a timid local functionary and three armed patriots in rough red caps and with pipes in their mouths, who sat down on the bed.

"Emigrant," said the functionary, "I am going to send you on to Paris under an escort."

"Citizen, I desire nothing more than to get to Paris, though I could dispense with the escort."

"Silence!" growled a red-cap, striking at the coverlet with the butt-end of his musket. "Peace, aristocrat!"

"It is as the good patriot says," observed the timid functionary. "You are an aristocrat, and must have an escort—and must pay for it."

"I have no choice," said Charles Darnay.

"Choice! Listen to him!" cried the same scowling red-cap. "As if it was not a favour to be protected from the lamp-iron!"

"It is always as the good patriot says," observed the functionary. "Rise and dress yourself, emigrant."

Darnay complied, and was taken back to the guard-house, where other patriots in rough red caps were smoking, drinking, and sleeping by a watch-fire. Here he paid a heavy price for his escort, and hence he started with it on the wet, wet roads at three o'clock in the morning.

The escort were two mounted patriots in red caps and tricoloured cockades, armed with national muskets and sabres, who rode one on either side of him. The escorted governed his own horse, but a loose line was attached to his bridle, the end of which one of the patriots kept girded round his wrist. In this state they set forth with the sharp rain driving in their faces, clattering at a heavy dragoon trot over the uneven town pavement, and out upon the mire-deep roads. In this state they traversed without change, except of horses and pace, all the mire-deep leagues that lay between them and the capital.

They travelled in the night, halting an hour or two after daybreak, and lying by until the twilight fell. The escort were so wretchedly clothed that they twisted straw round their bare legs, and thatched their ragged shoulders to keep the wet off. Apart from the personal discomfort of being so attended, and apart from such considerations of present danger as arose from one of the patriots being chronically drunk, and carrying his musket very recklessly, Charles Darnay did not allow the restraint that was laid upon him to awaken any serious fears in his breast, for he reasoned with himself that it could have no reference to the merits of an individual case that was not yet stated,

"Down with the Emigrant!"

and of representations, confirmable by the prisoner in the Abbaye, that were not yet made.

But when they came to the town of Beauvais—which they did at eventide, when the streets were filled with people—he could not conceal from himself that the aspect of affairs was very alarming. An ominous crowd gathered to see him dismount at the posting-yard, and many voices called out loudly, "Down with the emigrant!"

He stopped in the act of swinging himself out of his saddle, and, resuming it as his safest place, said—

"Emigrant, my friends! Do you not see me here, in France, of my own will?"

"You are a cursed emigrant," cried a farrier, making at him in a furious manner through the press, hammer in hand, "and you are a cursed aristocrat!"

The postmaster interposed himself between this man and the rider's bridle (at which he was evidently making), and soothingly said, "Let him be; let him be! He will be judged at Paris."

"Judged!" repeated the farrier, swinging his hammer. "Ay! and condemned as a traitor." At this the crowd roared approval.

Checking the postmaster, who was for turning his horse's head to the yard (the drunken patriot sat composedly in his saddle looking on, with the line round his wrist), Darnay said, as soon as he could make his voice heard—

"Friends, you deceive yourselves, or you are deceived. I am not a traitor."

"He lies!" cried the smith. "He is a traitor since the decree. His life is forfeit to the people. His cursed life is not his own!"

At the instant when Darnay saw a rush in the eyes of the crowd, which another instant would have brought upon him, the postmaster turned his horse into the yard, the escort rode in close upon his horse's flanks, and the postmaster shut and barred the crazy double gates. The farrier struck a blow upon them with his hammer, and the crowd groaned; but no more was done.

"What is this decree that the smith spoke of?" Darnay asked the postmaster, when he had thanked him, and stood beside him in the yard.

"Truly, a decree for selling the property of emigrants."

"When passed?"

"On the fourteenth."

"The day I left England!"

"Everybody says it is but one of several, and that there will be others—if there are not already—banishing all emigrants, and condemning all to death who return. That is what he meant when he said your life was not your own."

"But there are no such decrees yet?"

"What do I know!" said the postmaster, shrugging his shoulders; "there may be, or there will be. It is all the same. What would you have?"

They rested on some straw in a loft until the middle of the night, and then rode forward again when all the town was asleep. Among the many wild changes observable on familiar things which made this wild ride unreal, not the least was the seeming rarity of sleep. After long and lonely spurring over dreary roads, they would come to a cluster of poor cottages, not steeped in darkness, but all glittering with lights, and would find the people, in a ghostly manner in the dead of the night, circling hand in hand round a shrivelled tree of Liberty, or all drawn up together singing a Liberty song. Happily, however, there was sleep in Beauvais that night to help them out of it, and they passed on once more into solitude and loneliness, jingling through the untimely cold and wet, among impoverished fields that had yielded no fruits of the earth that year, diversified by the blackened remains of burnt houses, and by the sudden emergence from ambuscade, and sharp reining up across their way, of patriot patrols on the watch on all the roads.

Daylight at last found them before the wall of Paris. The barrier was closed and strongly guarded when they rode up to it.

"Where are the papers of this prisoner?" demanded a resolute-looking man in authority, who was summoned out by the guard.

Naturally struck by the disagreeable word, Charles Darnay requested the speaker to take notice that he was a free traveller and French citizen, in charge of an escort which the disturbed state of the country had imposed upon him, and which he had paid for.

"Where," repeated the same personage, without taking any heed of him whatever, "are the papers of this prisoner?"

The drunken patriot had them in his cap, and produced them. Casting his eyes over Gabelle's letter, the same personage in authority showed some disorder and surprise, and looked at Darnay with a close attention.

He left escort and escorted without saying a word, however, and went into the guard-room; meanwhile they sat upon their horses outside the gate. Looking about him while in this state of suspense, Charles Darnay observed that the gate was held by a mixed guard of soldiers and patriots, the latter far outnumbering the former; and that while ingress into the city for peasants' carts, bringing in supplies, and for similar traffic and traffickers, was easy enough, egress, even for the homeliest people, was very difficult. A numerous medley of men and women, not to mention beasts and vehicles of various sorts, was waiting to issue forth; but the previous identification was so strict, that they filtered through the barrier very slowly. Some of these people knew their turn for examination to be so far off, that they lay down on the ground to sleep or smoke, while others talked together, or loitered about. The red cap and tricolour cockade were universal, both among men and women.

When he had sat in his saddle some half-hour, taking note of these things, Darnay found himself confronted by the same man in authority, who directed the guard to open the barrier. Then he delivered to the escort, drunk and sober, a receipt for the escorted, and requested him to dismount. He did so, and the two patriots, leading his tired horse, turned and rode away without entering the city.

He accompanied his conductor into a guard-room, smelling of common wine and tobacco, where certain soldiers and patriots, asleep and awake, drunk and sober, and in various neutral states between sleeping and waking, drunkenness and sobriety, were standing and lying about. The light in the guard-house, half derived from the waning oil-lamps of the night, and half from the overcast day, was in a correspondingly uncertain condition. Some registers were lying open on a desk, and an officer of a coarse, dark aspect presided over these.

" Citizen Defarge," said he to Darnay's conductor, as he took a slip of paper to write on. " Is this the emigrant Evremond ? "

" This is the man."

" Your age, Evremond ? "

" Thirty-seven."

" Married, Evremond ? "

" Yes."

" Where married ? "

" In England."

" Without doubt. Where is your wife, Evremond ? "

" In England."

" Without doubt. You are consigned, Evremond, to the prison of La Force."

" Just Heaven !" exclaimed Darnay. " Under what law, and for what offence ? "

The officer looked up from his slip of paper for a moment.

" We have new laws, Evremond, and new offences, since you were here." He said it with a hard smile, and went on writing.

" I entreat you to observe that I have come here voluntarily, in response to that written appeal of a fellow-countryman which lies before you. I demand no more than the opportunity to do so without delay. Is not that my right ? "

" Emigrants have no rights, Evremond," was the stolid reply. The officer wrote until he had finished, read over to himself what he had written, sanded it, and handed it to Defarge, with the words " In secret."

Defarge motioned with the paper to the prisoner that he must accompany him. The prisoner obeyed, and a guard of two armed patriots attended them.

" Is it you," said Defarge, in a low voice, as they went down the guard-house steps and turned into Paris, " who married the daughter of Doctor Manette, once a prisoner in the Bastille that is no more ? "

" Yes," replied Darnay, looking at him with surprise.

" My name is Defarge, and I keep a wine-shop in the Quarter Saint Antoine. Possibly you have heard of me."

" My wife came to your house to reclaim her father ? Yes ! "

The word " wife " seemed to serve as a gloomy reminder to Defarge, to say with sudden impatience, " In the name of that sharp female newly-born, and called La Guillotine, why did you come to France ? "

"You heard me say why, a minute ago. Do you not believe it is the truth?"

"A bad truth for you," said Defarge, speaking with knitted brows, and looking straight before him.

"Indeed I am lost here. All here is so unprecedented, so changed, so sudden and unfair, that I am absolutely lost. Will you render me a little help?"

"None." Defarge spoke, always looking straight before him.

"Will you answer me a single question?"

"Perhaps. According to its nature. You can say what it is."

"In this prison that I am going to so unjustly, shall I have some free communication with the world outside?"

"You will see."

"I am not to be buried there, prejudged, and without any means of presenting my case?"

"You will see. But, what then? Other people have been similarly buried in worse prisons, before now."

"But never by me, Citizen Defarge."

Defarge glanced darkly at him for answer, and walked on in a steady and set silence. The deeper he sank into this silence, the fainter hope there was—or so Darnay thought—of his softening in any slight degree. He therefore made haste to say—

"It is of the utmost importance to me (you know, Citizen, even better than I, of how much importance) that I should be able to communicate to Mr. Lorry of Tellson's Bank, an English gentleman who is now in Paris, the simple fact, without comment, that I have been thrown into the prison of La Force. Will you cause that to be done for me?"

"I will do," Defarge doggedly rejoined, "nothing for you. My duty is to my country and the People. I am the sworn servant of both, against you. I will do nothing for you."

Charles Darnay felt it hopeless to entreat him further, and his pride was touched besides. As they walked on in silence, he could not but see how used the people were to the spectacle of prisoners passing along the streets. The very children scarcely noticed him. A few passers turned their heads, and a few shook their fingers at him as an aristocrat; otherwise, that a man in good clothes should be going to prison was no more remarkable than that a labourer in working clothes should be going to work. In one narrow, dark, and dirty street through which they passed, an excited orator, mounted on a stool, was addressing an excited audience on the crimes against the people of the king and the royal family. The few words that he caught from this man's lips first made it known to Charles Darnay that the king was in prison, and that the foreign ambassadors had one and all left Paris. On the road (except at Beauvais) he had heard absolutely nothing. The escort and the universal watchfulness had completely isolated him.

That he had fallen among far greater dangers than those which had developed themselves when he left England, he of course knew now. That perils had thickened about him fast, and might thicken faster and faster yet, he of course knew now. He could not but admit to himself that he might not have made this journey, if he could have foreseen the events of a few days. And yet his misgivings were not so dark as, imagined by the light of this later time, they would appear. Troubled as the future was, it was the unknown future, and in its obscurity there was ignorant hope. The horrible massacre, days and nights long, which, within a few rounds of the clock, was to set a great mark of blood upon the blessed garnering time of harvest, was as far out of his knowledge as if it had been a hundred thousand years away. The "sharp female newly-born, and called La Guillotine," was hardly known to him, or to the generality of people, by name. The frightful deeds that were to be soon done were probably unimagined at that time in the brains of the doers. How could they have a place in the shadowy conceptions of a gentle mind?

Of unjust treatment in detention and hardship, and in cruel separation from his wife and child, he foreshadowed the likelihood, or the certainty; but, beyond this, he dreaded nothing distinctly. With this on his mind, which was enough to carry into a dreary prison court-yard, he arrived at the prison of La Force.

A man with a bloated face opened the strong wicket, to whom Defarge presented "The Emigrant Evremond."

"What the Devil! How many more of them!" exclaimed the man with the bloated face.

Defarge took his receipt without noticing the exclamation, and withdrew, with his two fellow-patriots.

"What the Devil, I say again!" exclaimed the jailer, left with his wife. "How many more!"

The jailer's wife, being provided with no answer to the question, merely replied, "One must have patience, my dear!" Three turnkeys who entered responsive to a bell she rang echoed the sentiment, and one added, "For the love of Liberty"; which sounded in that place like an inappropriate conclusion.

The prison of La Force was a gloomy prison, dark and filthy, and with a horrible smell of foul sleep in it. Extraordinary how soon the noisome flavour of imprisoned sleep becomes manifest in all such places that are ill cared for!

"In secret, too," grumbled the jailer, looking at the written paper. "As if I was not already full to bursting!"

He stuck the paper on a file, in an ill-humour, and Charles Darnay awaited his further pleasure for half an hour, sometimes pacing to and fro in the strong arched room, sometimes resting on a stone seat—in either case detained to be imprinted on the memory of the chief and his subordinates.

"Come!" said the chief, at length taking up his keys, "come with me, emigrant."

Through the dismal prison twilight his new charge accompanied him by corridor and staircase, many doors clanging and locking behind them, until they came into a large, low, vaulted chamber, crowded with prisoners of both sexes. The women were seated at a long table, reading and writing, knitting, sewing, and embroidering; the men were for the most part standing behind their chairs, or lingering up and down the room.

In the instinctive association of prisoners with shameful crime and disgrace, the newcomer recoiled from this company. But the crowning unreality of his long unreal ride was their all at once rising to receive him, with every refinement of manner known to the time, and with all the engaging graces and courtesies of life.

So strangely clouded were these refinements by the prison manners and gloom, so spectral did they become in the inappropriate squalor and misery through which they were seen, that Charles Darnay seemed to stand in a company of the dead. Ghosts all! The ghost of beauty, the ghost of stateliness, the ghost of elegance, the ghost of pride, the ghost of frivolity, the ghost of wit, the ghost of youth, the ghost of age, all waiting their dismissal from the desolate shore, all turning on him eyes that were changed by the death they had died in coming there.

It struck him motionless. The jailer standing at his side, and the other jailers moving about, who would have been well enough as to appearance in the ordinary exercise of their functions, looked so extravagantly coarse contrasted with sorrowing mothers and blooming daughters who were there—with the apparitions of the coquette, the young beauty, and the mature woman delicately bred—that the inversion of all experience and likelihood which the scene of shadows presented was heightened to its utmost. Surely, ghosts all. Surely, the long unreal ride some progress of disease that had brought him to these gloomy shades!

"In the name of the assembled companions in misfortune," said a gentleman of courtly appearance and address, coming forward, "I have the honour of giving you welcome to La Force, and of condoling with you on the calamity that has brought you among us. May it soon terminate happily! It would be an impertinence elsewhere, but it is not so here, to ask your name and condition."

Charles Darnay roused himself, and gave the required information, in words as suitable as he could find.

"But I hope," said the gentleman, following the chief jailer with his eyes, who moved across the room, "that you are not in secret?"

"I do not understand the meaning of the term, but I have heard them say so."

"Ah, what a pity! We so much regret it! But take courage; several members of our society have been in secret, at first, and it has lasted but a short time." Then he added, raising his voice, "I grieve to inform the society—in secret."

There was a murmur of commiseration as Charles Darnay crossed the room to a grated door, where the jailer awaited him, and many voices—among which the soft and compassionate voices of women were conspicuous—gave him good wishes and encouragement. He turned at the grated door, to render the thanks of his heart ; it closed under the jailer's hand ; and the apparitions vanished from his sight for ever.

The wicket opened on a stone staircase, leading upward. When they had ascended forty steps (the prisoner of half an hour already counted them), the jailer opened a low, black door, and they passed into a solitary cell. It struck cold and damp, but was not dark.

" Yours," said the jailer.

" Why am I confined alone ? "

" How do I know ! "

" I can buy pen, ink, and paper ? "

" Such are not my orders. You will be visited, and can ask then. At present you may buy your food, and nothing more."

There were in the cell a chair, a table, and a straw mattress. As the jailer made a general inspection of these objects, and of the four walls, before going out, a wandering fancy wandered through the mind of the prisoner leaning against the wall opposite to him, that this jailer was so unwholesomely bloated, both in face and person, as to look like a man who had been drowned and filled with water. When the jailer was gone, he thought in the same wandering way, " Now am I left, as if I were dead." Stopping then, to look down at the mattress, he turned from it with a sick feeling, and thought, "And here, in these crawling creatures, is the first condition of the body after death."

" Five paces by four and a half, five paces by four and a half, five paces by four and a half." The prisoner walked to and fro in his cell, counting its measurement, and the roar of the city arose like muffled drums with a wild swell of voices added to them. " He made shoes, he made shoes, he made shoes." The prisoner counted the measurement again, and paced faster, to draw his mind with him from that latter repetition. " The ghosts that vanished when the wicket closed. There was one among them, the appearance of a lady dressed in black, who was leaning in the embrasure of a window, and she had a light shining upon her golden hair, and she looked like . . . Let us ride on again, for God's sake, through the illuminated villages with the people all awake ! . . . He made shoes, he made shoes, he made shoes. . . . Five paces by four and a half." With such scraps tossing and rolling upward from the depths of his mind, the prisoner walked faster and faster, obstinately counting and counting ; and the roar of the city changed to this extent—that it still rolled in like muffled drums, but with the wail of voices that he knew in the swell that rose above them.

CHAPTER II

THE GRINDSTONE

TELLSON'S Bank, established in the Saint Germain Quarter of Paris, was in a wing of a large house, approached by a courtyard and shut off from the street by a high wall and a strong gate. The house belonged to a great nobleman who had lived in it until he made a flight from the troubles, in his own cook's dress, and got across the borders. A mere beast of the chase flying from hunters, he was still in his metempsychosis no other than the same Monseigneur the preparation of whose chocolate for whose lips had once occupied three strong men besides the cook in question.

Monseigneur gone, and the three strong men absolving themselves from the sin of having drawn his high wages by being more than ready and willing to cut his throat on the altar of the dawning Republic One and Indivisible, of Liberty, Equality, Fraternity, or Death, Monseigneur's house had been first sequestrated, and then confiscated. For all things moved so fast, and decree followed decree with such fierce precipitation, that now, upon the third night of the autumn month of September, patriot emissaries of the law were in possession of Monseigneur's house, and had marked it with the tricolour, and were drinking brandy in its state apartments.

A place of business in London like Tellson's place of business in Paris would soon have driven the House out of its mind and into the *Gazette*. For what would staid British responsibility and respectability have said to orange-trees in boxes in a Bank courtyard, and even to a Cupid over the counter ? Yet such things were. Tellson's had white-washed the Cupid, but he was still to be seen on the ceiling, in the coolest linen, aiming (as he very often does) at money from morning to night. Bankruptcy must inevitably have come of this young Pagan, in Lombard Street, London, and also of a curtained alcove in the rear of the immortal boy, and also of a looking-glass let into the wall, and also of clerks not at all old, who danced in public on the slightest provocation. Yet a French Tellson's could get on with these things exceedingly well, and as long as the times held together, no man had taken fright at them, and drawn out his money.

What money would be drawn out of Tellson's henceforth, and what would lie there, lost and forgotten ; what plate and jewels would tarnish in Tellson's hiding-places, while the depositors rusted in prisons, and when they should have violently perished ; how many accounts with Tellson's never to be balanced in this world must be carried over into the next, no man could have said, that night, any more than Mr. Jarvis Lorry could, though he thought heavily of these questions. He sat by a newly-lighted wood fire (the blighted and unfruitful year was prematurely cold), and on his honest and courageous face there was a deeper shade than the pendent lamp could throw, or any object in the room distortedly reflect—a shade of horror.

He occupied rooms in the Bank, in his fidelity to the House of which he had grown to be a part, like strong root-ivy. It chanced that they derived a kind of security from the patriotic occupation of the main building, but the true-hearted old gentleman never calculated about that. All such circumstances were indifferent to him, so that he did his duty. On the opposite side of the courtyard, under a colonnade, was extensive standing for carriages—where, indeed, some carriages of Monseigneur yet stood. Against two of the pillars were fastened two great flaring flambeaux, and in the light of these, standing out in the open air, was a large grindstone : a roughly mounted thing which appeared to have hurriedly been brought there from some neighbouring smithy, or other workshop. Rising and looking out of window at these harmless objects, Mr. Lorry shivered, and retired to his seat by the fire. He had opened, not only the glass window, but the lattice blind outside it, and he had closed both again, and he shivered through his frame.

From the streets beyond the high wall and the strong gate there came the usual night hum of the city, with now and then an indescribable ring in it, weird and unearthly, as if some unwonted sounds of a terrible nature were going up to heaven.

"Thank God," said Mr. Lorry, clasping his hands, "that no one near and dear to me is in this dreadful town to-night. May He have mercy on all who are in danger ! "

Soon afterwards the bell at the great gate sounded, and he thought, "They have come back ! " and sat listening. But there was no loud irruption into the courtyard, as he had expected, and he heard the gate clash again, and all was quiet.

The nervousness and dread that were upon him inspired that vague uneasiness respecting the Bank which a great change would naturally awaken, with such feelings roused. It was well guarded, and he got up to go among the trusty people who were watching it, when his door suddenly opened, and two figures rushed in, at sight of which he fell back in amazement.

Lucie and her father ! Lucie with her arms stretched out to him, and with that old look of earnestness so concentrated and intensified, that it seemed as though it had been stamped upon her face expressly to give force and power to it in this one passage of her life.

"What is this ? " cried Mr. Lorry, breathless and confused. "What is the matter ? Lucie ! Manette ! What has happened ? What has brought you here ? What is it ? "

With the look fixed upon him, in her paleness and wildness, she panted out in his arms, imploringly, "Oh my dear friend ! My husband ! "

"Your husband, Lucie ? "

"Charles."

"What of Charles ? "

"Here."

"Here, in Paris?"

"Has been here some days—three or four—I don't know how many —I can't collect my thoughts. An errand of generosity brought him here unknown to us; he was stopped at the barrier, and sent to prison."

The old man uttered an irrepressible cry. Almost at the same moment the bell of the great gate rang again, and a loud noise of feet and voices came pouring into the courtyard.

"What is that noise?" said the Doctor, turning towards the window.

"Don't look!" cried Mr. Lorry. "Don't look out! Manette, for your life, don't touch the blind!"

The Doctor turned, with his hand upon the fastening of the window, and said, with a cool, bold smile—

"My dear friend, I have a charmed life in this city. I have been a Bastille prisoner. There is no patriot in Paris—in Paris?—in France —who, knowing me to have been a prisoner in the Bastille, would touch me, except to overwhelm me with embraces, or carry me in triumph. My old pain has given me a power that has brought us through the barrier and gained us news of Charles there, and brought us here. I knew it would be so; I knew I could help Charles out of all danger; I told Lucie so.—What is that noise?" His hand was again upon the window.

"Don't look!" cried Mr. Lorry, absolutely desperate. "No, Lucie, my dear, nor you!" He got his arm round her, and held her. "Don't be so terrified, my love. I solemnly swear to you that I know of no harm having happened to Charles; that I had no suspicion even of his being in this fatal place. What prison is he in?"

"La Force!"

"La Force! Lucie, my child, if ever you were brave and serviceable in your life—and you were always both—you will compose yourself now to do exactly as I bid you; for more depends upon it than you can think, or I can say. There is no help for you in any action on your part to-night; you cannot possibly stir out. I say this, because what I must bid you to do for Charles's sake is the hardest thing to do of all. You must instantly be obedient, still, and quiet. You must let me put you in a room at the back here. You must leave your father and me alone for two minutes, and as there are Life and Death in the world you must not delay."

"I will be submissive to you. I see in your face that you know I can do nothing else than this. I know you are true."

The old man kissed her, and hurried her into his room, and turned the key; then came hurrying back to the Doctor, and opened the window and partly opened the blind, and put his hand upon the Doctor's arm, and looked out with him into the courtyard.

Looked out upon a throng of men and women—not enough in number, or near enough, to fill the courtyard—not more than forty or fifty in all. The people in possession of the house had let them in at the gate, and they had rushed into work at the grindstone; it had evidently been set up there for their purpose, as in a convenient and retired spot.

But such awful workers, and such awful work!

The grindstone had a double handle, and turning at it madly were two men, whose faces, as their long hair flapped back when the whirlings of the grindstone brought their faces up, were more horrible and cruel than the visages of the wildest savages in their most barbarous disguise. False eyebrows and false moustaches were stuck upon them, and their hideous countenances were all bloody and sweaty, and all awry with howling, and all staring and glaring with beastly excitement and want of sleep. As these ruffians turned and turned, their matted locks now flung forward over their eyes, now flung backward over their necks, some women held wine to their mouths that they might drink; and what with dropping blood, and what with dropping wine, and what with the stream of sparks struck out of the stone, all their wicked atmosphere seemed gore and fire. The eye could not detect one creature in the group free from the smear of blood. Shouldering one another to get next at the sharpening-stone were men stripped to the waist, with the stain all over their limbs and bodies; men in all sorts of rags, with the stain upon those rags; men devilishly set off with spoils of women's lace and silk and ribbon, with the stain dyeing those trifles through and through. Hatchets, knives, bayonets, swords, all brought to be sharpened, were all red with it. Some of the hacked swords were tied to the wrists of those who carried them with strips of linen and fragments of dress—ligatures various in kind, but all deep of the one colour. And as the frantic wielders of these weapons snatched them from the stream of sparks and tore away into the streets, the same red hue was red in their frenzied eyes— eyes which any unbrutalised beholder would have given twenty years of life to petrify with a well-directed gun.

All this was seen in a moment, as the vision of a drowning man, or of any human creature at any very great pass, could see a world if it were there. They drew back from the window, and the Doctor looked for explanation in his friend's ashy face.

"They are," Mr. Lorry whispered the words, glancing fearfully round at the locked room, "murdering the prisoners. If you are sure of what you say; if you really have the power you think you have—as I believe you have—make yourself known to these devils, and get taken to La Force. It may be too late, I don't know, but let it not be a minute later!"

Doctor Manette pressed his hand, hastened bareheaded out of the room, and was in the courtyard when Mr. Lorry regained the blind.

His streaming white hair, his remarkable face, and the impetuous confidence of his manner, as he put the weapons aside like water, carried him in an instant to the heart of the concourse at the stone. For a few moments there was a pause, and a hurry, and a murmur, and the unintelligible sound of his voice; and then Mr. Lorry saw him, surrounded by all, and in the midst of a line of twenty men long, all linked shoulder to shoulder, and hand to shoulder, hurried out with cries of—" Live the Bastille prisoner! Help for the Bastille prisoner's kindred in La Force! Room for the Bastille prisoner in front there! Save the prisoner Evremond at La Force!" and a thousand answering shouts.

He closed the lattice again with a fluttering heart, closed the window and the curtain, hastened to Lucie, and told her that her father was assisted by the people, and gone in search of her husband. He found her child and Miss Pross with her; but it never occurred to him to be surprised by their appearance until a long time afterwards, when he sat watching them in such quiet as the night knew.

Lucie had, by that time, fallen into a stupor on the floor at his feet, clinging to his hand. Miss Pross had laid the child down on his own bed, and her head had gradually fallen on the pillow beside her pretty charge. Oh the long, long night, with the moans of the poor wife! And oh the long, long night, with no return of her father and no tidings!

Twice more in the darkness the bell at the great gate sounded, and the irruption was repeated, and the grindstone whirled and spluttered. "What is it?" cried Lucie, affrighted. "Hush! The soldiers' swords are sharpened there," said Mr. Lorry. "The place is national property now, and used as a kind of armoury, my love."

Twice more in all; but the last spell of work was feeble and fitful. Soon afterwards the day began to dawn, and he softly detached himself from the clasping hand, and cautiously looked out again. A man, so besmeared that he might have been a sorely wounded soldier creeping back to consciousness on a field of slain, was rising from the pavement by the side of the grindstone, and looking about him with a vacant air. Shortly this worn-out murderer descried in the imperfect light one of the carriages of Monseigneur, and staggering to that gorgeous vehicle, climbed in at the door, and shut himself up to take his rest on its dainty cushions.

The great grindstone, Earth, had turned when Mr. Lorry looked out again, and the sun was red on the courtyard. But the lesser grindstone stood alone there in the calm morning air, with a red upon it that the sun had never given, and would never take away.

CHAPTER III

THE SHADOW

ONE of the first considerations which arose in the business mind of Mr. Lorry when business hours came round was this—that he had no right to imperil Tellson's by sheltering the wife of an emigrant prisoner under the Bank roof. His own possessions, safety, life, he would have hazarded for Lucie and her child, without a moment's demur ; but the great trust he held was not his own, and as to that business charge he was a strict man of business.

At first his mind reverted to Defarge, and he thought of finding out the wine-shop again and taking counsel with its master in reference to the safest dwelling-place in the distracted state of the city. But the same consideration that suggested him repudiated him ; he lived in the most violent Quarter, and doubtless was influential there, and deep in its dangerous workings.

Noon coming, and the Doctor not returning, and every minute's delay tending to compromise Tellson's, Mr. Lorry advised with Lucie. She said that her father had spoken of hiring a lodging for a short term, in that Quarter, near the Banking-house. As there was no business objection to this, and as he foresaw that even if it were all well with Charles, and he were to be released, he could not hope to leave the city, Mr. Lorry went out in quest of such a lodging, and found a suitable one, high up in a removed by-street where the closed blinds in all the other windows of a high, melancholy square of buildings marked deserted homes.

To this lodging he at once removed Lucie and her child and Miss Pross, giving them what comfort he could, and much more than he had himself. He left Jerry with them, as a figure to fill a doorway that would bear considerable knocking on the head, and returned to his own occupations. A disturbed and doleful mind he brought to bear upon them, and slowly and heavily the day lagged on with him.

It wore itself out, and wore him out with it, until the Bank closed. He was again alone in his room of the previous night, considering what to do next, when he heard a foot upon the stair. In a few moments a man stood in his presence, who, with a keenly observant look at him, addressed him by his name.

"Your servant," said Mr. Lorry. "Do you know me?"

He was a strongly-made man with dark curling hair, from forty-five to fifty years of age. For answer he repeated, without any change of emphasis, the words—

"Do you know me?"

"I have seen you somewhere."

"Perhaps at my wine-shop?"

Much interested and agitated, Mr. Lorry said : "You come from Doctor Manette?"

"Yes. I come from Doctor Manette."

"And what says he? What does he send me?"

Defarge gave into his anxious hand an open scrap of paper. It bore the words in the Doctor's writing—

"Charles is safe, but I cannot safely leave this place yet. I have obtained the favour that the bearer has a short note from Charles to his wife. Let the bearer see his wife."

It was dated from La Force, within an hour.

"Will you accompany me," said Mr. Lorry, joyfully relieved after reading this note aloud, "to where his wife resides?"

"Yes," returned Defarge.

Scarcely noticing as yet in what a curiously reserved and mechanical way Defarge spoke, Mr. Lorry put on his hat and they went down into the courtyard. There they found two women; one, knitting.

"Madame Defarge, surely!" said Mr. Lorry, who had left her in exactly the same attitude some seventeen years ago.

"It is she," observed her husband.

"Does Madame go with us?" inquired Mr. Lorry, seeing that she moved as they moved.

"Yes. That she may be able to recognise the faces and know the persons. It is for their safety."

Beginning to be struck by Defarge's manner, Mr. Lorry looked dubiously at him, and led the way. Both the women followed; the second woman being The Vengeance.

They passed through the intervening streets as quickly as they might, ascended the staircase of the new domicile, were admitted by Jerry, and found Lucie weeping, alone. She was thrown into a transport by the tidings Mr. Lorry gave her of her husband, and clasped the hand that delivered his note—little thinking what it had been doing near him in the night, and might, but for a chance, have done to him.

"DEAREST—Take courage. I am well, and your father has influence around me. You cannot answer this. Kiss our child for me."

That was all the writing. It was so much, however, to her who received it, that she turned from Defarge to his wife, and kissed one of the hands that knitted. It was a passionate, loving, thankful, womanly action, but the hand made no response—dropped cold and heavy, and took to its knitting again.

There was something in its touch that gave Lucie a check. She stopped in the act of putting the note in her bosom, and, with her hands yet at her neck, looked terrified at Madame Defarge. Madame Defarge met the lifted eyebrows and forehead with a cold, impassive stare.

"My dear," said Mr. Lorry, striking in to explain, "there are frequent risings in the streets; and although it is not likely they will ever trouble you, Madame Defarge wishes to see those whom she has the power to protect at such times, to the end that she may know them—that she may identify them. I believe," said Mr. Lorry, rather halting in his reassuring words, as the stony manner of all the three impressed itself upon him more and more, "I state the case, Citizen Defarge?"

Defarge looked gloomily at his wife, and gave no other answer than a gruff sound of acquiescence.

"You had better, Lucie," said Mr. Lorry, doing all he could to propitiate, by tone and manner, "have the dear child here, and our good Pross. Our good Pross, Defarge, is an English lady, and knows no French."

The lady in question, whose rooted conviction, that she was more than a match for any foreigner, was not to be shaken by distress and danger, appeared with folded arms, and observed in English to The Vengeance, whom her eyes first encountered, "Well, I am sure, Boldface! I hope *you* are pretty well!" She also bestowed a British cough on Madame Defarge; but neither of the two took much heed of her.

"Is that his child?" said Madame Defarge, stopping in her work for the first time, and pointing her knitting-needle at little Lucie as if it were the finger of Fate.

"Yes, Madame," answered Mr. Lorry; "this is our poor prisoner's darling daughter, and only child."

The shadow attendant on Madame Defarge and her party seemed to fall so threatening and dark on the child, that her mother instinctively kneeled on the ground beside her, and held her to her breast. The shadow attendant on Madame Defarge and her party seemed then to fall, threatening and dark, on both the mother and the child.

"It is enough, my husband," said Madame Defarge. "I have seen them. We may go."

But the suppressed manner had enough of menace in it—not visible and presented, but indistinct and withheld—to alarm Lucie into saying, as she laid her appealing hand on Madame Defarge's dress—

"You will be good to my poor husband. You will do him no harm. You will help me to see him if you can?"

"Your husband is not my business here," returned Madame Defarge, looking down at her with perfect composure. "It is the daughter of your father who is my business here."

"For my sake, then, be merciful to my husband. For my child's sake! She will put her hands together and pray you to be merciful. We are more afraid of you than of these others."

Madame Defarge received it as a compliment, and looked at her husband. Defarge, who had been uneasily biting his thumb-nail and looking at her, collected his face into a sterner expression.

"What is it that your husband says in that little letter?" asked Madame Defarge, with a lowering smile. "Influence; he says something touching influence?"

"That my father," said Lucie, hurriedly taking the paper from her breast, but with her alarmed eyes on her questioner and not on it, "has much influence around him."

"Surely it will release him!" said Madame Defarge. "Let it do so."

"As a wife and mother," cried Lucie, most earnestly, "I implore you to have pity on me and not to exercise any power that you possess against my innocent husband, but to use it in his behalf. Oh sister-woman, think of me. As a wife and mother!"

Madame Defarge looked, coldly as ever, at the suppliant, and said, turning to her friend The Vengeance—

"The wives and mothers we have been used to see, since we were as little as this child, and much less, have not been greatly considered? We have known *their* husbands and fathers laid in prison and kept from them, often enough? All our lives we have seen our sister-women suffer, in themselves and in their children, poverty, nakedness, hunger, thirst, sickness, misery, oppression and neglect of all kinds?"

"We have seen nothing else," returned The Vengeance.

"We have borne this a long time," said Madame Defarge, turning her eyes again upon Lucie. "Judge you! Is it likely that the trouble of one wife and mother would be much to us now?"

She resumed her knitting and went out. The Vengeance followed. Defarge went last, and closed the door.

"Courage, my dear Lucie," said Mr. Lorry, as he raised her. "Courage, courage! So far all goes well with us—much, much better than it has of late gone with many poor souls. Cheer up, and have a thankful heart."

"I am not thankless, I hope, but that dreadful woman seems to throw a shadow on me and on all my hopes."

"Tut, tut!" said Mr. Lorry; "what is this despondency in the brave little breast? A shadow indeed! No substance in it, Lucie."

But the shadow of the manner of these Defarges was dark upon himself, for all that, and in his secret mind it troubled him greatly.

CHAPTER IV

CALM IN STORM

DOCTOR MANETTE did not return until the morning of the fourth day of his absence. So much of what had happened in that dreadful time as could be kept from the knowledge of Lucie was so well concealed from her, that not until long afterwards, when France and she were far apart, did she know that eleven hundred defenceless prisoners of both sexes and all ages had been killed by the populace; that four days and nights had been darkened by this deed of horror; and that the air around her had been tainted by the slain. She only knew that there had been an attack upon the prisons, that all political prisoners had been in danger, and that some had been dragged out by the crowd and murdered.

To Mr. Lorry the Doctor communicated, under an injunction of secrecy on which he had no need to dwell, that the crowd had taken him through a scene of carnage to the prison of La Force. That in the prison he had found a self-appointed Tribunal sitting, before which the prisoners were brought singly, and by which they were rapidly ordered to be put forth to be massacred, or to be released, or (in a few cases) to be sent back to their cells. That, presented by his conductors to this Tribunal, he had announced himself by name and profession as having been for eighteen years a secret and unaccused prisoner in the Bastille ; that one of the body so sitting in judgment had risen and identified him, and that this man was Defarge.

That hereupon he had ascertained, through the registers on the table, that his son-in-law was among the living prisoners, and had pleaded hard to the Tribunal—of whom some members were asleep and some awake, some dirty with murder and some clean, some sober and some not—for his life and liberty. That, in the first frantic greetings lavished on himself as a notable sufferer under the overthrown system, it had been accorded to him to have Charles Darnay brought before the lawless Court, and examined. That he seemed on the point of being at once released, when the tide in his favour met with some unexplained check (not intelligible to the Doctor), which led to a few words of secret conference. That the man sitting as President had then informed Doctor Manette that the prisoner must remain in custody, but should, for his sake, be held inviolate in safe custody. That immediately, on a signal, the prisoner was removed to the interior of the prison again ; but that he, the Doctor, had then so strongly pleaded for permission to remain and assure himself that his son-in-law was, through no malice or mischance, delivered to the concourse whose murderous yells outside the gate had often drowned the proceedings, that he had obtained the permission, and had remained in that Hall of Blood until the danger was over.

The sights he had seen there, with brief snatches of food and sleep by intervals, shall remain untold. The mad joy over the prisoners who were saved had astounded him scarcely less than the mad ferocity against those who were cut to pieces. One prisoner there was, he said, who had been discharged into the street free, but at whom a mistaken savage had thrust a pike as he passed out. Being besought to go to him and dress the wound, the Doctor had passed out at the same gate, and had found him in the arms of a company of Samaritans, who were seated on the bodies of their victims. With an inconsistency as monstrous as anything in this awful nightmare they had helped the healer, and tended the wounded man with the gentlest solicitude— had made a litter for him and escorted him carefully from the spot—had then caught up their weapons and plunged anew into a butchery so dreadful, that the Doctor had covered his eyes with his hands, and swooned away in the midst of it.

As Mr. Lorry received these confidences, and as he watched the face of his friend, now sixty-two years of age, a misgiving arose within him that such dread experiences would revive the old danger. But he had never seen his friend in his present aspect ; he had never at all known him in his present character. For the first time the Doctor felt, now, that his suffering was strength and power. For the first time he felt that in that sharp fire he had slowly forged the iron which could break the prison door of his daughter's husband, and deliver him. "It all tended to a good end, my friend; it was not mere waste and ruin. As my beloved child was helpful in restoring me to myself, I will be helpful now in restoring the dearest part of herself to her; by the aid of Heaven I will do it!" Thus, Doctor Manette. And when Jarvis Lorry saw the kindled eyes, the resolute face, the calm strong look and bearing of the man whose life always seemed to him to have been stopped, like a clock, for so many years, and then set going again with an energy which had lain dormant during the cessation of its usefulness, he believed.

Greater things than the Doctor had at that time to contend with would have yielded before his persevering purpose. While he kept himself in his place, as a physician, whose business was with all degrees of mankind, bond and free, rich and poor, bad and good, he used his personal influence so wisely, that he was soon the inspecting physician of three prisons, and among them of La Force. He could now assure Lucie that her husband was no longer confined alone, but was mixed with the general body of prisoners; he saw her husband weekly, and brought sweet messages to her, straight from his lips; sometimes her husband himself sent a letter to her (though never by the Doctor's hand), but she was not permitted to write to him; for among the many wild suspicions of plots in the prisons, the wildest of all pointed at emigrants who were known to have made friends or permanent connections abroad.

This new life of the Doctor's was an anxious life, no doubt; still the sagacious Mr. Lorry saw that there was a new sustaining pride in it. Nothing unbecoming tinged the pride; it was a natural and worthy one; but he observed it as a curiosity. The Doctor knew that up to that time his imprisonment had been associated in the minds of his daughter and his friend with his personal affliction, deprivation, and weakness. Now that this was changed, and he knew himself to be invested through that old trial with forces to which they both looked for Charles's ultimate safety and deliverance, he became so far exalted by the change, that he took the lead and direction, and required them, as the weak, to trust to him as the strong. The preceding relative positions of himself and Lucie were reversed, yet only as the liveliest gratitude and affection could reverse them, for he could have had no pride but in rendering some service to her who had rendered so much to him. "All curious to see," thought Mr. Lorry, in his amiably shrewd way, "but all natural and right; so take the lead, my dear friend, and keep it; it couldn't be in better hands."

But though the Doctor tried hard, and never ceased trying, to get Charles Darnay set at liberty, or at least to get him brought to trial, the public current of the time set too strong and fast for him. The new era began; the king was tried, doomed, and beheaded; the Republic of Liberty, Equality, Fraternity, or Death, declared for victory or death against the world in arms; the black flag waved night and day from the great towers of Notre Dame ; three hundred thousand men, summoned to rise against the tyrants of the earth, rose from all the varying soils of France, as if the dragon's teeth had been sown broadcast, and had yielded fruit equally on hill and plain, on rock, in gravel, and alluvial mud, under the bright sky of the South and under the clouds of the North, in fell and forest, in the vineyards and the olive-grounds and among the cropped grass and the stubble of the corn, along the fruitful banks of the broad rivers, and in the sand of the sea-shore. What private solicitude could rear itself against the deluge of the Year One of Liberty—the deluge rising from below, not falling from above, and with the windows of Heaven shut, not opened !

There was no pause, no pity, no peace, no interval of relenting rest, no measurement of time. Though days and nights circled as regularly as when time was young, and the evening and morning were the first day, other count of time there was none. Hold of it was lost in the raging fever of a nation, as it is in the fever of one patient. Now, breaking the unnatural silence of a whole city, the executioner showed the people the head of the king—and now, it seemed almost in the same breath, the head of his fair wife, which had had eight weary months of imprisoned widowhood and misery to turn it gray.

And yet, observing the strange law of contradiction which obtains in all such cases, the time was long, while it flamed by so fast. A revolutionary tribunal in the capital, and forty or fifty thousand revolutionary committees all over the land ; a law of the Suspected, which struck away all security for liberty or life, and delivered over any good and innocent person to any bad and guilty one ; prisons gorged with people who had committed no offence, and could obtain no hearing : these things became the established order and nature of appointed things, and seemed to be ancient usage before they were many weeks old. Above all, one hideous figure grew as familiar as if it had been before the general gaze from the foundations of the world—the figure of the sharp female called La Guillotine.

It was the popular theme for jests ; it was the best cure for headache ; it infallibly prevented the hair from turning gray ; it imparted a peculiar delicacy to the complexion ; it was the National Razor which shaved close ; who kissed La Guillotine looked through the little window and sneezed into the sack. It was the sign of the regeneration of the human race. It superseded the Cross. Models of it were worn on breasts from which the Cross was discarded, and it was bowed down to and believed in where the Cross was denied.

It sheared off heads so many, that it, and the ground it most polluted, were a rotten red. It was taken to pieces, like a toy-puzzle for a young Devil, and was put together again when the occasion wanted it. It hushed the eloquent, struck down the powerful, abolished the beautiful and good. Twenty-two friends of high public mark, twenty-one living and one dead, it had lopped the heads off, in one morning, in as many minutes. The name of the strong man of Old Scripture had descended to the chief functionary who worked it ; but, so armed, he was stronger than his namesake, and blinder, and tore away the gates of God's own Temple every day.

Among these terrors, and the brood belonging to them, the Doctor walked with a steady head, confident in his power, cautiously persistent in his end, never doubting that he would save Lucie's husband at last. Yet the current of the time swept by, so strong and deep, and carried the time away so fiercely, that Charles had lain in prison one year and three months when the Doctor was thus steady and confident. So much more wicked and distracted had the Revolution grown in that December month, that the rivers of the South were encumbered with the bodies of the violently drowned by night, and prisoners were shot in lines and squares under the southern wintry sun. Still the Doctor walked among the terrors with a steady head. No man better known than he in Paris at that day ; no man in a stranger situation. Silent, humane, indispensable in hospital and prison, using his art equally among assassins and victims, he was a man apart. In the exercise of his skill, the appearance and the story of the Bastille Captive removed him from all other men. He was not suspected or brought in question, any more than if he had indeed been recalled to life some eighteen years before, or were a Spirit moving among mortals.

CHAPTER V

THE WOOD-SAWYER

ONE year and three months. During all that time Lucie was never sure, from hour to hour, but that the Guillotine would strike off her husband's head next day. Every day, through the stony streets, the tumbrils now jolted heavily, filled with Condemned. Lovely girls ; bright women, brown-haired, black-haired, and gray; youths ; stalwart men and old ; gentle born and peasant born : all red wine for La Guillotine, all daily brought into light from the dark cellars of the loathsome prisons, and carried to her through the streets to slake her devouring thirst. Liberty, Equality, Fraternity, or Death—the last much the easiest to bestow, oh Guillotine !

If the suddenness of her calamity, and the whirling wheels of the time, had stunned the Doctor's daughter into awaiting the result in idle despair, it would but have been with her as it was with many. But from the hour when she had taken the white head to her fresh young bosom in the garret of Saint Antoine, she had been true to her duties. She was truest to them in the season of trial, as all the quietly loyal and good will always be.

As soon as they were established in their new residence, and her father had entered on the routine of his avocations, she arranged the little household as exactly as if her husband had been there. Everything had its appointed place and its appointed time. Little Lucie she taught as regularly as if they had all been united in their English home. The slight devices with which she cheated herself into the show of a belief that they would soon be reunited—the little preparations for his speedy return, the setting aside of his chair and his books—these, and the solemn prayer at night for one dear prisoner especially, among the many unhappy souls in prison and the shadow of death—were almost the only outspoken reliefs of her heavy mind.

She did not greatly alter in appearance. The plain dark dresses, akin to mourning dresses, which she and her child wore, were as neat and as well attended to as the brighter clothes of happy days. She lost her colour, and the old and intent expression was a constant, not an occasional thing; otherwise she remained very pretty and comely. Sometimes at night, on kissing her father, she would burst into the grief she had repressed all day, and would say that her sole reliance, under Heaven, was on him. He always resolutely answered: "Nothing can happen to him without my knowledge, and I know that I can save him, Lucie."

They had not made the round of their changed life many weeks, when her father said to her, on coming home one evening—

" My dear, there is an upper window in the prison to which Charles can sometimes gain access at three in the afternoon. When he can get to it—which depends on many uncertainties and incidents—he might see you in the street, he thinks, if you stood in a certain place that I can show you. But you will not be able to see him, my poor child, and, even if you could, it would be unsafe for you to make a sign of recognition."

"Oh, show me the place, my father, and I will go there every day."

From that time, in all weathers, she waited there two hours. As the clock struck two she was there, and at four she turned resignedly away. When it was not too wet or inclement for her child to be with her, they went together; at other times she was alone; but she never missed a single day.

It was the dark and dirty corner of a small winding street. The hovel of a cutter of wood into lengths for burning was the only house at that end; all else was wall. On the third day of her being there, he noticed her.

"Good-day, citizeness."

"Good-day, citizen."

This mode of address was now prescribed by decree. It had been established voluntarily some time ago among the more thorough patriots; but was now law for everybody.

"Walking here again, citizeness?"

"You see me, citizen!"

The wood-sawyer, who was a little man with a redundancy of gesture (he had once been a mender of roads), cast a glance at the prison, pointed at the prison, and, putting his ten fingers before his face to represent bars, peeped through them jocosely.

"But it's not my business," said he, and went on sawing his wood.

Next day he was looking out for her, and accosted her the moment she appeared.

"What? Walking here again, citizeness?"

"Yes, citizen."

"Ah! A child too! Your mother, is it not, my little citizeness?"

"Do I say yes, mamma?" whispered little Lucie, drawing close to her.

"Yes, dearest."

"Yes, citizen."

"Ah! But it's not my business. My work is my business. See my saw! I call it my Little Guillotine. La, la, la; La, la, la! And off his head comes!"

The billet fell as he spoke, and he threw it into a basket.

"I call myself the Samson of the firewood guillotine. See here again! Loo, loo, loo; Loo, loo, loo! And off *her* head comes! Now, a child. Tickle, tickle; Pickle, pickle! And off *its* head comes. All the family!"

Lucie shuddered as he threw two more billets into his basket, but it was impossible to be there while the wood-sawyer was at work and not be in his sight. Thenceforth, to secure his goodwill, she always spoke to him first, and often gave him drink-money, which he readily received.

He was an inquisitive fellow, and sometimes, when she had quite forgotten him in gazing at the prison roof and grates, and in lifting her heart up to her husband, she would come to herself to find him looking at her, with his knee on his bench and his saw stopped in its work. "But it's not my business!" he would generally say at those times, and would briskly fall to his sawing again.

In all weathers, in the snow and frost of winter, in the bitter winds of spring, in the hot sunshine of summer, in the rains of autumn, and again in the snow and frost of winter, Lucie passed two hours of every day at this place; and every day on leaving it she kissed the prison wall. Her husband saw her (so she learned from her father) it might be once in five or six times; it might be twice or thrice running; it might be, not for a week or a fortnight together. It was enough that he could and did see her when the chances served, and on that possibility she would have waited out the day, seven days a week.

These occupations brought her round to the December month, wherein her father walked among the terrors with a steady head. On a lightly-snowing afternoon she arrived at the usual corner. It was a day of some wild rejoicing, and a festival. She had seen the houses, as she came along, decorated with little pikes, and with little red caps stuck upon them; also, with tricoloured ribbons; also, with the standard inscription (tricoloured letters were the favourite), Republic One and Indivisible. Liberty, Equality, Fraternity, or Death!

The miserable shop of the wood-sawyer was so small that its whole

Lucie

surface furnished very indifferent space for this legend. He had got somebody to scrawl it up for him, however, who had squeezed Death in with most inappropriate difficulty. On his house-top he displayed pike and cap, as a good citizen must, and in a window he had stationed his saw inscribed as his "Little Sainte Guillotine"—for the great sharp female was by that time popularly canonised. His shop was shut and he was not there, which was a relief to Lucie, and left her quite alone.

But he was not far off, for presently she heard a troubled movement and a shouting coming along, which filled her with fear. A moment afterwards and a throng of people came pouring round the corner by the prison wall, in the midst of whom was the wood-sawyer hand in hand with The Vengeance. There could not be fewer than five hundred people, and they were dancing like five thousand demons. There was no other music than their own singing. They danced to the popular Revolution song, keeping a ferocious time that was like a gnashing of teeth in unison. Men and women danced together, women danced together, men danced together, as hazard had brought them together. At first they were a mere storm of coarse red caps and coarse woollen rags; but as they filled the place, and stopped to dance about Lucie, some ghastly apparition of a dance-figure gone raving mad arose among them. They advanced, retreated, struck at one another's hands, clutched at one another's heads, spun round alone, caught one another and spun round in pairs, until many of them dropped. While those were down, the rest linked hand in hand, and all spun round together; then the ring broke, and in separate rings of two and four they turned and turned until they all stopped at once, began again, struck, clutched, and tore, and then reversed the spin, and all spun round another way. Suddenly they stopped again, paused, struck out the time afresh, formed into lines the width of the public way, and, with their heads low down and their hands high up, swooped screaming off. No fight could have been half so terrible as this dance. It was so emphatically a fallen sport—a something, once innocent, delivered over to all devilry—a healthy pastime changed into a means of angering the blood, bewildering the senses, and steeling the heart. Such grace as was visible in it made it the uglier, showing how warped and perverted all things good by nature were become. The maidenly bosom bared to this, the pretty almost child's head thus distracted, the delicate foot mincing in this slough of blood and dirt, were types of the disjointed time.

This was the Carmagnole. As it passed, leaving Lucie frightened and bewildered in the doorway of the wood-sawyer's house, the feathery snow fell as quietly and lay as white and soft as if it had never been.

"Oh my father!" for he stood before her when she lifted up the eyes she had momentarily darkened with her hand; "such a cruel, bad sight."

"I know, my dear, I know. I have seen it many times. Don't be frightened! Not one of them would harm you."

"I am not frightened for myself, my father. But when I think of my husband, and the mercies of these people——"

"We will set him above their mercies very soon. I left him climbing to the window, and I came to tell you. There is no one here to see. You may kiss your hand towards that highest shelving roof."

"I do so, father, and I send him my Soul with it!"

"You cannot see him, my poor dear?"

"No, father," said Lucie, yearning and weeping as she kissed her hand, "no."

A footstep in the snow. Madame Defarge. "I salute you, citizeness," from the Doctor. "I salute you, citizen." This in passing. Nothing more. Madame Defarge gone, like a shadow over the white road.

"Give me your arm, my love. Pass from here with an air of cheerfulness and courage, for his sake. That was well done"—they had left the spot—"it shall not be in vain. Charles is summoned for to-morrow."

"For to-morrow!"

"There is no time to lose. I am well prepared, but there are precautions to be taken that could not be taken until he was actually summoned before the Tribunal. He has not received the notice yet, but I know that he will presently be summoned for to-morrow, and removed to the Conciergerie; I have timely information. You are not afraid?"

She could scarcely answer, "I trust in you."

"Do so, implicitly. Your suspense is nearly ended, my darling; he shall be restored to you within a few hours; I have encompassed him with every protection. I must see Lorry."

He stopped. There was a heavy lumbering of wheels within hearing. They both knew too well what it meant. One. Two. Three. Three tumbrils faring away with their dread loads over the hushing snow.

"I must see Lorry," the Doctor repeated, turning her another way.

The staunch old gentleman was still in his trust; had never left it. He and his books were in frequent requisition as to property confiscated and made national. What he could save for the owners, he saved. No better man living to hold fast by what Tellson's had in keeping, and to hold his peace.

A murky red and yellow sky, and a rising mist from the Seine, denoted the approach of darkness. It was almost dark when they arrived at the Bank. The stately residence of Monseigneur was altogether blighted and deserted. Above a heap of dust and ashes in the court ran the letters: National Property. Republic One and Indivisible. Liberty, Equality, Fraternity, or Death!

Who could that be with Mr. Lorry—the owner of the riding-coat upon the chair—who must not be seen? From whom newly arrived did he come out, agitated and surprised, to take his favourite in his arms? To whom did he appear to repeat her faltering words, when, raising his voice and turning his head towards the door of the room from which he had issued, he said: "Removed to the Conciergerie, and summoned for to-morrow"?

CHAPTER VI

TRIUMPH

THE dread Tribunal of five Judges, Public Prosecutor, and determined Jury, sat every day. Their lists went forth every evening, and were read out by the jailers of the various prisons to their prisoners. The standard jailer-joke was, " Come out and listen to the Evening Paper, you inside there ! "

" Charles Evremond, called Darnay ! "

So at last began the Evening Paper at La Force.

When a name was called its owner stepped apart into a spot reserved for those who were announced as being thus fatally recorded. Charles Evremond, called Darnay, had reason to know the usage ; he had seen hundreds pass away so.

His bloated jailer, who wore spectacles to read with, glanced over them to assure himself that he had taken his place, and went through the list, making a similar short pause at each name. There were twenty-three names, but only twenty were responded to ; for one of the prisoners so summoned had died in jail and been forgotten, and two had already been guillotined and forgotten. The list was read in the vaulted chamber where Darnay had seen the associated prisoners on the night of his arrival. Every one of those had perished in the massacre ; every human creature he had since cared for and parted with had died on the scaffold.

There were hurried words of farewell and kindness, but the parting was soon over. It was the incident of every day, and the society of La Force were engaged in the preparation of some games of forfeits and a little concert for that evening. They crowded to the grates and shed tears there ; but twenty places in the projected entertainments had to be refilled, and the time was, at best, short to the lock-up hour, when the common rooms and corridors would be delivered over to the great dogs who kept watch there through the night. The prisoners were far from insensible or unfeeling : their ways arose out of the condition of the time. Similarly, though with a subtle difference, a species of fervour or intoxication, known, without doubt, to have led some persons to brave the guillotine unnecessarily, and to die by it, was not mere boastfulness, but a wild infection of the wildly shaken public mind. In seasons of pestilence some of us will have a secret attraction to the disease—a terrible passing inclination to die of it. And all of us have like wonders hidden in our breasts, only needing circumstances to evoke them.

The passage to the Conciergerie was short and dark ; the night in its vermin-haunted cells was long and cold. Next day fifteen prisoners were put to the bar before Charles Darnay's name was called. All the fifteen were condemned, and the trials of the whole occupied an hour and a half.

"Charles Evremond, called Darnay," was at length arraigned.

His judges sat upon the Bench in feathered hats ; but the rough red cap and tricoloured cockade was the head-dress otherwise prevailing. Looking at the Jury and the turbulent audience, he might have thought that the usual order of things was reversed, and that the felons were trying the honest men. The lowest, cruelest, and worst populace of a city, never without its quantity of low, cruel, and bad, were the directing spirits of the scene : noisily commenting, applauding, disapproving, anticipating, and precipitating the result, without a check. Of the men, the greater part were armed in various ways ; of the women, some wore knives, some daggers, some ate and drank as they looked on, many knitted. Among these last was one with a spare piece of knitting under her arm as she worked. She was in a front row, by the side of a man whom he had never seen since his arrival at the Barrier, but whom he directly remembered as Defarge. He noticed that she once or twice whispered in his ear, and that she seemed to be his wife ; but what he most noticed in the two figures was, that although they were posted as close to himself as they could be, they never looked towards him. They seemed to be waiting for something with a dogged determination, and they looked at the Jury, but at nothing else. Under the President sat Doctor Manette, in his usual quiet dress. As well as the prisoner could see, he and Mr. Lorry were the only men there, unconnected with the Tribunal, who wore their usual clothes, and had not assumed the coarse garb of the Carmagnole.

Charles Evremond, called Darnay, was accused by the Public Prosecutor as an emigrant, whose life was forfeit to the Republic, under the decree which banished all emigrants on pain of Death. It was nothing that the decree bore date since his return to France. There he was, and there was the decree ; he had been taken in France, and his head was demanded.

"Take off his head !" cried the audience. "An enemy to the Republic !"

The President rang his bell to silence those cries, and asked the prisoner whether it was not true that he had lived many years in England ?

Undoubtedly it was.

Was he not an emigrant then ? What did he call himself ?

Not an emigrant, he hoped, within the sense and spirit of the law.

Why not ? the President desired to know.

Because he had voluntarily relinquished a title that was distasteful to him, and a station that was distasteful to him, and had left his country — he submitted before the word emigrant in the present acceptation by the Tribunal was in use—to live by his own industry in England, rather than on the industry of the overladen people of France.

What proof had he of this ?

He handed in the names of two witnesses : Théophile Gabelle and Alexandre Manette.

But he had married in England ? the President reminded him.

True, but not an English woman.

A citizeness of France?

Yes. By birth.

Her name and family?

" Lucie Manette, only daughter of Doctor Manette, the good physician who sits there."

This answer had a happy effect upon the audience. Cries in exaltation of the well-known good physician rent the hall. So capriciously were the people moved, that tears immediately rolled down several ferocious countenances which had been glaring at the prisoner a moment before as if with impatience to pluck him out into the streets and kill him.

On these few steps of his dangerous way Charles Darnay had set his foot according to Doctor Manette's reiterated instructions. The same cautious counsel directed every step that lay before him, and had prepared every inch of his road

The President asked, why had he returned to France when he did, and not sooner?

He had not returned sooner, he replied, simply because he had no means of living in France, save those he had resigned ; whereas, in England, he lived by giving instruction in the French language and literature. He had returned when he did on the pressing and written entreaty of a French citizen, who represented that his life was endangered by his absence. He had come back to save a citizen's life, and to bear his testimony, at whatever personal hazard, to the truth. Was that criminal in the eyes of the Republic?

The populace cried enthusiastically, " No!" and the President rang his bell to quiet them, which it did not, for they continued to cry " No!" until they left off of their own will.

The President required the name of that citizen. The accused explained that the citizen was his first witness. He also referred with confidence to the citizen's letter, which had been taken from him at the Barrier, but which he did not doubt would be found among the papers then before the President.

The Doctor had taken care that it should be there—had assured him that it would be there—and at this stage of the proceedings it was produced and read. Citizen Gabelle was called to confirm it, and did so. Citizen Gabelle hinted, with infinite delicacy and politeness, that in the pressure of business imposed on the Tribunal by the multitude of enemies of the Republic with which it had to deal, he had been slightly overlooked in his prison of the Abbaye—in fact, had rather passed out of the Tribunal's patriotic remembrance—until three days ago, when he had been summoned before it, and had been set at liberty on the Jury's declaring themselves satisfied that the accusation against him was answered, as to himself, by the surrender of the citizen Evremond, called Darnay.

Doctor Manette was next questioned. His high personal popularity, and the clearness of his answers, made a great impression ; but as he proceeded, as he showed that the accused was his first friend on his release from his long imprisonment; that the accused had remained in England, always faithful and devoted to his daughter and himself in their exile; that, so far from being in favour with the Aristocrat government there, he had actually been tried for his life by it, as the foe of England and friend of the United States—as he brought these circumstances into view, with the greatest discretion and with the straightforward force of truth and earnestness, the Jury and the populace became one. At last, when he appealed by name to Monsieur Lorry, an English gentleman then and there present, who, like himself, had been a witness on that English trial and could corroborate his account of it, the Jury declared that they had heard enough, and that they were ready with their votes if the President were content to receive them.

At every vote (the Jurymen voted aloud and individually) the populace set up a shout of applause. All the voices were in the prisoner's favour, and the President declared him free.

Then began one of those extraordinary scenes with which the populace sometimes gratified their fickleness, or their better impulses towards generosity and mercy, or which they regarded as some set-off against their swollen account of cruel rage. No man can decide now to which of these motives such extraordinary scenes were referable; it is probable, to a blending of all the three, with the second predominating. No sooner was the acquittal pronounced, than tears were shed as freely as blood at another time, and such fraternal embraces were bestowed upon the prisoner by as many of both sexes as could rush at him, that after his long and unwholesome confinement he was in danger of fainting from exhaustion; none the less because he knew very well that the very same people, carried by another current, would have rushed at him with the very same intensity to rend him to pieces and strew him over the streets.

His removal, to make way for other accused persons who were to be tried, rescued him from these caresses for the moment. Five were to be tried together, next, as enemies of the Republic, forasmuch as they had not assisted it by word or deed. So quick was the Tribunal to compensate itself and the nation for a chance lost, that these five came down to him before he left the place, condemned to die within twenty-four hours. The first of them told him so, with the customary prison sign of Death—a raised finger—and they all added in words, "Long live the Republic!"

The five had had, it is true, no audience to lengthen their proceedings, for when he and Doctor Manette emerged from the gate, there was a great crowd about it, in which there seemed to be every face he had seen in court—except two, for which he looked in vain. On his coming out, the concourse made at him anew, weeping, embracing, and shouting, all by turns and all together, until the very tide of the river on the bank of which the mad scene was acted seemed to run mad, like the people on the shore.

They put him into a great chair they had among them, and which they had taken either out of the court itself, or one of its rooms or passages. Over the chair they had thrown a red flag, and to the back of it they had bound a pike with a red cap on its top. In this car of triumph, not even the Doctor's entreaties could prevent his being carried to his home on men's shoulders, with a confused sea of red caps heaving about him, and casting up to sight from the stormy deep such wrecks of faces, that he more than once misdoubted his mind being in confusion, and that he was in the tumbril on his way to the guillotine.

In wild dreamlike procession, embracing whom they met and pointing him out, they carried him on. Reddening the snowy streets with the prevailing Republican colour, in winding and tramping through them, as they had reddened them below the snow with a deeper dye, they carried him thus into the courtyard of the building where he lived. Her father had gone on before, to prepare her, and when her husband stood upon his feet, she dropped insensible in his arms.

As he held her to his heart and turned her beautiful head between his face and the brawling crowd, so that his tears and her lips might come together unseen, a few of the people fell to dancing. Instantly all the rest fell to dancing, and the courtyard overflowed with the Carmagnole. Then they elevated into the vacant chair a young woman from the crowd to be carried as the Goddess of Liberty, and then, swelling and overflowing out into the adjacent streets, and along the river's bank, and over the bridge, the Carmagnole absorbed them every one and whirled them away.

After grasping the Doctor's hand, as he stood victorious and proud before him; after grasping the hand of Mr. Lorry, who came panting in breathless from his struggle against the waterspout of the Carmagnole; after kissing little Lucie, who was lifted up to clasp her arms round his neck; and after embracing the ever zealous and faithful Pross, who lifted her, he took his wife in his arms, and carried her up to their rooms.

"Lucie! My own! I am safe."

"Oh dearest Charles, let me thank God for this on my knees as I have prayed to Him."

They all reverently bowed their heads and hearts. When she was again in his arms, he said to her—

"And now speak to your father, dearest. No other man in all this France could have done what he has done for me."

She laid her head upon her father's breast, as she had laid his poor head on her own breast, long, long ago. He was happy in the return he had made her, he was recompensed for his suffering, he was proud of his strength. "You must not be weak, my darling," he remonstrated; "don't tremble so. I have saved him."

CHAPTER VII

A KNOCK AT THE DOOR

" I HAVE saved him." It was not another of the dreams in which he had often come back ; he was really here. And yet his wife trembled, and a vague but heavy fear was upon her.

All the air around was so thick and dark, the people were so passionately revengeful and fitful, the innocent were so constantly put to death on vague suspicion and black malice, it was so impossible to forget that many as blameless as her husband and as dear to others as he was to her, every day shared the fate from which he had been clutched, that her heart could not be as lightened of its load as she felt it ought to be. The shadows of the wintry afternoon were beginning to fall, and even now the dreadful carts were rolling through the streets. Her mind pursued them, looking for him among the Condemned ; and then she clung closer to his real presence and trembled more.

Her father, cheering her, showed a compassionate superiority to this woman's weakness which was wonderful to see. No garret, no shoemaking, no One Hundred and Five, North Tower, now ! He had accomplished the task he had set himself ; his promise was redeemed ; he had saved Charles. Let them all lean upon him.

Their housekeeping was of a very frugal kind : not only because that was the safest way of life, involving the least offence to the people, but because they were not rich, and Charles, throughout his imprisonment, had had to pay heavily for his bad food, and for his guard, and towards the living of the poorer prisoners. Partly on this account, and partly to avoid a domestic spy, they kept no servant ; the citizen and citizeness who acted as porters at the courtyard gate rendered them occasional service ; and Jerry (almost wholly transferred to them by Mr. Lorry) had become their daily retainer, and had his bed there every night.

It was an ordinance of the Republic One and Indivisible of Liberty, Equality, Fraternity, or Death, that on the door or doorpost of every house the name of every inmate must be legibly inscribed in letters of a certain size, at a certain convenient height from the ground. Mr. Jerry Cruncher's name, therefore, duly embellished the doorpost down below ; and, as the afternoon shadows deepened, the owner of that name himself appeared, from overlooking a painter whom Doctor Manette had employed to add to the list the name of Charles Evremond, called Darnay.

In the universal fear and distrust that darkened the time, all the usual harmless ways of life were changed. In the Doctor's little household, as in very many others, the articles of daily consumption that were wanted were purchased every evening, in small quantities and at various small shops.   To avoid attracting notice, and to give as little occasion as possible for talk and envy, was the general desire.

For some months past Miss Pross and Mr. Cruncher had discharged the office of purveyors : the former carrying the money ; the latter, the basket.   Every afternoon at about the time when the public lamps were lighted they fared forth on this duty, and made and brought home such purchases as were needful.   Although Miss Pross, through her long association with a French family, might have known as much of their language as of her own, if she had had a mind, she had no mind in that direction ; consequently she knew no more of that "nonsense" (as she was pleased to call it) than Mr. Cruncher did.   So her manner of marketing was to plump a noun-substantive at the head of a shopkeeper without any introduction in the nature of an article, and if it happened not to be the name of the thing she wanted, to look round for that thing, lay hold of it, and hold on by it until the bargain was concluded.   She always made a bargain for it, by holding up, as a statement of its just price, one finger less than the merchant held up, whatever his number might be.

"Now, Mr. Cruncher," said Miss Pross, whose eyes were red with felicity, "if you are ready, I am."

Jerry hoarsely professed himself at Miss Pross's service.   He had worn all his rust off long ago, but nothing would file his spiky head down.

"There's all manner of things wanted," said Miss Pross, "and we shall have a precious time of it.   We want wine, among the rest.   Nice toasts these Redheads will be drinking, wherever we buy it."

"It will be much the same to your knowledge, Miss, I should think," retorted Jerry, "whether they drink your health or the Old Un's."

"Who's he ? " said Miss Pross.

Mr. Cruncher, with some diffidence, explained himself as meaning "Old Nick's."

"Ha ! " said Miss Pross, "it doesn't need an interpreter to explain the meaning of these creatures.   They have but one, and it's Midnight Murder, and Mischief."

"Hush, dear !   Pray, pray, be cautious ! " cried Lucie.

"Yes, yes, yes, I'll be cautious," said Miss Pross ; "but I may say among ourselves, that I do hope there will be no oniony and tobaccoey smotherings, in the form of embracings all round, going on in the streets.   Now, Ladybird, never you stir from that fire till I come back !   Take care of the dear husband you have recovered, and don't move your pretty head from his shoulder, as you have it now, till you see me again !   May I ask a question, Doctor Manette, before I go ? "

"I think you may take that liberty," the Doctor answered, smiling.

"For gracious sake, don't talk about Liberty ; we have quite enough of that," said Miss Pross.

"Hush, dear !   Again ? " Lucie remonstrated.

"Well, my sweet," said Miss Pross, nodding her head emphatically, "the short and the long of it is, that I am a subject of His Most

(M 982)   15

Gracious Majesty King George the Third"—Miss Pross curtseyed at the name—"and as such, my maxim is, Confound their politics, Frustrate their knavish tricks, On him our hopes we fix, God save the King!"

Mr. Cruncher, in an access of loyalty, growlingly repeated the words after Miss Pross, like somebody at church.

"I am glad you have so much of the Englishman in you, though I wish you had never taken that cold in your voice," said Miss Pross, approvingly. "But the question, Doctor Manette. Is there"—it was the good creature's way to affect to make light of anything that was a great anxiety with them all, and to come at it in this chance manner—"is there any prospect yet of our getting out of this place?"

"I fear not yet. It would be dangerous for Charles yet."

"Heigh-ho-hum!" said Miss Pross, cheerfully repressing a sigh as she glanced at her darling's golden hair in the light of the fire, "then we must have patience and wait,—that's all. We must hold up our heads and fight low, as my brother Solomon used to say. Now, Mr. Cruncher!—Don't you move, Ladybird!"

They went out, leaving Lucie, and her husband, her father, and the child, by a bright fire. Mr. Lorry was expected back presently from the Banking House. Miss Pross had lighted the lamp, but had put it aside in a corner, that they might enjoy the firelight undisturbed. Little Lucie sat by her grandfather with her hands clasped through his arm; and he, in a tone not rising much above a whisper, began to tell her a story of a great and powerful Fairy who had opened a prison-wall and let out a captive who had once done the Fairy a service. All was subdued and quiet, and Lucie was more at ease than she had been.

"What is that?" she cried, all at once.

"My dear!" said her father, stopping in his story, and laying his hand on hers, "command yourself. What a disordered state you are in! The least thing—nothing—startles you! *You*, your father's daughter!"

"I thought, my father," said Lucie, excusing herself, with a pale face and in a faltering voice, "that I heard strange feet upon the stairs."

"My love, the staircase is as still as Death."

As he said the word, a blow was struck upon the door.

"Oh father, father! What can this be? Hide Charles. Save him!"

"My child," said the Doctor, rising, and laying his hand upon her shoulder, "I *have* saved him. What weakness is this, my dear! Let me go to the door."

He took the lamp in his hand, crossed the two intervening outer rooms, and opened it. A rude clattering of feet over the floor, and four rough men in red caps, armed with sabres and pistols, entered the room.

"The Citizen Evremond, called Darnay," said the first.

"Who seeks him?" answered Darnay.

"I seek him. We seek him. I know you, Evremond; I saw

you before the Tribunal to-day. You are again the prisoner of the Republic."

The four surrounded him, where he stood with his wife and child clinging to him.

"Tell me how and why am I again a prisoner."

"It is enough that you return straight to the Conciergerie, and will know to-morrow. You are summoned for to-morrow."

Dr. Manette, whom this visitation had so turned into stone, that he stood with the lamp in his hand, as if he were a statue made to hold it, moved after these words were spoken, put the lamp down, and confronting the speaker, and taking him, not ungently, by the loose front of his red woollen shirt, said—

"You know him, you have said. Do you know me?"

"Yes, I know you, Citizen Doctor."

"We all know you, Citizen Doctor," said the other three.

He looked abstractedly from one to another, and said, in a lower voice, after a pause—

"Will you answer his question to me then? How does this happen?"

"Citizen Doctor," said the first, reluctantly, "he has been denounced to the Section of Saint Antoine. This citizen," pointing out the second who had entered, "is from Saint Antoine."

The citizen here indicated nodded his head, and added—

"He is accused by Saint Antoine."

"Of what?" asked the Doctor.

"Citizen Doctor," said the first, with his former reluctance, "ask no more. If the Republic demands sacrifices from you, without doubt you as a good patriot will be happy to make them. The Republic goes before all. The People is supreme. Evremond, we are pressed."

"One word," the Doctor entreated. "Will you tell me who denounced him?"

"It is against rule," answered the first; "but you can ask him of Saint Antoine here."

The Doctor turned his eyes upon that man, who moved uneasily on his feet, rubbed his beard a little, and at length said—

"Well! Truly it is against rule. But he is denounced—and gravely—by the Citizen and Citizeness Defarge. And by one other."

"What other?"

"Do _you_ ask, Citizen Doctor?"

"Yes."

"Then," said he of Saint Antoine, with a strange look, "you will be answered to-morrow. Now, I am dumb!"

CHAPTER VIII

A HAND AT CARDS

HAPPILY unconscious of the new calamity at home, Miss Pross threaded her way along the narrow streets and crossed the river by the bridge of the Pont-Neuf, reckoning in her mind the number of indispensable purchases she had to make. Mr. Cruncher, with the basket, walked at her side. They both looked to the right and to the left into most of the shops they passed, had a wary eye for all gregarious assemblages of people, and turned out of their road to avoid any very excited group of talkers. It was a raw evening, and the misty river, blurred to the eye with blazing lights and to the ear with harsh noises, showed where the barges were stationed in which the smiths worked, making guns for the Army of the Republic. Woe to the man who played tricks with *that* Army, or got undeserved promotion in it ! Better for him that his beard had never grown, for the National Razor shaved him close.

Having purchased a few small articles of grocery, and a measure of oil for the lamp, Miss Pross bethought herself of the wine they wanted. After peeping into several wine-shops, she stopped at the sign of The Good Republican Brutus of Antiquity, not far from the National Palace, once (and twice) the Tuileries, where the aspect of things rather took her fancy. It had a quieter look than any other place of the same description they had passed, and, though red with patriotic caps, was not so red as the rest. Sounding Mr. Cruncher, and finding him of her opinion, Miss Pross resorted to The Good Republican Brutus of Antiquity, attended by her cavalier.

Slightly observant of the smoky lights ; of the people, pipe in mouth, playing with limp cards and yellow dominoes ; of the one bare-breasted, bare-armed, soot-begrimed workman reading a journal aloud, and of the others listening to him ; of the weapons worn, or laid aside to be resumed ; of the two or three customers fallen forward asleep, who in the popular high-shouldered, shaggy black spencer looked, in that attitude, like slumbering bears or dogs, the two out-landish customers approached the counter and showed what they wanted.

As their wine was measuring out, a man parted from another man in a corner and rose to depart. In going he had to face Miss Pross. No sooner did he face her than Miss Pross uttered a scream and clapped her hands.

In a moment the whole company were on their feet. That some-body was assassinated by somebody vindicating a difference of opinion was the likeliest occurrence. Everybody looked to see somebody fall, but only saw a man and a woman standing staring at each other, the man with all the outward aspect of a Frenchman and a thorough Republican ; the woman evidently English.

What was said in this disappointing anti-climax by the disciples of The Good Republican Brutus of Antiquity, except that it was something very voluble and loud, would have been as so much Hebrew or Chaldean to Miss Pross and her protector, though they had been all ears. But they had no ears for anything in their surprise. For it must be recorded that not only was Miss Pross lost in amazement and agitation, but Mr. Cruncher—though it seemed on his own separate and individual account—was in a state of the greatest wonder.

"What is the matter?" said the man who had caused Miss Pross to scream, speaking in a vexed, abrupt voice (though in a low tone), and in English.

"Oh Solomon, dear Solomon!" cried Miss Pross, clapping her hands again. "After not setting eyes upon you or hearing of you for so long a time, do I find you here!"

"Don't call me Solomon. Do you want to be the death of me?" asked the man, in a furtive, frightened way.

"Brother, brother!" cried Miss Pross, bursting into tears, "have I ever been so hard with you that you should ask me such a cruel question?"

"Then hold your meddlesome tongue," said Solomon, "and come out if you want to speak to me. Pay for your wine, and come out. Who's this man?"

Miss Pross, shaking her loving and dejected head at her by no means affectionate brother, said through her tears, "Mr. Cruncher."

"Let him come out too," said Solomon. "Does he think me a ghost?"

Apparently Mr. Cruncher did, to judge from his looks. He said not a word, however, and Miss Pross, exploring the depths of her reticule through her tears with great difficulty, paid for her wine. As she did so, Solomon turned to the followers of The Good Republican Brutus of Antiquity, and offered a few words of explanation in the French language, and caused them all to relapse into their former places and pursuits.

"Now," said Solomon, stopping at the dark street corner, "what do you want?"

"How dreadfully unkind in a brother nothing has ever turned my love away from!" cried Miss Pross, "to give me such a greeting, and show me no affection."

"There. Con-found it! There," said Solomon, making a dab at Miss Pross's lips with his own. "Now are you content?"

Miss Pross only shook her head and wept in silence.

"If you expect me to be surprised," said her brother Solomon, "I am not surprised; I knew you were here; I know of most people who are here. If you really don't want to endanger my existence—which I half believe you do—go your ways as soon as possible, and let me go mine. I am busy. I am an official."

"My English brother Solomon," mourned Miss Pross, casting up her tear-fraught eyes, "that had the makings in him of one of the best and greatest of men in his native country, an official among foreigners, and such foreigners! I would almost sooner have seen the dear boy lying in his——"

"I said so!" cried her brother, interrupting. "I knew it. You want to be the death of me. I shall be rendered Suspected, by my own sister. Just as I am getting on!"

"The gracious and merciful Heavens forbid!" cried Miss Pross. "Far rather would I never see you again, dear Solomon, though I have ever loved you truly, and ever shall. Say but one affectionate word to me, and tell me there is nothing angry or estranged between us, and I will detain you no longer."

Good Miss Pross! As if the estrangement between them had come of any culpability of hers. As if Mr. Lorry had not known it for a fact, years ago, in the quiet corner in Soho, that this precious brother had spent her money and left her!

He was saying the affectionate word, however, with a far more grudging condescension and patronage than he could have shown if their relative merits and positions had been reversed (which is invariably the case all the world over), when Mr. Cruncher, touching him on the shoulder, hoarsely and unexpectedly interposed with the following singular question—

"I say! Might I ask the favour? As to whether your name is John Solomon, or Solomon John?"

The official turned towards him with sudden distrust. He had not previously uttered a word.

"Come!" said Mr. Cruncher. "Speak out, you know." (Which, by the way, was more than he could do himself.) "John Solomon, or Solomon John? She calls you Solomon, and she must know, being your sister. And *I* know you're John, you know. Which of the two goes first? And regarding that name of Pross, likewise. That warn't your name over the water."

"What do you mean?"

"Well, I don't know all I mean, for I can't call to mind what your name was, over the water."

"No?"

"No. But I'll swear it was a name of two syllables."

"Indeed?"

"Yes. T'other one's was one syllable. I know you. You was a spy-witness at the Bailey. What, in the name of the Father of Lies, own father to yourself, was you called at that time?"

"Barsad," said another voice, striking in.

"That's the name for a thousand pound!" cried Jerry.

The speaker who struck in was Sydney Carton. He had his hands behind him under the skirts of his riding-coat, and he stood at Mr. Cruncher's elbow as negligently as he might have stood at the Old Bailey itself.

"Don't be alarmed, my dear Miss Pross. I arrived at Mr. Lorry's, to his surprise, yesterday evening ; we agreed that I would not present myself elsewhere until all was well, or unless I could be useful ; I present myself here to beg a little talk with your brother. I wish you had a better employed brother than Mr. Barsad. I wish, for your sake, Mr. Barsad was not a Sheep of the Prisons."

Sheep was a cant word of the time for a spy, under the jailers. The spy, who was pale, turned paler, and asked him how he dared——

"I'll tell you," said Sydney. "I lighted on you, Mr. Barsad, coming out of the prison of the Conciergerie while I was contemplating the walls, an hour or more ago. You have a face to be remembered, and I remember faces well. Made curious by seeing you in that connection, and having a reason, to which you are no stranger, for associating you with the misfortunes of a friend now very unfortunate, I walked in your direction. I walked into the wine-shop here, close after you, and sat near you. I had no difficulty in deducing from your unreserved conversation, and the rumour openly going about among your admirers, the nature of your calling. And gradually what I had done at random seemed to shape itself into a purpose, Mr. Barsad."

"What purpose ? " the spy asked.

"It would be troublesome, and might be dangerous, to explain in the street. Could you favour me, in confidence, with some minutes of your company—at the office of Tellson's Bank, for instance ? "

"Under a threat ? "

"Oh ! Did I say that ? "

"Then, why should I go there ? "

"Really, Mr. Barsad, I can't say, if you can't."

"Do you mean that you won't say, sir ? " the spy irresolutely asked.

"You apprehend me very clearly, Mr. Barsad. I won't."

Carton's negligent recklessness of manner came powerfully in aid of his quickness and skill in such a business as he had in his secret mind, and with such a man as he had to do with. His practised eye saw it, and made the most of it.

"Now, I told you so," said the spy, casting a reproachful look at his sister ; "if any trouble comes of this, it's your doing."

"Come, come, Mr. Barsad ! " exclaimed Sydney. "Don't be ungrateful. But for my great respect for your sister, I might not have led up so pleasantly to a little proposal that I wish to make for our mutual satisfaction. Do you go with me to the Bank ? "

"I'll hear what you have got to say. Yes, I'll go with you."

"I propose that we first conduct your sister safely to the corner of her own street. Let me take your arm, Miss Pross. This is not a good city, at this time, for you to be out in, unprotected ; and as your escort knows Mr. Barsad, I will invite him to Mr. Lorry's with us. Are we ready ? Come then ! "

Miss Pross recalled soon afterwards, and to the end of her life remembered, that as she pressed her hands on Sydney's arm and looked up in his face, imploring him to do no hurt to Solomon, there was a braced purpose in the arm and a kind of inspiration in the eyes which not only contradicted his light manner, but changed and raised the man. She was too much occupied then with fears for the brother who so little deserved her affection, and with Sydney's friendly reassurances, adequately to heed what she observed.

They left her at the corner of the street, and Carton led the way to Mr. Lorry's, which was within a few minutes' walk. John Barsad, or Solomon Pross, walked at his side.

Mr. Lorry had just finished his dinner, and was sitting before a cheery little log or two of fire—perhaps looking into their blaze for the picture of that younger elderly gentleman from Tellson's, who had looked into the red coals at the Royal George at Dover, now a good many years ago. He turned his head as they entered, and showed the surprise with which he saw a stranger.

" Miss Pross's brother, sir," said Sydney. " Mr. Barsad."

" Barsad?" repeated the old gentleman, " Barsad? I have an association with the name—and with the face."

" I told you you had a remarkable face, Mr. Barsad," observed Carton, coolly. " Pray sit down."

As he took a chair himself, he supplied the link that Mr. Lorry wanted, by saying to him with a frown, " Witness at that trial." Mr. Lorry immediately remembered, and regarded his new visitor with an undisguised look of abhorrence.

" Mr. Barsad has been recognised by Miss Pross as the affectionate brother you have heard of," said Sydney, " and has acknowledged the relationship. I pass to worse news. Darnay has been arrested again."

Struck with consternation, the old gentleman exclaimed, " What do you tell me? I left him safe and free within these two hours, and am about to return to him !"

" Arrested for all that. When was it done, Mr. Barsad?"

" Just now, if at all."

" Mr. Barsad is the best authority possible, sir," said Sydney, " and I have it from Mr. Barsad's communication to a friend and brother Sheep over a bottle of wine, that the arrest has taken place. He left the messengers at the gate, and saw them admitted by the porter. There is no earthly doubt that he is retaken."

Mr. Lorry's business eye read in the speaker's face that it was loss of time to dwell upon the point. Confused, but sensible that something might depend on his presence of mind, he commanded himself, and was silently attentive.

" Now, I trust," said Sydney to him, " that the name and influence of Doctor Manette may stand him in as good stead to-morrow—you said he would be before the Tribunal again to-morrow, Mr. Barsad?——"

" Yes ; I believe so."

"—In as good stead to-morrow as to-day. But it may not be so. I own to you, I am shaken, Mr. Lorry, by Doctor Manette's not having had the power to prevent this arrest."

" He may not have known of it beforehand," said Mr. Lorry.

"But that very circumstance would be alarming, when we remember how identified he is with his son-in-law."

"That's true," Mr. Lorry acknowledged, with his troubled hand at his chin, and his troubled eyes on Carton.

"In short," said Sydney, "this is a desperate time, when desperate games are played for desperate stakes. Let the Doctor play the winning game; I will play the losing one. No man's life here is worth purchase. Any one carried home by the people to-day may be condemned to-morrow. Now, the stake I have resolved to play for, in case of the worst, is a friend in the Conciergerie. And the friend I purpose to myself to win is Mr. Barsad."

"You need have good cards, Sir," said the spy.

"I'll run them over. I'll see what I hold,—Mr. Lorry, you know what a brute I am; I wish you'd give me a little brandy."

It was put before him, and he drank off a glassful—drank off another glassful—pushed the bottle thoughtfully away.

"Mr. Barsad," he went on, in the tone of one who really was looking over a hand at cards: "Sheep of the Prisons, emissary of Republican committees, now turnkey, now prisoner, always spy and secret informer, so much the more valuable here for being English, that an Englishman is less open to suspicion of subornation in those characters than a Frenchman, represents himself to his employers under a false name. That's a very good card. Mr. Barsad, now in the employ of the Republican French government, was formerly in the employ of the aristocratic English government, the enemy of France and freedom. That's an excellent card. Inference clear as day, in this region of suspicion, that Mr. Barsad, still in the pay of the aristocratic English government, is the spy of Pitt, the treacherous foe of the Republic crouching in its bosom, the English traitor and agent of all mischief so much spoken of and so difficult to find. That's a card not to be beaten. Have you followed my hand, Mr. Barsad?"

"Not to understand your play," returned the spy, somewhat uneasily.

"I play my Ace, Denunciation of Mr. Barsad to the nearest Section Committee. Look over your hand, Mr. Barsad, and see what you have. Don't hurry."

He drew the bottle near, poured out another glassful of brandy, and drank it off. He saw that the spy was fearful of his drinking himself into a fit state for the immediate denunciation of him. Seeing it, he poured out and drank another glassful.

"Look over your hand carefully, Mr. Barsad. Take time."

It was a poorer hand than he suspected. Mr. Barsad saw losing cards in it that Sydney Carton knew nothing of. Thrown out of his honourable employment in England, through too much unsuccessful hard swearing there—not because he was not wanted there; our English reasons for vaunting our superiority to secrecy and spies are of very modern date—he knew that he had crossed the Channel and accepted service in France: first, as a tempter and an eavesdropper

among his own countrymen there; gradually, as a tempter and an
eavesdropper among the natives. He knew that under the overthrown
government he had been a spy upon Saint Antoine and Defarge's wine-
shop; had received from the watchful police such heads of information
concerning Doctor Manette's imprisonment, release, and history as
should serve him for an introduction to familiar conversation with the
Defarges; and tried them on Madame Defarge, and had broken down
with them signally. He always remembered with fear and trembling
that that terrible woman had knitted when he talked with her, and
had looked ominously at him as her fingers moved. He had since
seen her, in the Section of Saint Antoine, over and over again produce
her knitted registers, and denounce people whose lives the guillotine
then surely swallowed up. He knew, as every one employed as he
was did, that he was never safe; that flight was impossible; that he
was tied fast under the shadow of the axe; and that in spite of his
utmost tergiversation and treachery in furtherance of the reigning
terror, a word might bring it down upon him. Once denounced, and
on such grave grounds as had just now been suggested to his mind,
he foresaw that the dreadful woman, of whose unrelenting character
he had seen many proofs, would produce against him that fatal register,
and would quash his last chance of life. Besides that all secret men
are men soon terrified, here were surely cards enough of one black
suit to justify the holder in growing rather livid as he turned them
over.

"You scarcely seem to like your hand," said Sydney, with the
greatest composure. "Do you play?"

"I think, Sir," said the spy, in the meanest manner, as he turned
to Mr. Lorry, "I may appeal to a gentleman of your years and
benevolence, to put it to this other gentleman, so much your junior,
whether he can, under any circumstances, reconcile it to his station to
play that Ace of which he has spoken. I admit that *I* am a spy, and
that it is considered a discreditable station—though it must be filled by
somebody; but this gentleman is no spy, and why should he so demean
himself as to make himself one?"

"I play my Ace, Mr. Barsad," said Carton, taking the answer on
himself, and looking at his watch, "without any scruple, in a very few
minutes."

"I should have hoped, gentlemen both," said the spy, always
striving to hook Mr. Lorry into the discussion, "that your respect for
my sister——"

"I could not better testify my respect for your sister than by finally
relieving her of her brother," said Sydney Carton.

"You think not, Sir?"

"I have thoroughly made up my mind about it."

The smooth manner of the spy, curiously in dissonance with his
ostentatiously rough dress, and probably with his usual demeanour,
received such a check from the inscrutability of Carton—who was a
mystery to wiser and honester men than he—that it faltered here and

failed him.   While he was at a loss, Carton said, resuming his former
air of contemplating cards—

"And indeed, now I think again, I have a strong impression that
I have another good card here, not yet enumerated.   That friend and
fellow-Sheep, who spoke of himself as pasturing in the country prisons ;
who was he ? "

"French.   You don't know him," said the spy, quickly.

"French, eh ? " repeated Carton, musing, and not appearing to
notice him at all, though he echoed his word.   " Well ; he may be."

" Is, I assure you," said the spy ;   "though it's not important."

"Though it's not important," repeated Carton, in the same
mechanical way—"though it's not important.—No, it's not important.
No.   Yet I know the face."

"I think not.   I am sure not.   It can't be," said the spy.

"It—can't—be," muttered Sydney Carton, retrospectively, and
filling his glass (which fortunately was a small one) again.   "Can't—
be.   Spoke good French.   Yet like a foreigner, I thought ? "

"Provincial," said the spy.

"No.   Foreign ! " cried Carton, striking his open hand on the
table, as a light broke clearly on his mind.   "Cly ! Disguised, but
the same man.   We had that man before us at the Old Bailey."

"Now, there you are hasty, Sir," said Barsad, with a smile that
gave his aquiline nose an extra inclination to one side ; "there you
really give me an advantage over you.   Cly (who I will unreservedly
admit, at this distance of time, was a partner of mine) has been dead
several years.   I attended him in his last illness.   He was buried in
London, at the church of Saint Pancras-in-the-Fields.   His un-
popularity with the blackguard multitude at the moment prevented
my following his remains, but I helped to lay him in his coffin."

Here Mr. Lorry became aware, from where he sat, of a most remarkable goblin shadow on the wall.   Tracing it to its source, he
discovered it to be caused by a sudden extraordinary rising and stiffen-
ing of all the risen and stiff hair on Mr. Cruncher's head.

"Let us be reasonable," said the spy, "and let us be fair.   To show
you how mistaken you are, and what an unfounded assumption yours
is, I will lay before you a certificate of Cly's burial, which I happen to
have carried in my pocket-book,"—with a hurried hand he produced and
opened it—"ever since.   There it is.   Oh, look at it, look at it !   You
may take it in your hand ; it's no forgery."

Here Mr. Lorry perceived the reflection on the wall to elongate, and
Mr. Cruncher rose and stepped forward.   His hair could not have been
more violently on end if it had been that moment dressed by the Cow
with the crumpled horn in the house that Jack built.

Unseen by the spy, Mr. Cruncher stood at his side, and touched him
on the shoulder like a ghostly bailiff.

"That there Roger Cly, master," said Mr. Cruncher, with a taciturn
and iron-bound visage.   "So *you* put him in his coffin ? "

"I did."

"Who took him out of it?"

Barsad leaned back in his chair and stammered, "What do you mean?"

"I mean," said Mr. Cruncher, "that he warn't never in it. No! Not he! I'll have my head took off if he was ever in it."

The spy looked round at the two gentlemen; they both looked in unspeakable astonishment at Jerry.

"I tell you," said Jerry, "that you buried paving-stones and earth in that there coffin. Don't go and tell *me* that you buried Cly. It was a take in. Me and two more knows it."

"How do you know it?"

"What's that to you? Ecod!" growled Mr. Cruncher, "it's you I have got a old grudge agin, is it, with your shameful impositions upon tradesmen! I'd catch hold of your throat and choke you for half a guinea."

Sydney Carton, who, with Mr. Lorry, had been lost in amazement at this turn of the business, here requested Mr. Cruncher to moderate and explain himself.

"At another time, Sir," he returned, evasively; "the present time is ill-conwenient for explainin'. What I stand to is, that he knows well wot that there Cly was never in that there coffin. Let him say he was, in so much as a word of one syllable, and I'll either catch hold of his throat and choke him for half a guinea,"—Mr. Cruncher dwelt upon this as quite a liberal offer—"or I'll out and announce him."

"Humph! I see one thing," said Carton. "I hold another card, Mr. Barsad. Impossible, here in raging Paris, with Suspicion filling the air, for you to outlive denunciation, when you are in communication with another aristocratic spy of the same antecedents as yourself, who, moreover, has the mystery about him of having feigned death and come to life again! A plot in the prisons, of the foreigner against the Republic. A strong card—a certain Guillotine card! Do you play?"

"No!" returned the spy. "I throw up. I confess that we were so unpopular with the outrageous mob, that I only got away from England at the risk of being ducked to death, and that Cly was so ferreted up and down, that he never would have got away at all but for that sham. Though how this man knows it was a sham is a wonder of wonders to me."

"Never you trouble your head about this man," retorted the contentious Mr. Cruncher; "you'll have trouble enough with giving your attention to that gentleman. And look here! Once more!"—Mr. Cruncher could not be restrained from making rather an ostentatious parade of his liberality—"I'd catch hold of your throat and choke you for half a guinea."

The Sheep of the Prisons turned from him to Sydney Carton and said, with more decision, "It has come to a point. I go on duty soon, and can't overstay my time. You told me you had a proposal; what is it? Now, it is of no use asking too much of me. Ask me to do anything in my office, putting my head in great extra danger, and I had better trust my life to the chances of a refusal than the chances of consent. In short, I should make that choice. You talk of desperation. We are all desperate here. Remember! I may denounce you if I think proper, and I can swear my way through stone walls, and so can others. Now, what do you want with me?"

"Not very much. You are a turnkey at the Conciergerie?"

"I tell you once for all there is no such thing as an escape possible," said the spy, firmly.

"Why need you tell me what I have not asked? You are a turnkey at the Conciergerie?"

"I am sometimes."

"You can be when you choose?"

"I can pass in and out when I choose."

Sydney Carton filled another glass with brandy, poured it slowly out upon the hearth, and watched it as it dropped. It being all spent, he said, rising—

"So far, we have spoken before these two, because it was as well that the merits of the cards should not rest solely between you and me. Come into the dark room here, and let us have one final word alone."

CHAPTER IX

THE GAME MADE

WHILE Sydney Carton and the Sheep of the Prisons were in the adjoining dark room, speaking so low that not a sound was heard, Mr. Lorry looked at Jerry in considerable doubt and mistrust. That honest tradesman's manner of receiving the look did not inspire confidence; he changed the leg on which he rested, as often as if he had fifty of those limbs, and were trying them all; he examined his finger-nails with a very questionable closeness of attention; and whenever Mr. Lorry's eye caught his, he was taken with that peculiar kind of short cough requiring the hollow of a hand before it, which is seldom, if ever, known to be an infirmity attendant on perfect openness of character.

"Jerry," said Mr. Lorry. "Come here."

Mr. Cruncher came forward sideways, with one of his shoulders in advance of him.

"What have you been, besides a messenger?"

After some cogitation, accompanied with an intent look at his patron, Mr. Cruncher conceived the luminous idea of replying, "Agricultooral character."

"My mind misgives me much," said Mr. Lorry, angrily shaking a forefinger at him, "that you have used the respectable and great house of Tellson's as a blind, and that you have had an unlawful occupation of an infamous description. If you have, don't expect me to befriend you when you get back to England. If you have, don't expect me to keep your secret. Tellson's shall not be imposed upon."

"I hope, Sir," pleaded the abashed Mr. Cruncher, "that a gentleman like yourself wot I've had the honour of odd jobbing till I'm gray at it, would think twice about harming of me, even if it wos so—I don't say it is, but even if it wos. And which it is to be took into account that if it wos, it wouldn't, even then, be all o' one side. There'd be two sides to it. There might be medical doctors at the present hour, a-picking up their guineas where a honest tradesman don't pick up his fardens—fardens! no, nor yet his half fardens—half fardens! no, nor yet his quarter—a-banking away like smoke at Tellson's, and a-cocking their medical eyes at that tradesman on the sly, a-going in and going out to their own carriages—ah! equally like smoke, if not more so. Well, that 'ud be imposing, too, on Tellson's. For you cannot sarse the goose and not the gander. And here's Mrs. Cruncher, or leastways wos in the Old England times, and would be to-morrow, if cause given, a-floppin' agin the business to that degree as is ruinating—stark ruinating! Whereas them medical doctors' wives don't flop—catch 'em at it! Or, if they flop, their floppings goes in favour of more patients, and how can you rightly have one without the t'other? Then, wot with undertakers, and wot with parish clerks, and wot with sextons, and wot with private watchmen (all awaricious and all in it), a man wouldn't get much by it, even if it wos so. And wot little a man did get would never prosper with him, Mr. Lorry. He'd never have no good of it; he'd want all along to be out of the line, if he could see his way out, being once in—even if it wos so."

"Ugh!" cried Mr. Lorry, rather relenting, nevertheless. "I am shocked at the sight of you."

"Now, what I would humbly offer to you, Sir," pursued Mr. Cruncher, "even if it wos so, which I don't say it is——"

"Don't prevaricate," said Mr. Lorry.

"No, I will *not*, Sir," returned Mr. Cruncher, as if nothing were further from his thoughts or practice—"which I don't say it is—wot I would humbly offer to you, Sir, would be this. Upon that there stool, at that there Bar, sets that there boy of mine, brought up and growed up to be a man, wot will errand you, message you, general-light-job you, till your heels is where your head is, if such should be your wishes. If it wos so, which I still don't say it is (for I will not prewaricate to you, Sir), let that there boy keep his father's place, and take care of his mother; don't blow upon that boy's father—do not do it, Sir—and let that father go into the line of the reg'lar diggin', and make amends for what he would have un-dug—if it wos so—by diggin' of 'em in with a will, and with conwictions respectin' the futur' keepin' of 'em safe. That, Mr. Lorry," said Mr. Cruncher, wiping his forehead with his arm, as an announcement that he had arrived at the peroration of his discourse, "is wot I would respectfully offer to you, Sir. A man don't see all this here a-goin' on dreadful round him, in the way of Subjects without heads, dear me, plentiful enough fur to bring the price down to porterage and hardly that, without havin' his serious thoughts of things. And these here would be mine, if it wos so, entreatin' of you fur to bear in mind that wot I said just now, I up and said in the good cause when I might have kep' it back."

"That at least is true," said Mr. Lorry. "Say no more now. It may be that I shall yet stand your friend, if you deserve it, and repent in action—not in words. I want no more words."

Mr. Cruncher knuckled his forehead, as Sydney Carton and the spy returned from the dark room. "Adieu, Mr. Barsad," said the former; "our arrangement thus made, you have nothing to fear from me."

He sat down in a chair on the hearth, over against Mr. Lorry. When they were alone, Mr. Lorry asked him what he had done.

"Not much. If it should go ill with the prisoner, I have ensured access to him, once."

Mr. Lorry's countenance fell.

"It is all I could do," said Carton. "To propose too much would be to put this man's head under the axe, and, as he himself said, nothing worse could happen to him if he were denounced. It was obviously the weakness of the position. There is no help for it."

"But access to him," said Mr. Lorry, "if it should go ill before the Tribunal, will not save him."

"I never said it would."

Mr. Lorry's eyes gradually sought the fire; his sympathy with his darling, and the heavy disappointment of this second arrest, gradually weakened them; he was an old man now, overborne with anxiety of late, and his tears fell.

"You are a good man and a true friend," said Carton, in an altered voice. "Forgive me if I notice that you are affected. I could not see my father weep, and sit by, careless. And I could not respect your sorrow more if you were my father. You are free from that misfortune, however."

Though he said the last words with a slip into his usual manner, there was a true feeling and respect both in his tone and in his touch, that Mr. Lorry, who had never seen the better side of him, was wholly unprepared for. He gave him his hand, and Carton gently pressed it.

"To return to poor Darnay," said Carton. "Don't tell Her of this interview, or this arrangement. It would not enable Her to go to see him. She might think it was contrived, in case of the worst, to convey to him the means of anticipating the sentence."

Mr. Lorry had not thought of that, and looked quickly at Carton to see if it were in his mind. It seemed to be; he returned the look, and evidently understood it.

"She might think a thousand things," Carton said, "and any of them would only add to her trouble. Don't speak of me to her. As I said to you when I first came, I had better not see her. I can put my hand out, to do any little helpful work for her that my hand can find to do, without that. You are going to her, I hope? She must be very desolate to-night."

"I am going now, directly."

"I am glad of that. She has such a strong attachment to you and reliance on you. How does she look?"

"Anxious and unhappy, but very beautiful."

"Ah!"

It was a long, grieving sound, like a sigh—almost like a sob. It attracted Mr. Lorry's eyes to Carton's face, which was turned to the fire. A light, or a shade (the old gentleman could not have said which), passed from it as swiftly as a change will sweep over a hillside on a wild bright day, and he lifted his foot to put back one of the little flaming logs, which was tumbling forward. He wore the white riding-coat and top-boots then in vogue, and the light of the fire touching their light surfaces made him look very pale, with his long brown hair, all untrimmed, hanging loose about him. His indifference to fire was sufficiently remarkable to elicit a word of remonstrance from Mr. Lorry; his boot was still upon the hot embers of the flaming log when it had broken under the weight of his foot.

"I forgot it," he said.

Mr. Lorry's eyes were again attracted to his face. Taking note of the wasted air which clouded the naturally handsome features, and having the expression of prisoners' faces fresh in his mind, he was strongly reminded of that expression.

"And your duties here have drawn to an end, Sir?" said Carton, turning to him.

"Yes. As I was telling you last night when Lucie came in so unexpectedly, I have at length done all that I can do here. I hoped to have left them in perfect safety, and then to have quitted Paris. I have my Leave to Pass. I was ready to go."

They were both silent.

"Yours is a long life to look back upon, Sir?" said Carton, wistfully.

"I am in my seventy-eighth year."

"You have been useful all your life; steadily and constantly occupied; trusted, respected, and looked up to?"

"I have been a man of business ever since I have been a man. Indeed, I may say that I was a man of business when a boy."

"See what a place you fill at seventy-eight. How many people will miss you when you leave it empty!"

"A solitary old bachelor," answered Mr. Lorry, shaking his head. "There is nobody to weep for me."

"How can you say that? Wouldn't She weep for you? Wouldn't her child?"

"Yes, yes, thank God. I didn't quite mean what I said."

"It *is* a thing to thank God for; is it not?"

"Surely, surely."

"If you could say, with truth, to your own solitary heart, to-night, 'I have secured to myself the love and attachment, the gratitude or respect, of no human creature; I have won myself a tender place in no

regard; I have done nothing good or serviceable to be remembered by !'
your seventy-eight years would be seventy-eight heavy curses ; would
they not ? "

" You say truly, Mr. Carton ; I think they would be."

Sydney turned his eyes again upon the fire, and, after a silence of a
few moments, said—

" I should like to ask you—Does your childhood seem far off ? Do
the days when you sat at your mother's knee seem days of very long
ago ? "

Responding to his softened manner, Mr. Lorry answered—

" Twenty years back, yes ; at this time of my life, no. For, as I
draw closer and closer to the end, I travel in the circle, nearer and
nearer to the beginning. It seems to be one of the kind smoothings
and preparings of the way. My heart is touched now by many
remembrances, that had long fallen asleep, of my pretty young mother
(and I so old !), and by many associations of the days when what we
call the World was not so real with me, and my faults were not
confirmed in me."

" I understand the feeling ! " exclaimed Carton, with a bright flush.
" And you are the better for it ? "

" I hope so."

Carton terminated the conversation here, by rising to help him on
with his outer coat. " But you," said Mr. Lorry, reverting to the theme,
" you are young."

" Yes," said Carton. " I am not old, but my young way was never
the way to age. Enough of me."

" And of me, I am sure," said Mr. Lorry. " Are you going out ? "

" I'll walk with you to her gate. You know my vagabond and
restless habits. If I should prowl about the streets a long time, don't
be uneasy ; I shall reappear in the morning. You go to the court
to-morrow ? "

" Yes, unhappily."

" I shall be there, but only as one of the crowd. My Spy will find a
place for me. Take my arm, Sir."

Mr. Lorry did so, and they went down-stairs and out in the streets.
A few minutes brought them to Mr. Lorry's destination. Carton left
him there ; but lingered at a little distance, and turned back to the gate
again when it was shut, and touched it. He had heard of her going to
the prison every day. " She came out here," he said, looking about
him, " turned this way, must have trod on these stones often. Let me
follow in her steps."

It was ten o'clock at night when he stood before the prison of La
Force, where she had stood hundreds of times. A little wood-sawyer,
having closed his shop, was smoking his pipe at his shop-door.

" Good-night, citizen," said Sydney Carton, pausing in going by ;
for the man eyed him inquisitively.

" Good-night, citizen."

" How goes the Republic ? "

"You mean the Guillotine. Not ill. Sixty-three to-day. We shall mount to a hundred soon. Samson and his men complain sometimes of being exhausted. Ha, ha, ha! He is so droll, that Samson. Such a Barber!"

"Do you often go to see him——"

"Shave? Always. Every day. What a barber! You have seen him at work?"

"Never."

"Go and see him when he has a good batch. Figure this to yourself, citizen; he shaved the sixty-three to-day in less than two pipes! Less than two pipes. Word of honour!"

As the grinning little man held out the pipe he was smoking, to explain how he timed the executioner, Carton was so sensible of a rising desire to strike the life out of him, that he turned away.

"But you are not English," said the wood-sawyer, "though you wear English dress?"

"Yes," said Carton, pausing again, and answering over his shoulder.

"You speak like a Frenchman."

"I am an old student here."

"Aha, a perfect Frenchman! Good-night, Englishman."

"Good-night, citizen."

"But go and see that droll dog," the little man persisted, calling after him. "And take a pipe with you!"

Sydney had not gone far out of sight when he stopped in the middle of the street under a glimmering lamp, and wrote with his pencil on a scrap of paper. Then traversing with the decided step of one who remembered the way well several dark and dirty streets—much dirtier than usual, for the best public thoroughfares remained uncleansed in those times of terror—he stopped at a chemist's shop, which the owner was closing with his own hands. A small, dim, crooked shop, kept in a tortuous, uphill thoroughfare, by a small, dim, crooked man.

Giving this citizen, too, good-night, as he confronted him at his counter, he laid the scrap of paper before him. "Whew!" the chemist whistled softly, as he read it. "Hi! hi! hi!"

Sydney Carton took no heed, and the chemist said—

"For you, citizen?"

"For me."

"You will be careful to keep them separate, citizen? You know the consequences of mixing them?"

"Perfectly."

Certain small packets were made and given to him. He put them, one by one, in the breast of his inner coat, counted out the money for them, and deliberately left the shop. "There is nothing more to do," said he, glancing upward at the moon, "until to-morrow. I can't sleep."

It was not a reckless manner, the manner in which he said these words aloud under the fast-sailing clouds, nor was it more expressive of negligence than defiance. It was the settled manner of a tired man, who had wandered and struggled and got lost, but who at length struck into his road and saw its end.

Long ago, when he had been famous among his earliest competitors as a youth of great promise, he had followed his father to the grave. His mother had died years before. These solemn words, which had been read at his father's grave, arose in his mind as he went down the dark streets, among the heavy shadows, with the moon and the clouds sailing on high above him. "I am the resurrection and the life, saith the Lord : he that believeth in me, though he were dead, yet shall he live : and whosoever liveth and believeth in me, shall never die."

In a city dominated by the axe, alone at night, with natural sorrow rising in him for the sixty-three who had been that day put to death, and for to-morrow's victims then awaiting their doom in the prisons, and still of to-morrow's and to-morrow's, the chain of association that brought the words home, like a rusty old ship's anchor from the deep, might have been easily found. He did not seek it, but repeated them and went on.

With a solemn interest in the lighted windows where the people were going to rest, forgetful through a few calm hours of the horrors surrounding them ; in the towers of the churches, where no prayers were said, for the popular revulsion had even travelled that length of self-destruction from years of priestly impostors, plunderers, and profligates ; in the distant burial-places, reserved, as they wrote upon the gates, for Eternal Sleep ; in the abounding jails ; and in the streets along which the sixties rolled to a death which had become so common and material, that no sorrowful story of a haunting Spirit ever arose among the people out of all the working of the Guillotine ; with a solemn interest in the whole life and death of the city settling down to its short nightly pause in fury, Sydney Carton crossed the Seine again for the lighter streets.

Few coaches were abroad, for riders in coaches were liable to be suspected, and gentility hid its head in red nightcaps, and put on heavy shoes, and trudged. But the theatres were all well filled, and the people poured cheerfully out as he passed, and went chatting home. At one of the theatre-doors there was a little girl with her mother, looking for a way across the street through the mud. He carried the child over, and before the timid arm was loosed from his neck asked her for a kiss.

"I am the resurrection and the life, saith the Lord : he that believeth in me, though he were dead, yet shall he live : and whosoever liveth and believeth in me, shall never die."

Now that the streets were quiet and the night wore on, the words were in the echoes of his feet, and were in the air. Perfectly calm and steady, he sometimes repeated them to himself as he walked ; but he heard them always.

The night wore out, and as he stood upon the bridge listening to the water as it splashed the river-walls of the Island of Paris, where the picturesque confusion of houses and cathedral shone bright in the light of the moon, the day came coldly, looking like a dead face out of the sky. Then the night, with the moon and the stars, turned pale and died, and for a little while it seemed as if Creation were delivered over to Death's dominion.

But the glorious sun, rising, seemed to strike those words, that burden of the night, straight and warm to his heart in its long bright rays. And looking along them, with reverently shaded eyes, a bridge of light appeared to span the air between him and the sun, while the river sparkled under it.

The strong tide, so swift, so deep, and certain, was like a congenial friend in the morning stillness. He walked by the stream, far from the houses, and in the light and warmth of the sun fell asleep on the bank. When he awoke and was afoot again, he lingered there yet a little longer, watching an eddy that turned and turned purposeless, until the stream absorbed it, and carried it on to the sea—"Like me !"

A trading-boat, with a sail of the softened colour of a dead leaf, then glided into his view, floated by him, and died away. As its silent track in the water disappeared, the prayer that had broken up out of his heart for a merciful consideration of all his poor blindnesses and errors, ended in the words, "I am the resurrection and the life."

Mr. Lorry was already out when he got back, and it was easy to surmise where the good old man was gone. Sydney Carton drank nothing but a little coffee, ate some bread, and having washed and changed to refresh himself, went out to the place of trial.

The court was all astir and a-buzz, when the black sheep—whom many fell away from in dread—pressed him into an obscure corner among the crowd. Mr. Lorry was there, and Doctor Manette was there. She was there, sitting beside her father.

When her husband was brought in, she turned a look upon him, so sustaining, so encouraging, so full of admiring love and pitying tenderness, yet so courageous for his sake, that it called the healthy blood into his face, brightened his glance, and animated his heart. If there had been any eyes to notice the influence of her look, on Sydney Carton it would have been seen to be the same influence exactly.

Before that unjust Tribunal there was little or no order of procedure, ensuring to any accused person any reasonable hearing. There could have been no such Revolution, if all laws, forms, and ceremonies had not first been so monstrously abused, that the suicidal vengeance of the Revolution was to scatter them all to the winds.

Every eye was turned to the Jury. The same determined patriots and good republicans as yesterday and the day before, and to-morrow and the day after. Eager and prominent among them one man with a craving face, and his fingers perpetually hovering about his lips, whose appearance gave great satisfaction to the spectators. A life-thirsting, cannibal-looking, bloody-minded juryman, the Jacques Three of Saint Antoine. The whole Jury, as a jury of dogs impanelled to try the deer.

Every eye then turned to the five Judges and the Public Prosecutor. No favourable leaning in that quarter to-day. A fell, uncompromising, murderous business-meaning there. Every eye then sought some other eye in the crowd, and gleamed at it approvingly ; and heads nodded at one another, before bending forward with a strained attention.

Charles Evremond, called Darnay. Released yesterday. Re-accused and retaken yesterday. Indictment delivered to him last night. Suspected and Denounced enemy of the Republic, Aristocrat, one of a family of tyrants, one of a race proscribed, for that they had used their abolished privileges to the infamous oppression of the people. Charles Evremond, called Darnay, in right of such proscription, absolutely Dead in Law.

To this effect, in as few or fewer words, the Public Prosecutor.

The President asked, was the Accused openly denounced or secretly ?

" Openly, President."

" By whom ? "

" Three voices. Ernest Defarge, wine-vendor of Saint Antoine."

" Good."

" Thérèse Defarge, his wife."

" Good."

" Alexandre Manette, physician."

A great uproar took place in the court, and in the midst of it Doctor Manette was seen, pale and trembling, standing where he had been seated.

" President, I indignantly protest to you that this is a forgery and a fraud. You know the accused to be the husband of my daughter. My daughter and those dear to her are far dearer to me than my life. Who and where is the false conspirator who says that I denounce the husband of my child ? "

" Citizen Manette, be tranquil. To fail in submission to the authority of the Tribunal would be to put yourself out of Law. As to what is dearer to you than life, nothing can be so dear to a good citizen as the Republic."

Loud acclamations hailed this rebuke. The President rang his bell, and with warmth, resumed—

" If the Republic should demand of you the sacrifice of your child herself, you would have no duty but to sacrifice her. Listen to what is to follow. In the meanwhile, be silent ! "

Frantic acclamations were again raised. Doctor Manette sat down, with his eyes looking around and his lips trembling ; his daughter drew closer to him. The craving man on the Jury rubbed his hands together, and restored the usual hand to his mouth.

Defarge was produced when the court was quiet enough to admit of his being heard, and rapidly expounded the story of the imprisonment, and of his having been a mere boy in the Doctor's service, and of the release, and of the state of the prisoner when released and delivered to him. This short examination followed, for the court was quick with its work :—

"You did good service at the taking of the Bastille, citizen?"

"I believe so."

Here an excited woman screeched from the crowd: "You were one of the best patriots there. Why not say so? You were a cannonier that day there, and you were among the first to enter the accursed fortress when it fell. Patriots, I speak the truth!"

It was The Vengeance who, amidst the warm commendations of the audience, thus assisted the proceedings. The President rang his bell; but The Vengeance, warming with encouragement, shrieked, "I defy that bell!" wherein she was likewise much commended.

"Inform the Tribunal of what you did that day within the Bastille, citizen."

"I knew," said Defarge, looking down at his wife, who stood at the bottom of the steps on which he was raised, looking steadily up at him; "I knew that this prisoner, of whom I speak, had been confined in a cell known as One Hundred and Five, North Tower. I knew it from himself. He knew himself by no other name than One Hundred and Five, North Tower, when he made shoes under my care. As I serve my gun that day, I resolve, when the place shall fall, to examine that cell. It falls. I mount to the cell, with a fellow-citizen who is one of the Jury, directed by a jailer. I examine it very closely. In a hole in the chimney, where a stone has been worked out and replaced, I find a written paper. This is that written paper. I have made it my business to examine some specimens of the writing of Doctor Manette. This is the writing of Doctor Manette. I confide this paper, in the writing of Doctor Manette, to the hands of the President."

"Let it be read."

In a dead silence and stillness — the prisoner under trial looking lovingly at his wife, his wife only looking from him to look with solicitude at her father, Doctor Manette keeping his eyes fixed on the reader, Madame Defarge never taking hers from the prisoner, Defarge never taking his from his feasting wife, and all the other eyes there intent upon the Doctor, who saw none of them—the paper was read, as follows :—

CHAPTER X

THE SUBSTANCE OF THE SHADOW

"I, ALEXANDRE MANETTE, unfortunate physician, native of Beauvais, and afterwards resident in Paris, write this melancholy paper in my doleful cell in the Bastille, during the last month of the year 1767. I write it at stolen intervals, under every difficulty. I design to secrete it in the wall of the chimney, where I have slowly and laboriously made a place of concealment for it. Some pitying hand may find it there, when I and my sorrows are dust.

"These words are formed by the rusty iron point with which I write with difficulty in scrapings of soot and charcoal from the chimney, mixed with blood, in the last month of the tenth year of my captivity. Hope has quite departed from my breast. I know from terrible warnings I have noted in myself that my reason will not long remain unimpaired, but I solemnly declare that I am at this time in the possession of my right mind—that my memory is exact and circumstantial—and that I write the truth as I shall answer for these my last recorded words, whether they be ever read by men or not, at the Eternal Judgment-seat.

"One cloudy moonlight night, in the third week of December (I think the twenty-second of the month) in the year 1757, I was walking on a retired part of the quay by the Seine for the refreshment of the frosty air, at an hour's distance from my place of residence in the Street of the School of Medicine, when a carriage came along behind me, driven very fast. As I stood aside to let that carriage pass, apprehensive that it might otherwise run me down, a head was put out at the window, and a voice called to the driver to stop.

"The carriage stopped as soon as the driver could rein in his horses, and the same voice called to me by my name. I answered. The carriage was then so far in advance of me that two gentlemen had time to open the door and alight before I came up with it. I observed that they were both wrapped in cloaks, and appeared to conceal themselves. As they stood side by side near the carriage-door, I also observed that they both looked of about my own age, or rather younger, and that they were greatly alike in stature, manner, voice, and (as far as I could see) face too.

"'You are Doctor Manette?' said one.

"'I am.'

"'Doctor Manette, formerly of Beauvais,' said the other; 'the young physician, originally an expert surgeon, who within the last year or two has made a rising reputation in Paris?'

"'Gentlemen,' I returned, 'I am that Doctor Manette of whom you speak so graciously.'

"'We have been to your residence,' said the first, 'and not being so fortunate as to find you there, and being informed that you were probably walking in this direction, we followed, in the hope of overtaking you. Will you please to enter the carriage?'

"The manner of both was imperious, and they both moved, as these words were spoken, so as to place me between themselves and the carriage-door. They were armed. I was not.

"'Gentlemen,' said I, 'pardon me; but I usually inquire who does me the honour to seek my assistance, and what is the nature of the case to which I am summoned.'

"The reply to this was made by him who had spoken second. 'Doctor, your clients are people of condition. As to the nature of the case, our confidence in your skill assures us that you will ascertain it for yourself better than we can describe it. Enough. Will you please to enter the carriage?'

"I could do nothing but comply, and I entered it in silence. They both entered after me—the last springing in, after putting up the steps. The carriage turned about, and drove on at its former speed.

"I repeat this conversation exactly as it occurred. I have no doubt that it is, word for word, the same. I describe everything exactly as it took place, constraining my mind not to wander from the task. Where I make the broken marks that follow here, I leave off for the time, and put my paper in its hiding place. . . .

"The carriage left the streets behind, passed the North Barrier, and emerged upon the country road. At two-thirds of a league from the Barrier—I did not estimate the distance at that time, but afterwards when I traversed it—it struck out of the main avenue, and presently stopped at a solitary house. We all three alighted, and walked, by a damp soft footpath in a garden where a neglected fountain had overflowed, to the door of the house. It was not opened immediately, in answer to the ringing of the bell, and one of my two conductors struck the man who opened it with his heavy riding-glove, across the face.

"There was nothing in this action to attract my particular attention, for I had seen common people struck more commonly than dogs. But the other of the two, being angry likewise, struck the man in like manner with his arm ; the look and bearing of the brothers were then so exactly alike, that I then first perceived them to be twin brothers.

"From the time of our alighting at the outer gate (which we found locked, and which one of the brothers had opened to admit us, and had re-locked), I had heard cries proceeding from an upper chamber. I was conducted to this chamber straight, the cries growing louder as we ascended the stairs, and I found a patient in a high fever of the brain, lying on a bed.

"The patient was a woman of great beauty, and young ; assuredly not much past twenty. Her hair was torn and ragged, and her arms were bound to her sides with sashes and handkerchiefs. I noticed that these bonds were all portions of a gentleman's dress. On one of them, which was a fringed scarf for a dress of ceremony, I saw the armorial bearings of a noble, and the letter E.

"I saw this within the first minute of my contemplation of the patient ; for in her restless strivings she had turned over on her face on the edge of the bed, had drawn the end of the scarf into her mouth, and was in danger of suffocation. My first act was to put out my hand to relieve her breathing ; and in moving the scarf aside, the embroidery in the corner caught my sight.

"I turned her gently over, placed my hands upon her breast to calm her and keep her down, and looked into her face. Her eyes were dilated and wild, and she constantly uttered piercing shrieks, and repeated the words, 'My husband, my father, and my brother !' and then counted up to twelve, and said, 'Hush !' For an instant, and no more, she would pause to listen, and then the piercing shrieks would begin again, and she would repeat the cry, 'My husband, my father, and my brother !' and would count up to twelve, and say 'Hush !'

There was no variation in the order, or the manner. There was no cessation, but the regular moment's pause, in the utterance of these sounds.

" 'How long,' I asked, ' has this lasted ? '

" To distinguish the brothers, I will call them the elder and the younger ; by the elder, I mean him who exercised the most authority. It was the elder who replied, ' Since about this hour last night.'

" ' She has a husband, a father, and a brother ? '

" ' A brother.'

" ' I do not address her brother ? '

" He answered with great contempt, ' No.'

" She has some recent association with the number twelve ? '

" The younger brother impatiently rejoined, ' With twelve o'clock.'

" ' See, gentlemen,' said I, still keeping my hands upon her breast, ' how useless I am, as you have brought me ! If I had known what I was coming to see, I could have come provided. As it is, time must be lost. There are no medicines to be obtained in this lonely place.'

" The elder brother looked to the younger, who said, haughtily, ' There is a case of medicines here ' ; and brought it from a closet, and put it on the table. . . .

" I opened some of the bottles, smelt them, and put the stoppers to my lips. If I had wanted to use anything save narcotic medicines that were poisons in themselves, I would not have administered any of those.

" ' Do you doubt them ? ' asked the younger brother.

" ' You see, Monsieur, I am going to use them,' I replied, and said no more.

" I made the patient swallow, with great difficulty, and after many efforts, the dose that I desired to give. As I intended to repeat it after a while, and as it was necessary to watch its influence, I then sat down by the side of the bed. There was a timid and suppressed woman in attendance (wife of the man down-stairs), who had retreated into a corner. The house was damp and decayed, indifferently furnished— evidently recently occupied and temporarily used. Some thick old hangings had been nailed up before the windows, to deaden the sound of the shrieks. They continued to be uttered in their regular succession, with the cry, ' My husband, my father, and my brother !' the counting up to twelve, and ' Hush !' The frenzy was so violent that I had not unfastened the bandages restraining the arms ; but I had looked to them, to see that they were not painful. The only spark of encourage- ment in the case was, that my hand upon the sufferer's breast had this much soothing influence, that for minutes at a time it tranquillised the figure. It had no effect upon the cries ; no pendulum could be more regular.

" For the reason that my hand had this effect (I assume), I had sat by the side of the bed for half an hour, with the two brothers looking on, before the elder said—

" ' There is another patient.'

"I was startled, and asked, 'Is it a pressing case?'

"'You had better see,' he carelessly answered, and took up a light. . . .

"The other patient lay in a back room across a second staircase, which was a species of loft over a stable. There was a low plastered ceiling to a part of it ; the rest was open, to the ridge of the tiled roof, and there were beams across. Hay and straw were stored in that portion of the place, faggots for firing, and a heap of apples in sand. I had to pass through that part to get at the other. My memory is circumstantial and unshaken. I try it with these details, and I see them all, in this my cell in the Bastille, near the close of the tenth year of my captivity, as I saw them all that night.

"On some hay on the ground, with a cushion thrown under his head, lay a handsome peasant boy—a boy of not more than seventeen at the most. He lay on his back, with his teeth set, his right hand clenched on his breast, and his glaring eyes looking straight upward. I could not see where his wound was, as I kneeled on one knee over him ; but I could see that he was dying of a wound from a sharp point.

"'I am a doctor, my poor fellow,' said I. 'Let me examine it.'

"'I do not want it examined,' he answered ; 'let it be.'

"It was under his hand, and I soothed him to let me move his hand away. The wound was a sword-thrust, received from twenty to twenty-four hours before, but no skill could have saved him if it had been looked to without delay. He was then dying fast. As I turned my eyes to the elder brother, I saw him looking down at this handsome boy, whose life was ebbing out, as if he were a wounded bird, or hare, or rabbit ; not at all as if he were a fellow-creature.

"'How has this been done, Monsieur?' said I.

"'A crazed young common dog! A serf! Forced my brother to draw upon him, and has fallen by my brother's sword—like a gentleman.'

"There was no touch of pity, sorrow, or kindred humanity in this answer. The speaker seemed to acknowledge that it was inconvenient to have that different order of creature dying there, and that it would have been better if he had died in the usual obscure routine of his vermin kind. He was quite incapable of any compassionate feeling about the boy, or about his fate.

"The boy's eyes had slowly moved to him as he had spoken, and they now slowly moved to me.

"'Doctor, they are very proud, these nobles ; but we common dogs are proud too, sometimes. They plunder us, outrage us, beat us, kill us ; but we have a little pride left, sometimes. She—have you seen her, Doctor?'

"The shrieks and the cries were audible there, though subdued by the distance. He referred to them, as if she were lying in our presence.

"I said, 'I have seen her.'

"'She is my sister, Doctor. They have had their shameful rights, these nobles, in the modesty and virtue of our sisters, many years, but we have had good girls among us. I know it, and have heard my father say so. She was a good girl. She was betrothed to a good young man, too; a tenant of his. We were all tenants of his—that man's who stands there. The other is his brother, the worst of a bad race.'

"It was with the greatest difficulty that the boy gathered bodily force to speak; but his spirit spoke with a dreadful emphasis.

"'We were so robbed by that man who stands there, as all we common dogs are by those superior beings—taxed by him without mercy, obliged to work for him without pay, obliged to grind our corn at his mill, obliged to feed scores of his tame birds on our wretched crops, and forbidden for our lives to keep a single tame bird of our own, pillaged and plundered to that degree that when we chanced to have a bit of meat, we ate it in fear, with the door barred and the shutters closed, that his people should not see it and take it from us— I say, we were so robbed, and hunted, and were made so poor, that our father told us it was a dreadful thing to bring a child into the world, and that what we should most pray for was, that our women might be barren and our miserable race die out!'

"I had never before seen the sense of being oppressed bursting forth like a fire. I had supposed that it must be latent in the people somewhere; but I had never seen it break out, until I saw it in the dying boy.

"'Nevertheless, Doctor, my sister married. He was ailing at that time, poor fellow, and she married her lover, that she might tend and comfort him in our cottage—our dog-hut, as that man would call it. She had not been married many weeks, when that man's brother saw her and admired her, and asked that man to lend her to him—for what are husbands among us! He was willing enough, but my sister was good and virtuous, and hated his brother with a hatred as strong as mine. What did the two then, to persuade her husband to use his influence with her, to make her willing?'

"The boy's eyes, which had been fixed on mine, slowly turned to the looker-on, and I saw in the two faces that all he said was true. The two opposing kinds of pride confronting one another, I can see, even in this Bastille: the gentleman's, all negligent indifference; the peasant's, all trodden-down sentiment, and passionate revenge.

"'You know, Doctor, that it is among the Rights of these nobles to harness us common dogs to carts, and drive us. They so harnessed him and drove him. You know that it is among their Rights to keep us in their grounds all night, quieting the frogs, in order that their noble sleep may not be disturbed. They kept him out in the un-wholesome mists at night, and ordered him back into his harness in the day. But he was not persuaded. No! Taken out of harness one day at noon, to feed—if he could find food—he sobbed twelve times, once for every stroke of the bell, and died on her bosom.'

"Nothing human could have held life in the boy but his determination to tell all his wrong. He forced back the gathering shadows of death, as he forced his clenched right hand to remain clenched, and to cover his wound.

"'Then, with that man's permission and even with his aid, his brother took her away; in spite of what I know she must have told his brother—and what that is will not be long unknown to you, Doctor, if it is now—his brother took her away—for his pleasure and diversion, for a little while. I saw her pass me on the road. When I took the tidings home, our father's heart burst; he never spoke one of the words that filled it. I took my young sister (for I have another) to a place beyond the reach of this man, and where, at least, she will never be *his* vassal. Then I tracked the brother here, and last night climbed in—a common dog, but sword in hand.—Where is the loft window? It was somewhere here.'

"The room was darkening to his sight; the world was narrowing around him. I glanced about me, and saw that the hay and straw were trampled over the floor, as if there had been a struggle.

"'She heard me, and ran in. I told her not to come near us till he was dead. He came in and first tossed me some pieces of money; then struck at me with a whip. But I, though a common dog, so struck at him as to make him draw. Let him break into as many pieces as he will the sword that he stained with my common blood, he drew to defend himself—thrust at me with all his skill for his life.'

"My glance had fallen, but a few moments before, on the fragments of a broken sword, lying among the hay. That weapon was a gentleman's. In another place lay an old sword that seemed to have been a soldier's.

"'Now, lift me up, Doctor; lift me up. Where is he?'

"'He is not here,' I said, supporting the boy, and thinking that he referred to the brother.

"'He! Proud as these nobles are, he is afraid to see me. Where is the man who was here? Turn my face to him.'

"I did so, raising the boy's head against my knee. But, invested for the moment with extraordinary power, he raised himself completely, obliging me to rise too, or I could not have still supported him.

"'Marquis,' said the boy, turned to him with his eyes opened wide, and his right hand raised, 'in the day when all these things are to be answered for, I summon you and yours, to the last of your bad race, to answer for them. I mark this cross of blood upon you, as a sign that I do it. In the days when all these things are to be answered for, I summon your brother, the worst of the bad race, to answer for them separately. I mark this cross of blood upon him, as a sign that I do it.'

"Twice he put his hand to the wound in his breast, and with his forefinger drew a cross in the air. He stood for an instant with the finger yet raised, and, as it dropped, he dropped with it, and I laid him down dead. . . .

"When I returned to the bedside of the young woman, I found her raving in precisely the same order and continuity. I knew that this might last for many hours, and that it would probably end in the silence of the grave.

"I repeated the medicines I had given her, and I sat at the side of the bed until the night was far advanced. She never abated the piercing quality of her shrieks, never stumbled in the distinctness or the order of her words. They were always 'My husband, my father, and my brother! One, two, three, four, five, six, seven, eight, nine, ten, eleven, twelve. Hush!'

"This lasted twenty-six hours from the time when I first saw her. I had come and gone twice, and was again sitting by her, when she began to falter. I did what little could be done to assist that opportunity, and by and by she sank into a lethargy, and lay like the dead.

"It was as if the wind and rain had lulled at last, after a long and fearful storm. I released her arms, and called the woman to assist me to compose her figure and the dress she had torn. It was then that I knew her condition to be that of one in whom the first expectations of being a mother have arisen; and it was then that I lost the little hope I had had of her.

"'Is she dead?' asked the Marquis, whom I will still describe as the elder brother, coming booted into the room from his horse.

"'Not dead,' said I; 'but like to die.'

"'What strength there is in these common bodies!' he said, looking down at her with some curiosity.

"'There is prodigious strength,' I answered him, 'in sorrow and despair.'

"He first laughed at my words, and then frowned at them. He moved a chair with his foot near to mine, ordered the woman away, and said in a subdued voice—

"'Doctor, finding my brother in this difficulty with these hinds, I recommended that your aid should be invited. Your reputation is high, and, as a young man with your fortune to make, you are probably mindful of your interest. The things that you see here are things to be seen, and not spoken of.'

"I listened to the patient's breathing, and avoided answering.

"'Do you honour me with your attention, Doctor?'

"'Monsieur,' said I, 'in my profession, the communications of patients are always received in confidence.' I was guarded in my answer, for I was troubled in my mind with what I had heard and seen.

"Her breathing was so difficult to trace, that I carefully tried the pulse and the heart. There was life and no more. Looking round as I resumed my seat, I found both the brothers intent upon me. . . .

"I write with so much difficulty, the cold is so severe, I am so fearful of being detected and consigned to an underground cell and total darkness, that I must abridge this narrative. There is no confusion or failure in my memory; it can recall, and could detail, every word that was ever spoken between me and those brothers.

"She lingered for a week. Towards the last I could understand some few syllables that she said to me, by placing my ear close to her lips. She asked me where she was, and I told her; who I was, and I told her. It was in vain that I asked her for her family name. She faintly shook her head upon the pillow, and kept her secret, as the boy had done.

"I had no opportunity of asking her any question, until I had told the brothers she was sinking fast, and could not live another day. Until then, though no one was ever presented to her consciousness save the woman and myself, one or other of them had always jealously sat behind the curtain at the head of the bed when I was there. But when it came to that, they seemed careless what communication I might hold with her, as if—the thought passed through my mind—I were dying too.

"I always observed that their pride bitterly resented the younger brother's (as I call him) having crossed swords with a peasant, and that peasant a boy. The only consideration that appeared to affect the mind of either of them was the consideration that this was highly degrading to the family, and was ridiculous. As often as I caught the younger brother's eyes, their expression reminded me that he disliked me deeply for knowing what I knew from the boy. He was smoother and more polite to me than the elder; but I saw this. I also saw that I was an incumbrance in the mind of the elder, too.

"My patient died two hours before midnight—at a time, by my watch, answering almost to the minute when I had first seen her. I was alone with her, when her forlorn young head drooped gently on one side, and all her earthly wrongs and sorrows ended.

"The brothers were waiting in a room down-stairs, impatient to ride away. I had heard them, alone at the bedside, striking their boots with their riding-whips, and loitering up and down.

"'At last she is dead?' said the elder, when I went in.

"'She is dead,' said I.

"'I congratulate you, my brother,' were his words as he turned round.

"He had before offered me money, which I had postponed taking. He now gave me a rouleau of gold. I took it from his hand, but laid it on the table. I had considered the question, and had resolved to accept nothing.

"'Pray excuse me,' said I. 'Under the circumstances, no.'

"They exchanged looks, but bent their heads to me as I bent mine to them, and we parted without another word on either side. . . .

"I am weary, weary, weary—worn down by misery. I cannot read what I have written with this gaunt hand.

"Early in the morning the rouleau of gold was left at my door in a little box, with my name on the outside. From the first I had anxiously considered what I ought to do. I decided, that day, to write privately to the Minister, stating the nature of the two cases to which I had been summoned, and the place to which I had gone—in effect, stating all the circumstances. I knew what Court influence was, and what the immunities of the nobles were, and I expected that the matter would never be heard of; but I wished to relieve my own mind. I had kept the matter a profound secret, even from my wife; and this, too, I resolved to state in my letter. I had no apprehension whatever of my real danger; but I was conscious that there might be danger for others, if others were compromised by possessing the knowledge that I possessed.

"I was much engaged that day, and could not complete my letter that night. I rose long before my usual time next morning to finish it. It was the last day of the year. The letter was lying before me just completed, when I was told that a lady waited who wished to see me. . . .

"I am growing more and more unequal to the task I have set myself. It is so cold, so dark, my senses are so benumbed, and the gloom upon me is so dreadful.

"The lady was young, engaging, and handsome, but not marked for long life. She was in great agitation. She presented herself to me as the wife of the Marquis St. Evremond. I connected the title by which the boy had addressed the elder brother with the initial letter embroidered on the scarf, and had no difficulty in arriving at the conclusion that I had seen that nobleman very lately.

"My memory is still accurate, but I cannot write the words of our conversation. I suspect that I am watched more closely than I was, and I know not at what times I may be watched. She had in part suspected, and in part discovered, the main facts of the cruel story, of her husband's share in it, and my being resorted to. She did not know that the girl was dead. Her hope had been, she said, in great distress, to show her, in secret, a woman's sympathy. Her hope had been to avert the wrath of Heaven from a House that had long been hateful to the suffering many.

"She had reasons for believing that there was a young sister living, and her greatest desire was to help that sister. I could tell her nothing but that there was such a sister; beyond that I knew nothing. Her inducement to come to me, relying on my confidence, had been the hope that I could tell her the name and place of abode. Whereas, to this wretched hour, I am ignorant of both. . . .

"These scraps of paper fail me. One was taken from me, with a warning, yesterday. I must finish my record to-day.

"She was a good, compassionate lady, and not happy in her marriage. How could she be! The brother distrusted and disliked her, and his influence was all opposed to her; she stood in dread of him, and in dread of her husband too. When I handed her down to the door, there was a child, a pretty boy from two to three years old, in her carriage.

"'For his sake, Doctor,' she said, pointing to him in tears, 'I would do all I can to make what poor amends I can. He will never prosper in his inheritance otherwise. I have a presentiment that if no other innocent atonement is made for this, it will one day be required of him.   What I have left to call my own—it is little beyond the worth of a few jewels—I will make it the first charge of his life to bestow, with the compassion and lamenting of his dead mother, on this injured family, if the sister can be discovered.'

"She kissed the boy, and said, caressing him, 'It is for thine own dear sake.   Thou wilt be faithful, little Charles?'   The child answered her bravely, 'Yes!'   I kissed her hand, and she took him in her arms, and went away caressing him.   I never saw her more.

"As she had mentioned her husband's name in the faith that I knew it, I added no mention of it to my letter.   I sealed my letter, and, not trusting it out of my own hands, delivered it myself that day.

"That night, the last night of the year, towards nine o'clock, a man in a black dress rang at my gate, demanded to see me, and softly followed my servant, Ernest Defarge, a youth, up-stairs.   When my servant came into the room where I sat with my wife—oh my wife, beloved of my heart!   My fair young English wife!—we saw the man, who was supposed to be at the gate, standing silent behind him.

"An urgent case in the Rue St. Honoré, he said.   It would not detain me ; he had a coach in waiting.

"It brought me here ; it brought me to my grave.   When I was clear of the house, a black muffler was drawn tightly over my mouth from behind, and my arms were pinioned.   The two brothers crossed the road from a dark corner, and identified me with a single gesture. The Marquis took from his pocket the letter I had written, showed it me, burnt it in the light of a lantern that was held, and extinguished the ashes with his foot.   Not a word was spoken.   I was brought here ; I was brought to my living grave.

"If it had pleased God to put it in the hard heart of either of the brothers, in all these frightful years, to grant me any tidings of my dearest wife—so much as to let me know by a word whether alive or dead—I might have thought that He had not quite abandoned them. But now I believe that the mark of the red cross is fatal to them, and that they have no part in His mercies.   And them and their descendants, to the last of their race, I, Alexandre Manette, unhappy prisoner, do, this last night of the year 1767, in my unbearable agony, denounce to the times when all these things shall be answered for.   I denounce them to Heaven and to earth."

A terrible sound arose when the reading of this document was done. A sound of craving and eagerness that had nothing articulate in it but blood.   The narrative called up the most revengeful passions of the time, and there was not a head in the nation but must have dropped before it.

Little need, in presence of that Tribunal and that auditory, to show how the Defarges had not made the paper public, with the other captured Bastille memorials borne in procession, and had kept it, biding their time.   Little need to show that this detested family name had long been anathematised by Saint Antoine, and was wrought into the fatal register. The man never trod ground whose virtues and services would have sustained him in that place that day against such denunciation.

And all the worse for the doomed man that the denouncer was a well-known citizen, his own attached friend, the father of his wife. One of the frenzied aspirations of the populace was for imitations of the questionable public virtues of antiquity, and for sacrifices and self-immolations on the people's altar. Therefore when the President said (else had his own head quivered on his shoulders) that the good physician of the Republic would deserve better still of the Republic by rooting out an obnoxious family of Aristocrats, and would doubtless feel a sacred glow and joy in making his daughter a widow and her child an orphan, there was wild excitement, patriotic fervour, not a touch of human sympathy.

"Much influence around him has that Doctor?" murmured Madame Defarge, smiling to The Vengeance. "Save him now, my Doctor, save him!"

At every juryman's vote there was a roar. Another and another. Roar and roar.

Unanimously voted. At heart and by descent an Aristocrat, an enemy of the Republic, a notorious oppressor of the People. Back to the Conciergerie, and Death within four-and-twenty hours!

CHAPTER XI

DUSK

THE wretched wife of the innocent man thus doomed to die fell under the sentence as if she had been mortally stricken. But she uttered no sound; and so strong was the voice within her, representing that it was she of all the world who must uphold him in his misery and not augment it, that it quickly raised her, even from that shock.

The judges having to take part in a public demonstration out-of-doors, the Tribunal adjourned. The quick noise and movement of the court's emptying itself by many passages had not ceased, when Lucie stood stretching out her arms towards her husband, with nothing in her face but love and consolation.

"If I might touch him! If I might embrace him once! Oh, good citizens, if you would have so much compassion for us!"

There was but a jailer left, along with two of the four men who had taken him last night, and Barsad. The people had all poured out to the show in the streets. Barsad proposed to the rest, "Let her embrace him then; it is but a moment." It was silently acquiesced in, and they passed her over the seats in the hall to a raised place, where he, by leaning over the dock, could fold her in his arms.

"Farewell, dear darling of my soul. My parting blessing on my love. We shall meet again, where the weary are at rest!"

They were her husband's words, as he held her to his bosom.

"I can bear it, dear Charles. I am supported from above; don't suffer for me. A parting blessing for our child."

"I send it to her by you. I kiss her by you. I say farewell to her by you."

"My husband. No! A moment!" He was tearing himself apart from her. "We shall not be separated long. I feel that this will break my heart by and by; but I will do my duty while I can, and when I leave her, God will raise up friends for her, as He did for me."

Her father had followed her, and would have fallen on his knees to both of them, but that Darnay put out a hand and seized him, crying—

"No, no! What have you done, what have you done, that you should kneel to us? We know now what a struggle you made of old. We know now what you underwent when you suspected my descent, and when you knew it. We know now the natural antipathy you strove against, and conquered, for her dear sake. We thank you with all our hearts, and all our love and duty. Heaven be with you!"

Her father's only answer was to draw his hands through his white hair, and wring them with a shriek of anguish.

"It could not be otherwise," said the prisoner. "All things have worked together as they have fallen out. It was the always vain endeavour to discharge my poor mother's trust that first brought my fatal presence near you. Good could never come of such evil, a happier end was not in nature to so unhappy a beginning. Be comforted, and forgive me. Heaven bless you!"

As he was drawn away, his wife released him, and stood looking after him with her hands touching one another in the attitude of prayer, and with a radiant look upon her face, in which there was even a comforting smile. As he went out at the prisoner's door, she turned, laid her head lovingly on her father's breast, tried to speak to him, and fell at his feet.

Then, issuing from the obscure corner from which he had never moved, Sydney Carton came and took her up. Only her father and Mr. Lorry were with her. His arm trembled as it raised her, and supported her head. Yet there was an air about him that was not all of pity—that had a flush of pride in it.

"Shall I take her to a coach? I shall never feel her weight."

He carried her lightly to the door, and laid her tenderly down in a coach. Her father and their old friend got into it, and he took his seat beside the driver.

When they arrived at the gateway where he had paused in the dark not many hours before, to picture to himself on which of the rough stones of the street her feet had trodden, he lifted her again, and carried her up the staircase to their rooms. There he laid her down on a couch, where her child and Miss Pross wept over her.

"Don't recall her to herself," he said, softly, to the latter, "she is better so. Don't revive her to consciousness, while she only faints."

"Oh Carton, Carton, dear Carton!" cried little Lucie, springing up and throwing her arms passionately round him, in a burst of grief. "Now that you have come, I think you will do something to help mamma, something to save papa! Oh, look at her, dear Carton! Can you, of all the people who love her, bear to see her so?"

He bent over the child, and laid her blooming cheek against his face. He put her gently from him, and looked at her unconscious mother.

"Before I go," he said, and paused—"I may kiss her?"

It was remembered afterwards that when he bent down and touched her face with his lips he murmured some words. The child, who was nearest to him, told them afterwards, and told her grandchildren when she was a handsome old lady, that she heard him say, "A life you love."

When he had gone out into the next room, he turned suddenly on Mr. Lorry and her father, who were following, and said to the latter—

"You had great influence but yesterday, Doctor Manette; let it at least be tried. These judges, and all the men in power, are very friendly to you, and very recognisant of your services; are they not?"

"Nothing connected with Charles was concealed from me. I had the strongest assurances that I should save him; and I did." He returned the answer in great trouble, and very slowly.

"Try them again. The hours between this and to-morrow afternoon are few and short, but try."

"I intend to try. I will not rest a moment."

"That's well. I have known such energy as yours do great things before now—though never," he added, with a smile and a sigh together, "such great things as this. But try! Of little worth as life is when we misuse it, it is worth that effort. It would cost nothing to lay down if it were not."

"I will go," said Doctor Manette, "to the Prosecutor and the President straight, and I will go to others whom it is better not to name. I will write too, and—— But stay! There is a celebration in the streets, and no one will be accessible until dark."

"That's true. Well! It is a forlorn hope at the best, and not much the forlorner for being delayed till dark. I should like to know how you speed; though, mind, I expect nothing! When are you likely to have seen these dread powers, Doctor Manette?"

"Immediately after dark, I should hope. Within an hour or two from this."

"It will be dark soon after four. Let us stretch the hour or two. If I go to Mr. Lorry's at nine, shall I hear what you have done, either from our friend or from yourself?"

"Yes."

"May you prosper!"

Mr. Lorry followed Sydney to the outer door, and, touching him on the shoulder as he was going away, caused him to turn.

"I have no hope," said Mr. Lorry, in a low and sorrowful whisper.

"Nor have I."

"If any one of these men, or all of these men, were disposed to spare him—which is a large supposition ; for what is his life, or any man's to them ?—I doubt if they durst spare him after the demonstration in the court."

"And so do I. I heard the fall of the axe in that sound."

Mr. Lorry leaned his arm upon the doorpost, and bowed his face upon it.

"Don't despond," said Carton, very gently ; "don't grieve. I encouraged Doctor Manette in this idea, because I felt that it might one day be consolatory to her. Otherwise, she might think ' his life was wantonly thrown away or wasted,' and that might trouble her."

"Yes, yes, yes," returned Mr. Lorry, drying his eyes, "you are right. But he will perish ; there is no real hope."

"Yes. He will perish ; there is no real hope," echoed Carton. And walked with a settled step down-stairs.

CHAPTER XII

DARKNESS

SYDNEY CARTON paused in the street, not quite decided where to go. "At Tellson's banking-house at nine," he said, with a musing face. "Shall I do well, in the meantime, to show myself ? I think so. It is best that these people should know there is such a man as I here ; it is a sound precaution, and may be a necessary preparation. But care, care, care ! Let me think it out !"

Checking his steps, which had begun to tend towards an object, he took a turn or two in the already darkening street, and traced the thought in his mind to its possible consequences. His first impression was confirmed. "It is best," he said, finally resolved, "that these people should know there is such a man as I here." And he turned his face towards Saint Antoine.

Defarge had described himself, that day, as the keeper of a wine-shop in the Saint Antoine suburb. It was not difficult for one who knew the city well to find the house without asking any question. Having ascertained its situation, Carton came out of those closer streets again, and dined at a place of refreshment, and fell sound asleep after dinner. For the first time in many years he had no strong drink. Since last night he had taken nothing but a little light thin wine, and last night he had dropped the brandy slowly on Mr. Lorry's hearth, like a man who had done with it.

It was as late as seven o'clock when he awoke refreshed, and went out into the streets again. As he passed along towards Saint Antoine, he stopped at a shop-window where there was a mirror, and slightly altered the disordered arrangement of his loose cravat, and his coat-collar, and his wild hair. This done, he went on direct to Defarge's, and went in.

There happened to be no customer in the shop but Jacques Three, of the restless fingers and croaking voice. This man, whom he had seen upon the Jury, stood drinking at the little counter, in conversation with the Defarges, man and wife. The Vengeance assisted in the conversation, like a regular member of the establishment.

As Carton walked in, took his seat and asked (in very indifferent French) for a small measure of wine, Madame Defarge cast a careless glance at him, and then a keener, and then a keener, and then advanced to him herself, and asked him what it was he had ordered.

He repeated what he had already said.

" English ? " asked Madame Defarge, inquisitively raising her dark eyebrows.

After looking at her, as if the sound of even a single French word were slow to express itself to him, he answered, in his former strong foreign accent, " Yes, Madame, yes. I am English ! "

Madame Defarge returned to her counter to get the wine, and, as he took up a Jacobin journal and feigned to pore over it puzzling out its meaning, he heard her say, " I swear to you, like Evremond ! "

Defarge brought him the wine, and gave him good-evening.

" How ? "

" Good-evening."

" Oh ! Good-evening, citizen," filling his glass. " Ah ! and good wine. I drink to the Republic."

Defarge went back to the counter, and said, " Certainly, a little like." Madame sternly retorted, " I tell you, a good deal like." Jacques Three pacifically remarked, " He is so much in your mind, see you, Madame." The amiable Vengeance added, with a laugh, " Yes, my faith ! And you are looking forward with so much pleasure to seeing him once more to-morrow ! "

Carton followed the lines and words of his paper with a slow fore-finger, and with a studious and absorbed face. They were all leaning their arms on the counter close together, speaking low. After a silence of a few moments, during which they all looked towards him without disturbing his outward attention from the Jacobin editor, they resumed their conversation.

" It is true what Madame says," observed Jacques Three. " Why stop ? There is great force in that. Why stop ? "

" Well, well," reasoned Defarge, " but one must stop somewhere. After all, the question is still where ? "

" At extermination," said Madame.

" Magnificent ! " croaked Jacques Three. The Vengeance, also, highly approved.

" Extermination is good doctrine, my wife," said Defarge, rather troubled ; " in general, I say nothing against it. But this Doctor has suffered much ; you have seen him to-day ; you have observed his face when the paper was read."

"I have observed his face!" repeated Madame, contemptuously and angrily. "Yes. I have observed his face. I have observed his face to be not the face of a true friend of the Republic. Let him take care of his face!"

"And you have observed, my wife," said Defarge, in a deprecatory manner, "the anguish of his daughter, which must be a dreadful anguish to him!"

"I have observed his daughter," repeated Madame ; "yes, I have observed his daughter, more times than one. I have observed her to-day, and I have observed her other days. I have observed her in the court, and I have observed her in the street by the prison. Let me but lift my finger——!" She seemed to raise it (the listener's eyes were always on his paper), and to let it fall with a rattle on the ledge before her, as if the axe had dropped.

"The citizeness is superb!" croaked the Juryman.

"She is an angel!" said The Vengeance, and embraced her.

"As to thee," pursued Madame, implacably, addressing her husband, "if it depended on thee—which, happily, it does not—thou wouldst rescue this man even now."

"No!" protested Defarge. "Not if to lift this glass would do it! But I would leave the matter there. I say, stop there."

"See you then, Jacques," said Madame Defarge, wrathfully ; "and see you, too, my little Vengeance ; see you both! Listen! For other crimes as tyrants and oppressors, I have this race a long time on my register, doomed to destruction and extermination. Ask my husband, is that so."

"It is so," assented Defarge, without being asked.

"In the beginning of the great days, when the Bastille falls, he finds this paper of to-day, and he brings it home, and in the middle of the night, when this place is clear and shut, we read it, here on this spot, by the light of this lamp. Ask him, is that so."

"It is so," assented Defarge.

"That night, I tell him, when the paper is read through, and the lamp is burnt out, and the day is gleaming in above those shutters and between those iron bars, that I have now a secret to communicate. Ask him, is that so."

"It is so," assented Defarge again.

"I communicate to him that secret. I smite this bosom with these two hands as I smite it now, and I tell him, 'Defarge, I was brought up among the fishermen of the sea-shore, and that peasant family so injured by the two Evremond brothers, as that Bastille paper describes, is my family. Defarge, that sister of the mortally wounded boy upon the ground was my sister, that husband was my sister's husband, that unborn child was their child, that brother was my brother, that father was my father, those dead are my dead, and that summons to answer for those things descends to me!' Ask him, is that so."

"It is so," assented Defarge once more.

"Then tell Wind and Fire where to stop," returned Madame; "but don't tell me."

Both her hearers derived a horrible enjoyment from the deadly nature of her wrath—the listener could feel how white she was, without seeing her—and both highly commended it. Defarge, a weak minority, interposed a few words for the memory of the compassionate wife of the Marquis; but only elicited from his own wife a repetition of her last reply. "Tell the Wind and the Fire where to stop; not me!"

Customers entered, and the group was broken up. The English customer paid for what he had had, perplexedly counted his change, and asked, as a stranger, to be directed towards the National Palace. Madame Defarge took him to the door, and put her arm on his, in pointing out the road. The English customer was not without his reflections then, that it might be a good deed to seize that arm, lift it, and strike under it sharp and deep.

But he went his way, and was soon swallowed up in the shadow of the prison wall. At the appointed hour he emerged from it to present himself in Mr. Lorry's room again, where he found the old gentleman walking to and fro in restless anxiety. He said he had been with Lucie until just now, and had only left her for a few minutes to come and keep his appointment. Her father had not been seen since he quitted the banking-house towards four o'clock. She had some faint hopes that his mediation might save Charles, but they were very slight. He had been more than five hours gone: where could he be?

Mr. Lorry waited until ten; but Doctor Manette not returning, and he being unwilling to leave Lucie any longer, it was arranged that he should go back to her, and come to the banking-house again at midnight. In the meanwhile, Carton would wait alone by the fire for the Doctor.

He waited and waited and the clock struck twelve; but Doctor Manette did not come back. Mr. Lorry returned, and found no tidings of him, and brought none. Where could he be?

They were discussing this question, and were almost building up some weak structure of hope on his prolonged absence, when they heard him on the stairs. The instant he entered the room, it was plain that all was lost.

Whether he had really been to any one, or whether he had been all that time traversing the streets, was never known. As he stood staring at them, they asked him no question, for his face told them everything.

"I cannot find it," said he, "and I must have it. Where is it?"

His head and throat were bare, and as he spoke with a helpless look straying all around, he took his coat off, and let it drop on the floor.

"Where is my bench? I have been looking everywhere for my bench, and I can't find it. What have they done with my work? Time presses: I must finish those shoes."

They looked at one another, and their hearts died within them.

"Come, come!" said he, in a whimpering, miserable way; "let me go to work. Give me my work."

Receiving no answer, he tore his hair, and beat his feet upon the ground, like a distracted child.

"Don't torture a poor forlorn wretch," he implored them, with a dreadful cry; "but give me my work! What is to become of us, if those shoes are not done to-night?"

Lost, utterly lost!

It was so clearly beyond hope to reason with him, or try to restore him, that, as if by agreement, they each put a hand upon his shoulder, and soothed him to sit down before the fire, with a promise that he should have his work presently. He sank into the chair, and brooded over the embers, and shed tears. As if all that had happened since the garret time were a momentary fancy, or a dream, Mr. Lorry saw him shrink into the exact figure that Defarge had had in keeping.

Affected, and impressed with terror as they both were, by this spectacle of ruin, it was not a time to yield to such emotions. His lonely daughter, bereft of her final hope and reliance, appealed to them both too strongly. Again, as if by agreement, they looked at one another with one meaning in their faces. Carton was the first to speak—

"The last chance is gone: it was not much. Yes; he had better be taken to her. But, before you go, will you, for a moment, steadily attend to me? Don't ask me why I make the stipulations I am going to make, and exact the promise I am going to exact; I have a reason —a good one."

"I do not doubt it," answered Mr. Lorry. "Say on."

The figure in the chair between them was all the time monotonously rocking itself to and fro, and moaning. They spoke in such a tone as they would have used if they had been watching by a sick-bed in the night.

Carton stooped to pick up the coat, which lay almost entangling his feet. As he did so, a small case in which the Doctor was accustomed to carry the list of his day's duties fell lightly on the floor. Carton took it up, and there was a folded paper in it. "We should look at this!" he said. Mr. Lorry nodded his consent. He opened it, and exclaimed, "Thank God!"

"What is it?" asked Mr. Lorry, eagerly.

"A moment! Let me speak of it in its place. First," he put his hand in his coat, and took another paper from it, "that is the certificate which enables me to pass out of this city. Look at it. You see— Sydney Carton, an Englishman?"

Mr. Lorry held it open in his hand, gazing in his earnest face.

"Keep it for me until to-morrow. I shall see him to-morrow, you remember, and I had better not take it into the prison."

"Why not?"

"I don't know; I prefer not to do so. Now, take this paper that Doctor Manette has carried about him. It is a similar certificate, enabling him and his daughter and her child, at any time, to pass the barrier and the frontier. You see?"

"Yes!"

"Perhaps he obtained it as his last and utmost precaution against evil, yesterday. When is it dated? But no matter; don't stay to look; put it up carefully with mine and your own. Now, observe! I never doubted until within this hour or two that he had, or could have, such a paper. It is good, until recalled. But it may be soon recalled, and, I have reason to think, will be."

"They are not in danger?"

"They are in great danger. They are in danger of denunciation by Madame Defarge. I know it from her own lips. I have overheard words of that woman's, to-night, which have presented their danger to me in strong colours. I have lost no time, and since then I have seen the spy. He confirms me. He knows that a wood-sawyer, living by the prison-wall, is under the control of the Defarges, and has been rehearsed by Madame Defarge as to his having seen Her"—he never mentioned Lucie's name—"making signs and signals to prisoners. It is easy to foresee that the pretence will be the common one, a prison plot, and that it will involve her life—and perhaps her child's—and perhaps her father's—for both have been seen with her at that place. Don't look so horrified. You will save them all."

"Heaven grant I may, Carton! But how?"

"I am going to tell you how. It will depend on you, and it could depend on no better man. This new denunciation will certainly not take place until after to-morrow; probably not until two or three days afterwards; more probably a week afterwards. You know it is a capital crime to mourn for, or sympathise with, a victim of the Guillotine. She and her father would unquestionably be guilty of this crime, and this woman (the inveteracy of whose pursuit cannot be described) would wait to add that strength to her case, and make herself doubly sure. You follow me?"

"So attentively, and with so much confidence in what you say, that for the moment I lose sight," touching the back of the Doctor's chair, "even of this distress."

"You have money, and can buy the means of travelling to the sea-coast as quickly as the journey can be made. Your preparations have been completed for some days, to return to England. Early to-morrow have your horses ready, so that they may be in starting trim at two o'clock in the afternoon."

"It shall be done!"

His manner was so fervent and inspiring, that Mr. Lorry caught the flame, and was as quick as youth.

"You are a noble heart. Did I say we could depend upon no better man? Tell her, to-night, what you know of her danger as involving her child and her father. Dwell upon that, for she would lay her own fair head beside her husband's cheerfully." He faltered for an instant; then went on as before. "For the sake of her child and her father, press upon her the necessity of leaving Paris, with them and you, at that hour. Tell her that it was her husband's last arrangement. Tell her that more depends upon it than she dare believe, or hope. You think that her father, even in this sad state, will submit himself to her ; do you not ? "

" I am sure of it."

" I thought so. Quietly and steadily have all these arrangements made in the courtyard here, even to the taking of your own seat in the carriage. The moment I come to you, take me in, and drive away."

" I understand that I wait for you under all circumstances ? "

" You have my certificate in your hand with the rest, you know, and will reserve my place. Wait for nothing but to have my place occupied, and then for England ! "

" Why, then," said Mr. Lorry, grasping his eager but so firm and steady hand, " it does not all depend on one old man, but I shall have a young and ardent man at my side."

" By the help of Heaven you shall ! Promise me solemnly that nothing will influence you to alter the course on which we now stand pledged to one another."

" Nothing, Carton."

" Remember these words to-morrow : change the course, or delay in it—for any reason—and no life can possibly be saved, and many lives must inevitably be sacrificed."

" I will remember them. I hope to do my part faithfully."

" And I hope to do mine. Now, good-bye ! "

Though he said it with a grave smile of earnestness, and though he even put the old man's hand to his lips, he did not part from him then. He helped him so far to arouse the rocking figure before the dying embers, as to get a cloak and hat put upon it, and to tempt it forth to find where the bench and work were hidden that it still moaningly besought to have. He walked on the other side of it and protected it to the courtyard of the house where the afflicted heart—so happy in the memorable time when he had revealed his own desolate heart to it— outwatched the awful night. He entered the courtyard and remained there for a few moments alone, looking up at the light in the window of her room. Before he went away, he breathed a blessing towards it, and a Farewell.

CHAPTER XIII

FIFTY-TWO

In the black prison of the Conciergerie the doomed of the day awaited their fate. They were in number as the weeks of the year. Fifty-two were to roll that afternoon on the life-tide of the city to the boundless everlasting sea. Before their cells were quit of them, new occupants were appointed ; before their blood ran into the blood spilled yesterday, the blood that was to mingle with theirs to-morrow was already set apart.

Two score and twelve were told off. From the farmer-general of seventy, whose riches could not buy his life, to the seamstress of twenty, whose poverty and obscurity could not save her. Physical diseases, engendered in the vices and neglects of men, will seize on victims of all degrees ; and the frightful moral disorder, born of unspeakable suffering, intolerable oppression, and heartless indifference, smote equally without distinction.

Charles Darnay, alone in a cell, had sustained himself with no flattering delusion since he came to it from the Tribunal. In every line of the narrative he had heard, he had heard his condemnation. He had fully comprehended that no personal influence could possibly save him, that he was virtually sentenced by the millions, and that units could avail him nothing.

Nevertheless, it was not easy, with the face of his beloved wife fresh before him, to compose his mind to what it must bear. His hold on life was strong, and it was very, very hard to loosen ; by gradual efforts and degrees unclosed a little here, it clenched the tighter there ; and when he brought his strength to bear on that hand and it yielded, this was closed again. There was a hurry, too, in all his thoughts, a turbulent and heated working of his heart, that contended against resignation. If, for a moment, he did feel resigned, then his wife and child, who had to live after him, seemed to protest and to make it a selfish thing.

But all this was at first. Before long, the consideration that there was no disgrace in the fate he must meet, and that numbers went the same road wrongfully, and trod it firmly every day, sprang up to stimulate him. Next followed the thought that much of the future peace of mind enjoyable by the dear ones depended on his quiet fortitude. So by degrees he calmed into the better state, when he could raise his thoughts much higher, and draw comfort down.

Before it had set in dark on the night of his condemnation, he had travelled thus far on his last way. Being allowed to purchase the means of writing, and a light, he sat down to write until such time as the prison lamps should be extinguished.

He wrote a long letter to Lucie, showing her that he had known nothing of her father's imprisonment, until he had heard of it from herself, and that he had been as ignorant as she of his father's and uncle's responsibility for that misery, until the paper had been read. He had already explained to her that his concealment from herself of the name he had relinquished was the one condition—fully intelligible now—that her father had attached to their betrothal, and was the one promise he had still exacted on the morning of their marriage. He entreated her, for her father's sake, never to seek to know whether her father had become oblivious of the existence of the paper, or had had it recalled to him (for the moment, or for good) by the story of the Tower, on that old Sunday under the dear old plane-tree in the garden. If he had preserved any definite remembrance of it, there could be no doubt that he had supposed it destroyed with the Bastille, when he had found no mention of it among the relics of prisoners which the populace had discovered there, and which had been described to all the world. He besought her—though he added that he knew it was needless—to console her father, by impressing him through every tender means she could think of, with the truth that he had done nothing for which he could justly reproach himself, but had uniformly forgotten himself for their joint sakes. Next to her preservation of his own last grateful love and blessing, and her overcoming of her sorrow, to devote herself to their dear child, he adjured her, as they would meet in heaven, to comfort her father.

To her father himself he wrote in the same strain; but he told her father that he expressly confided his wife and child to his care. And he told him this, very strongly, with the hope of rousing him from any despondency or dangerous retrospect towards which he foresaw he might be tending.

To Mr. Lorry he commended them all, and explained his worldly affairs. That done, with many added sentences of grateful friendship and warm attachment, all was done. He never thought of Carton. His mind was so full of the others that he never once thought of him.

He had time to finish these letters before the lights were put out. When he lay down on his straw bed, he thought he had done with this world.

But it beckoned him back in his sleep, and showed itself in shining forms. Free and happy, back in the old house in Soho (though it had nothing in it like the real house), unaccountably released and light of heart, he was with Lucie again, and she told him it was all a dream, and he had never gone away. A pause of forgetfulness, and then he had even suffered, and had come back to her, dead and at peace, and yet there was no difference in him. Another pause of oblivion, and he awoke in the sombre morning, unconscious where he was or what had happened, until it flashed upon his mind, "this is the day of my death!"

Thus had he come through the hours, to the day when the fifty-two heads were to fall. And now, while he was composed, and hoped that he could meet the end with quiet heroism, a new action began in his waking thoughts, which was very difficult to master.

He had never seen the instrument that was to terminate his life. How high it was from the ground, how many steps it had, where he would be stood, how he would be touched, whether the touching hands would be dyed red, which way his face would be turned, whether he would be the first, or might be the last: these and many similar questions, in no wise directed by his will, obtruded themselves over and over again, countless times. Neither were they connected with fear; he was conscious of no fear. Rather, they originated in a strange besetting desire to know what to do when the time came; a desire gigantically disproportionate to the few swift moments to which it referred ; a wondering that was more like the wondering of some other spirit within his than his own.

The hours went on as he walked to and fro, and the clocks struck the numbers he would never hear again. Nine gone for ever, ten gone for ever, eleven gone for ever, twelve coming on to pass away. After a hard contest with that eccentric action of thought which had last perplexed him, he had got the better of it. He walked up and down, softly repeating their names to himself. The worst of the strife was over. He could walk up and down, free from distracting fancies, praying for himself and for them.

Twelve gone for ever.

He had been apprised that the final hour was Three, and he knew he would be summoned some time earlier, inasmuch as the tumbrils jolted heavily and slowly through the streets. Therefore he resolved to keep Two before his mind, as the hour, and so to strengthen himself in the interval that he might be able, after that time, to strengthen others.

Walking regularly to and fro with his arms folded on his breast, a very different man from the prisoner who had walked to and fro at La Force, he heard One struck away from him without surprise. The hour had measured like most other hours. Devoutly thankful to Heaven for this recovered self-possession, he thought, "There is but another now," and turned to walk again.

Footsteps in the stone passage outside the door. He stopped.

The key was put in the lock, and turned. Before the door was opened, or as it opened, a man said in a low voice, in English : "He has never seen me here ; I have kept out of his way. Go you in alone ; I wait near. Lose no time !"

The door was quickly opened and closed, and there stood before him, face to face, quiet, intent upon him, with the light of a smile on his features, and a cautionary finger on his lip, Sydney Carton.

There was something so bright and remarkable in his look, that, for the first moment, the prisoner misdoubted him to be an apparition of his own imagining. But he spoke, and it was his voice ; he took the prisoner's hand, and it was his real grasp.

"Of all the people upon earth, you least expected to see me ?" he said.

"I could not believe it to be you. I can scarcely believe it now. You are not"—the apprehension came suddenly into his mind—"a prisoner ?"

"No. I am accidentally possessed of a power over one of the keepers here, and in virtue of it I stand before you. I come from her —your wife, dear Darnay."

The prisoner wrung his hand.

"I bring you a request from her."

"What is it ?"

"A most earnest, pressing, and emphatic entreaty, addressed to you in the most pathetic tones of the voice so dear to you, that you well remember."

The prisoner turned his face partly aside.

"You have no time to ask me why I bring it, or what it means; I have no time to tell you. You must comply with it—take off those boots you wear, and draw on these of mine."

There was a chair against the wall of the cell, behind the prisoner. Carton, pressing forward, had already, with the speed of lightning, got him down into it, and stood over him, barefoot.

"Draw on these boots of mine. Put your hands to them; put your will to them. Quick!"

"Carton, there is no escaping from this place; it never can be done. You will only die with me. It is madness."

"It would be madness if I asked you to escape; but do I? When I ask you to pass out at that door, tell me it is madness and remain here. Change that cravat for this of mine, that coat for this of mine. While you do it, let me take this ribbon from your hair, and shake out your hair like this of mine!"

With wonderful quickness, and with a strength both of will and action that appeared quite supernatural, he forced all these changes upon him. The prisoner was like a young child in his hands.

"Carton! Dear Carton! It is madness. It cannot be accomplished, it never can be done, it has been attempted, and has always failed. I implore you not to add your death to the bitterness of mine."

"Do I ask you, my dear Darnay, to pass the door? When I ask that, refuse. There are pen and ink and paper on this table. Is your hand steady enough to write?"

"It was when you came in."

"Steady it again, and write what I shall dictate. Quick, friend, quick!"

Pressing his hand to his bewildered head, Darnay sat down at the table. Carton, with his right hand in his breast, stood close beside him.

"Write exactly as I speak."

"To whom do I address it?"

"To no one." Carton still had his hand in his breast.

"Do I date it?"

"No."

The prisoner looked up at each question. Carton, standing over him with his hand in his breast, looked down.

"'If you remember,'" said Carton, dictating, "'the words that passed between us, long ago, you will readily comprehend this when you see it. You do remember them, I know. It is not in your nature to forget them.'"

He was drawing his hand from his breast; the prisoner chancing to look up in his hurried wonder as he wrote, the hand stopped, closing upon something.

"Have you written 'forget them'?" Carton asked.

"I have. Is that a weapon in your hand?"

"No; I am not armed."

"What is it in your hand?"

"You shall know directly. Write on; there are but a few words more." He dictated again. "'I am thankful that the time has come when I can prove them. That I do so is no subject for regret or grief.'" As he said these words, with his eyes fixed on the writer, his hand slowly and softly moved down close to the writer's face.

The pen dropped from Darnay's fingers on the table, and he looked about him vacantly.

"What vapour is that?" he asked.

"Vapour?"

"Something that crossed me?"

"I am conscious of nothing; there can be nothing here. Take up the pen and finish. Hurry, hurry!"

As if his memory were impaired, or his faculties disordered, the prisoner made an effort to rally his attention. As he looked at Carton with clouded eyes and with an altered manner of breathing, Carton—his hand again in his breast—looked steadily at him.

"Hurry, hurry!"

The prisoner bent over the paper once more.

"'If it had been otherwise'"—Carton's hand was again watchfully and softly stealing down—"'I never should have used the longer opportunity. If it had been otherwise'"—the hand was at the prisoner's face—"'I should but have had so much the more to answer for. If it had been otherwise——'" Carton looked at the pen and saw it was trailing off into unintelligible signs.

Carton's hand moved back to his breast no more. The prisoner sprang up with a reproachful look, but Carton's hand was close and firm at his nostrils, and Carton's left arm caught him round the waist. For a few seconds he faintly struggled with the man who had come to lay down his life for him; but within a minute or so he was stretched insensible on the ground.

Quickly, but with hands as true to the purpose as his heart was, Carton dressed himself in the clothes the prisoner had laid aside, combed back his hair, and tied it with the ribbon the prisoner had worn. Then he softly called, "Enter there! Come in!" and the Spy presented himself.

"You see?" said Carton, looking up, as he kneeled on one knee beside the insensible figure, putting the paper in the breast: "is your hazard very great?"

"Mr. Carton," the Spy answered, with a timid snap of his fingers, "my hazard is not *that*, in the thick of business here, if you are true to the whole of your bargain."

"Don't fear me. I will be true to the death."

"You must be, Mr. Carton, if the tale of fifty-two is to be right. Being made right by you in that dress, I shall have no fear."

"Have no fear! I shall soon be out of the way of harming you,

and the rest will soon be far from here, please God! Now, get assistance and take me to the coach."

"You?" said the Spy, nervously.

"Him, man, with whom I have exchanged. You go out at the
gate by which you brought me in?"

"Of course."

"I was weak and faint when you brought me in, and I am fainter
now you take me out. The parting interview has overpowered me.
Such a thing has happened here, often, and too often. Your life is in
your own hands. Quick! Call assistance!"

"You swear not to betray me?" said the trembling Spy, as he
paused for a last moment.

"Man, man!" returned Carton, stamping his foot; "have I sworn
by no solemn vow already to go through with this, that you waste the
precious moments now? Take him yourself to the courtyard you
know of, place him yourself in the carriage, show him yourself to Mr.
Lorry, tell him yourself to give him no restorative but air, and to
remember my words of last night, and his promise of last night, and
drive away!"

The Spy withdrew, and Carton seated himself at the table, resting
his forehead on his hands. The Spy returned immediately with two
men.

"How, then?" said one of them, contemplating the fallen figure.
"So afflicted to find that his friend has drawn a prize in the lottery of
Sainte Guillotine?"

"A good patriot," said the other, "could hardly have been more
afflicted if the Aristocrat had drawn a blank."

They raised the unconscious figure, placed it on a litter they had
brought to the door, and bent to carry it away.

"The time is short, Evremond," said the Spy, in a warning voice.

"I know it well," answered Carton. "Be careful of my friend, I
entreat you, and leave me."

"Come, then, my children," said Barsad. "Lift him, and come
away!"

The door closed, and Carton was left alone. Straining his powers
of listening to the utmost, he listened for any sound that might denote
suspicion or alarm. There was none. Keys turned, doors clashed,
footsteps passed along distant passages: no cry was raised, or hurry
made, that seemed unusual. Breathing more freely in a little while,
he sat down at the table, and listened again until the clock struck
Two.

Sounds that he was not afraid of, for he divined their meaning, then
began to be audible. Several doors were opened in succession, and
finally his own. A jailer, with a list in his hand, looked in, merely
saying, "Follow me, Evremond!" and he followed into a large dark
room at a distance. It was a dark winter day, and what with the
shadows within, and what with the shadows without, he could but
dimly discern the others who were brought there to have their arms

bound. Some were standing—some seated. Some were lamenting and in restless motion; but these were few. The great majority were silent and still, looking fixedly at the ground.

As he stood by the wall in a dim corner, while some of the fifty-two were brought in after him, one man stopped in passing to embrace him, as having a knowledge of him. It thrilled him with a great dread of discovery; but the man went on. A very few moments after that a young woman, with a slight girlish form, a sweet spare face in which there was no vestige of colour, and large widely-opened patient eyes, rose from the seat where he had observed her sitting, and came to speak to him.

"Citizen Evremond," she said, touching him with her cold hand, "I am a poor little seamstress who was with you in La Force."

He murmured for answer, "True. I forget what you were accused of?"

"Plots. Though the just Heaven knows I am innocent of any. Is it likely? Who would think of plotting with a poor little weak creature like me?"

The forlorn smile with which she said it so touched him that tears started from his eyes.

"I am not afraid to die, Citizen Evremond, but I have done nothing. I am not unwilling to die if the Republic, which is to do so much good to us poor, will profit by my death; but I do not know how that can be, Citizen Evremond. Such a poor, weak, little creature!"

As the last thing on earth that his heart was to warm and soften to, it warmed and softened to this pitiable girl.

"I heard you were released, Citizen Evremond. I hoped it was true?"

"It was. But I was again taken and condemned."

"If I may ride with you, Citizen Evremond, will you let me hold your hand? I am not afraid, but I am little and weak, and it will give me more courage."

As the patient eyes were lifted to his face, he saw a sudden doubt in them, and then astonishment. He pressed the work-worn, hunger-worn young fingers, and touched his lips.

"Are you dying for him?" she whispered.

"And his wife and child. Hush! Yes."

"Oh, you will let me hold your brave hand, stranger?"

"Hush! Yes, my poor sister; to the last."

The same shadows that are falling on the prison are falling, in that same hour of the early afternoon, on the Barrier with the crowd about it, when a coach going out of Paris drives up to be examined.

"Who goes here? Whom have we within? Papers!"

The papers are handed out and read.

"Alexandre Manette. Physician. French. Which is he?"

This is he, this helpless, inarticulately murmuring, wandering old man pointed out.

"Apparently the Citizen-Doctor is not in his right mind? The Revolution-fever will have been too much for him?"

Greatly too much for him.

"Hah! Many suffer with it. Lucie. His daughter. French. Which is she?"

This is she.

"Apparently it must be. Lucie, the wife of Evremond; is it not?"

It is.

"Hah! Evremond has an assignation elsewhere. Lucie, her child. English. This is she?"

She and no other.

"Kiss me, child of Evremond. Now, thou hast kissed a good Republican; something new in thy family; remember it! Sydney Carton. Advocate. English. Which is he?"

He lies here, in this corner of the carriage. He, too, is pointed out.

"Apparently the English advocate is in a swoon?"

It is hoped he will recover in the fresher air. It is represented that he is not in strong health, and has separated sadly from a friend who is under the displeasure of the Republic.

"Is that all? It is not a great deal, that! Many are under the displeasure of the Republic, and must look out at the little window. Jarvis Lorry. Banker. English. Which is he?"

"I am he. Necessarily, being the last."

It is Jarvis Lorry who has replied to all the previous questions. It is Jarvis Lorry who has alighted and stands with his hand on the coach door, replying to a group of officials. They leisurely walk round the carriage and leisurely mount the box to look at what little luggage it carries on the roof; the country-people hanging about press nearer to the coach doors and greedily stare in; a little child, carried by its mother, has its short arm held out for it, that it may touch the wife of an Aristocrat who has gone to the Guillotine.

"Behold your papers, Jarvis Lorry, countersigned."

"One can depart, citizen?"

"One can depart. Forward, my postilions! A good journey!"

"I salute you, citizens.—And the first danger passed!"

These are again the words of Jarvis Lorry as he clasps his hands and looks upward. There is terror in the carriage, there is weeping, there is the heavy breathing of the insensible traveller.

"Are we not going too slowly? Can they not be induced to go faster?" asks Lucie, clinging to the old man.

"It would seem like flight, my darling. I must not urge them too much; it would rouse suspicion."

"Look back, look back, and see if we are pursued!"

"The road is clear, my dearest. So far, we are not pursued."

Houses in twos and threes pass by us, solitary farms, ruinous buildings, dye-works, tanneries, and the like, open country, avenues of leafless trees. The hard uneven pavement is under us, the soft deep mud is on either side. Sometimes we strike into the skirting mud to avoid the stones that clatter us and shake us; sometimes we stick in ruts and sloughs there. The agony of our impatience is then so great, that in our wild alarm and hurry we are for getting out and running—hiding—doing anything but stopping.

Out of the open country, in again among ruinous buildings, solitary farms, dye-works, tanneries, and the like, cottages in twos and threes, avenues of leafless trees. Have these men deceived us and taken us back by another road? Is not this the same place twice over? Thank Heaven, no. A village. Look back, look back, and see if we are pursued! Hush! the posting-house.

Leisurely our four horses are taken out; leisurely the coach stands in the little street, bereft of horses, and with no likelihood upon it of ever moving again; leisurely the new horses come into visible existence, one by one; leisurely the new postilions follow, sucking and plaiting the lashes of their whips; leisurely the old postilions count their money, make wrong additions, and arrive at dissatisfied results. All the time our overfraught hearts are beating at a rate that would far outstrip the fastest gallop of the fastest horses ever foaled.

At length the new postilions are in their saddles, and the old are left behind. We are through the village, up the hill, and down the hill, and on the low watery grounds. Suddenly the postilions exchange speech with animated gesticulation, and the horses are pulled up, almost on their haunches. We are pursued?

" Ho! Within the carriage there. Speak then!"

" What is it?" asks Mr. Lorry, looking out at window.

" How many did they say?"

" I do not understand you."

" —At the last post. How many to the Guillotine to-day?"

" Fifty-two."

" I said so! A brave number! My fellow-citizen here would have it forty-two; ten more heads are worth having. The Guillotine goes handsomely. I love it. Hi forward. Whoop!"

The night comes on dark. He moves more; he is beginning to revive, and to speak intelligibly; he thinks they are still together; he asks him, by his name, what he has in his hand. Oh pity us, kind Heaven, and help us! Look out, look out, and see if we are pursued.

The wind is rushing after us, and the clouds are flying after us, and the moon is plunging after us, and the whole wild night is in pursuit of us; but, so far, we are pursued by nothing else.

CHAPTER XIV

THE KNITTING DONE

IN that same juncture of time when the Fifty-Two awaited their fate, Madame Defarge held darkly ominous council with The Vengeance and Jacques Three of the Revolutionary Jury. Not in the wine-shop did Madame Defarge confer with these ministers, but in the shed of the wood-sawyer, erst a mender of roads. The sawyer himself did not participate in the conference, but abided at a little distance, like an outer satellite who was not to speak until required, or to offer an opinion until invited.

"But our Defarge," said Jacques Three, "is undoubtedly a good Republican? Eh?"

"There is no better," the voluble Vengeance protested in her shrill notes, "in France."

"Peace, little Vengeance," said Madame Defarge, laying her hand with a slight frown on her lieutenant's lips, "hear me speak. My husband, fellow-citizen, is a good Republican and a bold man; he has deserved well of the Republic, and possesses its confidence. But my husband has his weaknesses, and he is so weak as to relent towards this Doctor."

"It is a great pity," croaked Jacques Three, dubiously shaking his head, with his cruel fingers at his hungry mouth; "it is not quite like a good citizen; it is a thing to regret."

"See you," said Madame, "I care nothing for this Doctor, I. He may wear his head or lose it, for any interest I have in him; it is all one to me. But the Evremond people are to be exterminated, and the wife and child must follow the husband and father."

"She has a fine head for it," croaked Jacques Three. "I have seen blue eyes and golden hair there, and they looked charming when Samson held them up." Ogre that he was, he spoke like an epicure.

Madame Defarge cast down her eyes, and reflected a little.

"The child also," observed Jacques Three, with a meditative enjoyment of his words, "has golden hair and blue eyes. And we seldom have a child there. It is a pretty sight!"

"In a word," said Madame Defarge, coming out of her short abstraction, "I cannot trust my husband in this matter. Not only do I feel, since last night, that I dare not confide to him the details of my projects; but also I feel that if I delay, there is danger of his giving warning, and then they might escape."

"That must never be," croaked Jacques Three; "no one must escape. We have not half enough as it is. We ought to have six score a day."

"In a word," Madame Defarge went on, "my husband has not my reason for pursuing this family to annihilation, and I have not his reason for regarding this Doctor with any sensibility. I must act for myself, therefore. Come hither, little citizen."

The wood-sawyer, who held her in the respect, and himself in the submission, of mortal fear, advanced with his hand to his red cap.

"Touching those signals, little citizen," said Madame Defarge, sternly, "that she made to the prisoners; you are ready to bear witness to them this very day?"

"Ay, ay, why not!" cried the sawyer. "Every day, in all weathers, from two to four, always signalling, sometimes with the little one, sometimes without. I know what I know. I have seen with my eyes."

He made all manner of gestures while he spoke, as if in incidental imitation of some few of the great diversity of signals that he had never seen.

"Clearly plots," said Jacques Three.   "Transparently!"

"There is no doubt of the Jury?" inquired Madame Defarge, letting her eyes turn to him with a gloomy smile.

"Rely upon the patriotic Jury, dear citizeness. I answer for my fellow-Jurymen."

"Now, let me see," said Madame Defarge, pondering again. "Yet once more! Can I spare this Doctor to my husband? I have no feeling either way. Can I spare him?"

"He would count as one head," observed Jacques Three, in a low voice. "We really have not heads enough; it would be a pity, I think."

"He was signalling with her when I saw her," argued Madame Defarge; "I cannot speak of one without the other; and I must not be silent, and trust the case wholly to him, this little citizen here. For I am not a bad witness."

The Vengeance and Jacques Three vied with each other in their fervent protestations that she was the most admirable and marvellous of witnesses. The little citizen, not to be outdone, declared her to be a celestial witness.

"He must take his chance," said Madame Defarge. "No, I cannot spare him! You are engaged at three o'clock; you are going to see the batch of to-day executed.—You?"

The question was addressed to the wood-sawyer, who hurriedly replied in the affirmative, seizing the occasion to add that he was the most ardent of Republicans, and that he would be in effect the most desolate of Republicans, if anything prevented him from enjoying the pleasure of smoking his afternoon pipe in the contemplation of the droll national barber. He was so very demonstrative herein, that he might have been suspected (perhaps was, by the dark eyes that looked contemptuously at him out of Madame Defarge's head) of having his small individual fears for his own personal safety, every hour in the day.

"I," said Madame, "am equally engaged at the same place. After it is over—say at eight to-night—come you to me, in Saint Antoine, and we will give information against these people at my Section."

The wood-sawyer said he would be proud and flattered to attend the citizeness. The citizeness looking at him, he became embarrassed, evaded her glance, as a small dog would have done, retreated among his wood, and hid his confusion over the handle of his saw.

Madame Defarge beckoned the Juryman and The Vengeance a little nearer to the door, and there expounded her further views to them thus—

"She will now be at home, awaiting the moment of his death. She will be mourning and grieving. She will be in a state of mind to impeach the justice of the Republic. She will be full of sympathy with its enemies. I will go to her."

"What an admirable woman; what an adorable woman!" exclaimed Jacques Three, rapturously. "Ah, my cherished!" cried The Vengeance, and embraced her.

"Take you my knitting," said Madame Defarge, placing it in her lieutenant's hands, "and have it ready for me in my usual seat. Keep me my usual chair. Go you there, straight, for there will probably be a greater concourse than usual, to-day."

"I willingly obey the orders of my Chief," said The Vengeance, with alacrity, and kissing her cheek. "You will not be late?"

"I shall be there before the commencement."

"And before the tumbrils arrive. Be sure you are there, my soul," said The Vengeance, calling after her, for she had already turned into the street, "before the tumbrils arrive!"

Madame Defarge slightly waved her hand, to imply that she heard, and might be relied upon to arrive in good time, and so went through the mud, and round the corner of the prison-wall. The Vengeance and the Juryman, looking after her as she walked away, were highly appreciative of her fine figure, and her superb moral endowments.

There were many women at that time upon whom the time laid a dreadfully disfiguring hand; but there was not one among them more to be dreaded than this ruthless woman, now taking her way along the streets. Of a strong and fearless character, of shrewd sense and readiness, of great determination, of that kind of beauty which not only seems to impart to its possessor firmness and animosity, but to strike into others an instinctive recognition of those qualities, the troubled time would have heaved her up, under any circumstances. But imbued from her childhood with a brooding sense of wrong, and an inveterate hatred of a class, opportunity had developed her into a tigress. She was absolutely without pity. If she had ever had the virtue in her, it had quite gone out of her.

It was nothing to her that an innocent man was to die for the sins of his forefathers; she saw, not him, but them. It was nothing to her that his wife was to be made a widow and his daughter an orphan; that was insufficient punishment, because they were her natural enemies and her prey, and as such had no right to live. To appeal to her was made hopeless by her having no sense of pity, even for herself. If she had been laid low in the streets, in any of the many encounters in which she had been engaged, she would not have pitied herself; nor, if she had been ordered to the axe to-morrow, would she have gone to it with any softer feeling than a fierce desire to change places with the man who sent her there.

Such a heart Madame Defarge carried under her rough robe. Carelessly worn, it was a becoming robe enough, in a certain weird way, and her dark hair looked rich under her coarse red cap. Lying hidden in her bosom was a loaded pistol. Lying hidden at her waist was a sharpened dagger. Thus accoutred, and walking with the confident tread of such a character, and with the supple freedom of a woman who had habitually walked in her girlhood, bare-foot and bare-legged, on the brown sea-sand, Madame Defarge took her way along the streets.

Now, when the journey of the travelling coach, at that very moment
waiting for the completion of its load, had been planned out last night,
the difficulty of taking Miss Pross in it had much engaged Mr. Lorry's
attention.   It was not merely desirable to avoid overloading the coach,
but it was of the highest importance that the time occupied in examining
it and its passengers should be reduced to the utmost, since their
escape might depend on the saving of only a few seconds here and there.
Finally, he had proposed, after anxious consideration, that Miss Pross
and Jerry, who were at liberty to leave the city, should leave it at three
o'clock in the lightest-wheeled conveyance known to that period.
Unencumbered with luggage, they would soon overtake the coach,
and, passing it and preceding it on the road, would order its horses in
advance, and greatly facilitate its progress during the precious hours of
the night, when delay was the most to be dreaded.

Seeing in this arrangement the hope of rendering real service in that
pressing emergency, Miss Pross hailed it with joy.   She and Jerry had
beheld the coach start, had known who it was that Solomon brought,
had passed some ten minutes in tortures of suspense, and were now
concluding their arrangements to follow the coach, even as Madame
Defarge, taking her way through the streets, now drew nearer and
nearer to the else-deserted lodging in which they held their con-
sultation.

"Now what do you think, Mr. Cruncher," said Miss Pross, whose
agitation was so great that she could hardly speak, or stand, or move,
or live,—"what do you think of our not starting from this courtyard?
Another carriage having already gone from here to-day, it might
awaken suspicion."

"My opinion, Miss," returned Mr. Cruncher, "is as you're right.
Likewise wot I'll stand by you, right or wrong."

"I am so distracted with fear and hope for our precious creatures,"
said Miss Pross, wildly crying, "that I am incapable of forming any
plan.   Are *you* capable of forming any plan, my dear good Mr.
Cruncher?"

"Respectin' a future spear o' life, Miss," returned Mr. Cruncher, "I
hope so.   Respectin' any present use o' this here blessed old head o'
mine, I think not.   Would you do me the favour, Miss, to take notice
o' two promises and wows wot it is my wishes fur to record in this here
crisis?"

"Oh, for gracious sake!" cried Miss Pross, still wildly crying,
"record them at once, and get them out of the way, like an excellent
man."

"First," said Mr. Cruncher, who was all in a tremble, and who
spoke with an ashy and solemn visage, "them poor things well out o'
this, never no more will I do it, never no more!"

"I am quite sure, Mr. Cruncher," returned Miss Pross, "that you
never will do it again, whatever it is, and I beg you not to think it
necessary to mention more particularly what it is."

"No, Miss," returned Jerry, "it shall not be named to you.   Second:

them poor things well out o' this, and never no more will I interfere with Mrs. Cruncher's flopping, never no more ! "

"Whatever housekeeping arrangement that may be," said Miss Pross, striving to dry her eyes and compose herself, "I have no doubt it is best that Mrs. Cruncher should have it entirely under her own superintendence.—Oh, my poor darlings ! "

"I go so far as to say, Miss, morehover," proceeded Mr. Cruncher, with a most alarming tendency to hold forth as from a pulpit—"and let my words be took down and took to Mrs. Cruncher through your-self—that wot my opinions respectin' flopping has undergone a change, and that wot I only hope with all my heart as Mrs. Cruncher may be a-flopping at the present time."

"There, there, there ! I hope she is, my dear man," cried the distracted Miss Pross, "and I hope she finds it answering her expectations."

"Forbid it," proceeded Mr. Cruncher, with additional solemnity, additional slowness, and additional tendency to hold forth and hold out, "as anything wot I have ever said or done should be wisited on my earnest wishes for them poor creeturs now ! Forbid it as we shouldn't all flop (if it was anyways conwenient) to get 'em out o' this here dismal risk ! Forbid it, Miss ! Wot I say, for—BID it ! " This was Mr. Cruncher's conclusion after a protracted but vain endeavour to find a better one.

And still Madame Defarge, pursuing her way along the streets, came nearer and nearer.

"If we ever get back to our native land," said Miss Pross, "you may rely upon my telling Mrs. Cruncher as much as I may be able to remember and understand of what you have so impressively said ; and at all events you may be sure that I shall bear witness to your being thoroughly in earnest at this dreadful time. Now, pray let us think ! My esteemed Mr. Cruncher, let us think ! "

Still Madame Defarge, pursuing her way along the streets, came nearer and nearer.

"If you were to go before," said Miss Pross, "and stop the vehicle and horses from coming here, and were to wait somewhere for me ; wouldn't that be best ? "

Mr. Cruncher thought it might be best.

"Where could you wait for me ? " asked Miss Pross.

Mr. Cruncher was so bewildered that he could think of no locality but Temple Bar. Alas ! Temple Bar was hundreds of miles away, and Madame Defarge was drawing very near indeed.

"By the cathedral door," said Miss Pross. "Would it be much out of the way to take me in near the great cathedral door between the two towers ? "

"No, Miss," answered Mr. Cruncher.

"Then, like the best of men," said Miss Pross, "go to the posting-house straight, and make that change."

"I am doubtful," said Mr. Cruncher, hesitating and shaking his head, "about leaving of you, you see. We don't know what may happen."

"Heaven knows we don't," returned Miss Pross, "but have no fear of me. Take me in at the cathedral, at three o'clock, or as near it as you can, and I am sure it will be better than our going from here. I feel certain of it. There! Bless you, Mr. Cruncher! Think—not of me, but of the lives that may depend on both of us!"

This exordium, and Miss Pross's two hands in quite agonised entreaty clasping his, decided Mr. Cruncher. With an encouraging nod or two, he immediately went out to alter the arrangements, and left her by herself to follow as she had proposed.

The having originated a precaution which was already in course of execution was a great relief to Miss Pross. The necessity of composing her appearance so that it should attract no special notice in the streets was another relief. She looked at her watch, and it was twenty minutes past two. She had no time to lose, but must get ready at once.

Afraid, in her extreme perturbation, of the loneliness of the deserted rooms, and of half-imagined faces peeping from behind every open door in them, Miss Pross got a basin of cold water and began laving her eyes, which were swollen and red. Haunted by her feverish apprehensions, she could not bear to have her sight obscured for a minute at a time by the dripping water, but constantly paused and looked round to see that there was no one watching her. In one of those pauses she recoiled and cried out, for she saw a figure standing in the room.

The basin fell to the ground broken, and the water flowed to the feet of Madame Defarge. By strange stern ways, and through much staining blood, those feet had come to meet that water.

Madame Defarge looked coldly at her, and said, "The wife of Evremond; where is she?"

It flashed upon Miss Pross's mind that the doors were all standing open, and would suggest the flight. Her first act was to shut them. There were four in the room, and she shut them all. She then placed herself before the door of the chamber which Lucie had occupied.

Madame Defarge's dark eyes followed her through this rapid movement, and rested on her when it was finished. Miss Pross had nothing beautiful about her; years had not tamed the wildness or softened the grimness of her appearance; but she too was a determined woman in her different way, and she measured Madame Defarge with her eyes, every inch.

"You might, from your appearance, be the wife of Lucifer," said Miss Pross, in her breathing. "Nevertheless, you shall not get the better of me. I am an Englishwoman."

Madame Defarge looked at her scornfully, but still with something of Miss Pross's own perception that they two were at bay. She saw a tight, hard, wiry woman before her, as Mr. Lorry had seen in the same figure a woman with a strong hand in the years gone by. She knew full well that Miss Pross was the family's devoted friend ; Miss Pross knew full well that Madame Defarge was the family's malevolent enemy.

"On my way yonder," said Madame Defarge, with a slight movement of her hand towards the fatal spot, "where they reserve my chair and my knitting for me, I am come to make my compliments to her in passing. I wish to see her."

"I know that your intentions are evil," said Miss Pross, "and you may depend upon it, I'll hold my own against them."

Each spoke in her own language ; neither understood the other's words ; both were very watchful, and intent to deduce from look and manner what the unintelligible words meant.

"It will do her no good to keep herself concealed from me at this moment," said Madame Defarge. "Good patriots will know what that means. Let me see her. Go tell her that I wish to see her. Do you hear ? "

"If those eyes of yours were bed-winches," returned Miss Pross, "and I was an English four-poster, they shouldn't loose a splinter of me. No, you wicked foreign woman ; I am your match."

Madame Defarge was not likely to follow these idiomatic remarks in detail ; but she so far understood them as to perceive that she was set at naught.

"Woman imbecile and pig-like ! " said Madame Defarge, frowning, "I take no answer from you. I demand to see her. Either tell her that I demand to see her, or stand out of the way of the door and let me go to her ! " This, with an angry explanatory wave of her right arm.

"I little thought," said Miss Pross, "that I should ever want to understand your nonsensical language ; but I would give all I have, except the clothes I wear, to know whether you suspect the truth, or any part of it."

Neither of them for a single moment released the other's eyes. Madame Defarge had not moved from the spot where she stood when Miss Pross first became aware of her, but she now advanced one step.

"I am a Briton," said Miss Pross, "I am desperate. I don't care an English Twopence for myself. I know that the longer I keep you here, the greater hope there is for my Ladybird. I'll not leave a handful of that dark hair upon your head, if you lay a finger on me ! "

Thus Miss Pross, with a shake of her head and a flash of her eyes between every rapid sentence, and every rapid sentence a whole breath. Thus Miss Pross, who had never struck a blow in her life.

But her courage was of that emotional nature that it brought the irrepressible tears into her eyes. This was a courage that Madame Defarge so little comprehended as to mistake for weakness. "Ha, ha ! " she laughed, "you poor wretch ! What are you worth ? I address myself to that Doctor." Then she raised her voice and called out, "Citizen Doctor ! Wife of Evremond ! Child of Evremond ! Any person but this miserable fool, answer the Citizeness Defarge ! "

Perhaps the following silence, perhaps some latent disclosure in the expression of Miss Pross's face, perhaps a sudden misgiving apart from either suggestion, whispered to Madame Defarge that they were gone. Three of the doors she opened swiftly, and looked in.

"Those rooms are all in disorder, there has been hurried packing, there are odds and ends upon the ground. There is no one in that room behind you! Let me look."

"Never!" said Miss Pross, who understood the request as perfectly as Madame Defarge understood the answer.

"If they are not in that room, they are gone, and can be pursued and brought back," said Madame Defarge to herself.

"As long as you don't know whether they are in that room or not, you are uncertain what to do," said Miss Pross to *her*self; "and you shall not know that, if I can prevent your knowing it; and know that, or not know that, you shall not leave here while I can hold you."

"I have been in the streets from the first, nothing has stopped me; I will tear you to pieces, but I will have you from that door," said Madame Defarge.

"We are alone at the top of a high house in a solitary courtyard, we are not likely to be heard, and I pray for bodily strength to keep you here, while every minute you are here is worth a hundred thousand guineas to my darling," said Miss Pross.

Madame Defarge made at the door. Miss Pross, on the instinct of the moment, seized her round the waist in both her arms, and held her tight. It was in vain for Madame Defarge to struggle and to strike; Miss Pross, with the vigorous tenacity of love, always so much stronger than hate, clasped her tight, and even lifted her from the floor in the struggle that they had. The two hands of Madame Defarge buffeted and tore her face; but Miss Pross, with her head down, held her round the waist, and clung to her with more than the hold of a drowning woman.

Soon Madame Defarge's hands ceased to strike, and felt at her encircled waist. "It is under my arm," said Miss Pross, in smothered tones, "you shall not draw it. I am stronger than you, I bless Heaven for it. I'll hold you till one or other of us faints or dies!"

Madame Defarge's hands were at her bosom. Miss Pross looked up, saw what it was, struck at it, struck out a flash and a crash, and stood alone—blinded with smoke.

All this was in a second. As the smoke cleared, leaving an awful stillness, it passed out on the air, like the soul of the furious woman whose body lay lifeless on the ground.

In the first fright and horror of her situation, Miss Pross passed the body as far from it as she could, and ran down the stairs to call for fruitless help. Happily, she bethought herself of the consequences of what she did, in time to check herself and go back. It was dreadful to go in at the door again; but she did go in, and even went near it, to get the bonnet and other things that she must wear. These she put on, out on the staircase, first shutting and locking the door and taking away the key. She then sat down on the stairs a few moments to breathe and to cry, and then got up and hurried away.

By good fortune she had a veil on her bonnet, or she could hardly have gone along the streets without being stopped. By good fortune, too, she was naturally so peculiar in appearance as not to show disfigurement like any other woman. She needed both advantages, for the marks of gripping fingers were deep in her face, and her hair was torn, and her dress (hastily composed with unsteady hands) was clutched and dragged a hundred ways.

In crossing the bridge, she dropped the door-key in the river. Arriving at the cathedral some few minutes before her escort, and waiting there, she thought, what if the key were already taken in a net, what if it were identified, what if the door were opened and the remains discovered, what if she were stopped at the gate, sent to prison, and charged with murder! In the midst of these fluttering thoughts the escort appeared, took her in, and took her away.

"Is there any noise in the streets?" she asked him.

"The usual noises," Mr. Cruncher replied, and looked surprised by the question and by her aspect.

"I don't hear you," said Miss Pross. "What do you say?"

It was in vain for Mr. Cruncher to repeat what he said; Miss Pross could not hear him. "So I'll nod my head," thought Mr. Cruncher, amazed, "at all events she'll see that." And she did.

"Is there any noise in the streets now?" asked Miss Pross again, presently.

Again Mr. Cruncher nodded his head.

"I don't hear it."

"Gone deaf in a hour?" said Mr. Cruncher, ruminating, with his mind much disturbed; "wot's come to her?"

"I feel," said Miss Pross, "as if there had been a flash and a crash, and that crash was the last thing I should ever hear in this life."

"Blest if she ain't in a queer condition!" said Mr. Cruncher, more and more disturbed. "Wot can she have been a-takin', to keep her courage up? Hark! There's the roll of them dreadful carts! You can hear that, Miss?"

"I can hear," said Miss Pross, seeing that he spoke to her, "nothing. Oh, my good man, there was first a great crash, and then a great stillness, and that stillness seems to be fixed and unchangeable, never to be broken any more as long as my life lasts."

"If she don't hear the roll of those dreadful carts, now very nigh their journey's end," said Mr. Cruncher, glancing over his shoulder, "it's my opinion that indeed she never will hear anything else in this world."

And indeed she never did.

CHAPTER XV

THE FOOTSTEPS DIE OUT FOR EVER

ALONG the Paris streets the death-carts rumble, hollow and harsh. Six tumbrils carry the day's wine to La Guillotine. All the devouring and insatiate Monsters imagined since imagination could record itself are fused in the one realisation, Guillotine. And yet there is not in France, with its rich variety of soil and climate, a blade, a leaf, a root, a sprig, a peppercorn, which will grow to maturity under conditions more certain than those that have produced this horror. Crush humanity out of shape once more, under similar hammers, and it will twist itself into the same tortured forms. Sow the same seed of rapacious license and oppression over again, and it will surely yield the same fruit according to its kind.

Six tumbrils roll along the streets. Change these back again to what they were, thou powerful enchanter, Time, and they shall be seen to be the carriages of absolute monarchs, the equipages of feudal nobles, the toilets of flaring Jezebels, the churches that are not my father's house but dens of thieves, the huts of millions of starving peasants! No; the great magician who majestically works out the appointed order of the Creator, never reverses his transformations. "If thou be changed into this shape by the will of God," say the seers to the enchanted, in the wise Arabian stories, "then remain so! But if thou wear this form through mere passing conjuration, then resume thy former aspect!" Changeless and hopeless, the tumbrils roll along.

As the sombre wheels of the six carts go round, they seem to plough up a long crooked furrow among the populace in the streets. Ridges of faces are thrown to this side and to that, and the ploughs go steadily onward. So used are the regular inhabitants of the houses to the spectacle, that in many windows there are no people, and in some the occupation of the hands is not so much as suspended, while the eyes survey the faces in the tumbrils. Here and there the inmate has visitors to see the sight; then he points his finger, with something of the complacency of a curator or authorised exponent, to this cart and to this, and seems to tell who sat here yesterday, and who there the day before.

Of the riders in the tumbrils some observe these things, and all things on their last roadside, with an impassive stare; others, with a lingering interest in the ways of life and men. Some, seated with drooping heads, are sunk in silent despair; again, there are some so heedful of their looks that they cast upon the multitude such glances as they have seen in theatres, and in pictures. Several close their eyes, and think, or try to get their straying thoughts together. Only one, and he a miserable creature, of a crazed aspect, is so shattered and made drunk by horror, that he sings, and tries to dance. Not one of the whole number appeals by look or gesture to the pity of the people.

There is a guard of sundry horsemen riding abreast of the tumbrils, and faces are often turned up to some of them, and they are asked some question. It would seem to be always the same question, for it is always followed by a press of people towards the third cart. The horsemen abreast of that cart frequently point out one man in it with their swords. The leading curiosity is, to know which is he ; he stands at the back of the tumbril with his head bent down, to converse with a mere girl who sits on the side of the cart, and holds his hand. He has no curiosity or care for the scene about him, and always speaks to the girl. Here and there in the long street of St. Honoré, cries are raised against him. If they move him at all, it is only to a quiet smile, as he shakes his hair a little more loosely about his face. He cannot easily touch his face, his arms being bound.

On the steps of a church, awaiting the coming-up of the tumbrils, stands the Spy and prison-sheep. He looks into the first of them ; not there. He looks into the second ; not there. He already asks himself, " Has he sacrificed me ? " when his face clears as he looks into the third.

" Which is Evremonde ? " says a man behind him.

" That. At the back there."

" With his hand in the girl's ? "

" Yes."

The man cries, " Down, Evrmonde ! To the Guillotine all Aristocrats ! Down, Evremond ! "

" Hush, hush ! " the Spy entreats him, timidly.

" And why not, citizen ? "

" He is going to pay the forfeit : it will be paid in five minutes more. Let him be at peace."

But the man continuing to exclaim, " Down, Evremond ! " the face of Evremond is for a moment turned towards him. Evremond then sees the Spy, and looks attentively at him, and goes his way.

The clocks are on the stroke of three, and the furrow ploughed among the populace is turning round, to come on into the place of execution, and end. The ridges thrown to this side and to that now crumble in and close behind the last plough as it passes on, for all are following to the Guillotine. In the front of it, seated in chairs, as in a garden of public diversion, are a number of women, busily knitting. On one of the foremost chairs stands The Vengeance, looking about for her friend.

" Thérèse ! " she cries, in her shrill tones. " Who has seen her ? Thérèse Defarge ! "

" She never missed before," says a knitting-woman of the sisterhood.

" No ; nor will she miss now," cries The Vengeance, petulantly. " Thérèse."

" Louder," the woman recommends.

Ay ! Louder, Vengeance, much louder, and still she will scarcely hear thee. Louder yet, Vengeance, with a little oath or so added, and yet it will hardly bring her. Send other women up and down to seek her, lingering somewhere; and yet, although the messengers have done dread deeds, it is questionable whether of their own wills they will go far enough to find her!

"Bad Fortune!" cries The Vengeance, stamping her foot in the chair, "and here are the tumbrils! And Evremond will be dispatched in a wink, and she not here! See her knitting in my hand, and her empty chair ready for her. I cry with vexation and disappointment!"

As The Vengeance descends from her elevation to do it, the tumbrils begin to discharge their loads. The ministers of Sainte Guillotine are robed and ready. Crash!—A head is held up, and the knitting-women who scarcely lifted their eyes to look at it a moment ago when it could think and speak, count One.

The second tumbril empties and moves on; the third comes up. Crash!—And the knitting-women, never faltering or pausing in their work, count Two.

The supposed Evremond descends, and the seamstress is lifted out next after him. He has not relinquished her patient hand in getting out, but still holds it as he promised. He gently places her with her back to the crashing engine that constantly whirrs up and falls, and she looks into his face and thanks him.

"But for you, dear stranger, I should not be so composed, for I am naturally a poor little thing, faint of heart; nor should I have been able to raise my thoughts to Him who was put to death that we might have hope and comfort here to-day. I think you were sent to me by Heaven."

"Or you to me," says Sydney Carton. "Keep your eyes upon me, dear child, and mind no other object."

"I mind nothing while I hold your hand. I shall mind nothing when I let it go, if they are rapid."

"They will be rapid. Fear not!"

The two stand in the fast-thinning throng of victims, but they speak as if they were alone. Eye to eye, voice to voice, hand to hand, heart to heart, these two children of the Universal Mother, else so wide apart and differing, have come together on the dark highway, to repair home together, and to rest in her bosom.

"Brave and generous friend, will you let me ask you one last question? I am very ignorant, and it troubles me—just a little."

"Tell me what it is."

"I have a cousin, an only relative and an orphan, like myself, whom I love very dearly. She is five years younger than I, and she lives in a farmer's house in the south country. Poverty parted us, and she knows nothing of my fate—for I cannot write—and if I could, how should I tell her! It is better as it is."

"Yes, yes; better as it is."

"What I have been thinking as we came along, and what I am still thinking now, as I look into your kind strong face which gives me so

much support, is this :—If the Republic really does good to the poor,
and they come to be less hungry, and in all ways to suffer less, she
may live a long time : she may even live to be old."

"What then, my gentle sister?"

"Do you think"—the uncomplaining eyes in which there is so much
endurance fill with tears, and the lips part a little more and tremble—
"that it will seem long to me, while I wait for her in the better land
where I trust both you and I will be mercifully sheltered?"

"It cannot be, my child; there is no Time there, and no trouble
there."

"You comfort me so much! I am so ignorant. Am I to kiss you
now? Is the moment come?"

"Yes."

She kisses his lips; he kisses hers; they solemnly bless each other.
The spare hand does not tremble as he releases it; nothing worse than
a sweet, bright constancy is in the patient face. She goes next before
him—is gone; the knitting-women count Twenty-Two.

"I am the Resurrection and the Life, saith the Lord: he that
believeth in me, though he were dead, yet shall he live; and whosoever
liveth and believeth in me shall never die."

The murmuring of many voices, the upturning of many faces, the
pressing on of many footsteps in the outskirts of the crowd, so that it
swells forward in a mass, like one great heave of water, all flashes
away. Twenty-Three.

They said of him, about the city that night, that it was the peacefullest
man's face ever beheld there. Many added that he looked sublime and
prophetic.

One of the most remarkable sufferers by the same axe—a woman—
had asked at the foot of the same scaffold, not long before, to be allowed
to write down the thoughts that were inspiring her. If he had given
any utterance to his, and they were prophetic, they would have been
these—

"I see Barsad, and Cly, Defarge, The Vengeance, the Juryman, the
Judge, long ranks of the new oppressors who have risen on the
destruction of the old, perishing by this retributive instrument, before
it shall cease out of its present use. I see a beautiful city and a brilliant
people rising from this abyss, and, in their struggles to be truly free,
in their triumphs and defeats, through long, long years to come, I see
the evil of this time, and of the previous time of which this is the natural
birth, gradually making expiation for itself and wearing out.

"I see the lives for which I lay down my life, peaceful, useful,
prosperous and happy, in that England which I shall see no more.
I see Her with a child upon her bosom, who bears my name. I see
her father, aged and bent, but otherwise restored, and faithful to all
men in his healing office, and at peace. I see the good old man, so
long their friend, in ten years' time enriching them with all he has,
and passing tranquilly to his reward.

Twenty-three!

"I see that I hold a sanctuary in their hearts, and in the hearts of their descendants, generations hence. I see her, an old woman, weeping for me on the anniversary of this day. I see her and her husband, their course done, lying side by side in their last earthly bed, and I know that each was not more honoured and held sacred in the other's soul than I was in the souls of both.

"I see that child who lay upon her bosom and who bore my name, a man winning his way up in that path of life which once was mine. I see him winning it so well, that my name is made illustrious there by the light of his. I see the blots I threw upon it faded away. I see him, foremost of just judges and honoured men, bringing a boy of my name, with a forehead that I know and golden hair, to this place —then fair to look upon, with not a trace of this day's disfigurement— and I hear him tell the child my story, with a tender and a faltering voice.

"It is a far, far better thing that I do, than I have ever done; it is a far, far better rest that I go to than I have ever known."

THE
UNCOMMERCIAL TRAVELLER

CONTENTS

THE
UNCOMMERCIAL TRAVELLER

I

HIS GENERAL LINE OF BUSINESS

ALLOW me to introduce myself—first negatively.

No landlord is my friend and brother, no chambermaid loves me, no waiter worships me, no boots admires and envies me. No round of beef or tongue or ham is expressly cooked for me, no pigeon-pie is especially made for me, no hotel advertisement is personally addressed to me, no hotel-room tapestried with great-coats and railway wrappers is set apart for me, no house of public entertainment in the United Kingdom greatly cares for my opinion of its brandy or sherry. When I go upon my journeys, I am not usually rated at a low figure in the bill; when I come home from my journeys, I never get any commission. I know nothing about prices, and should have no idea, if I were put to it, how to wheedle a man into ordering something he doesn't want. As a town traveller, I am never to be seen driving a vehicle externally like a young and volatile pianoforte van, and internally like an oven in which a number of flat boxes are baking in layers. As a country traveller, I am rarely to be found in a gig, and am never to be encountered by a pleasure train, waiting on the platform of a branch station, quite a Druid in the midst of a light Stonehenge of samples.

And yet—proceeding now to introduce myself positively—I am both a town traveller and a country traveller, and am always on the road. Figuratively speaking, I travel for the great house of Human Interest Brothers, and have rather a large connection in the fancy goods way. Literally speaking, I am always wandering here and there from my rooms in Covent Garden, London—now about the city streets: now about the country byroads—seeing many little things, and some great things, which, because they interest me, I think may interest others.

These are my brief credentials as the Uncommercial Traveller.

II

THE SHIPWRECK

NEVER had I seen a year going out, or going on, under quieter circumstances. Eighteen hundred and fifty-nine had but another day to live, and truly its end was Peace on that sea-shore that morning.

So settled and orderly was everything seaward, in the bright light of the sun and under the transparent shadows of the clouds, that it was hard to imagine the bay otherwise, for years past or to come, than it was that very day. The Tug-steamer lying a little off the shore, the Lighter lying still nearer to the shore, the boat alongside the Lighter, the regularly-turning windlass aboard the Lighter, the methodical figures at work, all slowly and regularly heaving up and down with the breathing of the sea, all seemed as much a part of the nature of the place as the tide itself. The tide was on the flow, and had been for some two hours and a half; there was a slight obstruction in the sea within a few yards of my feet, as if the stump of a tree, with earth enough about it to keep it from lying horizontally on the water, had slipped a little from the land—and as I stood upon the beach and observed it dimpling the light swell that was coming in, I cast a stone over it.

So orderly, so quiet, so regular—the rising and falling of the Tug-steamer, the Lighter, and the boat—the turning of the windlass—the coming in of the tide—that I myself seemed, to my own thinking, anything but new to the spot. Yet I had never seen it in my life, a minute before, and had traversed two hundred miles to get at it. That very morning I had come bowling down, and struggling up, hill-country roads; looking back at snowy summits; meeting courteous peasants, well to do, driving fat pigs and cattle to market; noting the neat and thrifty dwellings, with their unusual quantity of clean white linen drying on the bushes; having windy weather suggested by every cotter's little rick, with its thatch straw-ridged and extra straw-ridged into overlapping compartments like the back of a rhinoceros. Had I not given a lift of fourteen miles to the Coast-guardsman (kit and all), who was coming to his spell of duty there, and had we not just now parted company? So it was; but the journey seemed to glide down into the placid sea, with other chafe and trouble, and for the moment nothing was so calmly and monotonously real under the sunlight as the gentle rising and falling of the water with its freight, the regular turning of the windlass aboard the Lighter, and the slight obstruction so very near my feet.

Oh reader, haply turning this page by the fireside at Home, and hearing the night wind rumble in the chimney, that slight obstruction was the uppermost fragment of the wreck of the *Royal Charter*. Australian trader and passenger ship, Homeward bound, that struck nere cn the terrible morning of the twenty-sixth of this October, broke into three parts, went down with her treasure of at least five hundred human lives, and has never stirred since !

From which point, or from which, she drove ashore, stern formost ; on which side, or on which, she passed the little Island in the bay, for ages henceforth to be aground certain yards outside her ; these are rendered bootless questions by the darkness of that night and the darkness of death. Here she went down.

Even as I stood on the beach with the words " Here she went down ! " in my ears, a diver in his grotesque dress dipped heavily over the side of the boat alongside the Lighter and dropped to the bottom. On the shore by the water's edge was a rough tent, made of fragments of wreck, where other divers and workmen sheltered themselves, and where they had kept Christmas-day with rum and roast beef, to the destruction of their frail chimney. Cast up among the stones and boulders of the beach were great spars of the lost vessel, and masses of iron twisted by the fury of the sea into the strangest forms. The timber was already bleached and iron rusted, and even these objects did no violence to the prevailing air the whole scene wore of having been exactly the same for years and years.

Yet only two short months had gone since a man, living on the nearest hill-top overlooking the sea, being blown out of bed at about daybreak by the wind that had begun to strip his roof off, and getting upon a ladder with his nearest neighbour to construct some temporary device for keeping his house over his head, saw from the ladder's elevation, as he looked down by chance towards the shore, some dark troubled object close in with the land. And he and the other, descending to the beach, and finding the sea mercilessly beating over a great broken ship, had clambered up the stony ways, like staircases without stairs, on which the wild village hangs in little clusters, as fruit hangs on boughs, and had given the alarm. And so, over the hill-slopes, and past the waterfall, and down the gullies where the land drains off into the ocean, the scattered quarrymen and fishermen inhabiting that part of Wales had come running to the dismal sight—their clergyman among them. And as they stood in the leaden morning, stricken with pity, leaning hard against the wind, their breath and vision often failing as the sleet and spray rushed at them from the ever-forming and dissolving mountains of sea, and as the wool which was a part of the vessel's cargo blew in with the salt foam and remained upon the land when the foam melted, they saw the ship's life-boat put off from one of the heaps of wreck ; and first there were three men in her, and in a moment she capsized, and there were but two ; and again she was struck by a vast mass of water, and there was but one ; and again she was thrown bottom upward, and that one, with his arm struck through the broken planks and waving as if for help that could never reach him, went down into the deep.

It was the clergyman himself from whom I heard this, while I stood on the shore, looking in his kind wholesome face as it turned to the spot where the boat had been. The divers were down then, and busy. They were "lifting" to-day the gold found yesterday—some five-and-twenty thousand pounds. Of three hundred and fifty thousand pounds' worth of gold, three hundred thousand pounds' worth, in round numbers, was at that time recovered. The great bulk of the remainder was surely and steadily coming up. Some loss of sovereigns there would be, of course ; indeed, at first sovereigns had drifted in with the sand, and been scattered far and wide over the beach, like sea-shells ; but most other golden treasure would be found. As it was brought up, it went aboard the Tug-steamer, where good account was taken of it. So tremendous had the force of the sea been when it broke the ship, that it had beaten one great ingot of gold deep into a strong and heavy piece of her solid iron-work, in which, also, several loose sovereigns that the ingot had swept in before it had been found, as firmly embedded as though the iron had been liquid when they were forced there. It had been remarked of such bodies come ashore, too, as had been seen by scientific men, that they had been stunned to death, and not suffocated. Observation, both of the internal change that had been wrought in them, and of their external expression, showed death to have been thus merciful and easy. The report was brought, while I was holding such discourse on the beach, that no more bodies had come ashore since last night. It began to be very doubtful whether many more would be thrown up, until the north-east winds of the early spring set in. Moreover, a great number of the passengers, and particularly the second-class women-passengers, were known to have been in the middle of the ship when she parted, and thus the collapsing wreck would have fallen upon them after yawning open, and would keep them down. A diver made known, even then, that he had come upon the body of a man, and had sought to release it from a great superincumbent weight ; but that, finding he could not do so without mutilating the remains, he had left it where it was.

It was the kind and wholesome face I have made mention of as being then beside me that I had purposed to myself to see when I left home for Wales. I had heard of that clergyman as having buried many scores of the shipwrecked people ; of his having opened his house and heart to their agonised friends ; of his having used a most sweet and patient diligence for weeks and weeks in the performance of the forlornest offices that Man can render to his kind ; of his having most tenderly and thoroughly devoted himself to the dead, and to those who were sorrowing for the dead. I had said to myself, "In the Christmas season of the year, I should like to see that man !" And he had swung the gate of his little garden in coming out to meet me not half an hour ago.

So cheerful of spirit and guiltless of affectation, as true practical Christianity ever is ! I read more of the New Testament in the fresh frank face going up the village beside me, in five minutes, than I have read in anathematising discourses (albeit put to press with enormous flourishing of trumpets) in all my life. I heard more of the Sacred

Book in the cordial voice that had nothing to say about its owner, than in all the would-be celestial pairs of bellows that have ever blown conceit at me.

We climbed towards the little church at a cheery pace, among the loose stones, the deep mud, the wet coarse grass, the outlying water, and other obstructions from which frost and snow had lately thawed. It was a mistake (my friend was glad to tell me, on the way) to suppose that the peasantry had shown any superstitious avoidance of the drowned ; on the whole, they had done very well, and had assisted readily. Ten shillings had been paid for the bringing of each body up to the church, but the way was steep, and a horse and cart (in which it was wrapped in a sheet) were necessary, and three or four men, and, all things considered, it was not a great price. The people were none the richer for the wreck, for it was the season of the herring-shoal— and who could cast nets for fish and find dead men and women in the draught ?

He had the church keys in his hand, and opened the churchyard gate, and opened the church door ; and we went in.

It is a little church of great antiquity ; there is reason to believe that some church has occupied the spot these thousand years or more. The pulpit was gone, and other things usually belonging to the church were gone, owing to its living congregation having deserted it for the neighbouring school-room, and yielded it up to the dead. The very Commandments had been shouldered out of their places, in the bringing in of the dead ; the black wooden tables on which they were painted were askew, and on the stone pavement below them, and on the stone pavement all over the church, were the marks and stains where the drowned had been laid down. The eye, with little or no aid from the imagination, could yet see how the bodies had been turned, and where the head had been and where the feet. Some faded traces of the wreck of the Australian ship may be discernible on the stone pavement of this little church, hundreds of years hence, when the digging for gold in Australia shall have long and long ceased out of the land.

Forty-four shipwrecked men and women lay here at one time, awaiting burial. Here, with weeping and wailing in every room of his house, my companion worked alone for hours, solemnly surrounded by eyes that could not see him, and by lips that could not speak to him, patiently examining the tattered clothing, cutting off buttons, hair, marks from linen, anything that might lead to subsequent identification, studying faces, looking for a scar, a bent finger, a crooked toe, comparing letters sent to him with the ruin about him. " My dearest brother had bright gray eyes and a pleasant smile," one sister wrote. Oh poor sister ! well for you to be far from here, and keep that as your last remembrance of him !

The ladies of the clergyman's family, his wife and two sisters-in-law, came in among the bodies often. It grew to be the business of their lives to do so. Any new arrival of a bereaved woman would stimulate their pity to compare the description brought with the dread realities.

Sometimes they would go back able to say, "I have found him," or, "I think she lies there." Perhaps the mourner, unable to bear the sight of all that lay in the church, would be led in blindfold. Conducted to the spot with many compassionate words, and encouraged to look, she would say, with a piercing cry, "This is my boy!" and drop insensible on the insensible figure.

He soon observed that in some cases of women, the identification of persons, though complete, was quite at variance with the marks upon the linen; this led him to notice that even the marks upon the linen were sometimes inconsistent with one another; and thus he came to understand that they had dressed in great haste and agitation, and that their clothes had become mixed together. The identification of men by their dress was rendered extremely difficult, in consequence of a large proportion of them being dressed alike—in clothes of one kind, that is to say, supplied by slopsellers and outfitters, and not made by single garments but by hundreds. Many of the men were bringing over parrots, and had receipts upon them for the price of the birds; others had bills of exchange in their pockets, or in belts. Some of these documents, carefully unwrinkled and dried, were little less fresh in appearance that day than the present page will be under ordinary circumstances after having been opened three or four times.

In that lonely place it had not been easy to obtain even such common commodities in towns as ordinary disinfectants. Pitch had been burnt in the church, as the readiest thing at hand, and the frying-pan in which it had bubbled over a brazier of coals was still there, with its ashes. Hard by the Communion Table were some boots that had been taken off the drowned, and preserved—a gold-digger's boot, cut down the leg for its removal—a trodden-down man's ankle-boot with a buff cloth top—and others—soaked and sandy, weedy and salt.

From the church we passed out into the churchyard. Here there lay, at that time, one hundred and forty-five bodies, that had come ashore from the wreck. He had buried them, when not identified, in graves containing four each. He had numbered each body in a register describing it, and had placed a corresponding number on each coffin, and over each grave. Identified bodies he had buried singly, in private graves, in another part of the churchyard. Several bodies had been exhumed from the graves of four, as relatives had come from a distance and seen his register; and, when recognised, these have been reburied in private graves, so that the mourners might erect separate headstones over the remains. In all such cases he had performed the funeral service a second time, and the ladies of his house had attended. There had been no offence in the poor ashes when they were brought again to the light of day; the beneficent Earth had already absorbed it. The drowned were buried in their clothes. To supply the great sudden demand for coffins, he had got all the neighbouring people handy at tools to work the livelong day, and Sunday likewise. The coffins were neatly formed —I had seen two, waiting for occupants, under the lee of the ruined walls of a stone hut on the beach, within call of the tent where the

Christmas Feast was held.   Similarly, one of the graves for four was lying open and ready, here, in the churchyard.   So much of the scanty space was already devoted to the wrecked people, that the villagers had begun to express uneasy doubts whether they themselves could lie in their own ground, with their forefathers and descendants, by and by. The churchyard being but a step from the clergyman's dwelling-house, we crossed to the latter ; the white surplice was hanging up near the door ready to be put on at any time for a funeral service.

The cheerful earnestness of this good Christian minister was as consolatory as the circumstances out of which it shone were sad.   I never have seen anything more delightfully genuine than the calm dismissal by himself and his household of all they had undergone, as a simple duty that was quietly done and ended.   In speaking of it, they spoke of it with great compassion for the bereaved ; but laid no stress upon their own hard share in those weary weeks, except as it had attached many people to them as friends, and elicited many touching expressions of gratitude.   This clergyman's brother—himself the clergyman of two adjoining parishes, who had buried thirty-four of the bodies in his own churchyard, and who had done to them all that his brother had done as to the larger number—must be understood as included in the family. He was there, with his neatly arranged papers, and made no more account of his trouble than anybody else did.   Down to yesterday's post outward, my clergyman alone had written one thousand and seventy-five letters to relatives and friends of the lost people.   In the absence of self-assertion, it was only through my now and then delicately putting a question as the occasion arose, that I became informed of these things. It was only when I had remarked again and again, in the church, on the awful nature of the scene of death he had been required so closely to familiarise himself with for the soothing of the living, that he had casually said, without the least abatement of his cheerfulness, " indeed, it had rendered him unable for a time to eat or drink more than a little coffee now and then, and a piece of bread."

In this noble modesty, in this beautiful simplicity, in this serene avoidance of the least attempt to " improve " an occasion which might be supposed to have sunk of its own weight into my heart, I seemed to have happily come, in a few steps, from the churchyard with its open grave, which was the type of Death, to the Christian dwelling side by side with it, which was the type of Resurrection.   I never shall think of the former without the latter.   The two will always rest side by side in my memory.   If I had lost any one dear to me in this unfortunate ship, if I had made a voyage from Australia to look at the grave in the churchyard, I should go away thankful to God that that house was so close to it, and that its shadow by day and its domestic lights by night fell upon the earth in which its Master had so tenderly laid my dear one's head.

The references that naturally arose out of our conversation to the descriptions sent down of shipwrecked persons, and to the gratitude of relations and friends, made me very anxious to see some of those letters.

I was presently seated before a shipwreck of papers, all bordered with black, and from them I made the following few extracts.

A mother writes—

"REVEREND SIR—Amongst the many who perished on your shore was numbered my beloved son. I was only just recovering from a severe illness, and this fearful affliction has caused a relapse, so that I am unable at present to go to identify the remains of the loved and lost. My darling son would have been sixteen on Christmas-day next. He was a most amiable and obedient child, early taught the way of salvation. We fondly hoped that as a British seaman he might be an ornament to his profession, but, 'it is well'; I feel assured my dear boy is now with the redeemed. Oh, he did not wish to go this last voyage! On the fifteenth of October, I received a letter from him from Melbourne, date August twelfth; he wrote in high spirits, and in conclusion he says: 'Pray for a fair breeze, dear mamma, and I'll not forget to whistle for it! and, God permitting, I shall see you and all my little pets again. Good-bye, dear mother—good-bye, dearest parents. Good-bye, dear brother.' Oh, it was indeed an eternal farewell. I do not apologise for thus writing you, for oh, my heart is so very sorrowful."

A husband writes—

"MY DEAR KIND SIR—Will you kindly inform me whether there are any initials upon the ring and guard you have in possession, found, as the *Standard* says, last Tuesday? Believe me, my dear sir, when I say that I cannot express my deep gratitude in words sufficiently for your kindness to me on that fearful and appalling day. Will you tell me what I can do for you, and will you write me a consoling letter to prevent my mind from going astray?"

A widow writes—

"Left in such a state as I am, my friends and I thought it best that my dear husband should be buried where he lies, and, much as I should have liked to have had it otherwise, I must submit. I feel, from all I have heard of you, that you will see it done decently and in order. Little does it signify to us, when the soul has departed, where this poor body lies, but we who are left behind would do all we can to show how we loved them. This is denied me, but it is God's hand that afflicts us, and I try to submit. Some day I may be able to visit the spot, and see where he lies, and erect a simple stone to his memory. Oh! it will be long, long before I forget that dreadful night! Is there such a thing in the vicinity, or any shop in Bangor, to which I could send for a small picture of Moelfra or Llanallgo church, a spot now sacred to me?"

Another widow writes—

"I have received your letter this morning, and do thank you most kindly for the interest you have taken about my dear husband, as well for the sentiments yours contains, evincing the spirit of a Christian who can sympathise with those who, like myself, are broken down with grief.

"May God bless and sustain you, and all in connection with you, in this great trial. Time may roll on and bear all its sons away, but your name as a disinterested person will stand in history, and, as successive years pass, many a widow will think of your noble conduct, and the tears of gratitude flow down many a cheek, the tribute of a thankful heart, when other things are forgotten for ever."

A father writes—

"I am at a loss to find words to sufficiently express my gratitude to you for your kindness to my son Richard upon the melancholy occasion of his visit to his dear brother's body, and also for your ready attention in pronouncing our beautiful burial service over my poor unfortunate son's remains. God grant that your prayers over him may reach the Mercy Seat, and that his soul may be received (through Christ's intercession) into heaven!

"His dear mother begs me to convey to you her heartfelt thanks."

Those who were received at the clergyman's house, write thus, after leaving it—

"DEAR AND NEVER-TO-BE-FORGOTTEN FRIENDS—I arrived here yesterday morning without accident, and am about to proceed to my home by railway.

"I am overpowered when I think of you and your hospitable home. No words could speak language suited to my heart. I refrain. God reward you with the same measure you have meted with!

"I enumerate no names, but embrace you all."

"MY BELOVED FRIENDS—This is the first day that I have been able to leave my bedroom since I returned, which will explain the reason of my not writing sooner.

"If I could only have had my last melancholy hope realised in recovering the body of my beloved and lamented son, I should have returned home somewhat comforted, and I think I could then have been comparatively resigned.

"I fear now there is but little prospect, and I mourn as one without hope.

"The only consolation to my distressed mind is in having been so feelingly allowed by you to leave the matter in your hands, by whom I well know that everything will be done that can be, according to arrangements made before I left the scene of the awful catastrophe, both as to the identification of my dear son, and also his interment.

"I feel most anxious to hear whether anything fresh has transpired since I left you; will you add another to the many deep obligations I am under to you by writing to me? And should the body of my dear and unfortunate son be identified, let me hear from you immediately, and I will come again.

" Words cannot express the gratitude I feel I owe to you all for your benevolent aid, your kindness, and your sympathy."

" MY DEARLY BELOVED FRIENDS—I arrived in safety at my house yesterday, and a night's rest has restored and tranquillised me. I must again repeat, that language has no words by which I can express my sense of obligation to you. You are enshrined in my heart of hearts.

" I have seen him ! and can now realise my misfortune more than I have hitherto been able to do. Oh, the bitterness of the cup I drink ! But I bow submissive. God *must* have done right. I do not want to feel less, but to acquiesce more simply."

There were some Jewish passengers on board the *Royal Charter*, and the gratitude of the Jewish people is feelingly expressed in the following letter bearing date from " the office of the Chief Rabbi "—

" REVEREND SIR—I cannot refrain from expressing to you my heart-felt thanks on behalf of those of my flock whose relatives have unfortunately been among those who perished at the late wreck of the *Royal Charter*. You have, indeed, like Boaz, 'not left off your kindness to the living and the dead.'

" You have not alone acted kindly towards the living by receiving them hospitably at your house, and energetically assisting them in their mournful duty, but also towards the dead, by exerting yourself to have our co-religionists buried in our ground, and according to our rites. May our heavenly Father reward you for your acts of humanity and true philanthropy ! "

The " Old Hebrew congregation of Liverpool " thus express themselves through their secretary—

" REVEREND SIR—The wardens of this congregation have learned with great pleasure that, in addition to those indefatigable exertions, at the scene of the late disaster to the *Royal Charter*, which have received universal recognition, you have very benevolently employed your valuable efforts to assist such members of our faith as have sought the bodies of lost friends to give them burial in our consecrated grounds, with the observances and rites prescribed by the ordinances of our religion.

" The wardens desire me to take the earliest available opportunity to offer to you, on behalf of our community, the expression of their warm acknowledgments and grateful thanks, and their sincere wishes for your continued welfare and prosperity."

A Jewish gentleman writes—

" REVEREND AND DEAR SIR—I take the opportunity of thanking you right earnestly for the promptness you displayed in answering my note with full particulars concerning my much-lamented brother, and I also herein beg to express my sincere regard for the willingness you displayed and for the facility you afforded for getting the remains of my poor brother exhumed. It has been to us a most sorrowful and painful event, but when we meet with such friends as yourself, it in a measure, somehow or other, abates that mental anguish, and makes the suffering so much easier to be borne. Considering the circumstances connected with my poor brother's fate, it does, indeed, appear a hard one. He had been away in all seven years; he returned four years ago to see his family. He was then engaged to a very amiable young lady. He had been very successful abroad, and was now returning to fulfil his sacred vow; he brought all his property with him in gold uninsured. We heard from him when the ship stopped at Queenstown, when he was in the highest of hope, and in a few short hours afterwards all was washed away."

Mournful in the deepest degree, but too sacred for quotation here, were the numerous references to those miniatures of women worn round the necks of rough men (and found there after death), those locks of hair, those scraps of letters, those many, many slight memorials of hidden tenderness. One man cast up by the sea bore about him, printed on a perforated lace card, the following singular (and unavailing) charm:

"A BLESSING

"May the blessing of God await thee. May the sun of glory shine around thy bed; and may the gates of plenty, honour, and happiness be ever open to thee. May no sorrow distress thy days; may no grief disturb thy nights. May the pillow of peace kiss thy cheek, and the pleasures of imagination attend thy dreams; and when length of years makes thee tired of earthly joys, and the curtain of death gently closes around thy last sleep of human existence, may the Angel of God attend thy bed, and take care that the expiring lamp of life shall not receive one rude blast to hasten on its extinction."

A sailor had these devices on his right arm. "Our Saviour on the Cross, the forehead of the Crucifix and the vesture stained red; on the lower part of the arm, a man and woman; on one side of the Cross, the appearance of a half-moon with a face; on the other side, the sun; on the top of the Cross, the letters I.H.S.; on the left arm, a man and woman dancing, with an effort to delineate the female's dress; under which, initials." Another seaman "had, on the lower part of the right arm, the device of a sailor and a female; the man holding the Union Jack with a streamer, the folds of which waved over her head, and the end of it was held in her hand. On the upper part of the arm, a device of Our Lord on the Cross, with stars surrounding the head of the Cross, and one large star on the side in Indian ink. On the left arm, a flag, a true lovers' knot, a face, and initials." This tatooing was found still plain, below the discoloured outer surface of a mutilated arm, when such surface was carefully scraped away with a knife. It is not improbable that the perpetuation of this marking custom among seamen may be referred back to their desire to be identified, if drowned and flung ashore.

It was some time before I could sever myself from the many interesting papers on the table, and then I broke bread and drank wine with the kind family before I left them. As I brought the Coast-guard down, so I took the Postman back, with his leathern wallet, walking-stick, bugle, and terrier dog. Many a heartbroken letter had he brought to the Rectory House within two months ; many a benignantly painstaking answer had he carried back.

As I rode along, I thought of the many people, inhabitants of this mother country, who would make pilgrimages to the little churchyard in the years to come ; I thought of the many people in Australia who would have an interest in such a shipwreck, and would find their way here when they visit the Old World ; I thought of the writers of all the wreck of letters I had left upon the table ; and I resolved to place this little record where it stands. Convocations, Conferences, Diocesan Epistles, and the like, will do a great deal for religion, I dare say, and Heaven send they may ! but I doubt if they will ever do their Master's service half so well, in all the time they last, as the heavens have seen it done in this bleak spot upon the rugged coast of Wales.

Had I lost the friend of my life in the wreck of the *Royal Charter;* had I lost my betrothed, the more than friend of my life ; had I lost my maiden daughter, had I lost my hopeful boy, had I lost my little child ; I would kiss the hands that worked so busily and gently in the church, and say, "None better could have touched the form, though it had lain at home." I could be sure of it, I could be thankful for it : I could be content to leave the grave near the house the good family pass in and out of every day, undisturbed, in the little churchyard where so many are so strangely brought together.

Without the name of the clergyman to whom—I hope, not without carrying comfort to some heart at some time—I have referred, my reference would be as nothing. He is the Reverend Stephen Roose Hughes, of Llanallgo, near Moelfra, Anglesey. His brother is the Reverend Hugh Robert Hughes, of Penrhos Alligwy.

III

WAPPING WORKHOUSE

My day's no-business beckoning me to the East end of London, I had turned my face to that point of the metropolitan compass on leaving Covent Garden, and had got past the India House, thinking in my idle manner of Tippoo-Sahib and Charles Lamb, and had got past my little wooden midshipman, after affectionately patting him on one leg of his knee-shorts for old acquaintance' sake, and had got past Aldgate Pump, and had got past the Saracen's Head (with an ignominious rash of posting bills disfiguring his swarthy countenance), and had strolled up the empty yard of his ancient neighbour the Black or Blue Boar, or Bull, who departed this life I don't know when, and whose coaches are all gone I don't know where; and I had come out again into the age of railways, and I had got past Whitechapel Church, and was—rather inappropriately for an Uncommercial Traveller—in the Commercial Road. Pleasantly wallowing in the abundant mud of that thorough-fare, and greatly enjoying the huge piles of building belonging to the sugar refiners, the little masts and vanes in small back gardens in back streets, the neighbouring canals and docks, the India vans lumbering along their stone tramway, and the pawnbrokers' shops where hard-up mates had pawned so many sextants and quadrants, that I should have bought a few cheap if I had the least notion how to use them, I at last began to file off to the right, towards Wapping.

Not that I intended to take boat at Wapping Old Stairs, or that I was going to look at the locality, because I believe (for I don't) in the constancy of the young woman who told her sea-going lover, to such a beautiful old tune, that she had ever continued the same since she gave him the 'baccer-box marked with his name; I am afraid he usually got the worst of those transactions, and was frightfully taken in. No, I was going to Wapping because an Eastern police magistrate had said, through the morning papers, that there was no classification at the Wapping workhouse for women, and that it was a disgrace and a shame, and divers other hard names, and because I wished to see how the fact really stood. For, that Eastern police magistrates are not always the wisest men of the East, may be inferred from their course of procedure respecting the fancy-dressing and pantomime-posturing at St. George's in that quarter: which is usually, to discuss the matter at issue, in a state of mind betokening the weakest perplexity, with all parties concerned and unconcerned, and, for a final expedient, to consult the complainant as to what he thinks ought to be done with the defendant, and take the defendant's opinion as to what he would recommend to be done with himself.

Long before I reached Wapping, I gave myself up as having lost my way, and, abandoning myself to the narrow streets in a Turkish frame of mind, relied on predestination to bring me somehow or other to the place I wanted if I were ever to get there. When I had ceased for an hour or so to take any trouble about the matter, I found myself on a swing-bridge looking down at some dark locks in some dirty water. Over against me stood a creature remotely in the likeness of a young man, with a puffed sallow face, and a figure all dirty and shiny and slimy, who may have been the youngest son of his filthy old father, Thames, or the drowned man about whom there was a placard on the granite post like a large thimble that stood between us.

I asked this apparition what it called the place. Unto which it replied, with a ghastly grin and a sound like gurgling water in its throat—

" Mister Baker's trap."

As it is a point of great sensitiveness with me on such occasions to be equal to the intellectual pressure of the conversation, I deeply considered the meaning of this speech, while I eyed the apparition—then engaged in hugging and sucking a horizontal iron bar at the top of the locks. Inspiration suggested to me that Mr. Baker was the acting coroner of that neighbourhood.

"A common place for suicide," said I, looking down at the locks.

"Sue?" returned the ghost, with a stare. "Yes! And Poll. Likeways Emly. And Nancy. And Jane;" he sucked the iron between each name; "and all the bileing. Ketches off their bonnets or shorls, takes a run, and headers down here, they doos. Always a-headerin' down here, they is. Like one o'clock."

"And at about that hour of the morning, I suppose?"

"Ah!" said the apparition. *They* an't partickler. Two 'ull do for *them*. Three. All times o' night. O'ny mind you!" Here the apparition rested his profile on the bar, and gurgled in a sarcastic manner. "There must be somebody comin'. They don't go a-headerin' down here wen there an't no Bobby nor gen'ral Cove fur to hear the splash."

According to my interpretation of these words, I was myself a General Cove, or member of the miscellaneous public. In which modest character I remarked—

"They are often taken out, are they, and restored?"

"I dunno about restored," said the apparition, who, for some occult reason, very much objected to that word; "they're carried into the werkiss and put into a 'ot bath, and brought round. But I dunno about restored," said the apparition; "blow *that!*"—and vanished.

As it had shown a desire to become offensive, I was not sorry to find myself alone, especially as the " werkiss " it had indicated with a twist of its matted head was close at hand. So I left Mr. Baker's terrible trap (baited with a scum that was like the soapy rinsing of sooty chimneys), and made bold to ring at the workhouse gate, where I was wholly unexpected and quite unknown.

A very bright and nimble little matron, with a bunch of keys in her hand, responded to my request to see the House. I began to doubt whether the police magistrate was quite right in his facts when I noticed her quick, active little figure and her intelligent eyes.

The Traveller (the matron intimated) should see the worst first. He was welcome to see everything. Such as it was, there it all was.

This was the only preparation for our entering "the Foul wards." They were in an old building squeezed away in a corner of a paved yard, quite detached from the more modern and spacious main body of the workhouse. They were in a building most monstrously behind the time—a mere series of garrets or lofts, with every inconvenient and objectionable circumstance in their construction, and only accessible by steep and narrow staircases, infamously ill-adapted for the passage up-stairs of the sick or down-stairs of the dead.

Abed in these miserable rooms, here on bedsteads, there (for a change, as I understood it) on the floor, were women in every stage of distress and disease. None but those who have attentively observed such scenes can conceive the extraordinary variety of expression still latent under the general monotony and uniformity of colour, attitude, and condition. The form a little coiled up and turned away, as though it had turned its back on this world for ever; the uninterested face at once lead-coloured and yellow, looking passively upward from the pillow; the haggard mouth a little dropped, the hand outside the coverlet, so dull and indifferent, so light, and yet so heavy; these were on every pallet; but when I stopped beside a bed, and said ever so slight a word to the figure lying there, the ghost of the old character came into the face, and made the Foul ward as various as the fair world. No one appeared to care to live, but no one complained; all who could speak, said that as much was done for them as could be done there, that the attendance was kind and patient, that their suffering was very heavy, but they had nothing to ask for. The wretched rooms were as clean and sweet as it is possible for such rooms to be; they would become a pest-house in a single week if they were ill-kept.

I accompanied the brisk matron up another barbarous staircase, into a better kind of loft devoted to the idiotic and imbecile. There was at least Light in it, whereas the windows in the former wards had been like sides of schoolboys' bird-cages. There was a strong grating over the fire here, and, holding a kind of state on either side of the hearth, separated by the breadth of this grating, were two old ladies in a condition of feeble dignity, which was surely the very last and lowest reduction of self-complacency to be found in this wonderful humanity of ours. They were evidently jealous of each other, and passed their whole time (as some people do, whose fires are not grated) in mentally disparaging each other, and contemptuously watching their neighbours. One of these parodies on provincial gentlewomen was extremely talkative, and expressed a strong desire to attend the service on Sundays, from which she represented herself to have derived the greatest interest and consolation when allowed that privilege. She gossiped so well, and looked altogether so cheery and harmless, that I began to think this a case for the Eastern magistrate, until I found that on the last occasion of her attending chapel she had secreted a small stick, and had caused some confusion in the responses by suddenly producing it and belabouring the congregation.

So these two old ladies, separated by the breadth of the grating— otherwise they would fly at one another's caps—sat all day long, suspecting one another, and contemplating a world of fits. For everybody else in the room had fits, except the wards-woman; an elderly, able-bodied pauperess, with a large upper lip, and an air of repressing and saving her strength, as she stood with her hands folded before her, and her eyes slowly rolling, biding her time for catching or holding somebody. This civil personage (in whom I regretted to identify a reduced member of my honourable friend Mrs. Gamp's family) said, "They has 'em continiwal, Sir. They drops without no more notice than if they was coach-horses dropped from the moon, Sir. And when one drops, another drops, and sometimes there'll be as many as four or five on 'em at once, dear me, a-rollin' and a-tearin', bless you !—this young woman, now, has 'em dreadful bad."

She turned up this young woman's face with her hand as she said it. This young woman was seated on the floor, pondering, in the foreground of the afflicted. There was nothing repellent either in her face or head. Many, apparently worse, varieties of epilepsy and hysteria were about her, but she was said to be the worst there. When I had spoken to her a little, she still sat with her face turned up, pondering, and a gleam of the mid-day sun shone in upon her.

—Whether this young woman, and the rest of these so sorely troubled, as they sit or lie pondering in their confused, dull way, ever get mental glimpses among the motes in the sunlight of healthy people and healthy things? Whether this young woman, brooding like this in the summer season, ever thinks that somewhere there are trees and flowers, even mountains and the great sea? Whether, not to go so far, this young woman ever has any dim revelation of that young woman —that young woman who is not here and never will come here ; who is courted, and caressed, and loved, and has a husband, and bears children, and lives in a home, and who never knows what it is to have this lashing and tearing coming upon her? And whether this young woman, God help her, gives herself up then and drops like a coach-horse from the moon?

I hardly knew whether the voices of infant children, penetrating into so hopeless a place, made a sound that was pleasant or painful to me. It was something to be reminded that the weary world was not all aweary, and was ever renewing itself; but this young woman was a child not long ago, and a child not long hence might be such as she. Howbeit, the active step and eye of the vigilant matron conducted me past the two provincial gentlewomen (whose dignity was ruffled by the children), and into the adjacent nursery.

There were many babies here, and more than one handsome young mother. There were ugly young mothers also, and sullen young mothers, and callous young mothers. But the babies had not appropriated to themselves any bad expression yet, and might have been, for anything that appeared to the contrary in their soft faces, Princes Imperial and Princesses Royal. I had the pleasure of giving a poetical commission to the baker's man to make a cake with all despatch and toss it into the oven for one red-headed young pauper and myself, and felt much the better for it. Without that refreshment, I doubt if I should have been in a condition for "the Refractories," towards whom my quick little matron—for whose adaptation to her office I had by this time conceived a genuine respect—drew me next, and marshalled me the way that I was going.

The Refractories were picking oakum, in a small room giving on a yard. They sat in line on a form, with their backs to a window ; before them, a table, and their work. The oldest Refractory was, say twenty ;

youngest Refractory, say sixteen. I have never yet ascertained in the course of my uncommercial travels why a Refractory habit should affect the tonsils and uvula; but I have always observed that Refractories of both sexes and every grade, between a Ragged School and the Old Bailey, have one voice, in which the tonsils and uvula gain a diseased ascendency.

"Five pound indeed! I hain't a-going fur to pick five pound," said the Chief of the Refractories, keeping time to herself with her head and chin. "More than enough to pick what we picks now, in sitch a place as this, and on wot we gets here!"

(This was in acknowledgment of a delicate intimation that the amount of work was likely to be increased. It certainly was not heavy then, for one Refractory had already done her day's task—it was barely two o'clock—and was sitting behind it, with a head exactly matching it.)

"A pretty Ouse this is, matron, ain't it?" said Refractory Two, "where a pleeseman's called in if a gal says a word!"

"And wen you're sent to prison for nothink or less!" said the Chief, tugging at her oakum as if it were the matron's hair. "But any place is better than this; that's one thing, and be thankful!"

A laugh of Refractories led by Oakum Head with folded arms—who originated nothing, but who was in command of the skirmishers outside the conversation.

"If any place is better than this," said my brisk guide, in the calmest manner, "it is a pity you left a good place when you had one."

"Ho, no, I didn't, matron," returned the Chief, with another pull at her oakum, and a very expressive look at the enemy's forehead. "Don't say that, matron, cos it's lies!"

Oakum Head brought up the skirmishers again, skirmished, and retired.

"And *I* warn't a-going," exclaimed Refractory Two, "though I was in one place for as long as four year—*I* warn't a-going fur to stop in a place that warn't fit for me—there! And where the fam'ly warn't 'spectable characters—there! And where I fort'nately or hunfort'nately, found that the people warn't what they pretended to make theirselves out to be—there! And where it wasn't their faults, by chalks, if I warn't made bad and ruinated—Hah!"

During this speech Oakum Head had again made a diversion with the skirmishers, and had again withdrawn.

The Uncommercial Traveller ventured to remark that he supposed Chief Refractory and Number One to be the two young women who had been taken before the magistrate.

"Yes!" said the Chief, "we har! and the wonder is that a pleeseman an't 'ad in now, and we took off agen. You can't open your lips here, without a pleeseman."

Number Two laughed (very uvularly), and the skirmishers followed suit.

"I'm sure I'd be thankful," protested the Chief, looking sideways at the Uncommercial, "if I could be got into a place, or got abroad. I'm sick and tired of this precious Ouse, I am, with reason."

So would be, and so was, Number Two. So would be, and so was, Oakum Head. So would be, and so were, skirmishers.

The Uncommercial took the liberty of hinting that he hardly thought it probable that any lady or gentleman in want of a likely young domestic of retiring manners would be tempted into the engagement of either of the two leading Refractories, on her own presentation of herself as per sample.

"It ain't no good being nothink else here," said the Chief.

The Uncommercial thought it might be worth trying.

"Oh no it ain't," said the Chief.

"Not a bit of good," said Number Two.

"And I'm sure I'd be very thankful to be got into a place, or got abroad," said the Chief.

"And so should I," said Number Two. "Truly thankful, I should."

Oakum Head then rose, and announced as an entirely new idea, the mention of which profound novelty might be naturally expected to startle her unprepared hearers, that she would be very thankful to be got into a place, or got abroad. And, as if she had then said, "Chorus, ladies!" all the skirmishers struck up to the same purpose. We left them, thereupon, and began a long walk among the women who were simply old and infirm; but whenever, in the course of this same walk, I looked out of any high window that commanded the yard, I saw Oakum Head and all the other Refractories looking out at their low window for me, and never failing to catch me the moment I showed my head.

In ten minutes I had ceased to believe in such fables of a golden time as youth, the prime of life, or a hale old age. In ten minutes all the lights of womankind seemed to have been blown out, and nothing in that way to be left this vault to brag of but the flickering and expiring snuffs.

And what was very curious was, that these dim old women had one company notion which was the fashion of the place. Every old woman who became aware of a visitor and was not in bed hobbled over a form into her accustomed seat, and became one of a line of dim old women confronting another line of dim old women across a narrow table. There was no obligation whatever upon them to range themselves in this way; it was their manner of "receiving." As a rule, they made no attempt to talk to one another, or to look at the visitor, or to look at anything, but sat silently working their mouths, like a sort of poor old cows. In some of these wards it was good to see a few green plants; in others an isolated Refractory acting as nurse, who did well enough in that capacity when separated from her compeers; every one of these wards, day-room, night-room, or both combined, was scrupulously clean and fresh. I have seen as many such places as most travellers in my line, and I never saw one such better kept.

Among the bedridden there was great patience, great reliance on the books under the pillow, great faith in God. All cared for sympathy, but none much cared to be encouraged with hope of recovery; on the whole, I should say, it was considered rather a distinction to have a complication of disorders, and to be in a worse way than the rest. From some of the windows the river could be seen with all its life and movement; the day was bright, but I came upon no one who was looking out.

In one large ward, sitting by the fire in arm-chairs of distinction, like the President and Vice of the good company, were two old women, upwards of ninety years of age. The younger of the two, just turned ninety, was deaf, but not very, and could easily be made to hear. In her early time she had nursed a child, who was now another old woman, more infirm that herself, inhabiting the very same chamber. She perfectly understood this when the matron told it, and, with sundry nods and motions of her forefinger, pointed out the woman in question. The elder of this pair, ninety-three, seated before an illustrated news-paper (but not reading it), was a bright-eyed old soul, really not deaf, wonderfully preserved, and amazingly conversational. She had not long lost her husband, and had been in that place little more than a year. At Boston, in the State of Massachusetts, this poor creature would have been individually addressed, would have been tended in her own room, and would have had her life gently assimilated to a comfort-able life out of doors. Would that be much to do in England for a woman who has kept herself out of a workhouse more than ninety rough long years? When Britain first, at Heaven's command, arose, with a great deal of allegorical confusion, from out the azure main, did her guardian angels positively forbid it in the Charter which has been so much besung?

The object of my journey was accomplished when the nimble matron had no more to show me. As I shook hands with her at the gate, I told her that I thought Justice had not used her very well, and that the wise men of the East were not infallible.

Now, I reasoned with myself, as I made my journey home again, concerning those Foul wards. They ought not to exist; no person of common decency and humanity can see them and doubt it. But what is this Union to do? The necessary alteration would cost several thousands of pounds; it has already to support three workhouses; its inhabitants work hard for their bare lives, and are already rated for the relief of the poor to the utmost extent of reasonable endurance. One poor parish in this very Union is rated to the amount of FIVE AND SIXPENCE in the pound, at the very same time when the rich parish of Saint George's, Hanover Square, is rated at about SEVENPENCE in the pound, Paddington at about FOURPENCE, Saint James's, Westminster, at about TENPENCE ! It is only through the equalisation of Poor Rates that what is left undone in this wise can be done. Much more is left undone, or is ill-done, than I have space to suggest in these notes of a single uncommercial journey; but the wise men of the East, before they can reasonably hold forth about it, must look to the North and South and West ; let them also, any morning before taking the seat of Solomon, look into the shops and dwellings all around the Temple, and first ask themselves " how much more can these poor people—many of whom keep themselves with difficulty enough out of the workhouse—bear ? "

I had yet other matter for reflection as I journeyed home, inasmuch as, before I altogether departed from the neighbourhood of Mr. Baker's trap, I had knocked at the gate of the workhouse of St. George's-in-the-East, and had found it to be an establishment highly creditable to those parts, and thoroughly well administered by a most intelligent master. I remarked in it an instance of the collateral harm that obstinate vanity and folly can do. " This was the Hall where those old paupers, male and female, whom I had just seen, met for the Church service, was it ? "—" Yes."—" Did they sing the Psalms to any instrument ? "—" They would like to, very much ; they would have an extraordinary interest in doing so."—" And could none be got ? "—" Well, a piano could even have been got for nothing, but these unfortunate dissensions——" Ah ! better, far better, my Christian friend in the beautiful garment, to have let the singing boys alone, and left the multitude to sing for themselves ! You should know better than I, but I think I have read that they did so, once upon a time, and that " when they had sung an hymn," Some one (not in a beautiful garment) went up unto the Mount of Olives.

It made my heart ache to think of this miserable trifling, in the streets of a city where every stone seemed to call to me, as I walked along, " Turn this way, man, and see what waits to be done ! " So I decoyed myself into another train of thought to ease my heart. But I don't know that I did it, for I was so full of paupers, that it was, after all, only a change to a single pauper, who took possession of my remembrance instead of a thousand.

" I beg your pardon, Sir," he had said, in a confidential manner, on another occasion, taking me aside ; " but I have seen better days."

" I am very sorry to hear it. '

" Sir, I have a complaint to make against the master."

" I have no power here, I assure you. And if I had——"

" But allow me, Sir, to mention it, as between yourself and a man who has seen better days, Sir. The master and myself are both masons, Sir, and I make him the sign continually ; but, because I am in this unfortunate position, Sir, he won't give me the countersign ! "

IV

TWO VIEWS OF A CHEAP THEATRE

As I shut the door of my lodging behind me, and came out into the streets at six on a drizzling Saturday evening in the last past month of January, all that neighbourhood of Covent Garden looked very desolate. It is so essentially a neighbourhood which has seen better days, that bad weather affects it sooner than another place which has not come down in the world. In its present reduced condition it bears a thaw almost worse than any place I know. It gets so dreadfully low-spirited when damp breaks forth. Those wonderful houses about Drury Lane Theatre, which in the palmy days of theatres were prosperous and long-settled places of business, and which now change hands every week, but never change their character of being divided and subdivided on the ground floor into mouldy dens of shops where an orange and half-a-dozen nuts, or a pomatum pot, one cake of fancy soap, and a cigar-box are offered for sale and never sold, were most ruefully contemplated that evening by the statue of Shakespeare, with the rain-drops coursing one another down its innocent nose. Those inscrutable pigeon-hole offices, with nothing in them (not so much as an inkstand) but a model of a theatre before the curtain, where, in the Italian Opera season, tickets at reduced prices are kept on sale by nomadic gentlemen in smeary hats too tall for them, whom one occasionally seems to have seen on race-courses, not wholly unconnected with strips of cloth of various colours and a rolling ball—those Bedouin establishments, deserted by the tribe, and tenantless, except when sheltering in one corner an irregular row of ginger-beer bottles, which would have made one shudder on such a night, but for its being plain that they had nothing in them, shrank from the shrill cries of the newsboys at their Exchange in the kennel of Catherine Street, like guilty things upon a fearful summons. At the pipe-shop in Great Russell Street, the Death's-head pipes were like theatrical *memento mori*, admonishing beholders of the decline of the playhouse as an Institution. I walked up Bow Street, disposed to be angry with the shops there, that were letting out theatrical secrets by exhibiting to workaday humanity the stuff of which diadems and robes of kings are made. I noticed that some shops which had once been in the dramatic line, and had struggled out of it, were not getting on prosperously—like some actors I have known, who took to business and failed to make it answer. In a word, those streets looked so dull, and, considered as theatrical streets, so broken and bankrupt, that the FOUND DEAD on the black board at the police station might have announced the decease of the Drama, and the pools of water outside the fire-engine makers at the corner of Long Acre might have been occasioned by his having brought out the whole of his stock to play upon its last smouldering ashes.

And yet, on such a night, in so degenerate a time, the object of my journey was theatrical. And yet within half an hour I was in an immense theatre, capable of holding nearly five thousand people.

What theatre? Her Majesty's? Far better. Royal Italian Opera? Far better. Infinitely superior to the latter for hearing in; infinitely superior to both for seeing in. To every part of this theatre spacious fireproof ways of ingress and egress. For every part of it convenient places of refreshment and retiring rooms. Everything to eat and drink carefully supervised as to quality, and sold at an appointed price; respectable female attendants ready for the commonest women in the audience; a general air of consideration, decorum, and supervision, most commendable; an unquestionably humanising influence in all the social arrangements of the place.

Surely a dear theatre, then? Because there were in London (not very long ago) theatres with entrance-prices up to half-a-guinea a head whose arrangements were not half so civilised. Surely, therefore, a dear theatre? Not very dear. A gallery at threepence, another gallery at fourpence, a pit at sixpence, boxes and pit-stalls at a shilling, and a few private boxes at half-a-crown.

My uncommercial curiosity induced me to go into every nook of this great place, and among every class of the audience assembled in it— amounting that evening, as I calculated, to about two thousand and odd hundreds. Magnificently lighted by a firmament of sparkling chandeliers, the building was ventilated to perfection. My sense of smell, without being particularly delicate, has been so offended in some of the commoner places of public resort, that I have often been obliged to leave them when I have made an uncommercial journey expressly to look on. The air of this theatre was fresh, cool, and wholesome. To help towards this end very sensible precautions had been used, ingeniously combining the experience of hospitals and railway stations. Asphalt pavements substituted for wooden floors, honest bare walls of glazed brick and tile—even at the back of the boxes—for plaster and paper, no benches stuffed, and no carpeting or baize used; a cool material with a light glazed surface being the covering of the seats.

These various contrivances are as well considered in the place in question as if it were a Fever Hospital; the result is, that it is sweet and healthful. It has been constructed from the ground to the roof with a careful reference to sight and sound in every corner; the result is, that its form is beautiful, and that the appearance of the audience, as seen from the proscenium—with every face in it commanding the stage, and the whole so admirably raked and turned to that centre, that a hand can scarcely move in the great assemblage without the movement being seen from thence—is highly remarkable in its union of vastness with compactness. The stage itself, and all its appurtenances of machinery, cellarage, height, and breadth, are on a scale more like the Scala at Milan, or the San Carlo at Naples, or the Grand Opera at Paris, than any notion a stranger would be likely to form of the Britannia Theatre at Hoxton, a mile north of St Luke's Hospital in the Old Street Road, London. The Forty Thieves might be played here, and every thief ride his real horse, and the disguised captain bring in his oil jars on a train of real camels, and nobody be put out of the way. This really extraordinary place is the achievement of one man's enterprise, and was erected on the ruins of an inconvenient old building in less than five months, at a round cost of five-and-twenty thousand pounds. To dismiss this part of my subject, and still to render to the proprietor the credit that is strictly his due, I must add that his sense of the responsibility upon him to make the best of his audience, and to do his best for them, is a highly agreeable sign of these times.

As the spectators at this theatre, for a reason I will presently show, were the object of my journey, I entered on the play of the night as one of the two thousand and odd hundreds, by looking about me at my neighbours. We were a motley assemblage of people, and we had a good many boys and young men among us ; we had also many girls and young women. To represent, however, that we did not include a very great number, and a very fair proportion of family groups, would be to make a gross misstatement. Such groups were to be seen in all parts of the house ; in the boxes and stalls particularly, they were composed of persons of very decent appearance, who had many children with them. Among our dresses there were most kinds of shabby and greasy wear, and much fustian and corduroy that was neither sound nor fragrant. The caps of our young men were mostly of a limp character, and we who wore them, slouched, high-shouldered, into our places with our hands in our pockets, and occasionally twisted our cravats about our necks like eels, and occasionally tied them down our breasts like links of sausages, and occasionally had a screw in our hair over each cheek-bone with a slight thief-flavour in it. Besides prowlers and idlers, we were mechanics, dock-labourers, costermongers, petty tradesmen, small clerks, milliners, stay-makers, shoe-binders, slop workers, poor workers in a hundred highways and byways. Many of us—on the whole, the majority—were not at all clean, and not at all choice in our lives or conversation. But we had all come together in a place where our convenience was well consulted, and where we were well looked after, to enjoy an evening's entertainment in common. We were not going to lose any part of what we had paid for through anybody's caprice, and as a community we had a character to lose. So we were closely attentive and kept excellent order ; and let the man or boy who did otherwise instantly get out from this place, or we would put him out with the greatest expedition.

We began at half-past six with a pantomime—with a pantomime so long, that before it was over I felt as if I had been travelling for six weeks—going to India, say, by the Overland Mail. The Spirit of Liberty was the principal personage in the Introduction, and the Four Quarters of the World came out of the globe, glittering, and discoursed with the Spirit, who sang charmingly. We were delighted to understand that there was no liberty anywhere but among ourselves, and we highly applauded the agreeable fact. In an allegorical way, which did as well as any other way, we and the Spirit of Liberty got into a kingdom of Needles and Pins, and found them at war with a potentate who called in to his aid their old arch-enemy Rust, and who would have got the better of them if the Spirit of Liberty had not in the nick of time transformed the leaders into Clown, Pantaloon, Harlequin, Columbine, Harlequina, and a whole family of Sprites, consisting of a remarkably stout father and three spineless sons. We all knew what was coming when the Spirit of Liberty addressed the king with a big face, and His Majesty backed to the side-scenes and began untying himself behind, with his big face all on one side. Our excitement at that crisis was great, and our delight unbounded. After this era in our existence, we went through all the incidents of a pantomime ; it was not by any means a savage pantomime, in the way of burning or boiling people, or throwing them out of window, or cutting them up ; was often very droll ; was always liberally got up, and cleverly presented. I noticed that the people who kept the shops, and who represented the passengers in the thoroughfares, and so forth, had no conventionality in them, but were unusually like the real thing—from which I infer that you may take that audience in (if you wish to) concerning Knights and Ladies, Fairies, Angels, or such like, but they are not to be done as to anything in the streets. I noticed, also, that when two young men, dressed in exact imitation of the eel-and-sausage-cravated portion of the audience, were chased by policemen, and, finding themselves in danger of being caught, dropped so suddenly as to oblige the policemen to tumble over them, there was great rejoicing among the caps—as though it were a delicate reference to something they had heard of before.

The Pantomime was succeeded by a Melodrama. Throughout the evening I was pleased to observe Virtue quite as triumphant as she usually is out of doors, and indeed I thought rather more so. We all agreed (for the time) that honesty was the best policy, and we were as hard as iron upon Vice, and we wouldn't hear of Villainy getting on in the world—no, not on any consideration whatever.

Between the pieces, we almost all of us went out and refreshed. Many of us went the length of drinking beer at the bar of the neighbouring public-house, some of us drank spirits, crowds of us had sandwiches and ginger-beer at the refreshment-bars established for us in the theatre. The sandwich—as substantial as was consistent with portability, and as cheap as possible—we hailed as one of our greatest institutions. It forced its way among us at all stages of the entertainment, and we were always delighted to see it ; its adaptability to the varying moods of our nature was surprising ; we could never weep so comfortably as when our tears fell on our sandwich ; we could never laugh so heartily as when we choked with sandwich ; Virtue never looked so beautiful or Vice so deformed as when we paused, sandwich in hand, to consider what would come of that resolution of Wickedness in boots, to sever Innocence in flowered chintz from Honest Industry in striped stockings. When the curtain fell for the night, we still fell back upon sandwich, to help us through the rain and mire, and home to bed.

This, as I have mentioned, was Saturday night. Being Saturday night, I had accomplished but the half of my uncommercial journey; for its object was to compare the play on Saturday evening with the preaching in the same theatre on Sunday evening.

Therefore, at the same hour of half-past six on the similarly damp and muddy Sunday evening, I returned to this theatre. I drove up to the entrance (fearful of being late, or I should have come on foot), and found myself in a large crowd of people who, I am happy to state, were put into excellent spirits by my arrival. Having nothing to look at but the mud and the closed doors, they looked at me, and highly enjoyed the comic spectacle. My modesty inducing me to draw off, some hundreds of yards, into a dark corner, they at once forgot me, and applied themselves to their former occupation of looking at the mud and looking in at the closed doors : which, being of grated iron-work, allowed the lighted passage within to be seen. They were chiefly people of respectable appearance, odd and impulsive as most crowds are, and making a joke of being there as most crowds do.

In the dark corner I might have sat a long while, but that a very obliging passer-by informed me that the theatre was already full, and that the people whom I saw in the street were all shut out for want of room. After that, I lost no time in worming myself into the building, and creeping to a place in a proscenium box that had been kept for me.

There must have been full four thousand people present. Carefully estimating the pit alone, I could bring it out as holding little less than fourteen hundred. Every part of the house was well filled, and I had not found it easy to make my way along the back of the boxes to where I sat. The chandeliers in the ceiling were lighted ; there was no light on the stage ; the orchestra was empty. The green curtain was down, and, packed pretty closely on chairs on the small space of stage before it, were some thirty gentlemen, and two or three ladies. In the centre of these, in a desk or pulpit covered with red baize, was the presiding minister. The kind of rostrum he occupied will be very well understood if I liken it to a boarded-up-fireplace turned towards the audience, with a gentleman in a black surtout standing in the stove and leaning forward over the mantelpiece.

A portion of Scripture was being read when I went in. It was followed by a discourse, to which the congregation listened with most exemplary attention and uninterrupted silence and decorum. My own attention comprehended both the auditory and the speaker, and shall turn to both in this recalling of the scene, exactly as it did at the time.

"A very difficult thing," I thought, when the discourse began, "to speak appropriately to so large an audience, and to speak with tact. Without it, better not to speak at all. Infinitely better, to read the New Testament well, and to let *that* speak. In this congregation there is indubitably one pulse ; but I doubt if any power short of genius can touch it as one, and make it answer as one."

I could not possibly say to myself as the discourse proceeded that the minister was a good speaker. I could not possibly say to myself that he expressed an understanding of the general mind and character of his audience. There was a supposititious working-man introduced into the homily, to make supposititious objections to our Christian religion and be reasoned down, who was not only a very disagreeable person, but remarkably unlike life—very much more unlike it than anything I had seen in the pantomime. The native independence of character this artisan was supposed to possess was represented by a suggestion of a dialect that I certainly never heard in my uncommercial travels, and with a coarse swing of voice and manner anything but agreeable to his feelings, I should conceive, considered in the light of a portrait, and as far away from the fact as a Chinese Tartar. There was a model pauper introduced in like manner, who appeared to me to be the most intolerably arrogant pauper ever relieved, and to show him-self in absolute want and dire necessity of a course of Stone Yard. For how did this pauper testify to his having received the gospel of humility ? A gentleman met him in the workhouse, and said (which I myself really thought good-natured of him), "Ah, John ! I am sorry to see you here. I am sorry to see you so poor." "Poor, Sir !" replied that man, draw-ing himself up, "I am the son of a Prince ! *My* father is the King of kings. *My* father is the Lord of lords. *My* father is the Ruler of all the princes of the earth !" etc. And this was what all the preacher's fellow-sinners might come to, if they would embrace this blessed book —which I must say it did some violence to my own feelings of reverence to see held out at arm's-length at frequent intervals and soundingly slapped, like a slow lot at a sale. Now, could I help asking myself the question whether the mechanic before me, who must detect the preacher as being wrong about the visible manner of himself and the like of himself, and about such a noisy lip-server as that pauper, might not, most unhappily for the usefulness of the occasion, doubt that preacher's being right about things not visible to human senses ?

Again. Is it necessary or advisable to address such an audience continually as "fellow-sinners"? Is it not enough to be fellow-creatures, born yesterday, suffering and striving to-day, dying to-morrow ? By our common humanity, my brothers and sisters, by our common capacities for pain and pleasure, by our common laughter and our common tears, by our common aspiration to reach something better than ourselves, by our common tendency to believe in something good, and to invest whatever we love or whatever we lose with some qualities that are superior to our own failings and weaknesses as we know them in our own poor hearts—by these, hear me !—Surely it is enough to be fellow-creatures. Surely it includes the other designation, and some touching meanings over and above.

Again. There was a personage introduced into the discourse (not an absolute novelty, to the best of my remembrance of my reading), who had been personally known to the preacher, and had been quite a Crichton in all the ways of philosophy, but had been an infidel. Many a time had the preacher talked with him on that subject, and many a time had he failed to convince that intelligent man. But he fell ill, and died, and before he died he recorded his conversion—in words which the preacher had taken down, my fellow-sinners, and would read to you from this piece of paper. I must confess that to me, as one of an uninstructed audience, they did not appear particularly edifying. I thought their tone extremely selfish, and I thought they had a spiritual vanity in them which was of the before-mentioned refractory pauper's family.

All slangs and twangs are objectionable everywhere, but the slang and twang of the conventicle—as bad in its way as that of the House of Commons, and nothing worse can be said of it—should be studiously avoided under such circumstances as I describe. The avoidance was not complete on this occasion. Nor was it quite agreeable to see the preacher addressing his pet " points " to his backers on the stage, as if appealing to those disciples to show him up, and testify to the multitude that each of those points was a clincher.

But, in respect of the large Christianity of his general tone ; of his renunciation of all priestly authority ; of his earnest and reiterated assurance to the people that the commonest among them could work out their own salvation if they would, by simply, lovingly, and dutifully following our Saviour, and that they needed the mediation of no erring man ; in these particulars this gentleman deserved all praise. Nothing could be better than the spirit, or the plain emphatic words of his discourse in these respects. And it was a most significant and encouraging circumstance that whenever he struck that chord, or whenever he described anything which Christ Himself had done, the array of faces before him was very much more earnest, and very much more expressive of emotion, than at any other time.

And now I am brought to the fact that the lowest part of the audience of the previous night *was not there*. There is no doubt about it. There was no such thing in that building that Sunday evening. I have been told since that the lowest part of the audience of the Victoria Theatre has been attracted to its Sunday services. I have been very glad to hear it, but on this occasion of which I write, the lowest part of the usual audience of the Britannia Theatre decidedly and unquestionably stayed away. When I first took my seat and looked at the house, my surprise at the change in its occupants was as great as my disappointment. To the most respectable class of the previous evening was added a great number of respectable strangers attracted by curiosity, and drafts from the regular congregations of various chapels. It was impossible to fail in identifying the character of these last, and they were very numerous. I came out in a strong, slow tide of them setting from the boxes. Indeed, while the discourse was in progress, the respectable character of the auditory was so manifest in their appearance, that when the minister addressed a supposititious

" outcast," one really felt a little impatient of it, as a figure of speech not justified by anything the eye could discover.

The time appointed for the conclusion of the proceedings was eight o'clock. The address having lasted until full that time, and it being the custom to conclude with a hymn, the preacher intimated in a few sensible words that the clock had struck the hour, and that those who desired to go before the hymn was sung could go now, without giving offence. No one stirred. The hymn was then sung, in good time and tune and unison, and its effect was very striking. A comprehensive benevolent prayer dismissed the throng, and in seven or eight minutes there was nothing left in the theatre but a light cloud of dust.

That these Sunday meetings in theatres are good things I do not doubt. Nor do I doubt that they will work lower and lower down in the social scale, if those who preside over them will be very careful on two heads : firstly, not to disparage the places in which they speak, or the intelligence of their hearers ; secondly, not to set themselves in antagonism to the natural inborn desire of the mass of mankind to re-create themselves and to be amused.

There is a third head, taking precedence of all others, to which my remarks on the discourse I heard have tended. In the New Testament there is the most beautiful and affecting history conceivable by man, and there are the terse models for all prayer and for all preaching. As to the models, imitate them, Sunday preachers—else why are they there, consider ? As to the history, tell it. Some people cannot read, some people will not read, many people (this especially holds among the young and ignorant) find it hard to pursue the verse-form in which the book is presented to them, and imagine that those breaks imply gaps and want of continuity. Help them over that first stumbling-block, by setting forth the history in narrative, with no fear of exhausting it. You will never preach so well, you will never move them so profoundly, you will never send them away with half so much to think of. Which is the better interest : Christ's choice of twelve poor men to help in those merciful wonders among the poor and rejected ; or the pious bullying of a whole Union-full of paupers ? What is your changed philosopher to wretched me, peeping in at the door out of the mud of the streets and of my life, when you have the widow's son to tell me about, the ruler's daughter, the other figure at the door when the brother of the two sisters was dead, and one of the two ran to the mourner, crying, " The Master is come and calleth for thee " ?—Let the preacher who will thoroughly forget himself and remember no individuality but one, and no eloquence but one, stand up before four thousand men and women at the Britannia Theatre any Sunday night, recounting that narrative to them as fellow-creatures, and he shall see a sight !

V

POOR MERCANTILE JACK

Is the sweet little cherub who sits smiling aloft and keeps watch on the life of poor Jack, commissioned to take charge of Mercantile Jack, as well as Jack of the national navy? If not, who is? What is the cherub about, and what are we all about, when poor Mercantile Jack is having his brains slowly knocked out by pennyweights, aboard the brig *Beelzebub*, or the barque *Bowie-knife*—when he looks his last at that infernal craft, with the first officer's iron boot-heel in his remaining eye, or with his dying body towed overboard in the ship's wake, while the cruel wounds in it do "the multitudinous seas incarnadine"?

Is it unreasonable to entertain a belief that if, aboard the brig *Beelzebub* or the barque *Bowie-knife*, the first officer did half the damage to cotton that he does to men, there would presently arise from both sides of the Atlantic so vociferous an invocation of the sweet little cherub who sits calculating aloft, keeping watch on the markets that pay, that such vigilant cherub would, with a winged sword, have that gallant officer's organ of destructiveness out of his head in the space of a flash of lightning?

If it be unreasonable, then am I the most unreasonable of men, for I believe it with all my soul.

This was my thought as I walked the dock-quays at Liverpool, keeping watch on poor Mercantile Jack. Alas for me! I have long outgrown the state of sweet little cherub; but there I was, and there Mercantile Jack was, and very busy he was, and very cold he was: the snow yet lying in the frozen furrows of the land, and the north-east winds snipping off the tops of the little waves in the Mersey, and rolling them into hailstones to pelt him with. Mercantile Jack was hard at it, in the hard weather: as he mostly is in all weathers, poor Jack. He was girded to ships' masts and funnels of steamers, like a forester to a great oak, scraping and painting; he was lying out on yards, furling sails that tried to beat him off; he was dimly discernible up in a world of giant cobwebs, reefing and splicing; he was faintly audible down in holds, stowing and unshipping cargo; he was winding round and round at capstans, melodious, monotonous, and drunk; he was of a diabolical aspect, with coaling for the Antipodes; he was washing decks barefoot, with the breast of his red shirt open to the blast, though it was sharper than the knife in his leathern girdle; he was looking over bulwarks, all eyes and hair; he was standing by at the shoot of the Cunard steamer, off to-morrow, as the stocks in trade of several butchers, poulterers, and fishmongers poured down into the ice-house; he was coming aboard of other vessels, with his kit in a tarpaulin bag, attended by plunderers to the very last moment of his shore-going existence. As though his senses when released from the uproar of the elements were under obligation to be confused by other turmoil, there was a rattling of wheels, a clattering of hoofs, a clashing of iron, a jolting of cotton and hides and casks and timber, an incessant deafening disturbance on the quays, that was the very madness of sound. And as, in the midst of it, he stood swaying about, with his hair blown all manner of wild ways, rather crazedly taking leave of his plunderers, all the rigging in the docks was shrill in the wind, and every little steamer coming and going across the Mersey was sharp in its blowing off, and every buoy in the river bobbed spitefully up and down, as if there were a general taunting chorus of "Come along, Mercantile Jack! Ill-lodged, ill-fed, ill-used, hocussed, entrapped, anticipated, cleaned out. Come along, Poor Mercantile Jack, and be tempest-tossed till you are drowned!"

The uncommercial transaction which had brought me and Jack together was this :—I had entered the Liverpool police-force, that I might have a look at the various unlawful traps which are every night set for Jack. As my term of service in that distinguished corps was short, and as my personal bias in the capacity of one of its members has ceased, no suspicion will attach to my evidence that it is an admirable force. Besides that it is composed, without favour, of the best men that can be picked, it is directed by an unusual intelligence. Its organisation against Fires I take to be much better than the metropolitan system, and in all respects it tempers its remarkable vigilance with a still more remarkable discretion.

Jack had knocked off work in the docks some hours, and I had taken, for purposes of identification, a photograph-likeness of a thief, in the portrait-room at our head police office (on the whole, he seemed rather complimented by the proceeding), and I had been on police parade, and the small hand of the clock was moving on to ten, when I took up my lantern to follow Mr. Superintendent to the traps that were set for Jack. In Mr. Superintendent I saw, as anybody might, a tall, well-looking, well set-up man of a soldierly bearing, with a cavalry air, a good chest, and a resolute but not by any means ungentle face. He carried in his hand a plain black walking-stick of hard wood ; and whenever and wherever, at any after-time of the night, he struck it on the pavement with a ringing sound, it instantly produced a whistle out of the darkness, and a policeman. To this remarkable stick I refer an air of mystery and magic which pervaded the whole of my perquisition among the traps that were set for Jack.

We began by diving into the obscurest streets and lanes of the port. Suddenly pausing in a flow of cheerful discourse, before a dead wall, apparently some ten miles long, Mr. Superintendent struck upon the ground, and the wall opened and shot out, with military salute of hand to temple, two policemen—not in the least surprised themselves, not in the least surprising Mr. Superintendent.

"All right, Sharpeye?"

"All right, Sir."

"All right, Trampfoot?"

"All right, Sir."

"Is Quickear there?"

"Here am I, Sir."

"Come with us."

"Yes, Sir."

So Sharpeye went before, and Mr. Superintendent and I went next, and Trampfoot and Quickear marched as rear-guard. Sharpeye, I soon had occasion to remark, had a skilful and quite professional way of opening doors—touched latches delicately, as if they were keys of musical instruments—opened every door he touched, as if he were perfectly confident that there was stolen property behind it—instantly insinuated himself, to prevent its being shut.

Sharpeye opened several doors of traps that were set for Jack, but Jack did not happen to be in any of them. They were all such miserable places that really, Jack, if I were you, I would give them a wider berth. In every trap somebody was sitting over a fire waiting for Jack. Now, it was a crouching old woman, like the picture of the Norwood Gipsy in the old sixpenny dream-books ; now, it was a crimp of the male sex, in a checked shirt and without a coat, reading a newspaper ; now, it was a man crimp and a woman crimp, who always introduced themselves as united in holy matrimony ; now, it was Jack's delight, his (un)lovely Nan ; but they were all waiting for Jack, and were all frightfully disappointed to see us.

"Who have you got up-stairs here?" says Sharpeye, generally. (In the Move-on tone.)

"Nobody, Surr ; sure not a blessed sowl !" (Irish feminine reply.)

"What do you mean by nobody? Didn't I hear a woman's step go up-stairs when my hand was on the latch?"

"Ah ! sure thin you're right, Surr, I forgot her ! 'Tis on'y Betsy White, Surr. Ah ! you know Betsy, Surr. Come down, Betsy darlin' and say the gintlemin."

Generally, Betsy looks over the banisters (the steep staircase is in the room) with a forcible expression in her protesting face of an intention to compensate herself for the present trial by grinding Jack finer than usual when he does come. Generally, Sharpeye turns to Mr. Superintendent, and says, as if the subjects of his remarks were wax-work—

"One of the worst, Sir, this house is. This woman has been indicted three times. This man's a regular bad one likewise. His real name is Pegg. Gives himself out as Waterhouse."

"Never had sitch a name as Pegg near me back, thin, since I was in this house, bee the good Lard !" says the woman.

Generally, the man says nothing at all, but becomes exceedingly round-shouldered, and pretends to read his paper with rapt attention. Generally, Sharpeye directs our observation with a look to the prints and pictures that are invariably numerous on the walls. Always, Trampfoot and Quickear are taking notice on the doorstep. In default of Sharpeye being acquainted with the exact individuality of any gentleman encountered, one of these two is sure to proclaim from the outer air, like a gruff spectre, that Jackson is not Jackson, but knows himself to be Fogle ; or that Canlon is Walker's brother, against whom there was not sufficient evidence ; or that the man who says he never was at sea since he was a boy, came ashore from a voyage last Thursday, or sails to-morrow morning. "And that is a bad class of man, you see," says Mr. Superintendent, when he got out into the dark again, "and very difficult to deal with, who, when he has made this place too hot to hold him, enters himself for a voyage as steward or cook, and is out of knowledge for months, and then turns up again worse than ever."

When we had gone into many such houses, and had come out (always leaving everybody relapsing into waiting for Jack), we started off to a singing-house where Jack was expected to muster strong.

The vocalisation was taking place in a long, low room up-stairs ; at one end an orchestra of two performers, and a small platform ; across the room a series of open pews for Jack, with an aisle down the middle ; at the other end a larger pew than the rest, entitled SNUG, and reserved for mates and similar good company. About the room some amazing coffee-coloured pictures varnished an inch deep, and some stuffed creatures in cases ; dotted among the audience, in Snug and out of Snug, the "Professionals" ; among them the celebrated comic favourite Mr. Banjo Bones, looking very hideous with his blackened face and limp sugar-loaf hat ; beside him, sipping rum-and-water, Mrs. Banjo Bones, in her natural colours—a little heightened.

It was a Friday night, and Friday night was considered not a good night for Jack. At any rate, Jack did not show in very great force even here, though the house was one to which he much resorts, and where a good deal of money is taken. There was British Jack, a little maudlin and sleepy, lolling over his empty glass, as if he were trying to read his fortune at the bottom ; there was Loafing Jack of the Stars and Stripes, rather an unpromising customer, with his long nose, lank cheek, high cheek-bones, and nothing soft about him but his cabbage-leaf hat ; there was Spanish Jack, with curls of black hair, rings in his ears, and a knife not far from his hand, if you got into trouble with him ; there were Maltese Jack, and Jack of Sweden, and Jack the Finn, looming through the smoke of their pipes, and turning faces that looked as if they were carved out of dark wood, towards the young lady dancing the hornpipe, who found the platform so exceedingly small for it, that I had a nervous expectation of seeing her, in the backward steps, disappear through the window. Still, if all hands had been got together, they would not have more than half-filled the room. Observe, however, said Mr. Licensed Victualler, the host, that it was Friday night, and, besides, it was getting on for twelve, and Jack had gone aboard. A sharp and watchful man, Mr. Licensed Victualler, the host, with tight lips and a complete edition of Cocker's arithmetic in each eye. Attended to his business himself, he said. Always on the spot. When he heard of talent, trusted nobody's account of it, but went off by rail to see it. If true talent, engaged it. Pounds a week for talent —four pound—five pound. Banjo Bones was undoubted talent. Hear this instrument that was going to play—it was real talent! In truth it was very good; a kind of piano-accordion, played by a young girl of a delicate prettiness of face, figure, and dress, that made the audience look coarser. She sang to the instrument, too; first, a song about village bells, and how they chimed; then a song about how I went to sea; winding up with an imitation of the bagpipes, which Mercantile Jack seemed to understand much the best. A good girl, said Mr. Licensed Victualler. Kept herself select. Sat in Snug, not listening to the blandishments of mates. Lived with mother. Father dead. Once a merchant well to do, but over-speculated himself. On delicate inquiry as to salary paid for item of talent under consideration, Mr. Victualler's pounds dropped suddenly to shillings—still it was a very comfortable thing for a young person like that, you know; she only went on six times a night, and was only required to be there from six at night to twelve. What was more conclusive was Mr. Victualler's assurance that he "never allowed any language, and never suffered any disturbance." Sharpeye confirmed the statement, and the order that prevailed was the best proof of it that could have been cited. So I came to the conclusion that poor Mercantile Jack might do (as I am afraid he does) much worse than trust himself to Mr. Victualler, and pass his evenings here.

But we had not yet looked, Mr. Superintendent—said Trampfoot, receiving us in the street again with military salute—for Dark Jack. True, Trampfoot. Ring the wonderful stick, rub the wonderful lantern, and cause the spirits of the stick and lantern to convey us to the Darkies.

There was no disappointment in the matter of Dark Jack; *he* was producible. The Genii set us down in the little first floor of a little public-house, and there, in a stiflingly close atmosphere, were Dark Jack and Dark Jack's Delight, his *white* unlovely Nan, sitting against the wall all round the room. More than that: Dark Jack's Delight was the least unlovely Nan, both morally and physically, that I saw that night.

As a fiddle and tambourine band were sitting among the company, Quickear suggested why not strike up? "Ah, la'ads!" said a negro sitting by the door, "gib the jebblem a darnse. Tak' yah pardlers, jebblem, for 'um QUAD-rill."

This was the landlord, in a Greek cap, and a dress half Greek and half English. As master of the ceremonies, he called all the figures, and occasionally addressed himself parenthetically—after this manner. When he was very loud I use capitals.

"Now den! Hoy! ONE. Right and left. (Put a steam on, gib 'um powder.) LA-dies' chail. BAL-loon say. Lemonade! Two. AD-warnse and go back (gib 'ell a breakdown, shake it out o' yerselbs, keep a movil). SWING-corners, BAL-loon say, and Lemonade! (Hoy!) THREE. GENT come for'ard with a lady and go back, hoppersite come

for'ard and do what yer can. (Aeiohoy!) BAL-loon say, and leetle
lemonade (Dat hair nigger by 'um fireplace 'hind a' time, shake it out
o' yerselbs, gib 'ell a breakdown.) Now den! Hoy! FOUR! Lemonade. BAL-loon say, and swing. FOUR ladies meets in 'um middle,
FOUR gents goes round 'um ladies, FOUR gents passes out under 'um
ladies' arms, SWING—and Lemonade till 'a moosic can't play no more!
(Hoy, Hoy!)"

The male dancers were all blacks, and one was an unusually powerful man of six feet three or four. The sound of their flat feet on the
floor was as unlike the sound of white feet as their faces were unlike
white faces. They toed and heeled, shuffled, double-shuffled, double-
double-shuffled, covered the buckle, and beat the time out, rarely,
dancing with a great show of teeth, and with a childish good-humoured
enjoyment that was very prepossessing. They generally kept together,
these poor fellows, said Mr. Superintendent, because they were at a
disadvantage singly, and liable to slights in the neighbouring streets.
But if I were Light Jack, I should be very slow to interfere oppressively
with Dark Jack, for, whenever I have had to do with him I have found
him a simple and a gentle fellow. Bearing this in mind, I asked his
friendly permission to leave him restoration of beer, in wishing him
good-night, and thus it fell out that the last words I heard him say as
I blundered down the worn stairs were, "Jebblem's elth! Ladies
drinks fust!"

The night was now well on into the morning, but for miles and
hours we explored a strange world, where nobody ever goes to bed,
but everybody is eternally sitting up, waiting for Jack. This exploration was among a labyrinth of dismal courts and blind alleys, called
Entries, kept in wonderful order by the police, and in much better order
than by the corporation, the want of gaslight in the most dangerous
and infamous of these places being quite unworthy of so spirited a
town. I need describe but two or three of the houses in which Jack
was waited for, as specimens of the rest. Many we attained by noisome
passages so profoundly dark that we felt our way with our hands.
Not one of the whole number we visited was without its show of prints
and ornamental crockery; the quantity of the latter set forth on little
shelves and in little cases, in otherwise wretched rooms, indicating that
Mercantile Jack must have an extraordinary fondness for crockery, to
necessitate so much of that bait in his traps.

Among such garniture, in one front parlour in the dead of the night,
four women were sitting by a fire. One of them had a male child in
her arms. On a stool among them was a swarthy youth with a guitar,
who had evidently stopped playing when our footsteps were heard.

"Well! how do *you* do?" says Mr. Superintendent, looking about
him.

"Pretty well, Sir, and hope you gentlemen are going to treat us
ladies, now you have come to see us."

"Order there!" says Sharpeye.

"None of that!" says Quickear.

Trampfoot, outside, is heard to confide to himself, " Meggisson's lot this is. And a bad 'un ! "

" Well ! " says Mr. Superintendent, laying his hand on the shoulder of the swarthy youth, " and who's this ? "

" Antonio, Sir."

" And what does *he* do here ? "

" Come to give us a bit of music. No harm in that, I suppose ? "

" A young foreign sailor ? "

" Yes. He's a Spaniard. You're a Spaniard, ain't you, Antonio ? "

" Me Spanish."

" And he don't know a word you say, not he ; not if you was to talk to him till doomsday." (Triumphantly, as if it redounded to the credit of the house.)

" Will he play something ? "

" Oh, yes, if you like. Play something, Antonio. *You* ain't ashamed to play something, are you ? "

The cracked guitar raises the feeblest ghost of a tune, and three of the women keep time to it with their heads, and the fourth with the child. If Antonio has brought any money in with him, I am afraid he will never take it out, and it even strikes me that his jacket and guitar may be in a bad way. But the look of the young man and the tinkling of the instrument so change the place in a moment to a leaf out of *Don Quixote*, that I wonder where his mule is stabled, until he leaves off.

I am bound to acknowledge (as it tends rather to my uncommercial confusion) that I occasioned a difficulty in this establishment by having taken the child in my arms. For on my offering to restore it to a ferocious joker not unstimulated by rum, who claimed to be its mother, that unnatural parent put her hands behind her, and declined to accept it ; backing into the fire-place, and very shrilly declaring, regardless of remonstrance from her friends, that she knowed it to be Law, that whoever took a child from its mother of his own will was bound to stick to it. The uncommercial sense of being in a rather ridiculous position with the poor little child beginning to be frightened was relieved by my worthy friend and fellow-constable, Trampfoot ; who, laying hands on the article as if it were a Bottle, passed it on to the nearest woman, and bade her " take hold of that." As we came out, the Bottle was passed to the ferocious joker, and they all sat down as before, including Antonio and the guitar. It was clear that there was no such thing as a nightcap to this baby's head, and that even he never went to bed, but was always kept up—and would grow up, kept up— waiting for Jack.

Later still in the night we came (by the court " where the man was murdered," and by the other court across the street, into which his body was dragged) to another parlour in another Entry, where several people were sitting round a fire in just the same way. It was a dirty and offensive place, with some ragged clothes drying in it ; but there was a high shelf over the entrance-door (to be out of the reach of marauding hands, possibly) with two large white loaves on it, and a great piece of Cheshire cheese.

"Well!" says Mr. Superintendent, with a comprehensive look all round. "How do *you* do?"

"Not much to boast of, Sir." From the curtseying woman of the house. "This is my good man, Sir."

"You are not registered as a common Lodging House?"

"No, Sir."

Sharpeye (in the Move-on tone) puts in the pertinent inquiry, "Then why ain't you?"

"Ain't got no one here, Mr. Sharpeye," rejoins the woman and my good man together, "but our own family."

"How many are you in family?"

The woman takes time to count, under pretence of coughing, and adds, as one scant of breath, "Seven, Sir."

But she has missed one, so Sharpeye, who knows all about it, says:

"Here's a young man here makes eight, who ain't of your family?"

"No, Mr. Sharpeye, he's a weekly lodger."

"What does he do for a living?"

The young man here takes the reply upon himself, and shortly answers, "Ain't got nothing to do."

The young man here is modestly brooding behind a damp apron pendent from a clothes-line. As I glance at him I become—but I don't know why—vaguely reminded of Woolwich, Chatham, Portsmouth, and Dover. When we get out, my respected fellow-constable Sharpeye addressing Mr. Superintendent, says:

"You noticed that young man, Sir, in at Darby's?"

"Yes. What is he?"

"Deserter, Sir."

Mr. Sharpeye further intimates that when we have done with his services he will step back and take that young man. Which in course of time he does: feeling at perfect ease about finding him, and knowing for a moral certainty that nobody in that region will be gone to bed.

Later still in the night we came to another parlour up a step or two from the street, which was very cleanly, neatly, even tastefully, kept, and in which, set forth on a draped chest of drawers masking the staircase, was such a profusion of ornamental crockery, that it would have furnished forth a handsome sale-booth at a fair. It backed up a stout old lady—HOGARTH drew her exact likeness more than once—and a boy who was carefully writing a copy in a copy-book.

"Well, ma'am, how do *you* do?"

Sweetly, she can assure the dear gentlemen, sweetly. Charmingly, charmingly. And overjoyed to see us!

"Why, this is a strange time for this boy to be writing his copy. In the middle of the night!"

"So it is, dear gentlemen, Heaven bless your welcome faces and send ye prosperous, but he has been to the Play with a young friend for his diversion, and he combinates his improvement with entertainment, by doing his school-writhing afterwards, God be good to ye ! "

The copy admonished human nature to subjugate the fire of every fierce desire. One might have thought it recommended stirring the fire, the old lady so approved it. There she sat, rosily beaming at the copy-book and the boy, and invoking showers of blessings on our heads, when we left her in the middle of the night, waiting for Jack.

Later still in the night, we came to a nauseous room with an earth floor, into which the refuse scum of an alley trickled. The stench of this habitation was abominable ; the seeming poverty of it, diseased and dire. Yet, here again, was visitor or lodger—a man sitting before the fire, like the rest of them elsewhere, and apparently not distasteful to the mistress's niece, who was also before the fire. The mistress herself had the misfortune of being in jail.

Three weird old women of transcendent ghastliness were at needle-work at a table in this room. Says Trampfoot to First Witch, " What are you making ? " Says she, " Money-bags."

" *What* are you making ? " retorts Trampfoot, a little off his balance.

" Bags to hold your money," says the witch, shaking her head, and setting her teeth ; " you as has got it."

She holds up a common cash-bag, and on the table is a heap of such bags. Witch Two laughs at us. Witch Three scowls at us. Witch sisterhood all, stitch, stitch. First Witch has a red circle round each eye. I fancy it like the beginning of the development of a perverted diabolical halo, and that when it spreads all round her head she will die in the odour of devilry.

Trampfoot wishes to be informed what First Witch has got behind the table, down by the side of her there ? Witches Two and Three croak angrily, " Show him the child ! "

She drags out a skinny little arm from a brown dustheap on the ground. Adjured not to disturb the child, she lets it drop again. Thus we find at last that there is one child in the world of Entries who goes to bed—if this be bed.

Mr. Superintendent asks how long are they going to work at those bags ?

How long ? First Witch repeats. Going to have supper presently. See the cups and saucers, and the plates.

" Late ? Aye ! But we has to 'arn our supper afore we eats it ! " Both the other witches repeat this after First Witch, and take the Uncommercial measurement with their eyes, as for a charmed winding-sheet. Some grim discourse ensues, referring to the mistress of the cave, who will be released from jail to-morrow. Witches pronounce Trampfoot " right there," when he deems it a trying distance for the old lady to walk ; she shall be fetched by niece in a spring-cart.

As I took a parting look at First Witch in turning away, the red marks round her eyes seemed to have already grown larger, and she hungrily and thirstily looked out beyond me into the dark doorway, to see if Jack were there. For Jack came even here, and the mistress had got into jail through deluding Jack.

When I at last ended this night of travel and got to bed, I failed to keep my mind on comfortable thoughts cf Seaman's Homes (not overdone with strictness), and improved dock regulations giving Jack greater benefit of fire and candle aboard ship, through my mind's wandering among the vermin I had seen. Afterwards the same vermin ran all over my sleep. Evermore, when on a breezy day I see Poor Mercantile Jack running into port with a fair wind under all sail, I shall think of the unsleeping host of devourers who never go to bed, and are always in their set traps waiting for him.

VI

REFRESHMENTS FOR TRAVELLERS

In the late high winds I was blown to a great many places—and indeed, wind or no wind, I generally have extensive transactions on hand in the article of Air—but I have not been blown to any English place lately, and I very seldom have blown to any English place in my life, where I could get anything good to eat and drink in five minutes, or where, if I sought it, I was received with a welcome.

This is a curious thing to consider. But before (stimulated by my own experiences and the representations of many fellow-travellers of every uncommercial and commercial degree) I consider it further, I must utter a passing word of wonder concerning high winds.

I wonder why metropolitan gales always blow so hard at Walworth. I cannot imagine what Walworth has done to bring such windy punishment upon itself, as I never fail to find recorded in the newspapers when the wind has blown at all hard. Brixton seems to have something on its conscience ; Peckham suffers more than a virtuous Peckham might be supposed to deserve ; the howling neighbour of Deptford figures largely in the accounts of the ingenious gentlemen who are out in every wind that blows, and to whom it is an ill high wind that blows no good ; but there can hardly be any Walworth left by this time. It must surely be blown away. I have read of more chimney-stacks and house-copings coming down with terrific smashes at Walworth, and of more sacred edifices being nearly (not quite) blown out to sea from the same accursed locality, than I have read of practised thieves with the appearance and manners of gentlemen—a popular phenomenon which never existed on earth out of fiction and a police report. Again : I wonder why people are always blown into the Surrey Canal, and into no other piece of water ! Why do people get up early and go out in groups, to be blown into the Surrey Canal ? Do they say to one another, "Welcome death, so that we get into the newspapers"? Even that would be an insufficient explanation, because even then they might sometimes put themselves in the way of being blown into the Regent's Canal, instead of always saddling Surrey for the field.   Some nameless policeman, too, is constantly, on the slightest provocation, getting himself blown into this same Surrey Canal.   Will Sir Richard Mayne see to it, and restrain that weak-minded and feeble-bodied constable?

To resume the consideration of the curious question of Refreshment. I am a Briton, and, as such, I am aware that I never will be a slave— and yet I have latent suspicion that there must be some slavery of wrong custom in this matter.

I travel by railroad.   I start from home at seven or eight in the morning, after breakfasting hurriedly.   What with skimming over the open landscape, what with mining in the damp bowels of the earth, what with banging, booming, and shrieking the scores of miles away, I am hungry when I arrive at the "Refreshment" station where I am expected.   Please to observe, expected.   I have said, I am hungry; perhaps I might say, with greater point and force, that I am to some extent exhausted, and that I need—in the expressive French sense of the word—to be restored.   What is provided for my restoration?   The apartment that is to restore me is a wind-trap, cunningly set to inveigle all the draughts in that country-side, and to communicate a special intensity and velocity to them as they rotate in two hurricanes: one, about my wretched head; one, about my wretched legs.   The training of the young ladies behind the counter who are to restore me has been from their infancy directed to the assumption of a defiant dramatic show that I am *not* expected.   It is in vain for me to represent to them by my humble and conciliatory manners that I wish to be liberal.   It is in vain for me to represent to myself, for the encouragement of my sinking soul, that the young ladies have a pecuniary interest in my arrival. Neither my reason nor my feelings can make head against the cold, glazed glare of eye with which I am assured that I am not expected, and not wanted.   The solitary man among the bottles would sometimes take pity on me, if he dared, but he is powerless against the rights and mights of Woman.   (Of the page I make no account, for he is a boy, and therefore the natural enemy of Creation.)   Chilling fast, in the deadly tornadoes to which my upper and lower extremities are exposed, and subdued by the moral disadvantage at which I stand, I turn my disconsolate eyes on the refreshments that are to restore me.   I find that I must either scald my throat by insanely ladling into it, against time and for no wager, brown hot water stiffened with flour; or I must make myself flaky and sick with Banbury cake; or I must stuff into my delicate organisation a currant pincushion which I know will swell into immeasurable dimensions when it has got there; or I must extort from an iron-bound quarry, with a fork, as if I were farming an inhospitable soil, some glutinous lumps of gristle and grease called pork-pie.   While thus forlornly occupied, I find that the depressing banquet on the table is, in every phase of its profoundly unsatisfactory character, so like the banquet at the meanest and shabbiest of evening parties, that I begin to think I must have "brought down" to supper the old lady unknown, blue with cold, who is setting her teeth on edge with a cool orange at my elbow — that the pastrycook who has compounded for the company on the lowest terms per head is a fraudulent bankrupt, redeeming his contract with the stale stock from his window—that, for some unexplained reason, the family giving the party have become my mortal foes, and have given it on purpose to affront me. Or I fancy that I am "breaking up" again, at the evening conversazione at school, charged two-and-sixpence in the half-year's bill ; or breaking down again at that celebrated evening party given at Mrs. Bogles's boarding-house when I was a boarder there, on which occasion Mrs. Bogles was taken in execution by a branch of the legal profession who got in as the harp, and was removed (with the keys and subscribed capital) to a place of durance, half an hour prior to the commencement of the festivities.

Take another case.

Mr. Grazinglands, of the Midland Counties, came to London by railroad one morning last week, accompanied by the amiable and fascinating Mrs. Grazinglands. Mr. G. is a gentleman of a comfortable property, and had a little business to transact at the Bank of England, which required the concurrence and signature of Mrs. G. Their business disposed of, Mr. and Mrs. Grazinglands viewed the Royal Exchange and the exterior of St. Paul's Cathedral. The spirits of Mrs. Grazinglands then gradually beginning to flag, Mr. Grazinglands (who is the tenderest of husbands) remarked with sympathy, "Arabella, my dear, I fear you are faint." Mrs. Grazinglands replied, "Alexander, I am rather faint ; but don't mind me, I shall be better presently." Touched by the feminine meekness of this answer, Mr. Grazinglands looked in at a pastrycook's window, hesitating as to the expediency of lunching at that establishment. He beheld nothing to eat but butter in various forms, slightly charged with jam, and languidly frizzling over tepid water. Two ancient turtle-shells, on which was inscribed the legend, "Soups," decorated a glass partition within, enclosing a stuffy alcove, from which a ghastly mockery of a marriage-breakfast spread on a rickety table warned the terrified traveller. An oblong box of stale and broken pastry at reduced prices, mounted on a stool, ornamented the doorway ; and two high chairs that looked as if they were performing on stilts embellished the counter. Over the whole a young lady presided, whose gloomy haughtiness, as she surveyed the street, announced a deep-seated grievance against society, and an implacable determination to be avenged. From a beetle-haunted kitchen below this institution fumes arose, suggestive of a class of soup which Mr. Grazinglands knew, from painful experience, enfeebles the mind, distends the stomach, forces itself into the complexion, and tries to ooze out at the eyes. As he decided against entering, and turned away, Mrs. Grazinglands becoming perceptibly weaker, repeated, "I am rather faint, Alexander, but don't mind me." Urged to new efforts by these words of resignation, Mr. Grazinglands looked in at a cold and floury baker's shop, where utilitarian buns, unrelieved by a currant, consorted with hard biscuits, a stone filter of cold water, a hard pale clock, and a hard little old woman with flaxen hair, of an undeveloped-farinaceous aspect, as if she had been fed upon seeds. He might have entered even here, but for the timely remembrance coming upon him that Jairing's was but round the corner.

Now Jairing's being an hotel for families and gentlemen, in high repute among the midland counties, Mr. Grazinglands plucked up a great spirit when he told Mrs. Grazinglands she should have a chop there. That lady likewise felt that she was going to see Life. Arriving on that gay and festive scene, they found the second waiter, in a flabby undress, cleaning the windows of the empty coffee-room ; and the first waiter, denuded of his white tie, making up his cruets behind the Post-Office Directory. The latter (who took them in hand) was greatly put out by their patronage, and showed his mind to be troubled by a sense of the pressing necessity of instantly smuggling Mrs. Grazinglands into the obscurest corner of the building. This slighted lady (who is the pride of her division of the county) was immediately conveyed, by several dark passages, and up and down several steps, into a peniten-tial apartment at the back of the house, where five invalided old plate-warmers leaned up against one another under a discarded old melancholy sideboard, and where the wintry leaves of all the dining-tables in the house lay thick. Also a sofa, of incomprehensible form regarded from any sofane point of view, murmured " Bed " ; while an air of mingled fluffiness and heeltaps added, " Second Waiter's." Secreted in this dismal hold, objects of a mysterious distrust and suspicion, Mr. Grazinglands and his charming partner waited twenty minutes for the smoke (for it never came to a fire), twenty-five minutes for the sherry, half-an-hour for the table-cloth, forty minutes for the knives and forks, three-quarters of an hour for the chops, and an hour for the potatoes. On settling the little bill—which was not much more than the day's pay of a Lieutenant in the navy—Mr. Grazinglands took heart to remonstrate against the general quality and cost of his reception. To whom the waiter replied, substantially, that Jairing's made it a merit to have accepted him on any terms : " for," added the waiter (unmistakably coughing at Mrs. Grazinglands, the pride of her division of the county), " when indiwiduals is not staying in the 'Ouse, their favours is not as a rule looked upon as making it worth Mr. Jairing's while ; nor is it, indeed, a style of business Mr. Jairing wishes." Finally, Mr. and Mrs. Grazinglands passed out of Jairing's hotel for Families and Gentlemen, in a state of the greatest depression, scorned by the bar ; and did not recover their self-respect for several days.

Or take another case. Take your own case.

You are going off by railway, from any terminus. You have twenty minutes for dinner before you go. You want your dinner, and like Dr. Johnson, Sir, you like to dine. You present to your mind a picture of the refreshment-table at that terminus. The conventional shabby evening-party supper—accepted as the model for all termini and all refreshment stations, because it is the last repast known to this state of existence of which any human creature would partake but in the direst extremity—sickens your contemplation, and your words are these : " I cannot dine on stale sponge-cakes that turn to sand in the mouth. I cannot dine on shining brown patties, composed of unknown animals within, and offering to my view the device of an indigestible star-fish in leaden pie-crust without. I cannot dine on a sandwich that has long been pining under an exhausted receiver. I cannot dine on barley-sugar. I cannot dine on toffee." You repair to the nearest hotel, and arrive, agitated, in the coffee-room.

It is a most astonishing fact that the waiter is very cold to you. Account for it how you may, smooth it over how you will, you cannot deny that he is cold to you. He is not glad to see you, he does not want you, he would much rather you hadn't come. He opposes to your flushed condition an immovable composure. As if this were not enough, another waiter, born, as it would seem, expressly to look at you in this passage of your life, stands at a little distance, with his napkin under his arm and his hands folded, looking at you with all his might. You impress on your waiter that you have ten minutes for dinner, and he proposes that you shall begin with a bit of fish which will be ready in twenty. That proposal declined, he suggests—as a neat originality—"a weal or mutton cutlet." You close with either cutlet, any cutlet, anything. He goes, leisurely, behind a door and calls down some unseen shaft. A ventriloquial dialogue ensues, tending finally to the effect that weal only is available on the spur of the moment. You anxiously call out, "Veal, then !" Your waiter having settled that point, returns to array your tablecloth, with a table napkin folded cocked-hat-wise (slowly, for something out of the window engages his eye), a white wine-glass, a green wine-glass, a blue finger-glass, a tumbler, and a powerful field battery of fourteen castors with nothing in them ; or at all events—which is enough for your purpose—with nothing in them that will come out. All this time the other waiter looks at you—with an air of mental comparison and curiosity, now, as if it had occurred to him that you are rather like his brother. Half your time gone, and nothing come but the jug of ale and the bread, you implore your waiter to " See after that cutlet, waiter ; pray do ! " He cannot go at once, for he is carrying in seventeen pounds of American cheese for you to finish with, and a small Landed Estate of celery and water-cresses. The other waiter changes his leg, and takes a new view of you—doubtfully, now, as if he had rejected the resemblance to his brother, and had begun to think you more like his aunt or his grandmother. Again you beseech your waiter with pathetic indignation to " see after that cutlet ! " He steps out to see after it, and by and by, when you are going away without it, comes back with it. Even then he will not take the sham silver cover off without a pause for a flourish, and a look at the musty cutlet as if he were surprised to see it—which cannot possibly be the case, he must have seen it so often before. A sort of fur has been produced upon its surface by the cook's art, and in a sham silver vessel staggering on two feet instead of three is a cutaneous kind of sauce, of brown pimples and pickled cucumber. You order the bill, but your waiter cannot bring your bill yet, because he is bringing, instead, three flinty-hearted potatoes and two grim head of broccoli, like the occasional ornaments on area railings, badly boiled. You know that you will never come to this pass, any more than to the cheese and celery, and you imperatively demand your bill ; but it takes time to get, even when gone for, because your waiter has to communicate with a lady who lives behind a sash-window in a corner, and who appears to have to refer to several Ledgers before she can make it out—as if you had been staying there a year. You become distracted to get away, and the other waiter, once more changing his leg, still looks at you—but suspiciously now, as if you had begun to remind him of the party who took the greatcoats last winter. Your bill at last brought and paid, at the rate of sixpence a mouthful, your waiter reproachfully reminds you that "attendance is not charged for a single meal," and you have to search in all your pockets for sixpence more. He has a worse opinion of you than ever, when you have given it to him, and lets you out into the street with the air of one saying to himself, as you cannot doubt he is, "I hope we shall never see *you* here again !"

Or take any other of the numerous travelling instances in which, with more time at your disposal, you are, have been, or may be, equally ill served. Take the old-established Bull's Head with its old-established knife-boxes on its old-established sideboards, its old-established flue under its old-established four-post bedsteads in its old-established airless rooms, its old-established frouziness up-stairs and down-stairs, its old-established cookery, and its old-established principles of plunder. Count up your injuries, in its side-dishes of ailing sweet-breads in white poultices, of apothecaries' powders in rice for curry, of pale stewed bits of calf ineffectually relying for an adventitious interest on forcemeat balls. You have had experience of the old-established Bull's Head stringy fowls, with lower extremities like wooden legs, sticking up out of the dish ; of its cannibalic boiled mutton, gushing horribly among its capers when carved ; of its little dishes of pastry— roofs of spermaceti ointment erected over half an apple or four goose-berries. Well for you if you have yet forgotten the old-established Bull's Head fruity port ; whose reputation was gained solely by the old-established price the Bull's Head put upon it, and by the old-established air with which the Bull's Head set the glasses and doilies on, and held that Liquid Gout to the three-and-sixpenny wax-candle, as if its old-established colour hadn't come from the dyer's.

Or lastly, take to finish with, two cases that we all know, every day.

We all know the new hotel near the station, where it is always gusty, going up the lane which is always muddy, where we are sure to arrive at night, and where we make the gas start awfully when we open the front door. We all know the flooring of the passages and staircases that is too new, and the walls that are too new, and the house that is haunted by the ghost of mortar. We all know the doors that have cracked, and the cracked shutters through which we get a glimpse of the disconsolate moon. We all know the new people who have come to keep the new hotel, and who wish they had never come, and who (inevitable result) wish *we* had never come. We all know how much too scant and smooth and bright the new furniture is, and how it has never settled down, and cannot fit itself into right places, and will get into wrong places. We all know how the gas, being lighted, shows maps of Damp upon the walls. We all know how the ghost of mortar passes into our sandwich, stirs our negus, goes up to bed with us, ascends the pale bedroom chimney, and prevents the smoke from following. We all know how a leg of our chair comes off at breakfast in the morning, and how the dejected waiter attributes the accident to a general greenness pervading the establishment, and informs us, in reply to a local inquiry, that he is thankful to say he is an entire stranger in that part of the country, and is going back to his own connection on Saturday.

We all know, on the other hand, the great station hotel belonging to the company of proprietors, which has suddenly sprung up in the back outskirts of any place we like to name, and where we look out of our palatial windows at little back-yards and gardens, old summer-houses, fowl-houses, pigeon-traps, and pig-sties. We all know this hotel in which we can get anything we want, after its kind, for money ; but where nobody is glad to see us, or sorry to see us, or minds (our bill paid) whether we come or go, or how, or when, or why, or cares about us. We all know this hotel, where we have no individuality, but put ourselves into the general post, as it were, and are sorted and disposed of according to our division. We all know that we can get on very well indeed at such a place, but still not perfectly well ; and this may be because the place is largely wholesale, and there is a lingering personal retail interest within us that asks to be satisfied.

To sum up. My uncommercial travelling has not yet brought me to the conclusion that we are close to perfection in these matters. And just as I do not believe that the end of the world will ever be near at hand, so long as any of the very tiresome and arrogant people who constantly predict that catastrophe are left in it, so I shall have small faith in the Hotel Millennium while any of the uncomfortable super-stitions I have glanced at remain in existence.

VII

TRAVELLING ABROAD

I GOT into the travelling chariot—it was of German make, roomy, heavy, and unvarnished—I got into the travelling chariot, pulled up the steps after me, shut myself in with a smart bang of the door, and gave the word, " Go on ! "

Immediately all that W. and S.W. division of London began to slide away at a pace so lively, that I was over the river, and past the Old Kent Road, and out on Blackheath, and even ascending Shooter's Hill, before I had had time to look about me in the carriage like a collected traveller.

I had two ample Imperials on the roof, other fitted storage for luggage in front, and other up behind ; I had a net for books overhead, great pockets to all the windows, a leathern pouch or two hung up for odds and ends, and a reading lamp fixed in the back of the chariot in case I should be benighted. I was amply provided in all respects, and had no idea where I was going (which was delightful), except that I was going abroad.

So smooth was the old high road, and so fresh were the horses, and so fast went I, that it was midway between Gravesend and Rochester, and the widening river was bearing the ships, white sailed or black-smoked, out to sea, when I noticed by the wayside a very queer small boy.

" Holloa ! " said I, to the very queer small boy, " where do you live ? "

" At Chatham," says he.

" What do you do there ? " says I.

" I go to school," says he.

I took him up in a moment, and we went on. Presently the very queer small boy says, " This is Gadshill we are coming to, where Falstaff went out to rob those travellers, and ran away."

" You know something about Falstaff, eh ? " said I.

" All about him," said the very queer small boy. " I am old (I am nine), and I read all sorts of books. But *do* let us stop at the top of the hill, and look at the house there, if you please ! "

" You admire that house ? " said I.

" Bless you, sir," said the very queer small boy, " when I was not more than half as old as nine, it used to be a treat for me to be brought to look at it. And now I am nine, I come by myself to look at it. And ever since I can recollect, my father, seeing me so fond of it, has often said to me, ' If you were to be very persevering and were to work hard, you might some day come to live in it.' Though that's impossible ! " said the very queer small boy, drawing a low breath, and now staring at the house out of window with all his might.

I was rather amazed to be told this by the very queer small boy ; for that house happens to be *my* house, and I have reason to believe that what he said was true.

Well ! I made no halt there, and I soon dropped the very queer small boy and went on. Over the road where the old Romans used to march, over the road where the old Canterbury pilgrims used to go, over the road where the travelling trains of the old imperious priests and princes used to jingle on horseback between the Continent and this Island through the mud and water, over the road where Shakespeare hummed to himself, " Blow, blow, thou winter wind," as he sat in the saddle at the gate of the inn-yard noticing the carriers; all among the cherry orchards, apple orchards, corn-fields, and hop-gardens; so went I, by Canterbury to Dover. There the sea was tumbling in, with deep sounds, after dark, and the revolving French light on Cape Grinez was seen regularly bursting out and becoming obscured, as if the head of a gigantic light-keeper in an anxious state of mind were interposed every half minute to look how it was burning.

Early in the morning I was on the deck of the steam-packet, and we were aiming at the bar in the usual intolerable manner, and the bar was aiming at us in the usual intolerable manner, and the bar got by far the best of it, and we got by far the worst—all in the usual intolerable manner.

But when I was clear of the Custom House on the other side, and when I began to make the dust fly on the thirsty French roads, and when the twigsome trees by the wayside (which, I suppose, will never grow leafy, for they never did) guarded here and there a dusty soldier, or field-labourer, baking on a heap of broken stones, sound asleep in a fiction of shade, I began to recover my travelling spirits. Coming upon the breaker of the broken stones, in a hard, hot shining hat, on which the sun played at a distance as on a burning-glass, I felt that now, indeed, I was in the dear old France of my affections. I should have known it without the well-remembered bottle of rough ordinary wine, the cold roast fowl, the loaf, and the pinch of salt, on which I lunched with unspeakable satisfaction, from one of the stuffed pockets of the chariot.

I must have fallen asleep after lunch, for when a bright face looked in at the window, I started, and said:

"Good God, Louis, I dreamed you were dead!"

My cheerful servant laughed, and answered:

"Me? Not at all, sir."

"How glad I am to wake! What are we doing, Louis?"

"We go to take relay of horses. Will you walk up the hill?"

"Certainly."

Welcome the old French hill, with the old French lunatic (not in the most distant degree related to Sterne's Maria) living in a thatched dog-kennel half-way up, and flying out with his crutch and his big head and extended nightcap, to be beforehand with the old men and women exhibiting crippled children, and with the children exhibiting old men and women, ugly and blind, who always seemed by resurrectionary process to be recalled out of the elements for the sudden peopling of the solitude!

"It is well," said I, scattering among them what small coin I had; "here comes Louis, and I am quite roused from my nap."

We journeyed on again, and I welcomed every new assurance that France stood where I had left it. There were the posting-houses, with their archways, dirty stable-yards, and clean post-masters' wives, bright women of business, looking on at the putting-to of the horses; there were the postilions counting what money they got into their hats, and never making enough of it; there were the standard population of gray horses of Flanders descent, invariably biting one another when they got a chance ; there were the fleecy sheepskins, looped on over their uniforms by the postilions, like bibbed aprons, when it blew and rained ; there were their jack-boots, and their cracking whips ; there were the cathedrals that I got out to see, as under some cruel bondage, in no wise desiring to see them ; there were the little towns that appeared to have no reason for being towns, since most of their houses were to let and nobody could be induced to look at them, except the people who couldn't let them and had nothing else to do but look at them all day. I lay a night upon the road and enjoyed delectable cookery of potatoes, and some other sensible things, adoption of which at home would inevitably be shown to be fraught with ruin, somehow or other, to that rickety national blessing, the British farmer ; and at last I was rattled, like a single pill in a box, over leagues of stones, until—madly cracking, plunging, and flourishing two gray tails about—I made my triumphal entry into Paris.

At Paris I took an upper apartment for a few days in one of the hotels of the Rue de Rivoli ; my front windows looking into the garden of the Tuileries (where the principal difference between the nursemaids and the flowers seemed to be that the former were locomotive and the latter not) ; my back windows looking at all the other back windows in the hotel, and deep down into a paved yard, where my German chariot had retired under a tight-fitting archway, to all appearance, for life, and where bells rang all day without anybody's minding them but certain chamberlains with feather brooms and green baize caps, who here and there leaned out of some high window placidly looking down, and where neat waiters with trays on their left shoulders passed and repassed from morning to night.

Whenever I am at Paris I am dragged by invisible force into the Morgue. I never want to go there, but am always pulled there. One Christmas Day, when I would rather have been anywhere else, I was attracted in, to see an old gray man lying all alone on his cold bed, with a tap of water turned on over his gray hair, and running, drip, drip, drip, down his wretched face until it got to the corner of his mouth, where it took a turn, and made him look sly. One New Year's Morning (by the same token, the sun was shining outside, and there was a mountebank balancing a feather on his nose within a yard of the gate) I was pulled in again to look at a flaxen-haired boy of eighteen, with a heart hanging on his breast—" from his mother " was engraven on it—who had come into the net across the river, with a bullet-wound in his fair forehead and his hands cut with a knife, but whence or how was a blank mystery. This time I was forced into the same dread place to see a large dark man whose disfigurement by water was, in a frightful manner, comic, and whose expression was that of a prize-fighter who had closed his eyelids under a heavy blow, but was going immediately to open them, shake his head, and " come up smiling ". Oh, what this large dark man cost me in that bright city !

It was very hot weather, and he was none the better for that, and I was much the worse. Indeed, a very neat and pleasant little woman, with the key of her lodging on her forefinger, who had been showing him to her little girl while she and the child ate sweetmeats, observed monsieur looking poorly as we came out together, and asked monsieur, with her wondering little eyebrows prettily raised, if there were anything the matter. Faintly replying in the negative, monsieur crossed the road to a wine-shop, got some brandy, and resolved to freshen himself with a dip in the great floating bath on the river.

The bath was crowded in the usual airy manner by a male population in striped drawers of various gay colours, who walked up and down arm in arm, drank coffee, smoked cigars, sat at little tables, conversed politely with the damsels who dispensed the towels, and every now and then pitched themselves into the river head foremost, and came out again to repeat this social routine. I made haste to participate in the water part of the entertainments, and was in the full enjoyment of a delightful bath, when all in a moment I was seized with an unreasonable idea that the large dark body was floating straight at me.

I was out of the river, and dressing instantly. In the shock I had taken some water into my mouth, and it turned me sick, for I fancied that the contamination of the creature was in it. I had got back to my cool darkened room in the hotel, and was lying on a sofa there, before I began to reason with myself.

Of course I knew perfectly well that the large dark creature was stone dead, and that I should no more come upon him out of the place where I had seen him dead, than I should come upon the cathedral of Notre Dame in an entirely new situation. What troubled me was the picture of the creature ; and that had so curiously and strongly painted itself upon my brain, that I could not get rid of it until it was worn out.

I noticed the peculiarities of this possession, while it was a real discomfort to me. That very day, at dinner, some morsel on my plate looked like a piece of him, and I was glad to get up and go out. Later in the evening, I was walking along the Rue St. Honoré, when I saw a bill at a public room there announcing small-sword exercise, broad-sword exercise, wrestling, and other such feats. I went in, and some of the sword-play being very skilful, remained. A specimen of our own national sport, The British Boaxe, was announced to be given at the close of the evening. In an evil hour I determined to wait for this Boaxe, as became a Briton. It was a clumsy specimen (executed by two English grooms out of place), but one of the combatants, receiving a straight right-hander with the glove between his eyes, did exactly what the large dark creature in the Morgue had seemed going to do—and finished me for that night.

There was rather a sickly smell (not at all an unusual fragrance in Paris) in the little ante-room of my apartment at the hotel. The large dark creature in the Morgue was by no direct experience associated with my sense of smell, because, when I came to the knowledge of him, he lay behind a wall of thick plate-glass, as good as a wall of steel or marble for that matter. Yet the whiff of the room never failed to reproduce him. What was more curious, was the capriciousness with which his portrait seemed to light itself up in my mind, elsewhere. I might be walking in the Palais Royal, lazily enjoying the shop windows, and might be regaling myself with one of the ready-made clothes shops that are set out there. My eyes, wandering over impossible-waisted dressing-gowns and luminous waistcoats, would fall upon the master, or the shopman, or even the very dummy at the door, and would suggest to me, "Something like him!"—and instantly I was sickened again.

This would happen at the theatre in the same manner. Often it would happen in the street, when I certainly was not looking for the likeness, and when probably there was no likeness there. It was not because the creature was dead that I was so haunted, because I know that I might have been (and I know it because I have been) equally attended by the image of a living aversion. This lasted about a week. The picture did not fade by degrees, in the sense that it became a whit less forcible and distinct, but in the sense that it obtruded itself less and less frequently. The experience may be worth considering by some who have the care of children. It would be difficult to overstate the intensity and accuracy of an intelligent child's observation. At that impressible time of life it must sometimes produce a fixed impression. If the fixed impression be of an object terrible to the child, it will be (for want of reasoning upon) inseparable from great fear. Force the child at such a time, be Spartan with it, send it into the dark against its will, leave it in a lonely bedroom against its will, and you had better murder it.

On a bright morning I rattled away from Paris, in the German chariot, and left the large dark creature behind me for good. I ought to confess, though, that I had been drawn back to the Morgue, after he was put underground, to look at his clothes, and that I found them frightfully like him—particularly his boots. However, I rattled away for Switzerland, looking forward and not backward, and so we parted company.

Welcome again the long, long spell of France, with the queer country inns, full of vases of flowers and clocks, in the dull little towns, and with the little population not at all dull on the little Boulevard in the evening, under the little trees! Welcome Monsieur the Curé, walking alone in the early morning a short way out of the town, reading that eternal Breviary of yours, which surely might be almost read, without book, by this time! Welcome Monsieur the Curé, later in the day, jolting through the highway dust (as if you had already ascended to the cloudy region), in a very big-headed cabriolet, with the dried mud of a dozen winters on it. Welcome again Monsieur the Curé, as we exchange salutations; you, straightening your back to look at the German chariot, while picking in your little village garden a vegetable or two for the day's soup; I, looking out of the German chariot window in that delicious traveller's trance which knows no cares, no yesterdays, no to-morrows, nothing but the passing objects and the passing scents and sounds! And so I came, in due course of delight, to Strasbourg, where I passed a wet Sunday evening at a window, while an idle trifle of a vaudeville was played for me at the opposite house.

How such a large house came to have only three people living in it was its own affair. There were at least a score of windows in its high roof alone; how many in its grotesque front I soon gave up counting. The owner was a shopkeeper, by name Straudenheim; by trade—I couldn't make out what by trade, for he had forborne to write that up, and his shop was shut.

At first, as I looked at Straudenheim's, through the steadily falling rain, I set him up in business in the goose-liver line. But inspection of Straudenheim, who became visible at a window on the second floor, convinced me that there was something more precious than liver in the case. He wore a black velvet skull-cap, and looked usurious and rich. A large-lipped, pear-nosed old man, with white hair, and keen eyes, though near-sighted. He was writing at a desk was Straudenheim, and ever and again left off writing, put his pen in his mouth, and went through actions with his right hand, like a man steadying piles of cash. Five-franc pieces, Straudenheim, or golden Napoleons? A jeweller, Straudenheim, a dealer in money, a diamond merchant, or what?

Below Straudenheim, at a window on the first floor, sat his house-keeper—far from young, but of a comely presence, suggestive of a well-matured foot and ankle. She was cheerily dressed, had a fan in her hand, and wore large gold earrings and a large gold cross. She would have been out holiday-making (as I settled it) but for the pestilent rain. Strasbourg had given up holiday-making for that once as a bad job, because the rain was jerking in gushes out of the old roof-spouts, and running in a brook down the middle of the street. The housekeeper, her arms folded on her bosom and her fan tapping her chin, was bright and smiling at her open window, but otherwise Straudenheim's house front was very dreary. The housekeeper's was the only open window in it; Straudenheim kept himself close, though it was a sultry evening when air is pleasant, and though the rain had brought into the town that vague, refreshing smell of grass which rain does bring in the summer-time.

The dim appearance of a man at Straudenheim's shoulder inspired me with a misgiving that somebody had come to murder that flourishing merchant for the wealth with which I had handsomely endowed him: the rather, as it was an excited man, lean and long of figure, and evidently stealthy of foot. But he conferred with Straudenheim instead of doing him a mortal injury, and then they both softly opened the other window of that room—which was immediately over the housekeeper's —and tried to see her by looking down. And my opinion of Straudenheim was much lowered when I saw that eminent citizen spit out of window, clearly with the hope of spitting on the housekeeper.

The unconscious housekeeper fanned herself, tossed her head, and laughed. Though unconscious of Straudenheim, she was conscious of somebody else—of me?—there was nobody else.

After leaning so far out of window that I confidently expected to see their heels tilt up, Straudenheim and the lean man drew their heads in and shut the window. Presently the house door secretly opened, and they slowly and spitefully crept forth into the pouring rain. They were coming over to me (I thought) to demand satisfaction for my looking at the housekeeper, when they plunged into a recess in the architecture under my window and dragged out the puniest of little soldiers, begirt with the most innocent of little swords. The tall, glazed head-dress of this warrior Straudenheim instantly knocked off, and out of it fell two sugar-sticks and three or four large lumps of sugar.

The warrior made no effort to recover his property or to pick up his shako, but looked with an expression of attention at Straudenheim when he kicked him five times, and also at the lean man when *he* kicked him five times, and again at Straudenheim when he tore the breast of his (the warrior's) little coat open, and shook all his ten fingers in his face, as if they were ten thousand. When these outrages had been committed, Straudenheim and his man went into the house again and barred the door. A wonderful circumstance was that the housekeeper, who saw it all (and who could have taken six such warriors to her buxom bosom at once), only fanned herself and laughed as she had laughed before, and seemed to have no opinion about it, one way or other.

But the chief effect of the drama was the remarkable vengeance taken by the little warrior. Left alone in the rain, he picked up his shako ; put it on, all wet and dirty as it was ; retired into a court, of which Straudenheim's house formed the corner ; wheeled about ; and bringing his two forefingers close to the top of his nose, rubbed them over one another, cross-wise, in derision, defiance, and contempt of Straudenheim. Although Straudenheim could not possibly be supposed to be conscious of this strange proceeding, it so inflated and comforted the little warrior's soul, that twice he went away, and twice came back into the court to repeat it, as though it must goad his enemy to madness. Not only that, but he afterwards came back with two other small warriors, and they all three did it together. Not only that—as I live to tell the tale !—but just as it was falling quite dark, the three came back, bringing with them a huge bearded Sapper, whom they moved, by recital of the original wrong, to go through the same performance, with the same complete absence of all possible knowledge of it on the part of Straudenheim. And then they all went away, arm in arm, singing.

I went away too, in the German chariot at sunrise, and rattled on, day after day, like one in a sweet dream ; with so many clear little bells on the harness of the horses, that the nursery rhyme about Banbury Cross and the venerable lady who rode in state there, was always in my ears. And now I came to the land of wooden houses, innocent cakes, thin butter soup, and spotless little inn bedrooms with a family likeness to Dairies. And now the Swiss marksmen were for ever rifle-shooting at marks across gorges, so exceedingly near my ear, that I felt like a new Gesler in a Canton of Tells, and went in highly-deserved danger of my tyrannical life. The prizes at these shootings were watches, smart handkerchiefs, hats, spoons, and (above all) tea-trays ; and at these contests I came upon a more than usually accomplished and amiable countryman of my own, who had shot himself deaf in whole years of competition, and had won so many tea-trays that he went about the country with his carriage full of them, like a glorified Cheap-Jack.

In the mountain country into which I had now travelled a yoke of oxen were sometimes hooked on before the post-horses, and I went lumbering up, up, up, through mist and rain, with the roar of falling water for change of music. Of a sudden, mist and rain would clear away, and I would come down into picturesque little towns with gleaming spires and odd towers, and would stroll afoot into market-places in steep winding streets, where a hundred women in bodices sold eggs and honey, butter and fruit, and suckled their children as they sat by their clean baskets, and had such enormous goitres (or glandular swellings in the throat) that it became a science to know where the nurse ended and the child began. About this time I deserted my German chariot for the back of a mule (in colour and consistency so very like a dusty old hair trunk I once had at school, that I half-expected to see my initials in brass-headed nails on his backbone), and went up a thousand rugged ways, and looked down at a thousand woods of fir and pine, and would on the whole have preferred my mule's keeping a little nearer to the inside, and not usually travelling with a hoof or two over the precipice—though much consoled by explanation that this was to be attributed to his great sagacity, by reason of his carrying broad loads of wood at other times, and not being clear but that I myself belonged to that station of life, and required as much room as they. He brought me safely, in his own wise way, among the passes of the Alps, and here I enjoyed a dozen climates a day ; being now (like Don Quixote on the back of the wooden horse) in the region of wind, now in the region of fire, now in the region of unmelting ice and snow. Here I passed over trembling domes of ice, beneath which the cataract was roaring ; and here was received under arches of icicles, of unspeakable beauty ; and here the sweet air was so bracing and so light, that at halting-times I rolled in the snow when I saw my mule do it, thinking that he must know best. At this part of the journey we would come, at mid-day, into half-an-hour's thaw : when the rough mountain inn would be found on an island of deep mud in a sea of snow, while the baiting strings of mules, and the carts full of casks and bales, which had been in an Arctic condition a mile off, would steam again. By such ways and means I would come to the cluster of châlets where I had to turn out of the track to see the waterfall ; and then uttering a howl like a young giant on espying a traveller—in other words, something to eat—coming up the steep, the idiot lying on the wood-pile who sunned himself and nursed his goitre, would rouse the woman-guide within the hut, who would stream out hastily, throwing her child over one of her shoulders and her goitre over the other as she came along.   I slept at religious houses, and bleak refuges of many kinds, on this journey, and by the stove at night heard stories of travellers who had perished within call, in wreaths and drifts of snow.   One night the stove within, and the cold outside, awakened childish associations long forgotten, and I dreamed I was in Russia—the identical serf out of a picture-book I had, before I could read it for myself—and that I was going to be knouted by a noble personage in a fur cap, and earrings, who, I think, must have come out of some melodrama.

Commend me to the beautiful waters among these mountains ! Though I was not of their mind : they, being inveterately bent on getting down into the level country, and I ardently desiring to linger where I was.   What desperate leaps they took, what dark abysses they plunged into, what rocks they wore away, what echoes they invoked ! In one part where I went they were pressed into the service of carrying wood down, to be burnt next winter, as costly fuel, in Italy.   But their fierce, savage nature was not to be easily constrained, and they fought with every limb of the wood ; whirling it round and round, stripping its bark away, dashing it against pointed corners, driving it out of the course, and roaring and flying at the peasants who steered it back again from the bank with long stout poles.   Alas ! concurrent streams of time and water carried *me* down fast, and I came, on an exquisitely clear day, to the Lausanne shore of the Lake of Geneva, where I stood looking at the bright blue water, the flushed white mountains opposite, and the boats at my feet with their furled Mediterranean sails, showing like enormous magnifications of this goose-quill pen that is now in my hand.

—The sky became overcast without any notice ; a wind very like the March east wind of England blew across me ; and a voice said, " How do you like it ?   Will it do ? "

I had merely shut myself, for half a minute, in a German travelling chariot that stood for sale in the Carriage Department of the London Pantechnicon.   I had a commission to buy it, for a friend who was going abroad ; and the look and manner of the chariot, as I tried the cushions and the springs, brought all these hints of travelling re-membrance before me.

" It will do very well," said I, rather sorrowfully, as I got out at the other door, and shut the carriage up.

VIII

THE "GREAT TASMANIA'S" CARGO

I travel constantly up and down a certain line of railway that has a terminus in London.   It is the railway for a large military depôt, and for other large barracks. To the best of my serious belief, I have never been on that railway by daylight without seeing some handcuffed deserters in the train.

It is in the nature of things that such an institution as our English army should have many bad and troublesome characters in it. But this is a reason for, and not against, its being made as acceptable as possible to well-disposed men of decent behaviour. Such men are assuredly not tempted into the ranks by the beastly inversion of natural laws, and the compulsion to live in worse than swinish foulness. Accordingly, when any such Circumlocutional embellishments of the soldier's condition have of late been brought to notice, we civilians, seated in outer darkness cheerfully meditating on an Income Tax, have considered the matter as being our business, and have shown a tendency to declare that we would rather not have it misregulated, if such declaration may, without violence to the Church Catechism, be hinted to those who are put in authority over us.

Any animated description of a modern battle, any private soldier's letter published in the newspapers, any page of the records of the Victoria Cross, will show that in the ranks of the army there exists, under all disadvantages, as fine a sense of duty as is to be found in any station on earth. Who doubts that if we all did our duty as faithfully as the soldier does his, this world would be a better place? There may be greater difficulties in our way than in the soldier's. Not disputed. But let us at least do our duty towards *him*.

I had got back again to that rich and beautiful port where I had looked after Mercantile Jack, and I was walking up a hill there, on a wild March morning. My conversation with my official friend Pangloss, by whom I was accidentally accompanied, took this direction as we took the up-hill direction, because the object of my uncommercial journey was to see some discharged soldiers who had recently come home from India. There were men of Havelock's among them; there were men who had been in many of the great battles of the great Indian campaign among them; and I was curious to note what our discharged soldiers looked like, when they were done with.

I was not the less interested (as I mentioned to my official friend Pangloss) because these men had claimed to be discharged when their right to be discharged was not admitted. They had behaved with unblemished fidelity and bravery; but a change of circumstances had arisen which, as they considered, put an end to their compact and entitled them to enter on a new one. Their demand had been blunderingly resisted by the authorities in India; but it is to be presumed that the men were not far wrong, inasmuch as the bungle had ended in their being sent home discharged, in pursuance of orders from home. (There was an immense waste of money, of course.)

Under these circumstances—thought I, as I walked up the hill, on which I accidentally encountered my official friend—under these circumstances of the men having successfully opposed themselves to the Pagoda Department of that great Circumlocution Office on which the sun never sets and the light of reason never rises, the Pagoda Department will have been particularly careful of the national honour. It will have shown these men, in the scrupulous good faith, not to say the generosity, of its dealing with them, that great national authorities can have no small retaliations and revenges. It will have made every provision for their health on the passage home, and will have landed them, restored from their campaigning fatigues by a sea-voyage, pure air, sound food, and good medicines. And I pleased myself with dwelling beforehand on the great accounts of their personal treatment which these men would carry into their various towns and villages, and on the increasing popularity of the service that would insensibly follow. I almost began to hope that the hitherto-never-failing deserters on my railroad would by and by become a phenomenon.

In this agreeable frame of mind I entered the workhouse of Liverpool. —For the cultivation of laurels in a sandy soil had brought the soldiers in question to *that* abode of Glory.

Before going into their wards to visit them, I inquired how they had made their triumphant entry there? They had been brought through the rain in carts, it seemed, from the landing-place to the gate, and had then been carried up-stairs on the backs of paupers. Their groans and pains during the performance of this glorious pageant had been so distressing as to bring tears into the eyes of spectators but too well accustomed to scenes of suffering. The men were so dreadfully cold, that those who could get near the fires were hard to be restrained from thrusting their feet in among the blazing coals. They were so horribly reduced that they were awful to look upon. Racked with dysentery and blackened with scurvy, one hundred and forty wretched soldiers had been revived with brandy and laid in bed.

My official friend Pangloss is lineally descended from a learned doctor of that name, who was once tutor to Candide, an ingenious young gentleman of some celebrity. In his personal character he is as humane and worthy a gentleman as any I know; in his official capacity he unfortunately preaches the doctrines of his renowned ancestor, by demonstrating on all occasions that we live in the best of all possible official worlds.

"In the name of Humanity," said I, "how did the men fall into this deplorable state? Was the ship well found in stores?"

"I am not here to asseverate that I know the fact of my own knowledge," answered Pangloss, "but I have grounds for asserting that the stores were the best of all possible stores."

A medical officer laid before us a handful of rotten biscuit and a handful of split peas. The biscuit was a honeycombed heap of maggots and the excrement of maggot. The peas were even harder than this filth. A similar handful had been experimentally boiled six hours, and had shown no signs of softening. These were the stores on which the soldiers had been fed.

"The beef——" I began, when Pangloss cut me short.

"Was the best of all possible beef," said he.

But, behold, there was laid before us certain evidence given at the Coroner's Inquest, holden on some of the men (who had obstinately died of their treatment), and from that evidence it appeared that the beef was the worst of all possible beef!

"Then I lay my hand upon my heart, and take my stand," said Pangloss, "by the pork, which was the best of all possible pork."

"But look at this food before our eyes, if one may so misuse the word," said I. "Would any Inspector who did his duty pass such abomination?"

"It ought not to have been passed," Pangloss admitted.

"Then the authorities out there——" I began, when Pangloss cut me short again.

"There would certainly seem to have been something wrong somewhere," said he; "but I am prepared to prove that the authorities out there are the best of all possible authorities."

I never heard of any impeached public authority in my life who was not the best public authority in existence.

"We are told of these unfortunate men being laid low by scurvy," said I. "Since lime-juice has been regularly stored and served out in our navy, surely that disease, which used to devastate it, has almost disappeared? Was there lime-juice aboard this transport?"

My official friend was beginning "the best of all possible——" when an inconvenient medical forefinger pointed out another passage in the evidence, from which it appeared that the lime-juice had been bad too. Not to mention that the vinegar had been bad too, the vegetables bad too, the cooking accommodation insufficient (if there had been anything worth mentioning to cook), the water-supply exceedingly inadequate, and the beer sour.

"Then the men," said Pangloss, a little irritated, "were the worst of all possible men."

"In what respect?" I asked.

"Oh! Habitual drunkards," said Pangloss.

But again the same incorrigible medical forefinger pointed out another passage in the evidence, showing that the dead men had been examined after death, and that they, at least, could not possibly have been habitual drunkards, because the organs within them which must have shown traces of that habit were perfectly sound.

"And besides," said the three doctors present, one and all, "habitual drunkards brought as low as these men have been could not recover under care and food, as the great majority of these men are recovering. They would not have strength of constitution to do it."

"Reckless and improvident dogs, then," said Pangloss. "Always are—nine times out of ten."

I turned to the master of the workhouse and asked him whether the men had any money.

"Money?" said he. "I have in my iron safe nearly four hundred pounds of theirs; the agents have nearly a hundred pounds more; and many of them have left money in Indian banks besides."

Ha!" said I to myself, as we went up-stairs, "this is not the best of all possible stories, I doubt!"

We went into a large ward, containing some twenty or five-and-twenty beds. We went into several such wards, one after another. I find it very difficult to indicate what a shocking sight I saw in them, without frightening the reader from the perusal of these lines, and defeating my object of making it known.

Oh, the sunken eyes that turned to me as I walked between the rows of beds, or —worse still—that glazedly looked at the white ceiling, and saw nothing and cared for nothing! Here lay the skeleton of a man so lightly covered with a thin unwholesome skin that not a bone in the anatomy was clothed, and I could clasp the arm above the elbow in my finger and thumb. Here lay a man with the black scurvy eating his legs away, his gums gone, and his teeth all gaunt and bare. This bed was empty, because gangrene had set in, and the patient had died but yesterday. That bed was a hopeless one, because its occupant was sinking fast, and could only be roused to turn the poor pinched mask of face upon the pillow with a feeble moan. The awful thinness of the fallen cheeks, the awful brightness of the deep-set eyes, the lips of lead, the hands of ivory, the recumbent human images lying in the shadow of death with a kind of solemn twilight on them, like the sixty who had died aboard the ship and were lying at the bottom of the sea, oh Pangloss, God forgive you!

In one bed lay a man whose life had been saved (as it was hoped) by deep incisions in the feet and legs. While I was speaking to him, a nurse came up to change the poultices which this operation had rendered necessary, and I had an instinctive feeling that it was not well to turn away merely to spare myself. He was sorely wasted and keenly susceptible, but the efforts he made to subdue any expression of impatience or suffering were quite heroic. It was easy to see, in the shrinking of the figure, and the drawing of the bed-clothes over the head, how acute the endurance was, and it made me shrink too, as if *I* were in pain; but when the new bandages were on, and the poor feet were composed again, he made an apology for himself (though he had not uttered a word), and said plaintively, "I am so tender and weak, you see, Sir!" Neither from him nor from any one sufferer of the whole ghastly number did I hear a complaint. Of thankfulness for present solicitude and care I heard much; of complaint, not a word.

I think I could have recognised in the dismalest skeleton there the ghost of a soldier. Something of the old air was still latent in the palest shadow of life I talked to. One emaciated creature, in the strictest literality worn to the bone, lay stretched on his back, looking so like death that I asked one of the doctors if he were not dying, or dead. A few kind words from the doctor in his ear, and he opened his eyes, and smiled—looked, in a moment, as if he would have made a salute, if he could. "We shall pull him through, please God," said the doctor. "Plase God, Surr, and thankye," said the patient. "You are much better to-day, are you not?" said the doctor.

" Plase God, Surr ; 'tis the slape I want, Surr ; 'tis my breathin'
makes the nights so long." " He is a careful fellow this, you must
know," said the doctor, cheerfully ; "it was raining hard when they put
him in the open cart to bring him here, and he had the presence of
mind to ask to have a sovereign taken out of his pocket that he had
there, and a cab engaged. Probably it saved his life." The patient
rattled out the skeleton of a laugh, and said, proud of the story,
" 'Deed, Surr, an open cairt was a comical means o' bringin' a dyin'
man here, and a clever way to kill him.' You might have sworn to
him for a soldier when he said it.

One thing had perplexed me very much in going from bed to bed—
a very significant and cruel thing. I could find no young man but
one. He had attracted my notice by having got up and dressed
himself in his soldier's jacket and trousers, with the intention of sitting
by the fire ; but he had found himself too weak, and had crept back to
his bed and laid himself down on the outside of it. I could have
pronounced him, alone, to be a young man aged by famine and sickness. As we were standing by the Irish soldier's bed I mentioned
my perplexity to the doctor. He took a board with an inscription on
it from the head of the Irishman's bed, and asked me what age I
supposed that man to be. I had observed him with attention while
talking to him, and answered, confidently, " Fifty." The doctor, with
a pitying glance at the patient, who had dropped into a stupor again,
put the board back, and said, " Twenty-four."

All the arrangements of the wards were excellent. They could not
have been more humane, sympathising, gentle, attentive, or wholesome.
The owners of the ship, too, had done all they could, liberally. There
were bright fires in every room, and the convalescent men were sitting
round them, reading various papers and periodicals. I took the liberty
of inviting my official friend Pangloss to look at those convalescent
men, and to tell me whether their faces and bearing were or were not,
generally, the faces and bearing of steady respectable soldiers. The
master of the workhouse, overhearing me, said he had had a pretty
large experience of troops, and that better conducted men than these
he had never had to do with. They were always (he added) as we saw
them. And of us visitors (I add) they knew nothing whatever, except
that we were there.

It was audacious in me, but I took another liberty with Pangloss.
Prefacing it with the observation that, of course, I knew beforehand
that there was not the faintest desire, anywhere, to hush up any part
of this dreadful business, and that the Inquest was the fairest of all
possible Inquests, I besought four things of Pangloss :—Firstly, to
observe that the Inquest *was not held in that place*, but at some distance
off. Secondly, to look round upon those helpless spectres in their beds.
Thirdly, to remember that the witnesses produced from among them
before that Inquest could not have been selected because they were
the men who had the most to tell it, but because they happened to be
in a state admitting of their safe removal. Fourthly, to say whether

the coroner and jury could have come there, to those pillows, and taken a little evidence. My official friend declined to commit himself to a reply.

There was a sergeant, reading, in one of the fireside groups. As he was a man of a very intelligent countenance, and as I have a great respect for non-commissioned officers as a class, I sat down on the nearest bed, to have some talk with him. (It was the bed of one of the grisliest of the poor skeletons, and he died soon afterwards.)

"I was glad to see, in the evidence of an officer at the Inquest, sergeant, that he never saw men behave better on board ship than these men."

"They did behave very well, Sir."

"I was glad to see, too, that every man had a hammock."

The sergeant gravely shook his head. "There must be some mistake, Sir. The men of my own mess had no hammocks. There were not hammocks enough on board, and the men of the two next messes laid hold of hammocks for themselves as soon as they got on board, and squeezed my men out, as I may say."

"Had the squeezed-out men none then?"

"None, Sir. As men died, their hammocks were used by other men, who wanted hammocks; but many men had none at all."

"Then you don't agree with the evidence on that point?"

"Certainly not, Sir. A man can't, when he knows to the contrary."

"Did any of the men sell their bedding for drink?"

"There is some mistake on that point too, Sir. Men were under the impression—I knew it for a fact at the time—that it was not allowed to take blankets or bedding on board, and so men who had things of that sort came to sell them purposely."

"Did any of the men sell their clothes for drink?"

"They did, Sir." (I believe there never was a more truthful witness than the sergeant. He had no inclination to make out a case.)

"Many?"

"Some, Sir" (considering the question). "Soldier-like. They had been long marching in the rainy season, by bad roads—no roads at all, in short—and when they got to Calcutta, men turned to and drank, before taking a last look at it. Soldier-like."

"Do you see any men in this ward, for example, who sold clothes for drink at that time?"

The sergeant's wan eye, happily just beginning to rekindle with health, travelled round the place and came back to me. "Certainly, Sir."

"The marching to Calcutta in the rainy season must have been severe?"

"It was very severe, Sir."

"Yet what with the rest and the sea air, I should have thought that the men (even the men who got drunk) would have soon begun to recover on board ship?"

"So they might; but the bad food told upon them, and when we got into a cold latitude, it began to tell more, and the men dropped."

"The sick had a general disinclination for food, I am told, sergeant?"

"Have you seen the food, Sir?"

"Some of it."

"Have you seen the state of their mouths, Sir?"

If the sergeant, who was a man of a few orderly words, had spoken the amount of this volume, he could not have settled that question better. I believe the sick could as soon have eaten the ship as the ship's provisions.

I took the additional liberty with my friend Pangloss, when I had left the sergeant with good wishes, of asking Pangloss whether he had ever heard of biscuit getting drunk and bartering its nutritious qualities for putrefaction and vermin; of peas becoming hardened in liquor; of hammocks drinking themselves off the face of the earth; of lime-juice, vegetables, vinegar, cooking accommodation, water-supply, and beer, all taking to drinking together and going to ruin. "If not (I asked him), what did he say in defence of the officers condemned by the Coroner's Jury, who, by signing the General Inspection report relative to the ship *Great Tasmania* chartered for these troops, had deliberately asserted all that bad and poisonous dunghill refuse to be good and wholesome food?" My official friend replied that it was a remarkable fact, that whereas some officers were only positively good, and other officers only comparatively better, those particular officers were superlatively the very best of all possible officers.

My hand and my heart fail me in writing my record of this journey. The spectacle of the soldiers in the hospital-beds of that Liverpool workhouse (a very good workhouse, indeed, be it understood), was so shocking and so shameful, that as an Englishman I blush to remember it. It would have been simply unbearable at the time, but for the consideration and pity with which they were soothed in their sufferings.

No punishment that our inefficient laws provide is worthy of the name when set against the guilt of this transaction. But if the memory of it die out unavenged, and if it do not result in the inexorable dismissal and disgrace of those who are responsible for it, their escape will be infamous to the Government (no matter of what party) that so neglects its duty, and infamous to the nation that tamely suffers such intolerable wrong to be done in its name.

IX

CITY OF LONDON CHURCHES

IF the confession that I have often travelled from this Covent Garden lodging of mine on Sundays should give offence to those who never travel on Sundays, they will be satisfied (I hope) by my adding that the journeys in question were made to churches.

Not that I have any curiosity to hear powerful preachers. Time was when I was dragged by the hair of my head, as one may say, to hear too many. On summer evenings, when every flower, and tree, and bird might have better addressed my soft young heart, I have in my day been caught in the palm of a female hand by the crown, have been violently scrubbed from the neck to the roots of the hair as a purification for the Temple, and have then been carried off, highly charged with saponaceous electricity, to be steamed like a potato in the unventilated breath of the powerful Boanerges Boiler and his congregation, until what small mind I had was quite steamed out of me. In which pitiable plight I have been haled out of the place of meeting, at the conclusion of the exercises, and catechised respecting Boanerges Boiler, his fifthly, his sixthly, and his seventhly, until I have regarded that reverend person in the light of a most dismal and oppressive Charade. Time was when I was carried off to platform assemblages at which no human child, whether of wrath or grace, could possibly keep its eyes open, and when I felt the fatal sleep stealing, stealing over me, and when I gradually heard the orator in possession, spinning and humming like a great top, until he rolled, collapsed, and tumbled over, and I discovered, to my burning shame and fear, that as to that last stage it was not he, but I. I have sat under Boanerges when he has specifically addressed himself to us—us, the infants—and at this present writing I hear his lumbering jocularity (which never amused us, though we basely pretended that it did), and I behold his big round face, and I look up the inside of his outstretched coat-sleeve as if it were a telescope with the stopper on, and I hate him with an unwholesome hatred for two hours. Through such means did it come to pass that I knew the powerful preacher from beginning to end, all over and all through, while I was very young, and that I left him behind at an early period of life. Peace be with him! More peace than he brought to me!

Now, I have heard many preachers since that time—not powerful; merely Christian, unaffected, and reverential—and I have had many such preachers on my roll of friends. But it was not to hear these, any more than the powerful class, that I made my Sunday journeys. They were journeys of curiosity to the numerous churches in the City of London. It came into my head one day, here had I been cultivating a familiarity with all the churches of Rome, and I knew nothing of the insides of the old churches of London! This befell on a Sunday morning. I began my expeditions that very same day, and they lasted me a year.

I never wanted to know the names of the churches to which I went, and to this hour I am profoundly ignorant in that particular of at least nine-tenths of them. Indeed, saving that I know the church of old Gower's tomb (he lies in effigy with his head upon his books) to be the church of Saint Saviour's, Southwark; and the church of Milton's

tomb to be the church of Cripplegate ; and the church on Cornhill with
the great golden keys to be the church of Saint Peter ; I doubt if I
could pass a competitive examination in any of the names.   No question
did I ever ask of living creature concerning these churches, and no
answer to any antiquarian question on the subject that I ever put to
books shall harass the reader's soul.   A full half of my pleasure in
them arose out of their mystery ; mysterious I found them ; mysterious
they shall remain for me.

Where shall I begin my round of hidden and forgotten old churches
in the City of London ?

It is twenty minutes short of eleven on a Sunday morning when I
stroll down one of the many narrow hilly streets in the City that tend
due south to the Thames.   It is my first experiment, and I have come
to the region of Whittington in an omnibus, and we have put down a
fierce-eyed, spare old woman, whose slate-coloured gown smells of herbs,
and who walked up Aldersgate Street to some chapel where she comforts
herself with brimstone doctrine, I warrant.   We have also put down a
stouter and sweeter old lady, with a pretty large prayer-book in an
unfolded pocket-handkerchief, who got out at a corner of a court near
Stationers' Hall, and who I think must go to church there because she
is the widow of some deceased old Company's Beadle.   The rest of our
freight were mere chance pleasure-seekers and rural walkers, and went
on to the Blackwall railway.   So many bells are ringing, when I stand
undecided at a street corner, that every sheep in the ecclesiastical fold
might be a bell-wether.   The discordance is fearful.   My state of
indecision is referable to, and about equally divisible among, four great
churches which are all within sight and sound, all within the space of
a few square yards.   As I stand at the street corner, I don't see as many
as four people at once going to church, though I see as many as four
churches with their steeples clamouring for people.   I choose my church,
and go up the flight of steps to the great entrance in the tower.   A
mouldy tower within, and like a neglected washhouse.   A rope comes
through the beamed roof, and a man in the corner pulls it and clashes the
bell—a whity-brown man, whose clothes were once black—a man with flue
on him, and cobweb.   He stares at me, wondering how I come there,
and I stare at him, wondering how he comes there.   Through a screen
of wood and glass I peep into the dim church.   About twenty people are
discernible, waiting to begin.   Christening would seem to have faded
out of this church long ago, for the font has the dust of desuetude thick
upon it, and its wooden cover (shaped like an old-fashioned tureen-cover)
looks as if it wouldn't come off, upon requirement.   I perceive the altar
to be rickety, and the Commandments damp.   Entering after this survey,
I jostle the clergyman in his canonicals, who is entering too from a
dark lane behind a pew of state with curtains, where nobody sits.   The
pew is ornamented with four blue wands, once carried by four somebodys,
I suppose, before somebody else, but which there is nobody now to hold
or receive honour from.   I open the door of a family pew, and shut
myself in ; if I could occupy twenty family pews at once, I might have

them. The clerk, a brisk young man (how does *he* come here?), glances at me knowingly, as who should say, "You have done it now; you must stop." Organ plays. Organ-loft is in a small gallery across the church; gallery congregation, two girls. I wonder within myself what will happen when we are required to sing.

There is a pale heap of books in the corner of my pew, and while the organ, which is hoarse and sleepy, plays in such fashion that I can hear more of the rusty working of the stops than of any music, I look at the books, which are mostly bound in faded baize and stuff. They belonged in 1754 to the Dowgate family; and who were they? Jane Comport must have married Young Dowgate, and come into the family that way; Young Dowgate was courting Jane Comport when he gave her her prayer-book, and recorded the presentation in the fly-leaf; if Jane were fond of Young Dowgate, why did she die and leave the book here? Perhaps at the rickety altar, and before the damp Commandments, she, Comport, had taken him, Dowgate, in a flush of youthful hope and joy, and perhaps it had not turned out in the long run as great a success as was expected.

The opening of the service recalls my wandering thoughts. I then find, to my astonishment, that I have been, and still am, taking a strong kind of invisible snuff, up my nose, into my eyes, and down my throat. I wink, sneeze, and cough. The clerk sneezes; the clergyman winks; the unseen organist sneezes and coughs (and probably winks); all our little party wink, sneeze, and cough. The snuff seems to be made of the decay of matting, wood, cloth, stone, iron, earth, and something else. Is the something else the decay of dead citizens in the vaults below? As sure as death it is! Not only in the cold damp February day do we cough and sneeze dead citizens, all through the service, but dead citizens have got into the very bellows of the organ, and half choked the same. We stamp our feet to warm them, and dead citizens arise in heavy clouds. Dead citizens stick upon the walls, and lie pulverised on the sounding-board over the clergyman's head, and, when a gust of air comes, tumble down upon him.

In this first experience I was so nauseated by too much snuff, made of the Dowgate family, the Comport branch, and other families and branches, that I gave but little heed to our dull manner of ambling through the service; to the brisk clerk's manner of encouraging us to try a note or two at psalm time; to the gallery-congregation's manner of enjoying a shrill duet, without a notion of time or tune; to the whity-brown man's manner of shutting the minister into the pulpit, and being very particular with the lock of the door, as if he were a dangerous animal. But I tried again next Sunday, and soon accustomed myself to the dead citizens when I found that I could not possibly get on without them among the City churches.

Another Sunday.

After being again rung for by conflicting bells, like a leg of mutton or a laced hat a hundred years ago, I make selection of a church oddly put away in a corner among a number of lanes—a smaller church than the last, and an ugly, of about the date of Queen Anne. As a congregation, we are fourteen strong : not counting an exhausted charity school in a gallery, which has dwindled away to four boys and two girls. In the porch is a benefaction of loaves of bread, which there would seem to be nobody left in the exhausted congregation to claim, and which I saw an exhausted beadle, long faded out of uniform, eating with his eyes for self and family when I passed in. There is also an exhausted clerk in a brown wig, and two or three exhausted doors and windows have been bricked up, and the service books are musty, and the pulpit cushions are threadbare, and the whole of the church furniture is in a very advanced stage of exhaustion. We are three old women (habitual), two young lovers (accidental), two tradesmen, one with a wife and one alone, an aunt and nephew, again two girls (these two girls dressed out for church with everything about them limp that should be stiff, and *vice versâ*, are an invariable experience), and three sniggering boys. The clergyman is, perhaps, the chaplain of a civic company ; he has the moist and vinous look, and eke the bulbous boots, of one acquainted with 'Twenty port, and comet vintages.

We are so quiet in our dulness that the three sniggering boys, who have got away into a corner by the altar-railing, give us a start, like crackers, whenever they laugh. And this reminds me of my own village church where, during sermon-time on bright Sundays when the birds are very musical indeed, farmers' boys patter out over the stone pavement, and the clerk steps out from his desk after them, and is distinctly heard in the summer repose to pursue and punch them in the churchyard, and is seen to return with a meditative countenance, making believe that nothing of the sort has happened. The aunt and nephew in this City church are much disturbed by the sniggering boys. The nephew is himself a boy, and the sniggerers tempt him to secular thoughts of marbles and string, by secretly offering such commodities to his distant contemplation. This young Saint Anthony for a while resists, but presently becomes a backslider, and in dumb show defies the sniggerers to " heave " a marble or two in his direction. Herein he is detected by the aunt (a rigorous, reduced gentlewoman who has the charge of offices), and I perceive that worthy relative to poke him in the side with the corrugated hooked handle of an ancient umbrella. The nephew revenges himself for this, by holding his breath and terrifying his kinswoman with the dread belief that he has made up his mind to burst. Regardless of whispers and shakes, he swells and becomes discoloured, and yet again swells and becomes discoloured, until the aunt can bear it no longer, but leads him out, with no visible neck, and with his eyes going before him like a prawn's. This causes the sniggerers to regard flight as an eligible move, and I know which of them will go out first, because of the over-devout attention that he suddenly concentrates on the clergyman. In a little while this hypocrite, with an elaborate demonstration of hushing his footsteps, and with a face generally expressive of having until now forgotten a religious appointment elsewhere, is gone. Number two gets out in the same way, but rather quicker. Number three, getting safely to the door, there turns reckless, and banging it open, flies forth with a Whoop ! that vibrates to the top of the tower above us.

The clergyman, who is of a prandial presence and a muffled voice, may be scant of hearing as well as of breath, but he only glances up, as having an idea that somebody has said Amen in a wrong place, and continues his steady jog-trot like a farmer's wife going to market. He does all he has to do in the same easy way, and gives us a concise sermon, still like the jog-trot of the farmer's wife on a level road. Its drowsy cadence soon lulls the three old woman asleep, and the un-married tradesman sits looking out at window, and the married tradesman sits looking at his wife's bonnet, and the lovers sit looking at one another, so superlatively happy, that I mind when I, turned of eighteen, went with my Angelica to a City church on account of a shower (by this special coincidence that it was in Huggin Lane), and when I said to my Angelica, "Let the blessed event, Angelica, occur at no altar but this ! " and when my Angelica consented that it should occur at no other—which it certainly never did, for it never occurred anywhere. And oh, Angelica, what has become of you, this present Sunday morning when I can't attend to the sermon ; and, more difficult question than that, what has become of Me as I was when I sat by your side ?

But we receive the signal to make that unanimous dive which surely is a little conventional—like the strange rustlings and settlings and clearings of throats and noses, which are never dispensed with, at certain points of the Church service, and are never held to be necessary under any other circumstances. In a minute more it is all over, and the organ expresses itself to be as glad of it as it can be of anything in its rheumatic state, and in another minute we are all of us out of the church, and Whity-brown has locked it up. Another minute or little more and, in the neighbouring churchyard—not the yard of that church, but of another—a churchyard like a great shabby old mignon-ette-box, with two trees in it and one tomb—I meet Whity-brown, in his private capacity, fetching a pint of beer for his dinner from the public-house in the corner, where the keys of the rotting fire-ladders are kept and were never asked for, and where there is a ragged, white-seamed, out-at-elbowed bagatelle-board on the first floor.

In one of these City churches, and only in one, I found an individual who might have been claimed as expressly a City personage. I remember the church by the feature that the clergyman couldn't get to his own desk without going through the clerk's, or couldn't get to the pulpit without going through the reading-desk—I forget which, and it is no matter—and by the presence of this personage among the exceedingly sparse congregation. I doubt if we were a dozen, and we had no exhausted charity school to help us out. The personage was dressed in black of square cut, and was stricken in years, and wore a black velvet cap and cloth shoes. He was of a staid, wealthy, and dissatisfied aspect. In his hand he conducted to church a mysterious child—a child of the feminine gender. The child had a beaver hat, with a stiff drab plume that surely never belonged to any bird of the air. The child was further attired in a nankeen frock and spencer, brown boxing-gloves, and a veil. It had a blemish, in the nature of currant jelly, on its chin ; and was a thirsty child. Insomuch that the personage carried in his pocket a green bottle, from which, when the first psalm was given out, the child was openly refreshed. At all other times throughout the service it was motionless, and stood on the seat of the large pew, closely fitted into the corner, like a rain-water pipe.

The personage never opened his book, and never looked at the clergyman. *He* never sat down either, but stood with his arms leaning on the top of the pew, and his forehead sometimes shaded with his right hand, always looking at the church door. It was a long church for a church of its size, and he was at the upper end, but he always looked at the door. That he was an old bookkeeper, or an old trader who had kept his own books, and that he might be seen at the Bank of England about Dividend times, no doubt. That he had lived in the City all his life and was disdainful of other localities, no doubt. Why he looked at the door I never absolutely proved, but it is my belief that he lived in expectation of the time when the citizens would come back to live in the City, and its ancient glories would be renewed. He appeared to expect that this would occur on a Sunday, and that the wanderers would first appear in the deserted churches, penitent and humbled. Hence he looked at the door which they never darkened. Whose child the child was, whether the child of a disinherited daughter, or some parish orphan whom the personage had adopted, there was nothing to lead up to. It never played, or skipped, or smiled. Once the idea occurred to me that it was an automaton, and that the personage had made it ; but following the strange couple out one Sunday, I heard the personage say to it, " Thirteen thousand pounds ; " to which it added in a weak human voice, " Seventeen and fourpence." Four Sundays I followed them out, and this is all I ever heard or saw them say. One Sunday I followed them home. They lived behind a pump, and the personage opened their abode with an exceeding large key. The one solitary inscription on their house related to a fire-plug. The house was partly undermined by a deserted and closed gateway ; its windows were blind with dirt ; and it stood with its face disconsolately turned to a wall. Five great churches and two small ones rang their Sunday bells between this house and the church the couple frequented, so they must have had some special reason for going a quarter of a mile to it. The last time I saw them was on this wise. I had been to explore another church at a distance, and happened to pass the church they frequented, at about two of the afternoon when that edifice was closed. But a little side-door, which I had never observed before, stood open, and disclosed certain cellarous steps. Methought " They are airing the vaults to-day," when the personage and the child silently arrived at the steps, and silently descended. Of course I came to the conclusion that the personage had at last despaired of the looked-for return of the penitent citizens, and that he and the child went down to get themselves buried.

In the course of my pilgrimages I came upon one obscure church which had broken out in the melodramatic style, and was got up with various tawdry decorations, much after the manner of the extinct London may-poles. These attractions had induced several young priests or deacons in black bibs for waistcoats, and several young ladies interested in that holy order (the proportion being, as I estimated, seventeen young ladies to a deacon), to come into the City as a new and odd excitement. It was wonderful to see how these young people played out their little play in the heart of the City, all among themselves, without the deserted City's knowing anything about it. It was as if you should take an empty counting-house on a Sunday and act one of the old Mysteries there. They had impressed a small school (from what neighbourhood I don't know) to assist in the performances, and it was pleasant to notice frantic garlands of inscription on the walls especially addressing those poor innocents in characters impossible for them to decipher. There was a remarkably agreeable smell of pomatum in this congregation.

But in other cases rot and mildew and dead citizens formed the uppermost scent, while infused into it in a dreamy way not at all displeasing was the staple character of the neighbourhood. In the churches about Mark Lane, for example, there was a dry whiff of wheat; and I accidentally struck an airy sample of barley out of an aged hassock in one of them. From Rood Lane to Tower Street, and thereabouts, there was often a subtle flavour of wine; sometimes of tea. One church near Mincing Lane smelt like a druggist's drawer. Behind the Monument the service had a flavour of damaged oranges, which, a little farther down towards the river, tempered into herrings, and gradually toned into a cosmopolitan blast of fish. In one church, the exact counterpart of the church in the Rake's Progress where the hero is being married to the horrible old lady, there was no speciality of atmosphere, until the organ shook a perfume of hides all over us from some adjacent warehouse.

Be the scent what it would, however, there was no speciality in the people. There were never enough of them to represent any calling or neighbourhood. They had all gone elsewhere over-night, and the few stragglers in the many churches languished there inexpressively.

Among the uncommercial travels in which I have engaged, this year of Sunday travel occupies its own place, apart from all the rest. Whether I think of the church where the sails of the oyster-boats in the river almost flapped against the windows, or of the church where the railroad made the bells hum as the train rushed by above the roof, I recall a curious experience. On summer Sundays, in the gentle rain or the bright sunshine—either, deepening the idleness of the idle City —I have sat, in that singular silence which belongs to resting-places usually astir, in scores of buildings at the heart of the world's metropolis, unknown to far greater numbers of people speaking the English tongue than the ancient edifices of the Eternal City, or the Pyramids of Egypt. The dark vestries and registries into which I have peeped, and the little hemmed-in churchyards that have echoed to my feet, have left impressions on my memory as distinct and quaint as any it has in that way received. In all those dusty registers that the worms are eating there is not a line but made some hearts leap, or some tears flow, in their day. Still and dry now, still and dry! and the old tree at the window with no room for its branches has seen them all out. So with the tomb of the old Master of the old Company on which it drips. His son restored it and died, his daughter restored it and died, and then he had been remembered long enough, and the tree took possession of him, and his name cracked out.

There are few more striking indications of the changes of manners and customs that two or three hundred years have brought about, than these deserted churches. Many of them are handsome and costly structures, several of them were designed by Wren, many of them arose from the ashes of the Great Fire, others of them outlived the Plague and the Fire too, to die a slow death in these later days. No one can be sure of the coming time; but it is not too much to say of it that it has no sign in its outsetting tides of the reflux to these churches of their congregations and uses. They remain like the tombs of the old citizens who lie beneath them and around them, Monuments of another age. They are worth a Sunday-exploration now and then, for they yet echo, not unharmoniously, to the time when the City of London really was London; when the 'Prentices and Trained Bands were of mark in the state; when even the Lord Mayor himself was a Reality—not a Fiction conventionally be-puffed on one day in the year by illustrious friends, who no less conventionally laugh at him on the remaining three hundred and sixty-four days.

X

SHY NEIGHBOURHOODS

So much of my travelling is done on foot, that if I cherished betting propensities, I should probably be found registered in sporting newspapers under some such title as the Elastic Novice, challenging all eleven-stone mankind to competition in walking. My last special feat was turning out of bed at two, after a hard day, pedestrian and otherwise, and walking thirty miles into the country to breakfast. The road was so lonely in the night, that I fell asleep to the monotonous sound of my own feet doing their regular four miles an hour. Mile after mile I walked, without the slightest sense of exertion, dozing heavily and dreaming constantly. It was only when I made a stumble like a drunken man, or struck out into the road to avoid a horseman close upon me on the path—who had no existence—that I came to myself and looked about. The day broke mistily (it was autumn time), and I could not disembarrass myself of the idea that I had to climb those heights and banks of cloud, and that there was an Alpine Convent somewhere behind the sun, where I was going to breakfast. This sleepy notion was so much stronger than such substantial objects as villages and haystacks, that, after the sun was up and bright, and when I was sufficiently awake to have a sense of pleasure in the prospect, I still occasionally caught myself looking about for wooden arms to point the right track up the mountain, and wondering there was no snow yet. It is a curiosity of broken sleep that I made immense quantities of verses on that pedestrian occasion (of course I never make any when I am in my right senses), and that I spoke a certain language once pretty familiar to me, but which I have nearly forgotten from disuse, with fluency. Of both these phenomena I have such frequent experience in the state between sleeping and waking, that I sometimes argue with myself that I know I cannot be awake, for, if I were, I should not be half so ready. The readiness is not imaginary, because I often recall long strings of the verses, and many turns of the fluent speech, after I am broad awake.

My walking is of two kinds : one, straight on end to a definite goal at a round pace ; one, objectless, loitering, and purely vagabond. In the latter state no gipsy on earth is a greater vagabond than myself ; it is so natural to me, and strong with me, that I think I must be the descendant, at no great distance, of some irreclaimable tramp.

One of the pleasantest things I have lately met with, in a vagabond course of shy metropolitan neighbourhoods and small shops, is the fancy of a humble artist, as exemplified in two portraits representing Mr. Thomas Sayers, of Great Britain, and Mr. John Heenan of the United States of America. These illustrious men are highly coloured in fighting trim, and fighting attitude. To suggest the pastoral and meditative nature of their peaceful calling, Mr. Heenan is represented on emerald sward, with primroses and other modest flowers springing up under the heels of his half-boots ; while Mr. Sayers is impelled to the administration of his favourite blow, the Auctioneer, by the silent eloquence of a village church. The humble homes of England, with their domestic virtues and honeysuckle porches, urge both heroes to go in and win ; and the lark and other singing birds are observable in the upper air ecstatically carolling their thanks to Heaven for a fight. On the whole, the associations entwined with the pugilistic art by this artist are much in the manner of Izaak Walton.

But it is with the lower animals of back streets and by-ways that my present purpose rests. For human notes we may return to such neighbourhoods when leisure and opportunity serve.

Nothing in shy neighbourhoods perplexes my mind more than the bad company birds keep. Foreign birds often get into good society, but British birds are inseparable from low associates. There is a whole street of them in St. Giles's ; and I always find them in poor and immoral neighbourhoods, convenient to the public-house and the pawnbroker's. They seem to lead people into drinking, and even the man who makes their cages usually gets into a chronic state of black eye. Why is this? Also, they will do things for people in short-skirted velveteen coats with bone buttons, or in sleeved waistcoats and fur caps, which they cannot be persuaded by the respectable orders of society to undertake. In a dirty court in Spitalfields, once, I found a goldfinch drawing his own water, and drawing as much of it as if he were in a consuming fever. That goldfinch lived at a bird-shop, and offered, in writing, to barter himself against old clothes, empty bottles, or even kitchen-stuff. Surely a low thing and a depraved taste in any finch! I bought that goldfinch for money. He was sent home and hung upon a nail over against my table. He lived outside a counterfeit dwelling-house, supposed (as I argued) to be a dyer's; otherwise it would have been impossible to account for his perch sticking out of the garret window. From the time of his appearance in my room, either he left off being thirsty—which was not in the bond—or he could not make up his mind to hear his little bucket drop back into his well when he let it go, a shock which in the best of times had made him tremble. He drew no water but by stealth and under the cloak of night. After an interval of futile and at length hopeless expectation, the merchant who had educated him was appealed to. The merchant was a bow-legged character, with a flat and cushiony nose, like the last new strawberry. He wore a fur cap, and shorts, and was of the velveteen race, velveteeny. He sent word that he would "look round." He looked round, appeared in the doorway of the room, and slightly cocked up his evil eye at the goldfinch. Instantly a raging thirst beset that bird; when it was appeased, he still drew several unnecessary buckets of water; and finally leaped about his perch and sharpened his bill, as if he had been to the nearest wine-vaults and got drunk.

Donkeys again. I know shy neighbourhoods where the donkey goes in at the street door, and appears to live up-stairs, for I have examined the back-yard from over the palings and have been unable to make him out. Gentility, nobility, royalty, would appeal to that donkey in vain to do what he does for a costermonger. Feed him with oats at the highest price, put an infant prince and princess in a pair of panniers on his back, adjust his delicate trappings to a nicety, take him to the softest slopes at Windsor, and try what pace you can get out of him. Then starve him, harness him anyhow to a truck with a flat tray on it, and see him bowl from Whitechapel to Bayswater. There appears to be no particular private understanding between birds and donkeys in a state of nature; but in the shy neighbourhood state you shall see them always in the same hands, and always developing their very best energies for the very worst company. I have known a donkey—by sight (we were not on speaking terms)—who lived over on the Surrey side of London Bridge, among the fastnesses of Jacob's Island and Dockhead. It was the habit of that animal, when his services were not in immediate requisition, to go out alone, idling. I have met him a mile from his place of residence, loitering about the streets ; and the expression of his countenance at such times was most degraded. He was attached to the establishment of an elderly lady who sold periwinkles, and he used to stand on Saturday nights with a cartful of those delicacies outside a gin-shop, pricking up his ears when a customer came to the cart, and too evidently deriving satisfaction from the knowledge that they got bad measure. His mistress was sometimes overtaken by inebriety. The last time I ever saw him (about five years ago) he was in circumstances of difficulty caused by this failing. Having been left alone with the cart of periwinkles, and forgotten, he went off idling. He prowled among his usual low haunts for some time, gratifying his depraved tastes, until, not taking the cart into his calculations, he endeavoured to turn up a narrow alley, and became greatly involved. He was taken into custody by the police, and the Green Yard of the district being near at hand, was backed into that place of durance. At that crisis I encountered him ; the stubborn sense he evinced of being—not to compromise the expression—a blackguard, I never saw exceeded in the human subject. A flaring candle in a paper shade, stuck in among his periwinkles, showed him, with his ragged harness broken and his cart extensively shattered, twitching his mouth and shaking his hanging head, a picture of disgrace and obduracy. I have seen boys being taken to station-houses who were as like him as his own brother.

The dogs of shy neighbourhoods I observe to avoid play, and to be conscious of poverty. They avoid work, too, if they can, of course ; that is in the nature of all animals. I have the pleasure to know a dog in a back street in the neighbourhood of Walworth who has greatly distinguished himself in the minor drama, and who takes his portrait with him, when he makes an engagement, for the illustration of the play-bill. His portrait (which is not at all like him) represents him in the act of dragging to the earth a recreant Indian, who is supposed to have tomahawked, or essayed to tomahawk, a British officer. The design is pure poetry, for there is no such Indian in the piece, and no such incident. He is a dog of the Newfoundland breed, for whose honesty I would be bail to any amount, but whose intellectual qualities in association with dramatic fiction I cannot rate high. Indeed, he is too honest for the profession he has entered. Being at a town in Yorkshire last summer, and seeing him posted in the bill of the night, I attended the performance. His first scene was eminently successful ; but as it occupied a second in its representation (and five lines in the bill), it scarcely afforded ground for a cool and deliberate judgment of his powers. He had merely to bark, run on, and jump through an inn window after a comic fugitive. The next scene of importance to the fable was a little marred in its interest by his over-anxiety ; forasmuch as while his master (a belated soldier in a den of robbers on a tempestuous night) was feelingly lamenting the absence of his faithful dog, and laying great stress on the fact that he was thirty leagues away, the faithful dog was barking furiously in the prompter's box, and clearly choking himself against his collar. But it was in his greatest scene of all that his honesty got the better of him. He had to enter a dense and trackless forest, on the trail of the murderer, and there to fly at the murderer when he found him resting at the foot of a tree, with his victim bound ready for slaughter. It was a hot night, and he came into the forest from an altogether unexpected direction, in the sweetest temper, at a very deliberate trot, not in the least excited; trotted to the foot-lights with his tongue out; and there sat down, panting, and amiably surveying the audience, with his tail beating on the boards, like a Dutch clock. Meanwhile the murderer, impatient to receive his doom, was audibly calling to him "Co-o-ome here!" while the victim, struggling with his bonds, assailed him with the most injurious expressions. It happened through these means, that when he was in course of time persuaded to trot up and rend the murderer limb from limb, he made it (for dramatic purposes) a little too obvious that he worked out that awful retribution by licking butter off his blood-stained hands.

In a shy street behind Long Acre two honest dogs live, who perform in Punch's shows. I may venture to say that I am on terms of intimacy with both, and that I never saw either guilty of the falsehood of failing to look down at the man inside the show during the whole performance. The difficulty other dogs have in satisfying their minds about these dogs appears to be never overcome by time. The same dogs must encounter them over and over again, as they trudge along in their off-minutes behind the legs of the show and beside the drum; but all dogs seem to suspect their frills and jackets, and to sniff at them as if they thought those articles of personal adornment an eruption—a something in the nature of mange, perhaps. From this Covent Garden window of mine I noticed a country dog, only the other day, who had come up to Covent Garden Market under a cart, and had broken his cord, an end of which he still trailed along with him. He loitered about the corners of the four streets commanded by my window; and bad London dogs came up, and told him lies that he didn't believe; and worse London dogs came up, and made proposals to him to go and steal in the market, which his principles rejected; and the ways of the town confused him, and he crept aside and lay down in a doorway. He had scarcely got a wink of sleep when up comes Punch with Toby. He was darting to Toby for consolation and advice, when he saw the frill, and stopped in the middle of the street, appalled. The show was pitched, Toby retired behind the drapery, the audience formed, the drum and pipes struck up. My country dog remained immovable, intently staring at these strange appearances, until Toby opened the drama by appearing on his ledge, and to him entered Punch, who put a tobacco-pipe into Toby's mouth. At this spectacle the country dog threw up his head, gave one terrible howl, and fled due west.

We talk of men keeping dogs, but we might often talk more expressively of dogs keeping men. I know a bull-dog in a shy corner of Hammersmith who keeps a man. He keeps him up a yard, and makes him go to public-houses and lay wagers on him, and obliges him to lean against posts and look at him, and forces him to neglect work for him, and keeps him under rigid coercion. I once knew a fancy terrier who kept a gentleman—a gentleman who had been brought up at Oxford, too. The dog kept the gentleman entirely for his glorification, and the gentleman never talked about anything but the terrier. This, however, was not in a shy neighbourhood, and is a digression consequently.

There are a great many dogs in shy neighbourhoods who keep boys. I have my eye on a mongrel in Somers Town who keeps three boys. He feigns that he can bring down sparrows and unburrow rats (he can do neither), and he takes the boys out on sporting pretences into all sorts of suburban fields. He has likewise made them believe that he possesses some mysterious knowledge of the art of fishing, and they consider themselves incompletely equipped for the Hampstead ponds, with a pickle-jar and a wide-mouthed bottle, unless he is with them and barking tremendously. There is a dog residing in the Borough of Southwark who keeps a blind man. He may be seen, most days, in Oxford Street, haling the blind man away on expeditions wholly un-contemplated by, and unintelligible to, the man—wholly of the dog's conception and execution. Contrariwise, when the man has projects, the dog will sit down in a crowded thoroughfare and meditate. I saw him yesterday, wearing the money-tray like an easy collar, instead of offering it to the public, taking the man against his will, on the invitation of a disreputable cur, apparently to visit a dog at Harrow—he was so intent on that direction. The north wall of Burlington House Gardens, between the Arcade and the Albany, offers a shy spot for appointments among blind men at about two or three o'clock in the afternoon. They sit (very uncomfortably) on a sloping stone there, and compare notes. Their dogs may always be observed at the same time openly disparaging the men they keep, to one another, and settling where they shall respectively take their men when they begin to move again. At a small butcher's, in a shy neighbourhood (there is no reason for suppressing the name ; it is by Notting Hill, and gives upon the district called the Potteries), I know a shaggy black and white dog who keeps a drover. He is a dog of an easy disposition and too frequently allows this drover to get drunk. On these occasions it is the dog's custom to sit outside the public-house, keeping his eye on a few sheep, and thinking. I have seen him with six sheep, plainly casting up in his mind how many he began with when he left the market, and at what places he has left the rest. I have seen him perplexed by not being able to account to himself for certain particular sheep. A light has gradually broken on him, he has remembered at what butcher's he left them, and in a burst of grave satisfaction has caught a fly off his nose, and shown himself much relieved. If I could at any time have doubted the fact that it was he who kept the drover, and not the drover who kept him, it would have been abundantly proved by his way of taking undivided charge of the six sheep when the drover came out besmeared with red ochre and beer, and gave him wrong directions, which he calmly disregarded. He has taken the sheep entirely into his own hands, has merely remarked with respectful firmness, "That instruction would place them under an omnibus; you had better confine your attention to yourself—you will want it all;" and has driven his charge away, with an intelligence of ears and tail, and a knowledge of business, that has left his lout of a man very, very far behind.

As the dogs of shy neighbourhoods usually betray a slinking consciousness of being in poor circumstances—for the most part manifested in an aspect of anxiety, an awkwardness in their play, and a misgiving that somebody is going to harness them to something, to pick up a living—so the cats of shy neighbourhoods exhibit a strong tendency to relapse into barbarism. Not only are they made selfishly ferocious by ruminating on the surplus population around them, and on the densely crowded state of all the avenues to cat's meat; not only is there a moral and politico-economical haggardness in them, traceable to these reflections; but they evince a physical deterioration. Their linen is not clean, and is wretchedly got up; their black turns rusty, like old mourning; they wear very indifferent fur, and take to the shabbiest cotton velvet instead of silk velvet. I am on terms of recognition with several small streets of cats, about the Obelisk in Saint George's Fields, and also in the vicinity of Clerkenwell Green, and also in the back settlements of Drury Lane. In appearance they are very like the women among whom they live. They seem to turn out of their unwholesome beds into the street without any preparation. They leave their young families to stagger about the gutters, unassisted, while they frouzily quarrel and swear and scratch and spit at street corners. In particular, I remark that when they are about to increase their families (an event of frequent recurrence) the resemblance is strongly expressed in a certain dusty dowdiness, down-at-heel self-neglect, and general giving up of things. I cannot honestly report that I have ever seen a feline matron of this class washing her face when in an interesting condition.

Not to prolong these notes of uncommercial travel among the lower animals of shy neighbourhoods, by dwelling at length upon the exasperated moodiness of the tom-cats, and their resemblance in many respects to a man and a brother, I will come to a close with a word on the fowls of the same localities.

That anything born of an egg and invested with wings should have got to the pass that it hops contentedly down a ladder into a cellar, and calls *that* going home, is a circumstance so amazing as to leave one nothing more in this connection to wonder at. Otherwise I might wonder at the completeness with which these fowls have become separated from all the birds of the air—have taken to grovelling in bricks and mortar and mud—have forgotten all about live trees, and make roosting-places of shop-boards, barrows, oyster-tubs, bulk-heads, and door-scrapers. I wonder at nothing concerning them, and take them as they are I accept as products of Nature and things of course, a reduced Bantam family of my acquaintance in the Hackney Road, who are incessantly at the pawnbroker's. I cannot say that they enjoy themselves, for they are of a melancholy temperament; but what enjoyment they are capable of they derive from crowding together in the pawnbroker's side-entry. Here they are always to be found in a feeble flutter, as if they were newly come down in the world, and were afraid of being identified. I know a low fellow, originally of a good family from Dorking, who takes his whole establishment of wives, in single file, in at the door of the Jug Department of a disorderly tavern near the Haymarket, manœuvres them among the company's legs, emerges with them at the Bottle Entrance, and so passes his life— seldom, in the season, going to bed before two in the morning. Over Waterloo Bridge there is a shabby old speckled couple (they belong to the wooden French-bedstead, washing-stand, and towel-horse-making trade) who are always trying to get in at the door of a chapel. Whether the old lady, under a delusion reminding one of Mrs. South-cott, has an idea of entrusting an egg to that particular denomination, or merely understands that she has no business in the building, and is consequently frantic to enter it, I cannot determine; but she is constantly endeavouring to undermine the principal door: while her partner, who is infirm upon his legs, walks up and down, encouraging her and defying the Universe. But the family I have been best acquainted with since the removal from this trying sphere of a Chinese circle at Brentford, reside in the densest part of Bethnal Green. Their abstraction from the objects among which they live, or rather their conviction that those objects have all come into existence in express subservience to fowls, has so enchanted me, that I have made them the subject of many journeys at divers hours. After careful observation of the two lords and the ten ladies of whom this family consists, I have come to the conclusion that their opinions are represented by the leading lord and leading lady,—the latter, as I judge, an aged personage, afflicted with a paucity of feather and visibility of quill, that gives her the appearance of a bundle of office pens. When a railway goods van that would crush an elephant comes round the corner, tearing over these fowls, they emerge unharmed from under the horses, perfectly satisfied that the whole rush was a passing property in the air, which may have left something to eat behind it. They look upon old shoes, wrecks of kettles and saucepans, and fragments of bonnets, as a kind of meteoric discharge for fowls to peck at. Peg-tops and hoops they account, I think, as a sort of hail; shuttlecocks, as rain, or dew. Gaslight comes quite as natural to them as any other light; and I have more than a suspicion that, in the minds of the two lords, the early public-house at the corner has superseded the sun. I have established it as a certain fact, that they always begin to crow when the public-house shutters begin to be taken down, and that they salute the pot-boy, the instant he appears to perform that duty, as if he were Phœbus in person.

XI

TRAMPS

THE chance use of the word " Tramp " in my last paper brought that numerous fraternity so vividly before my mind's eye, that I had no sooner laid down my pen than a compulsion was upon me to take it up again, and make notes of the Tramps whom I perceived on all the summer roads in all directions.

Whenever a tramp sits down to rest by the wayside, he sits with his legs in a dry ditch ; and whenever he goes to sleep (which is very often indeed), he goes to sleep on his back. Yonder, by the high road, glaring white in the bright sunshine, lies, on the dusty bit of turf under the bramble-bush that fences the coppice from the highway, the tramp of the order savage, fast asleep. He lies on the broad of his back, with his face turned up to the sky, and one of his ragged arms loosely thrown across his face. His bundle (what can be the contents of that mysterious bundle, to make it worth his while to carry it about ?) is thrown down beside him, and the waking woman with him sits with her legs in the ditch, and her back to the road. She wears her bonnet rakishly perched on the front of her head, to shade her face from the sun in walking, and she ties her skirts round her in conventionally tight tramp-fashion with a sort of apron. You can seldom catch sight of her, resting thus, without seeing her in a despondently defiant manner doing something to her hair or her bonnet, and glancing at you between her fingers. She does not often go to sleep herself in the daytime, but will sit for any length of time beside the man. And his slumberous propensities would not seem to be referable to the fatigue of carrying the bundle, for she carries it much oftener and farther than he. When they are afoot you will mostly find him slouching on ahead, in a gruff temper, while she lags heavily behind with the burden. He is given to person-ally correcting her, too—which phase of his character develops itself oftenest on benches outside ale-house doors—and she appears to become strongly attached to him for these reasons ; it may usually be noticed that when the poor creature has a bruised face she is the most affection-ate. He has no occupation whatever, this order of tramp, and has no object whatever in going anywhere. He will sometimes call himself a brickmaker, or a sawyer, but only when he takes an imaginative flight. He generally represents himself, in a vague way, as looking out for a job of work ; but he never did work, he never does, and he never will. It is a favourite fiction with him, however (as if he were the most industrious character on earth), that *you* never work ; and as he goes past your garden and sees you looking at your flowers, you will over-hear him growl, with a strong sense of contrast, " *You* are a lucky hidle devil, *you* are ! "

The slinking tramp is of the same hopeless order, and has the same injured conviction on him that you were born to whatever you possess, and never did anything to get it ; but he is of a less audacious disposition. He will stop before your gate, and say to his female companion with an air of constitutional humility and propitiation—to edify any one who may be within hearing behind a blind or a bush— " This is a sweet spot, ain't it ? A lovely spot ! And I wonder if they'd give two poor footsore travellers like me and you a drop of fresh water out of such a pretty gen-teel crib ? We'd take it wery koind on 'em, wouldn't us ? Wery koind, upon my word, us would ! " He has a quick sense of a dog in the vicinity, and will extend his modestly-injured propitiation to the dog chained up in your yard ; remarking, as he slinks at the yard gate, " Ah ! You are a foine breed o' dog, too, and *you* ain't kep for nothink ! I'd take it wery koind o' your master if he'd elp a traveller and his woife as envies no gentlefolk their good fortun, wi' a bit o' your broken wittles. He'd never know the want of it, nor more would you. Don't bark like that at poor persons as never done you no 'arm ; the poor is down-trodden and broke enough without that ; oh DON'T ! " He generally heaves a prodigious sigh in moving away, and always looks up the lane and down the lane, and up the road and down the road, before going on.

Both of these orders of tramp are of a very robust habit ; let the hard-working labourer at whose cottage-door they prowl and beg have the ague never so badly, these tramps are sure to be in good health.

There is another kind of tramp whom you encounter this bright summer day—say, on a road with the sea-breeze making its dust lively, and sails of ships in the blue distance beyond the slope of Down. As you walk enjoyingly on, you descry in the perspective at the bottom of a steep hill up which your way lies, a figure that appears to be sitting airily on a gate, whistling in a cheerful and disengaged manner. As you approach nearer to it, you observe the figure to slide down from the gate, to desist from whistling, to uncock its hat, to become tender of foot, to depress its head and elevate its shoulders, and to present all the characteristics of profound despondency. Arriving at the bottom of the hill and coming close to the figure, you observe it to be the figure of a shabby young man. He is moving painfully forward, in the direction in which you are going, and his mind is so preoccupied with his misfortunes that he is not aware of your approach until you are close upon him at the hill-foot. When he is aware of you, you discover him to be a remarkably well-behaved young man, and a remarkably well-spoken young man. You know him to be well-behaved by his respectful manner of touching his hat ; you know him to be well-spoken, by his smooth manner of expressing himself. He says in a flowing confidential voice, and without punctuation, " I ask your pardon Sir but if you would excuse the liberty of being so addressed upon the public I way by one who is almost reduced to rags though it as not always been so and by no fault of his own but through ill elth in his family and many un-merited sufferings it would be a great obligation Sir to know the time. " You give the well-spoken young man the time. The well-spoken young man, keeping well up with you, resumes : " I am aware Sir that it is a liberty to intrude a further question on a gentleman walking for his entertainment but might I make so bold as ask the favour of the way to Dover Sir and about the distance ? " You inform the well-spoken young man that the way to Dover is straight on, and the distance some eighteen miles. The well-spoken young man becomes greatly agitated. " In the condition to which I am reduced," says he, " I could not ope to reach Dover before dark even if my shoes were in a state to take me there or my feet were in a state to old out over the flinty road and were not on the bare ground of which any gentleman has the means to satisfy himself by looking Sir may I take the liberty of speaking to you ? " As the well-spoken young man keeps so well up with you that you can't prevent his taking the liberty of speaking to you, he goes on, with fluency : " Sir it is not begging that is my intention for I was brought up by the best of mothers and begging is not my trade I should not know Sir how to follow it as a trade if such were my shameful wishes for the best of mothers long taught otherwise and in the best of omes though now reduced to take the present liberty on the Iway Sir my business was the law-stationering and I was favourably known to the Solicitor-General the Attorney-General the majority of the Judges and the ole of the legal profession but through ill elth in my family and the treachery of a friend for whom I became security and he no other than my own wife's brother the brother of my own wife I was cast forth with my tender partner and three young children not to beg for I will sooner die of deprivation but to make my way to the seaport town of Dover where I have a relative i in respect not only that will assist me but that would trust me with untold gold Sir in appier times and hare this calamity fell upon me I made for my amusement when I little thought that I should ever need it excepting for my 'air this "—here the well-spoken young man puts his hand into his breast—" this comb ! Sir I implore you in the name of charity to purchase a tortoiseshell comb which is a genuine article at any price that your humanity may put upon it and may the blessings of a ouseless family awaiting with beating arts the return of a husband and a father from Dover upon the cold stone seats of London Bridge ever attend you Sir may I take the liberty of speaking to you I implore you to buy this comb ! " By this time, being a reasonably good walker, you will have been too much for the well-spoken young man, who will stop short and express his disgust and his want of breath in a long expectoration, as you leave him behind.

Towards the end of the same walk, on the same bright summer day, at the corner of the next little town or village, you may find another kind of tramp, embodied in the persons of a most exemplary couple whose only improvidence appears to have been, that they spent the last of their little All on soap. They are a man and woman, spotless to behold— John Anderson, with the frost on his short smock-frock instead of his " pow," attended by Mrs. Anderson. John is over-ostentatious of the frost upon his raiment, and wears a curious and, you would say, an almost unnecessary demonstration of girdle of white linen wound about his waist—a girdle snowy as Mrs. Anderson's apron. This cleanliness was the expiring effort of the respectable couple, and nothing then remained to Mr. Anderson but to get chalked upon his spade in snow-white copy-book characters, HUNGRY ! and to sit down here. Yes ; one thing more remained to Mr. Anderson—his character ; Monarchs could not deprive him of his hard-earned character. Accordingly, as you come up with this spectacle of virtue in distress, Mrs. Anderson rises, and with a decent curtsey presents for your consideration a certificate from a Doctor of Divinity, the reverend the Vicar of Upper Dodgington, who informs his Christian friends and all whom it may concern that the bearers, John Anderson and lawful wife, are persons to whom you cannot be too liberal. This benevolent pastor omitted no work of his hands to fit the good couple out, for with half an eye you can recognise his autograph on the spade.

Another class of tramp is a man the most valuable part of whose stock-in-trade is a highly perplexed demeanour. He is got up like a countryman, and you will often come upon the poor fellow, while he is endeavouring to decipher the inscription on a milestone—quite a fruit-less endeavour, for he cannot read. He asks your pardon, he truly does (he is very slow of speech, this tramp, and he looks in a bewildered way all round the prospect while he talks to you), but all of us shold do as we wold be done by, and he'll take it kind, if you'll put a power man in the right road fur to jine his eldest son as has broke his leg bad in the masoning, and is in this heere Orspit'l as is wrote down by Squire Pouncerby's own hand as wold not tell a lie fur no man. He then produces from under his dark frock (being always very slow and perplexed) a neat but worn old leathern purse, from which he takes a scrap of paper. On this scrap of paper is written, by Squire Pouncerby, of The Grove, " Please to direct the Bearer, a poor but very worthy man, to the Sussex County Hospital, near Brighton "—a matter of some difficulty at the moment, seeing that the request comes suddenly upon you in the depths of Hertfordshire. The more you endeavour to indicate where Brighton is—when you have with the greatest difficulty remembered—the less the devoted father can be made to comprehend, and the more obtusely he stares at the prospect ; whereby, being reduced to extremity, you recommend the faithful parent to begin by going to St. Albans, and present him with half-a-crown. It does him good, no doubt, but scarcely helps him forward, since you find him lying drunk that same evening in the wheelwright's sawpit under the shed where the felled trees are, opposite the sign of the Three Jolly Hedgers.

But the most vicious, by far, of all the idle tramps, is the tramp who pretends to have been a gentleman. " Educated," he writes, from the village beer-shop in pale ink of a ferruginous complexion ; " educated at Trin. Coll. Cam.—nursed in the lap of affluence—once in my small way the pattron of the Muses," etc. etc. etc.—surely a sympathetic mind will not withhold a trifle, to help him on to the market-town where he thinks of giving a Lecture to the *fruges consumere nati*, on things in general. This shameful creature lolling about hedge tap-rooms in his ragged clothes, now so far from being black that they look as if they never can have been black, is more selfish and insolent than even the savage tramp. He would sponge on the poorest boy for a farthing, and spurn him when he had got it ; he would interpose (if he could get anything by it) between the baby and the mother's breast. So much lower than the company he keeps, for his maudlin assumption of being higher, this pitiless rascal blights the summer road as he maunders on between the luxuriant hedges : where (to my thinking) even the wild convolvulus and rose and sweet-briar are the worse for his going by, and need time to recover from the taint of him in the air.

The young fellows who trudge along barefoot, five or six together, their boots slung over their shoulders, their shabby bundles under their arms, their sticks newly cut from some roadside wood, are not eminently prepossessing, but are much less objectionable. There is a tramp-fellowship among them. They pick one another up at resting stations, and go on in companies. They always go at a fast swing— though they generally limp too—and there is invariably one of the company who has much ado to keep up with the rest. They generally talk about horses, and any other means of locomotion than walking ; or one of the company relates some recent experiences of the road—which are always disputes and difficulties. As for example. " So as I'm a-standing at the pump in the market, blest if there don't come up a Beadle, and he ses, ' Musn't stand here,' he ses. ' Why not ? ' I ses. ' No beggars allowed in this town,' he ses. " Who's a beggar ? ' I ses. ' You are,' he ses. ' Who ever see *me* beg ? Did *you* ? ' I ses. ' Then you're a tramp,' he ses. ' I'd rather be that than a Beadle,' I ses." (The company express great approval.) " ' Would you ? ' he ses to me. ' Yes I would,' I ses to him. ' Well,' he ses, ' anyhow, get out of this town.' ' Why, blow your little town ! ' I ses, ' who wants to be in it ? Wot does your dirty little town mean by comin' and stickin' itself in the road to anywhere ? Why don't you get a shovel and a barrer, and clear your town out o' people's way ? ' " (The company expressing the highest approval and laughing aloud, they all go down the hill.)

Then there are the tramp handicraft men. Are they not all over England, in this Midsummer time ? Where does the lark sing, the corn grow, the mill turn, the river run, and they are not among the lights and shadows, tinkering, chair-mending, umbrella-mending, clock-mending-knife-grinding ? Surely, a pleasant thing, if we were in that condition of life, to grind our way through Kent, Sussex, and Surrey. For the first six weeks or so we should see the sparks we ground off fiery bright against a background of green wheat and green leaves. A little later and the ripe harvest would pale our sparks from red to yellow, until we got the dark newly-turned land for a background again, and they were red once more. By that time we should have ground our way to the sea-cliffs, and the whirr of our wheel would be lost in the breaking of the waves. Our next variety in sparks would be derived from contrast with the gorgeous medley of colours in the autumn woods, and, by the time we had ground our way round to the heathy lands between Reigate and Croydon, doing a prosperous stroke of business all along, we should show like a little firework in the light frosty air, and be the next best thing to the blacksmith's forge. Very agreeable, too, to go on a chair-mending tour. What judges we should be of rushes, and how knowingly (with a sheaf and a bottomless chair at our back) we should lounge on bridges, looking over at osier-beds. Among all the innumerable occupations that cannot possibly be transacted without the assistance of lookers-on, chair-mending may take a station in the first rank. When we sat down with our backs against the barn or the public-house, and began to mend, what a sense of popularity would grow upon us. When all the children came to look at us, and the tailor, and the general dealer, and the farmer who had been giving a small order at the little saddler's, and the groom from the great house, and the publican, and even the two skittle-players (and here note that, howsoever busy all the rest of village humankind may be, there will always be two people with leisure to play at skittles, wherever village skittles are), what encouragement would be on us to plait and weave ! (No one looks at us while we plait and weave these words.)—Clock-mending, again. Except for the slight inconvenience of carrying a clock under our arm, and the monotony of making the bell go whenever we came to a human habitation, what a pleasant privilege to give a voice to the dumb cottage clock, and set it talking to the cottage family again. Likewise we foresee great interest in going round by the park plantations, under the overhanging boughs (hares, rabbits, partridges, and pheasants scudding like mad across and across the chequered ground before us), and so over the park ladder, and through the wood, until we came to the Keeper's lodge. Then would the Keeper be discoverable at his door, in a deep nest of leaves, smoking his pipe. Then, on our accosting him in the way of our trade, would he call to Mrs. Keeper, respecting " t'ould clock " in the kitchen. Then would Mrs. Keeper ask us into the lodge, and on due examination we should offer to make a good job of it for eighteenpence ; which offer, being accepted, would set us tinkling and clinking among the chubby, awe-struck little Keepers for an hour and more. So completely to the family's satisfaction would we achieve our work, that the Keeper would mention how that there was something wrong with the bell of the turret stable-clock up at the Hall, and that if we thought good of going up to the housekeeper on the chance of that job too, why he would take us. Then should we go, among the branching oaks and the deep fern, by silent ways of mystery known to the Keeper, seeing the herd glancing here and there as we went along, until we came to the old Hall, solemn and grand. Under the Terrace Flower Garden, and round by the stables, would the Keeper take us in, and as we passed we should observe how spacious and stately the stables, and how fine the painting of the horses' names over their stalls, and how solitary all—the family being in London. Then should we find ourselves presented to the housekeeper, sitting, in hushed state, at needle-work, in a bay-window looking out upon a mighty grim red-brick quadrangle, guarded by stone lions disrespectfully throwing somer-saults over the escutcheons of the noble family. Then our services accepted, and we insinuated with a candle into the stable-turret, we should find it to be a mere question of pendulum, but one that would hold us until dark. Then should we fall to work, with a general im-pression of Ghosts being about, and of pictures indoors that of a certainty came out of their frames and "walked," if the family would only own it. Then should we work and work, until the day gradually turned to dusk, and even until the dusk gradually turned to dark. Our task at length accomplished, we should be taken into an enormous servants' hall, and there regaled with beef and bread, and powerful ale. Then, paid freely, we should be at liberty to go, and should be told by a pointing helper to keep round over yinder by the blasted ash, and so straight through the woods, till we should see the town lights right afore us. Then, feeling lonesome, should we desire upon the whole that the ash had not been blasted, or that the helper had had the manners not to mention it. However, we should keep on, all right, till suddenly the stable bell would strike ten in the dolefullest way, quite chilling our blood, though we had so lately taught him how to acquit himself. Then, as we went on, should we recall old stories, and dimly consider what it would be most advisable to do, in the event of a tall figure, all in white, with saucer eyes, coming up and saying, "I want you to come to a churchyard and mend a church clock. Follow me!" Then should we make a burst to get clear of the trees, and should soon find ourselves in the open, with the town lights bright ahead of us. So should we lie that night at the ancient sign of the Crispin and Crispanus, and rise early next morning to be betimes on tramp again.

Bricklayers often tramp, in twos and threes, lying by night at their "lodges," which are scattered all over the country. Bricklaying is another of the occupations that can by no means be transacted in rural parts without the assistance of spectators—of as many as can be con-vened. In thinly-peopled spots, I have known bricklayers on tramp, coming up with bricklayers at work, to be so sensible of the indispens-ability of lookers-on, that they themselves have set up in that capacity, and have been unable to subside into the acceptance of a proffered/ share in the job for two or three days together. Sometimes the "navvy" on tramp, with an extra pair of half-boots over his shoulder, a bag, a bottle, and a can, will take a similar part in a job of excava-tion, and will look at it without engaging in it until all his money is gone. The current of my uncommercial pursuits caused me only last summer to want a little body of workmen for a certain spell of work in a pleasant part of the country; and I was at one time honoured with the attendance of as many as seven-and-twenty, who were looking at six.

Who can be familiar with any rustic highway in the summer-time, without storing up knowledge of the many tramps who go from one oasis of town or village to another, to sell a stock in trade, apparently

not worth a shilling when sold? Shrimps are a favourite commodity
for this kind of speculation, and so are cakes of a soft and spongy
character, coupled with Spanish nuts and brandy balls. The stock is
carried on the head in a basket, and, between the head and the basket,
are the trestles on which the stock is displayed at trading times.
Fleet of foot, but a careworn class of tramp this, mostly; with a
certain stiffness of neck, occasioned by much anxious balancing of
baskets; and also with a long Chinese sort of eye, which an over-
weighted forehead would seem to have squeezed into that form.

On the hot dusty roads near seaport towns and great rivers, behold
the tramping Soldier. And if you should happen never to have asked
yourself whether his uniform is suited to his work, perhaps the poor
fellow's appearance, as he comes distressfully towards you, with his
absurdly tight jacket unbuttoned, his neck-gear in his hand, and his
legs well chafed by his trousers of baize, may suggest the personal
inquiry, how you think *you* would like it. Much better the tramping
Sailor, although his cloth is somewhat too thick for land service. But
why the tramping merchant-mate should put on a black velvet waistcoat, for a chalky country in the dog-days, is one of the great secrets
of nature that will never be discovered.

I have my eye upon a piece of Kentish road, bordered on either side
by a wood, and having on one hand, between the road-dust and the
trees, a skirting patch of grass. Wild flowers grow in abundance on
this spot, and it lies high and airy, with a distant river stealing steadily
away to the ocean, like a man's life. To gain the milestone here,
which the moss, primroses, violets, blue-bells, and wild roses would
soon render illegible but for peering travellers pushing them aside
with their sticks, you must come up a steep hill, come which way you
may. So all the tramps with carts or caravans—the Gipsy-tramp, the
Show-tramp, the Cheap-Jack—find it impossible to resist the tempta-
tions of the place, and all turn the horse loose when they come to it,
and boil the pot. Bless the place, I love the ashes of the vagabond
fires that have scorched its grass! What tramp children do I see here,
attired in a handful of rags, making a gymnasium of the shafts of the
cart, making a feather-bed of the flints and brambles, making a toy of
the hobbled old horse who is not much more like a horse than any
cheap toy would be! Here do I encounter the cart of mats and
brooms and baskets—with all thoughts of business given to the evening wind—with the stew made and being served out—with Cheap
Jack and Dear Jill striking soft music out of the plates that are rattled
like warlike cymbals when put up for auction at fairs and markets—
their minds so influenced (no doubt) by the melody of the nightingales,
as they begin to sing in the woods behind them, that if I were to propose to deal, they would sell me anything at cost price. On this
hallowed ground has it been my happy privilege (let me whisper it) to
behold the White-haired Lady with the pink eyes eating meat-pie with
the Giant; while, by the hedge-side, on the box of blankets which I
knew contained the snakes, were set forth the cups and saucers and

the teapot. It was on an evening in August that I chanced upon this ravishing spectacle, and I noticed that, whereas the Giant reclined half concealed beneath the overhanging boughs and seemed indifferent to Nature, the white hair of the gracious Lady streamed free in the breath of evening, and her pink eyes found pleasure in the landscape. I heard only a single sentence of her uttering, yet it bespoke a talent for modest repartee. The ill-mannered Giant—accursed be his evil race!—had interrupted the Lady in some remark, and, as I passed that enchanted corner of the wood, she gently reproved him, with the words, " Now, Cobby,"—Cobby! so short a name!—"ain't one fool enough to talk at a time?"

Within appropriate distance of this magic ground, though not so near it as that the song trolled from tap or bench at door can invade its woodland silence, is a little hostelry which no man possessed of a penny was ever known to pass in warm weather. Before its entrance are certain pleasant trimmed limes; likewise, a cool well, with so musical a bucket-handle that its fall upon the bucket rim will make a horse prick up his ears and neigh upon the droughty road half a mile off. This is a house of great resort for haymaking tramps and harvest tramps, insomuch that as they sit within, drinking their mugs of beer, their relinquished scythes and reaping-hooks glare out of the open windows, as if the whole establishment were a family war-coach of Ancient Britons. Later in the season the whole country-side, for miles and miles, will swarm with hopping tramps. They come in families, men, women, and children, every family provided with a bundle of bedding, an iron pot, a number of babies, and too often with some poor sick creature quite unfit for the rough life, for whom they suppose the smell of the fresh hop to be a sovereign remedy. Many of these hoppers are Irish, but many come from London. They crowd all the roads, and camp under all the hedges and on all the scraps of common-land, and live among and upon the hops until they are all picked, and the hop-gardens, so beautiful through the summer, look as if they had been laid waste by an invading army. Then there is a vast exodus of tramps out of the county; and if you ride or drive round any turn of any road, at more than a foot-pace, you will be bewildered to find that you have charged into the bosom of fifty families, and that there are splashing up all around you, in the utmost prodigality of confusion, bundles of bedding, babies, iron pots, and a good-humoured multitude of both sexes and all ages, equally divided between perspiration and intoxication.

XII

DULLBOROUGH TOWN

IT lately happened that I found myself rambling about the scenes among which my earliest days were passed—scenes from which I departed when I was a child, and which I did not revisit until I was a man. This is no uncommon chance, but one that befalls some of us any day ; perhaps it may not be quite uninteresting to compare notes with the reader respecting an experience so familiar and a journey so uncommercial.

I call my boyhood's home (and I feel like a Tenor in an English Opera when I mention it) Dullborough. Most of us come from Dullborough who come from a country town.

As I left Dullborough in the days when there were no railroads in the land, I left it in a stage-coach. Through all the years that have since passed, have I ever lost the smell of the damp straw in which I was packed—like game—and forwarded, carriage paid, to the Cross Keys, Wood Street, Cheapside, London ? There was no other inside passenger, and I consumed my sandwiches in solitude and dreariness, and it rained hard all the way, and I thought life sloppier than I had expected to find it.

With this tender remembrance upon me, I was cavalierly shunted back into Dullborough the other day, by train. My ticket had been previously collected, like my taxes, and my shining new portmanteau had had a great plaster stuck upon it, and I had been defied by Act of Parliament to offer an objection to anything that was done to it, or me, under a penalty of not less than forty shillings or more than five pounds, compoundable for a term of imprisonment. When I had sent my disfigured property on to the hotel, I began to look about me ; and the first discovery I made was, that the Station had swallowed up the playing-field.

It was gone. The two beautiful hawthorn-trees, the hedge, the turf, and all those buttercups and daisies, had given place to the stoniest of jolting roads ; while, beyond the Station, an ugly dark monster of a tunnel kept its jaws open, as if it had swallowed them and were ravenous for more destruction. The coach that had carried me away was melodiously called Timpson's Blue-Eyed Maid, and belonged to Timpson, at the coach-office up-street ; the locomotive engine that had brought me back was called severely No. 97, and belonged to S.E.R., and was spitting ashes and hot water over the blighted ground.

When I had been let out at the platform-door, like a prisoner whom his turnkey grudgingly released, I looked in again over the low wall at the scene of departed glories. Here, in the haymaking time, had I been delivered from the dungeons of Seringapatam, an immense pile (of haycock), by my countrymen, the victorious British (boy next door

and his two cousins), and had been recognised with ecstasy by my
affianced one (Miss Green), who had come all the way from England
(second house in the terrace) to ransom me, and marry me,   Here had
I first heard in confidence, from one whose father was greatly connected,
being under Government, of the existence of a terrible banditti, called
"The Radicals," whose principles were, that the Prince Regent wore
stays, and that nobody had a right to any salary, and that the army
and navy ought to be put down—horrors at which I trembled in my
bed, after supplicating that the Radicals might be speedily taken and
hanged.   Here, too, had we, the small boys of Boles's, had that cricket
match against the small boys of Coles's, when Boles and Coles had
actually met upon the ground, and when, instead of instantly hitting
out at one another with the utmost fury, as we had all hoped and
expected, those sneaks had said respectively, "I hope Mrs. Boles is
well," and "I hope Mrs. Coles and the baby are doing charmingly."
Could it be that, after all this, and much more, the Playing-field was a
Station, and No. 97 expectorated boiling water and red-hot cinders on
it, and the whole belonged by Act of Parliament to S.E.R. ?

As it could be, and was, I left the place with a heavy heart for a
walk all over the town. And first of Timpson's up-street. When I
departed from Dullborough in the strawy arms of Timpson's Blue-Eyed
Maid, Timpson's was a moderate-sized coach-office (in fact, a little
coach-office), with an oval transparency in the window, which looked
beautiful by night, representing one of Timpson's coaches in the act of
passing a milestone on the London Road with great velocity, completely
full inside and out, and all the passengers dressed in the first style of
fashion, and enjoying themselves tremendously. I found no such place
as Timpson's now—no such bricks and rafters, not to mention the
name—no such edifice on the teeming earth. Pickford had come and
knocked Timpson's down. Pickford had not only knocked Timpson's
down, but had knocked two or three houses down on each side of
Timpson's, and then had knocked the whole into one great establishment with a pair of big gates, in and out of which his (Pickford's)
waggons are, in these days, always rattling, with their drivers sitting
up so high that they look in at the second-floor windows of the old-
fashioned houses in the High Street as they shake the town. I have
not the honour of Pickford's acquaintance, but I felt that he had done
me an injury, not to say committed an act of boyslaughter, in running
over my childhood in this rough manner ; and if ever I meet Pickford
driving one of his own monsters, and smoking a pipe the while (which
is the custom of his men), he shall know by the expression of my eye,
if it catches his, that there is something wrong between us.

Moreover, I felt that Pickford had no right to come rushing into
Dullborough and deprive the town of a public picture. He is not
Napoleon Bonaparte. When he took down the transparent stage-coach
he ought to have given the town a transparent van. With a gloomy
conviction that Pickford is wholly utilitarian and unimaginative, I
proceeded on my way.

It is a mercy I have not a red and green lamp and a night-bell at my door, for in my very young days I was taken to so many lyings-in that I wonder I escaped becoming a professional martyr to them in after-life. I suppose I had a very sympathetic nurse, with a large circle of married acquaintance. However that was, as I continued my walk through Dullborough, I found many houses to be solely associated in my mind with this particular interest. At one little greengrocer's shop, down certain steps from the street, I remember to have waited on a lady who had had four children (I am afraid to write five, though I fully believe it was five) at a birth. This meritorious woman held quite a reception in her room on the morning when I was introduced there, and the sight of the house brought vividly to my mind how the four (five) deceased young people lay, side by side, on a clean cloth on a chest of drawers; reminding me by a homely association, which I suspect their complexion to have assisted, of pigs' feet as they are usually displayed at a neat tripe-shop. Hot caudle was handed round on the occasion, and I further remembered, as I stood contemplating the greengrocer's, that a subscription was entered into among the company, which became extremely alarming to my consciousness of having pocket-money on my person. This fact being known to my conductress, whoever she was, I was earnestly exhorted to contribute, but resolutely declined—therein disgusting the company, who gave me to understand that I must dismiss all expectations of going to heaven.

How does it happen that when all else is change wherever one goes, there yet seem, in every place, to be some few people who never alter? As the sight of the greengrocer's house recalled these trivial incidents of long ago, the identical greengrocer appeared on the steps, with his hands in his pockets, and leaning his shoulder against the door-post, as my childish eyes had seen him many a time; indeed, there was his old mark on the door-post yet, as if his shadow had become a fixture there. It was he himself; he might formerly have been an old-looking young man, or he might now be a young-looking old man, but there he was. In walking along the street, I had as yet looked in vain for a familiar face, or even a transmitted face; here was the very green-grocer who had been weighing and handling baskets on the morning of the reception. As he brought with him a dawning remembrance that he had had no proprietary interest in those babies, I crossed the road, and accosted him on the subject. He was not in the least excited or gratified, or in any way roused by the accuracy of my recollection, but said, Yes, summut out of the common—he didn't remember how many it was (as if half-a-dozen babes either way made no difference)—had happened to a Mrs. What's-her-name, as once lodged there—but he didn't call it to mind, particular. Nettled by this phlegmatic conduct, I informed him that I had left the town when I was a child. He slowly returned, quite unsoftened, and not without a sarcastic kind of complacency, *Had* I? Ah! And did I find it had got on tolerably well without me? Such is the difference (I thought, when I had left him a few hundred yards behind, and was by so much in a better temper) between going away from a place and remaining in it. I had no right, I reflected, to be angry with the greengrocer for his want of interest. I was nothing to him ; whereas he was the town, the cathedral, the bridge, the river, my childhood, and a large slice of my life, to me.

Of course the town had shrunk fearfully since I was a child there. I had entertained the impression that the High Street was at least as wide as Regent Street, London, or the Italian Boulevard at Paris. I found it little better than a lane. There was a public clock in it, which I had supposed to be the finest clock in the world ; whereas it now turned out to be as inexpressive, moon-faced, and weak a clock as ever I saw. It belonged to a Town Hall where I had seen an Indian (who I now suppose wasn't an Indian) swallow a sword (which I now suppose he didn't). The edifice had appeared to me in those days so glorious a structure, that I had set it up in my mind as the model on which the Genie of the Lamp built the palace for Aladdin. A mean little brick heap, like a demented chapel, with a few yawning persons in leather gaiters, and in the last extremity for something to do, lounging at the door with their hands in their pockets, and calling themselves a Corn Exchange !

The Theatre was in existence, I found, on asking the fishmonger, who had a compact show of stock in his window, consisting of a sole and a quart of shrimps—and I resolved to comfort my mind by going to look at it. Richard the Third, in a very uncomfortable cloak, had first appeared to me there, and had made my heart leap with terror by backing up against the stage-box in which I was posted, while struggling for life against the virtuous Richmond. It was within those walls that I had learnt, as from a page of English history, how that wicked King slept in war-time on a sofa much too short for him, and how fearfully his conscience troubled his boots. There, too, had I first seen the funny countryman, but countryman of noble principles, in a flowered waistcoat, crunch up his little hat and throw it on the ground, and pull off his coat, saying, " Dom thee, squire, coom on with thy fistes then ! " At which the lovely young woman who kept company with him (and who went out gleaning in a narrow white muslin apron with five beautiful bars of five different coloured ribbons across it) was so frightened for his sake that she fainted away. Many wondrous secrets of Nature had I come to the knowledge of in that sanctuary ; of which not the least terrific were, that the witches in *Macbeth* bore an awful resemblance to the Thanes and other proper inhabitants of Scotland ; and that the good King Duncan couldn't rest in his grave, but was constantly coming out of it and calling himself somebody else. To the Theatre, therefore, I repaired for consolation. But I found very little, for it was in a bad and a declining way. A dealer in wine and bottled beer had already squeezed his trade into the box-office, and the theatrical money was taken—when it came—in a kind of meat-safe in the passage. The dealer in wine and bottled beer must have insinuated himself under the stage too ; for he announced that he had various descriptions of alcoholic drinks "in the wood," and there was no possible stowage for the wood anywhere else. Evidently he was by degrees eating the establishment away to the core, and would soon have sole possession of it. It was To Let, and hopelessly so, for its old purposes; and there had been no entertainment within its walls for a long time, except a Panorama; and even that had been announced as "pleasingly instructive," and I know too well the fatal meaning and the leaden import of those terrible expressions. No, there was no comfort in the Theatre. It was mysteriously gone, like my own youth. Unlike my own youth, it might be coming back some day; but there was little promise of it.

As the town was placarded with references to the Dullborough Mechanics' Institution, I thought I would go and look at that establishment next. There had been no such thing in the town in my young day, and it occurred to me that its extreme prosperity might have brought adversity upon the Drama. I found the Institution with some difficulty, and should scarcely have known that I had found it if I had judged from its external appearance only; but this was attributable to its never having been finished, and having no front,—consequently it led a modest and retired existence up a stable-yard. It was (as I learnt on inquiry) a most flourishing Institution, and of the highest benefit to the town,—two triumphs which I was glad to understand were not at all impaired by the seeming drawbacks that no mechanics belonged to it, and that it was steeped in debt to the chimney-pots. It had a large room, which was approached by an infirm step-ladder, the builder having declined to construct the intended staircase without a present payment in cash, which Dullborough (though profoundly appreciative of the Institution) seemed unaccountably bashful about subscribing. The large room had cost—or would, when paid for—five hundred pounds; and it had more mortar in it and more echoes than one might have expected to get for the money. It was fitted up with a platform and the usual lecturing tools, including a large black-board of a menacing appearance. On referring to lists of the courses of lectures that had been given in this thriving Hall, I fancied I detected a shyness in admitting that human nature when at leisure has any desire whatever to be relieved and diverted; and a furtive sliding in of any poor make-weight piece of amusement shamefacedly and edgewise. Thus I observed that it was necessary for the members to be knocked on the head with Gas, Air, Water, Food, the Solar System, the Geological periods, Criticism on Milton, the Steam-engine, John Bunyan, and Arrow-headed Inscriptions, before they might be tickled by those unaccountable choristers, the negro singers in the court costume of the reign of George the Second. Likewise, that they must be stunned by a weighty inquiry whether there was internal evidence in Shakespeare's works to prove that his uncle by the mother's side lived for some years at Stoke Newington, before they were brought-to by a Miscellaneous Concert. But, indeed, the masking of entertainment, and pretending it was something else—as people mask bedsteads when they are obliged to have them in sitting-rooms, and make believe that they are bookcases, sofas, chests of drawers, anything rather than bedsteads—was manifest even in the pretence of dreariness that the unfortunate entertainers themselves felt obliged in decency to put forth when they came here. One very agreeable professional singer who travelled with two professional ladies knew better than to introduce either of those ladies to sing the ballad "Comin' through the Rye," without prefacing it himself with some general remarks on wheat and clover; and even then he dared not for his life call the song, a song, but disguised it in the bill as an "Illustration." In the library, also—fitted with shelves for three thousand books, and containing upwards of one hundred and seventy (presented copies mostly), seething their edges in damp plaster —there was such a painfully apologetic return of 62 offenders who had read Travels, Popular Biography, and mere Fiction descriptive of the aspirations of the hearts and souls of mere human creatures like themselves; and such an elaborate parade of 2 bright examples who had had down Euclid after the day's occupation and confinement; and 3 who had had down Metaphysics after ditto; and 1 who had had down Theology after ditto; and 4 who had worried Grammar, Political Economy, Botany, and Logarithms all at once after ditto; that I suspected the boasted class to be one man, who had been hired to do it.

Emerging from the Mechanics' Institution and continuing my walk about the town, I still noticed everywhere the prevalence, to an extraordinary degree, of this custom of putting the natural demand for amusement out of sight, as some untidy housekeepers put dust, and pretending that it was swept away. And yet it was ministered to, in a dull and abortive manner, by all who made this feint. Looking in at what is called in Dullborough "the serious bookseller's," where, in my childhood, I had studied the faces of numbers of gentlemen depicted in rostrums with a gaslight on each side of them, and casting my eyes over the open pages of certain printed discourses there, I found a vast deal of aiming at jocosity and dramatic effect even in them—yes, verily, even on the part of one very wrathful expounder who bitterly anathematised a poor little Circus. Similarly, in the reading provided for the young people enrolled in the Lasso of Love, and other excellent unions, I found the writers generally under a distressing sense that they must start (at all events) like story-tellers, and delude the young persons into the belief that they were going to be interesting. As I looked in at this window for twenty minutes by the clock, I am in a position to offer a friendly remonstrance—not bearing on this particular point—to the designers and engravers of the pictures in those publications. Have they considered the awful consequences likely to flow from their representations of Virtue? Have they asked themselves the question, whether the terrific prospect of acquiring that fearful chubbiness of head, unwieldiness of arm, feeble dislocation of leg, crispiness of hair, and enormity of shirt-collar, which they represent as inseparable from Goodness, may not tend to confirm sensitive waverers in Evil? A most impressive example (if I had believed it) of what a Dustman and a Sailor may come to, when they mend their ways, was presented to me in this same shop-window. When they were leaning (they were intimate friends) against a post, drunk and reckless, with surpassingly bad hats on, and their hair over their foreheads, they were rather picturesque, and looked as if they might be agreeable men if they would not be beasts. But when they had got over their bad propensities, and when, as a consequence, their heads had swelled alarmingly, their hair had got so curly that it lifted their blown-out cheeks up, their coat-cuffs were so long that they never could do any work, and their eyes were so wide open that they never could do any sleep, they presented a spectacle calculated to plunge a timid nature into the depths of Infamy.

But the clock that had so degenerated since I saw it last admonished me that I had stayed here long enough ; and I resumed my walk.

I had not gone fifty paces along the street when I was suddenly brought up by the sight of a man who got out of a little phaeton at the doctor's door, and went into the doctor's house. Immediately the air was filled with the scent of trodden grass, and the perspective of years opened, and at the end of it was a little likeness of this man keeping a wicket, and I said, " God bless my soul ! Joe Specks ! "

Through many changes and much work I had preserved a tenderness for the memory of Joe, forasmuch as we had made the acquaintance of Roderick Random together, and had believed him to be no ruffian, but an ingenuous and engaging hero. Scorning to ask the boy left in the phaeton whether it was really Joe, and scorning even to read the brass plate on the door—so sure was I—I rang the bell and informed the servant-maid that a stranger sought audience of Mr. Specks. Into a room, half surgery, half study, I was shown to await his coming, and I found it, by a series of elaborate accidents, bestrewn with testimonies to Joe. Portrait of Mr. Specks, bust of Mr. Specks, silver cup from grateful patient to Mr. Specks, presentation sermon from local clergymen, dedication poem from local poet, dinner-card from local nobleman, tract on balance of power from local refugee, inscribed *Hommage de l'auteur à Specks*.

When my old schoolfellow came in, and I informed him with a smile that I was not a patient, he seemed rather at a loss to perceive any reason for smiling in connection with that fact, and inquired to what was he to attribute the honour. I asked him, with another smile, could he remember me at all. He had not (he said) that pleasure. I was beginning to have but a poor opinion of Mr. Specks, when he said reflectively, " And yet there's a something too." Upon that, I saw a boyish light in his eyes that looked well, and I asked him if he could inform me, as a stranger who desired to know and had not the means of reference at hand, what the name of the young lady was who married Mr. Random. Upon that, he said " Narcissa," and, after staring for a moment, called me by my name, shook me by the hand, and melted into a roar of laughter. " Why, of course, you'll remember Lucy Green," he said, after we had talked a little. "Of course," said I. "Whom do you think she married?" said he. "You?" I hazarded. "Me," said Specks, "and you shall see her." So I saw her, and she was fat, and if all the hay in the world had been heaped upon her, it could scarcely have altered her face more than Time had altered it from my remembrance of the face that had once looked down upon me into the fragrant dungeons of Seringapatam. But when her youngest child came in after dinner (for I dined with them, and we had no other company than Specks, Junior, Barrister-at-Law, who went away as soon as the cloth was removed, to look after the young lady to whom he was going to be married next week), I saw again, in that little daughter, the little face of the hayfield, unchanged, and it quite touched my foolish heart. We talked immensely, Specks and Mrs. Specks and I, and we spoke of our old selves as though our old selves were dead and gone, and indeed, indeed they were—dead and gone as the playing-field that had become a wilderness of rusty iron, and the property of S. E. R.

Specks, however, illuminated Dullborough with the rays of interest that I wanted and should otherwise have missed in it, and linked its present to its past with a highly agreeable chain. And in Specks's society I had new occasion to observe what I had before noticed in similar communications among other men. All the schoolfellows and others of old, whom I inquired about, had either done superlatively well or superlatively ill—had either become uncertificated bankrupts, or been felonious and got themselves transported, or had made great hits in life, and done wonders. And this is so commonly the case, that I never can imagine what becomes of all the mediocre people of people's youth—especially considering that we find no lack of the species in our maturity. But I did not propound this difficulty to Specks, for no pause in the conversation gave me an occasion. Nor could I discover one single flaw in the good doctor—when he reads this, he will receive in a friendly spirit the pleasantly meant record—except that he had forgotten his *Roderick Random*, and that he confounded Strap with Lieutenant Hatchway, who never knew Random, howsoever intimate with Pickle.

When I went alone to the Railway to catch my train at night (Specks had meant to go with me, but was inopportunely called out), I was in a more charitable mood with Dullborough than I had been all day; and yet in my heart I had loved it all day too. Ah! who was I that I should quarrel with the town for being changed to me, when I myself had come back, so changed, to it! All my early readings and early imaginations dated from this place, and I took them away so full of innocent construction and guileless belief, and I brought them back so worn and torn, so much the wiser and so much the worse!

XIII

NIGHT WALKS

SOME years ago, a temporary inability to sleep, referable to a distressing impression, caused me to walk about the streets all night for a series of several nights. The disorder might have taken a long time to conquer if it had been faintly experimented on in bed ; but it was soon defeated by the brisk treatment of getting up directly after lying down, and going out, and coming home tired at sunrise.

In the course of those nights I finished my education in a fair amateur experience of houselessness. My principal object being to get through the night, the pursuit of it brought me into sympathetic relations with people who have no other object every night in the year.

The month was March, and the weather damp, cloudy, and cold. The sun not rising before half-past five, the night perspective looked sufficiently long at half-past twelve, which was about my time for confronting it.

The restlessness of a great city, and the way in which it tumbles and tosses before it can get to sleep, formed one of the first entertainments offered to the contemplation of us houseless people. It lasted about two hours. We lost a great deal of companionship when the late public-houses turned their lamps out, and when the potmen thrust the last brawling drunkards into the street ; but stray vehicles and stray people were left us after that. If we were very lucky, a policeman's rattle sprang and a fray turned up ; but, in general, surprisingly little of this diversion was provided. Except in the Haymarket, which is the worst kept part of London, and about Kent Street in the Borough, and along a portion of the line of the Old Kent Road, the peace was seldom violently broken. But it was always the case that London, as if in imitation of individual citizens belonging to it, had expiring fits and starts of restlessness. After all seemed quiet, if one cab rattled by, half-a-dozen would surely follow ; and Houselessness even observed that intoxicated people appeared to be magnetically attracted towards each other, so that we knew when we saw one drunken object staggering against the shutters of a shop, that another drunken object would stagger up before five minutes were out, to fraternise or fight with it. When we made a divergence from the regular species of drunkard, the thin-armed, puff-faced, leaden-lipped gin-drinker, and encountered a rarer specimen of a more decent appearance, fifty to one but that specimen was dressed in soiled mourning. As the street experience in the night, so the street experience in the day ; the common folk who come unexpectedly into a little property, come unexpectedly into a deal of liquor.

At length these flickering sparks would die away, worn out—the last veritable sparks of waking life trailed from some late pieman or hot potato man—and London would sink to rest. And then the yearning of the houseless mind would be for any sign of company, any lighted place, any movement, anything suggestive of any one being up—nay, even so much as awake, for the houseless eye looked out for lights in windows.

Walking the streets under the pattering rain, Houselessness would walk and walk and walk, seeing nothing but the interminable tangle of streets, save at a corner, here and there, two policemen in conversation, or the sergeant or inspector looking after his men. Now and then in the night—but rarely—Houselessness would become aware of a furtive head peering out of a doorway a few yards before him, and, coming up with the head, would find a man standing bolt upright to keep within the doorway's shadow, and evidently intent upon no particular service to society. Under a kind of fascination, and in a ghostly silence suitable to the time, Houselessness and this gentleman would eye one another from head to foot, and so, without exchange of speech, part, mutually suspicious. Drip, drip, drip, from ledge and coping, splash from pipes and water-spouts, and by and by the houseless shadow would fall upon the stones that pave the way to Waterloo Bridge, it being in the houseless mind to have a halfpennyworth of excuse for saying "Good-night" to the toll-keeper, and catching a glimpse of his fire. A good fire and a good great-coat and a good woollen neck-shawl were comfortable things to see in conjunction with the toll-keeper; also his brisk wakefulness was excellent company when he rattled the change of halfpence down upon that metal table of his, like a man who defied the night, with all its sorrowful thoughts, and didn't care for the coming of dawn. There was need of encouragement on the threshold of the bridge, for the bridge was dreary. The chopped-up murdered man had not been lowered with a rope over the parapet when those nights were; he was alive, and slept then quietly enough most likely, and undisturbed by any dream of where he was to come. But the river had an awful look, the buildings on the banks were muffled in black shrouds, and the reflected lights seemed to originate deep in the water, as if the spectres of suicides were holding them to show where they went down. The wild moon and clouds were as restless as an evil conscience in a tumbled bed, and the very shadow of the immensity of London seemed to lie oppressively upon the river.

Between the bridge and the two great theatres there was but the distance of a few hundred paces, so the theatres came next. Grim and black within, at night, those great dry Wells, and lonesome to imagine, with the rows of faces faded out, the lights extinguished, and the seats all empty. One would think that nothing in them knew itself at such a time but Yorick's skull. In one of my night walks, as the church steeples were shaking the March winds and rain with the strokes of Four, I passed the outer boundary of one of these great deserts, and entered it. With a dim lantern in my hand, I groped my well-known way to the stage and looked over the orchestra—which was like a great grave dug for a time of pestilence—into the void beyond. A dismal cavern of an immense aspect, with the chandelier gone dead like everything else, and nothing visible through mist and fog and space but tiers of winding-sheets. The ground at my feet where, when last there, I had seen the peasantry of Naples dancing among the vines, reckless of the burning mountain which threatened to overwhelm them, was now in possession of a strong serpent of engine-hose, watchfully lying in wait for the serpent Fire, and ready to fly at it if it showed its forked tongue. A ghost of a watchman, carrying a faint corpse-candle, haunted the distant upper gallery and flitted away. Retiring within the proscenium, and holding my light above my head towards the rolled-up curtain—green no more, but black as ebony—my sight lost itself in a gloomy vault, showing faint indications in it of a shipwreck of canvas and cordage. Methought I felt much as a diver might at the bottom of the sea.

In those small hours when there was no movement in the streets, it afforded matter for reflection to take Newgate in the way, and, touching its rough stone, to think of the prisoners in their sleep, and then to glance in at the lodge over the spiked wicket, and see the fire and light of the watching turnkeys on the white wall. Not an inappropriate time either to linger by that wicked little Debtors' Door —shutting tighter than any other door one ever saw—which has been Death's Door to so many. In the days of the uttering of forged one-pound notes by people tempted up from the country, how many hundreds of wretched creatures of both sexes—many quite innocent— swung out of a pitiless and inconsistent world, with the tower of yonder Christian church of Saint Sepulchre monstrously before their eyes! Is there any haunting of the Bank Parlour by the remorseful souls of old directors, in the nights of these later days, I wonder, or is it as quiet as this degenerate Aceldama of an Old Bailey?

To walk on to the Bank, lamenting the good old times and bemoaning the present evil period, would be an easy next step, so I would take it, and would make my houseless circuit of the Bank, and give a thought to the treasure within; likewise to the guard of soldiers passing the night there, and nodding over the fire. Next, I went to Billingsgate, in some hope of market-people, but it proving as yet too early, crossed London Bridge and got down by the water-side on the Surrey shore among the buildings of the great brewery. There was plenty going on at the brewery; and the reek, and the smell of grains, and the rattling of the plump dray horses at their mangers, were capital company. Quite refreshed by having mingled with this good society, I made a new start with a new heart, setting the old King's Bench prison before me for my next object, and resolving, when I should come to the wall, to think of poor Horace Kinch, and the Dry Rot in men.

A very curious disease the Dry Rot in men, and difficult to detect the beginning of. It had carried Horace Kinch inside the wall of the old King's Bench prison, and it had carried him out with his feet foremost. He was a likely man to look at, in the prime of life, well to do, as clever as he needed to be, and popular among many friends. He was suitably married, and had healthy and pretty children. But, like some fair-looking houses or fair-looking ships, he took the Dry Rot. The first strong external revelation of the Dry Rot in men is a tendency to lurk and lounge ; to be at street-corners without intelligible reason ; to be going anywhere when met ; to be about many places rather than at any ; to do nothing tangible, but to have an intention of performing a variety of intangible duties to-morrow or the day after. When this manifestation of the disease is observed, the observer will usually connect it with a vague impression once formed or received, that the patient was living a little too hard. He will scarcely have had leisure to turn it over in his mind and form the terrible suspicion " Dry Rot," when he will notice a change for the worse in the patient's appearance : a certain slovenliness and deteriora- tion, which is not poverty, nor dirt, nor intoxication, nor ill-health, but simply Dry Rot. To this succeeds a smell as of strong waters, in the morning ; to that, a looseness respecting money ; to that, a stronger smell as of strong waters, at all times ; to that, a looseness respecting everything ; to that, a trembling of the limbs, somnolency, misery, and crumbling to pieces. As it is in wood, so it is in men. Dry Rot advances at a compound usury quite incalculable. A plank is found infected with it, and the whole structure is devoted. Thus it had been with the unhappy Horace Kinch, lately buried by a small subscription. Those who knew him had not nigh done saying, " So well off, so comfortably established, with such hope before him—and yet, it is feared, with a slight touch of Dry Rot !" when lo ! the man was all Dry Rot and dust.

From the dead wall associated on those houseless nights with this too common story, I chose next to wander by Bethlehem Hospital ; partly because it lay on my road round to Westminster ; partly because I had a night fancy in my head which could be best pursued within sight of its walls and dome. And the fancy was this : Are not the sane and the insane equal at night as the sane lie a-dreaming ? Are not all of us outside this hospital, who dream, more or less in the condition of those inside it, every night of our lives ? Are we not nightly persuaded, as they daily are, that we associate preposterously with kings and queens, emperors and empresses, and notabilities of all sorts ? Do we not nightly jumble events and personages and times and places, as these do daily ? Are we not sometimes troubled by our own sleeping inconsistencies, and do we not vexedly try to account for them or excuse them, just as these do sometimes in respect of their waking delusions ? Said an afflicted man to me, when I was last in a hospital like this, " Sir, I can frequently fly." I was half ashamed to reflect that so could I—by night. Said a woman to me on the same occasion, " Queen Victoria frequently comes to dine with me, and her Majesty and I dine off peaches and macaroni in our night-gowns, and His Royal Highness the Prince Consort does us the honour to make a third on horseback in a Field-Marshal's uniform." Could I refrain from reddening with consciousness when I remembered the amazing royal parties I myself had given (at night), the unaccountable viands I had put on table, and my extraordinary manner of conducting myself on those distinguished occasions? I wonder that the great master who knew everything, when he called Sleep the death of each day's life, did not call Dreams the insanity of each day's sanity.

By this time I had left the Hospital behind me, and was again setting towards the river; and in a short breathing space I was on Westminster Bridge, regaling my houseless eyes with the external walls of the British Parliament—the perfection of a stupendous institution, I know, and the admiration of all surrounding nations and succeeding ages, I do not doubt, but perhaps a little the better now and then for being pricked up to its work. Turning off into Old Palace Yard, the Courts of Law kept me company for a quarter of an hour, hinting in low whispers what numbers of people they were keeping awake, and how intensely wretched and horrible they were rendering the small hours to unfortunate suitors. Westminster Abbey was fine gloomy society for another quarter of an hour, suggesting a wonderful procession of its dead among the dark arches and pillars, each century more amazed by the century following it than by all the centuries going before. And indeed in those houseless night walks—which even included cemeteries, where watchmen went round among the graves at stated times, and moved the tell-tale handle of an index which recorded that they had touched it at such an hour—it was a solemn consideration what enormous hosts of dead belong to one old great city, and how, if they were raised while the living slept, there would not be the space of a pin's point in all the streets and ways for the living to come out into. Not only that, but the vast armies of dead would overflow the hills and valleys beyond the city, and would stretch away all round it, God knows how far.

When a church clock strikes on houseless ears in the dead of the night, it may be at first mistaken for company and hailed as such. But as the spreading circles of vibration, which you may perceive at such a time with great clearness, go opening out, for ever and ever afterwards widening perhaps (as the philosopher has suggested) in eternal space, the mistake is rectified and the sense of loneliness is profounder. Once—it was after leaving the Abbey and turning my face north—I came to the great steps of Saint Martin's church as the clock was striking Three. Suddenly, a thing that in a moment more I should have trodden upon, without seeing, rose up at my feet with a cry of loneliness and houselessness, struck out of it by the bell, the like of which I never heard. We then stood face to face looking at one another, frightened by one another. The creature was like a beetle-browed, hair-lipped youth of twenty, and it had a loose bundle of rags on, which it held together with one of its hands. It shivered from head to foot, and its teeth chattered, and as it stared at me—persecutor, devil, ghost, whatever it thought me—it made with its whining mouth as if it were snapping at me, like a worried dog. Intending to give this ugly object money, I put out my hand to stay it—for it recoiled as it whined and snapped—and laid my hand upon its shoulder. Instantly it twisted out of its garment, like the young man in the New Testament, and left me standing alone with its rags in my hand.

Covent Garden Market, when it was market morning, was wonderful company. The great waggons of cabbages, with growers' men and boys lying asleep under them, and with sharp dogs from market-garden neighbourhoods looking after the whole, were as good as a party. But one of the worst night sights I know in London is to be found in the children who prowl about this place, who sleep in the baskets, fight for the offal, dart at any object they think they can lay their thieving hands on, dive under the carts and barrows, dodge the constables, and are perpetually making a blunt pattering on the pavement of the Piazza with the rain of their naked feet. A painful and unnatural result comes of the comparison one is forced to institute between the growth of corruption as displayed in the so much improved and cared for fruits of the earth, and the growth of corruption as displayed in these all uncared for (except inasmuch as ever-hunted) savages.

There was early coffee to be got about Covent Garden Market, and that was more company—warm company, too, which was better. Toast of a very substantial quality was likewise procurable, though the towzled-headed man who made it, in an inner chamber within the coffee-room, hadn't got his coat on yet, and was so heavy with sleep that in every interval of toast and coffee he went off anew behind the partition into complicated cross-roads of choke and snore, and lost his way directly. Into one of these establishments (among the earliest), near Bow Street, there came one morning, as I sat over my houseless cup, pondering where to go next, a man in a high and long snuff-coloured coat, and shoes, and, to the best of my belief, nothing else but a hat, who took out of his hat a large cold meat pudding; a meat pudding so large that it was a very tight fit, and brought the lining of the hat out with it. This mysterious man was known by his pudding, for, on his entering, the man of sleep brought him a pint of hot tea, a small loaf, and a large knife and fork, and plate. Left to himself in his box, he stood the pudding on the bare table, and, instead of cutting it, stabbed it, overhand, with the knife, like a mortal enemy; then took the knife out, wiped it on his sleeve, tore the pudding asunder with his fingers, and ate it all up. The remembrance of this man with the pudding remains with me as the remembrance of the most spectral person my houselessness encountered. Twice only was I in that establishment, and twice I saw him stalk in (as I should say, just out of bed, and presently going back to bed), take out his pudding, stab his pudding, wipe the dagger, and eat his pudding all up. He was a man whose figure promised cadaverousness, but who had an excessively red face, though shaped like a horse's. On the second occasion of my seeing him, he said huskily to the man of sleep, "Am I red to-night?"

"You are," he uncompromisingly answered. "My mother," said the spectre, "was a red-faced woman that liked drink, and I looked at her hard when she laid in her coffin, and I took the complexion." Somehow, the pudding seemed an unwholesome pudding after that, and I put myself in its way no more.

When there was no market, or when I wanted variety, a railway terminus with the morning mails coming in was remunerative company. But, like most of the company to be had in this world, it lasted only a very short time. The station lamps would burst out ablaze, the porters would emerge from places of concealment, the cabs and trucks would rattle to their places (the post-office carts were already in theirs), and, finally, the bell would strike up, and the train would come banging in. But there were few passengers and little luggage, and everything scuttled away with the greatest expedition. The locomotive post-offices, with their great nets—as if they had been dragging the country for bodies—would fly open as to their doors, and would disgorge a smell of lamp, an exhausted clerk, a guard in a red coat, and their bags of letters ; the engine would blow and heave and perspire, like an engine wiping its forehead and saying what a run it had had ; and within ten minutes the lamps were out, and I was houseless and alone again.

But now there were driven cattle on the high road near, wanting (as cattle always do) to turn into the midst of stone walls, and squeeze themselves through six inches' width of iron railing, and getting their heads down (also as cattle always do) for tossing-purchase at quite imaginary dogs, and giving themselves and every devoted creature associated with them a most extraordinary amount of unnecessary trouble. Now, too, the conscious gas began to grow pale with the knowledge that daylight was coming, and straggling workpeople were already in the streets, and, as waking life had become extinguished with the last pieman's sparks, so it began to be rekindled with the fires of the first street-corner breakfast-sellers. And so by faster and faster degrees, until the last degrees were very fast, the day came, and I was tired and could sleep. And it is not, as I used to think, going home at such times, the least wonderful thing in London that in the real desert region of the night the houseless wanderer is alone there. I knew well enough where to find Vice and Misfortune of all kinds, if I had chosen ; but they were put out of sight, and my houselessness had many miles upon miles of streets in which it could, and did, have its own solitary way.

XIV

CHAMBERS

HAVING occasion to transact some business with a solicitor who occupies a highly suicidal set of chambers in Gray's Inn, I afterwards took a turn in the large square of that stronghold of Melancholy, reviewing, with congenial surroundings, my experiences of Chambers.

I began, as was natural, with the Chambers I had just left. They were an upper set on a rotten staircase, with a mysterious bunk or bulkhead on the landing outside them, of a rather nautical and Screw Collier-like appearance than otherwise, and painted an intense black. Many dusty years have passed since the appropriation of this Davy Jones's locker to any purpose, and during the whole period within the memory of living man it has been hasped and padlocked. I cannot quite satisfy my mind whether it was originally meant for the reception of coals, or bodies, or as a place of temporary security for the plunder "looted" by laundresses; but I incline to the last opinion. It is about breast-high, and usually serves as a bulk for defendants in reduced circumstances to lean against and ponder at, when they come on the hopeful errand of trying to make an arrangement without money—under which auspicious circumstances it mostly happens that the legal gentleman they want to see is much engaged, and they pervade the staircase for a considerable period. Against this opposing bulk, in the absurdest manner, the tomb-like outer door of the solicitor's chambers (which is also of an intense black) stands in dark ambush, half open, and half shut, all day. The solicitor's apartments are three in number, consisting of a slice, a cell, and a wedge. The slice is assigned to the two clerks, the cell is occupied by the principal, and the wedge is devoted to stray papers, old game baskets from the country, a washing-stand, and a model of a patent Ship's Caboose which was exhibited in Chancery at the commencement of the present century on an application for an injunction to restrain infringement. At about half-past nine on every week-day morning, the younger of the two clerks (who, I have reason to believe, leads the fashion at Pentonville in the articles of pipes and shirts) may be found knocking the dust out of his official door-key on the bunk or locker before mentioned; and so exceedingly subject to dust is his key, and so very retentive of that superfluity, that in exceptional summer weather, when a ray of sunlight has fallen on the locker in my presence, I have noticed its inexpressive countenance to be deeply marked by a kind of Bramah erysipelas or smallpox.

This set of chambers (as I have gradually discovered, when I have had restless occasion to make inquiries or leave messages, after office hours) is under the charge of a lady named Sweeney, in figure extremely like an old family-umbrella, whose dwelling confronts a dead wall in a court off Gray's Inn Lane, and who is usually fetched into the passage of that bower, when wanted, from some neighbouring home of industry, which has the curious property of imparting an inflammatory appearance to her visage. Mrs. Sweeney is one of the race of professed laundresses, and is the compiler of a remarkable manuscript volume entitled " Mrs. Sweeney's Book," from which much curious statistical information may be gathered respecting the high prices and small uses of soda, soap, sand, firewood, and other such articles. I have created a legend in my mind—and consequently I believe it with the utmost pertinacity—that the late Mr. Sweeney was a ticket-porter under the Honourable Society of Gray's Inn, and that, in consideration of his long and valuable services, Mrs. Sweeney was appointed to her present post. For, though devoid of personal charms, I have observed this lady to exercise a fascination over the elderly ticket-porter mind (particularly under the gateway, and in corners and entries), which I can only refer to her being one of the fraternity, yet not competing with it. All that need be said concerning this set of chambers is said, when I have added that it is in a large double house in Gray's Inn Square, very much out of repair, and that the outer portal is ornamented in a hideous manner with certain stone remains, which have the appearance of the dismembered bust, torso, and limbs of a petrified bencher.

Indeed, I look upon Gray's Inn generally as one of the most depressing institutions in brick and mortar known to the children of men. Can anything be more dreary than its arid Square, Sahara Desert of the law, with the ugly old tiled-topped tenements, the dirty windows, the bills To Let, To Let, the doorposts inscribed like gravestones, the crazy gateway giving upon the filthy Lane, the scowling iron-barred, prison-like passage into Verulam Buildings, the mouldy, red-nosed ticket-porters with little coffin plates, and why with aprons, the dry, hard, atomy-like appearance of the whole dust-heap? When my uncommercial travels tend to this dismal spot, my comfort is its rickety state. Imagination gloats over the fulness of time, when the staircases shall have quite tumbled down—they are daily wearing into an ill-savoured powder, but have not quite tumbled down yet—when the last old prolix bencher all of the olden time shall have been got out of an upper window by means of a Fire Ladder, and carried off to the Holborn Union ; when the last clerk shall have engrossed the last parchment behind the last splash on the last of the mud-stained windows, which, all through the miry year, are pilloried out of recognition in Gray's Inn Lane. Then shall a squalid little trench, with rank grass and a pump in it, lying between the coffee-house and South Square, be wholly given up to cats and rats, and not, as now, have its empire divided between those animals and a few briefless bipeds—surely called to the Bar by voices of deceiving spirits, seeing that they are wanted there by no mortal—who glance down, with eyes better glazed than their casements, from their dreary and lack-lustre rooms. Then shall the way Nor'-Westward, now lying under a short grim colonnade where in summer-time pounce flies from law-stationering windows into the eyes of laymen, be choked with rubbish and happily become impassable. Then shall the gardens, where turf, trees, and gravel wear a legal livery of black, run rank, and pilgrims go to Gorhambury to see Bacon's effigy as he sat, and not come here (which in truth they seldom do) to see where he walked. Then, in a word, shall the old-established vendor of periodicals sit alone in his little crib of a shop behind the Holborn Gate, like that lumbering Marius among the ruins of Carthage, who has sat heavy on a thousand million of similes.

At one period of my uncommercial career I much frequented another set of chambers in Gray's Inn Square. They were what is familiarly called "a top set," and all the eatables and drinkables introduced into them acquired a flavour of Cockloft. I have known an unopened Strasbourg pâté, fresh from Fortnum and Mason's, to draw in this cockloft tone through its crockery dish, and become penetrated with cockloft to the core of its inmost truffle in three-quarters of an hour. This, however, was not the most curious feature of those chambers; that consisted in the profound conviction entertained by my esteemed friend Parkle (their tenant) that they were clean. Whether it was an inborn hallucination, or whether it was imparted to him by Mrs. Miggot, the laundress, I never could ascertain. But I believe he would have gone to the stake upon the question. Now, they were so dirty that I could take off the distinctest impression of my figure on any article of furniture by merely lounging upon it for a few moments; and it used to be a private amusement of mine to print myself off—if I may use the expression—all over the rooms. It was the first large circulation I had. At other times I have accidentally shaken a window curtain while in animated conversation with Parkle, and struggling insects which were certainly red, and were certainly not ladybirds, have dropped on the back of my hand. Yet Parkle lived in that top set years, bound body and soul to the superstition that they were clean. He used to say, when congratulated upon them, "Well, they are not like chambers in one respect, you know; they are clean." Concurrently, he had an idea which he could never explain, that Mrs. Miggot was in some way connected with the Church. When he was in particularly good spirits, he used to believe that a deceased uncle of hers had been a Dean; when he was poorly and low, he believed that her brother had been a Curate. I and Mrs. Miggot (she was a genteel woman) were on confidential terms, but I never knew her to commit herself to any distinct assertion on the subject; she merely claimed a proprietorship in the Church, by looking, when it was mentioned, as if the reference awakened the slumbering Past, and were personal. It may have been his amiable confidence in Mrs. Miggot's better days that inspired my friend with his delusion respecting the chambers, but he never wavered in his fidelity to it for a moment, though he wallowed in dirt seven years.

Two of the windows of these chambers looked down into the garden; and we have sat up there together many a summer evening, saying how pleasant it was, and talking of many things. To my intimacy with that top set I am indebted for three of my liveliest personal impressions of the loneliness of life in chambers. They shall follow here, in order : first, second, and third.

First. My Gray's Inn friend, on a time, hurt one of his legs, and it became seriously inflamed. Not knowing of his indisposition, I was on my way to visit him as usual, one summer evening, when I was much surprised by meeting a lively leech in Field Court, Gray's Inn, seemingly on his way to the West End of London. As the leech was alone, and was of course unable to explain his position, even if he had been inclined to do so (which he had not the appearance of being), I passed him and went on. Turning the corner of Gray's Inn Square, I was beyond expression amazed by meeting another leech—also entirely alone, and also proceeding in a westerly direction, though with less decision of purpose. Ruminating on this extraordinary circumstance, and endeavouring to remember whether I had ever read, in the Philosophical Transactions or any work on Natural History, of a migration of Leeches, I ascended to the top set, past the dreary series of closed outer doors of offices and an empty set or two, which intervened between that lofty region and the surface. Entering my friend's rooms, I found him stretched upon his back, like Prometheus Bound, with a perfectly demented ticket-porter in attendance on him instead of the Vulture, which helpless individual, who was feeble and frightened, had (my friend explained to me, in great choler) been endeavouring for some hours to apply leeches to his leg, and as yet had only got on two out of twenty. To this Unfortunate's distraction between a damp cloth on which he had placed the leeches to freshen them, and the wrathful adjurations of my friend to "Stick 'em on, Sir !" I referred the phenomenon I had encountered, the rather as two fine specimens were at that moment going out at the door, while a general insurrection of the rest was in progress on the table. After a while our united efforts prevailed, and, when the leeches came off and had recovered their spirits, we carefully tied them up in a decanter. But I never heard more of them than that they were all gone next morning, and that the Out-of-door young man of Bickle Bush and Bodger, on the ground floor, had been bitten and blooded by some creature not identified. They never "took" on Mrs. Miggot, the laundress ; but I have always preserved fresh the belief that she unconsciously carried several about her, until they gradually found openings in life.

Second. On the same staircase with my friend Parkle, and on the same floor, there lived a man of law who pursued his business elsewhere, and used those chambers as his place of residence. For three or four years Parkle rather knew of him than knew him, but after that—for Englishmen—short pause of consideration, they began to speak. Parkle exchanged words with him in his private character only, and knew nothing of his business ways, or means. He was a man a good deal about town, but always alone. We used to remark to one another, that although we often encountered him in theatres, concert-rooms, and similar public places, he was always alone. Yet he was not a gloomy man, and was of a decidedly conversational turn, insomuch that he would sometimes of an evening lounge with a cigar in his mouth, half in and half out of Parkle's rooms, and discuss the topics of the day by the hour. He used to hint on these occasions that he had four faults to find with life : firstly, that it obliged a man to be always winding up his watch ; secondly, that London was too small ; thirdly, that it therefore wanted variety ; fourthly, that there was too much dust in it. There was so much dust in his own faded chambers, certainly, that they reminded me of a sepulchre, furnished in prophetic anticipation of the present time, which had newly been brought to light, after having lain buried a few thousand years. One dry hot autumn evening at twilight, this man, being then five years turned of fifty, looked in upon Parkle in his usual lounging way, with his cigar in his mouth as usual, and said, " I am going out of town." As he never went out of town, Parkle said, " Oh indeed ! At last ? " " Yes," says he, " at last. For what is a man to do ? London is so small ! If you go West, you come to Hounslow. If you go East, you come to Bow. If you go South, there's Brixton or Norwood. If you go North, you can't get rid of Barnet. Then, the monotony of all the streets, streets, streets—and of all the roads, roads, roads—and the dust, dust, dust ! " When he had said this, he wished Parkle a good-evening, but came back again and said, with his watch in his hand, " Oh, I really cannot go on winding up this watch over and over again ; I wish you would take care of it." So Parkle laughed and consented, and the man went out of town. The man remainded out of town so long that his letter-box became choked, and no more letters could be got into it, and they began to be left at the lodge and to accumulate there. At last the head-porter decided, on conference with the steward, to use his master-key and look into the chambers, and give them the benefit of a whiff of air. Then it was found that he had hanged himself to his bedstead, and had left this written memorandum : " I should prefer to be cut down by my neighbour and friend (if he will allow me to call him so), H. Parkle, Esq." This was the end of Parkle's occupancy of chambers. He went into lodgings immediately.

Third. While Parkle lived in Gray's Inn, and I myself was uncommercially preparing for the Bar—which is done, as everybody knows, by having a frayed old gown put on in a pantry by an old woman in a chronic state of Saint Anthony's fire and dropsy, and, so decorated, bolting a bad dinner in a party of four, whereof each individual mistrusts the other three—I say, while these things were, there was a certain elderly gentleman who lived in a court of the Temple, and was a great judge and lover of port wine. Every day he dined at his club and drank his bottle or two of port wine, and every night came home to the Temple and went to bed in his lonely chambers. This had gone on many years without variation, when one night he had a fit on coming home, and fell and cut his head deep, but partly recovered and groped about in the dark to find the door. When he was afterwards discovered, dead, it was clearly established by the marks of his hands about the room that he must have done so. Now, this chanced on the night of Christmas Eve, and over him lived a young fellow who had sisters and young country-friends, and who gave them a little party that night, in the course of which they played at Blindman's Buff. They played that game, for their greater sport, by the light of the fire only ; and once, when they were all quietly rustling and stealing about, and the blindman was trying to pick out the prettiest sister (for which I am far from blaming him), somebody cried, Hark ! The man below must be playing Blindman's Buff by himself to-night ! They listened, and they heard sounds of some one falling about and stumbling against furniture, and they all laughed at the conceit, and went on with their play, more light-hearted and merry than ever. Thus those two so different games of life and death were played out together, blindfold, in the two sets of chambers.

Such are the occurrences which, coming to my knowledge, imbued me long ago with a strong sense of the loneliness of chambers. There was a fantastic illustration to much the same purpose implicitly believed by a strange sort of man now dead, whom I knew when I had not quite arrived at legal years of discretion, though I was already in the uncommercial line.

This was a man who, though not more than thirty, had seen the world in divers irreconcilable capacities—had been an officer in a South American regiment among other odd things—but had not achieved much in any way of life, and was in debt, and in hiding. He occupied chambers of the dreariest nature in Lyon's Inn ; his name, however, was not upon the door, or doorpost, but in lieu of it stood the name of a friend who had died in the chambers, and had given him the furniture. The story arose out of the furniture, and was to this effect :— Let the former holder of the chambers, whose name was still upon the door and doorpost, be Mr. Testator.

Mr. Testator took a set of chambers in Lyon's Inn when he had but very scanty furniture for his bedroom, and none for his sitting-room. He had lived some wintry months in this condition, and had found it very bare and cold. One night, past midnight, when he sat writing and still had writing to do that must be done before he went to bed, he found himself out of coals. He had coals down-stairs, but had never been to his cellar ; however, the cellar-key was on his mantelshelf, and if he went down and opened the cellar it fitted, he might fairly assume the coals in that cellar to be his. As to his laundress, she lived among the coal-waggons and Thames watermen—for there were Thames watermen at that time—in some unknown rat-hole by the river, down lanes and alleys on the other side of the Strand. As to any other person to meet him or obstruct him, Lyon's Inn was dreaming, drunk, maudlin, moody, betting, brooding over bill-discounting or renewing —asleep or awake, minding its own affairs. Mr. Testator took his coal-scuttle in one hand, his candle and key in the other, and descended to the dismallest underground dens of Lyon's Inn, where the late vehicles in the streets became thunderous, and all the water-pipes in the neighbourhood seemed to have Macbeth's Amen sticking in their throats, and to be trying to get it out. After groping here and there among low doors to no purpose, Mr. Testator at length came to a door with a rusty padlock which his key fitted. Getting the door open with much trouble, and looking in, he found, no coals, but a confused pile of furniture. Alarmed by this intrusion on another man's property, he locked the door again, found his own cellar, filled his scuttle, and returned up-stairs.

But the furniture he had seen ran on casters across and across Mr. Testator's mind incessantly, when, in the chill hour of five in the morning, he got to bed. He particularly wanted a table to write at, and a table expressly made to be written at had been the piece of furniture in the foreground of the heap. When his laundress emerged from her burrow in the morning to make his kettle boil, he artfully led up to the subject of cellars and furniture; but the two ideas had evidently no connection in her mind. When she left him, and he sat at his breakfast, thinking about the furniture, he recalled the rusty state of the padlock, and inferred that the furniture must have been stored in the cellars for a long time—was perhaps forgotten—owner dead, perhaps. After thinking it over a few days, in the course of which he could pump nothing out of Lyon's Inn about the furniture, he became desperate, and resolved to borrow that table. He did so that night. He had not had the table long, when he determined to borrow an easy-chair; he had not had that long, when he made up his mind to borrow a bookcase; then a couch; then a carpet and rug. By that time he felt he was "in furniture stepped in so far," as that it could be no worse to borrow it all. Consequently, he borrowed it all, and locked up the cellar for good. He had always locked it after every visit. He had carried up every separate article in the dead of night, and, at the best, had felt as wicked as a Resurrection Man. Every article was blue and furry when brought into his rooms, and he had had, in a murderous and guilty sort of way, to polish it up while London slept.

Mr. Testator lived in his furnished chambers two or three years, or more, and gradually lulled himself into the opinion that the furniture was his own. This was his convenient state of mind when, late one night, a step came up the stairs, and a hand passed over his door feeling for his knocker, and then one deep and solemn rap was rapped that might have been a spring in Mr. Testator's easy-chair to shoot him out of it, so promptly was it attended with that effect.

With a candle in his hand, Mr. Testator went to the door, and found there a very pale and very tall man; a man who stooped; a man with very high shoulders, a very narrow chest, and a very red nose; a shabby-genteel man. He was wrapped in a long threadbare black coat, fastened up the front with more pins than buttons, and under his arm he squeezed an umbrella without a handle, as if he were playing bagpipes. He said, "I ask your pardon, but can you tell me——" and stopped, his eyes resting on some object within the chambers.

"Can I tell you what?" asked Mr. Testator, noting this stoppage with quick alarm.

"I ask your pardon," said the stranger, "but—this is not the inquiry I was going to make—*do* I see in there any small article of property belonging to *me?*"

Mr. Testator was beginning to stammer that he was not aware— when the visitor slipped past him, into the chambers. There, in a goblin way which froze Mr. Testator to the marrow, he examined, first, the writing-table, and said, "Mine"; then the easy-chair, and said, "Mine"; then the bookcase, and said, "Mine"; then turned up a corner of the carpet, and said "Mine!" in a word, inspected every item of furniture from the cellar, in succession, and said, "Mine!" Towards the end of this investigation Mr. Testator perceived that he was sodden with liquor, and that the liquor was gin. He was not unsteady with gin, either in his speech or carriage; but he was stiff with gin in both particulars.

Mr. Testator was in a dreadful state, for (according to his making out of the story) the possible consequences of what he had done in recklessness and hardihood flashed upon him in their fulness for the first time. When they had stood gazing at one another for a little while, he tremulously began—

"Sir, I am conscious that the fullest explanation, compensation, and restitution, are your due. They shall be yours. Allow me to entreat that, without temper, without even natural irritation on your part, we may have a little——"

"Drop of something to drink," interposed the stranger. "I am agreeable."

Mr. Testator had intended to say, "a little quiet conversation," but with great relief of mind adopted the amendment. He produced a decanter of gin, and was bustling about for hot water and sugar, when he found that his visitor had already drunk half of the decanter's contents. With hot water and sugar the visitor drank the remainder before he had been an hour in the chambers by the chimes of the church of St. Mary in the Strand; and during the process he frequently whispered to himself, "Mine!"

The gin gone, and Mr. Testator wondering what was to follow it, the visitor rose and said, with increased stiffness, "At what hour of the morning, Sir, will it be convenient?" Mr. Testator hazarded, "At ten." "Sir," said the visitor, "at ten, to the moment, I shall be here." He then contemplated Mr. Testator somewhat at leisure, and said, "God bless you! How is your wife?" Mr. Testator (who never had a wife) replied with much feeling, "Deeply anxious, poor soul, but otherwise well." The visitor thereupon turned and went away, and fell twice in going down-stairs. From that hour he was never heard of. Whether he was a ghost, or a spectral illusion of conscience, or a drunken man who had no business there, or the drunken rightful owner of the furniture, with a transitory gleam of memory; whether he got safe home, or had no home to get to;

whether he died of liquor on the way, or lived in liquor ever afterwards, he never was heard of more. This was the story, received with the furniture and held to be as substantial, by its second possessor in an upper set of chambers in grim Lyon's Inn.

It is to be remarked of chambers in general, that they must have been built for chambers, to have the right kind of loneliness. You may make a great dwelling-house very lonely, by isolating suites of rooms and calling them chambers, but you cannot make the true kind of loneliness. In dwelling-houses there have been family festivals; children have grown in them, girls have bloomed into women in them, courtships and marriages have taken place in them. True chambers never were young, childish, maidenly; never had dolls in them, or rocking-horses, or christenings, or betrothals, or little coffins. Let Gray's Inn identify the child who first touched hands and hearts with Robinson Crusoe in any one of its many "sets," and that child's little statue, in white marble with a golden inscription, shall be at its service, at my cost and charge, as a drinking fountain for the spirit to freshen its thirsty square. Let Lincoln's produce from all its houses a twentieth of the procession derivable from any dwelling-house one-twentieth of its age, of fair young brides who married for love and hope, not settlements, and all the Vice-Chancellors shall thenceforward be kept in nosegays for nothing, on application to the writer hereof. It is not denied that on the terrace of the Adelphi, or in any of the streets of that subterranean-stable-haunted spot, or about Bedford Row, or James Street of that ilk (a gruesome place), or anywhere among the neighbourhoods that have done flowering and have run to seed, you may find chambers replete with the accommodations of Solitude, Closeness, and Darkness, where you may be as low-spirited as in the genuine article, and might be as easily murdered, with the placid reputation of having merely gone down to the sea-side. But the many waters of life did run musical in those dry channels once; among the Inns, never. The only popular legend known in relation to any one of the dull family of Inns is a dark Old Bailey whisper concerning Clement's, and importing how the black creature who holds the sun-dial there was a negro who slew his master and built the dismal pile out of the contents of his strong box—for which architectural offence alone he ought to have been condemned to live in it. But what populace would waste fancy upon such a place, or on New Inn, Staple Inn, Barnard's Inn, or any of the shabby crew?

The genuine laundress, too, is an institution not to be had in its entirety out of and away from the genuine chambers. Again, it is not denied that you may be robbed elsewhere. Elsewhere you may have —for money—dishonesty, drunkenness, dirt, laziness, and profound incapacity. But the veritable shining-red-faced, shameless laundress; the true Mrs. Sweeney—in figure, colour, texture, and smell, like the old damp family umbrella; the tip-top complicated abomination of stockings, spirits, bonnet, limpness, looseness, and larceny, is only to be drawn at the fountain-head. Mrs. Sweeney is beyond the reach of individual art. It requires the united efforts of several men to ensure that great result, and it is only developed in perfection under an Honourable Society and in an Inn of Court.

XV

NURSE'S STORIES

THERE are not many places that I find it more agreeable to revisit when I am in an idle mood than some places to which I have never been. For my acquaintance with those spots is of such long standing, and has ripened into an intimacy of so affectionate a nature, that I take a particular interest in assuring myself that they are unchanged.

I never was in Robinson Crusoe's Island, yet I frequently return there. The colony he established on it soon faded away, and it is uninhabited by any descendants of the grave and courteous Spaniards, or of Will Atkins and the other mutineers, and has relapsed into its original condition. Not a twig of its wicker houses remains, its goats have long run wild again, its screaming parrots would darken the sun with a cloud of many flaming colours if a gun were fired there, no face is ever reflected in the waters of the little creek which Friday swam across when pursued by his two brother cannibals with sharpened stomachs. After comparing notes with other travellers who have similarly revisited the Island and conscientiously inspected it, I have satisfied myself that it contains no vestige of Mr. Atkins's domesticity or theology, though his track on the memorable evening of his landing to set his captain ashore, when he was decoyed about and round about until it was dark, and his boat was stove, and his strength and spirits failed him, is yet plainly to be traced. So is the hill-top on which Robinson was struck dumb with joy when the reinstated captain pointed to the ship, riding within half a mile of the shore, that was to bear him away, in the nine-and-twentieth year of his seclusion in that lonely place. So is the sandy beach on which the memorable footstep was impressed, and where the savages hauled up their canoes when they came ashore for those dreadful public dinners which led to a dancing worse than speech-making. So is the cave where the flaring eyes of the old goat made such a goblin appearance in the dark. So is the site of the hut where Robinson lived with the dog and the parrot and the cat, and where he endured those first agonies of solitude, which—strange to say—never involved any ghostly fancies : a circumstance so very remarkable that perhaps he left out something in writing his record ? Round hundreds of such objects, hidden in the dense tropical foliage, the tropical sea breaks evermore ; and over them the tropical sky, saving in the short rainy season, shines bright and cloudless.

Neither was I ever belated among wolves on the borders of France and Spain ; nor did I ever, when night was closing in and the ground was covered with snow, draw up my little company among some felled trees which served as a breastwork, and there fire a train of gunpowder so dexterously that suddenly we had three or four score blazing wolves illuminating the darkness around us.   Nevertheless, I occasionally go back to that dismal region and perform the feat again, when indeed to smell the singeing and the frying of the wolves afire, and to see them setting one another alight as they rush and tumble, and to behold them rolling in the snow vainly attempting to put them-selves out, and to hear their howlings taken up by all the echoes as well as by all the unseen wolves within the woods, makes me tremble.

I was never in the robbers' cave where Gil Blas lived, but I often go back there and find the trap-door just as heavy to raise as it used to be, while that wicked old disabled Black lies everlastingly cursing in bed.   I was never in Don Quixote's study, where he read his books of chivalry until he rose and hacked at imaginary giants, and then refreshed himself with great draughts of water, yet you couldn't move a book in it without my knowledge, or with my consent.   I was never (thank Heaven) in company with the little old woman who hobbled out of the chest and told the merchant Abudah to go in search of the Talisman of Oromanes, yet I make it my business to know that she is well preserved and as intolerable as ever.   I was never at the school where the boy Horatio Nelson got out of bed to steal the pears—not because he wanted any, but because every other boy was afraid,—yet I have several times been back to this Academy to see him let down out of window with a sheet.   So with Damascus, and Bagdad, and Brob-dingnag (which has the curious fate of being usually misspelt when written), and Lilliput, and Laputa, and the Nile, and Abyssinia, and the Ganges, and the North Pole, and many hundreds of places—I was never at them, yet it is an affair of my life to keep them intact, and I am always going back to them.

But when I was in Dullborough one day, revisiting the associations of my childhood as recorded in previous pages of these notes, my experience in this wise was made quite inconsiderable and of no account by the quantity of places and people—utterly impossible places and people, but none the less alarmingly real—that I found I had been introduced to by my nurse before I was six years old, and used to be forced to go back to at night without at all wanting to go.   If we all knew our own minds (in a more enlarged sense than the popular acceptation of that phrase), I suspect we should find our nurses re-sponsible for most of the dark corners we are forced to go back to against our wills.

The first diabolical character who intruded himself on my peaceful youth (as I called to mind that day at Dullborough) was a certain Captain Murderer.   This wretch must have been an offshoot of the Blue Beard family, but I had no suspicion of the consanguinity in those times.   His warning name would seem to have awakened no general prejudice against him, for he was admitted into the best society and

possessed immense wealth. Captain Murderer's mission was matrimony, and the gratification of a cannibal appetite with tender brides.
On his marriage morning he always caused both sides of the way to
church to be planted with curious flowers ; and when his bride said,
" Dear Captain Murderer, I never saw flowers like these before ; what
are they called ? " he answered, " They are called Garnish for house-
lamb," and laughed at his ferocious practical joke in a horrid manner,
disquieting the minds of the noble bridal company with a very sharp
show of teeth, then displayed for the first time. He made love in a
coach and six, and married in a coach and twelve, and all his horses
were milk-white horses with one red spot on the back, which he caused
to be hidden by the harness. For the spot *would* come there, though
every horse was milk-white when Captain Murderer bought him. And
the spot was young bride's blood. (To this terrific point I am indebted
for my first personal experience of a shudder and cold beads on the
forehead.) When Captain Murderer had made an end of feasting and
revelry, and had dismissed the noble guests, and was alone with his
wife on the day month after their marriage, it was his whimsical
custom to produce a golden rolling-pin and a silver pie-board. Now
there was this special feature in the Captain's courtships, that he always
asked if the young lady could make pie-crust ; and if she couldn't by
nature or education, she was taught. Well. When the bride saw
Captain Murderer produce the golden rolling-pin and silver pie-board,
she remembered this, and turned up her laced silk sleeves to make a
pie. The Captain brought out a silver pie-dish of immense capacity,
and the Captain brought out flour and butter and eggs and all things
needful, except the inside of the pie ; of materials for the staple of the
pie itself the Captain brought out none. Then said the lovely bride,
" Dear Captain Murderer, what pie is this to be ? " He replied, " A
meat pie." Then said the lovely bride, " Dear Captain Murderer, I
see no meat." The Captain humorously retorted, " Look in the glass."
She looked in the glass, but still she saw no meat, and then the Captain
roared with laughter, and, suddenly frowning and drawing his sword,
bade her roll out the crust. So she rolled out the crust, dropping large
tears upon it all the time because he was so cross, and when she had
lined the dish with crust and had cut the crust all ready to fit the top,
the Captain called out, " *I* see the meat in the glass ! " And the bride
looked up at the glass, just in time to see the Captain cutting her head
off ; and he chopped her in pieces, and peppered her, and salted her,
and put her in the pie, and sent it to the baker's, and ate it all, and
picked the bones.
Captain Murderer went on in this way, prospering exceedingly, until
he came to choose a bride from two twin sisters, and at first didn't
know which to choose. For though one was fair and the other dark,
they were both equally beautiful. But the fair twin loved him, and
the dark twin hated him, so he chose the fair one. The dark twin
would have prevented the marriage if she could, but she couldn't ;
however, on the night before it, much suspecting Captain Murderer,

she stole out and climbed his garden wall, and looked in at his window through a chink in the shutter, and saw him having his teeth filed sharp. Next day she listened all day, and heard him make his joke about the house-lamb. And that day month he had the paste rolled out, and cut the fair twin's head off, and chopped her in pieces, and peppered her, and salted her, and put her in the pie, and sent it to the baker's, and ate it all, and picked the bones.

Now the dark twin had had her suspicions much increased by the filing of the Captain's teeth, and again by the house-lamb joke. Putting all things together when he gave out that her sister was dead, she divined the truth, and determined to be revenged. So she went up to Captain Murderer's house, and knocked at the knocker and pulled at the bell, and when the Captain came to the door, said : " Dear Captain Murderer, marry me next, for I always loved you and was jealous of my sister." The Captain took it as a compliment, and made a polite answer, and the marriage was quickly arranged. On the night before it, the bride again climbed to his window, and again saw him having his teeth filed sharp. At this sight she laughed such a terrible laugh at the chink in the shutter that the Captain's blood curdled, and he said : " I hope nothing has disagreed with me ! " At that she laughed again, a still more terrible laugh, and the shutter was opened and search made, but she was nimbly gone, and there was no one. Next day they went to church in a coach and twelve, and were married. And that day month she rolled the pie-crust out, and Captain Murderer cut her head off, and chopped her in pieces, and peppered her, and salted her, and put her in the pie, and sent it to the baker's, and ate it all, and picked the bones.

But before she began to roll out the paste she had taken a deadly poison of a most awful character, distilled from toads' eyes and spiders' knees ; and Captain Murderer had hardly picked her last bone, when he began to swell, and to turn blue, and to be all over spots, and to scream. And he went on swelling and turning bluer, and being more all over spots and screaming, until he reached from floor to ceiling and from wall to wall ; and then, at one o'clock in the morning, he blew up with a loud explosion. At the sound of it all the milk-white horses in the stables broke their halters and went mad, and then they galloped over everybody in Captain Murderer's house (beginning with the family blacksmith who had filed his teeth) until the whole were dead, and then they galloped away.

Hundreds of times did I hear this legend of Captain Murderer in my early youth, and added hundreds of times was there a mental compulsion upon me in bed to peep in at his window as the dark twin peeped, and to revisit his horrible house, and look at him in his blue and spotty and screaming stage, as he reached from floor to ceiling and from wall to wall. The young woman who brought me acquainted with Captain Murderer had a fiendish enjoyment of my terrors, and used to begin, I remember—as a sort of introductory overture—by clawing the air with both hands, and uttering a long, low, hollow groan. So acutely did I suffer from this ceremony in combination with this infernal Captain, that I sometimes used to plead I thought I was hardly strong enough and old enough to hear the story again just yet. But she never spared me one word of it, and indeed commended the awful chalice to my lips as the only preservative known to science against "The Black Cat"—a weird and glaring-eyed supernatural Tom, who was reputed to prowl about the world by night, sucking the breath of infancy, and who was endowed with a special thirst (as I was given to understand) for mine.

This female bard—may she have been repaid my debt of obligation to her in the matter of nightmares and perspirations !—reappears in my memory as the daughter of a shipwright. Her name was Mercy, though she had none on me. There was something of a shipbuilding flavour in the following story. As it always recurs to me in a vague association with calomel pills, I believe it to have been reserved for dull nights when I was low with medicine.

There was once a shipwright, and he wrought in a Government Yard, and his name was Chips. And his father's name before him was Chips, and *his* father's name before *him* was Chips, and they were all Chipses. And Chips the father had sold himself to the Devil for an iron pot and a bushel of tenpenny nails and half a ton of copper and a rat that could speak ; and Chips the grandfather had sold himself to the Devil for an iron pot and a bushel of tenpenny nails and half a ton of copper and a rat that could speak ; and Chips the great-grandfather had disposed of himself in the same direction on the same terms ; and the bargain had run in the family for a long, long time. So, one day when young Chips was at work in the Dock Slip all alone, down in the dark hold of an old Seventy-four that was haled up for repairs, the Devil presented himself, and remarked—

> " A Lemon has pips,
> And a Yard has ships,
> And *I*'ll have Chips !"

(I don't know why, but this fact of the Devil's expressing himself in rhyme was peculiarly trying to me.) Chips looked up when he heard the words, and there he saw the Devil with saucer eyes that squinted on a terrible great scale, and that struck out sparks of blue fire continually. And whenever he winked his eyes, showers of blue sparks came out, and his eyelashes made a clattering like flints and steels striking lights. And hanging over one of his arms by the handle was an iron pot, and under that arm was a bushel of tenpenny nails, and under his other arm was half a ton of copper, and sitting on one of his shoulders was a rat that could speak. So the Devil said again—

> " A Lemon has pips,
> And a Yard has ships,
> And *I*'ll have Chips !"

(The invariable effect of this alarming tautology on the part of the Evil Spirit was to deprive me of my senses for some moments.) So Chips answered never a word, but went on with his work. "What are you doing, Chips?" said the rat that could speak. "I am putting in new planks where you and your gang have eaten old away," said Chips. "But we'll eat them too," said the rat that could speak; "and we'll let in the water and drown the crew, and we'll eat them too." Chips, being only a shipwright, and not a Man-of-war's man, said, "You are welcome to it." But he couldn't keep his eyes off the half a ton of copper or the bushel of tenpenny nails; for nails and copper are a shipwright's sweethearts, and shipwrights will run away with them whenever they can. So the Devil said, "I see what you are looking at, Chips. You had better strike the bargain. You know the terms. Your father before you was well acquainted with them, and so were your grandfather and great-grandfather before him." Says Chips, "I like the copper, and I like the nails, and I don't mind the pot, but I don't like the rat." Says the Devil, fiercely, "You can't have the metal without him—and *he's* a curiosity. I'm going." Chips, afraid of losing the half a ton of copper and the bushel of nails, then said, "Give us hold!" So he got the copper and the nails and the pot and the rat that could speak, and the Devil vanished. Chips sold the copper, and he sold the nails, and he would have sold the pot; but whenever he offered it for sale, the rat was in it, and the dealers dropped it, and would have nothing to say to the bargain. So Chips resolved to kill the rat, and, being at work in the Yard one day with a great kettle of hot pitch on one side of him and the iron pot with the rat in it on the other, he turned the scalding pitch into the pot, and filled it full. Then he kept his eye upon it till it cooled and hardened, and then he let it stand for twenty days, and then he heated the pitch again and turned it back into the kettle, and then he sank the pot in water for twenty days more, and then he got the smelters to put it in the furnace for twenty days more, and then they gave it him out, red-hot, and looking like red-hot glass instead of iron—yet there was the rat in it, just the same as ever! And the moment it caught his eye, it said with a jeer—

> "A Lemon has pips,
> And a Yard has ships,
> And *I'*ll have Chips!"

(For this Refrain I had waited since its last appearance, with inexpressible horror, which now culminated.) Chips now felt certain in his own mind that the rat would stick to him; the rat, answering his thought, said, "I will—like pitch!"

Now as the rat leaped out of the pot when it had spoken, and made off, Chips began to hope that it wouldn't keep its word. But a terrible thing happened next day. For, when dinner-time came, and the Dock-bell rang to strike work, he put his rule into the long pocket at the side of his trousers, and there he found a rat—not that rat, but another rat. And in his hat he found another; and in his pocket-handkerchief another; and in the sleeves of his coat, when he pulled it on to go to dinner, two more. And from that time he found himself so frightfully intimate with all the rats in the Yard, that they climbed up his legs when he was at work, and sat on his tools while he used them. And they could all speak to one another, and he understood what they said. And they got into his lodging, and into his bed, and into his teapot, and into his beer, and into his boots. And he was going to be married to a corn-chandler's daughter ; and when he gave her a workbox he had himself made for her, a rat jumped out of it ; and when he put his arm round her waist, a rat clung about her ; so the marriage was broken off, though the banns were already twice put up—which the parish clerk well remembers, for, as he handed the book to the clergyman for the second time of asking, a large fat rat ran over the leaf. (By this time a special cascade of rats was rolling down my back, and the whole of my small listening person was overrun with them. At intervals ever since I have been morbidly afraid of my own pocket, lest my exploring hand should find a specimen or two of those vermin in it.)

You may believe that all this was very terrible to Chips ; but even all this was not the worst. He knew besides what the rats were doing, wherever they were. So sometimes he would cry aloud, when he was at his club at night, " Oh ! keep the rats out of the convicts' burying-ground ! Don't let them do that ! " Or, " There's one of them at the cheese down-stairs ! " Or, " There's two of them smelling at the baby in the garret ! " Or other things of that sort. At last he was voted mad, and lost his work in the Yard, and could get no other work. But King George wanted men, so before very long he got pressed for a sailor. And so he was taken off in a boat one evening to his ship, lying at Spithead, ready to sail. And so the first thing he made out in her as he got near her was the figure-head of the old Seventy-four, where he had seen the Devil. She was called the *Argonaut,* and they rowed right under the bowsprit where the figure-head of the *Argonaut,* with a sheepskin in his hand and a blue gown on, was looking out to sea ; and sitting staring on his forehead was the rat who could speak, and his exact words were these : " Chips ahoy ! Old boy ! We've pretty well eat them too, and we'll drown the crew, and will eat them too ! " (Here I always became exceedingly faint, and would have asked for water, but that I was speechless.)

The ship was bound for the Indies ; and if you don't know where that is, you ought to know it, and angels will never love you. (Here I felt myself an outcast from a future state.) The ship set sail that very night, and she sailed, and sailed, and sailed. Chips's feelings were dreadful. Nothing ever equalled his terrors. No wonder, At last, one day he asked leave to speak to the Admiral. The Admiral giv' leave. Chips went down on his knees in the Great State Cabin. " Your Honour, unless your Honour, without a moment's loss of time, makes sail for the nearest shore, this is a doomed ship, and her name is the Coffin ! " " Young man, your words are a madman's words." " Your Honour, no ; they are nibbling us away." " They ? " " Your Honour, them dreadful rats. Dust and hollowness where solid oak

ought to be ! Rats nibbling a grave for every man on board ! Oh !
Does your Honour love your Lady and your pretty children ? " " Yes,
my man, to be sure." " Then, for God's sake, make for the nearest
shore, for at this present moment the rats are all stopping in their work,
and are all looking straight towards you with bare teeth, and are all
saying to one another that you shall never, never, never, never see
your Lady and your children more." " My poor fellow, you are a case
for the doctor. Sentry, take care of this man ! "

So he was bled and he was blistered, and he was this and that, for
six whole days and nights. So then he again asked leave to speak to
the Admiral. The Admiral giv' leave. He went down on his knees in
the Great State Cabin. " Now, Admiral, you must die ! You took no
warning ; you must die ! The rats are never wrong in their calculations,
and they make out that they'll be through at twelve to-night. So you
must die !—With me and all the rest ! " And so at twelve o'clock there
was a great leak reported in the ship, and a torrent of water rushed in
and nothing could stop it, and they all went down, every living soul.
And what the rats—being water-rats—left of Chips, at last floated to
shore, and sitting on him was an immense overgrown rat, laughing,
that dived when the corpse touched the beach and never came up. And
there was a deal of seaweed on the remains. And if you get thirteen
bits of seaweed, and dry them and burn them in the fire, they will go
off like in these thirteen words as plain as plain can be—

> " A Lemon has pips,
> And a Yard has ships,
> And I've got Chips ! "

The same female bard—descended, possibly, from those terrible old
Scalds who seem to have existed for the express purpose of addling the
brains of mankind when they begin to investigate languages—made a
standing pretence which greatly assisted in forcing me back to a number
of hideous places that I would by all means have avoided. This
pretence was, that all her ghost stories had occurred to her own
relations. Politeness towards a meritorious family, therefore, forbade
my doubting them, and they acquired an air of authentication that
impaired my digestive powers for life. There was a narrative concerning an unearthly animal foreboding death, which appeared in the open
street to a parlour-maid who " went to fetch the beer " for supper : first
(as I now recall it) assuming the likeness of a black dog, and gradually
rising on its hind-legs and swelling into the semblance of some quadruped
greatly surpassing a hippopotamus : which apparition—not because I
deemed it in the least improbable, but because I felt it to be really too
large to bear—I feebly endeavoured to explain away. But, on Mercy's
retorting with wounded dignity that the parlour-maid was her own
sister-in-law, I perceived there was no hope, and resigned myself to this
zoological phenomenon as one of my many pursuers. There was another
narrative describing the apparition of a young woman who came out of
a glass case and haunted another young woman until the other young

woman questioned it and elicited that its bones (Lord ! To think of its being so particular about its bones !) were buried under the glass case, whereas she required them to be interred, with every Undertaking solemnity up to twenty-four pound ten, in another particular place. This narrative I considered I had a personal interest in disproving, because we had glass cases at home, and how, otherwise, was I to be guaranteed from the intrusion of young women requiring *me* to bury them up to twenty-four pound ten, when I had only twopence a week ? But my remorseless nurse cut the ground from under my tender feet, by informing me that She was the other young woman ; and I couldn't say " I don't believe you " ; it was not possible.

Such are a few of the uncommercial journeys that I was forced to make, against my will, when I was very young and unreasoning. And really, as to the latter part of them, it is not so very long ago—now I come to think of it—that I was asked to undertake them once again, with a steady countenance.

XVI

ARCADIAN LONDON

BEING in a humour for complete solitude and uninterrupted meditation this autumn, I have taken a lodging for six weeks in the most unfrequented part of England—in a word, in London.

The retreat into which I have withdrawn myself is Bond Street. From this lonely spot I make pilgrimages into the surrounding wilderness, and traverse extensive tracts of the Great Desert. The first solemn feeling of isolation overcome, the first oppressive consciousness of profound retirement conquered, I enjoy that sense of freedom, and feel reviving within me that latent wildness of the original savage, which has been (upon the whole somewhat frequently) noticed by Travellers.

My lodgings are at a hatter's—my own hatter's. After exhibiting no articles in his window for some weeks but sea-side wide-awakes, shooting-caps, and a choice of rough waterproof headgear for the moors and mountains, he has put upon the heads of his family as much of this stock as they could carry, and has taken them off to the Isle of Thanet. His young man alone remains—and remains alone—in the shop. The young man has let out the fire at which the irons are heated, and, saving his strong sense of duty, I see no reason why he should take the shutters down.

Happily for himself and for his country, the young man is a Volunteer ; most happily for himself, or I think he would become the prey of a settled melancholy. For to live surrounded by human hats, and alienated from human heads to fit them on, is surely a great endurance. But the young man, sustained by practising his exercise, and by constantly furbishing up his regulation plume (it is unnecessary to observe that, as a hatter, he is in a cock's-feather corps), is resigned and uncomplaining. On a Saturday, when he closes early and gets his Knickerbockers on, he is even cheerful. I am gratefully particular in this reference to him, because he is my companion through many peaceful hours. My hatter has a desk up certain steps behind his counter, enclosed like the clerk's desk at Church. I shut myself into this place of seclusion after breakfast and meditate. At such times I observe the young man loading an imaginary rifle with the greatest precision, and maintaining a most galling and destructive fire upon the national enemy. I thank him publicly for his companionship and his patriotism.

The simple character of my life, and the calm nature of the scenes by which I am surrounded, occasion me to rise early. I go forth in my slippers and promenade the pavement. It is pastoral to feel the freshness of the air in the uninhabited town, and to appreciate the shepherdess character of the few milkwomen who purvey so little milk that it would be worth nobody's while to adulterate it, if anybody were left to undertake the task. On the crowded sea-shore the great demand for milk, combined with the strong local temptation of chalk, would betray itself in the lowered quality of the article. In Arcadian London I derive it from the cow.

The Arcadian simplicity of the metropolis altogether, and the primitive ways into which it has fallen in this autumnal Golden Age, make it entirely new to me. Within a few hundred yards of my retreat is the house of a friend who maintains a most sumptuous butler. I never, until yesterday, saw that butler out of superfine black broadcloth. Until yesterday, I never saw him off duty, never saw him (he is the best of butlers) with the appearance of having any mind for anything but the glory of his master and his master's friends. Yesterday morning, walking in my slippers near the house of which he is the prop and ornament—a house now a waste of shutters—I encountered that butler, also in his slippers, and in a shooting suit of one colour, and in a low-crowned straw hat, smoking an early cigar. He felt that we had formerly met in another state of existence, and that we were translated into a new sphere. Wisely and well, he passed me without recognition. Under his arm he carried the morning paper, and shortly afterwards I saw him sitting on a rail in the pleasant open landscape of Regent Street, perusing it at his ease under the ripening sun.

My landlord having taken his whole establishment to be salted down, I am waited on by an elderly woman labouring under a chronic sniff, who, at the shadowy hour of half-past nine o'clock of every evening, gives admittance at the street door to a meagre and mouldy old man whom I have never yet seen detached from a flat pint of beer in a pewter pot. The meagre and mouldy old man is her husband, and the pair have a dejected consciousness that they are not justified in appearing on the surface of the earth. They come out of some hole when London empties itself, and go in again when it fills. I saw them arrive

on the evening when I myself took possession, and they arrived with
the flat pint of beer, and their bed in a bundle. The old man is a weak
old man, and appeared to me to get the bed down the kitchen stairs
by tumbling down with and upon it. They make their bed in the
lowest and remotest corner of the basement, and they smell of bed, and
have no possession but bed—unless it be (which I rather infer from an
undercurrent of flavour in them) cheese. I know their name through
the chance of having called the wife's attention, at half-past nine on
the second evening of our acquaintance, to the circumstance of there
being some one at the house door, when she apologetically explained,
"It's on'y Mr. Klem." What becomes of Mr. Klem all day, or when
he goes out, or why, is a mystery I cannot penetrate; but at half-past
nine he never fails to turn up on the doorstep with the flat pint of beer.
And the pint of beer, flat as it is, is so much more important than
himself, that it always seems to my fancy as if it had found him
drivelling in the street and had humanely brought him home. In
making his way below, Mr. Klem never goes down the middle of the
passage, like another Christian, but shuffles against the wall as if
entreating me to take notice that he is occupying as little space as
possible in the house; and whenever I come upon him face to face, he
backs from me in fascinated confusion. The most extraordinary
circumstance I have traced in connection with this aged couple is that
there is a Miss Klem, their daughter, apparently ten years older than
either of them, who has also a bed and smells of it, and carries it about
the earth at dusk and hides it in deserted houses. I came into this
piece of knowledge through Mrs. Klem's beseeching me to sanction
the sheltering of Miss Klem under that roof for a single night,
"between her takin' care of the upper part in Pall Mall which the
family of his back, and a 'ouse in Serjameses Street, which the family
of leaves towng termorrer." I gave my gracious consent (having
nothing that I know of to do with it), and in the shadowy hours Miss
Klem became perceptible on the doorstep, wrestling with a bed in a
bundle. Where she made it up for the night I cannot positively state,
but I think in a sink. I know that, with the instinct of a reptile or an
insect, she stowed it and herself away in deep obscurity. In the Klem
family I have noticed another remarkable gift of nature, and that is a
power they possess of converting everything into flue. Such broken
victuals as they take by stealth appear (whatever the nature of the
viands) invariably to generate flue; and even the nightly pint of beer,
instead of assimilating naturally, strikes me as breaking out in that
form, equally on the shabby gown of Mrs. Klem and the threadbare
coat of her husband.

Mrs. Klem has no idea of my name—as to Mr. Klem, he has no idea
of anything—and only knows me as her good gentleman. Thus, if
doubtful whether I am in my room or no, Mrs. Klem taps at the door
and says, " Is my good gentleman here ? " Or, if a messenger desiring
to see me were consistent with my solitude, she would show him in
with " Here is my good gentleman." I find this to be a generic custom.

For I meant to have observed before now, that in its Arcadian time all my part of London is indistinctly pervaded by the Klem species. They creep about with beds, and go to bed in miles of deserted houses. They hold no companionship, except that sometimes, after dark, two of them will emerge from opposite houses, and meet in the middle of the road as on neutral ground, or will peep from adjoining houses over an interposing barrier of area railings, and compare a few reserved mistrustful notes respecting their good ladies or their good gentlemen. This I have discovered in the course of various solitary rambles I have taken Northward from my retirement, along the awful perspectives of Wimpole Street, Harley Street, and similar frowning regions. Their effect would be scarcely distinguishable from that of the primeval forests, but for the Klem stragglers ; these may be dimly observed, when the heavy shadows fall, flitting to and fro, putting up the door-chain, taking in the pint of beer, lowering like phantoms at the dark parlour windows, or secretly consorting underground with the dust-bin and the water-cistern.

In the Burlington Arcade I observe, with peculiar pleasure, a primitive state of manners to have superseded the baneful influence of ultra-civilisation. Nothing can surpass the innocence of the ladies' shoe-shops, the artificial flower repositories, and the head-dress depôts. They are in strange hands at this time of year—hands of unaccustomed persons, who are imperfectly acquainted with the prices of the goods, and contemplate them with unsophisticated delight and wonder. The children of these virtuous people exchange familiarities in the Arcade, and temper the asperity of the two tall beadles. Their youthful prattle blends in an unwonted manner with the harmonious shade of the scene, and the general effect is as of the voices of birds in a grove. In this happy restoration of the golden time it has been my privilege even to see the bigger beadle's wife. She brought him his dinner in a basin, and he ate it in his arm-chair, and afterwards fell asleep like a satiated child. At Mr. Truefitt's, the excellent hairdresser's, they are learning French to beguile the time, and even the few solitaries left on guard at Mr. Atkinson's, the perfumer's round the corner (generally the most inexorable gentleman in London, and the most scornful of three-and-sixpence), condescend a little, as they drowsily bide or recall their turn for chasing the ebbing Neptune on the ribbed sea-sand. From Messrs. Hunt and Roskell's, the jewellers, all things are absent but the precious stones, and the gold and silver, and the soldierly pensioner at the door with his decorated breast. I might stand night and day for a month to come, in Saville Row, with my tongue out, yet not find a doctor to look at it for love or money. The dentists' instruments are rusting in their drawers, and their horrible cool parlours, where people pretend to read the Every-Day Book and not to be afraid, are doing penance for their grimness in white sheets. The light-weight of shrewd appearance, with one eye always shut up, as if he were eating a sharp gooseberry in all seasons, who usually stands at the gateway of the livery stables on very little legs under a very large waistcoat, has gone to Doncaster.

Of such undesigning aspect is his guileless yard now, with its gravel and scarlet beans, and the yellow Brake housed under a glass roof in a corner, that I almost believe I could not be taken in there if I tried. In the places of business of the great tailors the cheval-glasses are dim and dusty for lack of being looked into. Ranges of brown paper coat and waistcoat bodies look as funereal as if they were the hatchments of the customers with whose names they are inscribed ; the measuring tapes hang idle on the wall ; the order-taker, left on the hopeless chance of some one looking in, yawns in the last extremity over the books of patterns, as if he were trying to read that entertaining library. The hotels in Brook Street have no one in them, and the staffs of servants stare disconsolately for next season out of all the windows. The very man who goes about like an erect Turtle, between two boards recommendatory of the Sixteen Shilling Trousers, is aware of himself as a hollow mockery, and eats filberts while he leans his hinder shell against a wall.

Among these tranquillising objects it is my delight to walk and meditate. Soothed by the repose around me, I wander insensibly to considerable distances, and guide myself back by the stars. Thus I enjoy the contrast of a few still partially inhabited and busy spots where all the lights are not fled, where all the garlands are not dead, whence all but I have not departed. Then does it appear to me that in this age three things are clamorously required of Man in the miscellaneous thoroughfares of the metropolis. Firstly, that he have his boots cleaned. Secondly, that he eat a penny ice. Thirdly, that he get himself photographed. Then do I speculate, What have those seam-worn artists been who stand at the photograph doors in Greek caps, sample in hand, and mysteriously salute the public—the female public with a pressing tenderness—to come in and be " took " ? What did they do with their greasy blandishments before the era of cheap photography ? Of what class were their previous victims, and how victimised ? And how did they get, and how did they pay for, that large collection of likenesses, all purporting to have been taken inside, with the taking of none of which had that establishment any more to do than with the taking of Delhi ?

But these are small oases, and I am soon back again in metropolitan Arcadia. It is my impression that much of its serene and peaceful character is attributable to the absence of customary Talk. How do I know but there may be subtle influences in Talk, to vex the souls of men who don't hear it ? How do I know but that Talk, five, ten, twenty miles off, may get into the air and disagree with me ? If I rise from my bed, vaguely troubled and wearied and sick of my life, in the session of Parliament, who shall say that my noble friend, my right reverend friend, my right honourable friend, my honourable friend, my honourable and learned friend, or my honourable and gallant friend, may not be responsible for that effect upon my nervous system ? Too much Ozone in the air, I am informed and fully believe (though I have no idea what it is), would affect me in a marvellously disagreeable way ː

why may not too much Talk? I don't see or hear the Ozone; I don't see or hear the Talk. And there is so much Talk, so much too much; such loud cry, and such scant supply of wool; such a deal of fleecing, and so little fleece! Hence, in the Arcadian season, I find it a delicious triumph to walk down to deserted Westminster, and see the Courts shut up; to walk a little further and see the Two Houses shut up; to stand in the Abbey Yard, like the New Zealander of the grand English History (concerning which unfortunate man a whole rookery of mares' nests is generally being discovered), and gloat upon the ruins of Talk. Returning to my primitive solitude and lying down to sleep, my grateful heart expands with the consciousness that there is no adjourned Debate, no ministerial explanation, nobody to give notice of intention to ask the noble Lord at the head of her Majesty's Government five-and-twenty bootless questions in one, no term time with legal argument, no Nisi Prius with eloquent appeal to British Jury; that the air will to-morrow, and to-morrow, and to-morrow, remain untroubled by this super-abundant generating of Talk. In a minor degree it is a delicious triumph to me to go into the club, and see the carpets up, and the Bores and the other dust dispersed to the four winds. Again, New Zealander-like, I stand on the cold hearth, and say in the solitude, "Here I watched Bore A 1, with voice always mysteriously low and head always mysteriously drooped, whispering political secrets into the ears of Adam's confiding children. Accursed be his memory for ever and a day!"

But I have all this time been coming to the point, that the happy nature of my retirement is most sweetly expressed in its being the abode of Love. It is, as it were, an inexpensive Agapemone: nobody's speculation: everybody's profit. The one great result of the resumption of primitive habits, and (convertible terms) the not having much to do, is the abounding of Love.

The Klem species are incapable of the softer emotions; probably, in that low nomadic race, the softer emotions have all degenerated into flue. But with this exception, all the sharers of my retreat make love.

I have mentioned Saville Row. We all know the Doctor's servant. We all know what a respectable man he is, what a hard dry man, what a firm man, what a confidential man: how he lets us into the waiting-room, like a man who knows minutely what is the matter with us, but from whom the rack should not wring the secret. In the prosaic "season" he has distinctly the appearance of a man conscious of money in the savings bank, and taking his stand on his respectability with both feet. At that time it is as impossible to associate him with relaxation, or any human weakness, as it is to meet his eye without feeling guilty of indisposition. In the blest Arcadian time, how changed! I have seen him, in a pepper-and-salt jacket—jacket—and drab trousers, with his arm round the waist of a bootmaker's housemaid, smiling in open day. I have seen him at the pump by the Albany, unsolicitedly pumping for two fair young creatures, whose figures, as they bent over their cans, were—if I may be allowed an original expression—a model for the sculptor. I have seen him trying the piano in the Doctor's drawing-room with his forefinger, and have heard him humming tunes in praise of lovely woman. I have seen him seated on a fire-engine, and going (obviously in search of excitement) to a fire. I saw him, one moonlight evening when the peace and purity of our Arcadian west were at their height, polk with the lovely daughter of a cleaner of gloves, from the door-steps of his own residence, across Saville Row, round by Clifford Street and Old Burlington Street, back to Burlington Gardens. Is this the Golden Age revived, or Iron London ?

The Dentist's servant. Is that man no mystery to us, no type of invisible power ? The tremendous individual knows (who else does ?) what is done with the extracted teeth ; he knows what goes on in the little room where something is always being washed or filed ; he knows what warm spicy infusion is put into the comfortable tumbler from which we rinse our wounded mouth, with a gap in it that feels a foot wide ; he knows whether the thing we spit into is a fixture communicating with the Thames, or could be cleared away for a dance ; he sees the horrible parlour when there are no patients in it, and he could reveal, if he would, what becomes of the Every-Day Book then. The conviction of my coward conscience when I see that man in a professional light is, that he knows all the statistics of my teeth and gums, my double teeth, my single teeth, my stopped teeth, and my sound. In this Arcadian rest I am fearless of him as of a harmless, powerless creature in a Scotch cap, who adores a young lady in a voluminous crinoline, at a neighbouring billiard-room, and whose passion would be uninfluenced if every one of her teeth were false. They may be. He takes them all on trust.

In secluded corners of the place of my seclusion there are little shops withdrawn from public curiosity, and never two together, where servants' perquisites are bought. The cook may dispose of grease at these modest and convenient marts ; the butler, of bottles ; the valet and lady's maid, of clothes ; most servants, indeed, of most things they may happen to lay hold of. I have been told that in sterner times loving correspondence, otherwise interdicted, may be maintained by letter through the agency of some of these useful establishments. In the Arcadian autumn no such device is necessary. Everybody loves, and openly and blamelessly loves. My landlord's young man loves the whole of one side of the way of Old Bond Street, and is beloved several doors up New Bond Street besides. I never look out of window but I see kissing of hands going on all around me. It is the morning custom to glide from shop to shop and exchange tender sentiments ; it is the evening custom for couples to stand hand in hand at house doors, or roam, linked in that flowery manner, through the unpeopled streets. There is nothing else to do but love ; and what there is to do, is done.

In unison with this pursuit, a chaste simplicity obtains in the domestic habits of Arcadia. Its few scattered people dine early, live moderately, sup socially. and sleep soundly. It is rumoured that the

Beadles of the Arcade, from being the mortal enemies of boys, have signed with tears an address to Lord Shaftesbury, and subscribed to a ragged school.   No wonder !   For they might turn their heavy maces into crooks and tend sheep in the Arcade, to the purling of the water-carts as they give the thirsty streets much more to drink than they can carry.

A happy Golden Age, and a serene tranquillity.   Charming picture, but it will fade.   The Iron Age will return, London will come back to town, if I show my tongue then in Saville Row for half a minute I shall be prescribed for, the Doctor's man and the Dentist's man will then pretend that these days of unprofessional innocence never existed. Where Mr. and Mrs. Klem and their bed will be at that time passes human knowledge ; but my hatter hermitage will then know them no more, nor will it then know me.   The desk at which I have written these meditations will retributively assist at the making out of my account, and the wheels of gorgeous carriages and the hoofs of high-stepping horses will crush the silence out of Bond Street—will grind Arcadia away, and give it to the elements in granite powder.

XVII

THE ITALIAN PRISONER

The rising of the Italian people from under their unutterable wrongs, and the tardy burst of day upon them after the long, long night of oppression that has darkened their beautiful country, has naturally caused my mind to dwell often of late on my own small wanderings in Italy.   Connected with them is a curious little drama, in which the character I myself sustained was so very subordinate, that I may relate its story without any fear of being suspected of self-display.   It is strictly a true story.

I am newly arrived one summer evening in a certain small town on the Mediterranean.   I have had my dinner at the inn, and I and the mosquitoes are coming out into the streets together.   It is far from Naples ; but a bright, brown, plump little woman-servant at the inn is a Neapolitan, and is so vivaciously expert in pantomimic action, that in the single moment of answering my request to have a pair of shoes cleaned which I have left up-stairs, she plies imaginary brushes, and goes completely through the motions of polishing the shoes up and laying them at my feet.   I smile at the brisk little woman in perfect satisfaction with her briskness ; and the brisk little woman, amiably pleased with me because I am pleased with her, claps her hands and laughs delightfully.   We are in the inn-yard.   As the little woman's bright eyes sparkle on the cigarette I am smoking, I make bold to offer her one ; she accepts it none the less merrily because I touch a most charming little dimple in her fat cheek with its light paper end.

Glancing up at the many green lattices to assure herself that the mistress is not looking on, the little woman then puts her two little dimpled arms akimbo, and stands on tiptoe to light her cigarette at mine. "And now, dear little Sir," says she, puffing out smoke in a most innocent and cherubic manner, "keep quite straight on, take the first to the right, and probably you will see him standing at his door."

I have a commission to "him," and I have been inquiring about him. I have carried the commission about Italy several months. Before I left England there came to me one night a certain generous and gentle English nobleman (he is dead in these days when I relate the story, and exiles have lost their best British friend), with this request: "Whenever you come to such a town, will you seek out one Giovanni Carlavero, who keeps a little wine-shop there, mention my name to him suddenly, and observe how it affects him?" I accepted the trust, and am on my way to discharge it.

The sirocco has been blowing all day, and it is a hot unwholesome evening with no cool sea-breeze. Mosquitoes and fireflies are lively enough, but most other creatures are faint. The coquettish airs of pretty young women in the tiniest and wickedest of dolls' straw hats, who lean out at opened lattice blinds, are almost the only airs stirring. Very ugly and haggard old women with distaffs, and with a gray tow upon them that looks as if they were spinning out their own hair (I suppose they were once pretty, too, but it is very difficult to believe so), sit on the footway leaning against house walls. Everybody who has come for water to the fountain stays there, and seems incapable of any such energetic idea as going home. Vespers are over, though not so long but that I can smell the heavy resinous incense as I pass the church. No man seems to be at work, save the coppersmith. In an Italian town he is always at work, and always thumping in the deadliest manner.

I keep straight on, and come in due time to the first on the right: a narrow dull street, where I see a well-favoured man of good stature and military bearing, in a great cloak, standing at a door. Drawing nearer to this threshold, I see it is the threshold of a small wine-shop; and I can just make out, in the dim light, the inscription that it is kept by Giovanni Carlavero.

I touch my hat to the figure in the cloak, and pass in, and draw a stool to a little table. The lamp (just such another as they dig out of Pompeii) is lighted, but the place is empty. The figure in the cloak has followed me in, and stands before me.

"The master?"

"At your service, Sir."

"Please to give me a glass of the wine of the country."

He turns to a little counter to get it. As his striking face is pale, and his action is evidently that of an enfeebled man, I remark that I fear he has been ill. It is not much, he courteously and gravely answers, though bad while it lasts: the fever.

As he sets the wine on the little table, to his manifest surprise, I lay my hand on the back of his, look him in the face, and say in a low voice : "I am an Englishman, and you are acquainted with a friend of mine. Do you recollect ——? " and I mentioned the name of my generous countryman.

Instantly he utters a loud cry, bursts into tears, and falls on his knees at my feet, clasping my legs in both his arms and bowing his head to the ground.

Some years ago, this man at my feet, whose overfraught heart is heaving as if it would burst from his breast, and whose tears are wet upon the dress I wear, was a galley-slave in the North of Italy. He was a political offender, having been concerned in the then last rising, and was sentenced to imprisonment for life. That he would have died in his chains is certain, but for the circumstance that the Englishman happened to visit his prison.

It was one of the vile old prisons of Italy, and a part of it was below the waters of the harbour. The place of his confinement was an arched underground and under-water gallery, with a grill-gate at the entrance, through which it received such light and air as it got. Its condition was insufferably foul, and a stranger could hardly breathe in it, or see in it with the aid of a torch. At the upper end of this dungeon, and consequently in the worst position, as being the furthest removed from light and air, the Englishman first beheld him, sitting on an iron bed-stead to which he was chained by a heavy chain. His countenance impressed the Englishman as having nothing in common with the faces of the malefactors with whom he was associated, and he talked with him, and learnt how he came to be there.

When the Englishman emerged from the dreadful den into the light of day, he asked his conductor, the governor of the jail, why Giovanni Carlavero was put into the worst place.

"Because he is particularly recommended," was the stringent answer.

"Recommended, that is to say, for death?"

"Excuse me; particularly recommended," was again the answer.

"He has a bad tumour in his neck, no doubt occasioned by the hardship of his miserable life. If it continues to be neglected, and he remains where he is, it will kill him."

"Excuse me, I can do nothing. He is particularly recommended."

The Englishman was staying in that town, and he went to his home there ; but the figure of this man chained to the bedstead made it no home, and destroyed his rest and peace. He was an Englishman of an extraordinarily tender heart, and he could not bear the picture. He went back to the prison grate ; went back again and again, and talked to the man and cheered him. He used his utmost influence to get the man unchained from the bedstead, were it only for ever so short a time in the day, and permitted to come to the grate. It took a long time, but the Englishman's station, personal character, and steadiness of purpose wore out opposition so far, and that grace was at last accorded. Through the bars, when he could thus get light upon the tumour, the

Englishman lanced it, and it did well, and healed. His strong interest in the prisoner had greatly increased by this time, and he formed the desperate resolution that he would exert his utmost self-devotion and use his utmost efforts to get Carlavero pardoned.

If the prisoner had been a brigand and a murderer, if he had committed every non-political crime in the Newgate Calendar and out of it, nothing would have been easier than for a man of any court or priestly influence to obtain his release. As it was, nothing could have been more difficult. Italian authorities, and English authorities who had interest with them, alike assured the Englishman that his object was hopeless. He met with nothing but evasion, refusal, and ridicule. His political prisoner became a joke in the place. It was especially observable that English Circumlocution, and English Society on its travels, were as humorous on the subject as Circumlocution and Society may be on any subject without loss of caste. But the Englishman possessed (and proved it well in his life) a courage very uncommon among us ; he had not the least fear of being considered a bore, in a good humane cause. So he went on persistently trying, and trying, and trying, to get Giovanni Carlavero out. That prisoner had been rigorously re-chained after the tumour operation, and it was not likely that his miserable life could last very long.

One day, when all the town knew about the Englishman and his political prisoner, there came to the Englishman a certain sprightly Italian Advocate of whom he had some knowledge, and he made this strange proposal. "Give me a hundred pounds to obtain Carlavero's release. I think I can get him a pardon with that money. But I cannot tell you what I am going to do with the money, nor must you ever ask me the question if I succeed, nor must you ever ask me for an account of the money if I fail." The Englishman decided to hazard the hundred pounds. He did so, and heard not another word of the matter. For half a year and more the Advocate made no sign, and never once "took on" in any way, to have the subject on his mind. The Englishman was then obliged to change his residence to another and more famous town in the North of Italy. He parted from the poor prisoner with a sorrowful heart, as from a doomed man for whom there was no release but Death.

The Englishman lived in his new place of abode another half-year and more, and had no tidings of the wretched prisoner. At length, one day, he received from the Advocate a cool, concise, mysterious note, to this effect : "If you still wish to bestow that benefit upon the man in whom you were once interested, send me fifty pounds more, and I think it can be ensured." Now the Englishman had long settled in his mind that the Advocate was a heartless sharper, who had preyed upon his credulity and his interest in an unfortunate sufferer. So he sat down and wrote a dry answer, giving the Advocate to understand that he was wiser now than he had been formerly, and that no more money was extractable from his pocket.

He lived outside the city gates, some mile or two from the post-office, and was accustomed to walk into the city with his letters and post them himself. On a lovely spring day, when the sky was exquisitely blue, and the sea divinely beautiful, he took his usual walk, carrying this letter to the Advocate in his pocket. As he went along, his gentle heart was much moved by the loveliness of the prospect, and by the thought of the slowly-dying prisoner chained to the bedstead, for whom the universe had no delights. As he drew nearer and nearer to the city where he was to post the letter, he became very uneasy in his mind. He debated with himself, was it remotely possible, after all, that this sum of fifty pounds could restore the fellow-creature whom he pitied so much, and for whom he had striven so hard, to liberty? He was not a conventionally rich Englishman—very far from that—but he had a spare fifty pounds at the banker's. He resolved to risk it. Without doubt, God has recompensed him for the resolution.

He went to the banker's, and got a bill for the amount, and enclosed it in a letter to the Advocate that I wish I could have seen. He simply told the Advocate that he was quite a poor man, and that he was sensible it might be a great weakness in him to part with so much money on the faith of so vague a communication; but that there it was, and that he prayed the Advocate to make a good use of it. If he did otherwise, no good could ever come of it, and it would lie heavy on his soul one day.

Within a week, the Englishman was sitting at his breakfast, when he heard some suppressed sounds of agitation on the staircase, and Giovanni Carlavero leaped into the room and fell upon his breast, a free man!

Conscious of having wronged the Advocate in his own thoughts, the Englishman wrote him an earnest and grateful letter, avowing the fact, and entreating him to confide by what means and through what agency he had succeeded so well. The Advocate returned for answer through the post: "There are many things, as you know, in this Italy of ours, that are safest and best not even spoken of—far less written of. We may meet some day, and then I may tell you what you want to know; not here, and now." But the two never did meet again. The Advocate was dead when the Englishman gave me my trust; and how the man had been set free remained as great a mystery to the Englishman, and to the man himself, as it was to me.

But I knew this:—here was the man, this sultry night, on his knees at my feet, because I was the Englishman's friend; here were his tears upon my dress; here were his sobs choking his utterance; here were his kisses on my hands, because they had touched the hands that had worked out his release. He had no need to tell me it would be happiness to him to die for his benefactor; I doubt if I ever saw real, sterling, fervent gratitude of soul, before or since.

He was much watched and suspected, he said, and had had enough to do to keep himself out of trouble. This, and his not having prospered in his worldly affairs, had led to his having failed in his usual communications to the Englishman for—as I now remember the period—some two or three years. But his prospects were brighter, and his wife, who had been very ill, had recovered, and his fever had left him, and he had bought a little vineyard, and would I carry to his benefactor the first of its wine? Ay, that I would (I told him with enthusiasm), and not a drop of it should be spilled or lost!

He had cautiously closed the door before speaking of himself, and had talked with such excess of emotion, and in a provincial Italian so difficult to understand, that I had more than once been obliged to stop him, and beg him to have compassion on me and be slower and calmer. By degrees he became so, and tranquilly walked back with me to the hotel. There I sat down before I went to bed and wrote a faithful account of him to the Englishman, which I concluded by saying that I would bring the wine home, against any difficulties, every drop.

Early next morning, when I came out at the hotel door to pursue my journey, I found my friend waiting with one of those immense bottles in which the Italian peasants store their wine—a bottle holding some half-dozen gallons—bound round with basket-work for greater safety on the journey. I see him now, in the bright sunlight, tears of gratitude in his eyes, proudly inviting my attention to this corpulent bottle. (At the street-corner hard by, two high-flavoured able-bodied monks— pretending to talk together, but keeping their four evil eyes upon us.)

How the bottle had been got there did not appear; but the difficulty of getting it into the ramshackle vetturino carriage in which I was departing was so great, and it took up so much room when it was got in, that I elected to sit outside. The last I saw of Giovanni Carlavero was his running through the town by the side of the jingling wheels, clasping my hand as I stretched it down from the box, charging me with a thousand last loving and dutiful messages to his dear patron, and finally looking in at the bottle as it reposed inside, with an admiration of its honourable way of travelling that was beyond measure delightful.

And now, what disquiet of mind this dearly-beloved and highly-treasured Bottle began to cost me, no man knows. It was my precious charge through a long tour, and, for hundreds of miles, I never had it off my mind by day or by night. Over bad roads—and they were many —I clung to it with affectionate desperation. Up mountains, I looked in at it and saw it helplessly tilting over on its back, with terror. At innumerable inn-doors, when the weather was bad, I was obliged to be put into my vehicle before the Bottle could be got in, and was obliged to have the Bottle lifted out before human aid could come near me. The Imp of the same name, except that his associations were all evil and these associations were all good, would have been a less troublesome travelling companion. I might have served Mr. Cruikshank as a subject for a new illustration of the miseries of the Bottle. The National Temperance Society might have made a powerful Tract of me.

The suspicions that attached to this innocent Bottle greatly aggravated my difficulties. It was like the apple-pie in the child's book. Parma pouted at it, Modena mocked it, Tuscany tackled it, Naples nibbled it, Rome refused it, Austria accused it, Soldiers suspected it, Jesuits jobbed it. I composed a neat Oration, developing my inoffensive intentions in connection with this Bottle, and delivered it in an infinity of guard-houses, at a multitude of town gates, and on every drawbridge, angle, and rampart of a complete system of fortifications. Fifty times a day I got down to harangue an infuriated soldiery about the Bottle. Through the filthy degradation of the abject and vile Roman States I had as much difficulty in working my way with the Bottle as if it had bottled up a complete system of heretical theology. In the Neapolitan country, where everybody was a spy, a soldier, a priest, or a lazzarone, the shameless beggars of all four denominations incessantly pounced on the Bottle and made it a pretext for extorting money from me. Quires—quires do I say? Reams—of forms illegibly printed on whity-brown paper were filled up about the Bottle, and it was the subject of more stamping and sanding than I had ever seen before. In consequence of which haze of sand, perhaps, it was always irregular, and always latent with dismal penalties of going back or not going forward, which were only to be abated by the silver crossing of a base hand, poked shirtless out of a ragged uniform sleeve. Under all discouragements, however, I stuck to my Bottle, and held firm to my resolution that every drop of its contents should reach the Bottle's destination.

The latter refinement cost me a separate heap of troubles on its own separate account. What corkscrews did I see the military power bring out against that Bottle; what gimlets, spikes, divining rods, gauges, and unknown tests and instruments! At some places they persisted in declaring that the wine must not be passed, without being opened and tasted; I, pleading to the contrary, used then to argue the question seated on the Bottle lest they should open it in spite of me. In the southern parts of Italy more violent shrieking, face-making, and gesticulating, greater vehemence of speech and countenance and action went on about that Bottle than would attend fifty murders in a northern latitude. It raised important functionaries out of their beds in the dead of night. I have known half-a-dozen military lanterns to disperse themselves at all points of a great sleeping Piazza, each lantern summoning some official creature to get up, put on his cocked-hat instantly, and come and stop the Bottle. It was characteristic that while this innocent Bottle had such immense difficulty in getting from little town to town, Signor Mazzini and the fiery cross were traversing Italy from end to end.

Still I stuck to my Bottle, like any fine old English gentleman all of the olden time. The more the Bottle was interfered with, the stauncher I became (if possible) in my first determination that my countryman should have it delivered to him intact, as the man whom he had so nobly restored to life and liberty had delivered it to me. If ever I had been obstinate in my days—and I may have been, say, once or twice—I was obstinate about the Bottle. But I made it a rule always to keep a pocket full of small coin at its service, and never to be out of temper in its cause.   Thus I and the Bottle made our way. Once we had a break-down ; rather a bad break-down, on a steep high place with the sea below us, on a tempestuous evening when it blew great guns.   We were driving four wild horses abreast, Southern fashion, and there was some little difficulty in stopping them.   I was outside, and not thrown off ; but no words can describe my feelings when I saw the Bottle—travelling inside, as usual—burst the door open, and roll obesely out into the road.   A blessed Bottle with a charmed existence, he took no hurt, and we repaired damage, and went on triumphant.

A thousand representations were made to me that the Bottle must be left at this place, or that, and called for again.   I never yielded to one of them, and never parted from the Bottle, on any pretence, consideration, threat, or entreaty.   I had no faith in any official receipt for the Bottle, and nothing would induce me to accept one.   These unmanageable politics at last brought me and the Bottle, still triumph- ant, to Genoa.   There I took a tender and reluctant leave of him for a few weeks, and consigned him to a trusty English captain, to be conveyed to the Port of London by sea.

While the Bottle was on his voyage to England, I read the Shipping Intelligence as anxiously as if I had been an underwriter.   There was some stormy weather after I myself had got to England by way of Switzerland and France, and my mind greatly misgave me that the Bottle might be wrecked.   At last, to my great joy, I received notice of his safe arrival, and immediately went down to Saint Katharine's Docks, and found him in a state of honourable captivity in the Custom House.

The wine was mere vinegar when I set it down before the generous Englishman—probably it had been something like vinegar when I took it up from Giovanni Carlavero—but not a drop of it was spilled or gone. And the Englishman told me, with much emotion in his face and voice, that he had never tasted wine that seemed to him so sweet and sound. And long afterwards the Bottle graced his table.   And the last time I saw him in this world that misses him, he took me aside in a crowd, to say, with his amiable smile : " We were talking of you only to-day at dinner, and I wished you had been there, for I had some Claret up in Carlavero's Bottle."

XVIII

THE CALAIS NIGHT MAIL

It is an unsettled question with me whether I shall leave Calais something handsome in my will, or whether I shall leave it my malediction. I hate it so much, and yet I am always so very glad to see it, that I am in a state of constant indecision on this subject.

When I first made acquaintance with Calais, it was as a maundering young wretch in a clammy perspiration and dripping saline particles, who was conscious of no extremities but the one great extremity, sea-sickness—who was a mere bilious torso, with a mislaid headache somewhere in its stomach—who had been put into a horrible swing in Dover Harbour, and had tumbled giddily out of it on the French coast, or the Isle of Man, or anywhere. Times have changed, and now I enter Calais self-reliant and rational. I know where it is beforehand, I keep a look out for it, I recognize its landmarks when I see any of them, I am acquainted with its ways, and I know—and I can bear—its worst behaviour.

Malignant Calais! Low-lying alligator, evading the eyesight and discouraging hope! Dodging flat streak, now on this bow, now on that, now anywhere, now everywhere, now nowhere! In vain Cape Grinez, coming frankly forth into the sea, exhorts the failing to be stout of heart and stomach: sneaking Calais, prone behind its bar, invites emetically to despair. Even when it can no longer quite conceal itself in its muddy dock, it has an evil way of falling off, has Calais, which is more hopeless than its invisibility. The pier is all but on the bowsprit, and you think you are there—roll, roar, wash! —Calais has retired miles inland, and Dover has burst out to look for it. It has a last dip and slide in its character, has Calais, to be especially commended to the infernal gods. Thrice accursed be that garrison-town, when it dives under the boat's keel, and comes up a league or two to the right, with the packet shivering and spluttering and staring about for it!

Not but what I have my animosities towards Dover. I particularly detest Dover for the self-complacency with which it goes to bed. It always goes to bed (when I am going to Calais) with a more brilliant display of lamp and candle than any other town. Mr. and Mrs. Birmingham, host and hostess of the Lord Warden Hotel, are my much esteemed friends, but they are too conceited about the comforts of that establishment when the Night Mail is starting. I know it is a good house to stay at, and I don't want the fact insisted upon in all its warm bright windows at such an hour. I know the Warden is a stationary edifice that never rolls or pitches, and I object to its big outline seeming to insist upon that circumstance, and, as it were, to come over me with it, when I am reeling on the deck of the boat. Beshrew the Warden likewise, for obstructing that corner, and making the wind so angry as it rushes round. Shall I not know that it blows quite soon enough, without the officious Warden's interference?

As I wait here on board the night packet, for the South-Eastern Train to come down with the Mail, Dover appears to me to be illuminated for some intensely aggravating festivity in my personal dishonour. All its noises smack of taunting praises of the land, and dispraises of the gloomy sea, and of me for going on it. The drums upon the heights have gone to bed, or I know they would rattle taunts against me for having my unsteady footing on this slippery deck. The many gas eyes of the Marine Parade twinkle in an offensive manner, as if with derision. The distant dogs of Dover bark at me in my mis-shapen wrappers, as if I were Richard the Third.

A screech, a bell, and two red eyes come gliding down the Admiralty Pier with a smoothness of motion rendered more smooth by the heaving of the boat. The sea makes noises against the pier, as if several hippopotami were lapping at it, and were prevented by circumstances over which they had no control from drinking peaceably. We, the boat, become violently agitated—rumble, hum, scream, roar, and establish an immense family washing-day at each paddle-box. Bright patches break out in the train as the doors of the post-office vans are opened, and instantly stooping figures with sacks upon their backs begin to be beheld among the piles, descending as it would seem in ghostly procession to Davy Jones's Locker. The passengers come on board; a few shadowy Frenchmen, with hat-boxes shaped like the stoppers of gigantic case-bottles; a few shadowy Germans in immense fur coats and boots; a few shadowy Englishmen prepared for the worst and pretending not to expect it. I cannot disguise from my uncommercial mind the miserable fact that we are a body of outcasts; that the attendants on us are as scant in number as may serve to get rid of us with the least possible delay; that there are no night-loungers interested in us; that the unwilling lamps shiver and shudder at us; that the sole object is to commit us to the deep and abandon us. Lo, the two red eyes glaring in increasing distance, and then the very train itself has gone to bed before we are off!

What is the moral support derived by some sea-going amateurs from an umbrella? Why do certain voyagers across the Channel always put up that article, and hold it up with a grim and fierce tenacity? A fellow-creature near me—whom I only know to *be* a fellow-creature, because of his umbrella: without which he might be a dark bit of cliff, pier, or bulkhead—clutches that instrument with a desperate grasp, that will not relax until he lands at Calais. Is there any analogy, in certain constitutions, between keeping an umbrella up, and keeping the spirits up? A hawser thrown on board with a flop replies "Stand by!" "Stand by, below." "Half a turn ahead!" "Half a turn ahead!" "Half speed!" "Half speed!" "Port!" "Port!" "Steady!" "Steady!" "Go on!" "Go on!"

A stout wooden wedge driven in at my right temple and out at my left, a floating deposit of lukewarm oil in my throat, and a compression of the bridge of my nose in a blunt pair of pincers,—these are the personal sensations by which I know we are off, and by which I shall continue to know it until I am on the soil of France. My symptoms have scarcely established themselves comfortably, when two or three skating shadows that have been trying to walk or stand, get flung together, and other two or three shadows in tarpaulin slide with them into corners and cover them up. Then the South Foreland lights begin to hiccup at us in a way that bodes no good.

It is at about this period that my detestation of Calais knows no bounds. Inwardly I resolve afresh that I never will forgive that hated town. I have done so before, many times, but that is past. Let me register a vow. Implacable animosity to Calais everm—— that was an awkward sea, and the funnel seems of my opinion, for it gives a complaining roar.

The wind blows stiffly from the Nor'-East, the sea runs high, we ship a deal of water, the night is dark and cold, and the shapeless passengers lie about in melancholy bundles, as if they were sorted out for the laundress; but for my own uncommercial part I cannot pretend that I am much inconvenienced by any of these things. A general howling whistling flopping gurgling and scooping, I am aware of, and a general knocking about of Nature; but the impressions I receive are very vague. In a sweet faint temper, something like the smell of damaged oranges, I think I should feel languidly benevolent if I had time. I have not time, because I am under a curious compulsion to occupy myself with the Irish melodies. "Rich and rare were the gems she wore," is the particular melody to which I find myself devoted. I sing it to myself in the most charming manner and with the greatest expression. Now and then, I raise my head (I am sitting on the hardest of wet seats, in the most uncomfortable of wet attitudes, but I don't mind it,) and notice that I am a whirling shuttlecock between a fiery battledore of a lighthouse on the French coast and a fiery battledore of a lighthouse on the English coast; but I don't notice it particularly, except to feel envenomed in my hatred of Calais. Then I go on again, "Rich and rare were the ge-ems she-e-e-e wore, And a bright gold ring on her wa-and she bo-ore, But O her beauty was fa-a-a-a-r beyond"—I am particularly proud of my execution here, when I become aware of another awkward shock from the sea, and another protest from the funnel, and a fellow-creature at the paddle-box more audibly indisposed than I think he need be—"Her sparkling gems, or snow-white wand, But O her beauty was fa-a-a-a-r beyond"—another awkward one here, and the fellow-creature with the umbrella down and picked up, "Her spa-a-rkling ge-ems, or her Port! port! steady! steady! snow-white fellow-creature at the paddle-box very selfishly audible, bump roar wash white wand."

As my execution of the Irish melodies partakes of my imperfect perceptions of what is going on around me, so what is going on around me becomes something else than what it is. The stokers open the

furnace doors below, to feed the fires, and I am again on the box
of the old Exeter Telegraph fast coach, and that is the light of the
for ever extinguished coach-lamps, and the gleam on the hatches and
paddle-boxes is *their* gleam on cottages and haystacks, and the monotonous noise of the engines is the steady jingle of the splendid team.
Anon, the intermittent funnel roar of protest at every violent roll,
becomes the regular blast of a high-pressure engine, and I recognize the exceedingly explosive steamer in which I ascended the Mississippi when the American civil war was not, and when only its
causes were. A fragment of mast on which the light of a lantern
falls, an end of rope, and a jerking block or so, become suggestive of
Franconi's Circus at Paris where I shall be this very night mayhap
(for it must be morning now), and they dance to the self-same time
and tune as the trained steed, Black Raven. What may be the
speciality of these waves as they come rushing on, I cannot desert the
pressing demands made upon me by the gems she wore, to inquire,
but they are charged with something about Robinson Crusoe, and
I think it was in Yarmouth Roads that he first went a seafaring and
was near foundering (what a terrific sound that word had for me
when I was a boy!) in his first gale of wind. Still, through all this,
I must ask her (who *was* she I wonder!) for the fiftieth time, and
without ever stopping, Does she not fear to stray, So lone and lovely
through this bleak way, And are Erin's sons so good or so cold, As
not to be tempted by more fellow-creatures at the paddle-box or gold?
Sir Knight I feel not the least alarm, No son of Erin will offer me
harm, For though they love fellow-creature with umbrella down
again and golden store, Sir Knight they what a tremendous one love
honour and virtue more: For though they love Stewards with a
bull's eye bright, they'll trouble you for your ticket, sir—rough passage to-night!

I freely admit it to be a miserable piece of human weakness and
inconsistency, but I no sooner become conscious of those last words
from the steward than I begin to soften towards Calais. Whereas I
have been vindictively wishing that those Calais burghers who came
out of their town by a short cut into the History of England, with
those fatal ropes round their necks by which they have since been
towed into so many cartoons, had all been hanged on the spot, I now
begin to regard them as highly respectable and virtuous tradesmen.
Looking about me, I see the light of Cape Grinez well astern of the
boat on the davits to leeward, and the light of Calais Harbour un-
deniably at its old tricks, but still ahead and shining. Sentiments
of forgiveness of Calais, not to say of attachment to Calais, begin to
expand my bosom. I have weak notions that I will stay there a day
or two on my way back. A faded and recumbent stranger pausing in
a profound reverie over the rim of a basin, asks me what kind of place
Calais is? I tell him (Heaven forgive me!) a very agreeable place
indeed—rather hilly than otherwise.

So strangely goes the time, and on the whole so quickly—though

still I seem to have been on board a week—that I am bumped rolled
gurgled washed and pitched into Calais Harbour before her maiden
smile has finally lighted her through the Green Isle, When blest for
ever is she who relied, On entering Calais at the top of the tide.
For we have not to land to-night down among those slimy timbers—
covered with green hair as if it were the mermaids' favourite combing-
place—where one crawls to the surface of the jetty, like a stranded
shrimp, but we go steaming up the harbour to the Railway Station
Quay. And as we go, the sea washes in and out among piles and
planks, with dead heavy beats and in quite a furious manner (whereof
we are proud), and the lamps shake in the wind, and the bells of
Calais striking One seem to send their vibrations struggling against
troubled air, as we have come struggling against troubled water.
And now, in the sudden relief and wiping of faces, everybody on
board seems to have had a prodigious double-tooth out, and to be
this very instant free of the Dentist's hands. And now we all know
for the first time how wet and cold we are, and how salt we are; and
now I love Calais with my heart of hearts!

"Hôtel Dessin!" (but in this one case it is not a vocal cry; it is but
a bright lustre in the eyes of the cheery representative of that best of
inns). "Hôtel Meurice!" "Hôtel de France!" "Hôtel de Calais!"
"The Royal Hôtel, Sir, Angaishe ouse!" "You going to Parry, Sir?"
"Your baggage, registair froo, Sir?" Bless ye, my Touters, bless ye,
my commissionaires, bless ye, my hungry-eyed mysteries in caps of
a military form, who are always here, day or night, fair weather or
foul, seeking inscrutable jobs which I never see you get! Bless ye,
my Custom House officers in green and grey; permit me to grasp
the welcome hands that descend into my travelling-bag, one on each
side, and meet at the bottom to give my change of linen a peculiar
shake up, as if it were a measure of chaff or grain! I have nothing
to declare, Monsieur le Douanier, except that when I cease to breathe,
Calais will be found written on my heart. No article liable to local
duty have I with me, Monsieur l'Officier de l'Octroi, unless the overflowing of a breast devoted to your charming town should be in that
wise chargeable. Ah! see at the gangway by the twinkling lantern,
my dearest brother and friend, he once of the Passport Office, he who
collects the names! May he be for ever changeless in his buttoned
black surtout, with his note-book in his hand, and his tall black hat,
surmounting his round smiling patient face! Let us embrace, my
dearest brother. I am yours à tout jamais—for the whole of ever.

Calais up and doing at the railway station, and Calais down and
dreaming in its bed; Calais with something of "an ancient and fish-
like smell" about it, and Calais blown and sea-washed pure; Calais
represented at the Buffet by savoury roast fowls, hot coffee, cognac,
and Bordeaux; and Calais represented everywhere by flitting persons
with a monomania for changing money—though I never shall be able
to understand in my present state of existence how they live by it,
but I suppose I should, if I understood the currency question—Calais

en gros, and Calais *en détail*, forgive one who has deeply wronged you.—I was not fully aware of it on the other side, but I meant Dover.

Ding, ding! To the carriages, gentlemen the travellers. Ascend then, gentlemen the travellers, for Hazebroucke, Lille, Douai, Bruxelles, Arras, Amiens, and Paris! I, humble representative of the uncommercial interest, ascend with the rest. The train is light to-night, and I share my compartment with but two fellow-travellers; one, a compatriot in an obsolete cravat, who thinks it a quite unaccountable thing that they don't keep "London time" on a French railway, and who is made angry by my modestly suggesting the possibility of Paris time being more in their way; the other, a young priest, with a very small bird in a very small cage, who feeds the small bird with a quill, and then puts him up in the network above his head, where he advances twittering, to his front wires, and seems to address me in an electioneering manner. The compatriot (who crossed in the boat, and whom I judge to be some person of distinction, as he was shut up, like a stately species of rabbit, in a private hutch on deck) and the young priest (who joined us at Calais) are soon asleep, and then the bird and I have it all to ourselves.

A stormy night still; a night that sweeps the wires of the electric telegraph with a wild and fitful hand; a night so very stormy, with the added storm of the train-progress through it, that when the Guard comes clambering round to mark the tickets while we are at full speed (a really horrible performance in an express train, though he holds on to the open window by his elbows in the most deliberate manner), he stands in such a whirlwind that I grip him fast by the collar, and feel it next to manslaughter to let him go. Still, when he is gone, the small small bird remains at his front wires feebly twittering to me—twittering and twittering, until, leaning back in my place and looking at him in drowsy fascination, I find that he seems to jog my memory as we rush along.

Uncommercial travels (thus the small small bird) have lain in their idle thriftless way through all this range of swamp and dyke, as through many other odd places; and about here, as you very well know, are the queer old stone farm-houses, approached by drawbridges, and the windmills that you get at by boats. Here, are the lands where the women hoe and dig, paddling canoe-wise from field to field, and here are the cabarets and other peasant-houses where the stone dove-cotes in the littered yards are as strong as warders' towers in old castles. Here, are the long monotonous miles of canal, with the great Dutch-built barges garishly painted, and the towing girls, sometimes harnessed by the forehead, sometimes by the girdle and the shoulders, not a pleasant sight to see. Scattered through this country are mighty works of VAUBAN, whom you know about, and regiments of such corporals as you heard of once upon a time, and many a blue-eyed Bebelle. Through these flat districts, in the shining summer days, walk those long grotesque files of young novices in enormous shovel-hats, whom you remember blackening the ground checkered by the avenues of leafy trees.   And now that Hazebroucke slumbers certain kilometres ahead, recall the summer evening when your dusty feet strolling up from the station tended hap-hazard to a Fair there, where the oldest inhabitants were circling round and round a barrel-organ on hobby-horses, with the greatest gravity, and where the principal show in the Fair was a Religious Richardson's—literally, on its own announcement in great letters, THEATRE RELIGIEUX.   In which improving Temple, the dramatic representation was of "all the interesting events in the life of our Lord, from the Manger to the Tomb"; the principal female character, without any reservation or exception, being at the moment of your arrival, engaged in trimming the external Moderators (as it was growing dusk), while the next principal female character took the money, and the Young Saint John disported himself upside down on the platform.

Looking up at this point to confirm the small small bird in every particular he has mentioned, I find he has ceased to twitter, and has put his head under his wing.   Therefore, in my different way I follow the good example.

XIX

SOME RECOLLECTIONS OF MORTALITY

I HAD parted from the small bird at somewhere about four o'clock in the morning, when he had got out at Arras, and had been received by two shovel-hats in waiting at the station, who presented an appropriately ornithological and crow-like appearance.   My compatriot and I had gone on to Paris; my compatriot enlightening me occasionally with a long list of the enormous grievances of French railway travelling: every one of which, as I am a sinner, was perfectly new to me, though I have as much experience of French railways as most uncommercials.   I had left him at the terminus (through his conviction, against all explanation and remonstrance, that his baggage-ticket was his passenger-ticket), insisting in a very high temper to the functionary on duty, that in his own personal identity he was four packages weighing so many kilogrammes—as if he had been Cassim Baba!   I had bathed and breakfasted, and was strolling on the bright quays.   The subject of my meditations was the question whether it is positively in the essence and nature of things, as a certain school of Britons would seem to think it, that a Capital must be ensnared and enslaved before it can be made beautiful: when I lifted up my eyes and found that my feet, straying like my mind, had brought me to Notre-Dame.

That is to say, Notre-Dame was before me, but there was a large open space between us.   A very little while gone, I had left that space covered with buildings densely crowded; and now it was cleared for some new wonder in the way of public Street, Place, Garden, Fountain, or all four. Only the obscene little Morgue, slinking on the brink of the river and soon to come down, was left there, looking mortally ashamed of itself, and supremely wicked. I had but glanced at this old acquaintance, when I beheld an airy procession coming round in front of Notre-Dame, past the great hospital. It had something of a Masaniello look, with fluttering striped curtains in the midst of it, and it came dancing round the cathedral in the liveliest manner.

I was speculating on a marriage in Blouse-life, or a Christening, or some other domestic festivity which I would see out, when I found, from the talk of a quick rush of Blouses past me, that it was a Body coming to the Morgue. Having never before chanced upon this initiation, I constituted myself a Blouse likewise, and ran into the Morgue with the rest. It was a very muddy day, and we took in a quantity of mire with us, and the procession coming in upon our heels brought a quantity more. The procession was in the highest spirits, and consisted of idlers who had come with the curtained litter from its starting-place, and of all the reinforcements it had picked up by the way. It set the litter down in the midst of the Morgue, and then two Custodians proclaimed aloud that we were all "invited" to go out. This invitation was rendered the more pressing, if not the more flattering, by our being shoved out, and the folding-gates being barred upon us.

Those who have never seen the Morgue, may see it perfectly, by presenting to themselves an indifferently paved coach-house accessible from the street by a pair of folding-gates; on the left of the coach-house, occupying its width, any large London tailor's or linendraper's plate-glass window reaching to the ground; within the window, on two rows of inclined planes, what the coach-house has to show; hanging above, like irregular stalactites from the roof of a cave, a quantity of clothes—the clothes of the dead and buried shows of the coach-house.

We had been excited in the highest degree by seeing the Custodians pull off their coats and tuck up their shirt-sleeves, as the procession came along. It looked so interestingly like business. Shut out in the muddy street, we now became quite ravenous to know all about it. Was it river, pistol, knife, love, gambling, robbery, hatred, how many stabs, how many bullets, fresh or decomposed, suicide or murder? All wedged together, and all staring at one another with our heads thrust forward, we propounded these inquiries and a hundred more such. Imperceptibly, it came to be known that Monsieur the tall and sallow mason yonder, was acquainted with the facts. Would Monsieur the tall and sallow mason, surged at by a new wave of us, have the goodness to impart? It was but a poor old man, passing along the street under one of the new buildings, on whom a stone had fallen, and who had tumbled dead. His age? Another wave surged up against the tall and sallow mason, and our wave swept on and broke, and he was any age from sixty-five to ninety.

An old man was not much: moreover, we could have wished he had been killed by human agency—his own, or somebody's else: the latter, preferable—but our comfort was, that he had nothing about him to lead to his identification, and that his people must seek him here. Perhaps they were waiting dinner for him even now? We liked that. Such of us as had pocket-handkerchiefs took a slow intense protracted wipe at our noses, and then crammed our handkerchiefs into the breast of our blouses. Others of us who had no handkerchiefs administered a similar relief to our overwrought minds, by means of prolonged smears or wipes of our mouths on our sleeves. One man with a gloomy malformation of brow—a homicidal worker in white-lead, to judge from his blue tone of colour, and a certain flavour of paralysis pervading him—got his coat-collar between his teeth, and bit at it with an appetite. Several decent women arrived upon the outskirts of the crowd, and prepared to launch themselves into the dismal coach-house when opportunity should come; among them, a pretty young mother, pretending to bite the forefinger of her baby-boy, kept it between her rosy lips that it might be handy for guiding to point at the show. Meantime, all faces were turned towards the building, and we men waited with a fixed and stern resolution:—for the most part with folded arms. Surely, it was the only public French sight these uncommercial eyes had seen, at which the expectant people did not form *en queue*. But there was no such order of arrangement here; nothing but a general determination to make a rush for it, and a disposition to object to some boys who had mounted on the two stone posts by the hinges of the gates, with the design of swooping in when the hinges should turn.

Now, they turned, and we rushed! Great pressure, and a scream or two from the front. Then a laugh or two, some expressions of disappointment, and a slackening of the pressure and subsidence of the struggle.—Old man not there.

"But what would you have?" the Custodian reasonably argues, as he looks out at his little door. "Patience, patience! We make his toilette, gentlemen. He will be exposed presently. It is necessary to proceed according to rule. His toilette is not made all at a blow. He will be exposed in good time, gentlemen, in good time." And so retires, smoking, with a wave of his sleeveless arm towards the window, importing, "Entertain yourselves in the meanwhile with the other curiosities. Fortunately the Museum is not empty to-day."

Who would have thought of public fickleness even at the Morgue? But there it was, on that occasion. Three lately popular articles that had been attracting greatly when the litter was first descried coming dancing round the corner by the great cathedral, were so completely deposed now, that nobody save two little girls (one showing them to a doll) would look at them. Yet the chief of the three, the article in the front row, had received jagged injury of the left temple; and the

other two in the back row, the drowned two lying side by side with
their heads very slightly turned towards each other, seemed to be
comparing notes about it. Indeed, those two of the back row were
so furtive of appearance, and so (in their puffed way) assassinatingly
knowing as to the one of the front, that it was hard to think the three
had never come together in their lives, and were only chance companions after death. Whether or no this was the general, as it was
the uncommercial, fancy, it is not to be disputed that the group had
drawn exceedingly within ten minutes. Yet now, the inconstant
public turned its back upon them, and even leaned its elbows carelessly against the bar outside the window and shook off the mud from
its shoes, and also lent and borrowed fire for pipes.

Custodian re-enters from his door, "Again once, gentlemen, you are
invited——" No further invitation necessary. Ready dash into the
street. Toilette finished. Old man coming out.

This time, the interest was grown too hot to admit of toleration of
the boys on the stone posts. The homicidal white-lead worker made
a pounce upon one boy who was hoisting himself up, and brought him
to earth amidst general commendation. Closely stowed as we were,
we yet formed into groups—groups of conversation, without separation from the mass—to discuss the old man. Rivals of the tall and
sallow mason sprang into being, and here again was popular inconstancy. These rivals attracted audiences, and were greedily listened
to; and whereas they had derived their information solely from the
tall and sallow one, officious members of the crowd now sought to
enlighten *him* on their authority. Changed by this social experience
into an iron-visaged and inveterate misanthrope, the mason glared
at mankind, and evidently cherished in his breast the wish that the
whole of the present company could change places with the deceased
old man. And now listeners became inattentive, and people made a
start forward at a slight sound, and an unholy fire kindled in the
public eye, and those next the gates beat at them impatiently, as if
they were of the cannibal species and hungry.

Again the hinges creaked, and we rushed. Disorderly pressure for
some time ensued before the uncommercial unit got figured into the
front row of the sum. It was strange to see so much heat and uproar
seething about one poor spare white-haired old man, quiet for evermore. He was calm of feature and undisfigured, as he lay on his back
—having been struck upon the hinder part of the head, and thrown
forward—and something like a tear or two had started from the
closed eyes, and lay wet upon the face. The uncommercial interest,
sated at a glance, directed itself upon the striving crowd on either
side and behind: wondering whether one might have guessed, from
the expression of those faces merely, what kind of sight they were
looking at. The differences of expression were not many. There was
a little pity, but not much, and that mostly with a selfish touch in it—
as who would say, "Shall I, poor I, look like that, when the time
comes!" There was more of a secretly brooding contemplation and

curiosity, as "That man I don't like, and have the grudge against; would such be his appearance, if some one—not to mention names— by any chance gave him an ugly knock?" There was a wolfish stare at the object, in which the homicidal white-lead worker shone conspicuous. And there was a much more general, purposeless, vacant staring at it—like looking at waxworks, without a catalogue, and not knowing what to make of it. But all these expressions concurred in possessing the one underlying expression of *looking at something that could not return a look*. The uncommercial notice had established this as very remarkable, when a new pressure all at once coming up from the street pinioned him ignominiously, and hurried him into the arms (now sleeved again) of the Custodian smoking at his door, and answering questions, between-puffs, with a certain placid meritorious air of not being proud, though high in office. And mentioning pride, it may be observed, by the way, that one could not well help investing the original sole occupant of the front row with an air depreciatory of the legitimate attraction of the poor old man: while the two in the second row seemed to exult at his superseded popularity.

Pacing presently round the garden of the Tower of St. Jacques de la Boucherie, and presently again in front of the Hôtel de Ville, I called to mind a certain desolate open-air Morgue that I happened to light upon in London, one day in the hard winter of 1861, and which seemed as strange to me, at the time of seeing it, as if I had found it in China. Towards that hour of a winter's afternoon when the lamplighters are beginning to light the lamps in the streets a little before they are wanted, because the darkness thickens fast and soon, I was walking in from the country on the northern side of the Regent's Park—hard frozen and deserted—when I saw an empty Hansom cab drive up to the lodge at Gloucester Gate, and the driver with great agitation call to the man there: who quickly reached a long pole from a tree, and, deftly collared by the driver, jumped to the step of his little seat, and so the Hansom rattled out at the gate, galloping over the iron-bound road. I followed running, though not so fast but that when I came to the right-hand Canal Bridge, near the cross-path to Chalk Farm, the Hansom was stationary, the horse was smoking hot, the long pole was idle on the ground, and the driver and the park-keeper were looking over the bridge parapet. Looking over too, I saw, lying on the towing-path with her face turned up towards us, a woman, dead a day or two, and under thirty, as I guessed, poorly dressed in black. The feet were lightly crossed at the ankles, and the dark hair, all pushed back from the face, as though that had been the last action of her desperate hands, streamed over the ground. Dabbled all about her, was the water and the broken ice that had dropped from her dress, and had splashed as she was got out. The policeman who had just got her out, and the passing costermonger who had helped him, were standing near the body; the latter with that stare at it which I have likened to being at a waxwork exhibition without a catalogue; the former, looking over his stock, with pro-

fessional stiffness and coolness, in the direction in which the bearers
he had sent for were expected. So dreadfully forlorn, so dreadfully
sad, so dreadfully mysterious, this spectacle of our dear sister here
departed! A barge came up, breaking the floating ice and the silence,
and a woman steered it. The man with the horse that towed it,
cared so little for the body, that the stumbling hoofs had been among
the hair, and the tow-rope had caught and turned the head, before
our cry of horror took him to the bridle. At which sound the steering
woman looked up at us on the bridge, with contempt unutterable,
and then looking down at the body with a similar expression—as if
it were made in another likeness from herself, had been informed with
other passions, had been lost by other chances, had had another nature
dragged down to perdition—steered a spurning streak of mud at it,
and passed on.

A better experience, but also of the Morgue kind, in which chance
happily made me useful in a slight degree, arose to my remembrance
as I took my way by the Boulevard de Sébastopol into the brighter
scenes of Paris.

The thing happened, say five-and-twenty years ago. I was a modest
young uncommercial then, and timid and inexperienced. Many suns
and winds have browned me in the line, but those were my pale days.
Having newly taken the lease of a house in a certain distinguished
metropolitan parish—a house which then appeared to me to be a
frightfully first-class Family Mansion, involving awful responsibilities
—I became the prey of a Beadle. I think the Beadle must have seen
me going in or coming out, and must have observed that I tottered
under the weight of my grandeur. Or he may have been in hiding
under straw when I bought my first horse (in the desirable stable-yard
attached to the first-class Family Mansion), and when the vendor
remarked to me, in an original manner, on bringing him for approval, taking his cloth off and smacking him, "There Sir! *There's
a Orse!*" And when I said gallantly, "How much do you want for
him?" and when the vendor said, "No more than sixty guineas, from
you," and when I said smartly, "Why not more than sixty from *me*?"
And when he said crushingly, "Because upon my soul and body he'd
be considered cheap at seventy, by one who understood the subject—
but you don't."—I say, the Beadle may have been in hiding under
straw, when this disgrace befell me, or he may have noted that I was
too raw and young an Atlas to carry the first-class Family Mansion in
a knowing manner. Be this as it may, the Beadle did what Melancholy did to the youth in Gray's Elegy—he marked me for his own.
And the way in which the Beadle did it, was this; he summoned
me as a Juryman on his Coroners' Inquests.

In my first feverish alarm I repaired "for safety and for succour"
—like those sagacious Northern shepherds who, having had no previous reason whatever to believe in young Norval, very prudently did
not originate the hazardous idea of believing in him—to a deep house-
holder. This profound man informed me that the Beadle counted on

my buying him off; on my bribing him not to summon me; and that if I would attend an Inquest with a cheerful countenance, and profess alacrity in that branch of my country's service, the Beadle would be disheartened, and would give up the game.

I roused my energies, and the next time the wily Beadle summoned me, I went. The Beadle was the blankest Beadle I have ever looked on when I answered to my name; and his discomfiture gave me courage to go through with it.

We were impannelled to inquire concerning the death of a very little mite of a child. It was the old miserable story. Whether the mother had committed the minor offence of concealing the birth, or whether she had committed the major offence of killing the child, was the question on which we were wanted. We must commit her on one of the two issues.

The Inquest came off in the parish workhouse, and I have yet a lively impression that I was unanimously received by my brother Jurymen as a brother of the utmost conceivable insignificance. Also, that before we began, a broker who had lately cheated me fearfully in the matter of a pair of card-tables, was for the utmost rigour of the law. I remember that we sat in a sort of board-room, on such very large square horse-hair chairs that I wondered what race of Patagonians they were made for; and further, that an undertaker gave me his card when we were in the full moral freshness of having just been sworn, as "an inhabitant that was newly come into the parish, and was likely to have a young family". The case was then stated to us by the Coroner, and then we went down-stairs—led by the plotting Beadle—to view the body. From that day to this, the poor little figure, on which that sounding legal appellation was bestowed, has lain in the same place and with the same surroundings, to my thinking. In a kind of crypt devoted to the warehousing of the parochial coffins, and in the midst of a perfect Panorama of coffins of all sizes, it was stretched on a box; the mother had put it in her box—this box —almost as soon as it was born, and it had been presently found there. It had been opened, and neatly sewn up, and regarded from that point of view, it looked like a stuffed creature. It rested on a clean white cloth, with a surgical instrument or so at hand, and regarded from that point of view, it looked as if the cloth were "laid", and the Giant were coming to dinner. There was nothing repellent about the poor piece of innocence, and it demanded a mere form of looking at. So, we looked at an old pauper who was going about among the coffins with a foot rule, as if he were a case of Self-Measurement; and we looked at one another; and we said the place was well whitewashed anyhow; and then our conversational powers as a British Jury flagged, and the foreman said, "All right, gentlemen? Back again, Mr. Beadle!"

The miserable young creature who had given birth to this child within a very few days, and who had cleaned the cold wet door-steps immediately afterwards, was brought before us when we resumed our horse-hair chairs, and was present during the proceedings. She had a horse-hair chair herself, being very weak and ill; and I remember how she turned to the unsympathetic nurse who attended her, and who might have been the figure-head of a pauper-ship, and how she hid her face and sobs and tears upon that wooden shoulder. I remember, too, how hard her mistress was upon her (she was a servant-of-all-work), and with what a cruel pertinacity that piece of Virtue spun her thread of evidence double, by intertwisting it with the sternest thread of construction. Smitten hard by the terrible low wail from the utterly friendless orphan girl, which never ceased during the whole inquiry, I took heart to ask this witness a question or two, which hopefully admitted of an answer that might give a favourable turn to the case. She made the turn as little favourable as it could be, but it did some good, and the Coroner, who was nobly patient and humane (he was the late Mr. Wakley), cast a look of strong encouragement in my direction. Then, we had the doctor who had made the examination, and the usual tests as to whether the child was born alive; but he was a timid muddle-headed doctor, and got confused and contradictory, and wouldn't say this, and couldn't answer for that, and the immaculate broker was too much for him, and our side slid back again. However, I tried again, and the Coroner backed me again, for which I ever afterwards felt grateful to him as I do now to his memory; and we got another favourable turn, out of some other witness, some member of the family with a strong prepossession against the sinner; and I think we had the doctor back again; and I know that the Coroner summed up for our side, and that I and my British brothers turned round to discuss our verdict, and got ourselves into great difficulties with our large chairs and the broker. At that stage of the case I tried hard again, being convinced that I had cause for it; and at last we found for the minor offence of only concealing the birth; and the poor desolate creature, who had been taken out during our deliberation, being brought in again to be told of the verdict, then dropped upon her knees before us, with protestations that we were right—protestations among the most affecting that I have ever heard in my life—and was carried away insensible.

(In private conversation after this was all over, the Coroner showed me his reasons as a trained surgeon, for perceiving it to be impossible that the child could, under the most favourable circumstances, have drawn many breaths, in the very doubtful case of its having ever breathed at all; this, owing to the discovery of some foreign matter in the windpipe, quite irreconcilable with many moments of life.)

When the agonised girl had made those final protestations, I had seen her face, and it was in unison with her distracted heartbroken voice, and it was very moving. It certainly did not impress me by any beauty that it had, and if I ever see it again in another world I shall only know it by the help of some new sense or intelligence. But it came to me in my sleep that night, and I selfishly dismissed it in the most efficient way I could think of. I caused some extra care to be taken of her in the prison, and counsel to be retained for her defence when she was tried at the Old Bailey; and her sentence was lenient, and her history and conduct proved that it was right. In doing the little I did for her, I remember to have had the kind help of some gentle-hearted functionary to whom I addressed myself—but what functionary I have long forgotten—who I suppose was officially present at the Inquest.

I regard this as a very notable uncommercial experience, because this good came of a Beadle. And to the best of my knowledge, information, and belief, it is the only good that ever did come of a Beadle since the first Beadle put on his cocked hat.

XX

BIRTHDAY CELEBRATIONS

It came into my mind that I would recall in these notes a few of the many hostelries I have rested at in the course of my journeys; and, indeed, I had taken up my pen for the purpose, when I was baffled by an accidental circumstance. It was the having to leave off, to wish the owner of a certain bright face that looked in at my door, " many happy returns of the day ". Thereupon a new thought came into my mind, driving its predecessor out, and I began to recall—instead of Inns—the birthdays that I have put up at, on my way to this present sheet of paper.

I can very well remember being taken out to visit some peach-faced creature in a blue sash, and shoes to correspond, whose life I supposed to consist entirely of birthdays. Upon seed-cake, sweet wine, and shining presents, that glorified young person seemed to me to be exclusively reared. At so early a stage of my travels did I assist at the anniversary of her nativity (and become enamoured of her), that I had not yet acquired the recondite knowledge that a birthday is the common property of all who are born, but supposed it to be a special gift bestowed by the favouring Heavens on that one distinguished infant. There was no other company, and we sat in a shady bower— under a table, as my better (or worse) knowledge leads me to believe— and were regaled with saccharine substances and liquids, until it was time to part. A bitter powder was administered to me next morning, and I was wretched. On the whole, a pretty accurate foreshadowing of my more mature experiences in such wise!

Then came the time when, inseparable from one's own birthday, was a certain sense of merit, a consciousness of well-earned distinction. When I regarded my birthday as a graceful achievement of my own, a monument of my perseverance, independence, and good sense, redounding greatly to my honour. This was at about the period when Olympia Squires became involved in the anniversary. Olympia was most beautiful (of course), and I loved her to that degree, that I used to be obliged to get out of my little bed in the night, expressly to exclaim to Solitude, "O, Olympia Squires!" Visions of Olympia, clothed entirely in sage-green, from which I infer a defectively educated taste on the part of her respected parents, who were necessarily unacquainted with the South Kensington Museum, still arise before me. Truth is sacred, and the visions are crowned by a shining white beaver bonnet, impossibly suggestive of a little feminine postboy. My memory presents a birthday when Olympia and I were taken by an unfeeling relative—some cruel uncle, or the like—to a slow torture called an Orrery. The terrible instrument was set up at the local Theatre, and I had expressed a profane wish in the morning that it was a Play: for which a serious aunt had probed my conscience deep, and my pocket deeper, by reclaiming a bestowed half-crown. It was a venerable and a shabby Orrery, at least one thousand stars and twenty-five comets behind the age. Nevertheless, it was awful. When the low-spirited gentleman with a wand said, "Ladies and gentlemen" (meaning particularly Olympia and me), "the lights are about to be put out, but there is not the slightest cause for alarm," it was very alarming. Then the planets and stars began. Sometimes they wouldn't come on, sometimes they wouldn't go off, sometimes they had holes in them, and mostly they didn't seem to be good likenesses. All this time the gentleman with the wand was going on in the dark (tapping away at the heavenly bodies between whiles, like a wearisome woodpecker), about a sphere revolving on its own axis eight hundred and ninety-seven thousand millions of times—or miles —in two hundred and sixty-three thousand five hundred and twenty-four millions of something elses, until I thought if this was a birthday it were better never to have been born. Olympia, also, became much depressed, and we both slumbered and woke cross, and still the gentleman was going on in the dark—whether up in the stars, or down on the stage, it would have been hard to make out, if it had been worth trying—cyphering away about planes of orbits, to such an infamous extent that Olympia, stung to madness, actually kicked me. A pretty birthday spectacle, when the lights were turned up again, and all the schools in the town (including the National, who had come in for nothing, and serve them right, for they were always throwing stones) were discovered with exhausted countenances, screwing their knuckles into their eyes, or clutching their heads of hair. A pretty birthday speech when Dr. Sleek of the City-Free bobbed up his powdered head in the stage-box, and said that before this assembly dispersed he really must beg to express his entire approval of a lecture as improving, as informing, as devoid of anything that could call a blush into the cheek of youth, as any it had ever been his lot to hear delivered. A pretty birthday altogether, when Astronomy couldn't leave poor Small Olympia Squires and me alone, but must put an end to our loves! For, we never got over it; the threadbare Orrery outwore our mutual tenderness; the man with the wand was too much for the boy with the bow.

When shall I disconnect the combined smells of oranges, brown paper, and straw, from those other birthdays at school, when the coming hamper casts its shadow before, and when a week of social harmony—shall I add of admiring and affectionate popularity—led up to that Institution? What noble sentiments were expressed to me in the days before the hamper, what vows of friendship were sworn to me, what exceedingly old knives were given me, what generous avowals of having been in the wrong emanated from else obstinate spirits once enrolled among my enemies! The birthday of the potted game and guava jelly, is still made special to me by the noble conduct of Bully Globson. Letters from home had mysteriously inquired whether I should be much surprised and disappointed if among the treasures in the coming hamper I discovered potted game, and guava jelly from the Western Indies. I had mentioned those hints in confidence to a few friends, and had promised to give away, as I now see reason to believe, a handsome covey of partridges potted, and about a hundred-weight of guava jelly. It was now that Globson, Bully no more, sought me out in the playground. He was a big fat boy, with a big fat head and a big fat fist, and at the beginning of that Half had raised such a bump on my forehead that I couldn't get my hat of state on, to go to church. He said that after an interval of cool reflection (four months) he now felt this blow to have been an error of judgment, and that he wished to apologise for the same. Not only that, but holding down his big head between his two big hands in order that I might reach it conveniently, he requested me, as an act of justice which would appease his awakened conscience, to raise a retributive bump upon it, in the presence of witnesses. This handsome proposal I modestly declined, and he then embraced me, and we walked away conversing. We conversed respecting the West India islands, and in the pursuit of knowledge he asked me with much interest whether in the course of my reading I had met with any reliable description of the mode of manufacturing guava jelly; or whether I had ever happened to taste that conserve, which he had been given to understand was of rare excellence.

Seventeen, eighteen, nineteen, twenty; and then with the waning months came an ever augmenting sense of the dignity of twenty-one. Heaven knows I had nothing to "come into", save the bare birthday, and yet I esteemed it as a great possession. I now and then paved the way to my state of dignity, by beginning a proposition with the casual words, "say that a man of twenty-one", or by the incidental assumption of a fact that could not sanely be disputed, as, "for when a fellow comes to be a man of twenty-one". I gave a party on the occasion. She was there. It is unnecessary to name Her, more particularly; She was older than I, and had pervaded every chink and crevice of my mind for three or four years. I had held volumes of Imaginary Conversations with her mother on the subject of our union, and I had

written letters more in number than Horace Walpole's, to that discreet
woman, soliciting her daughter's hand in marriage. I had never had
the remotest intention of sending any of those letters; but to write
them, and after a few days tear them up, had been a sublime occupation. Sometimes, I had begun "Honoured Madam. I think that
a lady gifted with those powers of observation which I know you
to possess, and endowed with those womanly sympathies with the
young and ardent which it were more than heresy to doubt, can
scarcely have failed to discover that I love your adorable daughter,
deeply, devotedly." In less buoyant states of mind I had begun,
"Bear with me, Dear Madam, bear with a daring wretch who is
about to make a surprising confession to you, wholly unanticipated by
yourself, and which he beseeches you to commit to the flames as soon
as you have become aware to what a towering height his mad ambition
soars." At other times—periods of profound mental depression, when
She had gone out to balls where I was not—the draft took the affecting
form of a paper to be left on my table after my departure to the
confines of the globe. As thus: "For Mrs. Onowenever, these lines
when the hand that traces them shall be far away. I could not
bear the daily torture of hopelessly loving the dear one whom I
will not name. Broiling on the coast of Africa, or congealing on
the shores of Greenland, I am far far better there than here." (In
this sentiment my cooler judgment perceives that the family of the
beloved object would have most completely concurred.) "If I ever
emerge from obscurity, and my name is ever heralded by Fame, it
will be for her dear sake. If I ever amass Gold, it will be to pour
it at her feet. Should I on the other hand become the prey of
Ravens——" I doubt if I ever quite made up my mind what was
to be done in that affecting case; I tried "then it is better so";
but not feeling convinced that it would be better so, I vacillated
between leaving all else blank, which looked expressive and bleak,
or winding up with "Farewell!"

This fictitious correspondence of mine is to blame for the fore-
going digression. I was about to pursue the statement that on my
twenty-first birthday I gave a party, and She was there. It was
a beautiful party. There was not a single animate or inanimate
object connected with it (except the company and myself) that I
had ever seen before. Everything was hired, and the mercenaries
in attendance were profound strangers to me. Behind a door, in
the crumby part of the night when wine-glasses were to be found in
unexpected spots, I spoke to Her—spoke out to Her. What passed, I
cannot as a man of honour reveal. She was all angelical gentleness,
but a word was mentioned—a short and dreadful word of three letters,
beginning with a B—which, as I remarked at the moment, "scorched
my brain". She went away soon afterwards, and when the hollow
throng (though to be sure it was no fault of theirs) dispersed, I
issued forth, with a dissipated scorner, and, as I mentioned expressly
to him, "sought oblivion". It was found, with a dreadful headache

in it, but it didn't last; for, in the shaming light of next day's noon, I raised my heavy head in bed, looking back to the birthdays behind me, and tracking the circle by which I had got round, after all, to the bitter powder and the wretchedness again.

This reactionary powder (taken so largely by the human race that I am inclined to regard it as the Universal Medicine once sought for in Laboratories) is capable of being made up in another form for birthday use. Anybody's long-lost brother will do ill to turn up on a birthday. If I had a long-lost brother I should know beforehand that he would prove a tremendous fraternal failure if he appointed to rush into my arms on my birthday. The first Magic Lantern I ever saw, was secretly and elaborately planned to be the great effect of a very juvenile birthday; but it wouldn't act, and its images were dim. My experience of adult birthday Magic Lanterns may possibly have been unfortunate, but has certainly been similar. I have an illustrative birthday in my eye; a birthday of my friend Flipfield, whose birthdays had long been remarkable as social successes. There had been nothing set or formal about them; Flipfield having been accustomed merely to say, two or three days before, " Don't forget to come and dine, old boy, according to custom ";—I don't know what he said to the ladies he invited, but I may safely assume it *not* to have been " old girl ". Those were delightful gatherings, and were enjoyed by all participators. In an evil hour, a long-lost brother of Flipfield's came to light in foreign parts. Where he had been hidden, or what he had been doing, I don't know, for Flipfield vaguely informed me that he had turned up " on the banks of the Ganges "—speaking of him as if he had been washed ashore. The Long-lost was coming home, and Flipfield made an unfortunate calculation, based on the well-known regularity of the P. and O. Steamers, that matters might be so contrived as that the Long-lost should appear in the nick of time on his (Flipfield's) birthday. Delicacy commanded that I should repress the gloomy anticipations with which my soul became fraught when I heard of this plan. The fatal day arrived, and we assembled in force. Mrs. Flipfield senior formed an interesting feature in the group, with a blue-veined miniature of the late Mr. Flipfield round her neck, in an oval, resembling a tart from the pastrycook's: his hair powdered, and the bright buttons on his coat, evidently very like. She was accompanied by Miss Flipfield, the eldest of her numerous family, who held her pocket-handkerchief to her bosom in a majestic manner, and spoke to all of us (none of us had ever seen her before), in pious and condoning tones, of all the quarrels that had taken place in the family, from her infancy—which must have been a long time ago—down to that hour. The Long-lost did not appear. Dinner, half an hour later than usual, was announced, and still no Long-lost. We sat down to table. The knife and fork of the Long-lost made a vacuum in Nature, and when the champagne came round for the first time, Flipfield gave him up for the day, and had them removed. It was then that the Long-lost gained the height of his popularity with the company; for my own part, I felt convinced that I loved him dearly.   Flipfield's dinners are perfect, and he is the easiest and best of entertainers.   Dinner went on brilliantly, and the more the Long-lost didn't come, the more comfortable we grew, and the more highly we thought of him.   Flipfield's own man (who has a regard for me) was in the act of struggling with an ignorant stipendiary, to wrest from him the wooden leg of a Guinea-fowl which he was pressing on my acceptance, and to substitute a slice of the breast, when a ringing at the door-bell suspended the strife.   I looked round me, and perceived the sudden pallor which I knew my own visage revealed, reflected in the faces of the company.   Flipfield hurriedly excused himself, went out, was absent for about a minute or two, and then re-entered with the Long-lost.

I beg to say distinctly that if the stranger had brought Mont Blanc with him, or had come attended by a retinue of eternal snows, he could not have chilled the circle to the marrow in a more efficient manner. Embodied Failure sat enthroned upon the Long-lost's brow, and pervaded him to his Long-lost boots.   In vain Mrs. Flipfield senior, opening her arms, exclaimed, " My Tom !" and pressed his nose against the counterfeit presentment of his other parent.   In vain Miss Flipfield, in the first transports of this re-union, showed him a dint upon her maidenly cheek, and asked him if he remembered when he did that with the bellows?   We, the bystanders, were overcome, but overcome by the palpable, undisguisable, utter, and total break-down of the Long-lost.   Nothing he could have done would have set him right with us but his instant return to the Ganges.   In the very same moments it became established that the feeling was reciprocal, and that the Long-lost detested us.   When a friend of the family (not myself, upon my honour), wishing to set things going again, asked him, while he partook of soup—asked him with an amiability of intention beyond all praise, but with a weakness of execution open to defeat—what kind of river he considered the Ganges, the Long-lost, scowling at the friend of the family over his spoon, as one of an abhorrent race, replied, " Why a river of water, I suppose ", and spooned his soup into himself with a malignancy of hand and eye that blighted the amiable questioner.   Not an opinion could be elicited from the Long-lost, in unison with the sentiments of any individual present.   He contradicted Flipfield dead, before he had eaten his salmon.   He had no idea—or affected to have no idea—that it was his brother's birthday, and on the communication of that interesting fact to him, merely wanted to make him out four years older than he was.   He was an antipathetical being, with a peculiar power and gift of treading on everybody's tenderest place.   They talk in America of a man's " Platform ".   I should describe the Platform of the Long-lost as a Platform composed of other people's corns, on which he had stumped his way, with all his might and main, to his present position.   It is needless to add that Flipfield's great birthday went by the board, and that he was a wreck when I pretended at parting to wish him many happy returns of it.

There is another class of birthdays at which I have so frequently assisted, that I may assume such birthdays to be pretty well known to the human race. My friend Mayday's birthday is an example. The guests have no knowledge of one another except on that one day in the year, and are annually terrified for a week by the prospect of meeting one another again. There is a fiction among us that we have uncommon reasons for being particularly lively and spirited on the occasion, whereas deep despondency is no phrase for the expression of our feelings. But the wonderful feature of the case is, that we are in tacit accordance to avoid the subject—to keep it as far off as possible, as long as possible—and to talk about anything else, rather than the joyful event. I may even go so far as to assert that there is a dumb compact among us that we will pretend that it is NOT Mayday's birthday. A mysterious and gloomy Being, who is said to have gone to school with Mayday, and who is so lank and lean that he seriously impugns the Dietary of the establishment at which they were jointly educated, always leads us, as I may say, to the block, by laying his grisly hand on a decanter and begging us to fill our glasses. The devices and pretences that I have seen put in practice to defer the fatal moment, and to interpose between this man and his purpose, are innumerable. I have known desperate guests, when they saw the grisly hand approaching the decanter, wildly to begin, without any antecedent whatsoever, "That reminds me——" and to plunge into long stories. When at last the hand and the decanter come together, a shudder, a palpable perceptible shudder, goes round the table. We receive the reminder that it is Mayday's birthday, as if it were the anniversary of some profound disgrace he had undergone, and we sought to comfort him. And when we have drunk Mayday's health, and wished him many happy returns, we are seized for some moments with a ghastly blitheness, an unnatural levity, as if we were in the first flushed reaction of having undergone a surgical operation.

Birthdays of this species have a public as well as a private phase. My "boyhood's home", Dullborough, presents a case in point. An Immortal Somebody was wanted in Dullborough, to dimple for a day the stagnant face of the waters; he was rather wanted by Dullborough generally, and much wanted by the principal hotel-keeper. The County history was looked up for a locally Immortal Somebody, but the registered Dullborough worthies were all Nobodies. In this state of things, it is hardly necessary to record that Dullborough did what every man does when he wants to write a book or deliver a lecture, and is provided with all the materials except a subject. It fell back upon Shakespeare.

No sooner was it resolved to celebrate Shakespeare's birthday in Dullborough, than the popularity of the immortal bard became surprising. You might have supposed the first edition of his works to have been published last week, and enthusiastic Dullborough to have got half through them. (I doubt, by the way, whether it had ever done half that, but this is a private opinion.) A young gentleman with a sonnet, the retention of which for two years had enfeebled his mind and undermined his knees, got the sonnet into the Dullborough Warden, and gained flesh. Portraits of Shakespeare broke out in the bookshop windows, and our principal artist painted a large original portrait in oils for the decoration of the dining-room. It was not in the least like any of the other portraits, and was exceedingly admired, the head being much swollen. At the Institution, the Debating Society discussed the new question, Was there sufficient ground for supposing that the Immortal Shakespeare ever stole deer? This was indignantly decided by an overwhelming majority in the negative; indeed, there was but one vote on the Poaching side, and that was the vote of the orator who had undertaken to advocate it, and who became quite an obnoxious character—particularly to the Dullborough "roughs" who were about as well informed on the matter as most other people. Distinguished speakers were invited down, and very nearly came (but not quite). Subscriptions were opened, and committees sat, and it would have been far from a popular measure in the height of the excitement, to have told Dullborough that it wasn't Stratford-upon-Avon. Yet, after all these preparations, when the great festivity took place, and the portrait, elevated aloft, surveyed the company as if it were in danger of springing a mine of intellect and blowing itself up, it did undoubtedly happen, according to the inscrutable mysteries of things, that nobody could be induced, not to say to touch upon Shakespeare, but to come within a mile of him, until the crack speaker of Dullborough rose to propose the immortal memory. Which he did with the perplexing and astonishing result that before he had repeated the great name half a dozen times, or had been upon his legs as many minutes, he was assailed with a general shout of "Question".

XXI

BOUND FOR THE GREAT SALT LAKE

BEHOLD me on my way to an Emigrant Ship, on a hot morning early in June. My road lies through that part of London generally known to the initiated as "Down by the Docks". Down by the Docks, is home to a good many people—to too many, if I may judge from the overflow of local population in the streets—but my nose insinuates that the number to whom it is Sweet Home might be easily counted. Down by the Docks, is a region I would choose as my point of embarkation aboard ship if I were an emigrant. It would present my intention to me in such a sensible light; it would show me so many things to be run away from.

Down by the Docks, they eat the largest oysters and scatter the roughest oyster shells, known to the descendants of Saint George and the Dragon. Down by the Docks, they consume the slimiest of shell-fish, which seem to have been scraped off the copper bottoms of ships. Down by the Docks, the vegetables at greengrocers' doors acquire a saline and a scaly look, as if they had been crossed with fish and sea-weed. Down by the Docks, they "board seamen" at the eating-houses, the public-houses, the slop-shops, the coffee-shops, the tally-shops, all kinds of shops mentionable and unmentionable—board them, as it were, in the piratical sense, making them bleed terribly, and giving no quarter. Down by the Docks, the seamen roam in mid-street and mid-day, their pockets inside-out, and their heads no better. Down by the Docks, the daughters of wave-ruling Britannia also rove, clad in silken attire, with uncovered tresses streaming in the breeze, bandanna kerchiefs floating from their shoulders, and crinoline not wanting. Down by the Docks, you may hear the Incomparable Joe Jackson sing the Standard of England, with a hornpipe, any night; or any day may see at the waxwork, for a penny and no waiting, him as killed the policeman at Acton and suffered for it. Down by the Docks, you may buy polonies, saveloys, and sausage preparations various, if you are not particular what they are made of besides season-ing. Down by the Docks, the children of Israel creep into any gloomy cribs and entries they can hire, and hang slops there—pewter watches, sou'-wester hats, waterproof overalls—"firtht rate articleth, Thjack". Down by the Docks, such dealers exhibiting on a frame a complete nautical suit without the refinement of a waxen visage in the hat, present the imaginary wearer as drooping at the yard-arm, with his seafaring and earthfaring troubles over. Down by the Docks, the placards in the shops apostrophise the customer, knowing him familiarly beforehand, as, "Look here, Jack!" "Here's your sort, my lad!" "Try our sea-going mixed, at two and nine!" "The right kit for the British tar!" "Ship ahoy!" "Splice the main-brace, brother!" "Come, cheer up, my lads. We've the best liquors here, And you'll find something new In our wonderful Beer!" Down by the Docks, the pawnbroker lends money on Union-Jack pocket-handkerchiefs, on watches with little ships pitching fore and aft on the dial, on telescopes, nautical instruments in cases, and such-like. Down by the Docks, the apothecary sets up in business on the wretchedest scale—chiefly on lint and plaster for the strapping of wounds—and with no bright bottles, and with no little drawers. Down by the Docks, the shabby undertaker's shop will bury you for next to nothing, after the Malay or Chinaman has stabbed you for nothing at all: so you can hardly hope to make a cheaper end. Down by the Docks, anybody drunk will quarrel with anybody drunk or sober, and everybody else will have a hand in it, and on the shortest notice you may revolve in a whirlpool of red shirts, shaggy beards, wild heads of hair, bare tattooed arms, Britannia's daughters, malice, mud, maundering, and madness. Down by the Docks, scraping fiddles go in the public-houses all day long, and, shrill above their din and all the din, rises the screeching of innumerable parrots brought from foreign parts, who appear to be very much astonished by what they find on these native shores of ours. Possibly the parrots don't know, possibly they do, that Down by the Docks is the road to the Pacific Ocean, with its lovely islands, where the savage girls plait flowers, and the savage boys carve cocoa-nut shells, and the grim blind idols muse in their shady groves to exactly the same purpose as the priests and chiefs. And possibly the parrots don't know, possibly they do, that the noble savage is a wearisome impostor wherever he is, and has five hundred thousand volumes of indifferent rhyme, and no reason, to answer for.

Shadwell church! Pleasant whispers of there being a fresher air down the river than down by the Docks, go pursuing one another, playfully, in and out of the openings in its spire. Gigantic in the basin just beyond the church, looms my Emigrant Ship: her name, the Amazon. Her figure-head is not *dis*figured as those beauteous founders of the race of strong-minded women are fabled to have been, for the convenience of drawing the bow; but I sympathise with the carver:

> A flattering carver who made it his care
> To carve busts as they ought to be—not as they were.

My Emigrant Ship lies broadside-on to the wharf. Two great gangways made of spars and planks connect her with the wharf; and up and down these gangways, perpetually crowding to and fro and in and out, like ants, are the Emigrants who are going to sail in my Emigrant Ship. Some with cabbages, some with loaves of bread, some with cheese and butter, some with milk and beer, some with boxes beds and bundles, some with babies—nearly all with children—nearly all with bran-new tin cans for their daily allowance of water, uncomfortably suggestive of a tin flavour in the drink. To and fro, up and down, aboard and ashore, swarming here and there and everywhere, my Emigrants. And still as the Dock-Gate swings upon its hinges, cabs appear, and carts appear, and vans appear, bringing more of my Emigrants, with more cabbages, more loaves, more cheese and butter, more milk and beer, more boxes beds and bundles, more tin cans, and on those shipping investments accumulated compound interest of children.

I go aboard my Emigrant Ship. I go first to the great cabin, and find it in the usual condition of a Cabin at that pass. Perspiring landsmen, with loose papers, and with pens and inkstands, pervade it; and the general appearance of things is as if the late Mr. Amazon's funeral had just come home from the cemetery, and the disconsolate Mrs. Amazon's trustees found the affairs in great disorder, and were looking high and low for the will. I go out on the poop-deck, for air, and surveying the emigrants on the deck below (indeed they are crowded all about me, up there too), find more pens and inkstands in action, and more papers, and interminable complication respecting accounts with individuals for tin cans and what not. But nobody is in an ill-temper, nobody is the worse for drink, nobody swears an oath or uses a coarse word, nobody appears depressed, nobody is weeping, and down upon the deck in every corner where it is possible to find a few square feet to kneel, crouch, or lie in, people, in every unsuitable attitude for writing, are writing letters.

Now, I have seen emigrant ships before this day in June. And these people are so strikingly different from all other people in like circumstances whom I have ever seen, that I wonder aloud, "What *would* a stranger suppose these emigrants to be!"

The vigilant bright face of the weather-browned captain of the Amazon is at my shoulder, and he says, "What, indeed! The most of these came aboard yesterday evening. They came from various parts of England in small parties that had never seen one another before. Yet they had not been a couple of hours on board, when they established their own police, made their own regulations, and set their own watches at all the hatchways. Before nine o'clock, the ship was as orderly and as quiet as a man-of-war."

I looked about me again, and saw the letter-writing going on with the most curious composure. Perfectly abstracted in the midst of the crowd; while great casks were swinging aloft, and being lowered into the hold; while hot agents were hurrying up and down, adjusting the interminable accounts; while two hundred strangers were searching everywhere for two hundred other strangers, and were asking questions about them of two hundred more; while the children played up and down all the steps, and in and out among all the people's legs, and were beheld, to the general dismay, toppling over all the dangerous places; the letter-writers wrote on calmly. On the starboard side of the ship, a grizzled man dictated a long letter to another grizzled man in an immense fur cap: which letter was of so profound a quality, that it became necessary for the amanuensis at intervals to take off his fur cap in both his hands, for the ventilation of his brain, and stare at him who dictated, as a man of many mysteries who was worth looking at. On the larboard side, a woman had covered a belaying-pin with a white cloth to make a neat desk of it, and was sitting on a little box, writing with the deliberation of a bookkeeper. Down upon her breast on the planks of the deck at this woman's feet, with her head diving in under a beam of the bulwarks on that side, as an eligible place of refuge for her sheet of paper, a neat and pretty girl wrote for a good hour (she fainted at last), only rising to the surface occasionally for a dip of ink. Alongside the boat, close to me on the poop-deck, another girl, a fresh well-grown country girl, was writing another letter on the bare deck. Later in the day, when this self-same boat was filled with a choir who sang glees and catches for a long time, one of the singers, a girl, sang her part mechanically all the while, and wrote a letter in the bottom of the boat while doing so.

"A stranger would be puzzled to guess the right name for these people, Mr. Uncommercial," says the captain.

" Indeed he would."

" If you hadn't known, could you ever have supposed——?"

" How could I! I should have said they were in their degree, the pick and flower of England."

" So should I," says the captain.

" How many are they?"

" Eight hundred in round numbers."

I went between-decks, where the families with children swarmed in the dark, where unavoidable confusion had been caused by the last arrivals, and where the confusion was increased by the little preparations for dinner that were going on in each group. A few women here and there, had got lost, and were laughing at it, and asking their way to their own people, or out on deck again. A few of the poor children were crying; but otherwise the universal cheerfulness was amazing. " We shall shake down by to-morrow." " We shall come all right in a day or so." " We shall have more light at sea." Such phrases I heard everywhere, as I groped my way among chests and barrels and beams and unstowed cargo and ring-bolts and Emigrants, down to the lower-deck, and thence up to the light of day again, and to my former station.

Surely, an extraordinary people in their power of self-abstraction! All the former letter-writers were still writing calmly, and many more letter-writers had broken out in my absence. A boy with a bag of books in his hand and a slate under his arm, emerged from below, concentrated himself in my neighbourhood (espying a convenient sky-light for his purpose), and went to work at a sum as if he were stone deaf. A father and mother and several young children, on the main deck below me, had formed a family circle close to the foot of the crowded restless gangway, where the children made a nest for themselves in a coil of rope, and the father and mother, she suckling the youngest, discussed family affairs as peaceably as if they were in perfect retirement. I think the most noticeable characteristic in the eight hundred as a mass, was their exemption from hurry.

Eight hundred what? " Geese, villain?" EIGHT HUNDRED MORMONS. I, Uncommercial Traveller for the firm of Human Interest Brothers, had come aboard this Emigrant Ship to see what Eight hundred Latter-Day Saints were like, and I found them (to the rout and overthrow of all my expectations) like what I now describe with scrupulous exactness.

The Mormon Agent who had been active in getting them together, and in making the contract with my friends the owners of the ship to take them as far as New York on their way to the Great Salt Lake, was pointed out to me. A compactly-made handsome man in black, rather short, with rich-brown hair and beard, and clear bright eyes. From his speech, I should set him down as American. Probably, a man who had "knocked about the world" pretty much. A man with a frank open manner, and unshrinking look; withal a man of great quickness. I believe he was wholly ignorant of my Uncommercial individuality, and consequently of my immense Uncommercial importance.

UNCOMMERCIAL.   These are a very fine set of people you have brought together here.

MORMON AGENT.   Yes, sir, they are a *very* fine set of people.

UNCOMMERCIAL (looking about).   Indeed, I think it would be difficult to find Eight hundred people together anywhere else, and find so much beauty and so much strength and capacity for work among them.

MORMON AGENT (not looking about, but looking steadily at Uncommercial).   I think so.—We sent out about a thousand more, yes'day, from Liverpool.

UNCOMMERCIAL.   You are not going with these emigrants?

MORMON AGENT.   No, sir.   I remain.

UNCOMMERCIAL.   But you have been in the Mormon Territory?

MORMON AGENT.   Yes; I left Utah about three years ago.

UNCOMMERCIAL.   It is surprising to me that these people are all so cheery, and make so little of the immense distance before them.

MORMON AGENT.   Well, you see; many of 'em have friends out at Utah, and many of 'em look forward to meeting friends on the way.

UNCOMMERCIAL.   On the way?

MORMON AGENT.   This way 'tis.   This ship lands 'em in New York City.   Then they go on by rail right away beyond St. Louis, to that part of the Banks of the Missouri where they strike the Plains.   There, waggons from the settlement meet 'em to bear 'em company on their journey 'cross—twelve hundred miles about.   Industrious people who come out to the settlement soon get waggons of their own, and so the friends of some of these will come down in their own waggons to meet 'em.   They look forward to that, greatly.

UNCOMMERCIAL.   On their long journey across the Desert, do you arm them?

MORMON AGENT.   Mostly you would find they have arms of some kind or another already with them.   Such as had not arms we should arm across the Plains, for the general protection and defence.

UNCOMMERCIAL.   Will these waggons bring down any produce to the Missouri?

MORMON AGENT.   Well, since the war broke out, we've taken to growing cotton, and they'll likely bring down cotton to be exchanged for machinery.   We want machinery.   Also we have taken to growing indigo, which is a fine commodity for profit.   It has been found that the climate on the further side of the Great Salt Lake suits well for raising indigo.

UNCOMMERCIAL.   I am told that these people now on board are principally from the South of England?

MORMON AGENT.   And from Wales.   That's true.

UNCOMMERCIAL.   Do you get many Scotch?

MORMON AGENT.   Not many.

UNCOMMERCIAL.   Highlanders, for instance?

MORMON AGENT.   No, not Highlanders.   They ain't interested enough in universal brotherhood and peace and good will.

UNCOMMERCIAL.   The old fighting blood is strong in them?

MORMON AGENT.   Well, yes.   And besides; they've no faith.

UNCOMMERCIAL (who has been burning to get at the Prophet Joe Smith, and seems to discover an opening).   Faith in——!

MORMON AGENT (far too many for Uncommercial).   Well.—In anything!

Similarly on this same head, the Uncommercial underwent discomfiture from a Wiltshire labourer: a simple fresh-coloured farm-labourer, of eight-and-thirty, who at one time stood beside him looking on at new arrivals, and with whom he held this dialogue:

UNCOMMERCIAL.   Would you mind my asking you what part of the country you come from?

WILTSHIRE.   Not a bit.   Theer! (exultingly) I've worked all my life o' Salisbury Plain, right under the shadder o' Stonehenge.   You mightn't think it, but I haive.

UNCOMMERCIAL.   And a pleasant country too.

WILTSHIRE.   Ah!   'Tis a pleasant country.

UNCOMMERCIAL.   Have you any family on board?

WILTSHIRE.   Two children, boy and gal.   I am a widderer, *I* am, and I'm going out alonger my boy and gal.   That's my gal, and she's a fine gal o' sixteen (pointing out the girl who is writing by the boat).   I'll go and fetch my boy.   I'd like to show you my boy. (Here Wiltshire disappears, and presently comes back with a big shy boy of twelve, in a superabundance of boots, who is not at all glad to be presented.)   He is a fine boy too, and a boy fur to work! (Boy having undutifully bolted, Wiltshire drops him.)

UNCOMMERCIAL.   It must cost you a great deal of money to go so far, three strong.

WILTSHIRE.   A power of money.   Theer!   Eight shillen a week, eight shillen a week, eight shillen a week, put by out of the week's wages for ever so long.

UNCOMMERCIAL.   I wonder how you did it.

WILTSHIRE (recognising in this a kindred spirit).   See theer now! *I* wonder how I done it!   But what with a bit o' subscription heer, and what with a bit o' help theer, it were done at last, though I don't hardly know how.   Then it were unfort'net for us, you see, as we got kep' in Bristol so long—nigh a fortnight, it were—on accounts of a mistake wi' Brother Halliday.   Swaller'd up money, it did, when we might have come straight on.

UNCOMMERCIAL (delicately approaching Joe Smith).   You are of the Mormon religion, of course?

WILTSHIRE (confidently).   O yes, *I*'m a Mormon.   (Then reflectively.)   I'm a Mormon.   (Then, looking round the ship, feigns to descry a particular friend in an empty spot, and evades the Uncommercial for evermore.)

After a noontide pause for dinner, during which my Emigrants were nearly all between-decks, and the Amazon looked deserted, a general muster took place. The muster was for the ceremony of passing the Government Inspector and the Doctor. Those authorities held their temporary state amidships, by a cask or two; and, knowing that the whole Eight hundred emigrants must come face to face with them, I took my station behind the two. They knew nothing whatever of me, I believe, and my testimony to the unpretending gentleness and good nature with which they discharged their duty, may be of the greater worth. There was not the slightest flavour of the Circumlocution Office about their proceedings

The emigrants were now all on deck. They were densely crowded aft, and swarmed upon the poop-deck like bees. Two or three Mormon agents stood ready to hand them on to the Inspector, and to hand them forward when they had passed. By what successful means, a special aptitude for organisation had been infused into these people, I am, of course, unable to report. But I know that, even now, there was no disorder, hurry, or difficulty.

All being ready, the first group are handed on. That member of the party who is entrusted with the passenger-ticket for the whole, has been warned by one of the agents to have it ready, and here it is in his hand. In every instance through the whole eight hundred, without an exception, this paper is always ready.

INSPECTOR (reading the ticket). Jessie Jobson, Sophronia Jobson, Jessie Jobson again, Matilda Jobson, William Jobson, Jane Jobson, Matilda Jobson again, Brigham Jobson, Leonardo Jobson, and Orson Jobson. Are you all here? (glancing at the party, over his spectacles). JESSIE JOBSON NUMBER TWO. All here, sir.

This group is composed of an old grandfather and grandmother, their married son and his wife, and *their* family of children. Orson Jobson is a little child asleep in his mother's arms. The Doctor, with a kind word or so, lifts up the corner of the mother's shawl, looks at the child's face, and touches the little clenched hand. If we were all as well as Orson Jobson, doctoring would be a poor profession.

INSPECTOR. Quite right, Jessie Jobson. Take your ticket, Jessie, and pass on.

And away they go. Mormon agent, skilful and quiet, hands them on. Mormon agent, skilful and quiet, hands next party up.

INSPECTOR (reading ticket again). Susannah Cleverly and William Cleverly. Brother and sister, eh?

SISTER (young woman of business, hustling slow brother). Yes, sir.

INSPECTOR. Very good, Susannah Cleverly. Take your ticket, Susannah, and take care of it.

And away they go.

INSPECTOR (taking ticket again). Sampson Dibble and Dorothy Dibble (surveying a very old couple over his spectacles, with some surprise). Your husband quite blind, Mrs. Dibble?

MRS. DIBBLE. Yes, sir, he be stone-blind.

MR. DIBBLE (addressing the mast). Yes, sir, I be stone-blind.

INSPECTOR. That's a bad job. Take your ticket, Mrs. Dibble, and don't lose it, and pass on.

Doctor taps Mr. Dibble on the eyebrow with his forefinger, and away they go.

INSPECTOR (taking ticket again). Anastatia Weedle.

ANASTATIA (a pretty girl, in a bright Garibaldi, this morning elected by universal suffrage the Beauty of the Ship). That is me, sir.

INSPECTOR. Going alone, Anastatia?

ANASTATIA (shaking her curls). I am with Mrs. Jobson, sir, but I've got separated for the moment.

INSPECTOR. Oh! You are with the Jobsons? Quite right. That'll do, Miss Weedle. Don't lose your ticket.

Away she goes, and joins the Jobsons who are waiting for her, and stoops and kisses Brigham Jobson—who appears to be considered too young for the purpose, by several Mormons rising twenty, who are looking on. Before her extensive skirts have departed from the casks, a decent widow stands there with four children, and so the roll goes.

The faces of some of the Welsh people, among whom there were many old persons, were certainly the least intelligent. Some of these emigrants would have bungled sorely, but for the directing hand that was always ready. The intelligence here was unquestionably of a low order, and the heads were of a poor type. Generally the case was the reverse. There were many worn faces bearing traces of patient poverty and hard work, and there was great steadiness of purpose and much undemonstrative self-respect among this class. A few young men were going singly. Several girls were going, two or three together. These latter I found it very difficult to refer back, in my mind, to their relinquished homes and pursuits. Perhaps they were more like country milliners, and pupil teachers rather tawdrily dressed, than any other classes of young women. I noticed, among many little ornaments worn, more than one photograph-brooch of the Princess of Wales, and also of the late Prince Consort. Some single women of from thirty to forty, whom one might suppose to be embroiderers, or straw bonnet-makers, were obviously going out in quest of husbands, as finer ladies go to India. That they had any distinct notions of a plurality of husbands or wives, I do not believe. To suppose the family groups of whom the majority of emigrants were composed, polygamically possessed, would be to suppose an absurdity, manifest to any one who saw the fathers and mothers.

I should say (I had no means of ascertaining the fact) that most familiar kinds of handicraft trades were represented here. Farm-labourers, shepherds, and the like, had their full share of representation, but I doubt if they preponderated. It was interesting to see how the leading spirit in the family circle never failed to show itself, even in the simple process of answering to the names as they were called, and checking off the owners of the names. Sometimes it was the father, much oftener the mother, sometimes a quick little girl second or third in order of seniority. It seemed to occur for the first time to some heavy fathers, what large families they had; and their eyes rolled about, during the calling of the list, as if they half-misdoubted some other family to have been smuggled into their own. Among all the fine handsome children, I observed but two with marks upon their necks that were probably scrofulous. Out of the whole number of emigrants, but one old woman was temporarily set aside by the doctor, on suspicion of fever; but even she afterwards obtained a clean bill of health.

When all had "passed", and the afternoon began to wear on, a black box became visible on deck, which box was in charge of certain personages also in black, of whom only one had the conventional air of an itinerant preacher. This box contained a supply of hymn-books, neatly printed and got up, published at Liverpool, and also in London at the "Latter-Day Saints' Book Depôt, 30, Florence Street". Some copies were handsomely bound; the plainer were the more in request, and many were bought. The title ran: "Sacred Hymns and Spiritual Songs for the Church of Jesus Christ of Latter-Day Saints". The Preface, dated Manchester, 1840, ran thus:—"The Saints in this country have been very desirous for a Hymn Book adapted to their faith and worship, that they might sing the truth with an understanding heart, and express their praise joy and gratitude in songs adapted to the New and Everlasting Covenant. In accordance with their wishes, we have selected the following volume, which we hope will prove acceptable until a greater variety can be added. With sentiments of high consideration and esteem, we subscribe ourselves your brethren in the New and Everlasting Covenant, BRIGHAM YOUNG, PARLEY P. PRATT, JOHN TAYLOR." From this book—by no means explanatory to myself of the New and Everlasting Covenant, and not at all making my heart an understanding one on the subject of that mystery—a hymn was sung, which did not attract any great amount of attention, and was supported by a rather select circle. But the choir in the boat was very popular and pleasant; and there was to have been a Band, only the Cornet was late in coming on board. In the course of the afternoon, a mother appeared from shore, in search of her daughter, "who had run away with the Mormons". She received every assistance from the Inspector, but her daughter was not found to be on board. The saints did not seem to me particularly interested in finding her.

Towards five o'clock, the galley became full of tea-kettles, and an agreeable fragrance of tea pervaded the ship. There was no scrambling or jostling for the hot water, no ill humour, no quarrelling. As the Amazon was to sail with the next tide, and as it would not be high water before two o'clock in the morning, I left her with her tea in full action, and her idle Steam Tug lying by, deputing steam and smoke for the time being to the Tea-kettles.

I afterwards learned that a Despatch was sent home by the captain before he struck out into the wide Atlantic, highly extolling the behaviour of these Emigrants, and the perfect order and propriety of all their social arrangements. What is in store for the poor people on the shores of the Great Salt Lake, what happy delusions they are labouring under now, on what miserable blindness their eyes may be opened then, I do not pretend to say. But I went on board their ship to bear testimony against them if they deserved it, as I fully believed they would; to my great astonishment they did not deserve it; and my predispositions and tendencies must not affect me as an honest witness. I went over the Amazon's side, feeling it impossible to deny that, so far, some remarkable influence had produced a remarkable result, which better known influences have often missed.[1]

XXII

THE CITY OF THE ABSENT

WHEN I think I deserve particularly well of myself, and have earned the right to enjoy a little treat, I stroll from Covent Garden into the City of London, after business-hours there, on a Saturday, or—better yet—on a Sunday, and roam about its deserted nooks and corners. It is necessary to the full enjoyment of these journeys that they should be made in summer-time, for then the retired spots that I love to haunt, are at their idlest and dullest. A gentle fall of rain is not objectionable, and a warm mist sets off my favourite retreats to decided advantage.

Among these, City Churchyards hold a high place. Such strange churchyards hide in the City of London; churchyards sometimes so entirely detached from churches, always so pressed upon by houses; so small, so rank, so silent, so forgotten, except by the few people who ever look down into them from their smoky windows. As I stand peeping in through the iron gates and rails, I can peel the rusty metal off, like bark from an old tree. The illegible tombstones are all lopsided, the grave-mounds lost their shape in the rains of a hundred years ago, the Lombardy Poplar or Plane-Tree that was once a drysalter's daughter and several common-councilmen, has withered like those worthies, and its departed leaves are dust beneath it. Con-

[1] After this Uncommercial Journey was printed, I happened to mention the experience it describes to Lord Houghton. That gentleman then showed me an article of his writing, in *The Edinburgh Review* for January, 1862, which is highly remarkable for its philosophical and literary research concerning these Latter-Day Saints. I find in it the following sentences:—"The Select Committee of the House of Commons on emigrant ships for 1854 summoned the Mormon agent and passenger-broker before it, and came to the conclusion that no ships under the provisions of the 'Passengers Act' could be depended upon for comfort and security in the same degree as those under his administration. The Mormon ship is a Family under strong and accepted discipline, with every provision for comfort, decorum, and internal peace."

tagion of slow ruin overhangs the place. The discoloured tiled roofs of the environing buildings stand so awry, that they can hardly be proof against any stress of weather. Old crazy stacks of chimneys seem to look down as they overhang, dubiously calculating how far they will have to fall. In an angle of the walls, what was once the tool-house of the grave-digger rots away, encrusted with toadstools. Pipes and spouts for carrying off the rain from the encompassing gables, broken or feloniously cut for old lead long ago, now let the rain drip and splash as it list, upon the weedy earth. Sometimes there is a rusty pump somewhere near, and, as I look in at the rails and meditate, I hear it working under an unknown hand with a creaking protest: as though the departed in the churchyard urged, " Let us lie here in peace; don't suck us up and drink us !"

One of my best beloved churchyards, I call the churchyard of Saint Ghastly Grim; touching what men in general call it, I have no information. It lies at the heart of the City, and the Blackwall Railway shrieks at it daily. It is a small small churchyard, with a ferocious strong spiked iron gate, like a jail. This gate is ornamented with skulls and cross-bones, larger than the life, wrought in stone; but it likewise came into the mind of Saint Ghastly Grim, that to stick iron spikes a-top of the stone skulls, as though they were impaled, would be a pleasant device. Therefore the skulls grin aloft horribly, thrust through and through with iron spears. Hence, there is attraction of repulsion for me in Saint Ghastly Grim, and, having often contemplated it in the daylight and the dark, I once felt drawn towards it in a thunderstorm at midnight. "Why not?" I said, in self-excuse. " I have been to see the Colosseum by the light of the moon; is it worse to go to see Saint Ghastly Grim by the light of the lightning?" I repaired to the Saint in a hackney cab, and found the skulls most effective, having the air of a public execution, and seeming, as the lightning flashed, to wink and grin with the pain of the spikes. Having no other person to whom to impart my satisfaction, I communicated it to the driver. So far from being responsive, he surveyed me—he was naturally a bottle-nosed red-faced man—with a blanched countenance. And as he drove me back, he ever and again glanced in over his shoulder through the little front window of his carriage, as mistrusting that I was a fare originally from a grave in the churchyard of Saint Ghastly Grim, who might have flitted home again without paying.

Sometimes, the queer Hall of some queer Company gives upon a churchyard such as this, and, when the Livery dine, you may hear them (if you are looking in through the iron rails, which you never are when I am) toasting their own Worshipful prosperity. Sometimes, a wholesale house of business, requiring much room for stowage, will occupy one or two or even all three sides of the enclosing space, and the backs of bales of goods will lumber up the windows, as if they were holding some crowded trade-meeting of themselves within. Sometimes, the commanding windows are all blank, and show no more sign of life than the graves below—not so much, for *they* tell of what once upon a time was life undoubtedly. Such was the surrounding of one City churchyard that I saw last summer, on a Volunteering Saturday evening towards eight of the clock, when with astonishment I beheld an old old man and an old old woman in it, making hay. Yes, of all occupations in this world, making hay! It was a very confined patch of churchyard lying between Gracechurch Street and the Tower, capable of yielding, say an apronful of hay. By what means the old man and woman had got into it, with an almost toothless haymaking rake, I could not fathom. No open window was within view; no window at all was within view, sufficiently near the ground to have enabled their old legs to descend from it; the rusty churchyard-gate was locked, the mouldy church was locked. Gravely among the graves, they made hay, all alone by themselves. They looked like Time and his wife. There was but the one rake between them, and they both had hold of it in a pastorally-loving manner, and there was hay on the old woman's black bonnet, as if the old man had recently been playful. The old man was quite an obsolete old man, in knee-breeches and coarse grey stockings, and the old woman wore mittens like unto his stockings in texture and in colour. They took no heed of me as I looked on, unable to account for them. The old woman was much too bright for a pew-opener, the old man much too meek for a beadle. On an old tombstone in the foreground between me and them, were two cherubim; but for those celestial embellishments being represented as having no possible use for knee-breeches, stockings, or mittens, I should have compared them with the haymakers, and sought a likeness. I coughed and awoke the echoes, but the haymakers never looked at me. They used the rake with a measured action, drawing the scanty crop towards them; and so I was fain to leave them under three yards and a half of darkening sky, gravely making hay among the graves, all alone by themselves. Perhaps they were Spectres, and I wanted a Medium.

In another City churchyard of similar cramped dimensions, I saw, that self-same summer, two comfortable charity children. They were making love—tremendous proof of the vigour of that immortal article, for they were in the graceful uniform under which English Charity delights to hide herself—and they were overgrown, and their legs (his legs at least, for I am modestly incompetent to speak of hers) were as much in the wrong as mere passive weakness of character can render legs. O it was a leaden churchyard, but no doubt a golden ground to those young persons! I first saw them on a Saturday evening, and, perceiving from their occupation that Saturday evening was their trysting-time, I returned that evening se'nnight, and renewed the contemplation of them. They came there to shake the bits of matting which were spread in the church aisles, and they afterwards rolled them up, he rolling up his end, she rolling hers, until they met, and over the two once divided now united rolls—sweet

emblem!—gave and received a chaste salute.   It was so refreshing
to find one of my faded churchyards blooming into flower thus, that
I returned a second time, and a third, and ultimately this befell:—
They had left the church door open, in their dusting and arranging.
Walking in to look at the church, I became aware, by the dim light,
of him in the pulpit, of her in the reading-desk, of him looking down,
of her looking up, exchanging tender discourse.   Immediately both
dived, and became as it were non-existent on this sphere.   With an
assumption of innocence I turned to leave the sacred edifice, when
an obese form stood in the portal, puffily demanding Joseph, or in
default of Joseph, Celia.   Taking this monster by the sleeve, and
luring him forth on pretence of showing him whom he sought, I
gave time for the emergence of Joseph and Celia, who presently
came towards us in the churchyard, bending under dusty matting,
a picture of thriving and unconscious industry.   It would be super-
fluous to hint that I have ever since deemed this the proudest passage
in my life.

But such instances, or any tokens of vitality, are rare indeed in
my City churchyards.   A few sparrows occasionally try to raise a
lively chirrup in their solitary tree—perhaps, as taking a different
view of worms from that entertained by humanity—but they are flat
and hoarse of voice, like the clerk, the organ, the bell, the clergyman,
and all the rest of the Church-works when they are wound up for
Sunday.   Caged larks, thrushes, or blackbirds, hanging in neighbouring courts, pour forth their strains passionately, as scenting the
tree, trying to break out, and see leaves again before they die, but
their song is Willow, Willow—of a churchyard cast.   So little light
lives inside the churches of my churchyards, when the two are co-
existent, that it is often only by an accident and after long acquaintance that I discover their having stained glass in some odd window.
The westering sun slants into the churchyard by some unwonted entry,
a few prismatic tears drop on an old tombstone, and a window that I
thought was only dirty, is for the moment all bejewelled.   Then the
light passes and the colours die.   Though even then, if there be room
enough for me to fall back so far as that I can gaze up to the top of
the Church Tower, I see the rusty vane new burnished, and seeming
to look out with a joyful flash over the sea of smoke at the distant
shore of country.

Blinking old men who are let out of workhouses by the hour, have
a tendency to sit on bits of coping stone in these churchyards, leaning
with both hands on their sticks and asthmatically gasping.   The
more depressed class of beggars too, bring hither broken meats, and
munch.   I am on nodding terms with a meditative turncock who
lingers in one of them, and whom I suspect of a turn for poetry; the
rather, as he looks out of temper when he gives the fire-plug a disparaging wrench with that large tuning-fork of his which would wear
out the shoulder of his coat, but for a precautionary piece of inlaid
leather.   Fire-ladders, which I am satisfied nobody knows anything

about, and the keys of which were lost in ancient times, moulder away in the larger churchyards, under eaves like wooden eyebrows; and so removed are those corners from the haunts of men and boys, that once on a fifth of November I found a "Guy" trusted to take care of himself there, while his proprietors had gone to dinner. Of the expression of his face I cannot report, because it was turned to the wall; but his shrugged shoulders and his ten extended fingers, appeared to denote that he had moralised in his little straw chair on the mystery of mortality until he gave it up as a bad job.

You do not come upon these churchyards violently; there are shades of transition in the neighbourhood. An antiquated news shop, or barber's shop, apparently bereft of customers in the earlier days of George the Third, would warn me to look out for one, if any discoveries in this respect were left for me to make. A very quiet court, in combination with an unaccountable dyer's and scourer's, would prepare me for a churchyard. An exceedingly retiring public-house, with a bagatelle-board shadily visible in a sawdusty parlour shaped like an omnibus, and with a shelf of punch-bowls in the bar, would apprise me that I stood near consecrated ground. A "Dairy", exhibiting in its modest window one very little milk-can and three eggs, would suggest to me the certainty of finding the poultry hard by, pecking at my forefathers. I first inferred the vicinity of Saint Ghastly Grim, from a certain air of extra repose and gloom pervading a vast stock of warehouses.

From the hush of these places, it is congenial to pass into the hushed resorts of business. Down the lanes I like to see the carts and waggons huddled together in repose, the cranes idle, and the warehouses shut. Pausing in the alleys behind the closed Banks of mighty Lombard Street, it gives one as good as a rich feeling to think of the broad counters with a rim along the edge, made for telling money out on, the scales for weighing precious metals, the ponderous ledgers, and, above all, the bright copper shovels for shovelling gold. When I draw money, it never seems so much money as when it is shovelled at me out of a bright copper shovel. I like to say, "In gold", and to see seven pounds musically pouring out of the shovel, like seventy; the Bank appearing to remark to me—I italicise *appearing*—"if you want more of this yellow earth, we keep it in barrows at your service". To think of the banker's clerk with his deft finger turning the crisp edges of the Hundred-Pound Notes he has taken in a fat roll out of a drawer, is again to hear the rustling of that delicious south-cash wind. "How will you have it?" I once heard this usual question asked at a Bank Counter of an elderly female, habited in mourning and steeped in simplicity, who answered, open-eyed, crook-fingered, laughing with expectation, "Anyhow!" Calling these things to mind as I stroll among the Banks, I wonder whether the other solitary Sunday man I pass, has designs upon the Banks. For the interest and mystery of the matter, I almost hope he may have, and that his confederate may be at this moment taking impressions of the keys of the iron closets in wax, and that a delightful robbery may be in course of transaction. About College Hill, Mark Lane, and so on towards the Tower, and Dockward, the deserted wine-merchants' cellars are fine subjects for consideration; but the deserted money-cellars of the Bankers, and their plate-cellars, and their jewel-cellars, what subterranean regions of the Wonderful Lamp are these! And again: possibly some shoeless boy in rags, passed through this street yesterday, for whom it is reserved to be a Banker in the fulness of time, and to be surpassing rich. Such reverses have been, since the days of Whittington; and were, long before. I want to know whether the boy has any foreglittering of that glittering fortune now, when he treads these stones, hungry. Much as I also want to know whether the next man to be hanged at Newgate yonder, had any suspicion upon him that he was moving steadily towards that fate, when he talked so much about the last man who paid the same great debt at the same small Debtors' Door.

Where are all the people who on busy working-days pervade these scenes? The locomotive banker's clerk, who carries a black portfolio chained to him by a chain of steel, where is he? Does he go to bed with his chain on—to church with his chain on—or does he lay it by? And if he lays it by, what becomes of his portfolio when he is unchained for a holiday? The wastepaper baskets of these closed counting-houses would let me into many hints of business matters if I had the exploration of them; and what secrets of the heart should I discover on the "pads" of the young clerks—the sheets of cartridge-paper and blotting-paper interposed between their writing and their desks! Pads are taken into confidence on the tenderest occasions, and oftentimes when I have made a business visit, and have sent in my name from the outer office, have I had it forced on my discursive notice that the officiating young gentleman has over and over again inscribed AMELIA, in ink of various dates, on corners of his pad. Indeed, the pad may be regarded as the legitimate modern successor of the old forest-tree: whereon these young knights (having no attainable forest nearer than Epping) engrave the names of their mistresses. After all, it is a more satisfactory process than carving, and can be oftener repeated. So these courts in their Sunday rest are courts of Love Omnipotent (I rejoice to bethink myself), dry as they look. And here is Garraway's, bolted and shuttered hard and fast! It is possible to imagine the man who cuts the sandwiches, on his back in a hayfield; it is possible to imagine his desk, like the desk of a clerk at church, without him; but imagination is unable to pursue the men who wait at Garraway's all the week for the men who never come. When they are forcibly put out of Garraway's on Saturday night—which they must be, for they never would go out of their own accord—where do they vanish until Monday morning? On the first Sunday that I ever strayed here, I expected to find them hovering about these lanes, like restless ghosts, and trying to peep into Garraway's through chinks in the shutters, if not endeavouring to turn the lock of the door with false keys, picks, and screw-drivers. But the wonder is, that they go clean away! And now I think of it, the wonder is, that every working-day pervader of these scenes goes clean away. The man who sells the dogs' collars and the little toy coal-scuttles, feels under as great an obligation to go afar off, as Glyn and Co., or Smith, Payne, and Smith. There is an old monastery-crypt under Garraway's (I have been in it among the port wine), and perhaps Garraway's, taking pity on the mouldy men who wait in its public-room all their lives, gives them cool house-room down there over Sundays; but the catacombs of Paris would not be large enough to hold the rest of the missing. This characteristic of London City greatly helps its being the quaint place it is in the weekly pause of business, and greatly helps my Sunday sensation in it of being the Last Man. In my solitude, the ticket-porters being all gone with the rest, I venture to breathe to the quiet bricks and stones my confidential wonderment why a ticket-porter, who never does any work with his hands, is bound to wear a white apron, and why a great Ecclesiastical Dignitary, who never does any work with his hands either, is equally bound to wear a black one.

XXIII

AN OLD STAGE-COACHING HOUSE

BEFORE the waitress had shut the door, I had forgotten how many stage-coaches she said used to change horses in the town every day. But it was of little moment; any high number would do as well as another. It had been a great stage-coaching town in the great stage-coaching times, and the ruthless railways had killed and buried it.

The sign of the house was the Dolphin's Head. Why only head, I don't know; for the Dolphin's effigy at full length, and upside down —as a Dolphin is always bound to be when artistically treated, though I suppose he is sometimes right side upward in his natural condition—graced the sign-board. The sign-board chafed its rusty hooks outside the bow-window of my room, and was a shabby work. No visitor could have denied that the Dolphin was dying by inches, but he showed no bright colours. He had once served another master; there was a newer streak of paint below him, displaying with inconsistent freshness the legend, By J. MELLOWS.

My door opened again, and J. Mellows's representative came back. I had asked her what I could have for dinner, and she now returned with the counter question, what would I like? As the Dolphin stood possessed of nothing that I do like, I was fain to yield to the suggestion of a duck, which I don't like. J. Mellows's representative was a mournful young woman, with one eye susceptible of guidance, and one uncontrollable eye; which latter, seeming to wander in quest of stage-coaches, deepened the melancholy in which the Dolphin was steeped.

This young woman had but shut the door on retiring again when I bethought me of adding to my order, the words, "with nice vegetables". Looking out at the door to give them emphatic utterance, I found her already in a state of pensive catalepsy in the deserted gallery, picking her teeth with a pin.

At the Railway Station seven miles off, I had been the subject of wonder when I ordered a fly in which to come here. And when I gave the direction "To the Dolphin's Head", I had observed an ominous stare on the countenance of the strong young man in velveteen, who was the platform servant of the Company. He had also called to my driver at parting, "All ri-ight! Don't hang yourself when you get there, Geo-o-rge!" in a sarcastic tone, for which I had entertained some transitory thoughts of reporting him to the General Manager.

I had no business in the town—I never have any business in any town—but I had been caught by the fancy that I would come and look at it in its degeneracy. My purpose was fitly inaugurated by the Dolphin's Head, which everywhere expressed past coachfulness and present coachlessness. Coloured prints of coaches, starting, arriving, changing horses, coaches in the sunshine, coaches in the snow, coaches in the wind, coaches in the mist and rain, coaches on the King's birthday, coaches in all circumstances compatible with their triumph and victory, but never in the act of breaking down or overturning, pervaded the house. Of these works of art, some, framed and not glazed, had holes in them; the varnish of others had become so brown and cracked, that they looked like overdone pie-crust; the designs of others were almost obliterated by the flies of many summers. Broken glasses, damaged frames, lopsided hanging, and consignment of incurable cripples to places of refuge in dark corners, attested the desolation of the rest. The old room on the ground floor where the passengers of the Highflyer used to dine, had nothing in it but a wretched show of twigs and flower-pots in the broad window to hide the nakedness of the land, and in a corner little Mellows's perambulator, with even its parasol-head turned despondently to the wall. The other room, where post-horse company used to wait while relays were getting ready down the yard, still held its ground, but was as airless as I conceive a hearse to be: insomuch that Mr. Pitt, hanging high against the partition (with spots on him like port wine, though it is mysterious how port wine ever got squirted up there), had good reason for perking his nose and sniffing. The stopperless cruets on the spindle-shanked sideboard were in a miserably dejected state: the anchovy sauce having turned blue some years ago, and the cayenne pepper (with a scoop in it like a small model of a wooden leg) having turned solid. The old fraudulent candles which were always being paid for and never used, were burnt out at last; but their tall stilts of candlesticks still lingered, and still outraged the human intellect by pretending to be silver. The mouldy old unreformed Borough Member, with his right hand buttoned up in the breast of his coat, and his back characteristically turned on bales of petitions from his constituents, was there too; and the poker which never had been among the fire-irons, lest post-horse company should overstir the fire, was *not* there, as of old.

Pursuing my researches in the Dolphin's Head, I found it sorely shrunken. When J. Mellows came into possession, he had walled off half the bar, which was now a tobacco-shop with its own entrance in the yard—the once glorious yard where the post-boys, whip in hand and always buttoning their waistcoats at the last moment, used to come running forth to mount and away. A "Scientific Shoeing-Smith and Veterinary Surgeon", had further encroached upon the yard; and a grimly satirical Jobber, who announced himself as having to Let "A neat one-horse fly, and a one-horse cart", had established his business, himself, and his family, in a part of the extensive stables. Another part was lopped clean off from the Dolphin's Head, and now comprised a chapel, a wheelwright's, and a Young Men's Mutual Improvement and Discussion Society (in a loft): the whole forming a back lane. No audacious hand had plucked down the vane from the central cupola of the stables, but it had grown rusty and stuck at N—Nil: while the score or two of pigeons that remained true to their ancestral traditions and the place, had collected in a row on the roof-ridge of the only outhouse retained by the Dolphin, where all the inside pigeons tried to push the outside pigeon off. This I accepted as emblematical of the struggle for post and place in railway times.

Sauntering forth into the town, by way of the covered and pillared entrance to the Dolphin's Yard, once redolent of soup and stable-litter, now redolent of musty disuse, I paced the street. It was a hot day, and the little sun-blinds of the shops were all drawn down, and the more enterprising tradesmen had caused their 'Prentices to trickle water on the pavement appertaining to their frontage. It looked as if they had been shedding tears for the stage-coaches, and drying their ineffectual pocket-handkerchiefs. Such weakness would have been excusable; for business was—as one dejected porkman who kept a shop which refused to reciprocate the compliment by keeping him, informed me—"bitter bad". Most of the harness-makers and corn-dealers were gone the way of the coaches, but it was a pleasant recognition of the eternal procession of Children down that old original steep Incline, the Valley of the Shadow, that those tradesmen were mostly succeeded by vendors of sweetmeats and cheap toys. The opposition house to the Dolphin, once famous as the New White Hart, had long collapsed. In a fit of abject depression, it had cast white-wash on its windows, and boarded up its front door, and reduced itself to a side entrance; but even that had proved a world too wide for the Literary Institution which had been its last phase; for the Institution had collapsed too, and of the ambitious letters of its inscription on the White Hart's front, all had fallen off but these:

L   Y   INS   T

—suggestive of Lamentably Insolvent. As to the neighbouring market-place, it seemed to have wholly relinquished marketing, to the dealer in crockery whose pots and pans straggled half across it, and to the Cheap Jack who sat with folded arms on the shafts of his cart, superciliously gazing around; his velveteen waistcoat, evidently harbouring grave doubts whether it was worth his while to stay a night in such a place.

The church bells began to ring as I left this spot, but they by no means improved the case, for they said, in a petulant way, and speaking with some difficulty in their irritation, "WHAT's-be-come-of-THE-coach-ES!" Nor would they (I found on listening) ever vary their emphasis, save in respect of growing more sharp and vexed, but invariably went on, "WHAT's-be-come-of-THE-coach-ES!"—always beginning the inquiry with an unpolite abruptness. Perhaps from their elevation they saw the railway, and it aggravated them.

Coming upon a coachmaker's workshop, I began to look about me with a revived spirit, thinking that perchance I might behold there some remains of the old times of the town's greatness. There was only one man at work—a dry man, grizzled, and far advanced in years, but tall and upright, who, becoming aware of me looking on, straightened his back, pushed up his spectacles against his brown paper cap, and appeared inclined to defy me. To whom I pacifically said:

"Good-day, sir!"

"What?" said he.

"Good-day, sir."

He seemed to consider about that, and not to agree with me.—"Was you a looking for anything?" he then asked, in a pointed manner.

"I was wondering whether there happened to be any fragment of an old stage-coach here."

"Is that all?"

"That's all."

"No, there ain't."

It was now my turn to say "Oh!" and I said it. Not another word did the dry and grizzled man say, but bent to his work again. In the coach-making days, the coach-painters had tried their brushes on a post beside him; and quite a Calendar of departed glories was to be read upon it, in blue and yellow and red and green, some inches thick. Presently he looked up again.

"You seem to have a deal of time on your hands," was his querulous remark.

I admitted the fact.

"I think it's a pity you was not brought up to something," said he.

I said I thought so too.

Appearing to be informed with an idea, he laid down his plane (for it was a plane he was at work with), pushed up his spectacles again, and came to the door.

"Would a po-shay do for you?" he asked.

"I am not sure that I understand what you mean."

"Would a po-shay," said the coachmaker, standing close before me, and folding his arms in the manner of a cross-examining counsel—"would a po-shay meet the views you have expressed? Yes, or no?"

"Yes."

"Then you keep straight along down there till you see one. *You'll* see one if you go fur enough."

With that, he turned me by the shoulder in the direction I was to take, and went in and resumed his work against a background of leaves and grapes. For, although he was a soured man and a discontented, his workshop was that agreeable mixture of town and country, street and garden, which is often to be seen in a small English town.

I went the way he had turned me, and I came to the Beer-shop with the sign of The First and Last, and was out of the town on the old London road. I came to the Turnpike, and I found it, in its silent way, eloquent respecting the change that had fallen on the road. The Turnpike-house was all overgrown with ivy; and the Turnpike-keeper, unable to get a living out of the tolls, plied the trade of a cobbler. Not only that, but his wife sold ginger-beer, and, in the very window of espial through which the Toll-takers of old times used with awe to behold the grand London coaches coming on at a gallop, exhibited for sale little barber's-poles of sweetstuff in a sticky lantern.

The political economy of the master of the turnpike thus expressed itself.

"How goes turnpike business, master?" said I to him, as he sat in his little porch, repairing a shoe.

"It don't go at all, master," said he to me. "It's stopped."

"That's bad," said I.

"Bad?" he repeated. And he pointed to one of his sunburnt dusty children who was climbing the turnpike-gate, and said, extending his open right hand in remonstrance with Universal Nature, "Five on 'em!"

"But how to improve Turnpike business?" said I.

"There's a way, master," said he, with the air of one who had thought deeply on the subject.

"I should like to know it."

"Lay a toll on everything as comes through; lay a toll on walkers. Lay another toll on everything as don't come through; lay a toll on them as stops at home."

"Would the last remedy be fair?"

"Fair? Them as stops at home, could come through if they liked; couldn't they?"

"Say they could."

"Toll 'em. If they don't come through, it's *their* look out. Anyways,—Toll 'em!"

Finding it was as impossible to argue with this financial genius as if he had been Chancellor of the Exchequer, and consequently the right man in the right place, I passed on meekly.

My mind now began to misgive me that the disappointed coach-maker had sent me on a wild-goose errand, and that there was no post-chaise in those parts. But coming within view of certain allotment-gardens by the roadside, I retracted the suspicion, and confessed that I had done him an injustice. For, there I saw, surely, the poorest superannuated post-chaise left on earth.

It was a post-chaise taken off its axletree and wheels, and plumped down on the clayey soil among a ragged growth of vegetables. It was a post-chaise not even set straight upon the ground, but tilted over, as if it had fallen out of a balloon. It was a post-chaise that had been a long time in those decayed circumstances, and against which scarlet beans were trained. It was a post-chaise patched and mended with old teatrays, or with scraps of iron that looked like them, and boarded up as to the windows, but having A KNOCKER on the off-side door. Whether it was a post-chaise used as tool-house, summer-house, or dwelling-house, I could not discover, for there was nobody at home at the post-chaise when I knocked; but it was certainly used for something, and locked up. In the wonder of this discovery, I walked round and round the post-chaise many times, and sat down by the post-chaise, waiting for further elucidation. None came. At last, I made my way back to the old London road by the further end of the allotment-gardens, and consequently at a point beyond that from which I had diverged. I had to scramble through a hedge and down a steep bank, and I nearly came down a-top of a little spare man who sat breaking stones by the roadside.

He stayed his hammer, and said, regarding me mysteriously through his dark goggles of wire:

"Are you aware, sir, that you've been trespassing?"

"I turned out of the way," said I, in explanation, "to look at that odd post-chaise. Do you happen to know anything about it?"

"I know it was many a year upon the road," said he.

"So I supposed. Do you know to whom it belongs?"

The stone-breaker bent his brows and goggles over his heap of stones, as if he were considering whether he should answer the question or not. Then, raising his barred eyes to my features as before, he said:

"To me."

Being quite unprepared for the reply, I received it with a sufficiently awkward "Indeed! Dear me!" Presently I added, "Do you——"

I was going to say "live there", but it seemed so absurd a question, that I substituted "live near here?"

The stone-breaker, who had not broken a fragment since we began to converse, then did as follows. He raised himself by poising his figure on his hammer, and took his coat, on which he had been seated, over his arm. He then backed to an easier part of the bank than that by which I had come down, keeping his dark goggles silently upon me all the time, and then shouldered his hammer, suddenly turned, ascended, and was gone. His face was so small, and his goggles were so large, that he left me wholly uninformed as to his countenance; but he left me a profound impression that the curved legs I had seen from behind as he vanished, were the legs of an old postboy. It was not until then that I noticed he had been working by a grass-grown milestone, which looked like a tombstone erected over the grave of the London road.

My dinner-hour being close at hand, I had no leisure to pursue the goggles or the subject then, but made my way back to the Dolphin's Head. In the gateway I found J. Mellows, looking at nothing, and apparently experiencing that it failed to raise his spirits.

"*I* don't care for the town," said J. Mellows, when I complimented him on the sanitary advantages it may or may not possess; "I wish I had never seen the town!"

"You don't belong to it, Mr. Mellows?"

"Belong to it!" repeated Mellows. "If I didn't belong to a better style of town than this, I'd take and drown myself in a pail." It then occurred to me that Mellows, having so little to do, was habitually thrown back on his internal resources—by which I mean the Dolphin's cellar.

"What we want," said Mellows, pulling off his hat, and making as if he emptied it of the last load of Disgust that had exuded from his brain, before he put it on again for another load; "what we want, is a Branch. The Petition for the Branch Bill is in the coffee-room. Would you put your name to it? Every little helps."

I found the document in question stretched out flat on the coffee-room table by the aid of certain weights from the kitchen, and I gave it the additional weight of my uncommercial signature. To the best of my belief, I bound myself to the modest statement that universal traffic, happiness, prosperity, and civilisation, together with unbounded national triumph in competition with the foreigner, would infallibly flow from the Branch.

Having achieved this constitutional feat, I asked Mr. Mellows if he could grace my dinner with a pint of good wine? Mr. Mellows thus replied:

"If I couldn't give you a pint of good wine, I'd—there!—I'd take and drown myself in a pail. But I was deceived when I bought this business, and the stock was higgledy-piggledy, and I haven't yet tasted my way quite through it with a view to sorting it. Therefore, if you order one kind and get another, change till it comes right. For what," said Mellows, unloading his hat as before, "what would you or any gentleman do, if you ordered one kind of wine and was required to drink another? Why, you'd (and naturally and properly, having the feelings of a gentleman), you'd take and drown yourself in a pail!"

XXIV

THE BOILED BEEF OF NEW ENGLAND

THE shabbiness of our English capital, as compared with Paris, Bordeaux, Frankfort, Milan, Geneva—almost any important town on the continent of Europe—I find very striking after an absence of any duration in foreign parts. London is shabby in contrast with Edinburgh, with Aberdeen, with Exeter, with Liverpool, with a bright little town like Bury St. Edmunds. London is shabby in contrast with New York, with Boston, with Philadelphia. In detail, one would say it can rarely fail to be a disappointing piece of shabbiness, to a stranger from any of those places. There is nothing shabbier than Drury Lane, in Rome itself. The meanness of Regent Street, set against the great line of Boulevarts in Paris, is as striking as the abortive ugliness of Trafalgar Square, set against the gallant beauty of the Place de la Concorde. London is shabby by daylight, and shabbier by gaslight. No Englishman knows what gaslight is, until he sees the Rue de Rivoli and the Palais Royal after dark.

The mass of London people are shabby. The absence of distinctive dress has, no doubt, something to do with it. The porters of the Vintners' Company, the draymen, and the butchers, are about the only people who wear distinctive dresses; and even these do not wear them on holidays. We have nothing which for cheapness, cleanliness, convenience, or picturesqueness, can compare with the belted blouse. As to our women;—next Easter or Whitsuntide, look at the bonnets at the British Museum or the National Gallery, and think of the pretty white French cap, the Spanish mantilla, or the Genoese mezzero.

Probably there are not more second-hand clothes sold in London than in Paris, and yet the mass of the London population have a second-hand look which is not to be detected on the mass of the Parisian population. I think this is mainly because a Parisian workman does not in the least trouble himself about what is worn by a Parisian idler, but dresses in the way of his own class, and for his own comfort. In London, on the contrary, the fashions descend; and you never fully know how inconvenient or ridiculous a fashion is, until you see it in its last descent. It was but the other day, on a race-course, that I observed four people in a barouche deriving great entertainment from the contemplation of four people on foot. The four people on foot were two young men and two young women; the four people in the barouche were two young men and two young women. The four young women were dressed in exactly the same style; the four young men were dressed in exactly the same style. Yet the two couples on wheels were as much amused by the two couples on foot, as if they were quite unconscious of having themselves set those fashions, or of being at that very moment engaged in the display of them.

Is it only in the matter of clothes that fashion descends here in London—and consequently in England—and thence shabbiness arises? Let us think a little, and be just. The "Black Country" round about Birmingham, is a very black country; but is it quite as black as it has been lately painted? An appalling accident happened at the People's Park near Birmingham, this last July, when it was crowded with people from the Black Country—an appalling accident consequent on a shamefully dangerous exhibition. Did the shamefully dangerous exhibition originate in the moral blackness of the Black Country and in the Black People's peculiar love of the excitement attendant on great personal hazard, which they looked on at, but in which they did not participate? Light is much wanted in the Black Country. O we are all agreed on that. But, we must not quite forget the crowds of gentlefolks who set the shamefully dangerous fashion, either. We must not quite forget the enterprising Directors of an Institution vaunting mighty educational pretences, who made the low sensation as strong as they possibly could make it, by hanging the Blondin rope as high as they possibly could hang it. All this must not be eclipsed in the Blackness of the Black Country. The reserved seats high up by the rope, the cleared space below it, so that no one should be smashed but the performer, the pretence of slipping and falling off, the baskets for the feet and the sack for the head, the·photographs everywhere, and the virtuous indignation nowhere—all this must not be wholly swallowed up in the blackness of the jet-black country.

Whatsoever fashion is set in England, is certain to descend. This is a text for a perpetual sermon on care in setting fashions. When you find a fashion low down, look back for the time (it will never be far off) when it was the fashion high up. This is the text for a perpetual sermon on social justice. From imitations of Ethiopian Serenaders, to imitations of Prince's coats and waistcoats, you will find the original model in St. James's Parish. When the Serenaders become tiresome, trace them beyond the Black Country; when the coats and waistcoats become insupportable, refer them to their source in the Upper Toady Regions.

Gentlemen's clubs were once maintained for purposes of savage party warfare; working men's clubs of the same day assumed the same character. Gentlemen's clubs became places of quiet inoffensive recreation; working men's clubs began to follow suit. If working men have seemed rather slow to appreciate advantages of combination which have saved the pockets of gentlemen, and enhanced their comforts, it is because working men could scarcely, for want of capital, originate such combinations without help; and because help has not been separable from that great impertinence, Patronage. The instinctive revolt of his spirit against patronage, is a quality much to be respected in the English working man. It is the base of the base of his best qualities. Nor is it surprising that he should be unduly suspicious of patronage, and sometimes resentful of it even where it is not, seeing what a flood of washy talk has been let loose on his devoted head, or with what complacent condescension the same devoted head has been smoothed and patted. It is a proof to me of his self-control that he never strikes out pugilistically, right and left, when addressed as one of " My friends", or " My assembled friends"; that he does not become inappeasable, and run amuck like a Malay, whenever he sees a biped in broadcloth getting on a platform to talk to him; that any pretence of improving his mind, does not instantly drive him out of his mind, and cause him to toss his obliging patron like a mad bull.

For, how often have I heard the unfortunate working man lectured, as if he were a little charity-child, humid as to his nasal development, strictly literal as to his Catechism, and called by Providence to walk all his days in a station in life represented on festive occasions by a mug of warm milk-and-water and a bun! What popguns of jokes have these ears tingled to hear let off at him, what asinine sentiments, what impotent conclusions, what spelling-book moralities, what adaptations of the orator's insufferable tediousness to the assumed level of his understanding! If his sledge-hammers, his spades and pick-axes, his saws and chisels, his paint-pots and brushes, his forges, furnaces, and engines, the horses that he drove at his work, and the machines that drove him at his work, were all toys in one little paper box, and he the baby who played with them, he could not have been discoursed to, more impertinently and absurdly than I have heard him discoursed to times innumerable. Consequently, not being a fool or a fawner, he has come to acknowledge his patronage by virtually saying: " Let me alone. If you understand me no better than *that*, sir and madam, let me alone. You mean very well, I dare say, but I don't like it, and I won't come here again to have any more of it."

Whatever is done for the comfort and advancement of the working man must be so far done by himself as that it is maintained by himself. And there must be in it no touch of condescension, no shadow of patronage. In the great working districts, this truth is studied and understood. When the American civil war rendered it necessary, first in Glasgow, and afterwards in Manchester, that the working people should be shown how to avail themselves of the advantages derivable from system, and from the combination of numbers, in the purchase and the cooking of their food, this truth was above all things borne in mind. The quick consequence was, that suspicion and reluctance were vanquished, and that the effort resulted in an astonishing and a complete success.

Such thoughts passed through my mind on a July morning of this summer, as I walked towards Commercial Street (not Uncommercial Street), Whitechapel. The Glasgow and Manchester system had been lately set a-going there, by certain gentlemen who felt an interest in its diffusion, and I had been attracted by the following hand-bill printed on rose-coloured paper:

SELF-SUPPORTING

COOKING DEPÔT

FOR THE WORKING CLASSES,

Commercial Street, Whitechapel,

Where Accommodation is provided for Dining comfortably 300 Persons at a time.

Open from 7 A.M. till 7 P.M.

PRICES.

All Articles of the BEST QUALITY.

Cup of Tea or Coffee	...	...	...	One Penny
Bread and Butter...	...	...	...	One Penny
Bread and Cheese	...	...	...	One Penny
Slice of Bread...One half-penny or			...	One Penny
Boiled Egg	...	...	...	One Penny
Ginger Beer	...	...	...	One Penny

The above Articles always ready.

Besides the above may be had, from 12 to 3 o'clock,

Bowl of Scotch Broth	...	...	...	One Penny
Bowl of Soup	...	...	...	One Penny
Plate of Potatoes ...	...	...	...	One Penny
Plate of Minced Beef	...	...	...	Twopence
Plate of Cold Beef	...	...	...	Twopence
Plate of Cold Ham	...	...	...	Twopence
Plate of Plum Pudding or Rice	...		...	One Penny

As the Economy of Cooking depends greatly upon the simplicity of the arrangements with which a great number of persons can be served at one time, the Upper Room of this Establishment will be especially set apart for a

PUBLIC DINNER EVERY DAY

From 12 till 3 o'clock.

Consisting of the following Dishes:

Bowl of Broth, or Soup,
Plate of Cold Beef or Ham,
Plate of Potatoes,
Plum Pudding, or Rice,

FIXED CHARGE, 4½d.

THE DAILY PAPERS PROVIDED.

N.B.—This Establishment is conducted on the strictest business principles, with the full intention of making it self-supporting, so that every one may frequent it with a feeling of perfect independence.

The assistance of all frequenting the Depôt is confidently expected in checking anything interfering with the comfort, quiet, and regularity of the establishment.

Please do not destroy this Hand Bill, but hand it to some other person whom it may interest.

This Self-Supporting Cooking Depôt (not a very good name, and one would rather give it an English one) had hired a newly-built warehouse that it found to let; therefore it was not established in premises specially designed for the purpose. But, at a small cost they were exceedingly well adapted to the purpose: being light, well ventilated, clean, and cheerful. They consisted of three large rooms. That on the basement story was the kitchen; that on the ground floor was the general dining-room; that on the floor above was the Upper Room referred to in the hand-bill, where the Public Dinner at fourpence-halfpenny a head was provided every day. The cooking was done, with much economy of space and fuel, by American cooking-stoves, and by young women not previously brought up as cooks; the walls and pillars of the two dining-rooms were agreeably brightened with ornamental colours; the tables were capable of accommodating six or eight persons each; the attendants were all young women, becomingly and neatly dressed, and dressed alike. I think the whole staff was female, with the exception of the steward or manager.

My first inquiries were directed to the wages of this staff; because, if any establishment claiming to be self-supporting, live upon the spoliation of anybody or anything, or eke out a feeble existence by poor mouths and beggarly resources (as too many so-called Mechanics' Institutions do), I make bold to express my Uncommercial opinion that it has no business to live, and had better die. It was made clear to me by the account books, that every person employed was properly paid. My next inquiries were directed to the quality of the provisions purchased, and to the terms on which they were bought. It was made equally clear to me that the quality was the very best, and that all bills were paid weekly. My next inquiries were directed to the balance-sheet for the last two weeks—only the third and fourth of the establishment's career. It was made equally clear to me, that after everything bought was paid for, and after each week was charged with its full share of wages, rent and taxes, depreciation of plant in use, and interest on capital at the rate of four per cent. per annum, the last week had yielded a profit of (in round numbers) one pound ten; and the previous week a profit of six pounds ten. By this time I felt that I had a healthy appetite for the dinners.

It had just struck twelve, and a quick succession of faces had already begun to appear at a little window in the wall of the partitioned space where I sat looking over the books. Within this little window like a pay-box at a theatre, a neat and brisk young woman presided to take money and issue tickets. Every one coming in must take a ticket. Either the fourpence-halfpenny ticket for the upper room (the most popular ticket, I think), or a penny ticket for a bowl of soup, or as many penny tickets as he or she chose to buy. For three penny tickets one had quite a wide range of choice. A plate of cold boiled beef and potatoes; or a plate of cold ham and potatoes; or a plate of hot minced beef and potatoes; or a bowl of soup, bread and cheese, and a plate of plum-pudding. Touching what they should have, some customers on taking their seats fell into a reverie—became mildly distracted—postponed decision, and said in bewilderment, they would think of it. One old man I noticed when I sat among the tables in the lower room, who was startled by the bill of fare, and sat contemplating it as if it were something of a ghostly nature. The decision of the boys was as rapid as their execution, and always included pudding.

There were several women among the diners, and several clerks and shopmen. There were carpenters and painters from the neighbouring buildings under repair, and there were nautical men, and there were, as one diner observed to me, "some of most sorts". Some were solitary, some came two together, some dined in parties of three or four, or six. The latter talked together, but assuredly no one was louder than at my club in Pall-Mall. One young fellow whistled in rather a shrill manner while he waited for his dinner, but I was gratified to observe that he did so in evident defiance of my Uncommercial individuality. Quite agreeing with him, on consideration, that I had no business to be there, unless I dined like the rest, I "went in", as the phrase is, for fourpence-halfpenny.

The room of the fourpence-halfpenny banquet had, like the lower room, a counter in it, on which were ranged a great number of cold portions ready for distribution. Behind this counter, the fragrant soup was steaming in deep cans, and the best-cooked of potatoes were fished out of similar receptacles. Nothing to eat was touched with the hand. Every waitress had her own tables to attend to. As soon as she saw a new customer seat himself at one of her tables, she took from the counter all his dinner—his soup, potatoes, meat, and pudding—piled it up dexterously in her two hands, set it before him, and took his ticket. This serving of the whole dinner at once, had been found greatly to simplify the business of attendance, and was also popular with the customers: who were thus enabled to vary the meal by varying the routine of dishes: beginning with soup to-day, putting soup in the middle to-morrow, putting soup at the end the day after to-morrow, and ringing similar changes on meat and pudding. The rapidity with which every new comer got served, was remarkable; and the dexterity with which the waitresses (quite new to the art a month before) discharged their duty, was as agreeable to see, as the neat smartness with which they wore their dress and had dressed their hair.

If I seldom saw better waiting, so I certainly never ate better meat, potatoes, or pudding. And the soup was an honest and stout soup, with rice and barley in it, and "little matters for the teeth to touch", as had been observed to me by my friend below stairs already quoted. The dinner-service, too, was neither conspicuously hideous for High Art nor for Low Art, but was of a pleasant and pure appearance. Concerning the viands and their cookery, one last remark. I dined at my club in Pall-Mall aforesaid, a few days afterwards, for exactly twelve times the money, and not half as well.

The company thickened after one o'clock struck, and changed pretty quickly. Although experience of the place had been so recently attainable, and although there was still considerable curiosity out in the street and about the entrance, the general tone was as good as could be, and the customers fell easily into the ways of the place. It was clear to me, however, that they were there to have what they paid for, and to be on an independent footing. To the best of my judgment, they might be patronised out of the building in a month. With judicious visiting, and by dint of being questioned, read to, and talked at, they might even be got rid of (for the next quarter of a century) in half the time.

This disinterested and wise movement is fraught with so many wholesome changes in the lives of the working people, and with so much good in the way of overcoming that suspicion which our own unconscious impertinence has engendered, that it is scarcely gracious to criticise details as yet; the rather, because it is indisputable that the managers of the Whitechapel establishment most thoroughly feel that they are upon their honour with the customers, as to the minutest points of administration. But, although the American stoves cannot roast, they can surely boil one kind of meat as well as another, and need not always circumscribe their boiling talents within the limits of ham and beef. The most enthusiastic admirer of those substantials, would probably not object to occasional inconstancy in respect of pork and mutton: or, especially in cold weather, to a little innocent trifling with Irish stews, meat pies, and toads in holes. Another drawback on the Whitechapel establishment, is the absence of beer. Regarded merely as a question of policy, it is very impolitic, as having a tendency to send the working men to the public-house, where gin is reported to be sold. But, there is a much higher ground on which this absence of beer is objectionable. It expresses distrust of the working man. It is a fragment of that old mantle of patronage in which so many estimable Thugs, so darkly wandering up and down the moral world, are sworn to muffle him. Good beer is a good thing for him, he says, and he likes it; the Depôt could give it him good, and he now gets it bad. Why does the Depôt not give it him good? Because he would get drunk. Why does the Depôt not let him have a pint with his dinner, which would not make him drunk? Because he might have had another pint, or another two pints, before he came. Now, this distrust is an affront, is exceedingly inconsistent with the confidence the managers express in their hand-bills, and is a timid stopping-short upon the straight highway. It is unjust and unreasonable, also. It is unjust, because it punishes the sober man for the vice of the drunken man. It is unreasonable, because any one at all experienced in such things knows that the drunken workman does not get drunk where he goes to eat and drink, but where he goes to drink—expressly to drink. To suppose that the working man cannot state this question to himself quite as plainly as I state it here, is to suppose that he is a baby, and is again to tell him in the old wearisome condescending patronising way that he must be goody-poody, and do as he is toldy-poldy, and not be a manny-panny or a voter-poter, but fold his handy-pandys, and be a childy-pildy.

I found from the accounts of the Whitechapel Self-Supporting Cooking Depôt, that every article sold in it, even at the prices I have quoted, yields a certain small profit! Individual speculators are of course already in the field, and are of course already appropriating the name. The classes for whose benefit the real depôts are designed, will distinguish between the two kinds of enterprise.

XXV

CHATHAM DOCKYARD

THERE are some small out-of-the-way landing-places on the Thames and the Medway, where I do much of my summer idling. Running water is favourable to day-dreams, and a strong tidal river is the best of running water for mine. I like to watch the great ships standing out to sea or coming home richly laden, the active little steam-tugs confidently puffing with them to and from the sea-horizon, the fleet of barges that seem to have plucked their brown and russet sails from the ripe trees in the landscape, the heavy old colliers, light in ballast, floundering down before the tide, the light screw barks and schooners imperiously holding a straight course while the others patiently tack and go about, the yachts with their tiny hulls and great white sheets of canvas, the little sailing-boats bobbing to and fro on their errands of pleasure or business, and—as it is the nature of little people to do—making a prodigious fuss about their small affairs. Watching these objects, I still am under no obligation to think about them, or even so much as to see them, unless it perfectly suits my humour. As little am I obliged to hear the plash and flop of the tide, the ripple at my feet, the clinking windlass afar off, or the humming steam-ship paddles further away yet. These, with the creaking little jetty on which I sit, and the gaunt high-water marks and low-water marks in the mud, and the broken causeway, and the broken bank, and the broken stakes and piles leaning forward as if they were vain of their personal appearance and looking for their reflection in the water, will melt into any train of fancy. Equally adaptable to any purpose or to none, are the pasturing sheep and kine upon the marshes, the gulls that wheel and dip around me, the crows (well out of gunshot) going home from the rich harvest-fields, the heron that has been out a-fishing and looks as melancholy, up there in the sky, as if it hadn't agreed with him. Everything within the range of the senses will, by the aid of the running water, lend itself to everything beyond that range, and work into a drowsy whole, not unlike a kind of tune, but for which there is no exact definition.

One of these landing-places is near an old fort (I can see the Nore Light from it with my pocket-glass), from which fort mysteriously emerges a boy, to whom I am much indebted for additions to my scanty stock of knowledge. He is a young boy, with an intelligent face burnt to a dust colour by the summer sun, and with crisp hair of the same hue. He is a boy in whom I have perceived nothing incompatible with habits of studious inquiry and meditation, unless an evanescent black eye (I was delicate of inquiring how occasioned) should be so considered. To him am I indebted for ability to identify a Custom-house boat at any distance, and for acquaintance with all the forms and ceremonies observed by a homeward-bound Indiaman coming up the river, when the Custom-house officers go aboard her. But for him, I might never have heard of "the dumb-ague", respecting which malady I am now learned. Had I never sat at his feet, I might have finished my mortal career and never known that when I see a white horse on a barge's sail, that barge is a lime barge. For precious secrets in reference to beer, am I likewise beholden to him, involving warning against the beer of a certain establishment, by reason of its having turned sour through failure in point of demand: though my young sage is not of opinion that similar deterioration has befallen the ale. He has also enlightened me touching the mushrooms of the marshes, and has gently reproved my ignorance in having supposed them to be impregnated with salt. His manner of imparting information, is thoughtful, and appropriate to the scene. As he reclines beside me, he pitches into the river, a little stone or piece of grit, and then delivers himself oracularly, as though he spoke out of the centre of the spreading circle that it makes in the water. He never improves my mind without observing this formula.

With the wise boy—whom I know by no other name than the Spirit of the Fort—I recently consorted on a breezy day when the river leaped about us and was full of life. I had seen the sheaved corn carrying in the golden fields as I came down to the river; and the rosy farmer, watching his labouring-men in the saddle on his cob, had told me how he had reaped his two hundred and sixty acres of long-strawed corn last week, and how a better week's work he had never done in all his days. Peace and abundance were on the country-side in beautiful forms and beautiful colours, and the harvest seemed even to be sailing out to grace the never-reaped sea in the yellow-laden barges that mellowed the distance.

It was on this occasion that the Spirit of the Fort, directing his remarks to a certain floating iron battery lately lying in that reach of the river, enriched my mind with his opinions on naval architecture, and informed me that he would like to be an engineer. I found him up to everything that is done in the contracting line by Messrs. Peto and Brassey—cunning in the article of concrete—mellow in the matter of iron—great on the subject of gunnery. When he spoke of pile-driving and sluice-making, he left me not a leg to stand on, and I can never sufficiently acknowledge his forbearance with me in my disabled state. While he thus discoursed, he several times directed his eyes to one distant quarter of the landscape, and spoke with vague mysterious awe of "the Yard". Pondering his lessons after we had parted, I bethought me that the Yard was one of our large public Dockyards, and that it lay hidden among the crops down in the dip behind the windmills, as if it modestly kept itself out of view in peaceful times, and sought to trouble no man. Taken with this modesty on the part of the Yard, I resolved to improve the Yard's acquaintance.

My good opinion of the Yard's retiring character was not dashed by nearer approach. It resounded with the noise of hammers beating upon iron; and the great sheds or slips under which the mighty men-of-war are built, loomed business-like when contemplated from the opposite side of the river. For all that, however, the Yard made no display, but kept itself snug under hill-sides of corn-fields, hop-gardens, and orchards; its great chimneys smoking with a quiet—almost a lazy—air, like giants smoking tobacco; and the great Shears moored off it, looking meekly and inoffensively out of proportion, like the Giraffe of the machinery creation. The store of cannon on the neighbouring gun-wharf, had an innocent toy-like appearance, and the one red-coated sentry on duty over them was a mere toy figure, with a clock-work movement. As the hot sunlight sparkled on him he might have passed for the identical little man who had the little gun, and whose bullets they were made of lead, lead, lead.

Crossing the river and landing at the Stairs, where a drift of chips and weed had been trying to land before me and had not succeeded, but had got into a corner instead, I found the very street posts to be cannon, and the architectural ornaments to be shells. And so I came to the Yard, which was shut up tight and strong with great folded gates, like an enormous patent safe. These gates devouring me, I became digested into the Yard; and it had, at first, a clean-swept holiday air, as if it had given over work till next war-time. Though indeed a quantity of hemp for rope was tumbling out of store-houses, even there, which would hardly be lying like so much hay on the white stones if the Yard were as placid as it pretended.

Ding, Clash, Dong, BANG, Boom, Rattle, Clash, BANG, Clink, BANG, Dong, BANG, Clatter, BANG BANG BANG! What on earth is this! This is, or soon will be, the Achilles, iron armour-plated ship. Twelve hundred men are working at her now; twelve hundred men working on stages over her sides, over her bows, over her stern, under her keel, between her decks, down in her hold, within her and without, crawling and creeping into the finest curves of her lines wherever it is possible for men to twist. Twelve hundred hammerers, measurers, caulkers, armourers, forgers, smiths, shipwrights; twelve hundred dingers, clashers, dongers, rattlers, clinkers, bangers bangers bangers! Yet all this stupendous uproar around the rising Achilles is as nothing to the reverberations with which the perfected Achilles shall resound upon the dreadful day when the full work is in hand for which this is but note of preparation—the day when the scuppers that are now fitting like great dry thirsty conduit-pipes, shall run red. All these busy figures between decks, dimly seen bending at their work in smoke and fire, are as nothing to the figures that shall do work here of another kind in smoke and fire, that day. These steam-worked engines alongside, helping the ship by travelling to and fro, and wafting tons of iron plates about, as though they were so many leaves of trees, would be rent limb from limb if they stood by her for a minute then. To think that this Achilles, monstrous compound of iron tank and oaken chest, can ever swim or roll! To think that any force of wind and wave could ever break her! To think that wherever I see a glowing red-hot iron point thrust out of her side from within—as I do now, there, and there, and there!—and two watching men on a stage without, with bared arms and sledge-hammers, strike at it fiercely, and repeat their blows until it is black and flat, I see a rivet being driven home, of which there are many in every iron plate, and thousands upon thousands in the ship! To think that the difficulty I experience in appreciating the ship's size when I am on board, arises from her being a series of iron tanks and oaken chests, so that internally she is ever finishing and ever beginning, and half of her might be smashed, and yet the remaining half suffice and be sound. Then, to go over the side again and down among the ooze and wet to the bottom of the dock, in the depths of the subterranean forest of dog-shores and stays that hold her up, and to see the immense mass bulging out against the upper light, and tapering down towards me, is, with great pains and much clambering, to arrive at an impossibility of realising that this is a ship at all, and to become possessed by the fancy that it is an enormous immovable edifice set up in an ancient amphitheatre (say, that at Verona), and almost filling it! Yet what would even these things be, without the tributary workshops and the mechanical powers for piercing the iron plates—four inches and a half thick—for rivets, shaping them under hydraulic pressure to the finest tapering turns of the ship's lines, and paring them away, with knives shaped like the beaks of strong and cruel birds, to the nicest require-ments of the design! These machines of tremendous force, so easily directed by one attentive face and presiding hand, seem to me to have in them something of the retiring character of the Yard. "Obedient monster, please to bite this mass of iron through and through, at equal distances, where these regular chalk-marks are, all round." Monster looks at its work, and lifting its ponderous head, replies, "I don't particularly want to do it; but if it must be done——!" The solid metal wriggles out, hot from the monster's crunching tooth, and it *is* done. "Dutiful monster, observe this other mass of iron. It is required to be pared away, according to this delicately lessening and arbitrary line, which please to look at." Monster (who has been in a reverie) brings down its blunt head, and, much in the manner of Doctor Johnson, closely looks along the line—very closely, being somewhat near-sighted. "I don't particularly want to do it; but if it must be done——!" Monster takes another near-sighted look, takes aim, and the tortured piece writhes off, and falls, a hot tight-twisted snake, among the ashes. The making of the rivets is merely a pretty round game, played by a man and a boy, who put red-hot barley sugar in a Pope Joan board, and immediately rivets fall out of window; but the tone of the great machines is the tone of the great Yard and the great country: "We don't particularly want to do it; but if it must be done——!"

How such a prodigious mass as the Achilles can ever be held by such comparatively little anchors as those intended for her and lying near her here, is a mystery of seamanship which I will refer to the wise boy. For my own part, I should as soon have thought of tethering an elephant to a tent-peg, or the larger hippopotamus in the Zoological Gardens to my shirt-pin. Yonder in the river, alongside a hulk, lie two of this ship's hollow iron masts. *They* are large enough for the eye, I find, and so are all her other appliances. I wonder why only her anchors look small.

I have no present time to think about it, for I am going to see the workshops where they make all the oars used in the British Navy. A pretty large pile of building, I opine, and a pretty long job! As to the building, I am soon disappointed, because the work is all done in one loft. And as to a long job—what is this? Two rather large mangles with a swarm of butterflies hovering over them? What can there be in the mangles that attracts butterflies?

Drawing nearer, I discern that these are not mangles, but intricate machines, set with knives and saws and planes, which cut smooth and straight here, and slantwise there, and now cut such a depth, and now miss cutting altogether, according to the predestined requirements of the pieces of wood that are pushed on below them: each of which pieces is to be an oar, and is roughly adapted to that purpose before it takes its final leave of far-off forests, and sails for England. Likewise I discern that the butterflies are not true butterflies, but wooden shavings, which, being spirted up from the wood by the violence of the machinery, and kept in rapid and not equal movement by the impulse of its rotation on the air, flutter and play, and rise and fall, and conduct themselves as like butterflies as heart could wish. Suddenly the noise and motion cease, and the butterflies drop dead. An oar has been made since I came in, wanting the shaped handle. As quickly as I can follow it with my eye and thought, the same oar is carried to a turning lathe. A whirl and a Nick! Handle made. Oar finished.

The exquisite beauty and efficiency of this machinery need no illustration, but happen to have a pointed illustration to-day. A pair of oars of unusual size chance to be wanted for a special purpose, and they have to be made by hand. Side by side with the subtle and facile machine, and side by side with the fast-growing pile of oars on the floor, a man shapes out these special oars with an axe. Attended by no butterflies, and chipping and dinting, by comparison as leisurely as if he were a labouring Pagan getting them ready against his decease at threescore and ten, to take with him as a present to Charon for his boat, the man (aged about thirty) plies his task. The machine would make a regulation oar while the man wipes his forehead. The man might be buried in a mound made of the strips of thin broad wooden ribbon torn from the wood whirled into oars as the minutes from the clock, before he had done a forenoon's work with his axe.

Passing from this wonderful sight to the Ships again—for my heart, as to the Yard, is where the ships are—I notice certain unfinished wooden walls left seasoning on the stocks, pending the solution of the merits of the wood and iron question, and having an air of biding their time with surly confidence. The names of these worthies are set up beside them, together with their capacity in guns—a custom highly conducive to ease and satisfaction in social intercourse, if it could be adapted to mankind. By a plank more gracefully pendulous than substantial, I make bold to go aboard a transport ship (iron screw) just sent in from the contractor's yard to be inspected and passed. She is a very gratifying experience, in the simplicity and humanity of her arrangements for troops, in her provision for light and air and cleanliness, and in her care for women and children. It occurs to me, as I explore her, that I would require a handsome sum of money to go aboard her, at midnight by the Dockyard bell, and stay aboard alone till morning; for surely she must be haunted by a crowd of ghosts of obstinate old martinets, mournfully flapping their cherubic epaulettes over the changed times. Though still we may learn from the astounding ways and means in our Yards now, more highly than ever to respect the forefathers who got to sea, and fought the sea, and held the sea, without them. This remembrance putting me in the best of tempers with an old hulk, very green as to her copper, and generally dim and patched, I pull off my hat to her. Which salutation a callow and downy-faced young officer of Engineers, going by at the moment, perceiving, appropriates—and to which he is most heartily welcome, I am sure.

Having been torn to pieces (in imagination) by the steam circular saws, perpendicular saws, horizontal saws, and saws of eccentric action, I come to the sauntering part of my expedition, and consequently to the core of my Uncommercial pursuits.

Everywhere, as I saunter up and down the Yard, I meet with tokens of its quiet and retiring character. There is a gravity upon its red brick offices and houses, a staid pretence of having nothing worth mentioning to do, an avoidance of display, which I never saw out of England. The white stones of the pavement present no other trace of Achilles and his twelve hundred banging men (not one of whom strikes an attitude) than a few occasional echoes. But for a whisper in the air suggestive of sawdust and shavings, the oar-making and the saws of many movements might be miles away. Down below here, is the great reservoir of water where timber is steeped in various temperatures, as a part of its seasoning process. Above it, on a tramroad supported by pillars, is a Chinese Enchanter's Car, which fishes the logs up, when sufficiently steeped, and rolls smoothly away with them to stack them. When I was a child (the Yard being then familiar to me) I used to think that I should like to play at Chinese Enchanter, and to have that apparatus placed at my disposal for the purpose by a beneficent country. I still think that I should rather like to try the effect of writing a book in it. Its retirement is complete, and to go gliding to and fro among the stacks of timber would be a convenient kind of travelling in foreign countries—among the forests of North America, the sodden Honduras swamps, the dark pine woods, the Norwegian frosts, and the tropical heats, rainy seasons, and thunder-storms. The costly store of timber is stacked and stowed away in sequestered places, with the pervading avoidance of flourish or effect. It makes as little of itself as possible, and calls to no one "Come and look at me!" And yet it is picked out from the trees of the world; picked out for length, picked out for breadth, picked out for straightness, picked out for crookedness, chosen with an eye to every need of ship and boat. Strangely twisted pieces lie about, precious in the sight of shipwrights. Sauntering through these groves, I come upon an open glade where workmen are examining some timber recently delivered. Quite a pastoral scene, with a background of river and windmill! and no more like War than the American States are at present like an Union.

Sauntering among the ropemaking, I am spun into a state of blissful indolence, wherein my rope of life seems to be so untwisted by the process as that I can see back to very early days indeed, when my bad dreams—they were frightful, though my more mature understanding has never made out why—were of an interminable sort of ropemaking, with long minute filaments for strands, which, when they were spun home together close to my eyes, occasioned screaming. Next, I walk among the quiet lofts of stores—of sails, spars, rigging, ships' boats—determined to believe that somebody in authority wears a girdle and bends beneath the weight of a massive bunch of keys, and that, when such a thing is wanted, he comes telling his keys like Blue Beard, and opens such a door. Impassive as the long lofts look, let the electric battery send down the word, and the shutters and doors shall fly open, and such a fleet of armed ships, under steam and

under sail, shall burst forth as will charge the old Medway—where
the merry Stuart let the Dutch come, while his not so merry sailors
starved in the streets—with something worth looking at to carry to
the sea. Thus I idle round to the Medway again, where it is now
flood tide; and I find the river evincing a strong solicitude to force
a way into the dry dock where Achilles is waited on by the twelve
hundred bangers, with intent to bear the whole away before they are
ready.

To the last, the Yard puts a quiet face upon it; for I make my way
to the gates through a little quiet grove of trees, shading the quaintest
of Dutch landing-places, where the leaf-speckled shadow of a shipwright just passing away at the further end might be the shadow of
Russian Peter himself. So, the doors of the great patent safe at last
close upon me, and I take boat again : somehow, thinking as the oars
dip, of braggart Pistol and his brood, and of the quiet monsters of the
Yard, with their "We don't particularly want to do it; but if it must
be done————!" Scrunch.

XXVI

IN THE FRENCH-FLEMISH COUNTRY

"IT is neither a bold nor a diversified country," said I to myself,
"this country which is three-quarters Flemish, and a quarter French;
yet it has its attractions too. Though great lines of railway traverse
it, the trains leave it behind, and go puffing off to Paris and the South,
to Belgium and Germany, to the Northern Sea-Coast of France, and
to England, and merely smoke it a little in passing. Then I don't
know it, and that is a good reason for being here; and I can't pronounce half the long queer names I see inscribed over the shops, and
that is another good reason for being here, since I surely ought to
learn how." In short, I was "here", and I wanted an excuse for not
going away from here, and I made it to my satisfaction, and stayed
here.

What part in my decision was borne by Monsieur P. Salcy, is of no
moment, though I own to encountering that gentleman's name on a
red bill on the wall, before I made up my mind. Monsieur P. Salcy,
"par permission de M. le Maire", had established his theatre in the
whitewashed Hôtel de Ville, on the steps of which illustrious edifice
I stood. And Monsieur P. Salcy, privileged director of such theatre,
situate in "the first theatrical arrondissement of the department of
the North", invited French-Flemish mankind to come and partake of
the intellectual banquet provided by his family of dramatic artists,
fifteen subjects in number. "La Famille P. SALCY, composée d'artistes
dramatiques, au nombre de 15 sujets".

Neither a bold nor a diversified country, I say again, and withal an
untidy country, but pleasant enough to ride in, when the paved roads

over the flats and through the hollows, are not too deep in black mud. A country so sparely inhabited, that I wonder where the peasants who till and sow and reap the ground, can possibly dwell, and also by what invisible balloons they are conveyed from their distant homes into the fields at sunrise and back again at sunset. The occasional few poor cottages and farms in this region, surely cannot afford shelter to the numbers necessary to the cultivation, albeit the work is done so very deliberately, that on one long harvest day I have seen, in twelve miles, about twice as many men and women (all told) reaping and binding. Yet have I seen more cattle, more sheep, more pigs, and all in better case, than where there is purer French spoken, and also better ricks—round swelling peg-top ricks, well thatched: not a shapeless brown heap, like the toast of a Giant's toast-and-water, pinned to the earth with one of the skewers out of his kitchen. A good custom they have about here, likewise, of prolonging the sloping tiled roof of farm or cottage, so that it overhangs three or four feet, carrying off the wet, and making a good drying place wherein to hang up herbs, or implements, or what not. A better custom than the popular one of keeping the refuse-heap and puddle close before the house door: which, although I paint my dwelling never so brightly blue (and it cannot be too blue for me, hereabouts), will bring fever inside my door. Wonderful poultry of the French-Flemish country, why take the trouble to *be* poultry? Why not stop short at eggs in the rising generation, and die out and have done with it? Parents of chickens have I seen this day, followed by their wretched young families, scratching nothing out of the mud with an air—tottering about on legs so scraggy and weak, that the valiant word drumsticks becomes a mockery when applied to them, and the crow of the lord and master has been a mere dejected case of croup. Carts have I seen, and other agricultural instruments, unwieldy, dislocated, monstrous. Poplar-trees by the thousand fringe the fields and fringe the end of the flat landscape, so that I feel, looking straight on before me, as if, when I pass the extremest fringe on the low horizon, I shall tumble over into space. Little whitewashed black holes of chapels, with barred doors and Flemish inscriptions, abound at roadside corners, and often they are garnished with a sheaf of wooden crosses, like children's swords; or, in their default, some hollow old tree with a saint roosting in it, is similarly decorated, or a pole with a very diminutive saint enshrined aloft in a sort of sacred pigeon-house. Not that we are deficient in such decoration in the town here, for, over at the church yonder, outside the building, is a scenic representation of the Crucifixion, built up with old bricks and stones, and made out with painted canvas and wooden figures: the whole surmounting the dusty skull of some holy personage (perhaps), shut up behind a little ashy iron grate, as if it were originally put there to be cooked, and the fire had long gone out. A windmilly country this, though the windmills are so damp and rickety, that they nearly knock themselves off their legs at every turn of their sails, and creak in loud complaint. A weaving country, too, for in the wayside cottages the loom goes wearily—rattle and click, rattle and click—and, looking in, I see the poor weaving peasant, man or woman, bending at the work, while the child, working too, turns a little handwheel put upon the ground to suit its height. An unconscionable monster, the loom in a small dwelling, asserting himself ungenerously as the bread-winner, straddling over the children's straw beds, cramping the family in space and air, and making himself generally objectionable and tyrannical. He is tributary, too, to ugly mills and factories and bleaching-grounds, rising out of the sluiced fields in an abrupt bare way, disdaining, like himself, to be ornamental or accommodating. Surrounded by these things, here I stood on the steps of the Hôtel de Ville, persuaded to remain by the P. Salcy family, fifteen dramatic subjects strong.

There was a Fair besides. The double persuasion being irresistible, and my sponge being left behind at the last Hotel, I made the tour of the little town to buy another. In the small sunny shops—mercers, opticians, and druggist-grocers, with here and there an emporium of religious images—the gravest of old spectacled Flemish husbands and wives sat contemplating one another across bare counters, while the wasps, who seemed to have taken military possession of the town, and to have placed it under wasp-martial law, executed warlike manœuvres in the windows. Other shops the wasps had entirely to themselves, and nobody cared and nobody came when I beat with a five-franc piece upon the board of custom. What I sought was no more to be found than if I had sought a nugget of Californian gold: so I went, spongeless, to pass the evening with the Family P. Salcy.

The members of the Family P. Salcy were so fat and so like one another—fathers, mothers, sisters, brothers, uncles, and aunts—that I think the local audience were much confused about the plot of the piece under representation, and to the last expected that everybody must turn out to be the long-lost relative of everybody else. The Theatre was established on the top story of the Hôtel de Ville, and was approached by a long bare staircase, whereon, in an airy situation, one of the P. Salcy Family—a stout gentleman imperfectly repressed by a belt—took the money. This occasioned the greatest excitement of the evening; for, no sooner did the curtain rise on the introductory Vaudeville, and reveal in the person of the young lover (singing a very short song with his eyebrows) apparently the very same identical stout gentleman imperfectly repressed by a belt, than everybody rushed out to the paying-place, to ascertain whether he could possibly have put on that dress-coat, that clear complexion, and those arched black vocal eyebrows, in so short a space of time. It then became manifest that this was another stout gentleman imperfectly repressed by a belt: to whom, before the spectators had recovered their presence of mind, entered a third stout gentleman imperfectly repressed by a belt, exactly like him. These two "subjects", making with the money-taker three of the announced fifteen, fell into conversation

touching a charming young widow: who, presently appearing, proved
to be a stout lady altogether irrepressible by any means—quite a
parallel case to the American Negro—fourth of the fifteen subjects,
and sister of the fifth who presided over the check-department. In
good time the whole of the fifteen subjects were dramatically presented, and we had the inevitable Ma Mère, Ma Mère! and also the
inevitable malédiction d'un père, and likewise the inevitable Marquis,
and also the inevitable provincial young man, weak-minded but faithful, who followed Julie to Paris, and cried and laughed and choked
all at once. The story was wrought out with the help of a virtuous
spinning-wheel in the beginning, a vicious set of diamonds in the
middle, and a rheumatic blessing (which arrived by post) from Ma
Mère towards the end; the whole resulting in a small sword in the
body of one of the stout gentlemen imperfectly repressed by a belt,
fifty thousand francs per annum and a decoration to the other stout
gentleman imperfectly repressed by a belt, and an assurance from
everybody to the provincial young man that if he were not supremely
happy—which he seemed to have no reason whatever for being—he
ought to be. This afforded him a final opportunity of crying and
laughing and choking all at once, and sent the audience home senti-
mentally delighted. Audience more attentive or better behaved there
could not possibly be, though the places of second rank in the Theatre
of the Family P. Salcy were sixpence each in English money, and the
places of first rank a shilling. How the fifteen subjects ever got so fat
upon it, the kind Heavens know.

What gorgeous china figures of knights and ladies, gilded till they
gleamed again, I might have bought at the Fair for the garniture
of my home, if I had been a French-Flemish peasant, and had had
the money! What shining coffee-cups and saucers I might have won
at the turntables, if I had had the luck! Ravishing perfumery also,
and sweetmeats, I might have speculated in, or I might have fired for
prizes at a multitude of little dolls in niches, and might have hit the
doll of dolls, and won francs and fame. Or, being a French-Flemish
youth, I might have been drawn in a hand-cart by my compeers, to
tilt for municipal rewards at the water-quintain; which, unless I sent
my lance clean through the ring, emptied a full bucket over me; to
fend off which, the competitors wore grotesque old scarecrow hats.
Or, being French-Flemish man or woman, boy or girl, I might have
circled all night on my hobby-horse in a stately cavalcade of hobby-
horses four abreast, interspersed with triumphal cars, going round
and round and round and round, we the goodly company singing a
ceaseless chorus to the music of the barrel-organ, drum, and cymbals.
On the whole, not more monotonous than the Ring in Hyde Park,
London, and much merrier; for when do the circling company sing
chorus, *there*, to the barrel-organ, when do the ladies embrace their
horses round the neck with both arms, when do the gentlemen fan
the ladies with the tails of their gallant steeds? On all these revolving delights, and on their own especial lamps and Chinese lanterns

revolving with them, the thoughtful weaver-face brightens, and the Hôtel de Ville sheds an illuminated line of gaslight: while above it, the Eagle of France, gas-outlined and apparently afflicted with the prevailing infirmities that have lighted on the poultry, is in a very undecided state of policy, and as a bird moulting. Flags flutter all around. Such is the prevailing gaiety that the keeper of the prison sits on the stone steps outside the prison-door, to have a look at the world that is not locked up; while that agreeable retreat, the wine-shop opposite to the prison in the prison-alley (its sign La Tranquillité, because of its charming situation), resounds with the voices of the shepherds and shepherdesses who resort there this festive night. And it reminds me that only this afternoon, I saw a shepherd in trouble, tending this way, over the jagged stones of a neighbouring street. A magnificent sight it was, to behold him in his blouse, a feeble little jog-trot rustic, swept along by the wind of two immense gendarmes, in cocked hats for which the street was hardly wide enough, each carrying a bundle of stolen property that would not have held his shoulder-knot, and clanking a sabre that dwarfed the prisoner.

"Messieurs et Mesdames, I present to you at this Fair, as a mark of my confidence in the people of this so-renowned town, and as an act of homage to their good sense and fine taste, the Ventriloquist, the Ventriloquist! Further, Messieurs et Mesdames, I present to you the Face-Maker, the Physiognomist, the great Changer of Countenances, who transforms the features that Heaven has bestowed upon him into an endless succession of surprising and extraordinary visages, comprehending, Messieurs et Mesdames, all the contortions, energetic and expressive, of which the human face is capable, and all the passions of the human heart, as Love, Jealousy, Revenge, Hatred, Avarice, Despair! Hi hi, Ho ho, Lu lu, Come in!" To this effect, with an occasional smite upon a sonorous kind of tambourine—bestowed with a will, as if it represented the people who won't come in—holds forth a man of lofty and severe demeanour; a man in stately uniform, gloomy with the knowledge he possesses of the inner secrets of the booth. "Come in, come in! Your opportunity presents itself to-night; to-morrow it will be gone for ever. To-morrow morning by the Express Train the railroad will reclaim the Ventriloquist and the Face-Maker! Algeria will reclaim the Ventriloquist and the Face-Maker! Yes! For the honour of their country they have accepted propositions of a magnitude incredible, to appear in Algeria. See them for the last time before their departure! We go to commence on the instant. Hi hi! Ho ho! Lu lu! Come in! Take the money that now ascends, Madame; but after that, no more, for we commence! Come in!"

Nevertheless, the eyes both of the gloomy Speaker and of Madame receiving sous in a muslin bower, survey the crowd pretty sharply after the ascending money has ascended, to detect any lingering sous at the turning-point. "Come in, come in! Is there any more money,

Madame, on the point of ascending? If so, we wait for it. If not, we commence!" The orator looks back over his shoulder to say it, lashing the spectators with the conviction that he beholds through the folds of the drapery into which he is about to plunge, the Ventriloquist and the Face-Maker. Several sous burst out of pockets, and ascend. "Come up, then, Messieurs!" exclaims Madame in a shrill voice, and beckoning with a bejewelled finger. "Come up! This presses. Monsieur has commanded that they commence!" Monsieur dives into his Interior, and the last half-dozen of us follow. His Interior is comparatively severe; his Exterior also. A true Temple of Art needs nothing but seats, drapery, a small table with two moderator lamps hanging over it, and an ornamental looking-glass let into the wall. Monsieur in uniform gets behind the table and surveys us with disdain, his forehead becoming diabolically intellectual under the moderators. "Messieurs et Mesdames, I present to you the Ventriloquist. He will commence with the celebrated Experience of the bee in the window. The bee, apparently the veritable bee of Nature, will hover in the window, and about the room. He will be with difficulty caught in the hand of Monsieur the Ventriloquist—he will escape—he will again hover—at length he will be recaptured by Monsieur the Ventriloquist, and will be with difficulty put into a bottle. Achieve then, Monsieur!" Here the proprietor is replaced behind the table by the Ventriloquist, who is thin and sallow, and of a weakly aspect. While the bee is in progress, Monsieur the Proprietor sits apart on a stool, immersed in dark and remote thought. The moment the bee is bottled, he stalks forward, eyes us gloomily as we applaud, and then announces, sternly waving his hand: "The magnificent Experience of the child with the whooping-cough!" The child disposed of, he starts up as before. "The superb and extraordinary Experience of the dialogue between Monsieur Tatambour in his dining-room, and his domestic, Jerome, in the cellar; concluding with the songsters of the grove, and the Concert of domestic Farmyard animals." All this done, and well done, Monsieur the Ventriloquist withdraws, and Monsieur the Face-Maker bursts in, as if his retiring-room were a mile long instead of a yard. A corpulent little man in a large white waistcoat, with a comic countenance, and with a wig in his hand. Irreverent disposition to laugh, instantly checked by the tremendous gravity of the Face-Maker, who intimates in his bow that if we expect that sort of thing we are mistaken. A very little shaving-glass with a leg behind it is handed in, and placed on the table before the Face-Maker. "Messieurs et Mesdames, with no other assistance than this mirror and this wig, I shall have the honour of showing you a thousand characters." As a preparation, the Face-Maker with both hands gouges himself, and turns his mouth inside out. He then becomes frightfully grave again, and says to the Proprietor, "I am ready!" Proprietor stalks forth from baleful reverie, and announces "The Young Conscript!" Face-Maker claps his wig on, hind side before, looks in the glass, and appears above it as a conscript so very imbecile, and squinting so extremely hard, that I should think the State would never get any good of him. Thunders of applause. Face-Maker dips behind the looking-glass, brings his own hair forward, is himself again, is awfully grave. "A distinguished inhabitant of the Faubourg St. Germain." Face-Maker dips, rises, is supposed to be aged, blear-eyed, toothless, slightly palsied, supernaturally polite, evidently of noble birth. "The oldest member of the Corps of Invalides on the fête-day of his master." Face-Maker dips, rises, wears the wig on one side, has become the feeblest military bore in existence, and (it is clear) would lie frightfully about his past achievements, if he were not confined to pantomime. "The Miser!" Face-Maker dips, rises, clutches a bag, and every hair of the wig is on end to express that he lives in continual dread of thieves. "The Genius of France!" Face-Maker dips, rises, wig pushed back and smoothed flat, little cocked hat (artfully concealed till now) put a-top of it, Face-Maker's white waistcoat much advanced, Face-Maker's left hand in bosom of white waistcoat, Face-Maker's right hand behind his back. Thunders. This is the first of three positions of the Genius of France. In the second position, the Face-Maker takes snuff; in the third, rolls up his right hand, and surveys illimitable armies through that pocket-glass. The Face-Maker then, by putting out his tongue, and wearing the wig nohow in particular, becomes the Village Idiot. The most remarkable feature in the whole of his ingenious performance, is, that whatever he does to disguise himself, has the effect of rendering him rather more like himself than he was at first.

There were peep-shows in this Fair, and I had the pleasure of recognising several fields of glory with which I became well acquainted a year or two ago as Crimean battles, now doing duty as Mexican victories. The change was neatly effected by some extra smoking of the Russians, and by permitting the camp followers free range in the foreground to despoil the enemy of their uniforms. As no British troops had ever happened to be within sight when the artist took his original sketches, it followed fortunately that none were in the way now.

The Fair wound up with a ball. Respecting the particular night of the week on which the ball took place, I decline to commit myself; merely mentioning that it was held in a stable-yard so very close to the railway, that it is a mercy the locomotive did not set fire to it. (In Scotland, I suppose it would have done so.) There, in a tent prettily decorated with looking-glasses and a myriad of toy flags, the people danced all night. It was not an expensive recreation, the price of a double ticket for a cavalier and lady being one and threepence in English money, and even of that small sum fivepence was reclaimable for "consummation": which word I venture to translate into refreshments of no greater strength, at the strongest, than ordinary wine made hot, with sugar and lemon in it. It was a ball of great good humour and of great enjoyment, though very many of the dancers must have been as poor as the fifteen subjects of the P. Salcy Family.

In short, not having taken my own pet national pint pot with me to this Fair, I was very well satisfied with the measure of simple enjoyment that it poured into the dull French-Flemish country life. How dull that is, I had an opportunity of considering when the Fair was over—when the tri-coloured flags were withdrawn from the windows of the houses on the Place where the Fair was held—when the windows were close shut, apparently until next Fair-time—when the Hôtel de Ville had cut off its gas and put away its eagle—when the two paviours, whom I take to form the entire paving population of the town, were ramming down the stones which had been pulled up for the erection of decorative poles—when the jailer had slammed his gate, and sulkily locked himself in with his charges. But then, as I paced the ring which marked the track of the departed hobby-horses on the market-place, pondering in my mind how long some hobby-horses do leave their tracks in public ways, and how difficult they are to erase, my eyes were greeted with a goodly sight. I beheld four male personages thoughtfully pacing the Place together, in the sunlight, evidently not belonging to the town, and having upon them a certain loose cosmopolitan air of not belonging to any town. One was clad in a suit of white canvas, another in a cap and blouse, the third in an old military frock, the fourth in a shapeless dress that looked as if it had been made out of old umbrellas. All wore dust-coloured shoes. My heart beat high; for, in those four male personages, although complexionless and eyebrowless, I beheld four subjects of the Family P. Salcy. Blue-bearded though they were, and bereft of the youthful smoothness of cheek which is imparted by what is termed in Albion a " Whitechapel shave " (and which is, in fact, whitening, judiciously applied to the jaws with the palm of the hand), I recognised them. As I stood admiring, there emerged from the yard of a lowly Cabaret, the excellent Ma Mère, Ma Mère, with the words, " The soup is served "; words which so elated the subject in the canvas suit, that when they all ran in to partake, he went last, dancing with his hands stuck angularly into the pockets of his canvas trousers, after the Pierrot manner. Glancing down the Yard, the last I saw of him was, that he looked in through a window (at the soup, no doubt) on one leg.

Full of this pleasure, I shortly afterwards departed from the town, little dreaming of an addition to my good fortune. But more was in reserve. I went by a train which was heavy with third-class carriages, full of young fellows (well guarded) who had drawn unlucky numbers in the last conscription, and were on their way to a famous French garrison town where much of the raw military material is worked up into soldiery. At the station they had been sitting about, in their threadbare homespun blue garments, with their poor little bundles under their arms, covered with dust and clay, and the various soils of France; sad enough at heart, most of them, but putting a good face upon it, and slapping their breasts and singing choruses on the smallest provocation; the gayer spirits shouldering half loaves of black bread speared upon their walking-sticks. As we went along, they were audible at every station, chorusing wildly out of tune, and feigning the highest hilarity. After a while, however, they began to leave off singing, and to laugh naturally, while at intervals there mingled with their laughter the barking of a dog. Now, I had to alight short of their destination, and, as that stoppage of the train was attended with a quantity of horn blowing, bell ringing, and proclamation of what Messieurs les Voyageurs were to do, and were not to do, in order to reach their respective destinations, I had ample leisure to go forward on the platform to take a parting look at my recruits, whose heads were all out at window, and who were laughing like delighted children. Then I perceived that a large poodle with a pink nose, who had been their travelling companion and the cause of their mirth, stood on his hind-legs presenting arms on the extreme verge of the platform, ready to salute them as the train went off. This poodle wore a military shako (it is unnecessary to add, very much on one side over one eye), a little military coat, and the regulation white gaiters. He was armed with a little musket and a little sword-bayonet, and he stood presenting arms in perfect attitude, with his unobscured eye on his master or superior officer, who stood by him. So admirable was his discipline, that, when the train moved, and he was greeted with the parting cheers of the recruits, and also with a shower of centimes, several of which struck his shako, and had a tendency to discompose him, he remained staunch on his post, until the train was gone. He then resigned his arms to his officer, took off his shako by rubbing his paw over it, dropped on four legs, bringing his uniform coat into the absurdest relations with the overarching skies, and ran about the platform in his white gaiters, wagging his tail to an exceeding great extent. It struck me that there was more waggery than this in the poodle, and that he knew that the recruits would neither get through their exercises, nor get rid of their uniforms, as easily as he; revolving which in my thoughts, and seeking in my pockets some small money to bestow upon him, I casually directed my eyes to the face of his superior officer, and in him beheld the Face-Maker! Though it was not the way to Algeria, but quite the reverse, the military poodle's Colonel was the Face-Maker in a dark blouse, with a small bundle dangling over his shoulder at the end of an umbrella, and taking a pipe from his breast to smoke as he and the poodle went their mysterious way.

XXVII

MEDICINE MEN OF CIVILISATION

My voyages (in paper boats) among savages often yield me matter for reflection at home. It is curious to trace the savage in the civilised man, and to detect the hold of some savage customs on conditions of society rather boastful of being high above them.

I wonder, is the Medicine Man of the North American Indians never to be got rid of, out of the North American country? He comes into my Wigwam on all manner of occasions, and with the absurdest "Medicine". I always find it extremely difficult, and I often find it simply impossible, to keep him out of my Wigwam. For his legal "Medicine" he sticks upon his head the hair of quadrupeds, and plasters the same with fat, and dirty white powder, and talks a gibberish quite unknown to the men and squaws of his tribe. For his religious "Medicine" he puts on puffy white sleeves, little black aprons, large black waistcoats of a peculiar cut, collarless coats with Medicine button-holes, Medicine stockings and gaiters and shoes, and tops the whole with a highly grotesque Medicinal hat. In one respect, to be sure, I am quite free from him. On occasions when the Medicine Men in general, together with a large number of the miscellaneous inhabitants of his village, both male and female, are presented to the principal Chief, his native "Medicine" is a comical mixture of old odds and ends (hired of traders) and new things in antiquated shapes, and pieces of red cloth (of which he is particularly fond), and white and red and blue paint for the face. The irrationality of this particular Medicine culminates in a mock battle-rush, from which many of the squaws are borne out, much dilapidated. I need not observe how unlike this is to a Drawing Room at St. James's Palace.

The African magician I find it very difficult to exclude from my Wigwam too. This creature takes cases of death and mourning under his supervision, and will frequently impoverish a whole family by his preposterous enchantments. He is a great eater and drinker, and always conceals a rejoicing stomach under a grieving exterior. His charms consist of an infinite quantity of worthless scraps, for which he charges very high. He impresses on the poor bereaved natives, that the more of his followers they pay to exhibit such scraps on their persons for an hour or two (though they never saw the deceased in their lives, and are put in high spirits by his decease), the more honourably and piously they grieve for the dead. The poor people, submitting themselves to this conjurer, an expensive procession is formed, in which bits of sticks, feathers of birds, and a quantity of other unmeaning objects besmeared with black paint, are carried in a certain ghastly order of which no one understands the meaning, if it ever had any, to the brink of the grave, and are then brought back again.

In the Tonga Islands everything is supposed to have a soul, so that when a hatchet is irreparably broken, they say, "His immortal part has departed; he is gone to the happy hunting-plains". This belief leads to the logical sequence that when a man is buried, some of his eating and drinking vessels, and some of his warlike implements, must be broken and buried with him. Superstitious and wrong, but surely a more respectable superstition than the hire of antic scraps for a show that has no meaning based on any sincere belief.

Let me halt on my Uncommercial road, to throw a passing glance on some funeral solemnities that I have seen where North American Indians, African Magicians, and Tonga Islanders, are supposed not to be.

Once, I dwelt in an Italian city, where there dwelt with me for a while, an Englishman of an amiable nature, great enthusiasm, and no discretion. This friend discovered a desolate stranger, mourning over the unexpected death of one very dear to him, in a solitary cottage among the vineyards of an outlying village. The circumstances of the bereavement were unusually distressing; and the survivor, new to the peasants and the country, sorely needed help, being alone with the remains. With some difficulty, but with the strong influence of a purpose at once gentle, disinterested, and determined, my friend— Mr. Kindheart—obtained access to the mourner, and undertook to arrange the burial.

There was a small Protestant cemetery near the city walls, and as Mr. Kindheart came back to me, he turned into it and chose the spot. He was always highly flushed when rendering a service unaided, and I knew that to make him happy I must keep aloof from his ministration. But when at dinner he warmed with the good action of the day, and conceived the brilliant idea of comforting the mourner with "an English funeral", I ventured to intimate that I thought that institution, which was not absolutely sublime at home, might prove a failure in Italian hands. However, Mr. Kindheart was so enraptured with his conception, that he presently wrote down into the town requesting the attendance with to-morrow's earliest light of a certain little upholsterer. This upholsterer was famous for speaking the unintelligible local dialect (his own) in a far more unintelligible manner than any other man alive.

When from my bath next morning I overheard Mr. Kindheart and the upholsterer in conference on the top of an echoing staircase; and when I overheard Mr. Kindheart rendering English Undertaking phrases into very choice Italian, and the upholsterer replying in the unknown Tongues; and when I furthermore remembered that the local funerals had no resemblance to English funerals; I became in my secret bosom apprehensive. But Mr. Kindheart informed me at breakfast that measures had been taken to ensure a signal success.

As the funeral was to take place at sunset, and as I knew to which of the city gates it must tend, I went out at that gate as the sun descended, and walked along the dusty, dusty road. I had not walked far, when I encountered this procession :

1. Mr. Kindheart, much abashed, on an immense grey horse.

2. A bright yellow coach and pair, driven by a coachman in bright red velvet knee-breeches and waistcoat. (This was the established local idea of State.) Both coach doors kept open by the coffin, which was on its side within, and sticking out at each.

3. Behind the coach, the mourner, for whom the coach was intended, walking in the dust.

4. Concealed behind a roadside well for the irrigation of a garden, the unintelligible Upholsterer, admiring.

It matters little now. Coaches of all colours are alike to poor Kindheart, and he rests far North of the little cemetery with the cypress-trees, by the city walls where the Mediterranean is so beautiful.

My first funeral, a fair representative funeral after its kind, was that of the husband of a married servant, once my nurse. She married for money. Sally Flanders, after a year or two of matrimony, became the relict of Flanders, a small master builder; and either she or Flanders had done me the honour to express a desire that I should "follow". I may have been seven or eight years old ;—young enough, certainly, to feel rather alarmed by the expression, as not knowing where the invitation was held to terminate, and how far I was expected to follow the deceased Flanders. Consent being given by the heads of houses, I was jobbed up into what was pronounced at home decent mourning (comprehending somebody else's shirt, unless my memory deceives me), and was admonished that if, when the funeral was in action, I put my hands in my pockets, or took my eyes out of my pocket-handkerchief, I was personally lost, and my family disgraced. On the eventful day, having tried to get myself into a disastrous frame of mind, and having formed a very poor opinion of myself because I couldn't cry, I repaired to Sally's. Sally was an excellent creature, and had been a good wife to old Flanders, but the moment I saw her I knew that she was not in her own real natural state. She formed a sort of Coat of Arms, grouped with a smelling-bottle, a handkerchief, an orange, a bottle of vinegar, Flanders's sister, her own sister, Flanders's brother's wife, and two neighbouring gossips—all in mourning, and all ready to hold her whenever she fainted. At sight of poor little me she became much agitated (agitating me much more), and having exclaimed, "O here's dear Master Uncommercial!" became hysterical, and swooned as if I had been the death of her. An affecting scene followed, during which I was handed about and poked at her by various people, as if I were the bottle of salts. Reviving a little, she embraced me, said, "You knew him well, dear Master Uncommercial, and he knew you!" and fainted again: which, as the rest of the Coat of Arms soothingly said, "done her credit". Now, I knew that she needn't have fainted unless she liked, and that she wouldn't have fainted unless it had been expected of her, quite as well as I know it at this day. It made me feel uncomfortable and hypocritical besides.

I was not sure but that it might be manners in *me* to faint next, and I resolved to keep my eye on Flanders's uncle, and if I saw any signs of his going in that direction, to go too, politely. But Flanders's uncle (who was a weak little old retail grocer) had only one idea, which was that we all wanted tea; and he handed us cups of tea all round incessantly, whether we refused or not. There was a young nephew of Flanders's present, to whom Flanders, it was rumoured, had left nineteen guineas. He drank all the tea that was offered him, this nephew—amounting, I should say, to several quarts—and ate as much plum-cake as he could possibly come by; but he felt it to be decent mourning that he should now and then stop in the midst of a lump of cake, and appear to forget that his mouth was full, in the contemplation of his uncle's memory. I felt all this to be the fault of the undertaker, who was handing us gloves on a tea-tray as if they were muffins, and tying us into cloaks (mine had to be pinned up all round, it was so long for me), because I knew that he was making game. So, when we got out into the streets, and I constantly disarranged the procession by tumbling on the people before me because my handkerchief blinded my eyes, and tripping up the people behind me because my cloak was so long, I felt that we were all making game. I was truly sorry for Flanders, but I knew that it was no reason why we should be trying (the women with their heads in hoods like coal-scuttles with the black side outward) to keep step with a man in a scarf, carrying a thing like a mourning spy-glass, which he was going to open presently and sweep the horizon with. I knew that we should not all have been speaking in one particular key-note struck by the undertaker, if we had not been making game. Even in our faces we were every one of us as like the undertaker as if we had been his own family, and I perceived that this could not have happened unless we had been making game. When we returned to Sally's, it was all of a piece. The continued impossibility of getting on without plum-cake; the ceremonious apparition of a pair of decanters containing port and sherry and cork; Sally's sister at the tea-table, clinking the best crockery and shaking her head mournfully every time she looked down into the teapot, as if it were the tomb; the Coat of Arms again, and Sally as before; lastly, the words of consolation administered to Sally when it was considered right that she should "come round nicely": which were, that the deceased had had "as com-for-ta-ble a fu-ne-ral as comfortable could be!"

Other funerals have I seen with grown-up eyes, since that day, of which the burden has been the same childish burden. Making game. Real affliction, real grief and solemnity, have been outraged, and the funeral has been "performed". The waste for which the funeral customs of many tribes of savages are conspicuous, has attended these civilised obsequies; and once, and twice, have I wished in my soul that if the waste must be, they would let the undertaker bury the money, and let me bury the friend.

In France, upon the whole, these ceremonies are more sensibly regulated, because they are upon the whole less expensively regulated. I cannot say that I have ever been much edified by the custom of tying a bib and apron on the front of the house of mourning, or that I would myself particularly care to be driven to my grave in a nodding and bobbing car, like an infirm four-post bedstead, by an inky fellow-creature in a cocked hat. But it may be that I am constitutionally insensible to the virtues of a cocked hat. In provincial France, the solemnities are sufficiently hideous, but are few and cheap. The friends and townsmen of the departed, in their own dresses and not masquerading under the auspices of the African Conjurer, surround the hand-bier, and often carry it. It is not considered indispensable to stifle the bearers, or even to elevate the burden on their shoulders; consequently it is easily taken up, and easily set down, and is carried through the streets without the distressing floundering and shuffling that we see at home. A dirty priest or two, and a dirtier acolyte or two, do not lend any especial grace to the proceedings; and I regard with personal animosity the bassoon, which is blown at intervals by the big-legged priest (it is always a big-legged priest who blows the bassoon), when his fellows combine in a lugubrious stalwart drawl. But there is far less of the Conjurer and the Medicine Man in the business than under like circumstances here. The grim coaches that we reserve expressly for such shows, are non-existent; if the cemetery be far out of the town, the coaches that are hired for other purposes of life are hired for this purpose; and although the honest vehicles make no pretence of being overcome, I have never noticed that the people in them were the worse for it. In Italy, the hooded Members of Confraternities who attend on funerals, are dismal and ugly to look upon; but the services they render are at least voluntarily rendered, and impoverish no one, and cost nothing. Why should high civilisation and low savagery ever come together on the point of making them a wantonly wasteful and contemptible set of forms?

Once I lost a friend by death, who had been troubled in his time by the Medicine Man and the Conjurer, and upon whose limited resources there were abundant claims. The Conjurer assured me that I must positively "follow", and both he and the Medicine Man entertained no doubt that I must go in a black carriage, and must wear "fittings". I objected to fittings as having nothing to do with my friendship, and I objected to the black carriage as being in more senses than one a job. So, it came into my mind to try what would happen if I quietly walked, in my own way, from my own house to my friend's burial-place, and stood beside his open grave in my own dress and person, reverently listening to the best of Services. It satisfied my mind, I found, quite as well as if I had been disguised in a hired hatband and scarf both trailing to my very heels, and as if I had cost the orphan children, in their greatest need, ten guineas.

Can any one who ever beheld the stupendous absurdities attendant on "A message from the Lords" in the House of Commons, turn upon the Medicine Man of the poor Indians? Has he any "Medicine" in that dried skin pouch of his, so supremely ludicrous as the two Masters in Chancery holding up their black petticoats and butting their ridiculous wigs at Mr. Speaker? Yet there are authorities innumerable to tell me—as there are authorities innumerable among the Indians to tell them—that the nonsense is indispensable, and that its abrogation would involve most awful consequences. What would any rational creature who had never heard of judicial and forensic "fittings", think of the Court of Common Pleas on the first day of Term? Or with what an awakened sense of humour would LIVINGSTONE'S account of a similar scene be perused, if the fur and red cloth and goats' hair and horse hair and powdered chalk and black patches on the top of the head, were all at Tala Mungongo instead of Westminster? That model missionary and good brave man found at least one tribe of blacks with a very strong sense of the ridiculous, insomuch that although an amiable and docile people, they never could see the Missionaries dispose of their legs in the attitude of kneeling, or hear them begin a hymn in chorus, without bursting into roars of irrepressible laughter. It is much to be hoped that no member of this facetious tribe may ever find his way to England and get committed for contempt of Court.

In the Tonga Island already mentioned, there are a set of personages called Mataboos—or some such name—who are the masters of all the public ceremonies, and who know the exact place in which every chief must sit down when a solemn public meeting takes place: a meeting which bears a family resemblance to our own Public Dinner, in respect of its being a main part of the proceedings that every gentleman present is required to drink something nasty. These Mataboos are a privileged order, so important is their avocation, and they make the most of their high functions. A long way out of the Tonga Islands, indeed, rather near the British Islands, was there no calling in of the Mataboos the other day to settle an earth-convulsing question of precedence; and was there no weighty opinion delivered on the part of the Mataboos which, being interpreted to that unlucky tribe of blacks with the sense of the ridiculous, would infallibly set the whole population screaming with laughter?

My sense of justice demands the admission, however, that this is not quite a one-sided question. If we submit ourselves meekly to the Medicine Man and the Conjurer, and are not exalted by it, the savages may retort upon us that we act more unwisely than they in other matters wherein we fail to imitate them. It is a widely diffused custom among savage tribes, when they meet to discuss any affair of public importance, to sit up all night making a horrible noise, dancing, blowing shells, and (in cases where they are familiar with fire-arms) flying out into open places and letting off guns. It is questionable whether our legislative assemblies might not take a hint from this. A shell is not a melodious wind-instrument, and it is monotonous; but it is as musical as, and not more monotonous than, my Honourable friend's own trumpet, or the trumpet that he blows so hard for the Minister. The uselessness of arguing with any supporter of a Government or of an Opposition, is well known. Try dancing. It is a better exercise, and has the unspeakable recommendation that it couldn't be reported. The honourable and savage member who has a loaded gun, and has grown impatient of debate, plunges out of doors, fires in the air, and returns calm and silent to the Palaver. Let the honourable and civilised member similarly charged with a speech, dart into the cloisters of Westminster Abbey in the silence of night, let his speech off, and come back harmless. It is not at first sight a very rational custom to paint a broad blue stripe across one's nose and both cheeks, and a broad red stripe from the forehead to the chin, to attach a few pounds of wood to one's under lip, to stick fish-bones in one's ears and a brass curtain-ring in one's nose, and to rub one's body all over with rancid oil, as a preliminary to entering on business. But this is a question of taste and ceremony, and so is the Windsor Uniform. The manner of entering on the business itself is another question. A council of six hundred savage gentlemen entirely independent of tailors, sitting on their hams in a ring, smoking, and occasionally grunting, seem to me, according to the experience I have gathered in my voyages and travels, somehow to do what they come together for; whereas that is not at all the general experience of a council of six hundred civilised gentlemen very dependent on tailors and sitting on mechanical contrivances. It is better that an Assembly should do its utmost to envelop itself in smoke, than that it should direct its endeavours to enveloping the public in smoke; and I would rather it buried half a hundred hatchets than buried one subject demanding attention.

XXVIII

TITBULL'S ALMS-HOUSES

By the side of most railways out of London, one may see Alms-Houses and Retreats (generally with a Wing or a Centre wanting, and ambitious of being much bigger than they are), some of which are newly-founded Institutions, and some old establishments transplanted. There is a tendency in these pieces of architecture to shoot upward unexpectedly, like Jack's bean-stalk, and to be ornate in spires of Chapels and lanterns of Halls, which might lead to the embellishment of the air with many castles of questionable beauty but for the restraining consideration of expense. However, the managers, being always of a sanguine temperament, comfort themselves with plans and elevations of Loomings in the future, and are influenced in the present by philanthropy towards the railway passengers. For, the question how prosperous and promising the buildings can be made to look in their eyes, usually supersedes the lesser question how they can be turned to the best account for the inmates.

Why none of the people who reside in these places ever look out of window, or take an airing in the piece of ground which is going to be a garden by-and-by, is one of the wonders I have added to my always-lengthening list of the wonders of the world. I have got it into my mind that they live in a state of chronic injury and resentment, and on that account refuse to decorate the building with a human interest. As I have known legatees deeply injured by a bequest of five hundred pounds because it was not five thousand, and as I was once acquainted with a pensioner on the Public to the extent of two hundred a year, who perpetually anathematised his Country because he was not in the receipt of four, having no claim whatever to sixpence: so perhaps it usually happens, within certain limits, that to get a little help is to get a notion of being defrauded of more. "How do they pass their lives in this beautiful and peaceful place?" was the subject of my speculation with a visitor who once accompanied me to a charming rustic retreat for old men and women: a quaint ancient foundation in a pleasant English county, behind a picturesque church and among rich old convent gardens. There were but some dozen or so of houses, and we agreed that we would talk with the inhabitants, as they sat in their groined rooms between the light of their fires and the light shining in at their latticed windows, and would find out. They passed their lives in considering themselves mulcted of certain ounces of tea by a deaf old steward who lived among them in the quadrangle. There was no reason to suppose that any such ounces of tea had ever been in existence, or that the old steward so much as knew what was the matter;—he passed *his* life in considering himself periodically defrauded of a birch-broom by the beadle.

But it is neither to old Alms-Houses in the country, nor to new Alms-Houses by the railroad, that these present Uncommercial notes relate. They refer back to journeys made among those common-place smoky-fronted London Alms-Houses, with a little paved court-yard in front enclosed by iron railings, which have got snowed up, as it were, by bricks and mortar; which were once in a suburb, but are now in the densely populated town; gaps in the busy life around them, parentheses in the close and blotted texts of the streets.

Sometimes, these Alms-Houses belong to a Company or Society. Sometimes, they were established by individuals, and are maintained out of private funds bequeathed in perpetuity long ago. My favourite among them is Titbull's, which establishment is a picture of many. Of Titbull I know no more than that he deceased in 1723, that his Christian name was Sampson, and his social designation Esquire, and that he founded these Alms-Houses as Dwellings for Nine Poor Women and Six Poor Men by his Will and Testament. I should not know even this much, but for its being inscribed on a grim stone very difficult to read, let into the front of the centre house of Titbull's Alms-Houses, and which stone is ornamented a-top with a piece of sculptured drapery resembling the effigy of Titbull's bath-towel.

Titbull's Alms-Houses are in the east of London, in a great highway, in a poor busy and thronged neighbourhood. Old iron and fried fish, cough drops and artificial flowers, boiled pigs'-feet and household furniture that looks as if it were polished up with lip-salve, umbrellas full of vocal literature and saucers full of shell-fish in a green juice which I hope is natural to them when their health is good, garnish the paved sideways as you go to Titbull's. I take the ground to have risen in those parts since Titbull's time, and you drop into his domain by three stone steps. So did I first drop into it, very nearly striking my brows against Titbull's pump, which stands with its back to the thoroughfare just inside the gate, and has a conceited air of reviewing Titbull's pensioners.

"And a worse one," said a virulent old man with a pitcher, "there isn't nowhere. A harder one to work, nor a grudginer one to yield, there isn't nowhere!" This old man wore a long coat, such as we see Hogarth's Chairmen represented with, and it was of that peculiar green-pea hue without the green, which seems to come of poverty. It had also that peculiar smell of cupboard which seems to come of poverty.

"The pump is rusty, perhaps," said I.

"Not *it*," said the old man, regarding it with undiluted virulence in his watery eye. "It never were fit to be termed a pump. That's what's the matter with *it*."

"Whose fault is that?" said I.

The old man, who had a working mouth which seemed to be trying to masticate his anger and to find that it was too hard and there was too much of it, replied, "Them gentlemen".

"What gentlemen?"

"Maybe you're one of 'em?" said the old man, suspiciously.

"The trustees?"

"I wouldn't trust 'em myself," said the virulent old man.

"If you mean the gentlemen who administer this place, no, I am not one of them; nor have I ever so much as heard of them."

"I wish *I* never heard of them," gasped the old man: "at my time of life—with the rheumatics—drawing water—from that thing!" Not to be deluded into calling it a Pump, the old man gave it another virulent look, took up his pitcher, and carried it into a corner dwelling-house, shutting the door after him.

Looking around and seeing that each little house was a house of two little rooms; and seeing that the little oblong court-yard in front was like a graveyard for the inhabitants, saving that no word was engraven on its flat dry stones; and seeing that the currents of life and noise ran to and fro outside, having no more to do with the place than if it were a sort of low-water mark on a lively beach; I say, seeing this and nothing else, I was going out at the gate when one of the doors opened.

"Was you looking for anything, sir?" asked a tidy well-favoured woman.

Really, no; I couldn't say I was.

" Not wanting any one, sir?"

" No—at least I—pray what is the name of the elderly gentleman who lives in the corner there?"

The tidy woman stepped out to be sure of the door I indicated, and she and the pump and I stood all three in a row with our backs to the thoroughfare.

" Oh! *His* name is Mr. Battens," said the tidy woman, dropping her voice.

" I have just been talking with him."

" Indeed?" said the tidy woman. " Ho! I wonder Mr. Battens talked!"

" Is he usually so silent?"

" Well, Mr. Battens is the oldest here—that is to say, the oldest of the old gentlemen—in point of residence."

She had a way of passing her hands over and under one another as she spoke, that was not only tidy but propitiatory; so I asked her if I might look at her little sitting-room? She willingly replied Yes, and we went into it together: she leaving the door open, with an eye as I understood to the social proprieties. The door opening at once into the room without any intervening entry, even scandal must have been silenced by the precaution.

It was a gloomy little chamber, but clean, and with a mug of wall-flower in the window. On the chimney-piece were two peacock's feathers, a carved ship, a few shells, and a black profile with one eyelash; whether this portrait purported to be male or female passed my comprehension, until my hostess informed me that it was her only son, and " quite a speaking one".

" He is alive, I hope?"

" No, sir," said the widow, " he were cast away in China." This was said with a modest sense of its reflecting a certain geographical distinction on his mother.

" If the old gentlemen here are not given to talking," said I, " I hope the old ladies are?—not that you are one."

She shook her head. " You see they get so cross."

" How is that?"

" Well, whether the gentlemen really do deprive us of any little matters which ought to be ours by rights, I cannot say for certain; but the opinion of the old ones is they do. And Mr. Battens he do even go so far as to doubt whether credit is due to the Founder. For Mr. Battens he do say, anyhow he got his name up by it and he done it cheap."

" I am afraid the pump has soured Mr. Battens."

" It may be so," returned the tidy widow, " but the handle does go very hard. Still, what I say to myself is, the gentlemen *may* not pocket the difference between a good pump and a bad one, and I would wish to think well of them. And the dwellings," said my hostess, glancing round her room; " perhaps they were convenient dwellings in the Founder's time, considered *as* his time, and therefore he should not be blamed. But Mrs. Saggers is very hard upon them."

" Mrs. Saggers is the oldest here?"

" The oldest but one. Mrs. Quinch being the oldest, and have totally lost her head."

" And you?"

" I am the youngest in residence, and consequently am not looked up to. But when Mrs. Quinch makes a happy release, there will be one below me. Nor is it to be expected that Mrs. Saggers will prove herself immortal."

" True. Nor Mr. Battens."

" Regarding the old gentlemen," said my widow slightingly, " they count among themselves. They do not count among us. Mr. Battens is that exceptional that he have written to the gentlemen many times and have worked the case against them. Therefore he have took a higher ground. But we do not, as a rule, greatly reckon the old gentlemen."

Pursuing the subject, I found it to be traditionally settled among the poor ladies that the poor gentlemen, whatever their ages, were all very old indeed, and in a state of dotage. I also discovered that the juniors and new comers preserved, for a time, a waning disposition to believe in Titbull and his trustees, but that as they gained social standing they lost this faith, and disparaged Titbull and all his works.

Improving my acquaintance subsequently with this respected lady, whose name was Mrs. Mitts, and occasionally dropping in upon her with a little offering of sound Family Hyson in my pocket, I gradually became familiar with the inner politics and ways of Titbull's Alms-Houses. But I never could find out who the trustees were, or where they were: it being one of the fixed ideas of the place that those authorities must be vaguely and mysteriously mentioned as " the gentlemen " only. The secretary of " the gentlemen " was once pointed out to me, evidently engaged in championing the obnoxious pump against the attacks of the discontented Mr. Battens; but I am not in a condition to report further of him than that he had the sprightly bearing of a lawyer's clerk. I had it from Mrs. Mitts's lips in a very confidential moment, that Mr. Battens was once " had up before the gentlemen " to stand or fall by his accusations, and that an old shoe was thrown after him on his departure from the building on this dread errand;—not ineffectually, for, the interview resulting in a plumber, was considered to have encircled the temples of Mr. Battens with the wreath of victory.

In Titbull's Alms-Houses, the local society is not regarded as good society. A gentleman or lady receiving visitors from without, or going out to tea, counts, as it were, accordingly; but visitings or tea-drinkings interchanged among Titbullians do not score. Such interchanges, however, are rare, in consequence of internal dissensions occasioned by Mrs. Saggers's pail: which household article has split Titbull's into almost as many parties as there are dwellings in that precinct. The extremely complicated nature of the conflicting articles of belief on the subject prevents my stating them here with my usual perspicuity, but I think they have all branched off from the root-and-trunk question, Has Mrs. Saggers any right to stand her pail outside her dwelling? The question has been much refined upon, but roughly stated may be stated in those terms.

There are two old men in Titbull's Alms-Houses who, I have been given to understand, knew each other in the world beyond its pump and iron railings, when they were both " in trade ". They make the best of their reverses, and are looked upon with great contempt. They are little stooping blear-eyed old men of cheerful countenance, and they hobble up and down the court-yard wagging their chins and talking together quite gaily. This has given offence, and has, moreover, raised the question whether they are justified in passing any other windows than their own. Mr. Battens, however, permitting them to pass *his* windows, on the disdainful ground that their imbecility almost amounts to irresponsibility, they are allowed to take their walk in peace. They live next door to one another, and take it by turns to read the newspaper aloud (that is to say, the newest newspaper they can get), and they play cribbage at night. On warm and sunny days they have been known to go so far as to bring out two chairs and sit by the iron railings, looking forth; but this low conduct, being much remarked upon throughout Titbull's, they were deterred by an outraged public opinion from repeating it. There is a rumour—but it may be malicious—that they hold the memory of Titbull in some weak sort of veneration, and that they once set off together on a pilgrimage to the parish churchyard to find his tomb. To this, perhaps, might be traced a general suspicion that they are spies of "the gentlemen": to which they were supposed to have given colour in my own presence on the occasion of the weak attempt at justification of the pump by the gentlemen's clerk; when they emerged bare-headed from the doors of their dwellings, as if their dwellings and themselves constituted an old-fashioned weather-glass of double action with two figures of old ladies inside, and deferentially bowed to him at intervals until he took his departure. They are understood to be perfectly friendless and relationless. Unquestionably the two poor fellows make the very best of their lives in Titbull's Alms-Houses, and unquestionably they are (as before mentioned) the subjects of unmitigated contempt there.

On Saturday nights, when there is a greater stir than usual outside, and when itinerant vendors of miscellaneous wares even take their stations and light up their smoky lamps before the iron railings, Titbull's becomes flurried. Mrs. Saggers has her celebrated palpitations of the heart, for the most part on Saturday nights. But Titbull's is unfit to strive with the uproar of the streets in any of its phases.

It is religiously believed at Titbull's that people push more than they used, and likewise that the foremost object of the population of England and Wales is to get you down and trample on you. Even of railroads they know, at Titbull's, little more than the shriek (which Mrs. Saggers says goes through her, and ought to be taken up by Government); and the penny postage may even yet be unknown there, for I have never seen a letter delivered to any inhabitant. But there is a tall straight sallow lady resident in Number Seven, Titbull's, who never speaks to anybody, who is surrounded by a superstitious halo of lost wealth, who does her household work in housemaid's gloves, and who is secretly much deferred to, though openly cavilled at; and it has obscurely leaked out that this old lady has a son, grandson, nephew, or other relative, who is "a Contractor", and who would think it nothing of a job to knock down Titbull's, pack it off into Cornwall, and knock it together again. An immense sensation was made by a gipsy-party calling in a spring-van, to take this old lady up to go for a day's pleasure into Epping Forest, and notes were compared as to which of the company was the son, grandson, nephew, or other relative, the Contractor. A thick-set personage with a white hat and a cigar in his mouth, was the favourite: though as Titbull's had no other reason to believe that the Contractor was there at all, than that this man was supposed to eye the chimney stacks as if he would like to knock them down and cart them off, the general mind was much unsettled in arriving at a conclusion. As a way out of this difficulty, it concentrated itself on the acknowledged Beauty of the party, every stitch in whose dress was verbally unripped by the old ladies then and there, and whose "goings on" with another and a thinner personage in a white hat might have suffused the pump (where they were principally discussed) with blushes, for months afterwards. Herein Titbull's was to Titbull's true, for it has a constitutional dislike of all strangers. As concerning innovations and improvements, it is always of opinion that what it doesn't want itself, nobody ought to want. But I think I have met with this opinion outside Titbull's.

Of the humble treasures of furniture brought into Titbull's by the inmates when they establish themselves in that place of contemplation for the rest of their days, by far the greater and more valuable part belongs to the ladies. I may claim the honour of having either crossed the threshold, or looked in at the door, of every one of the nine ladies, and I have noticed that they are all particular in the article of bedsteads, and maintain favourite and long-established bedsteads and bedding as a regular part of their rest. Generally an antiquated chest of drawers is among their cherished possessions; a tea-tray always is. I know of at least two rooms in which a little tea-kettle of genuine burnished copper, vies with the cat in winking at the fire; and one old lady has a tea-urn set forth in state on the top of her chest of drawers, which urn is used as her library, and contains four duodecimo volumes, and a black-bordered newspaper giving an account of the funeral of Her Royal Highness the Princess

Charlotte. Among the poor old gentlemen there are no such niceties. Their furniture has the air of being contributed, like some obsolete Literary Miscellany, "by several hands"; their few chairs never match; old patchwork coverlets linger among them; and they have an untidy habit of keeping their wardrobes in hat-boxes. When I recall one old gentleman who is rather choice in his shoe-brushes and blacking-bottle, I have summed up the domestic elegances of that side of the building.

On the occurrence of a death in Titbull's, it is invariably agreed among the survivors—and it is the only subject on which they do agree—that the departed did something "to bring it on". Judging by Titbull's, I should say the human race need never die, if they took care. But they don't take care, and they do die, and when they die in Titbull's they are buried at the cost of the Foundation. Some provision has been made for the purpose, in virtue of which (I record this on the strength of having seen the funeral of Mrs. Quinch) a lively neighbouring undertaker dresses up four of the old men, and four of the old women, hustles them into a procession of four couples, and leads off with a large black bow at the back of his hat, looking over his shoulder at them airily from time to time to see that no member of the party has got lost, or has tumbled down; as if they were a company of dim old dolls.

Resignation of a dwelling is of very rare occurrence in Titbull's. A story does obtain there, how an old lady's son once drew a prize of Thirty Thousand Pounds in the Lottery, and presently drove to the gate in his own carriage, with French Horns playing up behind, and whisked his mother away, and left ten guineas for a Feast. But I have been unable to substantiate it by any evidence, and regard it as an Alms-House Fairy Tale. It is curious that the only proved case of resignation happened within my knowledge.

It happened on this wise. There is a sharp competition among the ladies respecting the gentility of their visitors, and I have so often observed visitors to be dressed as for a holiday occasion, that I suppose the ladies to have besought them to make all possible display when they come. In these circumstances much excitement was one day occasioned by Mrs. Mitts receiving a visit from a Greenwich Pensioner. He was a Pensioner of a bluff and warlike appearance, with an empty coat-sleeve, and he was got up with unusual care; his coat-buttons were extremely bright, he wore his empty coat-sleeve in a graceful festoon, and he had a walking-stick in his hand that must have cost money. When, with the head of his walking-stick, he knocked at Mrs. Mitts's door—there are no knockers in Titbull's—Mrs. Mitts was overheard by a next-door neighbour to utter a cry of surprise expressing much agitation; and the same neighbour did afterwards solemnly affirm that when he was admitted into Mrs. Mitts's room, she heard a smack. Heard a smack which was not a blow.

There was an air about this Greenwich Pensioner when he took his departure, which imbued all Titbull's with the conviction that he was coming again. He was eagerly looked for, and Mrs. Mitts was closely watched. In the meantime, if anything could have placed the unfortunate six old gentlemen at a greater disadvantage than that at which they chronically stood, it would have been the apparition of this Greenwich Pensioner. They were well shrunken already, but they shrunk to nothing in comparison with the Pensioner. Even the poor old gentlemen themselves seemed conscious of their inferiority, and to know submissively that they could never hope to hold their own against the Pensioner with his warlike and maritime experience in the past, and his tobacco money in the present; his chequered career of blue water, black gunpowder, and red bloodshed for England home and beauty.

Before three weeks were out, the Pensioner reappeared. Again he knocked at Mrs. Mitts's door with the handle of his stick, and again was he admitted. But not again did he depart alone; for Mrs. Mitts, in a bonnet identified as having been re-embellished, went out walking with him, and stayed out till the ten o'clock beer, Greenwich time.

There was now a truce, even as to the troubled waters of Mrs. Saggers's pail; nothing was spoken of among the ladies but the conduct of Mrs. Mitts and its blighting influence on the reputation of Titbull's. It was agreed that Mr. Battens "ought to take it up", and Mr. Battens was communicated with on the subject. That unsatisfactory individual replied "that he didn't see his way yet", and it was unanimously voted by the ladies that aggravation was in his nature.

How it came to pass, with some appearance of inconsistency, that Mrs. Mitts was cut by all the ladies and the Pensioner admired by all the ladies, matters not. Before another week was out, Titbull's was startled by another phenomenon. At ten o'clock in the forenoon appeared a cab, containing not only the Greenwich Pensioner with one arm, but, to boot, a Chelsea Pensioner with one leg. Both dismounting to assist Mrs. Mitts into the cab, the Greenwich Pensioner bore her company inside, and the Chelsea Pensioner mounted the box by the driver; his wooden leg sticking out after the manner of a bowsprit, as if in jocular homage to his friend's seagoing career. Thus the equipage drove away. No Mrs. Mitts returned that night.

What Mr. Battens might have done in the matter of taking it up, goaded by the infuriated state of public feeling next morning, was anticipated by another phenomenon. A Truck, propelled by the Greenwich Pensioner and the Chelsea Pensioner, each placidly smoking a pipe, and pushing his warrior breast against the handle.

The display on the part of the Greenwich Pensioner of his "marriage-lines", and his announcement that himself and friend had looked in for the furniture of Mrs. G. Pensioner, late Mitts, by no means reconciled the ladies to the conduct of their sister; on the contrary, it is said that they appeared more than ever exasperated. Nevertheless, my stray visits to Titbull's since the date of this occurrence, have confirmed me in an impression that it was a wholesome fillip. The nine ladies are smarter, both in mind and dress, than they used to be, though it must be admitted that they despise the six gentlemen to the last extent. They have a much greater interest in the external thoroughfare too, than they had when I first knew Titbull's. And whenever I chance to be leaning my back against the pump or the iron railings, and to be talking to one of the junior ladies, and to see that a flush has passed over her face, I immediately know without looking round that a Greenwich Pensioner has gone past.

XXIX

AMONG THE SHORT-TIMERS

"WITHIN so many yards of this Covent Garden lodging of mine, as within so many yards of Westminster Abbey, Saint Paul's Cathedral, the Houses of Parliament, the Prisons, the Courts of Justice, all the Institutions that govern the land, I can find—*must* find, whether I will or no—in the open streets, shameful instances of neglect of children, intolerable toleration of the engenderment of paupers, idlers, thieves, races of wretched and destructive cripples both in body and mind, a misery to themselves, a misery to the community, a disgrace to civilisation, and an outrage on Christianity. I know it to be a fact as easy of demonstration as any sum in any of the elementary rules of arithmetic, that if the State would begin its work and duty at the beginning, and would with the strong hand take those children out of the streets, while they are yet children, and wisely train them, it would make them a part of England's glory, not its shame— of England's strength, not its weakness—would raise good soldiers and sailors, and good citizens, and many great men, out of the seeds of its criminal population. Yet I go on bearing with the enormity as if it were nothing, and I go on reading the Parliamentary Debates as if they were something, and I concern myself far more about one railway-bridge across a public thoroughfare, than about a dozen generations of scrofula, ignorance, wickedness, prostitution, poverty, and felony. I can slip out at my door, in the small hours after any midnight, and, in one circuit of the purlieus of Covent Garden Market, can behold a state of infancy and youth, as vile as if a Bourbon sat upon the English throne; a great police force looking on with authority to do no more than worry and hunt the dreadful vermin into corners, and there leave them. Within the length of a few streets I can find a workhouse, mismanaged with that dull short-sighted obstinacy that its greatest opportunities as to the children it receives are lost, and yet not a farthing saved to any one. But the wheel goes round, and round, and round; and because it goes round—so I am told by the politest authorities—it goes well."

Thus I reflected, one day in the Whitsun week last past, as I floated down the Thames among the bridges, looking—not inappropriately—at the drags that were hanging up at certain dirty stairs to hook the drowned out, and at the numerous conveniences provided to facilitate their tumbling in. My object in that uncommercial journey called up another train of thought, and it ran as follows:

"When I was at school, one of seventy boys, I wonder by what secret understanding our attention began to wander when we had pored over our books for some hours. I wonder by what ingenuity we brought on that confused state of mind when sense became nonsense, when figures wouldn't work, when dead languages wouldn't construe, when live languages wouldn't be spoken, when memory wouldn't come, when dulness and vacancy wouldn't go. I cannot remember that we ever conspired to be sleepy after dinner, or that we ever particularly wanted to be stupid, and to have flushed faces and hot beating heads, or to find blank hopelessness and obscurity this afternoon in what would become perfectly clear and bright in the freshness of to-morrow morning. We suffered for these things, and they made us miserable enough. Neither do I remember that we ever bound ourselves by any secret oath or other solemn obligation, to find the seats getting too hard to be sat upon after a certain time; or to have intolerable twitches in our legs, rendering us aggressive and malicious with those members; or to be troubled with a similar uneasiness in our elbows, attended with fistic consequences to our neighbours; or to carry two pounds of lead in the chest, four pounds in the head, and several active blue-bottles in each ear. Yet, for certain, we suffered under those distresses, and were always charged at for labouring under them, as if we had brought them on, of our own deliberate act and deed. As to the mental portion of them being my own fault in my own case—I should like to ask any well-trained and experienced teacher, not to say psychologist. And as to the physical portion—I should like to ask PROFESSOR OWEN."

It happened that I had a small bundle of papers with me, on what is called "The Half-Time System" in schools. Referring to one of those papers I found that the indefatigable MR. CHADWICK had been beforehand with me, and had already asked Professor Owen: who had handsomely replied that I was not to blame, but that, being troubled with a skeleton, and having been constituted according to certain natural laws, I and my skeleton were unfortunately bound by those laws—even in school—and had comported ourselves accordingly. Much comforted by the good Professor's being on my side, I read on to discover whether the indefatigable Mr. Chadwick had taken up the mental part of my afflictions. I found that he had, and that he had gained on my behalf, SIR BENJAMIN BRODIE, SIR DAVID WILKIE, SIR WALTER SCOTT, and the common sense of mankind. For which I beg Mr. Chadwick, if this should meet his eye, to accept my warm acknowledgments.

Up to that time I had retained a misgiving that the seventy

unfortunates of whom I was one, must have been, without knowing it, leagued together by the spirit of evil in a sort of perpetual Guy Fawkes Plot, to grope about in vaults with dark lanterns after a certain period of continuous study. But now the misgiving vanished, and I floated on with a quieted mind to see the Half-Time System in action. For that was the purpose of my journey, both by steam-boat on the Thames, and by very dirty railway on the shore. To which last institution, I beg to recommend the legal use of coke as engine-fuel, rather than the illegal use of coal; the recommendation is quite disinterested, for I was most liberally supplied with small coal on the journey, for which no charge was made. I had not only my eyes, nose, and ears filled, but my hat, and all my pockets, and my pocket-book, and my watch.

The V.D.S.C.R.C. (or Very Dirty and Small Coal Railway Company) delivered me close to my destination, and I soon found the Half-Time System established in spacious premises, and freely placed at my convenience and disposal.

What would I see first of the Half-Time System? I chose Military Drill. "Atten-tion!" Instantly a hundred boys stood forth in the paved yard as one boy; bright, quick, eager, steady, watchful for the look of command, instant and ready for the word. Not only was there complete precision—complete accord to the eye and to the ear—but an alertness in the doing of the thing which deprived it, curiously, of its monotonous or mechanical character. There was perfect uniformity, and yet an individual spirit and emulation. No spectator could doubt that the boys liked it. With non-commissioned officers varying from a yard to a yard and a half high, the result could not possibly have been attained otherwise. They marched, and counter-marched, and formed in line and square, and company, and single file and double file, and performed a variety of evolutions; all most admirably. In respect of an air of enjoyable understanding of what they were about, which seems to be forbidden to English soldiers, the boys might have been small French troops. When they were dismissed and the broadsword exercise, limited to a much smaller number, succeeded, the boys who had no part in that new drill, either looked on attentively, or disported themselves in a gymnasium hard by. The steadiness of the broadsword boys on their short legs, and the firmness with which they sustained the different positions, was truly remarkable.

The broadsword exercise over, suddenly there was great excitement and a rush. Naval Drill!

In a corner of the ground stood a decked mimic ship, with real masts, yards, and sails—mainmast seventy feet high. At the word of command from the Skipper of this ship—a mahogany-faced Old Salt, with the indispensable quid in his cheek, the true nautical roll, and all wonderfully complete—the rigging was covered with a swarm of boys: one, the first to spring into the shrouds, outstripping all the others, and resting on the truck of the main-topmast in no time.

And now we stood out to sea, in a most amazing manner; the Skipper himself, the whole crew, the Uncommercial, and all hands present, implicitly believing that there was not a moment to lose, that the wind had that instant chopped round and sprung up fair, and that we were away on a voyage round the world. Get all sail upon her! With a will, my lads! Lay out upon the main-yard there! Look alive at the weather earing! Cheery, my boys! Let go the sheet now! Stand by at the braces, you! With a will, aloft there! Belay, starboard watch! Fifer! Come aft, fifer, and give 'em a tune! Forthwith, springs up fifer, fife in hand—smallest boy ever seen—big lump on temple, having lately fallen down on a paving-stone —gives 'em a tune with all his might and main. Hooroar, fifer! With a will, my lads! Tip 'em a livelier one, fifer! Fifer tips 'em a livelier one, and excitement increases. Shake 'em out, my lads! Well done! There you have her! Pretty, pretty! Every rag upon her she can carry, wind right astern, and ship cutting through the water fifteen knot an hour!

At this favourable moment of her voyage, I gave the alarm, "A man overboard!" (on the gravel), but he was immediately recovered, none the worse. Presently, I observed the Skipper overboard, but forebore to mention it, as he seemed in no wise disconcerted by the accident. Indeed, I soon came to regard the Skipper as an amphibious creature, for he was so perpetually plunging overboard to look up at the hands aloft, that he was oftener in the bosom of the ocean than on deck. His pride in his crew on those occasions was delightful, and the conventional unintelligibility of his orders in the ears of uncommercial land-lubbers and loblolly boys, though they were always intelligible to the crew, was hardly less pleasant. But we couldn't expect to go on in this way for ever; dirty weather came on, and then worse weather, and when we least expected it we got into tremendous difficulties. Screw loose in the chart perhaps—something certainly wrong somewhere—but here we were with breakers ahead, my lads, driving head on, slap on a lee shore! The Skipper broached this terrific announcement in such great agitation, that the small fifer, not fifeing now, but standing looking on near the wheel with his fife under his arm, seemed for the moment quite unboyed, though he speedily recovered his presence of mind. In the trying circumstances that ensued, the Skipper and the crew proved worthy of one another. The Skipper got dreadfully hoarse, but otherwise was master of the situation. The man at the wheel did wonders; all hands (except the fifer) were turned up to wear ship; and I observed the fifer, when we were at our greatest extremity, to refer to some document in his waist-coat-pocket, which I conceived to be his will. I think she struck. I was not myself conscious of any collision, but I saw the Skipper so very often washed overboard and back again, that I could only impute it to the beating of the ship. I am not enough of a seaman to describe the manœuvres by which we were saved, but they made the Skipper very hot (French polishing his mahogany face) and the crew very nimble, and succeeded to a marvel; for, within a few minutes of the first alarm, we had wore ship and got her off, and were all a-tauto—which I felt very grateful for: not that I knew what it was, but that I perceived that we had not been all a-tauto lately. Land now appeared on our weather-bow, and we shaped our course for it, having the wind abeam, and frequently changing the man at the helm, in order that every man might have his spell. We worked into harbour under prosperous circumstances, and furled our sails, and squared our yards, and made all ship-shape and handsome, and so our voyage ended. When I complimented the Skipper at parting on his exertions and those of his gallant crew, he informed me that the latter were provided for the worst, all hands being taught to swim and dive; and he added that the able seaman at the maintopmast truck especially, could dive as deep as he could go high.

The next adventure that befell me in my visit to the Short-Timers, was the sudden apparition of a military band. I had been inspecting the hammocks of the crew of the good ship, when I saw with astonishment that several musical instruments, brazen and of great size, appeared to have suddenly developed two legs each, and to be trotting about a yard. And my astonishment was heightened when I observed a large drum, that had previously been leaning helpless against a wall, taking up a stout position on four legs. Approaching this drum and looking over it, I found two boys behind it (it was too much for one), and then I found that each of the brazen instruments had brought out a boy, and was going to discourse sweet sounds. The boys—not omitting the fifer, now playing a new instrument—were dressed in neat uniform, and stood up in a circle at their music-stands, like any other Military Band. They played a march or two, and then we had Cheer, Boys, Cheer, and then we had Yankee Doodle, and we finished, as in loyal duty bound, with God Save the Queen. The band's proficiency was perfectly wonderful, and it was not at all wonderful that the whole body corporate of Short-Timers listened with faces of the liveliest interest and pleasure.

What happened next among the Short-Timers? As if the band had blown me into a great class-room out of their brazen tubes, *in* a great class-room I found myself now, with the whole choral force of Short-Timers singing the praises of a summer's day to the harmonium, and my small but highly-respected friend the fifer blazing away vocally, as if he had been saving up his wind for the last twelvemonth; also the whole crew of the good ship Nameless swarming up and down the scale as if they had never swarmed up and down the rigging. This done, we threw our whole power into God bless the Prince of Wales, and blessed his Royal Highness to such an extent that, for my own Uncommercial part, I gasped again when it was over. The moment this was done, we formed, with surpassing freshness, into hollow squares, and fell to work at oral lessons, as if we never did, and had never thought of doing, anything else.

Let a veil be drawn over the self-committals into which the Uncommercial Traveller would have been betrayed but for a discreet reticence, coupled with an air of absolute wisdom on the part of that artful personage. Take the square of five, multiply it by fifteen, divide it by three, deduct eight from it, add four dozen to it, give me the result in pence, and tell me how many eggs I could get for it at three farthings apiece. The problem is hardly stated, when a dozen small boys pour out answers. Some wide, some very nearly right, some worked as far as they go with such accuracy, as at once to show what link of the chain has been dropped in the hurry. For the moment, none are quite right; but behold a labouring spirit beating the buttons on its corporeal waistcoat, in a process of internal calculation, and knitting an accidental bump on its corporeal forehead in a concentration of mental arithmetic! It is my honourable friend (if he will allow me to call him so) the fifer. With right arm eagerly extended in token of being inspired with an answer, and with right leg foremost, the fifer solves the mystery: then recalls both arm and leg, and with bump in ambush awaits the next poser. Take the square of three, multiply it by seven, divide it by four, add fifty to it, take thirteen from it, multiply it by two, double it, give me the result in pence, and say how many halfpence. Wise as the serpent is the four feet of performer on the nearest approach to that instrument, whose right arm instantly appears, and quenches this arithmetical fire. Tell me something about Great Britain, tell me something about its principal productions, tell me something about its ports, tell me something about its seas and rivers, tell me something about coal, iron, cotton, timber, tin, and turpentine. The hollow square bristles with extended right arms; but ever faithful to fact is the fifer, ever wise as the serpent is the performer on that instrument, ever prominently buoyant and brilliant are all members of the band. I observe the player of the cymbals to dash at a sounding answer now and then rather than not cut in at all; but I take that to be in the way of his instrument. All these questions, and many such, are put on the spur of the moment, and by one who has never examined these boys. The Uncommercial, invited to add another, falteringly demands how many birthdays a man born on the twenty-ninth of February will have had on completing his fiftieth year? A general perception of trap and pitfall instantly arises, and the fifer is seen to retire behind the corduroys of his next neighbours, as perceiving special necessity for collecting himself and communing with his mind. Meanwhile, the wisdom of the serpent suggests that the man will have had only one birthday in all that time, for how can any man have more than one, seeing that he is born once and dies once? The blushing Uncommercial stands corrected, and amends the formula. Pondering ensues, two or three wrong answers are offered, and Cymbals strikes up "Six!" but doesn't know why. Then modestly emerging from his Academic Grove of corduroys appears the fifer, right arm extended, right leg foremost, bump irradiated. "Twelve, and two over!"

The feminine Short-Timers passed a similar examination, and very creditably too. Would have done better perhaps, with a little more geniality on the part of their pupil-teacher; for a cold eye, my young friend, and a hard abrupt manner, are not by any means the powerful engines that your innocence supposes them to be. Both girls and boys wrote excellently, from copy and dictation; both could cook; both could mend their own clothes; both could clean up everything about them in an orderly and skilful way, the girls having womanly household knowledge superadded. Order and method began in the songs of the Infant School which I visited likewise, and they were even in their dwarf degree to be found in the Nursery, where the Uncommercial walking-stick was carried off with acclamations, and where "the Doctor"—a medical gentleman of two, who took his degree on the night when he was found at an apothecary's door—did the honours of the establishment with great urbanity and gaiety.

These have long been excellent schools; long before the days of the Short-Time. I first saw them, twelve or fifteen years ago. But since the introduction of the Short-Time system it has been proved here that eighteen hours a week of book-learning are more profitable than thirty-six, and that the pupils are far quicker and brighter than of yore. The good influences of music on the whole body of children have likewise been surprisingly proved. Obviously another of the immense advantages of the Short-Time system to the cause of good education is the great diminution of its cost, and of the period of time over which it extends. The last is a most important consideration, as poor parents are always impatient to profit by their children's labour.

It will be objected: Firstly, that this is all very well, but special local advantages and special selection of children must be necessary to such success. Secondly, that this is all very well, but must be very expensive. Thirdly, that this is all very well, but we have no proof of the results, sir, no proof.

On the first head of local advantages and special selection. Would Limehouse Hole be picked out for the site of a Children's Paradise? Or would the legitimate and illegitimate pauper children of the long-shore population of such a riverside district, be regarded as unusually favourable specimens to work with? Yet these schools are at Lime-house, and are the Pauper Schools of the Stepney Pauper Union.

On the second head of expense. Would sixpence a week be considered a very large cost for the education of each pupil, including all salaries of teachers and rations of teachers? But supposing the cost were not sixpence a week, not fivepence? It is FOURPENCE-HALFPENNY.

On the third head of no proof, sir, no proof. Is there any proof in the facts that Pupil Teachers more in number, and more highly qualified, have been produced here under the Short-Time system than under the Long-Time system? That the Short-Timers, in a writing competition, beat the Long-Timers of a first-class National School? That the sailor-boys are in such demand for merchant ships, that whereas, before they were trained, 10*l.* premium used to be given with each boy—too often to some greedy brute of a drunken skipper, who disappeared before the term of apprenticeship was out, if the ill-used boy didn't—captains of the best character now take these boys more than willingly, with no premium at all? That they are also much esteemed in the Royal Navy, which they prefer, "because everything is so neat and clean and orderly"? Or, is there any proof in Naval captains writing, "Your little fellows are all that I can desire"? Or, is there any proof in such testimony as this: "The owner of a vessel called at the school, and said that as his ship was going down Channel on her last voyage, with one of the boys from the school on board, the pilot said, 'It would be as well if the royal were lowered; I wish it were down'. Without waiting for any orders, and unobserved by the pilot, the lad, whom they had taken on board from the school, instantly mounted the mast and lowered the royal, and at the next glance of the pilot to the masthead, he perceived that the sail had been let down. He exclaimed, 'Who's done that job?' The owner, who was on board, said, 'That was the little fellow whom I put on board two days ago'. The pilot immediately said, 'Why, where could he have been brought up?' That boy had never seen the sea or been on a real ship before?" Or, is there any proof in these boys being in greater demand for Regimental Bands than the Union can meet? Or, in ninety-eight of them having gone into Regimental Bands in three years? Or, in twelve of them being in the band of one regiment? Or, in the colonel of that regiment writing, "We want six more boys; they are excellent lads"? Or, in one of the boys having risen to be band-corporal in the same regiment? Or, in employers of all kinds chorusing, "Give us drilled boys, for they are prompt, obedient, and punctual"? Other proofs I have myself beheld with these Uncommercial eyes, though I do not regard myself as having a right to relate in what social positions they have seen respected men and women who were once pauper children of the Stepney Union.

Into what admirable soldiers others of these boys have the capabilities for being turned, I need not point out. Many of them are always ambitious of military service; and once upon a time when an old boy came back to see the old place, a cavalry soldier all complete, *with his spurs on*, such a yearning broke out to get into cavalry regiments and wear those sublime appendages, that it was one of the greatest excitements ever known in the school. The girls make excellent domestic servants, and at certain periods come back, a score or two at a time, to see the old building, and to take tea with the old teachers, and to hear the old band, and see the old ship with her masts towering up above the neighbouring roofs and chimneys. As to the physical health of these schools, it is so exceptionally remarkable (simply because the sanitary regulations are as good as the other educational arrangements), that when Mr. TUFNELL, the Inspector, first stated it in a report, he was supposed, in spite of his high character, to have been betrayed into some extraordinary mistake or exaggeration. In the moral health of these schools—where corporal punishment is unknown—Truthfulness stands high. When the ship was first erected, the boys were forbidden to go aloft, until the nets, which are now always there, were stretched as a precaution against accidents. Certain boys, in their eagerness, disobeyed the injunction, got out of window in the early daylight, and climbed to the mast-head. One boy unfortunately fell, and was killed. There was no clue to the others; but all the boys were assembled, and the chairman of the Board addressed them. "I promise nothing; you see what a dreadful thing has happened; you know what a grave offence it is that has led to such a consequence; I cannot say what will be done with the offenders; but, boys, you have been trained here, above all things, to respect the truth. I want the truth. Who are the delinquents?" Instantly, the whole number of boys concerned, separated from the rest, and stood out.

Now, the head and heart of that gentleman (it is needless to say, a good head and a good heart) have been deeply interested in these schools for many years, and are so still; and the establishment is very fortunate in a most admirable master, and moreover the schools of the Stepney Union cannot have got to be what they are, without the Stepney Board of Guardians having been earnest and humane men, strongly imbued with a sense of their responsibility. But what one set of men can do in this wise, another set of men can do; and this is a noble example to all other Bodies and Unions, and a noble example to the State. Followed, and enlarged upon by its enforcement on bad parents, it would clear London streets of the most terrible objects they smite the sight with—myriads of little children who awfully reverse our Saviour's words, and are not of the Kingdom of Heaven, but of the Kingdom of Hell.

Clear the public streets of such shame, and the public conscience of such reproach? Ah! Almost prophetic, surely, the child's jingle:

> When will that be,
> Say the bells of Step-ney.

XXX

THE RUFFIAN

I ENTERTAIN so strong an objection to the euphonious softening of Ruffian into Rough, which has lately become popular, that I restore the right word to the heading of this paper; the rather, as my object is to dwell upon the fact that the Ruffian is tolerated among us to an extent that goes beyond all unruffianly endurance. I take the liberty to believe that if the Ruffian besets my life, a professional Ruffian at large in the open streets of a great city, notoriously having no other calling than that of Ruffian, and of disquieting and despoiling me as

I go peacefully about my lawful business, interfering with no one, then the Government under which I have the great constitutional privilege, supreme honour and happiness, and all the rest of it, to exist, breaks down in the discharge of any Government's most simple elementary duty.

What did I read in the London daily papers, in the early days of this last September? That the Police had "AT LENGTH SUCCEEDED IN CAPTURING TWO OF THE NOTORIOUS GANG THAT HAVE SO LONG INFESTED THE WATERLOO ROAD". Is it possible? What a wonderful Police! Here is a straight, broad, public thoroughfare of immense resort; half a mile long; gas-lighted by night; with a great gas-lighted railway station in it, extra the street lamps; full of shops; traversed by two popular cross thoroughfares of considerable traffic; itself the main road to the South of London; and the admirable Police have, after long infestment of this dark and lonely spot by a gang of Ruffians, actually got hold of two of them. Why, can it be doubted that any man of fair London knowledge and common resolution, armed with the powers of the Law, could have captured the whole confederacy in a week?

It is to the saving up of the Ruffian class by the Magistracy and Police—to the conventional preserving of them, as if they were Partridges—that their number and audacity must be in great part referred. Why is a notorious Thief and Ruffian ever left at large? He never turns his liberty to any account but violence and plunder, he never did a day's work out of gaol, he never will do a day's work out of gaol. As a proved notorious Thief he is always consignable to prison for three months. When he comes out, he is surely as notorious a Thief as he was when he went in. Then send him back again. "Just Heaven!" cries the Society for the protection of re-monstrant Ruffians. "This is equivalent to a sentence of perpetual imprisonment!" Precisely for that reason it has my advocacy. I demand to have the Ruffian kept out of my way, and out of the way of all decent people. I demand to have the Ruffian employed, per-force, in hewing wood and drawing water somewhere for the general service, instead of hewing at her Majesty's subjects and drawing their watches out of their pockets. If this be termed an unreasonable demand, then the tax-gatherer's demand on me must be far more unreasonable, and cannot be otherwise than extortionate and unjust.

It will be seen that I treat of the Thief and Ruffian as one. I do so, because I know the two characters to be one, in the vast majority of cases, just as well as the Police know it. (As to the Magistracy, with a few exceptions, they know nothing about it but what the Police choose to tell them.) There are disorderly classes of men who are not thieves; as railway-navigators, brickmakers, wood-sawyers, coster-mongers. These classes are often disorderly and troublesome; but it is mostly among themselves, and at any rate they have their indus-trious avocations, they work early and late, and work hard. The generic Ruffian—honourable member for what is tenderly called the

Rough Element—is either a Thief, or the companion of Thieves. When he infamously molests women coming out of chapel on Sunday evenings (for which I would have his back scarified often and deep) it is not only for the gratification of his pleasant instincts, but that there may be a confusion raised by which either he or his friends may profit, in the commission of highway robberies or in picking pockets. When he gets a police-constable down and kicks him helpless for life, it is because that constable once did his duty in bringing him to justice. When he rushes into the bar of a public-house and scoops an eye out of one of the company there, or bites his ear off, it is because the man he maims gave evidence against him. When he and a line of comrades extending across the footway—say of that solitary mountain-spur of the Abruzzi, the Waterloo Road—advance towards me "skylarking" among themselves, my purse or shirt-pin is in predestined peril from his playfulness. Always a Ruffian, always a Thief. Always a Thief, always a Ruffian.

Now, when I, who am not paid to know these things, know them daily on the evidence of my senses and experience; when I know that the Ruffian never jostles a lady in the street, or knocks a hat off, but in order that the Thief may profit, is it surprising that I should require from those who *are* paid to know these things, prevention of them?

Look at this group at a street corner. Number one is a shirking fellow of five-and-twenty, in an ill-favoured and ill-savoured suit, his trousers of corduroy, his coat of some indiscernible groundwork for the deposition of grease, his neckerchief like an eel, his complexion like dirty dough, his mangy fur cap pulled low upon his beetle brows to hide the prison cut of his hair. His hands are in his pockets. He puts them there when they are idle, as naturally as in other people's pockets when they are busy, for he knows that they are not roughened by work, and that they tell a tale. Hence, whenever he takes one out to draw a sleeve across his nose—which is often, for he has weak eyes and a constitutional cold in his head—he restores it to its pocket immediately afterwards. Number two is a burly brute of five-and-thirty, in a tall stiff hat; is a composite as to his clothes of betting-man and fighting-man; is whiskered; has a staring pin in his breast, along with his right hand; has insolent and cruel eyes; large shoulders; strong legs, booted and tipped for kicking. Number three is forty years of age; is short, thick-set, strong, and bow-legged; wears knee cords and white stockings, a very long-sleeved waistcoat, a very large neckerchief doubled or trebled round his throat, and a crumpled white hat crowns his ghastly parchment face. This fellow looks like an executed postboy of other days, cut down from the gallows too soon, and restored and preserved by express diabolical agency. Numbers five, six, and seven, are hulking, idle, slouching young men, patched and shabby, too short in the sleeves and too tight in the legs, slimily clothed, foul-spoken, repulsive wretches inside and out. In all the party there obtains a certain twitching character of mouth and furtiveness of eye, that hint how the coward is lurking under the bully. The hint is quite correct, for they are a slinking sneaking set, far more prone to lie down on their backs and kick out, when in difficulty, than to make a stand for it. (This may account for the street mud on the backs of Numbers five, six, and seven, being much fresher than the stale splashes on their legs.)

These engaging gentry a Police-constable stands contemplating. His Station, with a Reserve of assistance, is very near at hand. They cannot pretend to any trade, not even to be porters or messengers. It would be idle if they did, for he knows them, and they know that he knows them, to be nothing but professed Thieves and Ruffians. He knows where they resort, knows by what slang names they call one another, knows how often they have been in prison, and how long, and for what. All this is known at his Station, too, and is (or ought to be) known at Scotland Yard, too. But does he know, or does his Station know, or does Scotland Yard know, or does anybody know, why these fellows should be here at liberty, when, as reputed Thieves to whom a whole Division of Police could swear, they might all be under lock and key at hard labour? Not he; truly he would be a wise man if he did! He only knows that these are members of the "notorious gang", which, according to the newspaper Police-office reports of this last past September, "have so long infested" the awful solitudes of the Waterloo Road, and out of which almost impregnable fastnesses the Police have at length dragged Two, to the unspeakable admiration of all good civilians.

The consequences of this contemplative habit on the part of the Executive—a habit to be looked for in a hermit, but not in a Police System—are familiar to us all. The Ruffian becomes one of the established orders of the body politic. Under the playful name of Rough (as if he were merely a practical joker) his movements and successes are recorded on public occasions. Whether he mustered in large numbers, or small; whether he was in good spirits, or depressed; whether he turned his generous exertions to very prosperous account, or Fortune was against him; whether he was in a sanguinary mood, or robbed with amiable horse-play and a gracious consideration for life and limb; all this is chronicled as if he were an Institution. Is there any city in Europe, out of England, in which these terms are held with the pests of Society? Or in which, at this day, such violent robberies from the person are constantly committed as in London?

The Preparatory Schools of Ruffianism are similarly borne with. The young Ruffians of London—not Thieves yet, but training for scholarships and fellowships in the Criminal Court Universities— molest quiet people and their property, to an extent that is hardly credible. The throwing of stones in the streets has become a dangerous and destructive offence, which surely could have got to no greater height though we had had no Police but our own riding-whips and walking-sticks—the Police to which I myself appeal on these occasions. The throwing of stones at the windows of railway carriages in motion—an act of wanton wickedness with the very Arch-

Fiend's hand in it—had become a crying evil, when the railway companies forced it on Police notice. Constabular contemplation had until then been the order of the day.

Within these twelve months, there arose among the young gentlemen of London aspiring to Ruffianism, and cultivating that much-encouraged social art, a facetious cry of "I'll have this!" accompanied with a clutch at some article of a passing lady's dress. I have known a lady's veil to be thus humorously torn from her face and carried off in the open streets at noon; and I have had the honour of myself giving chase, on Westminster Bridge, to another young Ruffian, who, in full daylight early on a summer evening, had nearly thrown a modest young woman into a swoon of indignation and confusion, by his shameful manner of attacking her with this cry as she harmlessly passed along before me. Mr. CARLYLE, some time since, awakened a little pleasantry by writing of his own experience of the Ruffian of the streets. I have seen the Ruffian act in exact accordance with Mr. Carlyle's description, innumerable times, and I never saw him checked.

The blaring use of the very worst language possible, in our public thoroughfares—especially in those set apart for recreation—is another disgrace to us, and another result of constabular contemplation, the like of which I have never heard in any other country to which my uncommercial travels have extended. Years ago, when I had a near interest in certain children who were sent with their nurses, for air and exercise, into the Regent's Park, I found this evil to be so abhorrent and horrible there, that I called public attention to it, and also to its contemplative reception by the Police. Looking afterwards into the newest Police Act, and finding that the offence was punishable under it, I resolved, when striking occasion should arise, to try my hand as prosecutor. The occasion arose soon enough, and I ran the following gauntlet.

The utterer of the base coin in question was a girl of seventeen or eighteen, who, with a suitable attendance of blackguards, youths, and boys, was flaunting along the streets, returning from an Irish funeral, in a Progress interspersed with singing and dancing. She had turned round to me and expressed herself in the most audible manner, to the great delight of that select circle. I attended the party, on the opposite side of the way, for a mile further, and then encountered a Police-constable. The party had made themselves merry at my expense until now, but seeing me speak to the constable, its male members instantly took to their heels, leaving the girl alone. I asked the constable did he know my name? Yes, he did. "Take that girl into custody, on my charge, for using bad language in the streets." He had never heard of such a charge. I had. Would he take my word that he should get into no trouble? Yes, sir, he would do that. So he took the girl, and I went home for my Police Act.

With this potent instrument in my pocket, I literally as well as figuratively "returned to the charge", and presented myself at the Police Station of the district. There, I found on duty a very intelligent Inspector (they are all intelligent men), who, likewise, had never heard of such a charge. I showed him my clause, and we went over it together twice or thrice. It was plain, and I engaged to wait upon the suburban Magistrate to-morrow morning at ten o'clock.

In the morning, I put my Police Act in my pocket again, and waited on the suburban Magistrate. I was not quite so courteously received by him as I should have been by The Lord Chancellor or The Lord Chief Justice, but that was a question of good breeding on the suburban Magistrate's part, and I had my clause ready with its leaf turned down. Which was enough for *me*.

Conference took place between the Magistrate and clerk respecting the charge. During conference I was evidently regarded as a much more objectionable person than the prisoner;—one giving trouble by coming there voluntarily, which the prisoner could not be accused of doing. The prisoner had been got up, since I last had the pleasure of seeing her, with a great effect of white apron and straw bonnet. She reminded me of an elder sister of Red Riding Hood, and I seemed to remind the sympathising Chimney Sweep by whom she was attended, of the Wolf.

The Magistrate was doubtful, Mr. Uncommercial Traveller, whether this charge could be entertained. It was not known. Mr. Uncommercial Traveller replied that he wished it were better known, and that, if he could afford the leisure, he would use his endeavours to make it so. There was no question about it, however, he contended. Here was the clause.

The clause was handed in, and more conference resulted. After which I was asked the extraordinary question: "Mr. Uncommercial, do you really wish this girl to be sent to prison?" To which I grimly answered, staring: "If I didn't, why should I take the trouble to come here?" Finally, I was sworn, and gave my agreeable evidence in detail, and White Riding Hood was fined ten shillings, under the clause, or sent to prison for so many days. "Why, Lord bless you, sir," said the Police-officer, who showed me out, with a great enjoyment of the jest of her having been got up so effectively, and caused so much hesitation: "if she goes to prison, that will be nothing new to *her*. She comes from Charles Street, Drury Lane!"

The Police, all things considered, are an excellent force, and I have borne my small testimony to their merits. Constabular contemplation is the result of a bad system; a system which is administered, not invented, by the man in constable's uniform, employed at twenty shillings a week. He has his orders, and would be marked for discouragement if he overstepped them. That the system is bad, there needs no lengthened argument to prove, because the fact is self-evident. If it were anything else, the results that have attended it could not possibly have come to pass. Who will say that under a good system, our streets could have got into their present state?

The objection to the whole Police system, as concerning the Ruffian, may be stated, and its failure exemplified, as follows. It is well known that on all great occasions, when they come together in numbers, the mass of the English people are their own trustworthy Police. It is well known that wheresoever there is collected together any fair general representation of the people, a respect for law and order, and a determination to discountenance lawlessness and disorder, may be relied upon. As to one another, the people are a very good Police, and yet are quite willing in their good-nature that the stipendiary Police should have the credit of the people's moderation. But we are all of us powerless against the Ruffian, because we submit to the law, and it is his only trade, by superior force and by violence, to defy it. Moreover, we are constantly admonished from high places (like so many Sunday-school children out for a holiday of buns and milk-and-water) that we are not to take the law into our own hands, but are to hand our defence over to it. It is clear that the common enemy to be punished and exterminated first of all is the Ruffian. It is clear that he is, of all others, *the* offender for whose repressal we maintain a costly system of Police. Him, therefore, we expressly present to the Police to deal with, conscious that, on the whole, we can, and do, deal reasonably well with one another. Him the Police deal with so inefficiently and absurdly that he flourishes, and multiplies, and, with all his evil deeds upon his head as notoriously as his hat is, pervades the streets with no more let or hindrance than ourselves.

XXXI

ABOARD SHIP

MY journeys as Uncommercial Traveller for the firm of Human-Interest Brothers have not slackened since I last reported of them, but have kept me continually on the move. I remain in the same idle employment. I never solicit an order, I never get any commission, I am the rolling stone that gathers no moss,—unless any should by chance be found among these samples.

Some half a year ago, I found myself in my idlest, dreamiest, and least accountable condition altogether, on board ship, in the harbour of the city of New York, in the United States of America. Of all the good ships afloat, mine was the good steamship "RUSSIA", CAPT. COOK, Cunard Line, bound for Liverpool. What more could I wish for?

I had nothing to wish for but a prosperous passage. My salad-days, when I was green of visage and sea-sick, being gone with better things (and no worse), no coming event cast its shadow before.

I might but a few moments previously have imitated Sterne, and said, "'And yet, methinks, Eugenius,'—laying my forefinger wistfully on his coat-sleeve, thus,—'and yet, methinks, Eugenius, 'tis but sorry work to part with thee, for what fresh fields, . . . my dear Eugenius, . . . can be fresher than thou art, and in what pastures new shall I find Eliza, or call her, Eugenius, if thou wilt, Annie?'"—I say I might have done this; but Eugenius was gone, and I hadn't done it.

I was resting on a skylight on the hurricane-deck, watching the working of the ship very slowing about, that she might head for England. It was high-noon on a most brilliant day in April, and the beautiful bay was glorious and glowing. Full many a time, on shore there, had I seen the snow come down, down, down (itself like down), until it lay deep in all the ways of men, and particularly, as it seemed, in my way, for I had not gone dry-shod many hours for months. Within two or three days last past had I watched the feathery fall setting in with the ardour of a new idea, instead of dragging at the skirts of a worn-out winter, and permitting glimpses of a fresh young spring. But a bright sun and a clear sky had melted the snow in the great crucible of nature; and it had been poured out again that morning over sea and land, transformed into myriads of gold and silver sparkles.

The ship was fragrant with flowers. Something of the old Mexican passion for flowers may have gradually passed into North America, where flowers are luxuriously grown, and tastefully combined in the richest profusion; but, be that as it may, such gorgeous farewells in flowers had come on board, that the small officer's cabin on deck, which I tenanted, bloomed over into the adjacent scuppers, and banks of other flowers that it couldn't hold made a garden of the unoccupied tables in the passengers' saloon. These delicious scents of the shore, mingling with the fresh airs of the sea, made the atmosphere a dreamy, an enchanting one. And so, with the watch aloft setting all the sails, and with the screw below revolving at a mighty rate, and occasionally giving the ship an angry shake for resisting, I fell into my idlest ways, and lost myself.

As, for instance, whether it was I lying there, or some other entity even more mysterious, was a matter I was far too lazy to look into. What did it signify to me if it were I? or to the more mysterious entity, if it were he? Equally as to the remembrances that drowsily floated by me, or by him, why ask when or where the things happened? Was it not enough that they befell at some time, somewhere?

There was that assisting at the church service on board another steamship, one Sunday, in a stiff breeze. Perhaps on the passage out. No matter. Pleasant to hear the ship's bells go as like church-bells as they could; pleasant to see the watch off duty mustered and come in: best hats, best Guernseys, washed hands and faces, smoothed heads. But then arose a set of circumstances so rampantly comical, that no check which the gravest intentions could put upon them would hold them in hand. Thus the scene. Some seventy passengers assembled at the saloon tables. Prayer-books on tables. Ship rolling heavily. Pause. No minister. Rumour has related that a modest young clergyman on board has responded to the captain's request that he will officiate. Pause again, and very heavy rolling.

Closed double doors suddenly burst open, and two strong stewards skate in, supporting minister between them. General appearance as of somebody picked up drunk and incapable, and under conveyance to station-house. Stoppage, pause, and particularly heavy rolling. Stewards watch their opportunity, and balance themselves, but cannot balance minister; who, struggling with a drooping head and a backward tendency, seems determined to return below, while they are as determined that he shall be got to the reading-desk in mid-saloon. Desk portable, sliding away down a long table, and aiming itself at the breasts of various members of the congregation. Here the double doors, which have been carefully closed by other stewards, fly open again, and worldly passenger tumbles in, seemingly with pale-ale designs : who, seeking friend, says "Joe!" Perceiving incongruity, says, "Hullo! Beg yer pardon!" and tumbles out again. All this time the congregation have been breaking up into sects,—as the manner of congregations often is,—each sect sliding away by itself, and all pounding the weakest sect which slid first into the corner. Utmost point of dissent soon attained in every corner, and violent rolling. Stewards at length make a dash; conduct minister to the mast in the centre of the saloon, which he embraces with both arms; skate out; and leave him in that condition to arrange affairs with flock.

There was another Sunday, when an officer of the ship read the service. It was quiet and impressive, until we fell upon the dangerous and perfectly unnecessary experiment of striking up a hymn. After it was given out, we all rose, but everybody left it to somebody else to begin. Silence resulting, the officer (no singer himself) rather reproachfully gave us the first line again, upon which a rosy pippin of an old gentleman, remarkable throughout the passage for his cheerful politeness, gave a little stamp with his boot (as if he were leading off a country dance), and blithely warbled us into a show of joining. At the end of the first verse we became, through these tactics, so much refreshed and encouraged, that none of us, howsoever unmelodious, would submit to be left out of the second verse; while as to the third we lifted up our voices in a sacred howl that left it doubtful whether we were the more boastful of the sentiments we united in professing, or of professing them with a most discordant defiance of time and tune.

"Lord bless us!" thought I, when the fresh remembrance of these things made me laugh heartily alone in the dead water-gurgling waste of the night, what time I was wedged into my berth by a wooden bar, or I must have rolled out of it, "what errand was I then upon, and to what Abyssinian point had public events then marched? No matter as to me. And as to them, if the wonderful popular rage for a plaything (utterly confounding in its inscrutable unreason) had not then lighted on a poor young savage boy, and a poor old screw of a horse, and hauled the first off by the hair of his princely head to 'inspect' British volunteers, and hauled the second off by the hair of his equine tail to the Crystal Palace, why so much the better for all of us outside Bedlam!"

So, sticking to the ship, I was at the trouble of asking myself would I like to show the grog distribution in "the fiddle" at noon to the Grand United Amalgamated Total Abstinence Society? Yes, I think I should. I think it would do them good to smell the rum, under the circumstances. Over the grog, mixed in a bucket, presides the boatswain's mate, small tin can in hand. Enter the crew, the guilty consumers, the grown-up brood of Giant Despair, in contradistinction to the band of youthful angel Hope. Some in boots, some in leggings, some in tarpaulin overalls, some in frocks, some in pea-coats, a very few in jackets, most with sou'wester hats, all with something rough and rugged round the throat; all, dripping salt water where they stand; all pelted by weather, besmeared with grease, and blackened by the sooty rigging.

Each man's knife in its sheath in his girdle, loosened for dinner. As the first man, with a knowingly kindled eye, watches the filling of the poisoned chalice (truly but a very small tin mug, to be prosaic), and, tossing back his head, tosses the contents into himself, and passes the empty chalice and passes on, so the second man with an anticipatory wipe of his mouth on sleeve or handkerchief, bides his turn, and drinks and hands and passes on, in whom, and in each as his turn approaches, beams a knowingly kindled eye, a brighter temper, and a suddenly awakened tendency to be jocose with some shipmate. Nor do I even observe that the man in charge of the ship's lamps, who in right of his office has a double allowance of poisoned chalices, seems thereby vastly degraded, even though he empties the chalices into himself, one after the other, much as if he were delivering their contents at some absorbent establishment in which he had no personal interest. But vastly comforted, I note them all to be, on deck presently, even to the circulation of redder blood in their cold blue knuckles; and when I look up at them lying out on the yards, and holding on for life among the beating sails, I cannot for *my* life see the justice of visiting on them—or on me—the drunken crimes of any number of criminals arraigned at the heaviest of assizes.

Abetting myself in my idle humour, I closed my eyes, and recalled life on board of one of those mail-packets, as I lay, part of that day, in the Bay of New York, O! The regular life began—mine always did, for I never got to sleep afterwards—with the rigging of the pump while it was yet dark, and washing down of the decks. Any enormous giant at a prodigious hydropathic establishment, conscientiously undergoing the water-cure in all its departments, and extremely particular about cleaning his teeth, would make those noises.

Swash, splash, scrub, rub, toothbrush, bubble, swash, splash, bubble, toothbrush, splash, splash, bubble, rub. Then the day would break, and, descending from my berth by a graceful ladder composed of half-opened drawers beneath it, I would reopen my outer dead-light and my inner sliding window (closed by a watchman during the water-cure), and would look out at the long-rolling, lead-coloured, white-topped waves over which the dawn, on a cold winter morning, cast a level, lonely glance, and through which the ship fought her melancholy way at a terrific rate. And now, lying down again, awaiting the season for broiled ham and tea, I would be compelled to listen to the voice of conscience,—the screw.

It might be, in some cases, no more than the voice of stomach; but I called it in my fancy by the higher name. Because it seemed to me that we were all of us, all day long, endeavouring to stifle the voice. Because it was under everybody's pillow, everybody's plate, everybody's camp-stool, everybody's book, everybody's occupation. Because we pretended not to hear it, especially at meal-times, evening whist, and morning conversation on deck; but it was always among us in an under monotone, not to be drowned in pea-soup, not to be shuffled with cards, not to be diverted by books, not to be knitted into any pattern, not to be walked away from. It was smoked in the weediest cigar, and drunk in the strongest cocktail; it was conveyed on deck at noon with limp ladies, who lay there in their wrappers until the stars shone; it waited at table with the stewards; nobody could put it out with the lights. It was considered (as on shore) ill-bred to acknowledge the voice of conscience. It was not polite to mention it. One squally day an amiable gentleman in love gave much offence to a surrounding circle, including the object of his attachment, by saying of it, after it had goaded him over two easy-chairs and a skylight, " Screw !"

Sometimes it would appear subdued. In fleeting moments, when bubbles of champagne pervaded the nose, or when there was " hot pot " in the bill of fare, or when an old dish we had had regularly every day was described in that official document by a new name,—under such excitements, one would almost believe it hushed. The ceremony of washing plates on deck, performed after every meal by a circle as of ringers of crockery triple-bob majors for a prize, would keep it down. Hauling the reel, taking the sun at noon, posting the twenty-four hours' run, altering the ship's time by the meridian, casting the waste food overboard, and attracting the eager gulls that followed in our wake,—these events would suppress it for awhile. But the instant any break or pause took place in any such diversion, the voice would be at it again, importuning us to the last extent. A newly married young pair, who walked the deck affectionately some twenty miles per day, would, in the full flush of their exercise, suddenly become stricken by it, and stand trembling, but otherwise immovable, under its reproaches.

When this terrible monitor was most severe with us was when

the time approached for our retiring to our dens for the night; when the lighted candles in the saloon grew fewer and fewer; when the deserted glasses with spoons in them grew more and more numerous; when waifs of toasted cheese and strays of sardines fried in batter slid languidly to and fro in the table-racks; when the man who always read had shut up his book, and blown out his candle; when the man who always talked had ceased from troubling; when the man who was always medically reported as going to have delirium tremens had put it off till to-morrow; when the man who every night devoted himself to a midnight smoke on deck two hours in length, and who every night was in bed within ten minutes afterwards, was buttoning himself up in his third coat for his hardy vigil: for then, as we fell off one by one, and, entering our several hutches, came into a peculiar atmosphere of bilge-water and Windsor soap, the voice would shake us to the centre. Woe to us when we sat down on our sofa, watching the swinging candle for ever trying and re-trying to stand upon his head! or our coat upon its peg, imitating us as we appeared in our gymnastic days by sustaining itself horizontally from the wall, in emulation of the lighter and more facile towels! Then would the voice especially claim us for its prey, and rend us all to pieces.

Lights out, we in our berths, and the wind rising, the voice grows angrier and deeper. Under the mattress and under the pillow, under the sofa and under the washing-stand, under the ship and under the sea, seeming to arise from the foundations under the earth with every scoop of the great Atlantic (and oh! why scoop so?), always the voice. Vain to deny its existence in the night season; impossible to be hard of hearing; screw, screw, screw! Sometimes it lifts out of the water, and revolves with a whirr, like a ferocious firework,—except that it never expends itself, but is always ready to go off again; sometimes it seems to be aguish, and shivers; sometimes it seems to be terrified by its last plunge, and has a fit which causes it to struggle, quiver, and for an instant stop. And now the ship sets in rolling, as only ships so fiercely screwed through time and space, day and night, fair weather and foul, *can* roll.

Did she ever take a roll before like that last? Did she ever take a roll before like this worse one that is coming now? Here is the partition at my ear down in the deep on the lee side. Are we ever coming up again together? I think not; the partition and I are so long about it that I really do believe we have overdone it this time. Heavens, what a scoop! What a deep scoop, what a hollow scoop, what a long scoop! Will it ever end, and can we bear the heavy mass of water we have taken on board, and which has let loose all the table furniture in the officers' mess, and has beaten open the door of the little passage between the purser and me, and is swashing about, even there and even here? The purser snores reassuringly, and the ship's bells striking, I hear the cheerful "All's well!" of the watch musically given back the length of the deck, as the lately diving partition, now high in air, tries (unsoftened by what we have gone through together) to force me out of bed and berth.

"All's well!" Comforting to know, though surely all might be better. Put aside the rolling and the rush of water, and think of darting through such darkness with such velocity. Think of any other similar object coming in the opposite direction!

Whether there may be an attraction in two such moving bodies out at sea, which may help accident to bring them into collision? Thoughts, too, arise (the voice never silent all the while, but marvellously suggestive) of the gulf below; of the strange unfruitful mountain ranges and deep valleys over which we are passing; of monstrous fish midway; of the ship's suddenly altering her course on her own account, and with a wild plunge settling down, and making *that* voyage with a crew of dead discoverers. Now, too, one recalls an almost universal tendency on the part of passengers to stumble, at some time or other in the day, on the topic of a certain large steamer making this same run, which was lost at sea, and never heard of more. Everybody has seemed under a spell, compelling approach to the threshold of the grim subject, stoppage, discomfiture, and pretence of never having been near it. The boatswain's whistle sounds! A change in the wind, hoarse orders issuing, and the watch very busy. Sails come crashing home overhead, ropes (that seem all knot) ditto; every man engaged appears to have twenty feet, with twenty times the average amount of stamping power in each. Gradually the noise slackens, the hoarse cries die away, the boatswain's whistle softens into the soothing and contented notes, which rather reluctantly admit that the job is done for the time, and the voice sets in again.

Thus come unintelligible dreams of up hill and down, and swinging and swaying, until consciousness revives of atmospherical Windsor soap and bilge-water, and the voice announces that the giant has come for the water-cure again.

Such were my fanciful reminiscences as I lay, part of that day, in the Bay of New York, O! Also as we passed clear of the Narrows, and got out to sea; also in many an idle hour at sea in sunny weather! At length the observations and computations showed that we should make the coast of Ireland to-night. So I stood watch on deck all night to-night, to see how we made the coast of Ireland.

Very dark, and the sea most brilliantly phosphorescent. Great way on the ship, and double look-out kept. Vigilant captain on the bridge, vigilant first officer looking over the port side, vigilant second officer standing by the quarter-master at the compass, vigilant third officer posted at the stern rail with a lantern. No passengers on the quiet decks, but expectation everywhere nevertheless. The two men at the wheel very steady, very serious, and very prompt to answer orders. An order issued sharply now and then, and echoed back; otherwise the night drags slowly, silently, and with no change.

All of a sudden, at the blank hour of two in the morning, a vague movement of relief from a long strain expresses itself in all hands;

the third officer's lantern twinkles, and he fires a rocket, and another rocket. A sullen solitary light is pointed out to me in the black sky yonder. A change is expected in the light, but none takes place. "Give them two more rockets, Mr. Vigilant." Two more, and a blue-light burnt. All eyes watch the light again. At last a little toy sky-rocket is flashed up from it; and, even as that small streak in the darkness dies away, we are telegraphed to Queenstown, Liverpool, and London, and back again under the ocean to America.

Then up come the half-dozen passengers who are going ashore at Queenstown, and up comes the mail-agent in charge of the bags, and up come the men who are to carry the bags into the mail-tender that will come off for them out of the harbour. Lamps and lanterns gleam here and there about the decks, and impeding bulks are knocked away with handspikes; and the port-side bulwark, barren but a moment ago, bursts into a crop of heads of seamen, stewards, and engineers.

The light begins to be gained upon, begins to be alongside, begins to be left astern. More rockets, and, between us and the land, steams beautifully the Inman steamship City of Paris, for New York, outward bound. We observe with complacency that the wind is dead against her (it being *with* us), and that she rolls and pitches. (The sickest passenger on board is the most delighted by this circumstance.) Time rushes by as we rush on; and now we see the light in Queenstown Harbour, and now the lights of the mail-tender coming out to us. What vagaries the mail-tender performs on the way, in every point of the compass, especially in those where she has no business, and why she performs them, Heaven only knows! At length she is seen plunging within a cable's length of our port broadside, and is being roared at through our speaking-trumpets to do this thing, and not to do that, and to stand by the other, as if she were a very demented tender indeed. Then, we slackening amidst a deafening roar of steam, this much-abused tender is made fast to us by hawsers, and the men in readiness carry the bags aboard, and return for more, bending under their burdens, and looking just like the pasteboard figures of the miller and his men in the theatre of our boyhood, and comporting themselves almost as unsteadily. All the while the unfortunate tender plunges high and low, and is roared at. Then the Queenstown passengers are put on board of her, with infinite plunging and roaring, and the tender gets heaved up on the sea to that surprising extent that she looks within an ace of washing aboard of us, high and dry. Roared at with contumely to the last, this wretched tender is at length let go, with a final plunge of great ignominy, and falls spinning into our wake.

The voice of conscience resumed its dominion as the day climbed up the sky, and kept by all of us passengers into port; kept by us as we passed other lighthouses, and dangerous islands off the coast, where some of the officers, with whom I stood my watch, had gone ashore in sailing-ships in fogs (and of which by that token they seemed to have quite an affectionate remembrance), and past the Welsh coast, and past the Cheshire coast, and past everything and everywhere lying between our ship and her own special dock in the Mersey. Off which at last, at nine of the clock, on a fair evening early in May, we stopped, and the voice ceased. A very curious sensation, not unlike having my own ears stopped, ensued upon that silence; and it was with a no less curious sensation that I went over the side of the good Cunard ship "Russia" (whom prosperity attend through all her voyages!) and surveyed the outer hull of the gracious monster that the voice had inhabited. So, perhaps, shall we all, in the spirit, one day survey the frame that held the busier voice from which my vagrant fancy derived this similitude.

XXXII

A SMALL STAR IN THE EAST

I HAD been looking, yesternight, through the famous "Dance of Death", and to-day the grim old woodcuts arose in my mind with the new significance of a ghastly monotony not to be found in the original. The weird skeleton rattled along the streets before me, and struck fiercely; but it was never at the pains of assuming a disguise. It played on no dulcimer here, was crowned with no flowers, waved no plume, minced in no flowing robe or train, lifted no wine-cup, sat at no feast, cast no dice, counted no gold. It was simply a bare, gaunt, famished skeleton, slaying its way along.

The borders of Ratcliff and Stepney, eastward of London, and giving on the impure river, were the scene of this uncompromising dance of death, upon a drizzling November day. A squalid maze of streets, courts, and alleys of miserable houses let out in single rooms. A wilderness of dirt, rags, and hunger. A mud-desert, chiefly inhabited by a tribe from whom employment has departed, or to whom it comes but fitfully and rarely. They are not skilled mechanics in any wise. They are but labourers,—dock-labourers, water-side labourers, coal-porters, ballast-heavers, such-like hewers of wood and drawers of water. But they have come into existence, and they propagate their wretched race.

One grisly joke alone, methought, the skeleton seemed to play off here. It had stuck election-bills on the walls, which the wind and rain had deteriorated into suitable rags. It had even summed up the state of the poll, in chalk, on the shutters of one ruined house. It adjured the free and independent starvers to vote for Thisman and vote for Thatman; not to plump, as they valued the state of parties and the national prosperity (both of great importance to them, I think); but, by returning Thisman and Thatman, each naught without the other, to compound a glorious and immortal whole. Surely the skeleton is nowhere more cruelly ironical in the original monkish idea!

Pondering in my mind the far-seeing schemes of Thisman and Thatman, and of the public blessing called Party, for staying the degeneracy, physical and moral, of many thousands (who shall say how many?) of the English race; for devising employment useful to the community for those who want but to work and live; for equalising rates, cultivating waste lands, facilitating emigration, and, above all things, saving and utilising the oncoming generations, and thereby changing ever-growing national weakness into strength: pondering in my mind, I say, these hopeful exertions, I turned down a narrow street to look into a house or two.

It was a dark street with a dead wall on one side. Nearly all the outer doors of the houses stood open. I took the first entry, and knocked at a parlour-door. Might I come in? I might, if I plased, sur.

The woman of the room (Irish) had picked up some long strips of wood, about some wharf or barge; and they had just now been thrust into the otherwise empty grate to make two iron pots boil. There was some fish in one, and there were some potatoes in the other. The flare of the burning wood enabled me to see a table, and a broken chair or so, and some old cheap crockery ornaments about the chimney-piece. It was not until I had spoken with the woman a few minutes, that I saw a horrible brown heap on the floor in a corner, which, but for previous experience in this dismal wise, I might not have suspected to be "the bed". There was something thrown upon it; and I asked what that was.

"'Tis the poor craythur that stays here, sur; and 'tis very bad she is, and 'tis very bad she's been this long time, and 'tis better she'll never be, and 'tis slape she does all day, and 'tis wake she does all night, and 'tis the lead, sur."

"The what?"

"The lead, sur. Sure 'tis the lead-mills, where the women gets took on at eighteen-pence a day, sur, when they makes applicaytion early enough, and is lucky and wanted; and 'tis lead-pisoned she is, sur, and some of them gets lead-pisoned soon, and some of them gets lead-pisoned later, and some, but not many, niver; and 'tis all according to the constitooshun, sur, and some constitooshuns is strong, and some is weak; and her constitooshun is lead-pisoned, bad as can be, sur; and her brain is coming out at her ear, and it hurts her dreadful; and that's what it is, and niver no more, and niver no less, sur."

The sick young woman moaning here, the speaker bent over her, took a bandage from her head, and threw open a back door to let in the daylight upon it, from the smallest and most miserable back-yard I ever saw.

"That's what cooms from her, sur, being lead-pisoned; and it cooms from her night and day, the poor, sick craythur; and the pain of it is dreadful; and God he knows that my husband has walked the sthreets these four days, being a labourer, and is walking

them now, and is ready to work, and no work for him, and no fire
and no food but the bit in the pot, and no more than ten shillings
in a fortnight; God be good to us! and it is poor we are, and dark
it is and could it is indeed."

Knowing that I could compensate myself thereafter for my self-
denial, if I saw fit, I had resolved that I would give nothing in the
course of these visits. I did this to try the people. I may state at
once that my closest observation could not detect any indication whatever of an expectation that I would give money: they were grateful
to be talked to about their miserable affairs, and sympathy was plainly
a comfort to them; but they neither asked for money in any case, nor
showed the least trace of surprise or disappointment or resentment at
my giving none.

The woman's married daughter had by this time come down from
her room on the floor above, to join in the conversation. She herself
had been to the lead-mills very early that morning to be "took on",
but had not succeeded. She had four children; and her husband,
also a water-side labourer, and then out seeking work, seemed in no
better case as to finding it than her father. She was English, and
by nature of a buxom figure and cheerful. Both in her poor dress
and in her mother's there was an effort to keep up some appearance
of neatness. She knew all about the sufferings of the unfortunate
invalid, and all about the lead-poisoning, and how the symptoms
came on, and how they grew,—having often seen them. The very
smell when you stood inside the door of the works was enough to
knock you down, she said: yet she was going back again to get
"took on". What could she do? Better be ulcerated and paralysed
for eighteen-pence a day, while it lasted, than see the children
starve.

A dark and squalid cupboard in this room, touching the back door
and all manner of offence, had been for some time the sleeping place
of the sick young woman. But the nights being now wintry, and
the blankets and coverlets "gone to the leaving shop", she lay all
night where she lay all day, and was lying then. The woman of the
room, her husband, this most miserable patient, and two others, lay
on the one brown heap together for warmth.

"God bless you, sir, and thank you!" were the parting words from
these people,—gratefully spoken too,—with which I left this place.

Some streets away, I tapped at another parlour-door on another
ground-floor. Looking in, I found a man, his wife, and four children,
sitting at a washing-stool by way of table, at their dinner of bread
and infused tea-leaves. There was a very scanty cinderous fire in
the grate by which they sat; and there was a tent bedstead in the
room with a bed upon it and a coverlet. The man did not rise
when I went in, nor during my stay, but civilly inclined his head
on my pulling off my hat, and, in answer to my inquiry whether I
might ask him a question or two, said, "Certainly". There being
a window at each end of this room, back and front, it might have

been ventilated; but it was shut up tight, to keep the cold out, and was very sickening.

The wife, an intelligent, quick woman, rose and stood at her husband's elbow; and he glanced up at her as if for help. It soon appeared that he was rather deaf. He was a slow, simple fellow of about thirty.

"What was he by trade?"

"Gentleman asks what are you by trade, John?"

"I am a boilermaker;" looking about him with an exceedingly perplexed air, as if for a boiler that had unaccountably vanished.

"He ain't a mechanic, you understand, sir," the wife put in; "he's only a labourer."

"Are you in work?"

He looked up at his wife again. "Gentleman says are you in work, John?"

"In work!" cried this forlorn boilermaker, staring aghast at his wife, and then working his vision's way very slowly round to me: "Lord, no!"

"Ah, he ain't indeed!" said the poor woman, shaking her head, as she looked at the four children in succession, and then at him.

"Work!" said the boilermaker, still seeking that evaporated boiler, first in my countenance, then in the air, and then in the features of his second son at his knee: "I wish I *was* in work! I haven't had more than a day's work to do this three weeks."

"How have you lived?"

A faint gleam of admiration lighted up the face of the would-be boilermaker, as he stretched out the short sleeve of his threadbare canvas jacket, and replied, pointing her out, "On the work of the wife".

I forget where boilermaking had gone to, or where he supposed it had gone to; but he added some resigned information on that head, coupled with an expression of his belief that it was never coming back.

The cheery helpfulness of the wife was very remarkable. She did slop-work; made pea-jackets. She produced the pea-jacket then in hand, and spread it out upon the bed,—the only piece of furniture in the room on which to spread it. She showed how much of it she made, and how much was afterwards finished off by the machine. According to her calculation at the moment, deducting what her trimming cost her, she got for making a pea-jacket tenpence-half-penny, and she could make one in something less than two days.

But, you see, it come to her through two hands, and of course it didn't come through the second hand for nothing. Why did it come through the second hand at all? Why, this way. The second hand took the risk of the given-out work, you see. If she had money enough to pay the security deposit,—call it two pound,—she could get the work from the first hand, and so the second would not have to be deducted for. But, having no money at all, the second hand come in and took its profit, and so the whole worked down to ten-pence-halfpenny. Having explained all this with great intelligence, even with some little pride, and without a whine or murmur, she folded her work again, sat down by her husband's side at the washing-stool, and resumed her dinner of dry bread. Mean as the meal was, on the bare board, with its old gallipots for cups, and what not other sordid makeshifts; shabby as the woman was in dress, and toning down towards the Bosjesman colour, with want of nutriment and washing,—there was positively a dignity in her, as the family anchor just holding the poor shipwrecked boilermaker's bark. When I left the room, the boilermaker's eyes were slowly turned towards her, as if his last hope of ever again seeing that vanished boiler lay in her direction.

These people had never applied for parish relief but once; and that was when the husband met with a disabling accident at his work.

Not many doors from here, I went into a room on the first floor. The woman apologised for its being in "an untidy mess". The day was Saturday, and she was boiling the children's clothes in a sauce-pan on the hearth. There was nothing else into which she could have put them. There was no crockery, or tinware, or tub, or bucket. There was an old gallipot or two, and there was a broken bottle or so, and there were some broken boxes for seats. The last small scraping of coals left was raked together in a corner of the floor. There were some rags in an open cupboard, also on the floor. In a corner of the room was a crazy old French bedstead, with a man lying on his back upon it in a ragged pilot jacket, and rough oil-skin fantail hat. The room was perfectly black. It was difficult to believe, at first, that it was not purposely coloured black, the walls were so begrimed.

As I stood opposite the woman boiling the children's clothes,—she had not even a piece of soap to wash them with,—and apologising for her occupation, I could take in all these things without appearing to notice them, and could even correct my inventory. I had missed, at the first glance, some half a pound of bread in the otherwise empty safe, an old red ragged crinoline hanging on the handle of the door by which I had entered, and certain fragments of rusty iron scattered on the floor, which looked like broken tools and a piece of stove-pipe. A child stood looking on. On the box nearest to the fire sat two younger children; one a delicate and pretty little creature, whom the other sometimes kissed.

This woman, like the last, was wofully shabby, and was degenerat-ing to the Bosjesman complexion. But her figure, and the ghost of a certain vivacity about her, and the spectre of a dimple in her cheek, carried my memory strangely back to the old days of the Adelphi Theatre, London, when Mrs. Fitzwilliam was the friend of Victorine.

" May I ask you what your husband is?"

" He's a coal-porter, sir,"—with a glance and a sigh towards the bed.

"Is he out of work?"

"Oh, yes, sir! and work's at all times very, very scanty with him; and now he's laid up."

"It's my legs," said the man upon the bed. "I'll unroll 'em." And immediately began.

"Have you any older children?"

"I have a daughter that does the needle-work, and I have a son that does what he can. She's at her work now, and he's trying for work."

"Do they live here?"

"They sleep here. They can't afford to pay more rent, and so they come here at night. The rent is very hard upon us. It's rose upon us too, now,—sixpence a week,—on account of these new changes in the law, about the rates. We are a week behind; the landlord's been shaking and rattling at that door frightful; he says he'll turn us out. I don't know what's to come of it."

The man upon the bed ruefully interposed, "Here's my legs. The skin's broke, besides the swelling. I have had a many kicks, working, one way and another."

He looked at his legs (which were much discoloured and misshapen) for a while, and then appearing to remember that they were not popular with his family, rolled them up again, as if they were something in the nature of maps or plans that were not wanted to be referred to, lay hopelessly down on his back once more with his fantail hat over his face, and stirred not.

"Do your eldest son and daughter sleep in that cupboard?"

"Yes," replied the woman.

"With the children?"

"Yes. We have to get together for warmth. We have little to cover us."

"Have you nothing by you to eat but the piece of bread I see there?"

"Nothing. And we had the rest of the loaf for our breakfast, with water. I don't know what's to come of it."

"Have you no prospect of improvement?"

"If my eldest son earns anything to-day, he'll bring it home. Then we shall have something to eat to-night, and may be able to do something towards the rent. If not, I don't know what's to come of it."

"This is a sad state of things."

"Yes, sir; it's a hard, hard life. Take care of the stairs as you go, sir,—they're broken,—and good-day, sir!"

These people had a mortal dread of entering the workhouse, and received no out-of-door relief.

In another room, in still another tenement, I found a very decent woman with five children,—the last a baby, and she herself a patient of the parish doctor,—to whom, her husband being in the hospital, the Union allowed for the support of herself and family, four shillings a week and five loaves. I suppose when Thisman, M.P., and That-man, M.P., and the Public-blessing Party, lay their heads together in course of time, and come to an equalization of rating, she may go down the dance of death to the tune of sixpence more.

I could enter no other houses for that one while, for I could not bear the contemplation of the children. Such heart as I had summoned to sustain me against the miseries of the adults failed me when I looked at the children. I saw how young they were, how hungry, how serious and still. I thought of them, sick and dying in those lairs. I could think of them dead without anguish; but to think of them so suffering and so dying quite unmanned me.

Down by the river's bank in Ratcliff, I was turning upward by a side-street, therefore, to regain the railway, when my eyes rested on the inscription across the road, "East London Children's Hospital". I could scarcely have seen an inscription better suited to my frame of mind; and I went across and went straight in.

I found the Children's Hospital established in an old sail-loft or storehouse, of the roughest nature, and on the simplest means. There were trap-doors in the floors, where goods had been hoisted up and down; heavy feet and heavy weights had started every knot in the well-trodden planking; inconvenient bulks and beams and awkward staircases perplexed my passage through the wards. But I found it airy, sweet, and clean. In its seven and thirty beds I saw but little beauty; for starvation in the second or third generation takes a pinched look: but I saw the sufferings both of infancy and child-hood tenderly assuaged; I heard the little patients answering to pet playful names, the light touch of a delicate lady laid bare the wasted sticks of arms for me to pity; and the claw-like little hands, as she did so, twined themselves lovingly around her wedding-ring.

One baby mite there was as pretty as any of Raphael's angels. The tiny head was bandaged for water on the brain; and it was suffering with acute bronchitis too, and made from time to time a plaintive, though not impatient or complaining, little sound. The smooth curve of the cheeks and of the chin was faultless in its condensation of infantine beauty, and the large bright eyes were most lovely. It happened as I stopped at the foot of the bed, that these eyes rested upon mine with that wistful expression of wondering thoughtfulness which we all know sometimes in very little children. They remained fixed on mine, and never turned from me while I stood there. When the utterance of that plaintive sound shook the little form, the gaze still remained unchanged. I felt as though the child implored me to tell the story of the little hospital in which it was sheltered to any gentle heart I could address. Laying my world-worn hand upon the little unmarked clasped hand at the chin, I gave it a silent promise that I would do so.

A gentleman and lady, a young husband and wife, have bought and fitted up this building for its present noble use, and have quietly settled themselves in it as its medical officers and directors. Both have had considerable practical experience of medicine and surgery; he as house-surgeon of a great London hospital; she as a very earnest student, tested by severe examination, and also as a nurse of the sick poor during the prevalence of cholera.

With every qualification to lure them away, with youth and accomplishments and tastes and habits that can have no response in any breast near them, close begirt by every repulsive circumstance inseparable from such a neighbourhood, there they dwell. They live in the hospital itself, and their rooms are on its first floor. Sitting at their dinner-table, they could hear the cry of one of the children in pain. The lady's piano, drawing-materials, books, and other such evidences of refinement are as much a part of the rough place as the iron bedsteads of the little patients. They are put to shifts for room, like passengers on board ship. The dispenser of medicines (attracted to them not by self-interest, but by their own magnetism and that of their cause) sleeps in a recess in the dining-room, and has his washing apparatus in the sideboard.

Their contented manner of making the best of the things around them, I found so pleasantly inseparable from their usefulness! Their pride in this partition that we put up ourselves, or in that partition that we took down, or in that other partition that we moved, or in the stove that was given us for the waiting-room, or in our nightly conversion of the little consulting-room into a smoking-room! Their admiration of the situation, if we could only get rid of its one objectionable incident, the coal-yard at the back! "Our hospital carriage, presented by a friend, and very useful." That was my presentation to a perambulator, for which a coach-house had been discovered in a corner down-stairs, just large enough to hold it. Coloured prints, in all stages of preparation for being added to those already decorating the wards, were plentiful; a charming wooden phenomenon of a bird, with an impossible top-knot, who ducked his head when you set a counter weight going, had been inaugurated as a public statue that very morning; and trotting about among the beds, on familiar terms with all the patients, was a comical mongrel dog, called Poodles. This comical dog (quite a tonic in himself) was found characteristically starving at the door of the institution, and was taken in and fed, and has lived here ever since. An admirer of his mental endowments has presented him with a collar bearing the legend, "Judge not Poodles by external appearances". He was merrily wagging his tail on a boy's pillow when he made this modest appeal to me.

When this hospital was first opened, in January of the present year, the people could not possibly conceive but that somebody paid for the services rendered there; and were disposed to claim them as a right, and to find fault if out of temper. They soon came to understand the case better, and have much increased in gratitude. The mothers of the patients avail themselves very freely of the visiting rules; the fathers often on Sundays. There is an unreasonable (but still, I think, touching and intelligible) tendency in the parents to take a child away to its wretched home, if on the point of death. One boy who had been thus carried off on a rainy night, when in a violent state of inflammation, and who had been afterwards brought back, had been recovered with exceeding difficulty; but he was a jolly boy, with a specially strong interest in his dinner, when I saw him.

Insufficient food and unwholesome living are the main causes of disease among these small patients. So nourishment, cleanliness, and ventilation are the main remedies. Discharged patients are looked after, and invited to come and dine now and then; so are certain famishing creatures who never were patients. Both the lady and the gentleman are well acquainted, not only with the histories of the patients and their families, but with the characters and circumstances of great numbers of their neighbours: of these they keep a register. It is their common experience, that people, sinking down by inches into deeper and deeper poverty, will conceal it, even from them, if possible, unto the very last extremity.

The nurses of this hospital are all young,—ranging, say, from nineteen to four and twenty. They have even within these narrow limits, what many well-endowed hospitals would not give them, a comfortable room of their own in which to take their meals. It is a beautiful truth, that interest in the children and sympathy with their sorrows bind these young women to their places far more strongly than any other consideration could. The best skilled of the nurses came originally from a kindred neighbourhood, almost as poor; and she knew how much the work was needed. She is a fair dressmaker. The hospital cannot pay her as many pounds in the year as there are months in it; and one day the lady regarded it as a duty to speak to her about her improving her prospects and following her trade. " No," she said: she could never be so useful or so happy elsewhere any more; she must stay among the children. And she stays. One of the nurses, as I passed her, was washing a baby-boy. Liking her pleasant face, I stopped to speak to her charge,—a common, bullet-headed, frowning charge enough, laying hold of his own nose with a slippery grasp, and staring very solemnly out of a blanket. The melting of the pleasant face into delighted smiles, as this young gentleman gave an unexpected kick, and laughed at me, was almost worth my previous pain.

An affecting play was acted in Paris years ago, called " The Children's Doctor ". As I parted from my children's doctor, now in question, I saw in his easy black necktie, in his loose buttoned black frock-coat, in his pensive face, in the flow of his dark hair, in his eyelashes, in the very turn of his moustache, the exact realisation of the Paris artist's ideal as it was presented on the stage. But no romancer that I know of has had the boldness to prefigure the life and home of this young husband and young wife in the Children's Hospital in the east of London.

I came away from Ratcliff by the Stepney railway station to the terminus at Fenchurch Street. Any one who will reverse that route may retrace my steps.

XXXIII

A LITTLE DINNER IN AN HOUR

It fell out on a day in this last autumn, that I had to go down from London to a place of seaside resort, on an hour's business, accompanied by my esteemed friend Bullfinch. Let the place of seaside resort be, for the nonce, called Namelesston.

I had been loitering about Paris in very hot weather, pleasantly breakfasting in the open air in the garden of the Palais Royal or the Tuileries, pleasantly dining in the open air in the Elysian Fields, pleasantly taking my cigar and lemonade in the open air on the Italian Boulevard towards the small hours after midnight. Bullfinch—an excellent man of business—had summoned me back across the Channel, to transact this said hour's business at Namelesston; and thus it fell out that Bullfinch and I were in a railway carriage together on our way to Namelesston, each with his return-ticket in his waistcoat-pocket.

Says Bullfinch, "I have a proposal to make. Let us dine at the Temeraire."

I asked Bullfinch, did he recommend the Temeraire? inasmuch as I had not been rated on the books of the Temeraire for many years.

Bullfinch declined to accept the responsibility of recommending the Temeraire, but on the whole was rather sanguine about it. He "seemed to remember", Bullfinch said, that he had dined well there. A plain dinner, but good. Certainly not like a Parisian dinner (here Bullfinch obviously became the prey of want of confidence), but of its kind very fair.

I appeal to Bullfinch's intimate knowledge of my wants and ways to decide whether I was usually ready to be pleased with any dinner, or—for the matter of that—with anything that was fair of its kind and really what it claimed to be. Bullfinch doing me the honour to respond in the affirmative, I agreed to ship myself as an able trencherman on board the Temeraire.

"Now, our plan shall be this," says Bullfinch, with his forefinger at his nose. "As soon as we get to Namelesston, we'll drive straight to the Temeraire, and order a little dinner in an hour. And as we shall not have more than enough time in which to dispose of it comfortably, what do you say to giving the house the best opportunities of serving it hot and quickly by dining in the coffee-room?"

What I had to say was, Certainly. Bullfinch (who is by nature of a hopeful constitution) then began to babble of green geese. But I checked him in that Falstaffian vein, urging considerations of time and cookery.

In due sequence of events we drove up to the Temeraire, and alighted. A youth in livery received us on the door-step. "Looks well," said Bullfinch confidentially. And then aloud, "Coffee-room!"

The youth in livery (now perceived to be mouldy) conducted us to the desired haven, and was enjoined by Bullfinch to send the waiter at once, as we wished to order a little dinner in an hour. Then Bullfinch and I waited for the waiter, until, the waiter continuing to wait in some unknown and invisible sphere of action, we rang for the waiter; which ring produced the waiter, who announced himself as not the waiter who ought to wait upon us, and who didn't wait a moment longer.

So Bullfinch approached the coffee-room door, and melodiously pitching his voice into a bar where two young ladies were keeping the books of the Temeraire, apologetically explained that we wished to order a little dinner in an hour, and that we were debarred from the execution of our inoffensive purpose by consignment to solitude.

Hereupon one of the young ladies rang a bell, which reproduced— at the bar this time—the waiter who was not the waiter who ought to wait upon us; that extraordinary man, whose life seemed consumed in waiting upon people to say that he wouldn't wait upon them, repeated his former protest with great indignation, and retired.

Bullfinch, with a fallen countenance, was about to say to me, "This won't do", when the waiter who ought to wait upon us left off keeping us waiting at last. "Waiter," said Bullfinch piteously, "we have been a long time waiting." The waiter who ought to wait upon us laid the blame upon the waiter who ought not to wait upon us, and said it was all that waiter's fault.

"We wish," said Bullfinch, much depressed, "to order a little dinner in an hour. What can we have?"

"What would you like to have, gentlemen?"

Bullfinch, with extreme mournfulness of speech and action, and with a forlorn old fly-blown bill of fare in his hand which the waiter had given him, and which was a sort of general manuscript index to any cookery-book you please, moved the previous question.

We could have mock-turtle soup, a sole, curry, and roast duck. Agreed. At this table by this window. Punctually in an hour.

I had been feigning to look out of this window; but I had been taking note of the crumbs on all the tables, the dirty table-cloths, the stuffy, soupy, airless atmosphere, the stale leavings everywhere about, the deep gloom of the waiter who ought to wait upon us, and the stomach-ache with which a lonely traveller at a distant table in a corner was too evidently afflicted. I now pointed out to Bullfinch the alarming circumstance that this traveller had *dined*. We hurriedly debated whether, without infringement of good breeding, we could ask him to disclose if he had partaken of mock-turtle, sole, curry, or roast duck? We decided that the thing could not be politely done, and that we had set our own stomachs on a cast, and they must stand the hazard of the die.

I hold phrenology, within certain limits, to be true; I am much of the same mind as to the subtler expressions of the hand; I hold physiognomy to be infallible; though all these sciences demand rare qualities in the student. But I also hold that there is no more certain index to personal character than the condition of a set of casters is to the character of any hotel. Knowing, and having often tested this theory of mine, Bullfinch resigned himself to the worst, when, laying aside any remaining veil of disguise, I held up before him in succession the cloudy oil and furry vinegar, the clogged cayenne, the dirty salt, the obscene dregs of soy, and the anchovy sauce in a flannel waistcoat of decomposition.

We went out to transact our business. So inspiriting was the relief of passing into the clean and windy streets of Namelesston from the heavy and vapid closeness of the coffee-room of the Temeraire, that hope began to revive within us. We began to consider that perhaps the lonely traveller had taken physic, or done something injudicious to bring his complaint on. Bullfinch remarked that he thought the waiter who ought to wait upon us had brightened a little when suggesting curry; and although I knew him to have been at that moment the express image of despair, I allowed myself to become elevated in spirits. As we walked by the softly-lapping sea, all the notabilities of Namelesston, who are for ever going up and down with the changelessness of the tides, passed to and fro in procession. Pretty girls on horseback, and with detested riding-masters; pretty girls on foot; mature ladies in hats,—spectacled, strong-minded, and glaring at the opposite or weaker sex. The Stock Exchange was strongly represented, Jerusalem was strongly represented, the bores of the prosier London clubs were strongly represented. Fortune-hunters of all denominations were there, from hirsute insolvency, in a curricle, to closely buttoned-up swindlery in doubtful boots, on the sharp look-out for any likely young gentleman disposed to play a game at billiards round the corner. Masters of languages, their lessons finished for the day, were going to their homes out of sight of the sea; mistresses of accomplishments, carrying small portfolios, likewise tripped homeward; pairs of scholastic pupils, two and two, went languidly along the beach, surveying the face of the waters as if waiting for some Ark to come and take them off. Spectres of the George the Fourth days flitted unsteadily among the crowd, bearing the outward semblance of ancient dandies, of every one of whom it might be said, not that he had one leg in the grave, or both legs, but that he was steeped in grave to the summit of his high shirt-collar, and had nothing real about him but his bones. Alone stationary in the midst of all the movement, the Namelesston boatmen leaned against the railings and yawned, and looked out to sea, or looked at the moored fishing-boats and at nothing. Such is the unchanging manner of life with this nursery of our hardy seamen; and very dry nurses they are, and always wanting something to drink. The only two nautical personages detached from the railing were the two fortunate possessors of the celebrated monstrous unknown barking-fish, just caught (frequently just caught off Namelesston), who carried him about in a hamper, and pressed the scientific to look in at the lid.

The sands of the hour had all run out when we got back to the Temeraire. Says Bullfinch, then, to the youth in livery, with bold-ness, "Lavatory!"

When we arrived at the family vault with a skylight, which the youth in livery presented as the institution sought, we had already whisked off our cravats and coats; but finding ourselves in the pre-sence of an evil smell, and no linen but two crumpled towels newly damp from the countenances of two somebody elses, we put on our cravats and coats again, and fled unwashed to the coffee-room.

There the waiter who ought to wait upon us had set forth our knives and forks and glasses, on the cloth whose dirty acquaintance we had already had the pleasure of making, and whom we were pleased to recognise by the familiar expression of its stains. And now there occurred the truly surprising phenomenon, that the waiter who ought not to wait upon us swooped down upon us, clutched our loaf of bread, and vanished with the same.

Bullfinch, with distracted eyes, was following this unaccountable figure "out at the portal", like the ghost in Hamlet, when the waiter who ought to wait upon us jostled against it, carrying a tureen.

"Waiter!" said a severe diner, lately finished, perusing his bill fiercely through his eye-glass.

The waiter put down our tureen on a remote side-table, and went to see what was amiss in this new direction.

"This is not right, you know, waiter. Look here! here's yesterday's sherry, one and eightpence, and here we are again, two shillings. And what does sixpence mean?"

So far from knowing what sixpence meant, the waiter protested that he didn't know what anything meant. He wiped the perspiration from his clammy brow, and said it was impossible to do it,—not particular-ising what,—and the kitchen was so far off.

"Take the bill to the bar, and get it altered," said Mr. Indignation Cocker, so to call him.

The waiter took it, looked intensely at it, didn't seem to like the idea of taking it to the bar, and submitted, as a new light upon the case, that perhaps sixpence meant six pence.

"I tell you again," said Mr. Indignation Cocker, "here's yesterday's sherry—can't you see it?—one and eightpence, and here we are again, two shillings. What do you make of one and eightpence and two shillings?"

Totally unable to make anything of one and eightpence and two shillings, the waiter went out to try if anybody else could; merely casting a helpless backward glance at Bullfinch, in acknowledgment of his pathetic entreaties for our soup-tureen. After a pause, during which Mr. Indignation Cocker read a newspaper and coughed defiant coughs, Bullfinch arose to get the tureen, when the waiter reappeared and brought it,—dropping Mr. Indignation Cocker's altered bill on Mr. Indignation Cocker's table as he came along.

"It's quite impossible to do it, gentlemen," murmured the waiter; "and the kitchen is so far off."

"Well, you don't keep the house; it's not your fault, we suppose. Bring some sherry."

"Waiter!" from Mr. Indignation Cocker, with a new and burning sense of injury upon him.

The waiter, arrested on his way to our sherry, stopped short, and came back to see what was wrong now.

"Will you look here? This is worse than before. *Do* you understand? Here's yesterday's sherry, one and eightpence, and here we are again two shillings. And what the devil does ninepence mean?"

This new portent utterly confounded the waiter. He wrung his napkin, and mutely appealed to the ceiling.

"Waiter, fetch that sherry," says Bullfinch, in open wrath and revolt.

"I want to know," persisted Mr. Indignation Cocker, "the meaning of ninepence. I want to know the meaning of sherry one and eightpence yesterday, and of here we are again two shillings. Send somebody."

The distracted waiter got out of the room under pretext of sending somebody, and by that means got our wine. But the instant he appeared with our decanter, Mr. Indignation Cocker descended on him again.

"Waiter!"

"You will now have the goodness to attend to our dinner, waiter," said Bullfinch, sternly.

"I am very sorry, but it's quite impossible to do it, gentlemen," pleaded the waiter; "and the kitchen——"

"Waiter!" said Mr. Indignation Cocker.

"—Is," resumed the waiter, "so far off, that——"

"Waiter!" persisted Mr. Indignation Cocker, "send somebody."

We were not without our fears that the waiter rushed out to hang himself; and we were much relieved by his fetching somebody,—in gracefully, flowing skirts and with a waist,—who very soon settled Mr. Indignation Cocker's business.

"Oh!" said Mr. Cocker, with his fire surprisingly quenched by this apparition; "I wished to ask about this bill of mine, because it appears to me that there's a little mistake here. Let me show you. Here's yesterday's sherry one and eightpence, and here we are again two shillings. And how do you explain ninepence?"

However it was explained, in tones too soft to be overheard. Mr. Cocker was heard to say nothing more than "Ah-h-h! Indeed; thank you! Yes," and shortly afterwards went out, a milder man.

The lonely traveller with the stomach-ache had all this time suffered severely, drawing up a leg now and then, and sipping hot brandy-and-water with grated ginger in it. When we tasted our (very) mock-turtle soup, and were instantly seized with symptoms of some disorder simulating apoplexy, and occasioned by the surcharge of the nose and brain with lukewarm dish-water holding in solution sour flour, poisonous condiments, and (say) seventy-five per cent of miscellaneous kitchen stuff rolled into balls, we were inclined to trace his disorder to that source. On the other hand, there was a silent anguish upon him too strongly resembling the results established within ourselves by the sherry, to be discarded from alarmed consideration. Again, we observed him, with terror, to be much overcome by our sole's being aired in a temporary retreat close to him, while the waiter went out (as we conceived) to see his friends. And when the curry made its appearance he suddenly retired in great disorder.

In fine, for the uneatable part of this little dinner (as contradistinguished from the undrinkable) we paid only seven shillings and sixpence each. And Bullfinch and I agreed unanimously, that no such ill-served, ill-appointed, ill-cooked, nasty little dinner could be got for the money anywhere else under the sun. With that comfort to our backs, we turned them on the dear old Temeraire, the charging Temeraire, and resolved (in the Scotch dialect) to gang nae mair to the flabby Temeraire.

XXXIV

MR. BARLOW

A GREAT reader of good fiction at an unusually early age, it seems to me as though I had been born under the superintendence of the estimable but terrific gentleman whose name stands at the head of my present reflections. The instructive monomaniac, Mr. Barlow, will be remembered as the tutor of Master Harry Sandford and Master Tommy Merton. He knew everything, and didactically improved all sorts of occasions, from the consumption of a plate of cherries to the contemplation of a starlight night. What youth came to without Mr. Barlow was displayed in the history of Sandford and Merton, by the example of a certain awful Master Mash. This young wretch wore buckles and powder, conducted himself with insupportable levity at the theatre, had no idea of facing a mad bull single-handed (in which I think him less reprehensible, as remotely reflecting my own character), and was a frightful instance of the enervating effects of luxury upon the human race.

Strange destiny on the part of Mr. Barlow, to go down to posterity as childhood's first experience of a bore! Immortal Mr. Barlow, boring his way through the verdant freshness of ages!

My personal indictment against Mr. Barlow is one of many counts. I will proceed to set forth a few of the injuries he has done me.

In the first place, he never made or took a joke. This insensibility on Mr. Barlow's part not only cast its own gloom over my boyhood, but blighted even the sixpenny jest-books of the time; for, groaning under a moral spell constraining me to refer all things to Mr. Barlow, I could not choose but ask myself in a whisper when tickled by a printed jest, "What would *he* think of it? What would *he* see in it?" The point of the jest immediately became a sting, and stung my conscience. For my mind's eye saw him stolid, frigid, perchance taking from its shelf some dreary Greek book, and translating at full length what some dismal sage said (and touched up afterwards, perhaps, for publication), when he banished some unlucky joker from Athens.

The incompatibility of Mr. Barlow with all other portions of my young life but himself, the adamantine inadaptability of the man to my favourite fancies and amusements, is the thing for which I hate him most. What right had he to bore his way into my Arabian Nights? Yet he did. He was always hinting doubts of the veracity of Sindbad the Sailor. If he could have got hold of the Wonderful Lamp, I knew he would have trimmed it and lighted it, and delivered a lecture over it on the qualities of sperm-oil, with a glance at the whale fisheries. He would so soon have found out—on mechanical principles—the peg in the neck of the Enchanted Horse, and would have turned it the right way in so workmanlike a manner, that the horse could never have got any height into the air, and the story couldn't have been. He would have proved, by map and compass, that there was no such kingdom as the delightful kingdom of Casgar, on the frontiers of Tartary. He would have caused that hypocritical young prig Harry to make an experiment—with the aid of a temporary building in the garden and a dummy,—demonstrating that you couldn't let a choked hunchback down an Eastern chimney with a cord, and leave him upright on the hearth to terrify the sultan's purveyor.

The golden sounds of the overture to the first metropolitan pantomime, I remember, were alloyed by Mr. Barlow. Click click, ting ting, bang bang, weedle weedle weedle, bang! I recall the chilling air that passed across my frame and cooled my hot delight, as the thought occurred to me, "This would never do for Mr. Barlow!" After the curtain drew up, dreadful doubts of Mr. Barlow's considering the costumes of the Nymphs of the Nebula as being sufficiently opaque, obtruded themselves on my enjoyment. In the clown I perceived two persons; one a fascinating unaccountable creature of a hectic complexion, joyous in spirits though feeble in intellect, with flashes of brilliancy; the other a pupil for Mr. Barlow. I thought how Mr. Barlow would secretly rise early in the morning, and butter the pavement for *him*, and, when he had brought him down, would look severely out of his study window and ask *him* how he enjoyed the fun.

I thought how Mr. Barlow would heat all the pokers in the house, and singe him with the whole collection, to bring him better acquainted with the properties of incandescent iron, on which he (Barlow) would fully expatiate. I pictured Mr. Barlow's instituting a comparison between the clown's conduct at his studies,—drinking up the ink, licking his copy-book, and using his head for blotting-paper,—and that of the already mentioned young prig of prigs, Harry, sitting at the Barlovian feet, sneakingly pretending to be in a rapture of useful knowledge. I thought how soon Mr. Barlow would smooth the clown's hair down, instead of letting it stand erect in three tall tufts; and how, after a couple of years or so with Mr. Barlow, he would keep his legs close together when he walked, and would take his hands out of his big loose pockets, and wouldn't have a jump left in him.

That I am particularly ignorant what most things in the universe are made of, and how they are made, is another of my charges against Mr. Barlow. With the dread upon me of developing into a Harry, and with the further dread upon me of being Barlowed if I made inquiries, by bringing down upon myself a cold shower-bath of explanations and experiments, I forbore enlightenment in my youth, and became, as they say in melodramas, "the wreck you now behold". That I consorted with idlers and dunces is another of the melancholy facts for which I hold Mr. Barlow responsible. That pragmatical prig, Harry, became so detestable in my sight, that, he being reported studious in the South, I would have fled idle to the extremest North. Better to learn misconduct from a Master Mash than science and statistics from a Sandford! So I took the path, which, but for Mr. Barlow, I might never have trodden. Thought I, with a shudder, "Mr. Barlow is a bore, with an immense constructive power of making bores. His prize specimen is a bore. He seeks to make a bore of me. That knowledge is power I am not prepared to gainsay; but, with Mr. Barlow, knowledge is power to bore." Therefore I took refuge in the caves of ignorance, wherein I have resided ever since, and which are still my private address.

But the weightiest charge of all my charges against Mr. Barlow is, that he still walks the earth in various disguises, seeking to make a Tommy of me, even in my maturity. Irrepressible, instructive monomaniac, Mr. Barlow fills my life with pitfalls, and lies hiding at the bottom to burst out upon me when I least expect him.

A few of these dismal experiences of mine shall suffice.

Knowing Mr. Barlow to have invested largely in the moving panorama trade, and having on various occasions identified him in the dark with a long wand in his hand, holding forth in his old way (made more appalling in this connection by his sometimes cracking a piece of Mr. Carlyle's own Dead-Sea fruit in mistake for a joke), I systematically shun pictorial entertainment on rollers. Similarly, I should demand responsible bail and guaranty against the appearance of Mr. Barlow, before committing myself to attendance at any assemblage of my fellow-creatures where a bottle of water and a note-book were conspicuous objects; for in either of those associations, I should expressly expect him. But such is the designing nature of the man, that he steals in where no reasonable precaution or prevision could expect him. As in the following case :—

Adjoining the Caves of Ignorance is a country town. In this country town the Mississippi Momuses, nine in number, were announced to appear in the town-hall, for the general delectation, this last Christmas week. Knowing Mr. Barlow to be unconnected with the Mississippi, though holding republican opinions, and deeming myself secure, I took a stall. My object was to hear and see the Mississippi Momuses in what the bills described as their "National ballads, plantation break-downs, nigger part-songs, choice conundrums, sparkling repartees, &c.". I found the nine dressed alike, in the black coat and trousers, white waistcoat, very large shirt-front, very large shirt-collar, and very large white tie and wristbands, which constitute the dress of the mass of the African race, and which has been observed by travellers to prevail over a vast number of degrees of latitude. All the nine rolled their eyes exceedingly, and had very red lips. At the extremities of the curve they formed, seated in their chairs, were the performers on the tambourine and bones. The centre Momus, a black of melancholy aspect (who inspired me with a vague uneasiness for which I could not then account), performed on a Mississippi instrument closely resembling what was once called in this island a hurdy-gurdy. The Momuses on either side of him had each another instrument peculiar to the Father of Waters, which may be likened to a stringed weather-glass held upside down. There were likewise a little flute and a violin. All went well for awhile, and we had had several sparkling repartees exchanged between the performers on the tambourine and bones, when the black of melancholy aspect, turning to the latter, and addressing him in a deep and improving voice as "Bones, sir", delivered certain grave remarks to him concerning the juveniles present, and the season of the year; whereon I perceived that I was in the presence of Mr. Barlow,—corked!

Another night—and this was in London—I attended the representation of a little comedy. As the characters were lifelike (and consequently not improving), and as they went upon their several ways and designs without personally addressing themselves to me, I felt rather confident of coming through it without being regarded as Tommy, the more so, as we were clearly getting close to the end. But I deceived myself. All of a sudden, and àpropos of nothing, everybody concerned came to a check and halt, advanced to the footlights in a general rally to take dead aim at me, and brought me down with a moral homily, in which I detected the dread hand of Barlow.

Nay, so intricate and subtle are the toils of this hunter, that on the very next night after that, I was again entrapped, where no vestige of a springe could have been apprehended by the timidest. It was a burlesque that I saw performed; an uncompromising burlesque, where everybody concerned, but especially the ladies, carried on at a very considerable rate indeed. Most prominent and active among the corps of performers was what I took to be (and she really gave me very fair opportunities of coming to a right conclusion) a young lady of a pretty figure. She was dressed as a picturesque young gentleman, whose pantaloons had been cut off in their infancy; and she had very neat knees and very neat satin boots. Immediately after singing a slang song and dancing a slang dance, this engaging figure approached the fatal lamps, and, bending over them, delivered in a thrilling voice a random eulogium on, and exhortation to pursue, the virtues. "Great Heaven!" was my exclamation; "Barlow!"

There is still another aspect in which Mr. Barlow perpetually insists on my sustaining the character of Tommy, which is more unendurable yet, on account of its extreme aggressiveness. For the purposes of a review or newspaper, he will get up an abstruse subject with infinite pains, will Barlow, utterly regardless of the price of midnight oil, and indeed of everything else, save cramming himself to the eyes.

But mark. When Mr. Barlow blows his information off, he is not contented with having rammed it home, and discharged it upon me, Tommy, his target, but he pretends that he was always in possession of it, and made nothing of it—that he imbibed it with mother's milk, —and that I, the wretched Tommy, am most abjectly behindhand in not having done the same. I ask, why is Tommy to be always the foil of Mr. Barlow to this extent? What Mr. Barlow had not the slightest notion of himself, a week ago, it surely cannot be any very heavy backsliding in me not to have at my fingers' ends to-day! And yet Mr. Barlow systematically carries it over me with a high hand, and will tauntingly ask me, in his articles, whether it is possible that I am not aware that every school-boy knows that the fourteenth turning on the left in the steppes of Russia will conduct to such and such a wandering tribe? with other disparaging questions of like nature. So, when Mr. Barlow addresses a letter to any journal as a volunteer correspondent (which I frequently find him doing), he will previously have gotten somebody to tell him some tremendous technicality, and will write in the coolest manner, "Now, sir, I may assume that every reader of your columns, possessing average information and intelligence, knows as well as I do that "—say that the draught from the touch-hole of a cannon of such a calibre bears such a proportion in the nicest fractions to the draught from the muzzle; or some equally familiar little fact. But whatever it is, be certain that it always tends to the exaltation of Mr. Barlow, and the depression of his enforced and enslaved pupil.

Mr. Barlow's knowledge of my own pursuits I find to be so profound, that my own knowledge of them becomes as nothing. Mr. Barlow (disguised and bearing a feigned name, but detected by me) has occasionally taught me, in a sonorous voice, from end to end of a long dinner-table, trifles that I took the liberty of teaching him five-and-twenty years ago. My closing article of impeachment against Mr. Barlow is, that he goes out to breakfast, goes out to dinner, goes out everywhere, high and low, and that he WILL preach to me, and that I CAN'T get rid of him. He makes of me a Promethean Tommy, bound; and he is the vulture that gorges itself upon the liver of my uninstructed mind.

XXXV

ON AN AMATEUR BEAT

IT is one of my fancies, that even my idlest walk must always have its appointed destination. I set myself a task before I leave my lodging in Covent Garden on a street expedition, and should no more think of altering my route by the way, or turning back and leaving a part of it unachieved, than I should think of fraudulently violating an agreement entered into with somebody else. The other day, finding myself under this kind of obligation to proceed to Lime-house, I started punctually at noon, in compliance with the terms of the contract with myself to which my good faith was pledged.

On such an occasion, it is my habit to regard my walk as my beat, and myself as a higher sort of police-constable doing duty on the same. There is many a ruffian in the streets whom I mentally collar and clear out of them, who would see mighty little of London, I can tell him, if I could deal with him physically.

Issuing forth upon this very beat, and following with my eyes three hulking garrotters on their way home,—which home I could confidently swear to be within so many yards of Drury Lane, in such a narrowed and restricted direction (though they live in their lodging quite as undisturbed as I in mine),—I went on duty with a consideration which I respectfully offer to the new Chief Commissioner,—in whom I thoroughly confide as a tried and efficient public servant. How often (thought I) have I been forced to swallow, in police-reports, the intolerable stereotyped pill of nonsense, how that the police-constable informed the worthy magistrate how that the associates of the prisoner did, at that present speaking, dwell in a street or court which no man dared go down, and how that the worthy magistrate had heard of the dark reputation of such street or court, and how that our readers would doubtless remember that it was always the same street or court which was thus edifyingly discoursed about, say once a fortnight.

Now, suppose that a Chief Commissioner sent round a circular to every division of police employed in London, requiring instantly the names in all districts of all such much-puffed streets or courts which no man durst go down; and suppose that in such circular he gave plain warning, "If those places really exist, they are a proof of police inefficiency which I mean to punish; and if they do not exist, but are a conventional fiction, then they are a proof of lazy tacit police connivance with professional crime, which I also mean to punish"— what then? Fictions or realities, could they survive the touchstone of this atom of common sense? To tell us in open court, until it has become as trite a feature of news as the great gooseberry, that a costly police-system such as was never before heard of, has left in London, in the days of steam and gas and photographs of thieves and electric telegraphs, the sanctuaries and stews of the Stuarts! Why, a parity of practice, in all departments, would bring back the Plague in two summers, and the Druids in a century!

Walking faster under my share of this public injury, I overturned a wretched little creature, who, clutching at the rags of a pair of trousers with one of its claws, and at its ragged hair with the other, pattered with bare feet over the muddy stones. I stopped to raise and succour this poor weeping wretch, and fifty like it, but of both sexes, were about me in a moment, begging, tumbling, fighting, clamouring, yelling, shivering in their nakedness and hunger. The piece of money I had put into the claw of the child I had overturned was clawed out of it, and was again clawed out of that wolfish gripe, and again out of that, and soon I had no notion in what part of the obscene scuffle in the mud, of rags and legs and arms and dirt, the money might be. In raising the child, I had drawn it aside out of the main thoroughfare, and this took place among some wooden hoardings and barriers and ruins of demolished buildings, hard by Temple Bar.

Unexpectedly, from among them emerged a genuine police-constable, before whom the dreadful brood dispersed in various directions, he making feints and darts in this direction and in that, and catching nothing. When all were frightened away, he took off his hat, pulled out a handkerchief from it, wiped his heated brow, and restored the handkerchief and hat to their places, with the air of a man who had discharged a great moral duty,—as indeed he had, in doing what was set down for him. I looked at him, and I looked about at the disorderly traces in the mud, and I thought of the drops of rain and the footprints of an extinct creature, hoary ages upon ages old, that geologists have identified on the face of a cliff; and this speculation came over me: If this mud could petrify at this moment, and could lie concealed here for ten thousand years, I wonder whether the race of men then to be our successors on the earth could, from these or any marks, by the utmost force of the human intellect, unassisted by tradition, deduce such an astounding inference as the existence of a polished state of society that bore with the public savagery of neglected children in the streets of its capital city, and was proud of its power by sea and land, and never used its power to seize and save them!

After this, when I came to the Old Bailey and glanced up it towards Newgate, I found that the prison had an inconsistent look. There seemed to be some unlucky inconsistency in the atmosphere that day; for though the proportions of St. Paul's Cathedral are very beautiful, it had an air of being somewhat out of drawing, in my eyes. I felt as though the cross were too high up, and perched upon the intervening golden ball too far away.

Facing eastward, I left behind me Smithfield and Old Bailey,—

fire and fagot, condemned hold, public hanging, whipping through the city at the cart-tail, pillory, branding-iron, and other beautiful ancestral landmarks, which rude hands have rooted up, without bringing the stars quite down upon us as yet,—and went my way upon my beat, noting how oddly characteristic neighbourhoods are divided from one another, hereabout, as though by an invisible line across the way. Here shall cease the bankers and the money-changers; here shall begin the shipping interest and the nautical-instrument shops; here shall follow a scarcely perceptible flavouring of groceries and drugs; here shall come a strong infusion of butchers; now, small hosiers shall be in the ascendant; henceforth, everything exposed for sale shall have its ticketed price attached. All this as if specially ordered and appointed.

A single stride at Houndsditch Church, no wider than sufficed to cross the kennel at the bottom of the Canongate, which the debtors in Holyrood sanctuary were wont to relieve their minds by skipping over, as Scott relates, and standing in delightful daring of catchpoles on the free side,—a single stride, and everything is entirely changed in grain and character. West of the stride, a table, or a chest of drawers on sale, shall be of mahogany and French-polished; east of the stride, it shall be of deal, smeared with a cheap counterfeit resembling lip-salve. West of the stride, a penny loaf or bun shall be compact and self-contained; east of the stride, it shall be of a sprawling and splay-footed character, as seeking to make more of itself for the money. My beat lying round by Whitechapel Church, and the adjacent sugar-refineries,—great buildings, tier upon tier, that have the appearance of being nearly related to the dock-warehouses at Liverpool,—I turned off to my right, and, passing round the awkward corner on my left, came suddenly on an apparition familiar to London streets afar off.

What London peripatetic of these times has not seen the woman who has fallen forward, double, through some affection of the spine, and whose head has of late taken a turn to one side, so that it now droops over the back of one of her arms at about the wrist? Who does not know her staff, and her shawl, and her basket, as she gropes her way along, capable of seeing nothing but the pavement, never begging, never stopping, for ever going somewhere on no business? How does she live, whence does she come, whither does she go, and why? I mind the time when her yellow arms were naught but bone and parchment. Slight changes steal over her; for there is a shadowy suggestion of human skin on them now. The Strand may be taken as the central point about which she revolves in a half-mile orbit. How comes she so far east as this? And coming back too! Having been how much farther? She is a rare spectacle in this neighbourhood. I receive intelligent information to this effect from a dog,—a lop-sided mongrel with a foolish tail, plodding along with his tail up, and his ears pricked, and displaying an amiable interest in the ways of his fellow-men,—if I may be allowed the expression. After pausing at a pork-shop, he is jogging eastward like myself, with a benevolent countenance and a watery mouth, as though musing on the many excellences of pork, when he beholds this doubled-up bundle approaching. He is not so much astonished at the bundle (though amazed by that), as at the circumstance that it has within itself the means of locomotion. He stops, pricks his ears higher, makes a slight point, stares, utters a short, low growl, and glistens at the nose,—as I conceive with terror. The bundle continuing to approach, he barks, turns tail, and is about to fly, when, arguing with himself that flight is not becoming in a dog, he turns, and once more faces the advancing heap of clothes. After much hesitation, it occurs to him that there may be a face in it somewhere. Desperately resolving to undertake the adventure, and pursue the inquiry, he goes slowly up to the bundle, goes slowly round it, and coming at length upon the human countenance down there where never human countenance should be, gives a yelp of horror, and flies for the East India Docks.

Being now in the Commercial Road district of my beat, and be-thinking myself that Stepney station is near, I quicken my pace that I may turn out of the road at that point, and see how my small eastern star is shining.

The Children's Hospital, to which I gave that name, is in full force. All its beds occupied. There is a new face on the bed where my pretty baby lay, and that sweet little child is now at rest for ever. Much kind sympathy has been here since my former visit, and it is good to see the walls profusely garnished with dolls. I wonder what Poodles may think of them, as they stretch out their arms above the beds, and stare, and display their splendid dresses. Poodles has a greater interest in the patients. I find him making the round of the beds, like a house-surgeon, attended by another dog, —a friend,—who appears to trot about with him in the character of his pupil dresser. Poodles is anxious to make me known to a pretty little girl looking wonderfully healthy, who has had a leg taken off for cancer of the knee. A difficult operation, Poodles intimates, wagging his tail on the counterpane, but perfectly successful, as you see, dear sir! The patient, patting Poodles, adds with a smile, "The leg was so much trouble to me, that I am glad it's gone". I never saw anything in doggery finer than the deportment of Poodles, when another little girl opens her mouth to show a peculiar enlarge-ment of the tongue. Poodles (at that time on a table, to be on a level with the occasion) looks at the tongue (with his own sym-pathetically out) so very gravely and knowingly, that I feel inclined to put my hand in my waistcoat-pocket, and give him a guinea, wrapped in paper.

On my beat again, and close to Limehouse Church, its termination, I found myself near to certain "Lead-Mills". Struck by the name, which was fresh in my memory, and finding, on inquiry, that these same lead-mills were identical with those same lead-mills of which I made mention when I first visited the East London Children's

Hospital and its neighbourhood as Uncommercial Traveller, I resolved to have a look at them.

Received by two very intelligent gentlemen, brothers, and partners with their father in the concern, and who testified every desire to show their works to me freely, I went over the lead-mills. The purport of such works is the conversion of pig-lead into white-lead. This conversion is brought about by the slow and gradual effecting of certain successive chemical changes in the lead itself. The processes are picturesque and interesting,—the most so, being the burying of the lead, at a certain stage of preparation, in pots, each pot containing a certain quantity of acid besides, and all the pots being buried in vast numbers, in layers, under tan, for some ten weeks.

Hopping up ladders, and across planks, and on elevated perches, until I was uncertain whether to liken myself to a bird or a bricklayer, I became conscious of standing on nothing particular, looking down into one of a series of large cocklofts, with the outer day peeping in through the chinks in the tiled roof above. A number of women were ascending to, and descending from, this cockloft, each carrying on the upward journey a pot of prepared lead and acid, for deposition under the smoking tan. When one layer of pots was completely filled, it was carefully covered in with planks, and those were carefully covered with tan again, and then another layer of pots was begun above; sufficient means of ventilation being preserved through wooden tubes. Going down into the cockloft then filling, I found the heat of the tan to be surprisingly great, and also the odour of the lead and acid to be not absolutely exquisite, though I believe not noxious at that stage. In other cocklofts, where the pots were being exhumed, the heat of the steaming tan was much greater, and the smell was penetrating and peculiar. There were cocklofts in all stages; full and empty, half filled and half emptied; strong, active women were clambering about them busily; and the whole thing had rather the air of the upper part of the house of some immensely rich old Turk, whose faithful seraglio were hiding his money because the sultan or the pasha was coming.

As is the case with most pulps or pigments, so in the instance of this white-lead, processes of stirring, separating, washing, grinding, rolling, and pressing succeed. Some of these are unquestionably inimical to health, the danger arising from inhalation of particles of lead, or from contact between the lead and the touch, or both. Against these dangers, I found good respirators provided (simply made of flannel and muslin, so as to be inexpensively renewed, and in some instances washed with scented soap), and gauntlet gloves, and loose gowns. Everywhere, there was as much fresh air as windows, well placed and opened, could possibly admit. And it was explained that the precaution of frequently changing the women employed in the worst parts of the work (a precaution originating in their own experience or apprehension of its ill effects) was found salutary. They had a mysterious and singular appearance, with the mouth and nose covered, and the loose gown on, and yet bore out the simile of the old Turk and the seraglio all the better for the disguise.

At last this vexed white-lead, having been buried and resuscitated, and heated and cooled and stirred, and separated and washed and ground, and rolled and pressed, is subjected to the action of intense fiery heat. A row of women, dressed as above described, stood, let us say, in a large stone bakehouse, passing on the baking-dishes as they were given out by the cooks, from hand to hand, into the ovens. The oven, or stove, cold as yet, looked as high as an ordinary house, and was full of men and women on temporary footholds, briskly passing up and stowing away the dishes. The door of another oven, or stove, about to be cooled and emptied, was opened from above, for the uncommercial countenance to peer down into. The uncommercial countenance withdrew itself, with expedition and a sense of suffocation, from the dull-glowing heat and the overpowering smell. On the whole, perhaps the going into these stoves to work, when they are freshly opened, may be the worst part of the occupation.

But I made it out to be indubitable that the owners of these lead-mills honestly and sedulously try to reduce the dangers of the occupation to the lowest point.

A washing-place is provided for the women (I thought there might have been more towels), and a room in which they hang their clothes, and take their meals, and where they have a good fire-range and fire, and a female attendant to help them, and to watch that they do not neglect the cleansing of their hands before touching their food. An experienced medical attendant is provided for them, and any premonitory symptoms of lead-poisoning are carefully treated. Their teapots and such things were set out on tables ready for their afternoon meal, when I saw their room; and it had a homely look. It is found that they bear the work much better than men: some few of them have been at it for years, and the great majority of those I observed were strong and active. On the other hand, it should be remembered that most of them are very capricious and irregular in their attendance.

American inventiveness would seem to indicate that before very long white-lead may be made entirely by machinery. The sooner, the better. In the meantime, I parted from my two frank conductors over the mills, by telling them that they had nothing there to be concealed, and nothing to be blamed for. As to the rest, the philosophy of the matter of lead-poisoning and workpeople seems to me to have been pretty fairly summed up by the Irishwoman whom I quoted in my former paper: "Some of them gits lead-pisoned soon, and some of them gets lead-pisoned later, and some, but not many, niver; and 'tis all according to the constitooshun, sur; and some constitooshuns is strong and some is weak."

Retracing my footsteps over my beat, I went off duty.

XXXVI

A FLY-LEAF IN A LIFE

ONCE upon a time (no matter when), I was engaged in a pursuit (no matter what), which could be transacted by myself alone; in which I could have no help; which imposed a constant strain on the attention, memory, observation, and physical powers; and which involved an almost fabulous amount of change of place and rapid railway travelling. I had followed this pursuit through an exceptionally trying winter in an always trying climate, and had resumed it in England after but a brief repose. Thus it came to be prolonged until, at length—and, as it seemed, all of a sudden—it so wore me out that I could not rely, with my usual cheerful confidence, upon myself to achieve the constantly recurring task, and began to feel (for the first time in my life) giddy, jarred, shaken, faint, uncertain of voice and sight and tread and touch, and dull of spirit. The medical advice I sought within a few hours, was given in two words: "Instant rest". Being accustomed to observe myself as curiously as if I were another man, and knowing the advice to meet my only need, I instantly halted in the pursuit of which I speak, and rested.

My intention was, to interpose, as it were, a fly-leaf in the book of my life, in which nothing should be written from without for a brief season of a few weeks. But some very singular experiences recorded themselves on this same fly-leaf, and I am going to relate them literally. I repeat the word: literally.

My first odd experience was of the remarkable coincidence between my case, in the general mind, and one Mr. Merdle's as I find it recorded in a work of fiction called LITTLE DORRIT. To be sure, Mr. Merdle was a swindler, forger, and thief, and my calling had been of a less harmful (and less remunerative) nature; but it was all one for that.

Here is Mr. Merdle's case:

"At first, he was dead of all the diseases that ever were known, and of several bran-new maladies invented with the speed of Light to meet the demand of the occasion. He had concealed a dropsy from infancy, he had inherited a large estate of water on the chest from his grandfather, he had had an operation performed upon him every morning of his life for eighteen years, he had been subject to the explosion of important veins in his body after the manner of fire-works, he had had something the matter with his lungs, he had had something the matter with his heart, he had had something the matter with his brain. Five hundred people who sat down to break-fast entirely uninformed on the whole subject, believed before they had done breakfast, that they privately and personally knew Physician to have said to Mr. Merdle, 'You must expect to go out, some day, like the snuff of a candle;' and that they knew Mr. Merdle to have said to Physician, 'A man can die but once.' By about eleven o'clock in the forenoon, something the matter with the brain, became the favourite theory against the field; and by twelve the something had been distinctly ascertained to be 'Pressure'.

"Pressure was so entirely satisfactory to the public mind, and seemed to make every one so comfortable, that it might have lasted all day but for Bar's having taken the real state of the case into Court at half-past nine. Pressure, however, so far from being overthrown by the discovery, became a greater favourite than ever. There was a general moralising upon Pressure, in every street. All the people who had tried to make money and had not been able to do it, said, There you were! You no sooner began to devote yourself to the pursuit of wealth, than you got Pressure. The idle people improved the occasion in a similar manner. See, said they, what you brought yourself to by work, work, work! You persisted in working, you overdid it, Pressure came on, and you were done for! This consideration was very potent in many quarters, but nowhere more so than among the young clerks and partners who had never been in the slightest danger of overdoing it. These, one and all declared, quite piously, that they hoped they would never forget the warning as long as they lived, and that their conduct might be so regulated as to keep off Pressure, and preserve them, a comfort to their friends, for many years."

Just my case—if I had only known it—when I was quietly basking in the sunshine in my Kentish meadow!

But while I so rested, thankfully recovering every hour, I had experiences more odd than this. I had experiences of spiritual conceit, for which, as giving me a new warning against that curse of mankind, I shall always feel grateful to the supposition that I was too far gone to protest against playing sick lion to any stray donkey with an itching hoof. All sorts of people seemed to become vicariously religious at my expense. I received the most uncompromising warning that I was a Heathen: on the conclusive authority of a field preacher, who, like the most of his ignorant and vain and daring class, could not construct a tolerable sentence in his native tongue or pen a fair letter. This inspired individual called me to order roundly, and knew in the freest and easiest way where I was going to, and what would become of me if I failed to fashion myself on his bright example, and was on terms of blasphemous confidence with the Heavenly Host. He was in the secrets of my heart, and in the lowest soundings of my soul—he!—and could read the depths of my nature better than his A B C, and could turn me inside out, like his own clammy glove. But what is far more extraordinary than this—for such dirty water as this could alone be drawn from such a shallow and muddy source—I found from the information of a beneficed clergyman, of whom I never heard and whom I never saw, that I had not, as I rather supposed I had, lived a life of some reading, contemplation, and inquiry; that I had not studied, as I rather supposed I had, to inculcate some Christian lessons in books; that I had never tried, as I rather supposed I had, to turn a child or two tenderly towards the knowledge and love of our Saviour; that I had never had, as I rather supposed I had had, departed friends, or stood beside open graves; but that I had lived a life of "uninterrupted prosperity", and that I needed this "check, overmuch", and that the way to turn it to account was to read these sermons and these poems, enclosed, and written and issued by my correspondent! I beg it may be understood that I relate facts of my own uncommercial experience, and no vain imaginings. The documents in proof lie near my hand.

Another odd entry on the fly-leaf, of a more entertaining character, was the wonderful persistency with which kind sympathisers assumed that I had injuriously coupled with the so suddenly relinquished pursuit, those personal habits of mine most obviously incompatible with it, and most plainly impossible of being maintained, along with it. As, all that exercise, all that cold bathing, all that wind and weather, all that uphill training—all that everything else, say, which is usually carried about by express trains in a portmanteau and hat-box, and partaken of under a flaming row of gaslights in the company of two thousand people. This assuming of a whole case against all fact and likelihood, struck me as particularly droll, and was an oddity of which I certainly had had no adequate experience in life until I turned that curious fly-leaf.

My old acquaintances the begging-letter writers came out on the fly-leaf, very piously indeed. They were glad, at such a serious crisis, to afford me another opportunity of sending that Post-office order. I needn't make it a pound, as previously insisted on; ten shillings might ease my mind. And Heaven forbid that they should refuse, at such an insignificant figure, to take a weight off the memory of an erring fellow-creature! One gentleman, of an artistic turn (and copiously illustrating the books of the Mendicity Society), thought it might soothe my conscience in the tender respect of gifts misused, if I would immediately cash up in aid of his lowly talent for original design—as a specimen of which he enclosed me a work of art which I recognized as a tracing from a woodcut originally published in the late Mrs. Trollope's book on America, forty or fifty years ago. The number of people who were prepared to live long years after me, untiring benefactors to their species, for fifty pounds a piece down, was astonishing. Also, of those who wanted bank notes for stiff penitential amounts, to give away:—not to keep, on any account.

Divers wonderful medicines and machines insinuated recommendations of themselves into the fly-leaf that was to have been so blank. It was specially observable that every prescriber, whether in a moral or physical direction, knew me thoroughly—knew me from head to heel, in and out, through and through, upside down. I was a glass piece of general property, and everybody was on the most surprisingly intimate terms with me. A few public institutions had complimentary

perceptions of corners in my mind, of which, after considerable self-
examination, I have not discovered any indication. Neat little printed
forms were addressed to those corners, beginning with the words:
" I give and bequeath ".

Will it seem exaggerative to state my belief that the most honest,
the most modest, and the least vain-glorious of all the records upon
this strange fly-leaf, was a letter from the self-deceived discoverer of
the recondite secret " how to live four or five hundred years "? Doubtless it will seem so, yet the statement is not exaggerative by any
means, but is made in my serious and sincere conviction. With this,
and with a laugh at the rest that shall not be cynical, I turn the Fly-
leaf, and go on again.

XXXVII

A PLEA FOR TOTAL ABSTINENCE

ONE day this last Whitsuntide, at precisely eleven o'clock in the
forenoon, there suddenly rode into the field of view commanded by
the windows of my lodging an equestrian phenomenon. It was a
fellow-creature on horseback, dressed in the absurdest manner. The
fellow-creature wore high boots; some other (and much larger) fellow-
creature's breeches, of a slack-baked doughy colour and a baggy form;
a blue shirt, whereof the skirt, or tail, was puffily tucked into the
waist-band of the said breeches; no coat; a red shoulder-belt; and a
demi-semi-military scarlet hat, with a feathered ornament in front,
which, to the uninstructed human vision, had the appearance of a
moulting shuttlecock. I laid down the newspaper with which I had
been occupied, and surveyed the fellow-man in question with astonishment. Whether he had been sitting to any painter as a frontispiece
for a new edition of " Sartor Resartus "; whether " the husk or shell
of him ", as the esteemed Herr Teufelsdroch might put it, were
founded on a jockey, on a circus, on General Garibaldi, on cheap
porcelain, on a toy-shop, on Guy Fawkes, on wax-work, on gold-
digging, on Bedlam, or on all,—were doubts that greatly exercised
my mind. Meanwhile, my fellow-man stumbled and slided, excessively against his will, on the slippery stones of my Covent Garden
street, and elicited shrieks from several sympathetic females, by convulsively restraining himself from pitching over his horse's head. In
the very crisis of these evolutions, and indeed at the trying moment
when his charger's tail was in a tobacconist's shop, and his head
anywhere about town, this cavalier was joined by two similar portents,
who, likewise stumbling and sliding, caused him to stumble and slide
the more distressingly. At length this Gilpinian triumvirate effected
a halt, and, looking northward, waved their three right hands as commanding unseen troops, to " Up, guards ! and at 'em ". Hereupon a
brazen band burst forth, which caused them to be instantly bolted

with to some remote spot of earth in the direction of the Surrey Hills.

Judging from these appearances that a procession was under way, I threw up my window, and, craning out, had the satisfaction of beholding it advancing along the street. It was a Teetotal procession, as I learnt from its banners, and was long enough to consume twenty minutes in passing. There were a great number of children in it, some of them so very young in their mothers' arms as to be in the act of practically exemplifying their abstinence from fermented liquors, and attachment to an unintoxicating drink, while the procession defiled. The display was, on the whole, pleasant to see, as any good-humoured holiday assemblage of clean, cheerful, and well-conducted people should be. It was bright with ribbons, tinsel, and shoulder-belts, and abounded in flowers, as if those latter trophies had come up in profusion under much watering. The day being breezy, the insubordination of the large banners was very reprehensible. Each of these being borne aloft on two poles and stayed with some half-dozen lines, was carried, as polite books in the last century used to be written, by "various hands", and the anxiety expressed in the upturned faces of those officers,—something between the anxiety attendant on the balancing art, and that inseparable from the pastime of kite-flying, with a touch of the angler's quality in landing his scaly prey,—much impressed me. Suddenly, too, a banner would shiver in the wind, and go about in the most inconvenient manner. This always happened oftenest with such gorgeous standards as those representing a gentleman in black, corpulent with tea and water, in the laudable act of summarily reforming a family, feeble and pinched with beer. The gentleman in black distended by wind would then conduct himself with the most unbecoming levity, while the beery family, growing beerier, would frantically try to tear themselves away from his ministration. Some of the inscriptions accompanying the banners were of a highly determined character, as "We never, never will give up the temperance cause", with similar sound resolutions rather suggestive to the profane mind of Mrs. Micawber's "I never will desert Mr. Micawber", and of Mr. Micawber's retort, "Really, my dear, I am not aware that you were ever required by any human being to do anything of the sort".

At intervals, a gloom would fall on the passing members of the procession, for which I was at first unable to account. But this I discovered, after a little observation, to be occasioned by the coming on of the executioners,—the terrible official beings who were to make the speeches by-and-by,—who were distributed in open carriages at various points of the cavalcade. A dark cloud and a sensation of dampness, as from many wet blankets, invariably preceded the rolling on of the dreadful cars containing these headsmen; and I noticed that the wretched people who closely followed them, and who were in a manner forced to contemplate their folded arms, complacent countenances, and threatening lips, were more overshadowed by the cloud and damp than those in front. Indeed, I perceived in some of these so moody an implacability towards the magnates of the scaffold, and so plain a desire to tear them limb from limb, that I would respectfully suggest to the managers the expediency of conveying the executioners to the scene of their dismal labours by unfrequented ways, and in closely-tilted carts next Whitsuntide.

The procession was composed of a series of smaller processions, which had come together, each from its own metropolitan district. An infusion of allegory became perceptible when patriotic Peckham advanced. So I judged, from the circumstance of Peckham's unfurling a silken banner that fanned heaven and earth with the words, "The Peckham Lifeboat". No boat being in attendance, though life, in the likeness of "a gallant, gallant crew", in nautical uniform, followed the flag, I was led to meditate on the fact that Peckham is described by geographers as an inland settlement, with no larger or nearer shore-line than the towing-path of the Surrey Canal, on which stormy station I had been given to understand no lifeboat exists. Thus I deduced an allegorical meaning, and came to the conclusion, that if patriotic Peckham picked a peck of pickled poetry, this *was* the peck of pickled poetry which patriotic Peckham picked.

I have observed that the aggregate procession was on the whole pleasant to see. I made use of that qualified expression with a direct meaning, which I will now explain. It involves the title of this paper, and a little fair trying of teetotalism by its own tests. There were many people on foot, and many people in vehicles of various kinds. The former were pleasant to see, and the latter were not pleasant to see; for the reason that I never, on any occasion or under any circumstances, have beheld heavier overloading of horses than in this public show. Unless the imposition of a great van laden with from ten to twenty people on a single horse be a moderate tasking of the poor creature, then the temperate use of horses was immoderate and cruel. From the smallest and lightest horse to the largest and heaviest, there were many instances in which the beast of burden was so shamefully overladen, that the Society for the Prevention of Cruelty to Animals has frequently interposed in less gross cases.

Now, I have always held that there may be, and that there unquestionably is, such a thing as use without abuse, and that therefore the total abolitionists are irrational and wrong-headed. But the procession completely converted me. For so large a number of the people using draught-horses in it were clearly unable to use them without abusing them, that I perceived total abstinence from horseflesh to be the only remedy of which the case admitted. As it is all one to teetotalers whether you take half a pint of beer or half a gallon, so it was all one here whether the beast of burden were a pony or a cart-horse. Indeed, my case had the special strength that the half-pint quadruped underwent as much suffering as the half-gallon quadruped. Moral: total abstinence from horseflesh through the whole length and breadth of the scale. This pledge will be in course of administration to all teetotal processionists, not pedestrians, at the publishing office of "All the Year Round", on the 1st day of April, 1870.

Observe a point for consideration. This procession comprised many persons in their gigs, broughams, tax-carts, barouches, chaises, and what not, who were merciful to the dumb beasts that drew them, and did not overcharge their strength. What is to be done with those unoffending persons? I will not run amuck and vilify and defame them, as teetotal tracts and platforms would most assuredly do, if the question were one of drinking instead of driving: I merely ask what is to be done with them? The reply admits of no dispute whatever. Manifestly, in strict accordance with teetotal doctrines, THEY must come in too, and take the total abstinence from horseflesh pledge. It is not pretended that those members of the procession misused certain auxiliaries which in most countries and all ages have been bestowed upon man for his use, but it is undeniable that other members of the procession did. Teetotal mathematics demonstrate that the less includes the greater; that the guilty include the innocent, the blird the seeing, the deaf the hearing, the dumb the speaking, the drunken the sober. If any of the moderate users of draughtcattle in question should deem that there is any gentle violence done to their reason by these elements of logic, they are invited to come out of the procession next Whitsuntide, and look at it from my window.